T0367272

Unhappily Ever After

Unhappily Ever After

A Novel

Norman I. Gelman

iUniverse, Inc.
New York   Bloomington

This is a work of fiction. All of the characters, names, incidents,
organizations, and dialogue in this novel are either the products
of the author's imagination or are used fictitiously.

iUniverse books may be ordered through booksellers or by contacting:

iUniverse
1663 Liberty Drive
Bloomington, IN 47403
www.iuniverse.com
1-800-Authors (1-800-288-4677)

Because of the dynamic nature of the Internet, any Web addresses or links
contained in this book may have changed since publication and may no longer be
valid. The views expressed in this work are solely those of the author and do not
necessarily reflect the views of the publisher, and the publisher hereby disclaims
any responsibility for them.

ISBN: 978-1-4401-8164-1 (sc)
ISBN: 978-1-4401-8171-9 (dj)
ISBN: 978-1-4401-8172-6 (ebook)

Library of Congress Control Number: 2009910340

Printed in the United States of America

iUniverse rev. date: 10/28/2009

PART I

RACHEL'S STORY

Gregor Mendel was right about people as well as peas. To be convinced of that, all I've ever had to do is to look in the mirror. I inherited tallness-and-thinness genes. The tactful way to describe me as a kid would have been to say: "She looks exactly like you." That could have been directed with equal accuracy to either of my parents. Mom—Hanna—was twenty-three when I was born, five feet ten inches, rail-thin, and flat-chested. My father—Hillel—was twenty-five, six feet two inches, and, as my grandmother once told me, "shaped pretty much like the blade of a Swiss Army knife."

Shortly before I was born, my folks moved from the East Coast to Southern California. They found an apartment atop the bluff overlooking the highway along the beach in Santa Monica, west of Los Angeles. My dad brought with him a screenplay that he wrote in film school. With help from one of his professors, he'd succeeded in selling it to one of the studios. He was already working on a second script.

After New York City, with its cold winters and humid summers, Mom and Daddy loved being in the outdoors year-round. It was just a short distance downhill from our apartment to the beach. Alongside the beach is a paved path stretching many miles to the south for walking, biking, and roller-skating. Bike riding was their favorite pastime. Even when I was an infant, they took me along on weekend bike rides, strapped into a low-slung trailer that hung off the frame of

1

Mom's bike. During the week, Mom liked to go running in the cool of morning, pushing me ahead of her in the sleek little carriage with big, wide-set wheels on the rear end and a smaller wheel in front. It was just the thing for parental joggers and bike riders. From infancy, I was an outdoors kid, a typical child of Southern California.

Mom and Daddy found everything they wanted in Santa Monica. When Mom became pregnant for the second time, they bought a house, with help from Daddy's parents, in the area north of Montana Avenue. Less than three blocks away stood Roosevelt Elementary School, where I would later go to school. Ours was a big house, with a sizable sunroom in the rear that Mom converted into a studio where she could paint and store her art supplies. We had five bedrooms, one serving as Daddy's office. I had my own large room. Mom decorated it in bright colors and functional furniture, including a double bed. She would be able to lie down beside me and read to me. If necessary, she could even sleep with me when I was sick. That was very rarely required. Thin as I was, I had a sturdy constitution.

Like all small children, I had stuffed animals—including a plush bear that I usually slept with, which I cleverly named Mr. Bear. A six-foot-tall giraffe, which my father named Wilt Chamberlain, stood in the corner of my room, probably thinking about the tasty leaves on the high branches of the tree outside my window. I had no dolls, nor was I encouraged to play dress-up. Mom was determined that I not be raised to conform to the stereotypical "little girl" profile. She did not own much jewelry, wore no lipstick, and used very little makeup. Mom was one of those bra-burning sixties' feminists who believed that cosmetics encourage males to think of women as less than equal. I was being raised to be a little person, not a little girl. If Daddy had an opinion different from Mom's on the subject, I never heard it.

The first toy I was really passionate about was my tricycle. That was the type of gender-neutral equipment acceptable under Mom's child-rearing doctrine. By then, I was three. I'm told that I was a happy, alert little kid. I was certainly accustomed, like other Southern California children, to being unconfined. My parents brought my trike along to Santa Monica Beach where they usually rode on weekends. They allowed me to pretend that I was a big girl, going biking with my parents. They took turns riding up and down the beach, so that one was always there to bike along slowly, waiting for me to catch up or to get tired of pedaling. My twin brothers, David and Noah, now occupied bicycle trailers, while I was allowed to act big sister.

And I *was* big, though in one dimension only. In the pictures taken of me when I was three or four, I must have been almost as tall as a yardstick, and only slightly wider. I had narrow shoulders and no hips at all. I was so thin that all my ribs stood out like the keys on a xylophone. Although I wasn't yet ready to play basketball alongside the real Wilt Chamberlain, I was off the charts in height-for-age. If my parents and I had been bronzed while standing together, we could easily have doubled for a Giacometti sculpture—all length and no breadth.

By the time I was ready for playmates, the kids my own age living on our block were all boys. Mom did not think it was necessary to search out little girls for me to play with: I was still being raised as a little person. I suppose she figured that boys were people, too. Besides, I really didn't know a thing about being a little girl. I was a natural tomboy. Biking, climbing trees, and running were my passions. I was quick. I was elusive. I learned to throw a ball overhand like a boy, though not as hard and not as far. I learned how to swing a bat, and I usually made contact with the ball. I learned how to dribble a soccer ball and to kick it accurately and with as much authority as a child my age could muster. I made a good show of being fearless—which was, of course, a deception but a successful one. Pretending to be brave when you aren't is a significant part of being a boy. I had it down just right.

I knew quite well that boys were different from me. I had twin brothers, after all. But I determinedly ignored it. At five, I got my clothes wet in the lawn sprinkler system while running around in his backyard with Jerry Schwartz, my next door neighbor. I simply stripped myself naked. Jerry's mother called Mom, and I got seriously yelled at, which startled me so much that I began crying. Then Mom sat me down. Tears ran down my cheeks. In the same voice that the Lord must have used on Mt. Sinai, Mom informed me that I was never, ever to undress in front of the boys. I really didn't understand why. I wasn't required to be clothed in front of my father or my brothers. I was permitted to walk in on Daddy while he was getting dressed. However, I knew instinctively that questioning a commandment might invite divine retribution. So, except for residual sniveling, I kept my silence.

*   *   *

The lone television set in our house was used for news and special programs, never for cartoons. My parents were readers. They took turns reading to me every night before I went to sleep. By the time I was ready for kindergarten, I was able to read on my own—and not just isolated words. I remember reading Dr. Seuss books and learning about dinosaurs. At seven, I was reading books about Greek and Roman mythology—simple books but advanced for my age. Daddy was teaching me mathematical tricks. My schoolwork came easily. Mom thought it came too easily. She felt I was becoming bored by school and suggested that I skip second grade. The school authorities didn't like the idea much—it was decidedly unfashionable. But they gave me a battery of tests that seem to have shown that Mom was right. In any case, I moved directly from first grade into third.

I had no trouble adjusting academically. However, the girls in my new class, knowing that I was a year younger, acted as if I was a baby. That only strengthened my resolve to be one of the guys. I showed the same disdain for girls that the boys felt. I hated girls' games. At recess, I avoided the groups playing hopscotch and went to play catch with the guys. After school, I joined the pickup softball games. I wasn't the first chosen, but I usually wasn't the last. The boys—the "other" boys— knew that I was a good second baseman and a better-than-average hitter. They didn't think about me as a girl. I was just another member of the gang of kids that hung out together, playing ball, pretending to be cops or robbers, running all over the neighborhood.

When our little group began to get into mischief so my friends could prove their manhood, which seems to be a necessary stage for all boys, I was an eager participant. I accepted dares that I would probably have refused if I had been an actual boy. I didn't want the guys to think I was a sissy. They might have said, "What can you *expect* from a girl?" That was a verdict I dreaded and was determined to prevent. One episode I remember with particular clarity. It got me in serious trouble because it intruded on Mom's art.

Mom painted abstracts mainly, but she often started with real objects. They included still lifes carefully arranged under lights on a table in front of her easel. She'd first draw them meticulously in charcoal, emphasizing the shapes and angles. Then she would change those shapes into geometries of intense color, deliberately making the objects themselves unrecognizable. Sometimes she'd let me and my friends watch her work. That was good for about five minutes' entertainment.

I remember to this very moment the particular painting that she was working on the day I accepted the wrong dare. She had made an arrangement of four pears, two grapefruit, and an old alarm clock. We watched her set it up. She hadn't yet started sketching when Billy Hanson dared me to substitute an apple for one of the pears. Big-shot tomboy, I accepted the dare. I imagined that Mom wouldn't notice. I didn't know until later that the painting was to be named *Alarm Clock with Pears and Grapefruit*. The name would have been a signal even to eight-year-old me that the replacement of a pear with an apple would not escape detection.

Anyway, I made the substitution while the boys watched through a side window. I swaggered pretty good the rest of the morning. Rachel, the Daredevil. Mom summoned me into the studio that afternoon and asked what had happened to her still life. I compounded my felony, first by denying that any change had been made and, second, by asserting that, if it had, somebody else must have done it, perhaps our cleaning woman, maybe the Martians. Rachel, the Stupid. The services of the local district attorney were not required to secure a conviction.

Mom was angry with me for having disturbed her still life and, even more so, for trying to lie my way out of it. Although my parents did not believe officially in corporal punishment, my Mom had experienced it as a child and apparently thought this was the appropriate occasion to apply it. She marched me into the master bedroom and administered a sound spanking to my bare behind. I cried pretty hard. The twins, who heard all the smacking and crying, managed to sneak a peek before Mom chased them away.

When I emerged from the back of the house, they started chanting, "We saw your *tushie*, we saw your *tushie*." Rebecca, the baby of the family, little more than a toddler then, joined in the chorus, though I suspect she hadn't the slightest idea why the twins were serenading my *tushie* when they had never serenaded hers.

I was humiliated and probably angrier at that moment than I'd ever been in my life. I went after the twins in full fury. The Pentagon never had a clearer plan than the one I had instantly formed. Killing one of the twins, I didn't care which, was my first objective. Killing the other twin would be the second. My brothers had seen me naked many times before, but I felt this was entirely different. Mom caught me before I could get to either twin. She promised me that if I touched either one of them, I'd regret it.

"Leave your sister alone, or you'll get what she got," Mom said to the twins. "Do you hear me?" The boys said "yes'm" and went on to other things. I vowed silently to obliterate the twins when Mom wasn't looking. I didn't think for one moment about what would happen afterward. My pride was injured. I wasn't about to "forgive and forget," the advice Mom usually gave when we were angry with one another. My tomboy soul demanded revenge, and to hell with the consequences.

Hours later, I found my opportunity. Through my bedroom window, I saw David alone in the backyard playing on the swing set that Daddy had installed for me a couple of years earlier. David didn't even see me coming. I pulled him backward off the swing, sat on his chest, and began pummeling him. Noah flew out of the house to David's aid. I kicked his feet out from under him. On the soccer field, under a referee's eye, I would have earned a red card for that. With Noah down, I went back to beating poor David. I was a lot stronger than he was in those days.

Noah gave up on Tarzan-to-the-rescue and ran crying for Mom. She came out of the house in a hail of fire. She grabbed me by the arm, dragged me off David, marched me into the house, and took me into the master bedroom. She told me, "I don't know what you were thinking, young lady, but you're going to pay for it."

I was defiant. Even though I was desperately afraid of what was coming, I said, "I don't care."

Mom gave up threatening. She made me sit exactly where I was on the big bed and went to get a hairbrush. I'm sure Mom wasn't really angry when she spanked me after the still life episode. All she used on me then was her hand, and she made no attempt to force me to beg for mercy. Boy, oh boy, was it different this time. She was blazing. She walloped my bare butt with the hairbrush until my resistance was completely broken and I was shedding tears like a waterfall. She required me to admit my guilt and promise never, never to do it or anything like it again. When it was over, she allowed me to pull up my underpants and jeans and then ordered me to my room, where I was to remain until ready to apologize to David and Noah.

Darned if I was ever going to do that. I was the injured party. I was convinced that Mom always sided with the twins. I'd only given David what he deserved. I hadn't done anything—yet—to Noah. I was determined not to apologize—not then and not ever. Even if I had to remain in my room a million trillion years or until the end of time, whichever came first.

I did without dinner. Before bedtime, Daddy brought me a glass of milk and a plate of cookies. Good old Daddy, I thought. He had never hit me and never would. He held me close. I thought *Daddy's on my side. Him and me against Mommy and the twins.*

But then he said, "I'm very disappointed in you, Rachel." I couldn't believe it. I began crying, differently than when I was getting spanked, but uncontrollably. "I don't care how angry you are," continued Daddy. "Fighting is not allowed in this family. Noah and David were wrong to tease you, and I've spoken to them about that. But what you did was unforgivable."

At that moment, I felt like I was alone in the world.

"I expect you to think tonight about what you did. In the morning, I expect you to apologize to the whole family, not just to the twins but to Mommy and me also. And then, we'll forgive the unforgivable. Can you do that for me?"

I couldn't speak. I hung onto him and wet his shirt with my tears while he patted my back. My anger was gone. I felt just awful. The next morning, I came out of my room and told the twins I was sorry. I almost meant it. I asked Mom to forgive me and received a hug and kiss in return. I told Daddy I loved him. He took me into his lap and held me tight. He called me "*Scheinkeit*," and I felt reborn.

Another few months passed before I got into my next serious scrape. On a dare from other members of the gang, augmented by a wager of five dollars each, two of my pals and I went skinny-dipping one warm summer evening in the pool behind a neighbor's house down the block. We'd been told by the boys who made the dare and offered the bet that the neighbors were away on vacation. This was what spies call "disinformation" —the owners of the pool were merely out to dinner.

The boys and I disrobed side by side, jumped into the pool, and splashed noisily about, feeling like we deserved medals for bravery. When the lights around the pool suddenly came on, the two boys grabbed their clothes and disappeared over the fence before they could be cornered. But I was at the wrong end of the pool: I was destined for the slammer.

Mom wanted to apply the hairbrush again. Daddy, however, said that wasn't a good idea and, besides, it didn't seem to deter me. So instead they decreed that I would be confined to my room from after school until bedtime for the next three weeks. No phone calls in or out. The penalty, I was informed, included one week for the trespass and two weeks for skinny-dipping. No concurrent sentences in the Rothschild courtroom. I would also lose my allowance for an entire month.

I would have much preferred a spanking. I hadn't exactly been looking forward to one, but I'd steeled myself for it; and when a spanking was over, it was over. Confinement was much harder to bear. Every afternoon, I had to imagine what was happening that I wasn't allowed to be part of. I was more miserable than I could ever remember being. I begged for parole, promising to be good forever after.

I know that Mom also found the extended punishment difficult to deal with. Daddy, who by now did his writing in an office at the movie studio, didn't have to listen to me plead and whine, appealing the verdict. Like any criminal court judge, his exposure to the felon ended once the sentence was handed down. It was up to Mom, the warden, to deal with the prisoner and to put up with my pleading. That isn't precisely true. I saved a good deal of my whining until after dinner when Daddy was in the audience. But he was unmoved. "You need to learn your lesson, Rachel," he said. "That's all there is to it."

Mom argued in vain for reduction of the sentence to time served. Daddy's answer was: "I don't intend for the child to come away from this experience thinking she can wheedle her way out of the punishment she's earned."

The confinement seemed to go on forever. The days moved a millisecond at a time. I took a calendar from the kitchen and marked them off. Slowly, slowly, slowly my sentence crept to an end, and the prison gates at last swung open. I adopted the swagger of an ex-con rejoining the gang on release from San Quentin. I acted as if I'd been abused by the guards and fed on bread and water. I pretended that I'd served my sentence uncomplainingly. The guys admired my imaginary stoicism.

"That Rothschild," I'm sure they told one another. "She's got guts. She'll do anything." Oh, yeah.

But the fact was that my readiness to accept dares was on the wane—at least those dares that carried the threat of punishment. I had tasted the hairbrush and might have risked additional spankings. That wasn't what I was going to get if I kept on misbehaving. The idea of losing my freedom was more than I was willing to hazard for the fleeting admiration of my friends. My days as the Lead Lemming were over. If they weren't willing to follow me over the cliff, why should I jump?

My career as a tomboy was also nearing an end. The change would probably have come soon anyway, but it was initiated by events they and I didn't control. The boys were starting to join kid leagues. I simply wasn't invited—even if I was almost as good at softball and soccer as most of my pals. It was completely, totally, 100 percent unfair. I remember thinking that. I told Daddy, "I can't help being a girl."

He said, "I'm very sorry, Rache. In a perfect world, you're right. But those are the rules, and I can't change them."

The authorities told me I was welcome on the sidelines. At first, I went to the practices and most of the games to cheer my pals. But standing there when I wanted to be out on the field was simply too frustrating. So I stopped going. The guys continued to invite me to their birthday parties, but I was clearly slipping from the center of the gang to the periphery. I felt left out, and increasingly I was. Boys being boys, not a one of them understood how tormented I was. They were the only friends I had.

School became my principal source of satisfaction. I had always been an outstanding student, and I simply channeled my competitive energies into being the best—no one else was going to come close. The other kids found it difficult to take, even those who regarded me as a friend. They called me "the brain," sometimes to my face. I didn't like it much, but being the smartest kid in class was all I had.

Altogether, it was a very unhappy period for me. I'd lost my place in the world and hadn't found another. Mom could see that I was socially adrift. She began doing special things with me, leaving the other three kids behind with a sitter afternoons and with Daddy for at least a couple of hours each weekend. The twins certainly didn't miss me. All I did when I was home was to tease them or order them around. Rebecca, the baby of the family, liked being the focus of Daddy's attention.

Mommy and I—just the two of us—went bike riding on the path along the beach. Sometimes we went running together. Mommy took me to museums and to the movies, shopped with me on the Third Street Promenade, went on rides at Disneyland, and toured the movie studio where Daddy did most of his work. He arranged for us to visit the set of a movie being directed by one of his friends. I wrote a little report about it for school, but it was not like I had anyone special to tell.

One weekend, leaving the rest of the family behind, Mommy took me to San Francisco. We stayed at the St. Francis across from Union Square, rode the cable car up the steep slope of Powell Street to Nob Hill, took another cable car to shop at Ghirardelli Square, ate giant crab legs at Fisherman's Wharf. We went by taxi to the Pacific Ocean Palisade overlooking Seal Rock, where the animals climb out of the Pacific to sun themselves and fill the air with their barking.

We wandered through the narrow, crowded streets of Chinatown looking at the ducks hung upside down in the butcher shop windows and poking our heads into the shops selling trinkets made in Hong Kong and Taiwan. I was fascinated by the kids my age who chattered among themselves in Chinese but responded to questions asked of them in perfect, unaccented English.

We climbed Coit Tower to see the view of the delicate-looking Golden Gate Bridge in one direction and the long, heavy San Francisco-Oakland Bay Bridge in the other. Mom even took me on the ferry to Alcatraz. I imagined serving a sentence there, like the sentence I'd served for skinny-dipping. I don't think I would have done well at Alcatraz.

It was a golden weekend. I remembered each and every detail for the longest time. I hadn't been alone with Mom this much since I was an infant. I felt more like a little kid, a loved little kid, than I ever remembered feeling. The warmth I felt toward Mommy overwhelmed me. I hugged Mom like I used to hug Mr. Bear. Toward the end of the San Francisco trip, I climbed onto her lap and nuzzled her neck. "I love you, Mommy," I told her. "Thank you for bringing me."

Mom hugged me back, and I could see tears in her eyes. "I love you, too, Rache. You're my oldest baby, but you're still my baby." She could scarcely get the words out.

I came back to Santa Monica as happy as it was possible for me to be, given that I no longer knew anyone who would listen eagerly, or at all, to the wonders I'd seen and envy my good fortune. Having Mommy on my side was great, but alone was still alone.

*   *   *

Aside from my parents, the twins, and my sister Rebecca, we had no other family in California. My mother's parents lived in New York, but I only met them twice in my life. I was three the first time and have no memory of it. The second time was at my wedding and, to understate the matter, it was not a notable success. By the time I was born, Mom's relationship with her mother, father, and older brother Haim was strained almost to the point of nonexistence. I've never met Haim and his wife and five children, and I'm not likely to. I don't think Mom has ever seen Haim's wife or any of his kids.

Moishe and Sura Horowitz, my grandparents, fled Poland in 1938 and, through one accident and another, ended up in Shanghai. My Mom, originally Chana, was born there. Their other child, Haim—I can't think of him as my uncle—was born two years earlier than Mom at a way station en route to Shanghai.

My grandfather was a rabbi, ordained shortly before leaving Poland. When the family finally migrated to the United States in 1947, my grandfather got a job in Brooklyn teaching at an Ultra-Orthodox *yeshiva*, and Haim became a student there. Mom was sent to a girl's *yeshiva*. But educating her was not a family priority: Her parents planned on Mom's marrying into the Ultra-Orthodox community. She would live exactly like they did—in a Brooklyn *shtetl*, completely removed from the non-Jewish world.

Haim did what was expected of him. Mom, on the other hand, discovered America. She attended the local public schools, showed a talent for art, started making weekend visits to Greenwich Village, and began dressing like a hippie. *Curveh claide*, tart's clothing, her father called it. Desperate to hold onto their daughter, Mom's parents announced her betrothal at age seventeen to the son of an Ultra-Orthodox rabbi in an adjoining neighborhood. Mom would have none of it. She simply went to her room, packed a suitcase, and moved out. It was really an incredibly brave thing for her to do. She was not just going against her parents, she was defying the entire community. She lived with her art teacher for several weeks until her parents agreed to cancel the engagement and do it Mom's way. But it was an uneasy and temporary truce.

After she graduated from high school, Mom enrolled at Cooper Union to continue her art studies. She also began taking college classes at New York University, earning her way by working as a waitress at a restaurant near Union Square. It was not an easy life. She was nineteen when she met Daddy—in front of the rack where they both parked their bicycles. Daddy had transferred to NYU from Yale to pursue film studies. Mom was the nice Jewish Bohemian Daddy had hoped to meet in Greenwich Village. After a brief courtship, they moved in together. Mom didn't even bother to conceal it from her parents when she spoke with them, which was infrequently. They weren't mollified in the least by the fact that Daddy was Jewish. He was living with their daughter and, they soon discovered, ate *tref* and never went to *shul*. They also suspected him of smoking marijuana. None of it was acceptable. Daddy *certainly* wasn't acceptable.

By the time Mom announced her plans to marry Daddy, the rift with her parents had become a chasm. It was all my grandmother could do to persuade my grandfather to attend the wedding. The ceremony was performed at the big reform temple my father's family belonged to in Pittsburgh. *Rodef Shalom* was as distant from my grandfather's little Brooklyn synagogue as Paris is from Bucyrus, Ohio. It had paneled mahogany walls in the sanctuary, many stained-glass windows, marble floors in the halls, bronze sculptures all over the building, and worst of all, an organ with gleaming copper pipes positioned in plain sight above the *bimah*. An organ! Real Jews did not have organs. From my grandfather's standpoint, the wedding might just as well have taken place in a Catholic Church with the Archbishop presiding. Haim, of course, remained in Brooklyn and did not bother to send regrets.

Once Mom and Daddy moved to California, there was little communication between Mom and her parents. Mom had no use for Orthodox Judaism and not much for organized religion generally. The one Jewish holiday that she celebrated enthusiastically was Passover, always a major event in the Rothschild family.

My single visit to Mom's parents occurred when a dozen of her paintings were shown at a New York gallery managed by a classmate from Cooper Union. She flew East, taking me with her while the twins remained behind with Daddy. We went to my grandparents' home so Mom could show them their granddaughter. It ended in a bitter argument between Mom and her father. She walked out, never to return. There was no contact at all for a very long time. Mom finally invited them to my wedding, and they came. Why, I never understood.

Daddy's relationship with his family was entirely different—very warm and loving. His parents had moved to Israel before I was born. That was where their oldest child, my Aunt Shoshana, lived. The Rothschild family remained in constant touch, however. My grandparents called us weekly, and they sent us presents all the time. They came to visit once a year, and Daddy went there occasionally, usually with his other sister, Aunt Ruth, who lived in Colorado. His parents were from old German Jewish families that arrived in Pittsburgh in the middle of the nineteenth century. They owned department stores and became wealthy. By my grandfather's generation, however, the Rothschilds were in the professions.

My grandfather, Albert, was an orthopedic surgeon, a graduate of Johns Hopkins Medical School. Hilda, my grandmother, belonged to one of the wealthiest Jewish families in Pittsburgh. They fell in love when they were kids and married as soon as my grandfather got out of medical school. Albert and Hilda had three children—Shoshana, Ruth, and Daddy—but Daddy was actually the fourth child to be born. Another sister, Leah, died suddenly in infancy. Daddy was conceived to fill the void in my grandmother's heart.

Grandma and Grandpa were ardent Zionists, which was a rarity among German Jews in those days. All three of their kids were sent to Zionist camps when they were old enough. Aunt Shoshana and Aunt Ruth got no religious education, and Daddy got just enough to have a bar mitzvah. Zionism was my grandparents' Judaism. They believed that establishment of an independent Jewish state was the only escape from global anti-Semitism.

By the time Daddy moved to NYU from Yale, Aunt Shoshana had already made *aliyah*—emigrated—to Israel. She was in love with my uncle, Elliott Jacobson, whom she'd known since they met at camp outside Philadelphia where he was a counselor. Uncle El went to Israel straight out of college and was serving in the Israel Defense Forces at the time of the 1956 war with Egypt. Aunt Shoshana, panicked that he might die in the fighting, quit college immediately, landed in Tel Aviv the following week, and moved straight into Uncle El's Jerusalem apartment. They were married as quickly as it could be arranged. My grandparents were unable to attend the wedding, but they were immensely proud of Shoshana's Zionist resolve. Uncle El eventually changed his name to Eliezer Ben Ya'acov—Jacob's son in Hebrew.

The first time my grandparents visited Aunt Shoshana and Uncle El, they purchased an apartment in Tel Aviv, intending to make *aliyah* themselves. Israel needed surgeons, and Grandpa was a good one. However, they kept their big house in Pittsburgh until Aunt Ruth and Daddy were settled.

Aunt Ruth and Daddy, nearly four years apart in age, are friends as well as siblings. Aunt Ruth went to college at Brandeis, just outside Boston. That was where she met my uncle, Aaron Goodman, who was then at Harvard Law School. Even before my folks moved to California, Aunt Ruth finished college and followed Uncle Aaron to Boulder, Colorado, where he'd just been appointed to the law school faculty at the university. They got married after Aunt Ruth became pregnant with my cousin Devorah, known first as Devi and now as Dev. So there was nothing to keep my grandparents in Pittsburgh. They were moved permanently in Tel Aviv.

Aunt Ruth, Uncle Aaron, and their two kids have been constants in my life. My cousin Dev is four years older than me, more like a big sister. The second daughter, Ya'el—whom everyone but Aunt Ruth calls Yalie—is one year older than I am. She's also more than another cousin to me. I worshiped Devi, but Yalie was my soul mate. She was the only girl my age that I really liked as a child. For as long as I can remember, our families got together at least twice a year. For Passover in the spring, usually in California, and in Colorado to ski during the winter. Mom and Daddy learned to ski in their twenties, but I began at age four. Yalie and I tottered along at the base of the mountain on our short little skis with our parents taking turns supervising. We had an instructor, of course, but Devi was the one we copied. By the time she was ten, Devi was already a better skier than any of the adults in the family.

The first time I was ever with my Aunt Shoshana and Uncle El was when the entire American family, the Rothschilds and the Goodmans, went to Israel for their oldest son's bar mitzvah. I was four and a half, the twins two and a half. Daddy and Aunt Ruth had been to Israel several times already, but it was a first trip for the rest of us. Aunt Shoshana and Uncle El lived in Jerusalem in a crowded apartment building with stone floors that felt cold all day long. Their daughter, Avital, didn't speak English very well. However, when we played, she took directions from Devi the way Yalie and I did. The only other things I remember about the trip besides the stone floors are the tumult in the Old City and walking down the many flights of steps in the Jewish Quarter toward the plaza in front of the Western Wall. That memory is seared into my brain because I'd never seen Daddy with tears in his eyes until that moment.

We all went back to Israel two years later for the second son's bar mitzvah. Uncle El rented a small bus and took all of us visitors around the country, except for Mom who stayed behind in Jerusalem with my baby sister. We traveled to Tel Aviv, Caesarea, Haifa, Safed, the Galilee, Tiberias, Jericho, the Dead Sea. Only two things stuck in my mind from that second trip: getting oil and tar on my bare feet from the beach in Caesarea and looking straight down from the top of Mt. Carmel in Haifa to the golden Baha'i Temple with its colorful gardens and, way below that, the curve of the Mediterranean up the coast to the North beyond the port. Uncle El also gave us a special tour of the Israel Museum, where he worked as a biblical archeologist. I had that same tour again ten years later, when I began to understand what I had previously seen.

The only other time the whole Rothschild clan was together was at Devi's bat mitzvah two and a half years later in Boulder. We didn't go to Avital's bat mitzvah. Israeli bat mitzvahs are celebrated when the girl is twelve—and it isn't considered much of an occasion. However, our absence was a problem. Aunt Shoshana was miffed, and her family didn't come to Yalie's bat mitzvah or later on to mine.

I remember Yalie's bat mitzvah especially well, maybe because I knew I would be next. She did everything—read from the Torah, led much of the service, and gave a speech about being Jewish that she'd written by herself with only the smallest amount of help from Uncle Aaron. I was a gawky kid then, very tall for my age and extremely thin.

Yalie, however, was already a little green-eyed beauty, better looking even than Devi, whom everyone considered gorgeous.

Devi and Yalie had—and still have—an extraordinary relationship. I won't say that they never fought. After all, they are sisters. But Devi was always Yalie's protector. Mine, too. I was far closer to the two of them than to my younger sister.

*   *   *

Apart from Devi and Yalie, my first real girlfriend materialized at the beginning of sixth grade. Suzi Orbach arrived from Cleveland in late August, knowing no one. She was a shy kid, only a couple of inches shorter than me. She was another A student, given to lone bike rides, made to be left out of an inner circle. Meanwhile, I was lost in space between the boys and the girls, not yet across the divide. The meaner girls whispered behind my back. They called me a "slut" or other equally unpleasant names. Why else would I prefer the company of boys?

Still, I wasn't exactly an outcast. I had something many of the other girls wanted, the ability to talk naturally to guys in our class. Sometimes when the other girls weren't forward enough to approach the boys directly, they would ask me to tell one of them that "Jennifer thinks you're cool" or "Andrea really likes you." I usually obliged. I was the fifth-grade matchmaker, the *shatrun* as it's called in Yiddish.

Except when they wanted something from me, however, none of the girls ever phoned me at night. I wasn't on the girls' birthday circuit. No one rushed to my table in the lunchroom to share the latest gossip. I didn't belong to a clique—certainly not the one shadowing Heidi Bernstein, who was the high priestess of Roosevelt Elementary. Heidi was blond and beautiful, the envy of all the girls. She was already attracting boys like bears to honey, so she had no need for my services. In fact, she saw no need for me. My sins were that I was too tall and too smart. She told everybody I was a geek and an "easy lay." And, of course, the girls who were her acolytes concurred. I was dirt to Heidi's circle. They did their best to make me *feel* like dirt. And they pretty well succeeded. I stayed as far away from them as possible. Still, they often managed to hurt my feelings.

The other groupings of girls tolerated me because I was useful.

In addition to being class matchmaker, I always knew the answers at test time, and I was pitifully eager to share what I knew as a claim on friendship. However, the claim was almost never rewarded. Girls accepted favors from me, but they all belonged to groups, and none of the groups wanted me in their midst.

I was tarnished by the slanders that Heidi and her minions circulated. I was miserable, pathetic.

So there was Suzi Orbach, in search of a friend, and unpopular me. The main thing was that we could fulfill each other's needs. More than that, at that stage in our lives, we were pretty much the same person. We were both good students. I was the tallest girl in the class, and Suzi was the second tallest. We were both bike riders and the oldest kids in our families, and both of us were dying for companionship. We were in the same homeroom and going to the same classes at the temple.

Two weeks after we met, we were best friends, as if we'd known one another since infancy. We told each other our life stories, shared secrets, spent most of our waking hours together—at school, at temple, in one another's homes, out riding our bikes. The only thing I didn't tell Suzi was that I had skipped second grade and was a year younger than she was. I was ashamed of being younger than the other kids. I never said how old I was—not even on my birthday. Mom should probably have insisted I tell, but she didn't.

Mom and Daddy were delighted to see me come alive in Suzi's company. They felt Suzi was exactly the kind of girl I needed as a friend. She was smart, polite, sweet as May, and completely, utterly square. Even though my daredevil days were behind me, I think Mom and Daddy were reassured by seeing me in the company of a girl who was incapable of tempting me into a relapse.

Suzi's parents were relieved that their child had found a friend and stopped moping about the move from Cleveland required by her father's job. They encouraged the match every way they could, inviting me to stay for dinner or come for a weekend sleepover. We weren't exactly peas in a pod. I was comfortable around boys. Suzi wasn't. I was the better student. She looked as if she might turn out to be a girl someday. I looked like a piece of equipment that a pole-vaulter might find useful. Still, her parents and my parents thought we were made for each other.

By the time we graduated from Roosevelt Elementary School,

a year after we first met, Suzi and I were inseparable. We wouldn't be caught dead dressing alike, but, of course, to adults it must have seemed that we dressed exactly alike. We consulted each evening about what we would wear the next day and how we would fix our hair. When we didn't have to attend classes at the temple, we had long, repetitive discussions about what to do and where to do it. Sometimes the discussions went on so long they interfered with the doing.

Mom would ask, "Can't you two make up your minds about anything?"

And I would answer, "Oh, *Mother*, you don't understand."

Discussion was the whole point, of course. We needed to talk. It didn't really matter what we talked about. We were at the very center of each other's lives.

Then in our second year together, Suzi and I moved from Roosevelt Elementary to Lincoln Junior High. Other schools besides Roosevelt fed into Lincoln, and that disturbed the constellations we'd lived with all during elementary school. Heidi Bernstein was no longer the supreme arbiter. A couple of her faithful planets found other stars to circle, and my place in the universe was no longer fixed.

Suzi and I discovered a trio of other girls to become friends with. Arlene Becker, Laura Ludwig, and Jessica Sherman came to Lincoln from Franklin Elementary, which was on Montana Avenue, east of where we lived. Within easy biking distance by the less-trafficked roads. I had actually seen a couple of them around Santa Monica, but we'd never spoken. On the first day of classes, I was assigned the seat next to Jessica Sherman in seventh-grade social studies—an artifact of the alphabet. The teacher, Mrs. Robertson, spent the hour handing out our textbooks and telling us what we would be studying during the year. As we were leaving, Jessica held up the textbook and said dramatically: "Social Studies! Gosh. I don't think I can *stand* the excitement." I was her audience, and I started giggling. And that was the beginning of our friendship.

That afternoon I introduced Jessica to Suzi, and she introduced us to Arlene and Laura. Soon the five of us were flocking together in the lunchroom. Our new friends loved what we loved and loathed what we loathed. Where there had been two of us, now there were five. We gossiped in the corridors, passed notes in class, giggled in the school yard. After school, we usually congregated at my house. Mom, who worked in her studio in the morning, always had a snack waiting when we arrived and saw to it that we didn't neglect our schoolwork. We called each other every evening, often more than once, and we talked endlessly and breathlessly about boys—even me, though I didn't find guys as mysterious as the others did.

The phone at our house seemed never to stop ringing during the evening. The same was true at the Orbach house—and at Arlene's house and at Laura's house and at Jess Sherman's. The five of us were aspirants to teendom.

For the first time in my life, I got in trouble with my teachers, though never for academic reasons. I completed all my assignments, and my grades remained perfect. But I was frequently caught in the hall after the bell rang and was constantly being rebuked for talking to my girlfriends in class or passing notes between the girls and boys. I might have spent more time in detention than any other A student in the history of Western civilization.

Perhaps it was a relic of my days as a risk-taking tomboy. Although Suzi, Arlie, Laura, and Jess were also at fault, I was generally the one who made the extra comment after the teacher was thoroughly exasperated and demanded "no talking." I was usually the one who sailed a note in the form of a paper airplane to the back of the room just as the teacher turned around, or who mimicked the teacher behind her back, earning laughs from my classmates and a quick trip to the principal's office.

I came to realize many years later that the principal, Dr. Brooks—whom we called "Hermie-the-Hermit Brooks" because we discovered that her first name was Hermione—was really a very nice person. Though I certainly didn't know it at the time, she regarded all of us affectionately and recognized our need to rebel. But she clothed her affection for us in a no-nonsense, this-will-not-be-tolerated manner, and the disguise was perfect. None of us guessed then that Hermie-the-Hermit actually liked us. We thought she was an ogre who probably ate junior high school kids for dinner, maybe, like french fries, with a little ketchup on the side.

She lectured miscreants calmly and quietly for a first offense, concluding with a doomsday warning. Recidivists could count on punishment from then on, and the sentence was to be escalated every time they reappeared in her outer office. True to her code, Dr. Brooks was increasingly severe with me. Over the course of a semester, I was sentenced to detention, two days detention, three days, ultimately a week. A note to my parents, recommending denial of telephone privileges, finally got my attention. But I couldn't entirely help myself. It wasn't so much defiance as exuberance. Here I was, for the first time in my life, a girl among girls, indulging in girly preteen excess.

Mom sat me down one evening and informed me that if I didn't "clean up my act," my weekend trips to the Westwood Village with Suzi, Arlie, Laura, and Jess would come to an end. l didn't really think my mother was serious. My parents were plainly pleased with my newfound popularity. I couldn't believe they would do anything that risked harming it. However, I'd experienced tough parental discipline before, so I wasn't 100 percent certain.

I tried very hard to behave myself during the remainder of the year. I got into trouble only once, when my homeroom teacher, Mr. Williams, accused me of authoring and circulating something that Jessica Sherman, my pal Jess, had actually written. Done in elaborate calligraphy, it read:

Note to Mr. Williams from his girlfriend:
Roses are red,
Violets are blue.
I'd rather be dead,
Than go out with you.

I protested my innocence without identifying Jess as the culprit, but I was sent off to Dr. Brooks's office, where punishment awaited. I was seated on the chair next to Dr. Brooks's desk—the Prisoner's Dock, we called it—receiving the usual lecture about my misdeeds prior to sentencing when there was a knock on the door.

"Who is it?" Dr. Brooks barked.

"It's Jessica Sherman, Dr. Brooks," said a small voice from the other side of the door. "May I come in? Please."

"I'm busy. Wait there, or come back later, Jessica."

"Dr. Brooks. Please. I need to see you now. It's about Rachel."

Once she was inside the door, Jess said, "Dr. Brooks. Rachel didn't write that. I did. I can't let her take the blame."

I could see how terrified she was. She was trembling.

Dr. Brooks said, "Jessica, I appreciate your desire to save your friend from the punishment she deserves. But Mr. Williams says Rachel did it, and I believe him. All your confession means is that you will be punished along with Rachel. Do you still maintain that you wrote it?"

"Yes, Ma'am. I did it."

It was years before we discovered that Dr. Brooks admired Jess's honesty and was pleased to learn that I was not at fault. But her policy was never to overrule one of her teachers in front of students. So the official decision was that I was guilty and Jess was lying to protect me. Dr. Brooks sentenced us to two days detention each, breaking her usual rule. That would have required letting Jess, who was a first-time offender, off with a lecture and a warning. She did not, however, increase my punishment still further or send another note home to my folks. Happily, I never found out what might have happened to me if Jess hadn't confessed.

We were in eighth grade when Suzi, Arlie, Laura, and Jess realized that I was a year younger than they were. It was bat mitzvah time for Suzi, Arlie, and Laura—Jess was the lone non-Jew among the Fabulous Five, as we called ourselves. But there was no bat mitzvah in the offing for me. I had to admit that I was just turning twelve. I realized that Suzi felt betrayed by the fact that she knew everything there was to know about me but not how old I was. "I'm eleven" was almost the first thing she told me on the day we met. She didn't notice that I failed to respond. Although she was invited to my tenth birthday party and the next year to my eleventh birthday party, age was not specified on either occasion. As I said, I didn't want the others to know how young I was, and Mom agreed not to tell. Suzi simply assumed I was two months younger, not fourteen months.

Once they all knew that I'd deceived them, however, I was in big trouble. Suzi called me a liar, which made me cry. She made me get down on my knees and ask her to forgive me. But she refused to commit herself. She insisted that I write each of them a letter of apology and told me they would meet without me around to decide my fate. Those were the most tear-soaked letters anyone ever wrote. I pleaded. I begged. I said I'd do anything they demanded of me if they'd take me back.

They kept me waiting a couple of days. Then they summoned me to Suzi's house. Arlie, who had anointed herself, without opposition, as our leader, said I deserved to be expelled from the group. They all nodded their agreement. I began to cry once again. I pleaded for mercy. When they finally relented and told me that they'd decided to accept my apologies, I felt as if I'd just been spared the death penalty while already strapped into the electric chair. I was exhausted, exhilarated, humbled, contrite—all at once. I thanked them profusely. I told them I didn't deserve to have such friends. I promised them I'd never tell any of them another lie as long as I lived.

Suzi was slower to take me back than the others. She had me on probation and really made me suffer for about a week. She said she now understood why I was so babyish at times. But once Suzi relented and the ripples subsided, it was as if, on the surface at least, the rock had never been dropped into the pond. Life went on as before.

I celebrated my bat mitzvah at the beginning of ninth grade. The Goodmans came to Santa Monica for the occasion, just as we'd gone to Colorado the previous year for Yalie's. My grandmother and grandfather were there from Israel—alone.

I wanted to do what Yalie had done. I expected to lead the service, read from the Torah, do a Haftorah, and deliver a speech on Anwar Sadat's historic visit to Jerusalem. But we belonged to a Reform temple, and the rabbi considered my plan inappropriate. I was given relatively little to do. He said a speech about Israel and Egypt was out of the question. I couldn't possibly know enough. Especially since he didn't. All I would be allowed to do was to speak a few words about the portion for the week and to thank my parents and teachers. I wanted to be a little funny. He insisted I be entirely serious. Mom, who had little use for rabbis anyway, took the position that he was acting like a pompous fool. She informed him that I would not give any speech during the service but would reserve my talk for the bat mitzvah party afterward. Clearly, he did not appreciate the rebuke. On the day of the bat mitzvah, the tension on the *bimah* might not have been discernable from the audience, but it was palpable from where I was sitting. I did not perform particularly well under the circumstances; I was a nervous wreck the whole time.

Everyone was invited to the party—my closest friends, my next closest friends, girls I was not particularly close to, and all the boys who were my pals when we were younger. The boys, who were mostly at or near fourteen, had begun to grow, but I still towered over them. I was nearly five feet nine inches tall, wearing my first bra and beginning to develop the hint of an actual figure, though, at best, it was a stick figure. The adults all told me how beautiful I was. They were flattering me, of course. But I was straight-backed, proud of my height, and oval-faced. I had flashing dark eyes and curly brown hair. Grandma said that when I smiled, it lit the synagogue. That was *certainly* an exaggeration since I didn't do any smiling from the *bimah* that day.

Nevertheless, it was like a coming-out party for me. I was now officially a girl person. The guys I grew up with saw for the first time that I was somebody they could imagine going to a movie with and trying to kiss. And the other girls, the ones who hadn't always been my very best friends, recognized that I was someone of consequence, a boy magnet—at least for the taller boys. I was no longer trusted as a matchmaker because I might take the guy for myself.

Heidi Bernstein was not invited to my party. Beautiful as always, she remained a sworn enemy. She kept on slandering me mercilessly until I heard about it from one of the boys. I avenged myself by calling the Bernstein household and leaving a message on the answering machine inquiring sweetly whether Heidi's VD treatment was working. We'd never spoken on the phone, but I'm sure Heidi had no difficulty recognizing my voice. I wanted her to understand that if you struck Rachel Rothschild, Rachel Rothschild would strike back. I think she knew that the game was up, because she never troubled me again.

*   *   *

We were finished at Lincoln Junior High now and ready to enter Santa Monica High School. It was a huge, sprawling campus of playing fields and blocky, whitewashed two-story buildings that looked as if they might be inhabited by auto parts makers, clubbed together in a manufacturers' enclave. The school property comprised something like fifty acres of land about six blocks from Santa Monica Pier, across the road from the local government center. It had twice as many students as Lincoln.

No sooner had I begun classes than I was summoned to a meeting with the girls' basketball coach. I was the tallest girl in the entire school, and she wanted me to come out for the team. Though I'd never played basketball, it seemed at first like a great idea. I was a good athlete, I thought, and I could envision myself sauntering around campus in a letter sweater. *Rachel Rothschild—you know her, the all-star basketball player.* My career lasted less than a month. I'd never played basketball, and it showed. Practice turned out to be sweaty work. It took place in the afternoons, which cut into the time reserved for my girlfriends. The coach told me I was "promising." But I sprained my ankle during the third week of practice and had to use crutches. That was the end for me. *Forget about it!*

Apart from crutches, all I got out of my brief career as a basketball player was a lasting friendship with Lynetta Pearson, a smart, bright-eyed black girl. Like me, Lynetta was a newcomer to the school. That was our initial bond, but we also had lockers next to one another and practiced together on the second team. Lynetta enjoyed the game and was a quick study. By the time we were seniors, she was the team's leader.

I was still hobbling around on crutches, my high school athletic career behind me, when disaster struck. Five weeks after we first marched into our classes at the high school, Suzi—Suze by this time—came to our house acting like someone had died. At first she couldn't speak. All she could do was to cling to me and cry. She was so weepy that I also started to cry, not knowing what I was crying about. When Suze finally subsided a little, the story seeped out between sobs. Her father had received a big and unexpected promotion, and they were moving east again, to Cincinnati. Next month!

Then I began crying in earnest, not just in sympathy. We held onto each other and wept until we could weep no more. We had been best friends for four years, and we each thought that losing the other was the worst thing imaginable. We promised to write. We promised to stay best friends forever. All the girls were devastated. We convinced ourselves that life would never be the same without Suze.

When the time came to say our last good-byes, Mom drove me to the airport to see the Orbachs off, bringing Jess Sherman along. Arlie Becker and Laura Ludwig were also there, delivered by Arlie's mother. We clung to one another like vines to a trellis, unable to say a word. Suze's father finally separated Suze from the pack. We were all crying. Arlie, Laura, Jess, and I continued in a knot, clutching one another, with my crutch folded in. Suze followed her parents and her brother and sister through the entryway to the plane, her shoulders shaking.

When the plane was loaded and began to pull away from the gate, my friends and I stood at the window waving all the time it was on the runway. Then it took off and disappeared. Mom put her arm around me, something I did not normally allow. There was nothing for any of us to say, nothing at all.

Returning to equilibrium was not easy. I may have been the hardest hit, but the other members of the Fabulous ex-Five were also traumatized. A fixed part of our world had suddenly vanished, like Atlantis fallen into the sea.

Suze Orbach wasn't the smartest one in our little circle or the prettiest. I was considered the smartest because I got the best grades, and Jess was unquestionably the prettiest. Suze wasn't the dominant personality that Arlie Becker was, or the social tactician (Laura Ludwig's department) or the comedian (Jess Sherman's role). But she was the glue that held us all together, the foil for all the other personalities in the group. She spoke with each of us every evening, knew what each of us planned to wear the following day, kept everyone's calendar in her head, carried out Arlie's instructions, relayed Laura's advice, passed Jess's latest smart-aleck remark along, took pride in my academic achievements. Although she wasn't first in anything, she got very good grades, understood people, had grown in self-confidence, and had learned to be funny enough to make us all laugh.

We talked about the possibility of replacing Suze. My candidate was Lynetta Pearson. Although my basketball career had ended, Lynetta was in a couple of my classes, and I liked her a lot. It would have to be a group decision, of course, but I invited Lynetta one day to join us on a trip to Westwood Village. That would give the others a chance to get to know her. Her answer was that she didn't have time for just hanging out. Her mom was a schoolteacher and insisted that Lynetta study when she wasn't practicing. It wasn't until much later that I learned the real reason that Lynetta wasn't interested. She was afraid of being accused by her black classmates of wanting to be white. For different reasons, none of the other prospective candidates worked out either.

So the five become four, and sometimes we weren't quite enough for one another. I had lost my chief admirer, Arlie her executive officer, Laura her relay station, and Jess her most appreciative audience. Now that Suze was gone, there was no one to smooth over the tiny irritations, the annoyances, we sometimes felt toward one another. I hadn't previously minded Arlie's bossiness or Laura's manipulations or Jess's apparent inability to be serious. And the others hadn't been quite so bothered by my exaggerated opinion of my own intelligence. While Suze was around, her pleasure at my accomplishments was so genuine that I felt no need to boast. Now I couldn't wait to tell the other girls that I'd aced a history test or been praised by the math teacher.

No one in our circle had ever objected to my brainpower—until then. Now Jess began to make jokes at my expense. I was the Big Brain in the Bottle or HAL, the Supercomputer gone awry in *2001*. I was Albert Einstein's Stepdaughter. I was Dr. Know-It-All. Unlike most of Jess's other jokes, I didn't think this was at all funny. However, it was effective. I soon stopped patting myself on the back.

The four of us finally managed to settle down after a sleepover at Jess's house in which we exposed our grievances and our vulnerabilities, enjoyed a wholesale crying jag, and finally, in the early hours of the morning, proclaimed our undying love for one another. After that, we were a lot more careful about how we handled each other than when Suze was there to serve like a sheathed copper wire, acting both as insulator and go-between.

Jess, with her humor, was now our buffer. She gave each of us a nickname. Arlie, who spouted instructions as regularly as Old Faithful, was Big Boss Becker or simply Boss. Laura, our social counselor, was Dr. Lovelorn. I became Einstein, which was a somewhat kinder reference to my academic skills than Jess had tagged me with earlier. Jess referred to herself as Bozo the Clown, or simply Bozo, as in "Bozo wants to go to the Village after school. Is that okay, Boss?" The other kids at school heard these names often enough that they also began to employ them. I got used to being greeted with "Hey, Einstein" when I ran into a classmate in the hall.

Since Jess was satirizing herself as well as the rest of us, we all accepted it with good humor, though we each understood the implicit criticism inherent in the nicknames we were given. As Bozo, Jess remained free to continue clowning, but the rest of us understood our deficiencies far better than we had before Jess pinned us like butterflies in a scrapbook and gave us labels.

I was fourteen by now and in full throttle adolescence. Though I was willing to accept Arlie's direction, which now came wrapped in cotton, and to listen carefully to Laura's softly-delivered advice, I dismissed my mother's suggestions with unconcealed impatience. "Oh, *Mother*," I would say. "You're so Dark Ages. *Nobody* does X anymore" —X being the mathematical variable for wearing knee-length skirts to school or going to bed at 10 p.m. or arriving home before midnight on the weekend or not going out (actually, not being *allowed* to go out) with any guy over fifteen.

No one had a mother who interfered as much with a daughter's life as Mom did. *No* one had a more old-fashioned mother.

I tolerated Daddy, but he too acted as if I weren't fourteen and in high school. I thought my folks ought to be concentrating on the twins, who were such babies, or on Rebecca, who was always using my things and trying to listen in on my private phone conversations. *"Honestly,"* I told my friends, "parents are so *stupid*." Arlie, Laura, and Jess said they'd noticed the same thing about their parents.

My attitude exasperated Mom no end. With hindsight, I suspect it was all she could do not to smack me across the face when I rolled my eyes and challenged her to combat over what to eat, what to wear, when to get up, when to go to bed, where to be at what hour of the day or night. Mom tried to avoid getting into a test of wills with fourteen-year-old me. However, I was *always* ready for a fight, and Mom often obliged me. We shouted at one another a good deal, and it regularly ended with me screaming, "I hate you" and slamming the door to my room as hard as I could.

Though I was forbidden to smoke, I left cigarettes around where they could be discovered, as much to annoy my parents as for any other reason. I didn't even *like* tobacco. Confining me to my room had no effect—or at least no *beneficial* effect from my parents' standpoint. I sulked through my punishment, and when it was done found another way to offend. I talked often about running away from home, although I had no intention of doing so. Getting Mom's goat was my chief pleasure, and I collected an entire herd of Mom's goats—a large and ever-growing herd.

I also got into more serious trouble. My friends and I smoked marijuana and consumed three cases of beer at a weekend house party and left the place in a shambles. The boys at the party were chiefly responsible. But I got a thundering lecture from Daddy, and for once I neither talked back nor pretended indifference. Daddy's anger intimidated me. If I'd been a puppy, I would have hung my head and put my tail between my legs. I actually said, "I'm sorry." No one in the Rothschild household had heard those words from me in a very long time.

My friends and I hung out with guys now. When the phone rang, it was almost as likely to be a boy as one of my girlfriends. I was now considered slim instead of merely skinny. I was also very fashion-conscious in a style that might have been described as Montmartre-on-the-beach. When Mom didn't physically prevent it, I wore short skirts and tight sweaters (though, truth be told, I was far too flat-chested for the tightness to reveal much). I became very conscious of my powers over the boys I was interested in. Which is to say anyone who was a year or two older than me, was at least five feet ten inches tall, and had a penis. My friends and I talked a lot about boys and "doing it." I hadn't done it yet. I was fascinated … and afraid, though I wouldn't admit it.

I was almost fifteen when I had my first period. My girlfriends had gotten there way ahead of me—and it wasn't just that they were older than me. My doctor told me that it wasn't unusual for somebody with my build to begin relatively late. Still, I felt reassured when it happened. It was another reason to think about Doing It.

When I was barely fifteen, a Santa Monica policeman found me half-undressed with Arnie Haas, one of the tall boys I admired, in the back seat of his parents' parked car, which he was driving illegally. I begged the policeman not to tell my parents but, of course, he did. Mom was the one who stormed at me this time, and she cut right through my defenses. I simply wasn't prepared for the ferocity of the attack. I even agreed to a ban on further contact with Arnie.

Despite the fact that *It* didn't happen, I knew it soon would. I asked Laura, Dr. Lovelorn, what to do. She told me that she and Jess had already been to Planned Parenthood to obtain birth control pills. She advised me and Arlie to do the same. Arlie really wasn't ready, but she yielded to my entreaties to come along. I wouldn't have had the nerve to go alone. Once we arrived at the clinic, I had a hard time explaining what we doing there. It was pretty obvious to the woman in charge. She gave us the pills but advised us not to have sex prematurely. That was not an option, however. It was the Age, and I was the age.

Within weeks after beginning on the pill, I gave up my virginity to another of my high school friends—actually Charlie Harrison, one of my main pals from when I was eight and a tomboy—in the dark backyard of a neighbor who was on vacation. I felt it was a required event, something I had to do to keep pace with my girlfriends. Even while it was happening, I was thinking about what I would tell Arlie, Laura, and Jess—that is, Boss, Dr. Lovelorn, and Bozo. I thought I might even tell Suze. I owed her a letter, and I felt this was news worth communicating. But I certainly didn't enjoy the act itself. I was afraid of getting pregnant or catching a venereal disease. As a result, I was a belt-and-suspenders girl. I was taking The Pill, but I also insisted that he wear a condom. Let me tell you: Watching a guy roll a rubber onto his wienie is not exactly conducive to romance.

I "went all the way," which was how we described it, with two different guys in high school, maybe a total of six or seven times. I pretended to them and to my girlfriends that I craved sex. You were *supposed* to want it. I liked my childhood pal, Charlie Harrison, well enough, and for a while I convinced myself that I was in love with Adam Popkin, whom I went out with regularly during my senior year. But the truth is that both of them were lousy lovers, stingy with words, incompetent in foreplay, and quick to explode. I liked boys. I just didn't like having sex with them.

In this I was unlike Laura, who considered sex no big deal—just something girls and boys did to show they liked each other—or Jess, who argued that girls had as much right to orgasms as guys and practiced what she preached with her steady boyfriend, Michael Cohen.

We were nearly full grown now. Thin and flat-chested as I was, I had the bearing and gaunt good looks of a fashion model. It was that, not any of my features, not even my dark eyes and curly dark hair, that made people think of me as beautiful. Jess Sherman, the next tallest at five feet six inches, was slightly built and angular. But she had expressive brown eyes, dark wavy hair, cupid's-bow lips, an olive complexion, and a bright and constant smile. Jess was generally accounted gorgeous by everyone, male and female. She was still the class comedian. Arlie Becker, at five feet five inches and about a hundred pounds, was thinner even than I was and always on a diet. She appeared to have no body at all. In retrospect, she was probably anorexic. Arlie's outstanding characteristics were her quickness and her readiness to command. She told everybody what to do and was almost invariably the first to raise her hand in class, the first to finish every test, the first out of the room when the bell rang. Arlie went out with boys, but she had no one who could be considered a boyfriend. Laura Ludwig, the shortest member of our group at five feet two inches, had delicate features complemented by big dark eyes. Her face was framed by long dark hair, which she usually wore in a perky ponytail. With her nicely rounded chest and curvy behind, she was the most feminine and the sexiest member of our crowd. Laura was an indifferent student, but a dedicated friend. She might not have understood that boys were taking advantage of her, but she was very perceptive about me, Jess, and Arlie and, as always, she was extremely generous with her advice.

Our friendship was deeper than ever. At Arlie's insistence, we formed a book club—and read one book, Simone de Beauvoir's *The Second Sex*—before deciding we were too busy with schoolwork for additional reading assignments. We collaborated on an alternative school newspaper, a teenage feminist magazine, which we called *The Female Revolution*. Arlie, of course, was the editor. That went without saying. We published three issues before we lost interest. Nevertheless, I learned something important from that brief episode: I liked writing for an audience.

The four of us knew one another inside out. We knew each other's strengths, each other's weaknesses. We had accepted each other for who we were. I was insecure about a lot of things when I was fifteen, but never about Arlie, Laura, and Jess. I could always count on them, and they could count on me.

During spring vacation of our junior year, Yalie came alone to Santa Monica for a visit. Even beautiful Jess was in the shadows next to Yalie. Yalie was sixteen, and every boy's idea of the most gorgeous girl he'd ever seen outside the *Sports Illustrated* swimsuit issue. She had perfect features on a perfect face atop a perfectly formed female body with curves in all the places girls were supposed to have curves. She had green eyes and honey-blond hair that curled naturally into ringlets. At five feet six inches, the same as Jess, she was just the right height for most guys, neither too tall nor too short. Yet, perhaps because she was smarter than any of the guys and didn't bother to conceal it, Yalie had no boyfriends. She rarely dated. Boys were afraid to approach her. It was as if she were unattainable.

If we'd been in high school together, it's possible that Yalie and

I might have been rivals. We were both determined to be number one academically. But we weren't at school together, and we loved each other. Yalie fit quickly and easily into my circle of friends. In spite of her exceptional good looks, Yalie had no problem with other girls. Yes, she was prettier. Yes, she was smarter. But she was fun to be with (provided you were another girl), and she would never steal your boyfriend. She was as afraid of boys as they were of her. Unlike me, Yalie had no ongoing quarrel with Mom or Daddy, so she was more of a pleasure to have around the house than I was. Her presence had a calming influence on me. The household was unusually tranquil during the week she was around.

Mom had the twins and Rebecca to worry about, so she couldn't take Yalie around as much as she'd have liked. But Daddy took a day off to show Yalie more of Los Angeles than she'd previously had an opportunity to see. I asked if I could bring Arlie, Laura, and Jess along. So there were six of us in our family wagon. He drove us north up the beach to Malibu, then into Beverly Hills to gaze at the sumptuous homes of movie stars, then into the Hollywood Hills, then east on the busy freeways to Pasadena to see the Rose Bowl and the Norton Simon Museum with its wondrous collection of European art and sculpture. On the way back, he took us to see the La Brea Tar Pits and all those specimens of dinosaurs and other prehistoric creatures.

Some bits were new even to Arlie, Laura, Jess, and me. We pretended, of course, of course, to be unimpressed. But we *were* impressed, especially by the Rodin bronzes at the Norton Simon Museum, which none of us had ever seen. I think Daddy enjoyed chauffeuring a buzzing hive of young females, and I'm sure he learned more about us that day than he ever heard from me. He told me afterward that he discovered that my nickname was Einstein, that Arlie was called Boss, that Laura was Dr. Lovelorn, and that Jess was Bozo. I had to tell him how I got my nickname. That was embarrassing. When you're fifteen, *everything* is embarrassing.

Daddy was exposed to all the gossip and intimate exchanges that the five of us were capable of in seven hours together. I'm sure he found out more about me and Yalie than he would have in a month of police interrogation. We were having a marvelous time together. Daddy said he had a good time, too, though he'd heard enough squealing and giggling to last him the rest of his life—or at least until Rebecca was my age.

On other days, the five of us would go to Westwood Village to hang out, shop, eat lunch, go to the movies, and hang out some more. We played tennis together. We swam together. We went running together on the beach road. Even though we considered ourselves a bit too grown up for it, we even went bike riding. I gave Yalie my bike and borrowed Noah's. Jess gave Yalie a nickname, too. It started out as Harvard, and by the end of the week had progressed to Harvie.

On the last night of her visit, Yalie and I, lying side by side in my big bed, stayed up until 3:30 a.m. talking about our futures. That was when we decided to go to the same university and room together. We also decided to beg our parents to allow us to go to Israel together during the summer. If we had to, we'd enlist our grandparents in the cause.

It was a glorious week. My girlfriends really liked Yalie, and that brought two halves of my life together. I no longer had to agonize over whether Yalie was my best friend or Arlie, Laura, and Jess were my best friends. Now that they all knew each other, they could all be my best friends.

The process of persuading Mom and Daddy to allow me and Yalie to travel to Israel together began immediately. We found a program for teens, involving some time on a kibbutz, and tried to persuade our parents that it was just right for both of us. The first response from my parents was encouraging, but Mom told me that my attitude needed to improve "a lot" before she would grant me such a privilege. I didn't know it until later, but Daddy, meanwhile, talked with Aunt Ruth and Uncle Aaron about their willingness to let Yalie go. Then he called my grandparents in Tel Aviv to see if they could handle a visit from their two granddaughters in the summer.

My grandparents were past seventy now and beginning to slow down a little, but they were genuinely enthusiastic about the prospect of having us in Israel. Grandpa said he'd heard of the program we were considering. Since I'd never had a real job and Yalie had only helped out a little in a local dress shop, Grandpa thought the experience would be really good for us. He thought Avital, whom we hadn't seen in a number of years, might join us.

These arrangements were made, and the airplane tickets were

purchased without our being told. Our parents continued to use the trip as leverage to modify our behavior. I'd have to say that the strategy worked exceptionally well on me. I hadn't been this good or this thoughtful in years. I wore acceptable clothing, kept my curfew, and carefully ignored Mom and Daddy's deficiencies (which remained as plentiful as ever). Mom, no doubt, thought that someone had kidnapped her own Rachel and substituted a well-mannered look-alike. Yalie had never been much of a problem for her parents, but I know that she, too, did everything she possibly could to convince Uncle Aaron and Aunt Ruth that she deserved to go. By the beginning of May, we were starting to fret. I broke down in tears over dinner one evening, and that's when Mom and Daddy announced that we could go to Israel as soon as school ended. Jubilation reigned. I hugged and kissed them, having suddenly discovered that they were the best parents on earth.

Then I called Yalie. Her parents hadn't gotten around to telling her yet, so she was getting the news from me. She began screaming with joy. After she calmed down a little, we talked about everything from clothes we would take to what we intended to do when we got to Israel. That was the first of a half dozen phone conversations that we had covering essentially the same ground. I was more excited than I'd ever been.

I couldn't wait to tell my friends. Arlie had been to England, France, Germany, and Italy, but never to Israel. Jess had visited Hawaii, Mexico, and the Caribbean, and knew how to speak a little Spanish. Laura had been all over the western United States but, other than a short jaunt to the Yucatan, had never been out of the country. The four of us weren't normally jealous of one another, but I know they envied me. They would each have liked to have grandparents who lived abroad and invited them to come for the summer.

Yalie and I arrived in Israel the first week of June. Grandma and Grandpa met us at Ben Gurion Airport with hugs and kisses. They'd brought our cousin Avital along. Yalie and I hadn't seen her since we were in Israel nine years earlier for her second brother's bar mitzvah, so we were nearly strangers to one another. Although Daddy and Aunt Ruth had been to Israel a couple of times in the interim to visit my grandparents, neither Yalie nor I had gone on those trips. Avital was a very open, friendly kid, dark-eyed and dark-haired like me. In fact, though I was a lot taller than she was, people might still have mistaken us for sisters. On the way into Tel Aviv, she pointed the sights out to us and brought us up to date on her family. By the time we got to Grandma and Grandpa's apartment, we were friends. Her English was now pretty good. Not only had she taken it in school, she had English-speaking parents and grandparents around to help her with the accent.

Aunt Shoshana and Uncle El were waiting for us when we got to the apartment. Aunt Shoshana told us we were beautiful young ladies. I was taller than both my aunt and uncle, so they marveled at that. "You look just like a model," Aunt Shoshana said. That was typical adult flattery. On the other hand, when she told Yalie she was gorgeous, no exaggeration was required. "The boys must be mad for you," Aunt Shoshana said, and Yalie gave an embarrassed shrug.

"What was I supposed to say?" she asked me later. "'I'm sixteen years old and never been kissed?' 'Boys are usually mad *at* me, not mad *for* me.' Why do adults always assume boys are crazy about me? It's just not true." She was crying, and I tried to comfort her. I hadn't realized until then how sensitive Yalie was about her lack of popularity with the guys. My beautiful cousin at sixteen was afraid of boys. Just terrified. I told her they were nothing special—just horny little toads. Even my playmates from my tomboy days were horny little toads now. I had her laughing before we fell asleep that night.

With her sons fully grown and gone from the house, Aunt Shoshana was free to devote herself to Avital and us. She took us all over Tel Aviv and to the Port of Jaffa, an enclave of sophisticated shops, restaurants, and apartments adjacent to the old city of Jaffa and overlooking the Mediterranean. This was the first time that Yalie and I had walked the streets of Tel Aviv, and we loved the city's bustle, the sidewalk cafes filled with kids our age and a little older, the rock music blaring from storefronts, the dress shops filled with fashionable clothing. Numbers of people aside, Tel Aviv is a big city, whereas Jerusalem is just a collection of neighborhoods distributed among and around ancient buildings and holy spaces. Jerusalem is a beautiful city. Tel Aviv is kind of ugly. Jerusalem is history. Jerusalem is religion. Jerusalem is where people go to be awed by Israel. Tel Aviv is where they come to feel the spirit and energy of Israel.

After a week in Tel Aviv, Aunt Shoshana carted us off to Jerusalem.

I'm sure Grandpa and Grandma must have been exhausted by the time we left. Even though we'd tried to be a lot more considerate than we would have been in our own homes, we made a lot of extra work, and we were up late every night. I know they enjoyed having us, but I suspect they were also glad to see us go for a time.

In Jerusalem, Aunt Shoshana allowed Avital to take us around the Old City and the new city. Both of us had been to Jerusalem as children and remembered a little of it, but seeing it through the eyes of another teenager was very special. Avital took us to the *Mahane Yehuda*, the outdoor market where working-class Jews, the Ultra-Orthodox, and well-dressed bargain hunters from all over the city bought their necessities. It was a bit like the Farmers' Market back home, with fruits and vegetables piled in abundant mounds and bright-colored flower stands and shoppers crowded around. But these customers were entirely unlike any I'd ever encountered. They competed noisily for the attention of the vendors and then haggled with them over prices. There were swarthy "Oriental" Jews from Morocco and Syria—the Sephardim. There were bearded men, young and old, with their curled earlocks and black hats. But among the Ultra-Orthodox, at least, it was the women who did most of the shopping. They came in all shapes. Most wore very long, deliberately unfashionable dresses, with sleeves down to their wrists and kerchiefs or babushkas. Those without kerchiefs had wigs that covered their own hair, as is customary among the Orthodox. They weren't one little bit like the Jews Yalie and I knew back home.

Conversation took place in a free-floating mixture of Yiddish and Hebrew, with some Russian thrown in along with occasional French, German, or Polish. Through Mom, I understood a little Yiddish if it was spoken slowly and distinctly, and both Yalie and I could understand some Hebrew. But neither of us was capable of following a conversation when the words flowed rapidly, so we were dependent on Avital to explain what we were hearing as well as what we were seeing. We didn't buy anything at the *Mahane Yehuda*, but Avital also took us to the bazaar in the Old City, where Yalie and I bought souvenirs. When she took us to Ben Yehuda Street, the main shopping thoroughfare, I purchased a silver Star of David on a long silver chain.

Uncle El took us again to the Israel Museum, which we'd seen years earlier at the time of our cousin's bar mitzvah. I had only the vaguest memory of the previous visit, but this time Uncle El explained the significance of the artifacts we were looking at. He had studied biblical archeology at Hebrew University after the 1956 war, and he was an expert on the Second Temple period. I suspect Yalie and I enjoyed it a lot more than Avital did. She'd heard it all before and, besides, Uncle El was her father, so what could he possibly know that mattered to her?

After dark, there wasn't much to do, and, unlike Tel Aviv, Jerusalem was shut tight on Friday night and Saturday for Shabbat. The Ben Ya'acovs were no more religious than my folks or Yalie's were, but Uncle El took Avital and us on a synagogue tour of Central Jerusalem one Friday evening. Before we entered each synagogue, Uncle El explained what we were about to see. Once services began at the final stop on our tour, we had to separate, Uncle El to one side, the three of us to the other, as required by Orthodox religious practice. As a result, we had only a dim grasp of what was happening. We couldn't follow the service without page numbers being given from the *bimah*. No two congregants seemed to use the same prayer book, and there were no English translations. Avital was as mystified by the proceedings as Yalie and I were.

The week in Jerusalem ended, and Uncle El drove the three of us to the kibbutz in the Galilee where we'd been assigned for a month of labor. The place had been established not long after Israel's War of Independence: two hundred twenty families, about nine hundred people in all, living in one-story homes built out of cinder block, spread around a core of communal buildings. The business of the kibbutz was mainly farming, but there was also a small plastics factory, a guest house built to accommodate tourists, and a high school that served half a dozen kibbutzim in the area. The kids in the program numbered thirty, half girls and half boys. We were from all over. Avital was the only Israeli. More than half the kids were from the United States. They came from New York, Boston, Philadelphia, Cleveland, Chicago, and Washington, D.C. The group included another girl from Los Angeles and a boy from San Diego. In addition, there were kids from Canada, France, England, Argentina, and a couple of non-Jews from Germany and Sweden.

The kibbutznik in charge of the volunteers was Amichai Barat, a big, strongly built South African Jew, who was maybe forty-five years old and, like most Israelis his age, a veteran of both the Six Day War of June 1967 and the Yom Kippur War of 1973. He used English sparingly with us. He wanted us to become accustomed to hearing Hebrew. Except for a boy from Montreal who was fluent in the language, it was a real struggle. I was dependent on Avital to translate half of what Amichai said and to supplement my meager vocabulary. But with afternoon language classes, I was beginning to make genuine progress. I could almost follow a Hebrew conversation. At least I got the subject, and I could say a few simple sentences without stumbling all over myself.

Yalie didn't have to come to Avital for help. From the first hour of the first day, the boy from Montreal, Richard Axelrod—Axie—was at her side every moment. He was smitten, and Yalie was ripe for romance. Overripe, I'd say, like a squishy peach that's been left on the tree too long. They didn't exactly fall into bed together. Yalie wasn't like that. Axie plainly wanted her, but he wasn't crude about it the way lots of guys are. He came a-courtin', like Froggy in the song we sang as children. He charmed her. He was handsome, funny, and easy to like. By the end of the first week on the kibbutz, the two of them were spending every spare minute together, and Yalie was breathlessly in love. She hurriedly got a supply of birth control pills from the kibbutz infirmary. Although I was in Israel to be with Yalie, I didn't resent the time she spent with Axie. I was happy for her. She really needed to have a boy in love with her and to love him back.

They worked us extremely hard on the kibbutz. We arose at dawn each morning. We spent much of the day in the fields, doing whatever task we were assigned. Cleaning out the chicken houses was the job I disliked the most. It was filthy work, and the stench was awful. We also helped out a little in the communal kitchen and dining room, cutting vegetables, dishing out the food, and cleaning up. Yalie was good in the kitchen. I wasn't. Never had been. Mostly, I was assigned cleanup duties. Despite our long duty hours, Yalie somehow found the energy to spend evenings with Axie. But every night, I fell into bed exhausted and slept a dreamless sleep. It was by far the most physical labor I'd ever done. I was beginning to feel like a real kibbutznik.

A little over three weeks into our month-long program, Avital, Yalie, and I were summoned from the fields to the communal center. For the first time, our South African supervisor spoke to Avital in rapid

Hebrew and to Yalie and me in English. There had been an accident, we were told, and Avital's father had been injured. He didn't know the details. Grandpa was on the way to pick us up. I did the packing for all three of us. There was no other way. Avital was in too much distress to help, and I sent Yalie off to say good-bye to Axie. They needed the time together.

Yalie still hadn't returned when Grandpa arrived. Amichai had to go find her. Axie came with her. He had his arm around her, and Yalie was crying like I'd never seen her cry before. Amichai practically had to pry them apart to get Yalie into the car. Grandpa was pretty angry with her. "You ought to be a lot more concerned about Avital and a little less concerned about yourself, young lady," he said. I thought scolding her publicly was totally unfair. Yalie just cried harder. She said she was sorry but could barely get the words out.

Although he was tough on Yalie, Grandpa was very tender with Avital. He hugged her the whole time we were waiting for Yalie to show up. All we were told was that Uncle El had been in a car wreck and that he'd been badly injured. We didn't know until we got back to Jerusalem that he was dead, killed instantly in a pileup on the coast highway from Tel Aviv to Haifa.

On the drive back, Yalie was preoccupied with her own misery about being separated from Axie. Meanwhile, I did my best to comfort Avital. Uncle El had been wonderful to me. He was the one who first showed us Israel years ago. Only a couple of weeks earlier, he'd taken us through the Israel Museum and been our guide to the synagogues of Jerusalem.

Avital worked at being brave. She kept saying that Uncle El would be all right. He'd been through a couple of Israel's wars, and he was indestructible. I had to dig my fingernails into my palms to prevent myself from crying. I didn't want to undermine Avital's strength. When we got to Jerusalem, we were met in the street outside the family apartment by Avital's older brother. He was the one who broke the bad news. Avital insisted he had to be wrong. She said that her Abba, her father, couldn't be dead. Her brother just shook his head. There were tears in his eyes. Avital fell apart. I was crying, too, and for the first time Yalie began crying about Uncle El instead of about Axie. Between sobs, she told me that she was thoroughly ashamed of herself. Grandpa had been right. I told her not to blame herself. She couldn't know that

Uncle El was dead. Grandpa just didn't understand about being in love for the first time.

Once we were upstairs, Aunt Shoshana emerged from the bedroom where she'd been lying down and took Avital into her arms. Avital's wails caused everyone's composure to collapse. Aunt Shoshana was weeping. Grandma was weeping. The two sons held onto one another and sobbed. Grandpa, who had forced himself to hold his emotions in during the drive from the kibbutz, sat forlornly in the corner wiping his tears on his handkerchief. Yalie went over to him and asked to be forgiven, and he took her onto his lap. They sat there together with her crying and him patting her on the back. I sat there beside them, leaning on Grandpa's shoulder and holding Yalie's hand. It was the worst moment I'd ever experienced. The worst.

The apartment was filled with people I didn't know. Neighbors, friends of the family, Uncle El's coworkers from the Israel Museum, his buddies from the army. People were trying to comfort Aunt Shoshana, Avital, the boys, Grandma, Grandpa, even me and Yalie. A few were too preoccupied with their own grief to do much except sit or stand around in a state of shock.

Little by little, the worst of the crying subsided. Just a muffled sob here and there. A rabbi arrived to make funeral arrangements. The brothers handled that, sparing Aunt Shoshana.

Daddy and Aunt Ruth were on their way from the United States. A friend would meet them at the airport.

More friends arrived to offer condolences. Avital retreated to her bedroom. Aunt Shoshana moved back and forth between the new arrivals and her daughter. Grandma asked Yalie and me to help dish out the food that people had brought in. We welcomed having something useful to do. Since I was not to be trusted with full plates of food, Yalie did the carrying. I did the best I could with the dishing out.

Food was served. People ate. More tears were shed. Avital emerged from the back of the apartment looking the way she must have felt, her eyes bloodshot, a dazed look on her countenance. Grandma brought her a cup of hot tea, and suddenly she was crying again, her chest heaving, and then she was screaming *"lo, lo, lo"* —*no* in Hebrew—which trailed off into a high keening noise of utter misery. Aunt Shoshana sat down beside her and held her tightly around the shoulder until she subsided. Like vibrating strings on a violin, Yalie and I wept along with Avital.

Daddy and Aunt Ruth arrived, red-eyed from lack of sleep and from the shock. Aunt Shoshana fell on them and began crying again. So did Avital. And so did Yalie and I.

The funeral took place within hours after they arrived. When Uncle El's body was lowered into his grave, Avital broke down once again. She couldn't bear to say good-bye. One of her brothers hugged her to him and kissed her on the forehead. And then it was done.

Yalie and I returned to the United States three days later with Daddy and Aunt Ruth. I felt a lot older and a lot more experienced than I was when I'd left home six weeks earlier.

*   *   *

Uncle El's death left me numb. I went to Westwood Village with Arlie, Laura, and Jess, but it wasn't the same as it had always been. I felt as if I had entered a new phase. For the first time really, I was beginning to think seriously about what I would do with my life. Not daydreams, but thoughts about some kind of career. I had always known I would go to college, but going to college had been the goal, not what I would study there or what I would do after college.

When we were younger, my girlfriends and I had the usual discussions about "the meaning of life," but they'd usually ended with Jess saying something like "The meaning of life is shopping, so let's go shopping." It wasn't possible to talk about serious things for very long with Bozo as part of the conversation. Besides, the talk hadn't been real enough for any of us to tell Jess to stop fooling around. She always cracked us up.

But now I needed to talk about the future, and my friends weren't going to be a lot of help. Like me, they expected to go to college, and that was pretty much it. Arlie intended to apply to Stanford, where her father had gone, but she had no clear idea what she would study. Engineering maybe. Laura, our advice-giver, said she liked the idea of being a doctor, though all of us knew that the sight of blood made her nauseous. Jess, ever in character, said she intended to study "drinking beer, smoking pot, and getting laid" in college. Although it went against my principle of never asking parental advice, I asked Daddy how he decided to become a screenwriter.

He said, "The first thing is that I was a teenager. My father would have liked me to study medicine, and that was the one thing I was determined never to do. I wanted to be an actor. That drove my father crazy, which was one of the best reasons I had for wanting to be an actor."

I laughed because at that point in my life, not doing what my parents wanted me to do was also one of my chief motivations.

Daddy went on. "Then I got into Yale. Grandpa was sure I'd come to my senses there. But the reason I wanted Yale was because of its drama department. Problem was; I wasn't much of an actor. 'Rothschild,' my acting teacher said, 'you can't act worth a damn. If you keep at it, you'll ruin Yale's reputation. Why don't you go to the NYU film school and become a writer? If you're no good as a screenwriter, at least they'll blame NYU instead of Yale.' And the rest is history."

I laughed again but said, "Oh, Daddy. Seriously."

He said, "Okay, Rache. It wasn't quite like that. I went to Yale intending to be a playwright. One of the professors I worked with told me I had a good visual imagination and suggested I ought to think about writing for films. That's really how it happened. But it all started with my liking theater and the movies as a teenager. I had no desire to be a doctor like Grandpa, and he didn't try to push me in that direction. He let me find my own way."

I asked, "So, what do you think I ought to do, Daddy?"

He answered, "I can't decide for you, Rache. Tell you what I'll do, though. I'll arrange for you to talk to some people about career choices, and maybe that will suggest some directions."

So Daddy made up a schedule that called for me to talk with one of his lawyer friends and go to court with him, to meet with a guidance counselor at UCLA about academic careers, to tag along on hospital rounds with a surgeon Daddy knew, to learn about the film industry from one of his associates at the studio, and to visit the *Los Angeles Times* with a family friend who was one of the paper's top editors.

As it happened, the first item on the agenda was a visit to the *Los Angeles Times* newsroom with Amanda Collins, who'd been a friend of the family since I was a child. I had never been a particularly avid newspaper reader. Though I usually looked at the comics and read the gossip columns, I'd never cared much about "the news." I'd had a lot of fun working on the three issues of our little alternative high school newspaper, *The Female Revolution*, but that was just a lark. I had never given serious thought to a career in journalism. On the visit with Ms. Collins—Amanda—the glamour of the profession really caught me. It was early evening, and the place was humming with activity. There was this huge newsroom, filled with row on row of desks, all of them cluttered with paper, coffee cups, notebooks, copy pencils, and other paraphernalia. A couple dozen men and women were working the phones, scribbling notes and typing their stories. Reporters and editors were conferring. Copy boys and girls fetched and delivered—wire copy, files of clippings, fresh cups of coffee, a pizza. People at central desks shouted instructions to someone halfway across the room or demanded copy from another someone. It was like a living version of one of those Brueghel paintings that I'd often seen in Mom's collection of art books. A couple hundred different people doing a couple hundred different things.

Amanda arranged for me to talk to several reporters who weren't on deadline. One of them covered City Hall, another the police beat, and a third the Los Angeles Dodgers. She got one of the paper's editorial writers to tell me about the editorials and the Op Ed columns that would appear in the next morning's paper. Amanda explained to me how decisions were made about which articles would appear on the front page.

She showed me the list of stories being prepared for all sections of the next day's paper. She even took me into the room where the news tickers chattered bringing reports from around the country and around the world. I was allowed to sit beside a rewrite man as he took a story over the phone from a reporter in the field. I watched while headlines were written, the front page was assembled, and copy was proofread. Around 1:00 a.m., she took me into a glass enclosure in the press room so I could watch the presses begin to roll, shaking the floor, roaring like distant thunder. Then, freshly printed newspapers were brought into the newsroom, and there it all was—the day's news as it would appear in the morning on doorsteps all over the metropolitan area.

What I would do with my life became as clear that night as it had been murky that morning. I burned with desire to be a newspaper woman. I turned into a news junkie. I followed the bylines of the reporters I'd met, understanding a little now about the "beats" they covered. I talked so often with Amanda about developments in the news that Mom told me I had to stop being a pest. Amanda said it was no bother, that she was really pleased that I was interested because her own kids sure weren't. I guess teenagers are teenagers in every family.

I continued with the meetings Daddy had arranged for me, but none of the other visits made a favorable impression. I couldn't imagine defending criminals who deserved to go to jail or taking care of sick people or getting a Ph.D. in sociology or biology or history. I certainly didn't want to take a job in the movie industry where my father had a big reputation and I'd be known as "Hillel Rothschild's daughter."

When my senior year in high school began in September, I immediately signed up to work on the school newspaper, as Amanda had advised. The teacher who supervised its preparation and production showed me how to write a news lead and how to expand it into a complete story. She told me to make sure to get everybody's name spelled correctly and, if I was quoting someone, to get the words down exactly and not make anything up. The other seniors who worked on the paper had been at it for a couple of years, and they had the most desirable beats. I drew the assignment of covering girls' sports, a job that would normally fall to a sophomore or junior. But I dug in as if I'd been assigned to cover the White House. The first thing I did was to interview my ex-teammate, Lynetta Pearson, who was now a starting guard on the school's basketball team and its leader. I asked her in passing where she was planning to go to college. It was a subject on the mind of every senior.

"UCLA," she said. "They have a good premed program."

"You want to be a doctor?"

"That's the plan, girl. My father's head of the Santa Monica Health Department. Didn't you know? It's what I've wanted since I was a little girl."

"Are you going to try to play basketball, too?"

"If I'm good enough to make the team, why not? I can walk and chew gum at the same time."

That's the story I wrote. "The doctor's in," it began. "Lynetta (Doc) Pearson, point guard on the girl's basketball team, will be seeing patients in a few years. Right now she's using her patience to dissect opposing defenses. And this Doc really knows how to operate." Awfully corny, I'll admit, but it gave Lynetta a lasting nickname. It was also my first byline, and it thrilled me like nothing I'd ever done before. I felt like an actress must feel when her name goes up on a movie marquee for the very first time.

I couldn't explain it to Arlie, Laura, and Jess. They didn't understand why the newspaper was so important to me or why having a byline was such a big deal. For the first time in years, the ones I turned to for approval were Daddy and Mom. Daddy was a writer himself and knew the thrill of having your name appear on something you've written. Mom had worked for years to establish her reputation as a painter, so she understood, too. "I won a competition in high school when I was about your age," she told me, "and the winning painting was hung on the wall in a neighborhood restaurant. That was the most important thing that had ever happened to me, Rache. It showed me I could be a professional artist and maybe some day exhibit in a major gallery."

I mustered the nerve to visit the community newspaper to ask the editor whether he'd be interested in letting me report for free on a local government meeting. The editor, who had more space to fill than people to help him fill it, saw no harm in letting me try. So I headed off to an evening meeting of the city council. I hadn't read anything in advance about items on the agenda and had a hard time following the discussion. I was almost ready to cry by the end of the evening, but I stopped the city clerk and asked her to explain what had happened. I guess she took pity on me, because she must have spent half an hour telling me what I'd witnessed.

When I'd written it up, I showed it to the woman who supervised the high school newspaper. She told me that my story was too long and contained too much detail. It needed to be shortened and simplified. Furthermore, my sentences were too long, and my vocabulary was too literary. This wasn't what I had expected to be told. I was sure she would maybe change a couple of words and tell me I'd done a wonderful job. I couldn't help myself: I had tears rolling down my cheeks.

She said, "Rachel, I can tell you this story is perfect if that's what you want to hear. But it's not, and I wouldn't be helping you by telling you it is. You've got to be able to accept criticism. That's how you learn."

"I thought I did what you've been telling us to do," I said. "I tried to tell who, what, when, where, why, and how."

Her answer was, "Listen to me, Rachel. No one's born knowing how to write a news story. I'm not a journalist. I'm only a teacher. I wouldn't be taking the time to criticize your work if I didn't believe you can be a journalist—and a good one. If you're going to be a crybaby, you better find another profession because editors will be a lot tougher on you than I'm being. Do you understand me?"

I stood there and stupidly nodded my head. I didn't trust myself to speak. But I dried my tears, went home, and rewrote the story—and then I rewrote it again. When I was done, I could see for myself that it was much better than it had been the first time. Although I didn't need my teacher to tell me so, I took the story back to her. She changed one word. She substituted "said" for "declared" and handed it back smiling.

I turned it in, and the editor told me I'd done a good job. When the story appeared under my byline, I felt as if I'd taken a big step from high school journalism into the professional world. I had another one of my talks with Amanda Collins, who told me, "I'm proud of you, Rachel. Not many kids would have the guts to go right at it. And that's the best way to learn journalism." She went on to tell me that when I got to college, I should major in a subject area like political science, history, or biology—not in journalism. "You won't learn anything in J-school that you can't learn on the job," she said. "Journalism is about mechanics. It's a craft. Substance is a lot harder to learn on your own."

The next time the town council met, I read everything in advance. This time I understood what the discussion was about. I was careful to keep the story short and to make everything clear. When I took it to my teacher, I considered it just a formality. I was confident that I'd done it exactly right. So I was totally unprepared when she handed it back to me and said, "This is completely unsatisfactory, Rachel." I was too shocked to say anything. I'm sure I looked bewildered. She went on, "You're not telling what happened. You're giving your opinion about what happened. That's not your job."

I started to protest, but she pointed out a sentence that said: "Councilman Shanahan made a strong point about the likelihood that the proposed rezoning would increase traffic congestion on Montana Street," and another that said: "Only commercial interests supported the rezoning request." Yet another said, "Despite the persuasive case made by opponents, the council approved the zoning change, 4 to 3."

My teacher said, "The first story you wrote, you didn't fully understand what was happening, so you didn't have an opinion that got in the way. This time you reached a conclusion about what should happen, and you let that be the main story. Do you see the difference?"

I went home and rewrote the story. When I brought it back, my teacher said, "This is better, Rachel, but it needs more work. You've still stacked the deck for one side of the argument."

I argued, "But objectivity is a myth." I was quoting from an article about journalism that I'd just finished reading.

"That's the excuse that some reporters give for failing to try, Rachel," she said. "Yes, it's not possible for reporters to be opinion-free. But it's possible to achieve fairness and balance. It's possible to stick to the facts and not rub the reader's nose in your biases. When you get to write editorials, that's when you're entitled to an opinion. Now take this back and rewrite it again."

So I went back to my typewriter and rewrote the story once more. This time my teacher said, "That's more like it."

The editor of the paper, John Mussmano, told me he'd decided to pay me for my work. My byline from now on would read "staff writer." He waved my gratitude aside. "I'm doing this, kid, because I think you've got real promise," he told me. "Someday I'd like to be able to tell people that I gave Rachel Rothschild her first paying job in journalism."

Mr. Mussmano said he wanted me to interview the head of the planning board about a pending change in the zoning law, which the board opposed. This was the first time I had to prepare a set of questions. I read the existing law and the proposed amendment. I asked an aide to the amendment's sponsor why the change was being suggested. Then I made an appointment to see the planning board chief, telling his secretary proudly that I was "a reporter for the *Weekly Ledger*."

Herbert Woodson was older than my parents by about twenty years and an important figure in local government. When this sixteen-year-old high school girl walked into his office and began asking questions about zoning issues, I'm sure he couldn't believe it. He must have thought that the *Weekly Ledger* had no business sending a representative of the kiddie corps around to see him.

He spoke crossly to me: "I'm too busy, young woman, to help you write a term paper for your civics class."

I steeled myself. I don't know where I got the nerve to say it. "I'm going to write this story with or without you, Mr. Woodson. I'll report what Councilman Krohn has to say about his amendment, and I'll report that you declined to be interviewed. If the story is one-sided, that's your problem, not mine. Maybe Mr. Mussmano will want to write an editorial about your contempt for the press."

He looked at me kind of funny and then exploded in laughter. "I'll say this for you, young lady, you've got a lot of nerve. Okay, ask your questions, and if they're not too dumb to bother with, I'll answer them."

So I asked, and Mr. Woodson answered. The answers were grudging at first, but I had done my homework and I was asking appropriate questions. They weren't necessarily the best questions, however, so Mr. Woodson began to expand on his answers and point me toward the main issues as he saw them.

After most of an hour, when I was folding my notebook and getting ready to leave, Mr. Woodson said, "You know, girl, you're pretty damn good. I thought Mussmano was sending me someone fresh from the cradle. You did a lot of work preparing for this interview, and it showed. I'm sorry I mistreated you at the outset. No hard feelings, I hope. You can come see me anytime you want."

I left the interview feeling both drained and exhilarated. Writing up the interview and balancing Mr. Woodson's comments against Councilman Krohn's was hard work. I showed a draft to my high school teacher, who rearranged a couple of sentences and did some minor editing. "This is a good story, Rachel," she said when she handed it back. "You're really learning."

The next time she came to our home, Amanda Collins looked at the clippings I showed her and said, "Now, don't go getting a swelled head, Rachel. You're not quite ready to join our Washington bureau. But you are going to be a good journalist one day. I can tell." I was already at my full height, five feet eleven inches, and Ms. Collins was not quite five feet four inches, but she bestowed a motherly hug and kiss on me, her protege. I never felt prouder of myself than I did at that moment. The praise I got from my high school teacher meant a lot to me, but Amanda was an editor, a professional. It was what she did every day of her life.

I was now spending eight hours a week on my duties at the

Weekly Ledger—an evening at the council meeting, an afternoon at my typewriter, and another afternoon in the office. With my schoolwork added on, I didn't have a lot of time for the ritual evening phone calls with my girlfriends. I saw them at lunch every day, however, generally went to Westwood Village with them on Saturdays, and often double-dated or even triple-dated for a movie and pizza on Saturday night. I was going out pretty regularly with Adam Popkin, who'd been a year ahead of me at Santa Monica High School and was now a freshman at UCLA. Jess, beautiful Jess, went out unfailingly every Friday and Saturday night with her boyfriend, Michael Cohen; and sexy, flirty Laura had several boyfriends. Arlie was never out with us on those dates. She didn't have a boyfriend, and besides, she was off making visits to West Coast colleges and universities with her parents.

*   *   *

The next stage in our young lives was applying to college and waiting to get into the ones we wanted. Unless you planned to go East or attend one of the private schools, that shouldn't have been such a big deal when you lived where we lived. California has the best and most extensive system of public colleges and universities in the country, plus a junior college or community college in almost every city in the state of any size. There's a school for every kid capable of getting a higher education. But teenagers can manufacture angst even if there's no reason for it, and my friends and I manufactured plenty.

I wanted desperately to go to the University of Colorado (CU) with my cousin Yalie. My folks didn't like the idea much. They thought I was too young to be that far away from home. They allowed me to apply to CU, but they also insisted I apply to Stanford, the University of California at Berkeley, UCLA, and, as a safety valve, to UC-San Diego. Arlie was intent on going to Stanford, but she also applied to Reed College and Pacific University in Oregon, and to the University of Southern California. Jess thought she'd go to UC-Davis with Michael Cohen, her steady, although her parents didn't much care for him. They got her to apply to Mills College, where her mom had gone to school, and also to Berkeley and UCLA. Laura, who had the worst grades in our little clique, was interested in UC-Santa Cruz, where one of her several boyfriends, Bruce Levy, would be going, but she was also applying to Cal State-Fullerton and could always fall back on Santa Monica Community College.

I was a nervous wreck and so were my girlfriends until we heard back. I got into all the schools I applied to, and then I began to campaign in earnest to be allowed to go to CU-Boulder. Arlie had hurried through her SATs and hadn't done as well as she should have. She was wait-listed at Stanford but accepted at Reed. Arlie wasn't a waiter, so she decided on Reed. Quickly. The way she did everything. Jess got in everywhere. Left to herself, she might have gone to Davis with Michael. But she let herself be persuaded to go to Mills. Good old Bozo. She said, "If I go to a girls' school, I might actually get some studying done." Laura got into Santa Cruz, which surprised her, I know, since her grade point average was so mediocre, but she had done extremely well on her SATs. Laura was smart. She just hadn't worked very hard in high school.

All that remained for us then was our high school prom; and, of course, we decided to go as a group. The plan was for us to convene at Arlie's house since her parents would be out of town, have our dates pick us up there, go out to dinner and then to the dance, and afterwards come back to Arlie's for a post-prom party. Arlie's folks were a lot more trusting than they should have been.

My date for the night was Adam Popkin. We'd been going out regularly during my senior year. Jess, of course, would be going with Michael Cohen. Laura's escort for the evening was Bruce Levy, who'd gradually worked his way into the number one spot on her long list of admirers. Arlie's guy was Lowell Lippman, who was more of a family friend than a boyfriend. Arlie didn't have a real boyfriend.

Daddy dropped me off at the Beckers' house about 4:30 p.m. I had my makeup case, my gown in a big plastic bag, and a small overnight case. Arlie lived in quite a large house, but it was awfully darn crowded. Four teenage girls getting dressed for a big night is quite a few. Even though there were four bathrooms, it wasn't enough. We needed mirrors to see ourselves from the back as well as the front and, of course, we wanted one another's approval, so we kept running back and forth between the bedrooms and the bathrooms, one of which was downstairs on the main floor. Even Arlie, who always did things lickety-split, took a half hour applying her makeup. We were ready, all but Laura, by 6:00 p.m., when the boys began arriving. Laura—Dr.

Lovelorn—told us that being on time was inadvisable. She said we had to make them wait at least ten or fifteen minutes, and we went along with that.

Arlie called down and told the guys to "have a coke." Laura, our social strategist, had gotten her older brother to purchase a couple of cases of beer for us, and the Beckers' refrigerator was full. So that was the "coke" the guys consumed while they were waiting for us to appear.

They'd each had a couple by the time we came downstairs, and they'd also been smoking marijuana. So the evening began with our dates a little high and a little soused. The big white stretch limousine that we'd hired for the evening was outside in the driveway. We paired off and climbed in. The driver took us to Valentino's, which is generally considered the best Italian restaurant in the entire city of Los Angeles and one of the best in the country.

The food was spectacular, but the conversation sure wasn't. Michael Cohen insisted on telling us a couple of crude and sexist dirty jokes. Bruce Levy, Laura's date, offered a few double hentendres, which I'm certain he thought were clever but which were simply transparent and dumb. And Adam Popkin joined in, as did Lowell Lippman, Arlie's friend.

Jess asked them if they'd all graduated from the same charm school, but I don't think any of them understood what she meant, because they were all slightly drunk. Laura shushed her, and Arlie and I were too embarrassed to say anything.

As far as I was concerned, it got the evening off on the wrong foot. I know that Jess was peeved at Michael because she told me so when we went to the ladies' room. Later, when we got to the dance, she took him aside and I could see her giving him hell, but he must have apologized abjectly because that was the end of it. I never said anything to Adam, and he was oblivious. I just wasn't enjoying myself.

By the time the limo picked us up to take us back to Arlie's, Jess seemed to have forgiven Michael. She was sitting on his lap, and he had his hand up her dress. Laura and Bruce were all over one another. Adam had his arm around me and was breathing on my neck. I couldn't see Arlie and Lowell; they were in the seat behind me.

Once we got back to Arlie's house, it was like open season for sex. Bruce lit a joint for himself and Laura. He picked up a couple of beers, and they headed upstairs. Jess and Michael followed soon afterward. The zipper to her dress was down, and he was undoing her bra as they went. I wasn't at all pleased with Adam's behavior that evening, but he brought me a beer and I drank it, not liking the taste, and I relaxed a little. I'd had sex with Adam a few times before, and I knew that was how this night would end. So we went into the den, and I let him undress me. Once I was sure he had a condom on, we made love. I enjoyed it about as much as I usually did, which is to say not at all.

Meanwhile, Lowell was trying to corner Arlie. She told me all about it later. They each had a beer, and then he took another and gave her a couple of sips. Pretty soon he had his hand on her leg and began to move it up her thigh toward her middle. She got flustered and asked him to stop, but he wouldn't. When he got to the top of her thigh, she slapped his face and told him to leave her house. He apologized, but Arlie started crying and couldn't stop. He finally left.

When Adam and I came out of the den, Lowell was gone and Arlie was sitting there, still crying. I asked her what was wrong, and she had a hard time answering. She was nearly incoherent, but I understood enough. I kissed Adam good night. Jess and Laura were still upstairs with their boyfriends, but we went into Arlie's room. We both climbed into Arlie's bed, and she cried on me while I tried to comfort her. She told me she was still a virgin, as if that were a crime; and she'd never even really liked a boy, let alone loved one. We must have talked for a couple of hours once she stopped crying. I heard the other boys leave before the two of us fell asleep.

In the morning, I was the one who told Jess and Laura what happened. Unexpectedly, Jess took the blame on herself. "I saw what was happening when we were at Valentino's," she said. "Instead of trying to act like Bozo and make a joke out of it, I should have told the guys to stop it right there or we'd leave. All four of us. I was pissed at Michael for telling those crude goddam jokes, and I told him so afterwards. But I let him sweet-talk me into the sack again—as usual. It's a damn good thing I'm going to Mills. Maybe I'll grow up there and learn to be a person instead of a fucking idiot."

I'd always loved Jess, but that was when I finally began to understand how sensitive she was and how perceptive. She was a lot deeper than I'd given her credit for, and she understood herself better than any of us understood her. I never again thought about Jess as a shallow jokester, incapable of being serious.

*   *   *

My first choice for college was always the University of Colorado's main campus in Boulder. It wasn't the equal of Stanford or Berkeley academically, maybe not of UCLA. But it was a good school, and I'd been traveling to Colorado to ski since I was a toddler. I loved the place. More important, going to CU would allow me to room with Yalie and to be on campus with Dev, my "big sister." After I was accepted, however, it took almost a month to persuade Mom and Daddy to let me go. I must have shed a gallon of tears. Being with Yalie wasn't the winning argument. They didn't think Yalie was much more grown-up than they thought I was. However, they were reassured by the fact that Aunt Ruth and Uncle Aaron lived in Boulder and that Dev would be around to keep an eye on me. Dev was a grown-up.

Once Mom and Daddy agreed to let me go, they entered enthusiastically into my going-away-to-college adventure. Daddy bought me a used four-wheel-drive Jeep as a high school graduation present, a car I could use to go skiing. He drove with me to Boulder in it. The Jeep was loaded floor-to-ceiling with my clothes, my skis, my typewriter, my sound system, my records, my tapes—all my gear. In retrospect, buying me a car turned out to be an extremely bad decision. I really had no business having a car at school: I wasn't an experienced driver, and I was immature.

We arrived in Boulder in late August. Aunt Ruth and Yalie had already taken possession of our room in Farrand Hall, a large residential dormitory populated mostly by freshman women. I moved right in. Yalie and I were ecstatic. She was looking forward to rooming with me just as much as I was looking forward to rooming with her. Even though she was a year older than me, we'd been in the same class in school ever since I skipped second grade. I saw more of Arlie, Jess, and Laura as I was growing up, of course, but I knew everything there was to know about Yalie, and she knew everything there was to know about me. It was a perfect fit, we thought.

Once he'd unloaded the Jeep, Daddy kissed me good-bye and told me to be a good girl. I rolled my eyes for Yalie to see, though it was advice I should certainly have taken to heart. If I had, my life might have been different. Dev, who was beginning her senior year, took me on a walking tour of the campus. Yalie had lived in Boulder her entire life and didn't need the introduction, but she came along anyway.

It was late summer, and the great lawn on the quadrangle of the central campus was beginning to brown. Around the quadrangle stood buildings in the Tuscan Vernacular style, with its sandstone facing and red tile roofs, its arches and turrets and narrow windows, that gave the university its unified and distinctive appearance. As I would discover, the architecture also led to displaced, strangely shaped spaces and lots and lots of stairs. It was far prettier than it was functional.

But there were also buildings on the quadrangle erected before Tuscan Vernacular became *the* University of Colorado style. Old Main, where my journalism classes would meet, was an enormous red brick Victorian pile, rising three stories above a visible basement, with a bulky square tower centered over the entryway. It was the oldest university structure and impressive in its way, though graceless and, I thought, ugly beyond ugly. Behind it was Macky Auditorium, where visiting artists performed. Nearby was Varsity Lake, a small irregularly shaped, muddy-looking body of water overgrown with aquatic plants. It was a popular spot for moonlight romance, Devi said.

Norlin Library, at the eastern end of the quadrangle, had a graceful, long front and a pediment supported by a row of square cement pillars. Devi pointed out the words carved on the facing above the pillars: "Who Knows Only His Own Generation Remains Always a Child." She said, "You'll like the library. Lots of open shelf material. It's easy to use. There are some courses where the only way to get a good grade is to cite as much material off the supplementary reading list as you can on the final exam. You guys will spend a lot of time in there."

Devi led us into the massive student center and showed me the Alferd Packer grill, which, as Yalie was allowed to explain, wasn't a misspelling. It was named after the only man ever to be convicted of cannibalism in the history of the United States. Student humor. Devi also pointed out the campus bookstore inside the student center, where we would purchase our class texts. Yalie and I looked over the bulletin boards crammed with notices of rides wanted or offered, books and bikes for sale, rooms for rent, and events scheduled on and off the campus.

Devi told me that I would want a bicycle to get around on campus. The Jeep would be useful when I went "down the Hill" to the Pearl Street shops or elsewhere in Boulder and the surrounding area, but driving on campus was deliberately made difficult for the student population. So I jotted down the telephone numbers of a couple of people who wanted to sell their bikes. I didn't need a good bike. I had one at home and would bring it with me to Boulder when I was next in Santa Monica.

That evening the three of us went to dinner with Daddy, Aunt Ruth, and Uncle Aaron at a rustic restaurant up Boulder Canyon, west of town. The eastern part of Colorado where Boulder and Denver are situated is a high plains plateau, extending from the borders of Nebraska and Kansas to the front range of the Rocky Mountains. Denver has a panoramic view of the mountains running jaggedly all the way along the western horizon from north to south. Boulder, which is to the north and west of Denver, is nose to nose with the front range. Immediately west of the city, less than two minutes from downtown, the road running along Boulder Creek enters a steep-sided canyon and begins rising rapidly toward the town of Nederland, less than thirty miles away but almost three thousand feet above Boulder. The creek flows like a torrent here across its rock-laden bed, and at one point there is a special course for people wanting to practice white-water canoeing. I had been up Boulder Canyon before—on our way to ski country. I looked at it this time with new eyes. This was *my* canyon. I would hike up it along Boulder Creek. I would ride the bike I planned to buy up Boulder Canyon. I would go for cookouts in Boulder Canyon. This was my place, and I was in love with it.

When the evening came to an end and Yalie, Dev, and I were delivered back to the campus, I kissed Daddy good-bye. I was startled to find myself choked up, not able to speak. Daddy was the best father in the world, I felt. It was a thought I hadn't often had since I'd turned fourteen. But there it was. I hugged him a lot harder than he was accustomed to being hugged by his eldest child.

He wished me luck, kissed me good-bye, and headed off with Aunt Ruth and Uncle Aaron to spend the night before catching his plane in the morning back to Los Angeles.

Initially, things went very well for me at the University of Colorado. I wasn't too homesick. My aunt and uncle were nearby,

Devi's apartment was no more than five minutes away by bicycle, and I was rooming with Yalie, whom I'd known my entire life and loved with my whole heart. Yalie also had a bunch of girls she knew from Boulder High who quickly became my friends, too.

Yalie and I were quite a pair. We had both been straight A students all the way through high school. And, even if it sounds vain, I'd have to say that we were a couple of striking young women. I was tall and erect, had a slight, bony frame, and was unnaturally slim. People said I belonged on a runway in Paris or Milan. Other girls told me they envied my ability to look good in any kind of clothing—everything from blue jeans to a skirt and blouse to fancier clothing worn only to big dances. My dark brown hair came halfway down my back when it was not braided or gathered into a ponytail, and I had an oval face with a long, straight nose and dark, wide-set eyes. My chest might be a vertical cliff, but my body was mounted on the long legs of a dancer.

If I had glanced into a magic mirror, however, and inquired who was the most beautiful girl in Room 315 of Farrand Hall, I knew what the mirror would say. It wouldn't be *my* name. Yalie wasn't just good-looking. She was simply extraordinary. Everybody said so. Yet Yalie was still this odd combination of class beauty and wallflower. Her romance with Richie Axelrod—Axie—had fizzled after they returned from Israel, and it wasn't because of the distance between Boulder and Montreal, where Axie lived. They had written back and forth for a time and talked about the possibility of going to the same college. But doing physical labor together on a kibbutz and having sex didn't translate into genuine compatibility. Axie hadn't been accepted at CU. His scores weren't anywhere near good enough to get in, and that finished him in Yalie's eyes. She only wanted to be around the brainiest people.

That was also her big problem with the boys in high school. None of them was smart enough for Yalie, and she didn't bother concealing it. One of the boys in our freshman class, who'd gone to high school with her, told me she was "stuck up" and thought she was "too good" for the guys. They referred to her as "the ice princess" behind her back, he said. Boys may have fantasized about Yalie, but they simply didn't have the nerve to approach her. Yalie projected a sense of superiority, but she also had the social presence around guys her own age of your average twelve-year-old. The interlude on the kibbutz hadn't taught Yalie much. Outside the classroom, where she was this unbelievable whiz, she hadn't the least idea before she got to college of what to say or how to behave in a boy's presence.

Once school began, Yalie and I were inundated with work. Courses were far more demanding than they had been in high school, and the amount of reading required was staggering. We were more than a little anxious about the transition from high school to college, especially me. I wasn't quite as intellectually arrogant as Yalie was. However, we both got all A's on our midterm exams, and that eased our concern. The other kids in the dorm were awed by our joint achievement. "Brilliant" was the word on the two of us.

Midterm success put an end to my self-restraint. The next weekend I went with a guy I'd met in my journalism class to a "coke" party. It was held in a large fraternity house at the edge of campus. There were maybe ten couples and six or seven unattached boys in attendance. Unlike the night of my high school prom, "coke" wasn't a euphemism for beer and marijuana. What made it a "coke" party was that there was cocaine available to those who wanted it and rum and Coca-Cola for those who didn't. My date urged me to try the cocaine. He wanted to get me high and take me to bed. I declined the cocaine, though I thought I'd probably have sex with him after the party. I didn't like him all that much. It just seemed the thing to do. I was on my third rum and Coke and pretty darned woozy when the police burst in.

Several people, including my date, were arrested on drug charges. My name went to university authorities for underage drinking. Two days later, I was called into the Dean of Women's office to be reprimanded. Dean Simmons, a friend of my Aunt Ruth, had consulted with a couple of my professors and heard I was going to be a star academically. Underage drinking and use of marijuana were a common occurrence on campus, and I'd refused cocaine. I was let off with a warning. As it turned out, it would have been far better for me if I'd been severely punished for the first offense. My cousin Dev gave me the only piece of bad advice I ever got from her. She told me not to worry: "Everybody does it. Getting drunk and smoking Mary Janes is what freshmen do."

In mid-December, after finals were over and before I was due to go home for Christmas vacation, Yalie and I were invited by a couple of junior guys to a party "up the canyon." Yalie knew both of the guys from Boulder High School. They were twenty years old and had finally worked up the nerve to ask her out. I think they drew straws for who would invite Yalie. The loser would ask me. I was not being invited for my wit or beauty. The main reasons for including me were that I was Yalie's roommate and I had wheels. The party was being held in Ward, an old gold-mining town on the mountain road, the Peak to Peak Highway, north of Nederland, more than an hour from Boulder. My Jeep was how we would get there.

The party was already underway when we arrived. There were around twenty couples gathered in an old tavern adjoining what was the local whorehouse in gold-mining days. The setting promised marijuana, alcohol, and sex, which was also the agenda of the party planners. They were serving "purple passion," grape juice and grain alcohol. It was a lethal combination for two unwary freshman women. Yalie and I quickly got smashed. Around midnight, we wanted to go home. Neither of us was feeling entirely well, and we sure didn't want to go to bed with our dates. Yalie was totally drunk, and I was pretty far gone myself. I convinced the guys to take us back to Boulder and asked my date to do the driving because I knew I couldn't. My eyes weren't focusing.

I wouldn't let the boys take Yalie and me all the way to Farrand Hall. We didn't intend to invite them up to our room, and I didn't want them to have to hike back in the snow and icy chill to their place, which was further up the hill south of campus on Baseline Drive near the Chautauqua Park encampment.

So I got behind the wheel when the two guys got out. That was a serious mistake. Coming down the hill on the way to our dorm, I hit a patch of ice and lost control of the Jeep. It did a 180-degree arc, climbed a curb, glanced off a tree, and smashed into a parked sedan, totaling it. Yalie and I were bruised and badly shaken. The Jeep was a wreck. When the police arrived, they tested me with a breathalyzer, arrested me for drunken driving, and took me off to jail. I was hysterical. Yalie, cited for underage drinking, wasn't a lot calmer. She knew she was in trouble, too. But since there was no way she could avoid it, she called her father to come rescue us. Uncle Aaron arrived shortly afterwards. He gave Yalie an angry lecture, which she'd earned and expected, and told her to wait in an outer office while he arranged bail for me.

That took almost an hour. I was still crying when I emerged from my cell. I cried even harder when Uncle Aaron hugged me and then told me how stupid and how juvenile I was. Yalie had gone outside and was standing there retching when we left the police station. "Look at you," Uncle Aaron said to her. "You're nothing but a common drunk."

We were received a lot more tenderly by Aunt Ruth. She could see that we'd been chastened. She mothered us and left the hollering to Uncle Aaron. She helped us undress, tended to our bruises, and put us to bed. We were both distraught, and we both were nauseous from all the liquor.

Yalie, who had been a lot drunker than I was, understood that she was going to have to face Dean Simmons, but she also knew that I was in much more serious trouble. Though it was my own fault, she felt responsible.

Devi showed up the next morning, having heard about the accident from a friend of hers who was a proctor at Farrand Hall. I think she must have regretted coming home when she did because Uncle Aaron lit into her, too. Her fault was that she'd not been strict enough with the two of us. Devi protested that she hadn't known about the party, but Uncle Aaron said that only proved she wasn't a responsible adult. It was totally unfair, of course. But Uncle Aaron was really upset about what Yalie and I had done, and Devi just got in the way of his anger. I guess she knew that because she stood there and allowed herself to be scolded, instead of telling him to shove it as she had every right to do.

My parents, who learned of the misadventure from Aunt Ruth, were glad the two of us weren't seriously hurt, but they also yelled at me for my stupidity. "You think you're grown-up," Daddy said to me on the telephone, "but you're obviously not. You could have killed yourself. You could have killed Yalie. You could have killed another driver. You ought to be ashamed of yourself." I started crying again, and Yalie began crying, too. We had quite a little duet going.

What happened next was kept from me for a long time. The local prosecutor was a former student of Uncle Aaron. As he and Daddy agreed, Uncle Aaron arranged for me to plead guilty and accept the following "plea bargain": I would be sentenced to ninety days in jail and required to pay a one-thousand-dollar fine out of my personal funds. The jail time would be waived on condition that I do seven hundred fifty hours of community service. In addition, I had to agree that my California driver's license would be revoked and that I would not reapply for a period of two years. It was not until much later that I discovered that any competent criminal attorney could have gotten me off with a fine, probation, and a six-month suspension of my license.

Then Yalie and I had to face Dean Simmons. We went in together. She informed me that I was to be expelled from the university and could not reapply. If I agreed to withdraw "voluntarily," there would be no permanent record. Although I'd completed the first semester, my grades had not yet been reported. Therefore, I would receive no credit. That, too, was Daddy's decision executed through Aunt Ruth. Yalie was told that she would be allowed to continue at the university but would be on probation for the remainder of her freshman year. If there were a second offense of any sort, even of the most minor variety, she too would be expelled.

I was devastated. Less than three months earlier, I had been a happy kid at the beginning of my college career. Now I was leaving Boulder in complete disgrace. I felt as if all my hopes were in ruins. Yalie, Devi, and Aunt Ruth helped me pack and ship my stuff. Yalie was as miserable as I was. We both knew we'd screwed up. The dorm was almost empty. All the kids had gone home for Christmas. The campus seemed desolate, in line with my mood. I wept silently all the way home. I'd let everyone down—Mom and Daddy, Yalie, Dev, Aunt Ruth, Uncle Aaron, and myself most of all.

My personal bank account had been cleaned out by the fine (Daddy knew exactly how much I had). He informed me that I would lose my credit cards. He would pay my carfare and lunch money while I did my community service, but I would receive no other payment and no allowance. After the community service was ended, I would need to find a job to pay the deductible for the damage to the Jeep, which had been junked. I would be grounded on weekends.

Arlie, Laura, and Jess were already home from college, and I was allowed to see them "one night and one night only." It was the single concession to my normal life that Daddy said he would allow "for the duration."

On the only night we had together, I learned that Arlie loved being at Reed, which was an intense academic institution, but was also smaller than our high school. It was very supportive of freshmen. Arlie said she was glad she went there instead of Stanford, and she might actually have meant it. Laura wasn't so happy. She and Bruce Levy had broken up, and the Santa Cruz campus wasn't big enough for the two of them. She was hoping he'd transfer because, if he didn't, she would. Jess provided a minimum of information about Mills. I didn't know it until some time later, but boy-crazy Jess was having a lesbian affair with her roommate and wasn't ready to say anything because she wasn't ready to believe it herself. For the first time ever, Bozo was subdued, not doing her usual clowning.

But my plight was the big news, and it thoroughly dampened our reunion. The other girls tried to lighten my spirits, but that wasn't possible. I was really down on myself, and my parents agreed I ought to be.

My "probation officer"—a fiction Daddy had arranged with the Santa Monica police department through a friend—told me on the Friday after Christmas that I would do my community service mornings at a drug clinic about eighteen miles away from our house and late afternoons and evenings at a soup kitchen about ten miles closer. My hours at the drug clinic would be 7:30 a.m. to 1:30 p.m. and at the soup clinic from 5:30 p.m. to 8:30 or 9:00 p.m. Since I had to get around using public transportation—no small feat in the Los Angeles area—that meant I had to be out of the house by 6:00 a.m. and my day would not end until almost 10:00 p.m. I could come home between the drug clinic and the soup kitchen or spend a couple of hours at a public library near the soup kitchen. The magnitude of the penalty overwhelmed me. I was only getting what I deserved; I admitted that to myself. But I'd be working much harder than if I'd been sent to jail, and it would go on for a longer period of time. I spent the entire weekend in my room, weeping inconsolably.

On the first Monday in January, I took an early bus to the drug clinic and reported for work. The director, Shayanna Lee, a heavyset, big-breasted black woman from South Central L.A., made it clear that she didn't like me at all. She referred to me alternately as "Miss Rich Bitch from Santa Monica" and "The Princess." "This is Rachel Rothschild," she introduced me to the rest of the staff. "She's a rich little Jew girl from Santa Monica. Went shopping at the May Company instead of Saks, and she's being punished for it. She'll be slumming with us for a few months."

Despite that beginning, I thought I might do some useful work. I told Ms. Lee that I was an experienced writer and could handle correspondence for the clinic. She simply sneered. "Understand me, girl," she said, "I don't give a warm shit about your so-called skills. You're the maid around here. Get used to it. You're here to do exactly what I tell you to do."

Miss Lee, as she insisted on being called, told me to start by cleaning the restrooms. "I want you down on your hands and knees scrubbing the floor." I protested that I was wearing a short skirt and wouldn't be able to keep it under me. She said, "I don't give a fuck if everybody for miles around gets a close-up of your little white ass, girl. Scrubbing the floor is what you're going to do, and keep the restroom doors open while you do it. And then be sure you wash the toilet bowls and clean out the urinals, Princess. I may have you drink out of them later."

I tried to ignore what she'd said about keeping the restroom doors open while I worked, but she immediately threw the door open and screamed at me. "Hear me, Princess. Listen good. When I give you an order, you do exactly as I say, or I'll have your ass. This door is to remain open while you are in here. Do you hear me?"

I didn't say anything. So she said again, louder than before, "Do you hear me, girl?" I said yes, and she said, "Yes, Miss Lee. It's always 'Yes, Miss Lee.' Say it." So I said, "Yes, Miss Lee."

After that, I did my best to keep my front side to the open restroom doors as I washed the floors. It wasn't always possible. My "little white ass" might not have been seen by everyone from miles around, but my undies were certainly on view a good part of the time to anyone who happened by. Miss Lee "happened by" quite a lot and laughed maliciously at my predicament. My cheeks were red with the shame of it, and that was the point, of course. Miss Lee wanted me to suffer. When the job was completed, Miss Lee did an inspection and then informed me that cleaning the restrooms would be my job first thing every morning while I was there.

She assigned me all the menial jobs—picking up the cigarette butts and the soft drink cans left outside the front door, clearing out the trash, straightening up the treatment rooms after each client left, making coffee multiple times a day, running errands for the staff. When there wasn't a demeaning task that needed to be performed, she had me hand-deliver letters that could just as conveniently have gone through the mail, or she created other make-work to keep me busy.

Except for the short time I was allowed for lunch, Miss Lee made it her business to see that I never sat down. I was called to clean up every time anyone vomited, which was a common enough occurrence at the drug clinic. If clients tried to help clean up the mess, Miss Lee waved them off. "That's what The Princess is here for," she said.

I spent a lot of time on my hands and knees, gagging at the smells. I vomited myself the first time I was ordered to "clean it up, girl." After the first day, I never came to the drug clinic in a dress or skirt. I would have liked to be able to tell Miss Lee to shove it up her ass, but that wasn't an option. She was the one who had to sign my time sheet for five hours a day, five days a week. Together with the three hours I earned at the soup kitchen, that meant I would be following this routine for nineteen miserable, miserable weeks, from January until after the middle of May.

Miss Lee tried to humiliate me daily—and she succeeded daily. I wouldn't give her the satisfaction of seeing me in tears, however. I shed them freely on the way to and from the drug clinic, and I regularly cried myself to sleep knowing what awaited me the next morning. Despite Miss Lee's efforts to goad me, I succeeded pretty well in maintaining a surface stoicism.

Most of the counselors at the clinic weren't a lot nicer to me than Miss Lee. They knew I'd be going back to my comfortable life in a couple of months, and they resented it. The only one who took pity on me was Moe, Moses White, a hulky ex-football player, ex-heroin addict, and ex-jailbird. Even though I held in the tears, he saw that I was hurting. "Be cool, child," he said one morning. "Don't let the bitch get to you. This too will pass."

Moe's role at the clinic was to counsel young black men, trying hard to convince them that straight is better than crooked. He'd been there, done that, he told them, and regretted with his whole being that he'd ever taken drugs and robbed to support his habit. "There ain't no future in it, man," I heard him tell one kid. "You be dead young or in jail or on the street you whole life. Do like I say, not like I done." I don't know how many of Moe's clients heard his message. But if there was any good done at the clinic while I was there, he was the one doing it.

It was much better for me at the soup kitchen. The place was under the auspices of a nearby Baptist church. The man in charge, a fortyish social worker named Joe Lawrence, was kind to everyone. He called me "Miss Rachel" and asked me to do things instead of ordering me around. My job there was mainly kitchen duty. I peeled vegetables, helped serve, cleaned off the tables, washed the pots and pans, scrubbed the floors. It was tedious and exhausting, but no one was trying to humiliate me.

Some of the soup kitchen's clients were nice people down on their luck. They wore ragged clothing and lived in flophouses or public shelters. Some did a little work but weren't paid enough to get by. Others begged for money on the streets. The place also attracted folks with serious mental health problems. Some of these were docile, living on the street, carrying their belongings with them in grocery store carts. Others muttered angrily to themselves, occasionally directing their belligerency at others or at the walls. Men (and an occasional woman) who had drunk too much were not allowed inside the soup kitchen, but there was no ban on alcoholics in between drunken sprees. Sickness was on their faces and in the way they carried themselves. Among the regulars, there were also a couple of drug addicts much in need of Moe's caring lecture. They tended to be younger than the alcoholics and somewhat healthier looking on the surface, but only on the surface. While I was there, one of them died of a heroin overdose. I heard about it from one of my coworkers, a nice old man who was a member of the church and came in to help a couple of nights a week.

I had no resentment about the soup kitchen. But it was tough work. When I left there each night, I was ready to drop. It was into bed as soon as I got home and up at dawn the next morning. I was chronically tired.

The first two days on this schedule, I tried going home between the drug clinic and the soup kitchen, but it simply added more time to an already intolerable commute. My bus passed close to Westwood Village, where my girlfriends and I had spent so many spare hours when we were in junior high school and high school. But I didn't have any money for shopping or the movies or a snack, and just wandering through the area was no fun, even if I'd been in the mood for fun, which I wasn't. So I began spending the time between my two work assignments at the library. That wasn't particularly satisfactory either. Although I was usually an avid reader, I couldn't sink myself into anything I picked up. I often found myself dozing off in the middle of reading a short story or a magazine article. When that happened, I stepped outside and took a walk. I didn't even have enough cash to buy myself a cup of espresso. True to his word, Daddy kept me without pocket money all through my ordeal.

On weekends, I never slept less than ten hours a night. Daddy had forbidden me to date until my sentence was completed. But the fact that I was not allowed to go anywhere was not a particular hardship. I was much too tired to play. I took long walks or bike rides along the Santa Monica Beach most weekend days, but all I ever did by way of nighttime entertainment was to listen to music or watch TV. Noah and David asked what bands I was interested in and paid for tapes out of their allowances. The two of them and Rebecca felt sorry for me, and I loved them for it. I felt closer to them during the time I was being punished than I ever had when we were growing up.

Mom recognized how hard this was on me emotionally and questioned me occasionally on how the community service was coming. I chose not to complain about Miss Lee or the drug clinic. What could Mom do about it?

Daddy—another revelation that came later—kept track of what was happening through my phony probation officer to whom I reported each Friday by telephone in between the clinic and the soup kitchen and saw in person once a month.

The treatment I was receiving from Miss Lee was not unforeseen. Miss Lee had a reputation for abusing white girls from the West Side. I had been sent there deliberately to give me a taste of what it might be like to be in prison under the supervision of a guard who disliked me.

At one of those check-ins, I complained about how Miss Lee was treating me. My probation officer shrugged. "Don't come crying to me, kid. Maybe you'll learn to behave yourself. If there's a next time, you'll go to prison, and it will be a lot worse."

I'm sure I must have blanched. I was determined that there wouldn't be a next time. But it hadn't occurred to me that what I'd done might follow me around, that I had a criminal record. In fact, I didn't. Uncle Aaron had seen to that. But, of course, no one told me any of this until much later. As far as I knew at the moment, it was all real.

My sentence seemed to last forever. But even nineteen weeks of servitude eventually comes to an end. I can't say that I was elated when it was over. I was merely numb. I didn't even bother to tell Miss Lee what I thought of her. In some deep part of my soul, I felt I'd deserved it.

The rest of the "school year" was spent part-time at the *Weekly Ledger* and part-time flipping burgers at a nearby McDonald's. Mr. Mussmano was glad to have me back reporting on the local council but couldn't employ me full-time. I was at McDonald's from 10:00 a.m. to 7:00 p.m. three days a week and from 10:00 a.m. to 3:00 p.m. two days a week. I spent an evening a week at the council and was at the *Weekly Ledger* from 4:00 p.m. to 8:00 p.m. twice a week. In addition, I did an occasional weekend shift at McDonald's. It was a punishing schedule, and it would continue through mid-August. I owed Daddy a lot of money, and he wasn't in a hurry to forgive the debt. He was teaching me a lesson and, boy, was I learning it.

In the spring, while I was still doing community service, I applied for admission to UCLA. The only other option I had would be to enroll in the junior college. I had some nervous moments waiting to hear from UCLA because of my expulsion from Boulder. I actually wept when the letter of acceptance arrived.

When Arlie, Laura, and Jess came home to Santa Monica at the end of their freshman year, I was the one who felt left behind. Arlie had enjoyed a successful year at Reed. Laura was over her split with Bruce Levy. She had another boyfriend and would be returning to Santa Cruz even though Bruce would also be coming back. Jess had decided she wasn't a lesbian after all, and she was ready to be more forthcoming about life at Mills though not yet about her sexual misadventure. I told the other girls my woeful tale, including all the details about Miss Lee that I'd concealed from my parents. I relived the pain and humiliation and shed fresh tears. My friends told me they loved me. It was the best therapy I'd had since the whole thing happened.

I saw the three of them when I could during the summer, but it wasn't very often. I had a busy work schedule, and I still wasn't permitted to date, whereas Laura seemed to be out every night with one or another of her boyfriends and Jess was back with Michael Cohen, sleeping with him every chance she got. Arlie was the one I hung out with most. But I was trying very hard to save money, so I wasn't eager to go out to dinner or see a movie, and wandering through Westwood Village wasn't the attraction it had been when we were younger. Altogether, it wasn't a terribly satisfactory summer. I wanted September to come so I could go back to school.

When the fall semester began, my girlfriends returned to their campuses for their sophomore years. I entered UCLA as a freshman with no credit for the first semester at CU. My parents required me to live at home. I made no protest, and it wouldn't have helped if I had. I'd learned from experience that Daddy was unyielding about discipline. I would be required to prove that I was mature enough to regain the privileges I'd previously enjoyed.

College under these circumstances was an altogether different experience than being at CU. UCLA was just up the street from Westwood Village, where I'd hung out so often with my girlfriends. UCLA was simply college at the other end of the bus line. I knew it was a good school, maybe better than CU. But the territory was so familiar to me that it was almost like being back at Santa Monica High School, taking tougher courses.

My only real friend on campus was Lynetta Pearson, the girl I'd named Doc Pearson when I wrote her story for our high school newspaper. Lynetta had gotten past worrying whether black friends might object to seeing her regularly in the company of a white girl like me. We had coffee almost every afternoon. However, that was about it. Lynetta was a reserve on UCLA's basketball team and was working hard during the preseason to earn a starting job. With that and her premed studies, she was one busy lady. She was often exhausted.

"Why don't you make it easier on yourself and reduce your class schedule during basketball season?" I asked one afternoon.

"And be stereotyped as this black girl jock who can't handle her schoolwork? No thanks."

"C'mon, Doc. You're on the honor roll. Nobody's gonna stereotype you."

"Girlfriend, you haven't got a clue. The first time I volunteered an answer in my advanced biology class, you should have seen the surprise on the professor's face. If I get in med school—okay, *when* I get into med school—most of my classmates will think I got there because of affirmative action. I work hard because I intend to be better than *any* of them, rub their motherfucking noses in it."

"You really mean that, don't you?"

"Yeah, I do. I mask it pretty good most of the time, but I got a lot of rage inside. I'm this middle-class kid from Santa Monica, same as you. But I'm black, and that's all most people know about me."

"I'm sorry, lovey."

"No need for you to be sorry, Rache. It's just the way the world is. You didn't make it that way."

We didn't talk about it again. But I'd learned something from Lynetta. Her anger helped me understand why Shayanna Lee had crapped all over me. She had been rubbing *my* motherfucking nose in it, whatever "it" was in her particular case.

Lynetta Pearson wasn't the only person I knew on the Westwood Campus, of course. Several others of my high school classmates were also there. Like Lynetta, they were now a year ahead of me, including Heidi Bernstein, my nemesis in elementary school and junior high. Heidi had been a beautiful ten-year-old, but she was an ordinary-looking nineteen-year-old and she seemed lost without her retinue. She was no longer Miss High and Mighty. I almost felt sorry for her. If we hadn't had this previous history, we might actually have become friends. My old boyfriend, Adam Popkin, was in his junior year on campus, but we were no longer involved—and not just because I wasn't permitted to date. He'd found another girlfriend, someone who possibly loved him more than I ever did.

But Heidi, Adam, and the other kids from Santa Monica High simply weren't part of my life at UCLA. I had coffee with Lynetta. Sometimes I went to the gym with her to feed her the ball so she could practice shooting. (To look at us, me at five feet eleven inches, Lynetta at five feet five inches, people might have thought I was the player—until they watched Lynetta handle the ball.) Afterward, I went home and studied. That was my routine. My mood was very subdued.

Despite the advice I got when I was in high school from Amanda Collins, my friend at the *L.A. Times*, I had enrolled in a couple of journalism classes, same as I'd done at CU. However, the courses weren't very challenging, and I began to think that maybe Amanda was right, that I ought to find another major, possibly history or political science. I was doing very well academically—all A's.

Then, as winter break approached, Mom and Daddy told me I could go skiing in Colorado with my cousins. I cried when they announced it. Considering my tomboy childhood when crying would have been a disqualification, I was now remarkably generous with my tears. Uncle Aaron picked me up at the Denver airport and drove with me to Steamboat Springs. Aunt Ruth, Devi, and Yalie were already there. They greeted me with hugs and kisses. A year had passed since my summary dismissal from CU, and I'd paid my debt to society, so to speak. At least that's the way I felt. Devi was now in law school in Denver, and Yalie was in the middle of her sophomore year.

I learned from Devi on the second day of that visit that my "sentence" had been a charade. Dev—as she had become outside the family—was taking a class in criminal law and had asked Uncle Aaron about it. He admitted it. I was outraged and went to confront Uncle Aaron.

He said, "I'm sorry if you think you've been ill-used, Rache, but your Dad and I felt you needed to be taught a lesson, and we took the opportunity. You would have been expelled from the university in any case. The only difference was how much of a fine you'd have to pay and how long you'd have to do community service. We maximized it instead of minimizing it. Your parents think it's done you a world of good and so do I."

Though I was furious for several days and nursed a grievance against Uncle Aaron and Daddy for a long, long time afterward, I have to admit now that they were right. I was a much more responsible person than I had been as a freshman on the CU campus. I was certainly more mature.

Despite the anger I felt at being deceived, I had a good time in Steamboat Springs. Dev, Yalie, and I had become expert skiers over the years, and we skied the most difficult trails. They hadn't been responsible for deceiving me. Our time together was marred only a little by the knock on the knee I suffered in a fall on the final day of skiing. I cried again when I hugged Devi, Yalie, and my aunt good-bye. I was now a confirmed crybaby. (No hug for Uncle Aaron. He and Daddy were on my shit list.)

I went back to UCLA for the second semester feeling more like myself. I was allowed to date again and went out a couple of times each with three different guys. Once I double-dated with Lynetta and her boyfriend, Allen Jordan. I was once more having fun. Still, my grades remained excellent. When my freshman year ended, my parents decided that they would let me transfer to Berkeley if I wanted. I certainly wanted. Their decision was a vote of confidence in me, and I needed it. Maybe Daddy wasn't such a bad guy after all.

Over the summer, I worked at the *Weekly Ledger* and at a dress store on Montana Street, not far from my house. Daddy had forgiven the rest of my debt, but I was trying to earn extra spending money. I hoped to see as much of my girlfriends as was possible that summer, but most of them weren't around. Lynetta was working in San Diego and attending basketball camp. Laura, who'd never been much of a student in high school and seemed to lack ambition, had suddenly discovered that she had some talent as a writer. She was at a writer's workshop in North Carolina and would be gone much of the summer. Arlie was spending five weeks touring Scandinavia with her brother.

Jess was the only one of the Fabulous ex-Five around town, and she was tied to Michael. I'd always tried to be tolerant of Michael for Jess's sake, but I'd reached the point where I considered him a reptile. He had a dirty mouth, was much too possessive of Jess, and acted with his dark good looks as if he were God's gift to womankind. He was perfectly capable of making passes at other women while Jess was present. Including me. More than once. Being in his company for an evening was an ordeal. I tried to avoid it. As a result, I mostly saw Jess during daylight hours on Saturdays and Sundays. She was apologetic about Michael's behavior. "He's a prick," she said. "But he's my prick, if you know what I mean." That wasn't the Jess I knew. It wasn't funny. It was crude. And Jess Sherman wasn't a crude person. Michael's personality was rubbing off on her.

I said, "I probably shouldn't say this, Jess. Maybe you'll be angry with me. But, damn it, you're too good for Michael. Much too good. He's not the only guy around. You're a beautiful woman, Jess. You can have any guy you want."

Instead of being angry at me, Jess looked thoughtful and nodded. "Thanks, babe," she said. "We'll discuss this again in the fall when Michael isn't around."

That seemed awfully cryptic, but I let it go.

After Arlie returned from Scandinavia and Laura was back from North Carolina, we had a sleepover—just the four of us, no guys—at my house. Jess was her old self. "You know, Dr. Lovelorn," she said to Laura, "Einstein here has been poaching on your territory. Giving advice to the heart-struck instead of sticking to the theory of relativity. I wouldn't stand for it if I were you."

I'm sure Laura hadn't the least idea what Jess was talking about. I was the only one who understood—and I didn't understand completely either.

When the summer was over, Daddy drove me and my things to Berkeley, where I was beginning my sophomore year. I was thankful to be allowed the privilege of living on campus once again. I buckled down eagerly to my academic work. I was no longer studying journalism. I had concluded that Amanda Collins was right and was working toward a degree in political science with a minor in economics. I continued to get almost all A's.

Jess was a junior at Mills College in Oakland, and she and I were now within shouting distance. But Jess didn't have a car, and I didn't expect to get another one in this lifetime. So we talked on the phone quite often but didn't see one another much. When we finally came face-to-face, Jess said, "I know I was awfully mysterious this summer, Rache. Maybe I should have told you then. I had a lesbian affair my freshman year at Mills. It was over pretty quickly, but it took me a long, long time to sort it out. I was still sorting it out in my mind when you and I had the conversation about Michael. You had no way of knowing it, but what you said played a big part in resolving the issue for me."

I must have looked as startled as I felt because Jess said, "Your mouth is hanging open. You can shut it any time. I had this roommate from Seattle when I got to Mills, and she came on to me." Jess adopted a bantering tone. She was back to being Bozo. "I thought—what the hell—what's so great about outside plumbing? Think about it. Civilization's greatest accomplishment in umptybump centuries is inside plumbing. So why shouldn't I use it? But it turned out my girlfriend wasn't a very good boyfriend. She wanted *me* to take out the garbage and walk the dog. And we didn't even have a dog." I smiled. Jess continued, "Not a very good deal, I told myself. Men and women were put on earth for very different purposes. Men are here to take out the garbage and walk the dog. Women are here to have boyfriends. So I told her to get lost."

I understood that Jess was hiding a lot of pain behind her joking manner. "Was it tough?" is all I asked.

Jess, suddenly serious again, nodded a yes. "Lesbian relationships were the in thing when I got to Mills. We did it for several months. I was in the middle of it when I saw you all that Christmas after you got expelled from Boulder. I couldn't talk about it. I felt confused. I felt conflicted. I felt guilty. We lasted another month. Broke up because she cheated on me with a guy and admitted it. Turns out she was a fashionable lesbian, same as me."

"You okay now?" I asked.

Jess said, "Yeah. I spent that summer in bed with Michael. He cured me of girls. He may have been using me, but I was using him, too. Using his thingy to reassure myself that I was really hetero. When we got together again this past summer, I started seeing Michael for what he is. You helped me see it. A year ago, Michael cured me of lesbianism. This past summer, he cured me permanently of Michael Cohen. Now I'm looking for a new boyfriend." She added lightly, "Got any spares?"

I hugged her. "I had no idea what you were going through," I said. "I just didn't like Michael. Hadn't liked him for a long time."

"There's plenty not to like, Rache. He's going to make some unfortunate woman a philandering husband someday. But it isn't going to be me," she said. "He's history as far as I'm concerned. Like the battle of Thermopylae."

"Good. I'm glad," I said.

"Problem is," she went on, "Mills, being a girls' school, has a notable lack of young men. So it's up to you to help me find a new boyfriend."

I said that I didn't have a boyfriend myself. In truth, I'd *never* had a really serious boyfriend. Adam was just somebody I dated in high school and occasionally slept with.

Jess said, "Okay, not counting David and Noah, you know any twins? We'll submit a purchase order, one for you and one for me." It was part serious and part joke, but we did soon find a way to double-date. There was a guy in my world history class who liked me and, when I mentioned Jess, he had a friend for her. Jess's date, Sam Adams, had a car, and the four of us drove over to San Francisco for a meal in Chinatown. I hadn't been to Chinatown since I made the trip with Mom as a little girl. But I remembered going to this restaurant and looking in this store window and shopping in this store. Jess finally said, "Okay, Marco Polo, enough with the travelogue. Bozo's hungry. Let's eat."

Now that I was out with him, I didn't know what I saw in Craig Walker. He seemed so immature. The four and a half months I'd spent working at the drug clinic and the soup kitchen showed me a side of the world most of my classmates had never seen. I felt older than my nineteen years, and Craig seemed younger. But Jess had made a conquest. "My Revolutionary War hero," as she called Sam, was the son of a Fresno doctor, a premed student with wire-rim glasses, carrot-colored hair, a shy smile, and a quiet, introverted manner. He seemed uneasy around girls, and he sure as hell had never met anyone like Jess—not as pretty, not as spirited.

He called her constantly, wanted to take her out every weekend, and was willing to find another guy for me after I made it plain that once with Craig Walker was sufficient. Jess had been with Michael for so long that she wasn't used to being wooed, and I don't think she knew what to make of Sam initially. He was nothing at all like Michael. I didn't care for Michael one little bit, but he was exceptionally good-looking, as handsome as Jess was gorgeous. He carried himself like an athlete, though his only sport was sexual gymnastics. Sam, on the other hand, was sort of geeky-looking, not the kind of boy that girls normally went for, and he had a physique like "before" in an advertisement for bodybuilding. Jess and Michael had been this beautiful couple—golden Southern California kids—and that was what she was accustomed to.

However, on every other point of comparison, Sam was the clear winner. Michael always wanted to finish a date in the backseat of the car, having sex. Jess figured she might have to make the first move if she ever expected to make love with Sam. Aside from sex, Michael didn't have much on his mind. Sam's natural shyness disappeared when there was a book to discuss or a philosophical issue to debate. Jess always found it necessary to pretend around Michael that she wasn't as smart as he was. Sam was proud of her intelligence. Michael admired Jess's butt and her boobs. Sam appreciated her humor and her personality.

It wasn't long before Jess began to like Sam back. A little at first, and then a lot. "I can't explain it," she told me. "I feel like a total person around Sam. I never felt that way around Michael. Never. He was just this handsome guy I was fucking as often as I could."

At first, they usually invited me along when they went out on the weekend, but the guys Sam chose for me weren't my type. I was beginning to wonder whether I even had a type. Soon enough, Sam and Jess didn't require my company. The stars in Sam's eyes were as visible as the Big Dipper, and Jess was many miles along the road to being in love.

I thought Sam was the right guy for her—finally. "Sam's a sweetheart," I said, confirming Jess's own opinion. "You're lucky you found him. And if he needs to be told how lucky *he* is, just send him to me."

Now that Jess was busy with Sam, she and I talked less often, but I didn't mind. I was happy for her, and I was working very hard myself. I'd decided, moreover, to apply for a job on the student newspaper. The fact that I'd had some professional experience with the *Weekly Ledger* didn't much impress the woman editor who interviewed me. I was new at Berkeley, was only a sophomore, and wasn't in the journalism school. I wanted to report on university administration or student government, but that wasn't going to happen any time soon. Minor reporting assignments would be all I could look forward to for the first year.

I came to understand after a short time that Mira Clawson seriously disliked me. But that was not unusual. A guy on the staff, a fellow reporter, explained that Mira Clawson disliked most other women. He said she was pals with a couple of dumb, ugly women who willingly accepted her leadership—and she could tolerate pretty girls if they were stupid enough or smart girls if they were ugly enough, but a combination of brains and looks in other women offended her. "Your problem," he said, "is that you're intelligent and good-looking. That's a fatal combination in Mira's eyes."

No doubt she was blind to her prejudices. She was hard on me, I'm sure, because she thought I had it coming. I claimed I was a journalist. She seemed determined to show me that I wasn't.

She sent me to cover a talk by a visiting lecturer from Russia, and then she spiked the story. "No room," she told me, though there was plenty of room for stories written by Mira's favorites. I interviewed a jazz musician who was playing on campus, and she edited the story until it was unrecognizable before allowing it to be printed. I told her I didn't want my byline on it because I hadn't written it.

"So you don't like being edited," she said dismissively. "Well,

Rothschild, if you're going to act like an *artiste*, you'd better learn to write like one."

I sensed it was futile but decided to give it one more try. I intended to write a feature story about the care of the UC bell tower, the Campanile. I interviewed the university architect and the caretaker, got all the data about supplies required to maintain the tower and the bell, and talked to a knot of people listening to it tolling—what it did for them. When I finished writing it all up, I just *knew* it was good. Mira Clawson glanced at the story and tossed it aside. "Not printable" was her verdict.

I was furious. I went back to my dorm room and called Amanda Collins at the *L.A. Times* to get the name of an editor at the *San Francisco Chronicle* I could send the story to. Amanda offered to call him to tell him it was coming. Two weeks later, when the article was accepted for publication, I marched up to Mira Clawson's desk and told her in a voice loud enough for half the newspaper staff to hear, "You know that story about the Campanile that you rejected? It's going to appear in the *San Francisco Chronicle*. Which goes to show, Mira, that in addition to being a bitch, you're a fucking incompetent bitch." And I strode out, feeling triumphant. I'd had it with student journalism.

I spent the remainder of my sophomore year—most of it—on schoolwork. I was getting top grades and beginning to attract faculty attention. Professor Ferguson, with whom I was studying American politics, invited me into his office in late spring to suggest a junior seminar that he'd like to see me take next year. He gave me a long reading list for the summer. My economics professor told me I ought to consider changing my major to economics, that I was "very promising." Though I intended to stay in political science, it was very flattering.

A lot of people on campus had seen the story I'd written about the Campanile, and many of them had also heard about how I'd told the editor of the campus paper to go fuck herself. I'd become something of a sophomore celebrity. I was easy to recognize, a tall, thin girl with a long ponytail. Guys I didn't know would come up to me and say they'd read my story and would I like to have coffee or go somewhere for a pizza. I went on a few dates, but nothing clicked for me—or, let's face it, for them either. None of them wanted to talk about American politics or hear about the drug clinic on the east side of L.A., and I didn't have anything interesting to say on most other topics. I'd never been much good at flirty boy-girl talk, and I wasn't getting any better.

Jess, meanwhile, had taken Sam into her bed and was thinking about maybe living with him next year in an off-campus apartment. She didn't make jokes about Sam the way she did with Michael. "Bozo's in love," she told me. Sam, when he and Jess stopped by to visit, was no longer the shy, introverted guy I'd first met six months ago. He had this beautiful girl whom he loved and who loved him back. He'd been initiated into the mysteries of sex. He greeted me with a hug. "Jess and I are having dinner next weekend in San Francisco," he said. "Would you like to join us?"

I said I didn't have a date. "Jess and I don't care," Sam replied. "You brought us together. You're *our* friend, not just Jess's."

I said, "Thank you, but no." But they wouldn't allow me to refuse. So the following Saturday night, I went with them to an Italian restaurant in North Beach. When we were together at dinner, Jess and Sam tried to remember that I was along, but they couldn't keep their eyes or their hands off each other. I felt a little superfluous, but I couldn't have been happier for Jess. Michael Cohen was a shmuck and a people-user. Sam Adams might not have movie-star looks, but he was 100 percent real. And Jess, who'd always acted artificially dependent and dumb around Michael, was free to be her true self with Sam. I thought—make that, I *knew*—they were made for each other.

When the school year ended, Jess and Sam went off to Europe together. Sam's parents were none too happy about it, and Jess's voiced strenuous objections, but to no avail. Jess described the conversation. "Look, Mom," she said. "Sam and I are going to live together in the fall, and in case you think it's platonic, it's not. So you might as well get used to it." Mr. and Mrs. Sherman knew a sound argument when they heard one. They decided to get used to it. With Jess away, the Fab Four were down to three. Laura had changed boyfriends again. Arlie was still unattached, like me. Arlie suggested that she, Laura, and I go on a camping trip to Yosemite. She'd borrow her father's car. And Aunt Ruth had invited me to come to Colorado for a couple of weeks.

After some schedule juggling, I managed to do both. The trip to Yosemite was first. I asked Arlie and Laura if it would be okay to invite my friend Lynetta Pearson to come along.

Laura and Arlie were hesitant. "You asked her once if she'd join us after Suze Orbach left," Arlie said, "and her answer was no. She didn't want to be our friend. Why should we want her now?"

I said, "It may have looked like she rejected us, Arlie, but that wasn't it at all. She was afraid that if she hung with us, her black friends would accuse her of wanting to be white. That was a long time ago. She's grown up. She's comfortable with who she is now. I'd really like you guys to know each other better."

Laura and Arlie said okay a little reluctantly, and convincing Lynetta wasn't a lot easier. "You and I have a history, Rache. All I ever did with Arlie and Laura was to spurn an offer of friendship. I don't think it's a good idea."

"That was tenth grade, Lynnie. I think they understand now where you were coming from. Besides, they've said yes, and so will you." So Lynetta allowed herself to be persuaded.

Once we were in the car, it was a little awkward at first. But Lynetta handled it. "Look," she said, "back then I wasn't cool with the fact that you guys are white. I'm okay with it now." She laughed. "You can't help your color any more than I can help mine."

"It's a mauve world anyway," Laura said. "Especially in California. I'm glad you came."

"Me, too," Arlie said. And that was it.

Once we got to Yosemite, the four of us camped out, hiked the forest paths under an arched canopy of branches and greenery, rested beside cascading waterfalls, and told each other everything we had to tell.

Lynetta expected to be starting at point guard on the UCLA women's basketball team in the fall. She was still on track for medical school but was no longer involved with Allen Jordan, who'd been her boyfriend when she and I were on campus together. She said, "I'm 'playing the field,' as it's called. Translated, that means I study a lot on the weekends."

Laura had spent most of her spare time the past year writing short stories. She said they weren't good enough to show. "You know how you're supposed to throw away the first pancake because it has all the grease? I'm still in the first pancake stage. Don't know that I'll ever get past it. But I love doing the writing even if it's not very good."

We begged her to let us see her stuff, but she was adamant. "Don't rush me. When I've got something I'm satisfied with, you guys will be my first readers. Right now, I'm just doing exercises for the wastebasket. Okay?" We stopped pressing.

Arlie was beginning to think about graduate school. She said she'd like to study computer science. "I'm good at math. It's my best subject. And my professors have been encouraging me. They say they'll help me get into Stanford. Wouldn't that be a hoot? I couldn't get in there as a freshman. Maybe I'll get there to do a Ph.D."

"You would have gotten into Stanford if you'd taken more time on the SATs," I said. "You were always in such a hurry, Arlie. Are you still?"

"Afraid so. World-class conclusion jumper, that's me. I always feel like I'm in a race. I've got to be the first one to finish every test I ever take. It's not a very good habit, but I can't seem to break it. Just like I can't break the habit of telling everyone what to do. Jess sure had me pegged—Big Boss Becker still reigns."

"Jess had us all pegged," I said. "It took me awhile to realize it, but behind that Bozo mask is one very, very smart woman. Looking back on it, she was the one who held us together after Suzi left. We were getting on one another's nerves, and she kidded us out of it. We're very lucky to have her as a friend."

"Amen," said Laura, giving it the Hebrew pronunciation. "*Selah*," Arlie added.

Jess wasn't there physically, but she was with us nonetheless. No matter the distance between us, we were never far from one another.

Lynetta, of course, barely knew Jess, and all she'd ever experienced was the comic side. The only real link between them besides Santa Monica High School was that Jess's boyfriend, like Lynetta, was bound for medical school, but that was enough. Lynetta wanted to like my friends, and I was sure she and Jess would be great pals once they knew each other.

After we got back from Yosemite, it was off to Colorado for me. I spent two weeks at the Aspen Music Festival with Aunt Ruth, Uncle Aaron, Yalie, and Dev. Uncle Aaron had rented a house at the foot of Aspen Mountain, a block from the main ski lift, the Gondola, and close to the downtown shopping area. I still hadn't forgiven him.

Aspen, which had been a wealthy mining town, was Colorado's richest ski resort and had also become a culture center famous for its summer music festival and the Aspen Institute. With its mild summer climate—warm days and cool nights—Aspen was almost as much of a summer resort as a winter resort. Dev, Yalie, and I hiked and biked each day and went to concerts each evening with Aunt Ruth and Uncle Aaron. Okay, he was very nice to me.

Dev was now in law school at the University of Denver, and Yalie, who'd just completed her junior year at Boulder, was also planning to go to law school. When the three of us were alone, we talked about our disappointing love lives. Yalie had gotten over her shyness and, beauty that she was, had a swarm of fellows at her disposal. But she was looking for someone who was her intellectual equal, and he wasn't going to be easy to find.

Dev, who would be twenty-four in September, was very unhappy. She had been seeing a man who was a year ahead of her in law school. He'd left her for another man, and she was devastated. "Imagine sleeping with a guy for a couple of months," she said, "and then finding out he didn't want you, that you were the wrong sex for him. God, I felt awful. It took everything I had not to flunk out this past semester."

Yalie said, "Don't exaggerate, Dev. You're at the top of your class."

"Yeah," Dev responded, "and at the bottom of the barrel. I'll never be able to trust my heart to another man."

"You'll recover, Dev," I said. I didn't know whether to believe what I was saying. I wasn't yet twenty. What did I know about men? Hell, what did I know about life? "Were you really in love with him?"

"I don't know. I liked him enough to go to bed with him half a dozen times. Is that love? All I know is that when he told me he was gay, it was like somebody had dropped an anvil on me."

"Damn. When did this happen?" I asked.

"In February. Around Valentine's Day. Isn't that just perfect?" She gave a rueful little smile.

Yalie said, "You were in bad shape for a while, Dev, but you're over it. You know you are."

"You're wrong, Yalie. I'll never be over it completely. I'm just trying to get on with my life."

"Poor Dev," I said, and hugged her. "It's the times. We're living in the wrong generation. My friend Jess spent a couple of months as a lesbian. You had a homosexual boyfriend."

She smiled. "Wrong generation for sure. Twenty years ago, Tom Harriman would have had the decency to stay in the closet."

Yalie said, "A hundred years ago might be even better. There's a lot to be said for arranged marriages, don't you think? Stay a virgin. Never see the groom until your wedding day."

We played with that conceit for a while. Made obscene jokes about it. Dev's mood gradually brightened.

That evening we went to dinner at the Hotel Jerome with Aunt Ruth and Uncle Aaron, and then to a concert in the festival tent. By the time the trip to Aspen came to an end, Dev seemed to be herself again. At least she wasn't as doleful as she'd been at the beginning of the trip. I was still mad at Uncle Aaron—but beginning to soften.

Toward the end of the summer, Jess and Sam returned to Santa Monica from Germany, Switzerland, and France. They were staying at Jess's house, though not in the same bedroom. Mrs. Sherman wouldn't allow that.

According to Jess, her father told her, "Your mother's too young for R-rated movies, Jessica. So don't even go around holding hands in the house. Okay?"

Bozo replied, "Is tonsil hockey okay, Daddy?"

Sam needed to go home to Fresno before school started again, but Jess was eager for him to meet Laura and Arlie. Jess was an only child, and Arlie, Laura, and I were her chosen siblings. I had been telling Arlie and Laura how terrific Sam was, and they were prepared to love him for Jess's sake. Lynetta, who was at my house when we gathered, had that premed connection with Sam and knew how much Jess meant to me and the others.

But Laura's new boyfriend, Jake Shaffer, accompanied her to my place, and the chemistry wasn't good. Jake prided himself on being an athlete, though he was only a quarterback on one of the intramural teams. If there's one thing Sam wasn't, it was an athlete. Sam was headed for med school, as was Lynetta. Jake, who was also premed, would be lucky if he got accepted as a patient. Jake behaved like an asshole, which would no doubt be his profession after college. Neither of the two guys showed his best side.

Jess told me she'd never met anybody so full of himself with so little reason. "So he's got jock itch," she said. "That doesn't make him a Heisman Trophy candidate. Intramural football at Santa Cruz is just one step up from the Pop Warner League. Maybe only half a step.

Lynetta's the only real athlete among us, and she doesn't go around boasting about it."

I thought Jake was an idiot, but didn't want to say anything that would hurt Laura. Arlie wanted to be neutral, though she told me she considered Sam "cute" and Jake a blowhard. Laura was defensive about Jake. She was extremely unhappy with the way he'd been greeted. That was pretty obvious.

So the summer ended on a somewhat discordant note. But Jess soon took care of that. When she got back to college, she dropped Laura a note and apologized for anything she might have said or done that caused Laura pain. And she got Sam to add a line to her note saying he was sorry, too. I heard about it months later from Laura, who was very touched by Jess's gesture. It was one more proof, if any was needed, that Jess Sherman was becoming a genuine grown-up.

*   *   *

I was now beginning my second year at Berkeley, my junior year. The term had barely begun when I met Joshua Weiner. I was about to turn twenty. He was twenty-six and a senior at the Hastings College of Law in San Francisco. My political science professor, Tom Ferguson, invited me over to his house for a buffet dinner one Friday night, and JJ—which was what everybody called him—was there. A good-looking guy about as tall as I was, with curly brown hair and dark eyes, wearing a brown tweed jacket. Professor Ferguson introduced us: "Rachel," he said, "this is JJ. He needs instruction. JJ, Rachel is my prize student. She can teach you everything you failed to learn when you were in my classes. I've signed you up for her seminar."

JJ seemed to take the teasing in stride. "Okay, professor," he said to me. "Teach me all there is to know about American politics. I'll try to pay attention." Tom Ferguson began to leave us, and JJ added loudly enough for him to hear, "You're quite a bit prettier than Tom Ferguson is, although that isn't saying a lot."

I didn't know what I was supposed to do or say. Tom Ferguson surely wasn't inviting me to lecture this guy. My awkwardness must have been obvious because JJ said, "I think Tom means for us to get to know each other. That's all. He invited me here tonight especially to meet you. Said you were extraordinary. Smart as hell. Beautiful. Since

I have eyes, I can see he's right about beautiful. I'm willing to take his word about smart."

I blushed. I'm sure I blushed. I was uncharacteristically tongue-tied.

He said, "If you're not going to speak, I'll have to ask you to give back my assumption that you're smart."

I replied, "He told you about me? He didn't tell me anything about you."

"You're entitled to three facts," he said. "I graduated from Berkeley four years ago. I spent a year in Europe. I'm about to finish law school. Your serve now."

I said, "Okay. Might as well get it all out on the table. Despite my height, I'm not on the basketball team or the volleyball team. And, no, I don't have a serious boyfriend." Serious boyfriend? Hell, since arriving at Berkeley, I'd never been *invited out twice* by the same guy.

He said, "Preliminaries over. Down to basics. What do you think about the Reagan administration?"

"You're kidding me," I said. "I'm your average pointy-headed intellectual snob. I'm studying political science at Berkeley. At Berkeley! I don't know any Republicans. At least, none who would admit it."

He said, "That's good. I couldn't love a Republican. And Tom tells me I'm going to fall in love with you."

"Whoa," I answered. "It's a little early for that. I have to know a guy at least twenty minutes before he's allowed to fall in love with me."

"How long will it take you to love me back?" he asked.

"Not tonight," I answered.

The evening went on like that for several hours. Trying hard as I could to be witty, I purloined several of Jess's best lines. Everything I could remember. Witty was not my strength. When the evening was over, JJ left his car at the Fergusons' house and walked me back to my dorm. We sat on a bench outside the dorm in the cool September evening, continuing to talk. We were being serious now. I told JJ I wanted to be a journalist. I told him this was my second year at Berkeley, that I'd done my freshman year at UCLA. I didn't say anything about Boulder or my time at the drug clinic and soup kitchen. I wasn't ready to open the closet and show him my skeletons.

I didn't notice it at the time, but he didn't tell me any more about himself than he'd told me to begin with. He talked about his four years at Berkeley, where he'd gone during his year in Europe, what he'd studied in law school. He sure didn't say that his family was rich. I didn't discover that until much later, not before I'd agreed to marry him.

It was getting toward midnight. JJ said he'd enjoyed meeting me and hoped to see me again. I said "that would be nice." He asked me if I'd go to dinner with him the next evening. I said I was busy, which wasn't true. I just didn't want to seem too eager or too available. He asked if I'd like to go somewhere for a cup of coffee. I said I'd had a hard week and needed to get some sleep. That wasn't true either. I was intending to do at least an hour's reading before I went to sleep. He asked me for my telephone number. After I wrote it down for him, he kissed me on the cheek and said good night. I went upstairs and practiced saying "I do." I only hoped I'd made as much of an impression on him as he had on me.

I guess I did. He called me the next morning about dinner Sunday. I said I was busy—another lie.

He asked about dinner the following Friday. I didn't keep a social calendar because I didn't need one. For the next five weeks, all I had to do was go to class and study. But I said that I had dates Friday and Saturday night. I thought maybe we could go to breakfast on Sunday.

"And spend the day together," he suggested.

"We'll see about that," I said. Of course, we'd spend the day together. I was already mentally planning our wedding.

Why was I so sure that JJ was the one? I wasn't. At twenty, I was having a girlish fantasy. Like I've said, I didn't have a lot of suitors. I was attracted to JJ because he was attracted to me. I wanted a boyfriend. I needed a *serious* boyfriend. I was hoping. I was like those people who buy a lottery ticket and, before the drawing takes place, plan how to spend their millions. JJ was my lottery ticket. I was mentally cashing him in. I was ready to have what my friend Jess had—someone who would love me and whom I could love. That's the basic truth about how our relationship began. With his good looks, his interest in me, and my basic insecurity.

By Tuesday, I was regretting that I had lied about being busy Friday and Saturday nights. I couldn't concentrate on the reading I was supposed to be doing about the American presidency. I was preoccupied with making mental lists of people to invite to our wedding. I thought about calling JJ to say that my Friday night date had been canceled and we could go to dinner. But that would put me in the not-so-hard-to-get-after-all category, so I didn't. Instead, I spent Friday night and Saturday night preparing a menu for the wedding reception.

I was up before the sun rose Sunday morning. I hadn't had any more than three hours of solid sleep, and I should have been groggy. But I was full of nervous energy. JJ was supposed to pick me up at 9:00. I was dressed—the first time—before 7:00. I wore a dress, a lavender print, very flattering, I thought. Then I decided the outfit was too girly, so I changed into pants and a blouse. Then I went real casual: jeans and a sweater. Finally, I settled on the pants and the sweater. Something I "just threw on," of course. Eager? Acting like a giddy teenager? Guilty on both counts.

I didn't put on any makeup. Thought about it, of course. Settled for "the natural look." Put on a silver bracelet. Considered a necklace and decided against it. All my indecisive decision making consumed less than an hour. I was downstairs by 8:15 and beginning to be anxious by 8:55 when I saw him walking up the path toward the dorm. For a moment, I thought about going back upstairs and adopting Laura's prom night strategy of keep-them-waiting. But I settled on telling him that I'd just finished getting ready and had come down to meet him.

Liar. Liar. Liar. That was me. Rachel Rothschild, UC-Berkeley's liar in residence.

JJ asked if I'd mind going to San Francisco for breakfast. He wanted to take me to a restaurant on the Embarcadero that was famous for its Sunday brunch. I did him a favor. I said yes.

We drove over in his bright blue Porsche, the kind you see at auto dealerships in Beverly Hills selling for sixty to seventy thousand dollars. "College graduation present from my grandmother," he said.

"Oh," I said, cleverly processing the information. JJ had a rich grandmother. That was the fourth fact I knew about him.

All I learned about him on the way to San Francisco was a fifth fact—that he'd grown up in Denver, where his parents still lived. I told him that I had an aunt and uncle in Boulder, that one of my cousins was a senior at the university, that the other was in law school at the University of Denver, that I'd been skiing in Colorado since I was a little kid, that my parents lived in Santa Monica where my father was a screenwriter and my mother was an artist, that I had twin brothers and a little sister, that I had four best girlfriends, one of them at Mills, one at Reed, one at Santa Cruz, and one at UCLA. I told him about the courses I was taking. If there'd been enough time before we got to the restaurant, I probably would have told him about riding my tricycle on Santa Monica Beach.

He could already have written my biography, and I didn't yet know six facts about JJ Weiner. It wasn't as if he was closemouthed. We talked about politics while we ate. His choice of subject. He was very opinionated. But his opinions were pretty much the same as mine. For someone who must have been busy reading law books, he was extremely well-informed. I asked him how he found the time to keep up with the news. He said, "I'm interested, so I make the time. You can always find time for what interests you. For example, you interest me. I'll make time in my life for you."

I think I blushed again. I *must* have blushed again. I couldn't think of anything to say.

"Did you hear what I said?" he asked.

"Yes," I said. If I'd shaken my head any more vigorously, it might have fallen off my neck.

"Yes? Is that all?" He was laughing at me.

I said, "I'm not very good at this sort of thing. What I mean is 'yes, I'd like that.' There. Is that a good answer?"

He took my hand and kissed it. "It's a very good answer, Rachel. It's what I hoped you'd say."

I don't remember what I ate. I don't remember what we talked about after that. All I remember is thinking "He's going to be my boyfriend … he's gorgeous … he's wonderful … he's mine."

After breakfast, he drove me out to Golden Gate Park, and we walked around for what seemed like minutes but was actually a couple of hours. I don't remember seeing a thing. The famous San Francisco fog was sitting between my ears. I was euphoric. I was giddy. I was stupid—world-class stupid. I was already in love. In love on a first date with a boy I knew almost nothing about.

Before he took me back to my Berkeley dorm, we'd made plans for the following Friday and Saturday nights and for breakfast again on Sunday. I didn't pretend any longer than I needed to consult my calendar. Even if I'd had a social schedule to worry about, I would have swept it clean. This was the guy. This was *my* guy! I just knew it.

We began to see each other every weekend, and soon we were on the phone every night. Sometimes he'd show up at my dorm in the middle of the week, and we'd go out for coffee and talk until well past midnight even though I had work to do and might have to stay up all night to get it done.

He told me I was the most beautiful girl he'd ever seen. That was the sort of thing guys said to Yalie, not to me, not to Rachel Rothschild, girl skyscraper. The most beautiful girl he'd ever seen? C'mon. Yalie was gorgeous. My pal Jess was beautiful. My cousin Dev was really, really pretty. Laura was curvaceous and sexy. Lynetta had a perfect body. I wasn't in their league. There I was: all five feet eleven inches of me, all ironing-board chest of me. Maybe I finished a step ahead of Arlie, who was still thin as a number two pencil. Most beautiful girl he'd ever seen, hah! Who was lying now?

But did I argue with him? Not me. In the eye of the beholder, I thought. I was being beheld, and he was the beholder. So why not? Maybe my mirror was defective after all. Stomp on it. Toss it in the garbage. Go with the Judgment of Paris as handed down by JJ Weiner, soon to be JJ Weiner, Esq.

As for JJ, he was my Adonis. Even handsomer than that bastard Michael Cohen. JJ was my height, maybe a half inch taller. (I'd have to be careful never to wear high heels.) He had a full head of brown curls and amber-colored eyes and nice broad shoulders and arms that were just right for holding me close. And he was smart. I couldn't be in love with a guy who wasn't smart.

And, boy, was I in love. Totally in love. Fatuously in love. I could hardly think of anything else. I couldn't get through a day without hearing his voice. Even when I was in the middle of writing a paper or studying for exams, I had to talk with him. Never less than an hour at a time. What did we talk about? Nothing. Everything. It didn't matter.

We started going out in the middle of the week, as well as on weekends. I was beginning to fall behind on my schoolwork, and so was he. I suggested maybe we could study together instead of going to dinner or the movies. So he'd bring his lawbooks to Berkeley in the evenings, and we'd sit in the lounge downstairs in my dorm, usually on one of the long couches. I'd rest my back against his, and we'd sit that way for hours, reading and taking notes, scarcely exchanging a word. We just needed to be together.

We kissed and hugged a lot, but the one thing we didn't do was sleep together. Not that I wanted it so badly. I wasn't like Jess with her healthy animal appetites or Laura who had sex as easily as most girls have baths. The next time I enjoyed going to bed with a guy would be my first. But that was what guys wanted, and I was prepared to give it. JJ simply didn't ask. In high school, the boys I knew were hormonal excess in motion. Erections by the bushel basket. As near as I could tell, sex was what they thought about every waking moment. And while they slept, too, from what I understand. College guys were a little less obviously, shall we say, *aroused*. They didn't *always* walk around with sailboat masts in their pants. They might be spending as much as 2 percent of their time thinking about something other than sex.

I wondered if JJ were like Sam Adams. Would I have to make the first move? Was it possible that JJ didn't desire me that way? I remembered Dev's homosexual boyfriend. I thought maybe I ought to advertise my availability. I started wearing blouses that were open halfway down to my belly button. I trotted out the shortest skirts I owned. I actually went out and bought several pairs of sexy bikini panties—in red and sapphire and aquamarine. And I made sure he saw them. Rachel Rothschild, girl temptress, a new incarnation.

I might as well have been wearing a sandwich board saying "fuck me."

Finally one night when we'd finished dinner at Fisherman's Wharf in San Francisco and were driving back to Berkeley, JJ said with some irritation in his voice, "Look, Rachel. I'm not blind. I know what you're doing. I have to ask you, please, don't do it any more. Don't try to seduce me. I'd hate myself if I slept with you before things are settled between us."

I was dumbfounded. "What do you mean 'settled between us'?"

"You haven't guessed that I want to marry you?"

"What am I, a fucking mind reader?" I said. I was the one who was irritated now. "I know you like me, but you haven't said anything about getting married. You haven't even told me you love me."

"Well, I do. I love you, and I intend to marry you."

"Did I miss something? Aren't you supposed to ask?"

"Yes. I plan to."

"When?" I was getting angry. I'd never been angry at JJ.

"When I graduate law school."

"And then will things be 'settled between us'?"

"No, they won't. I don't intend to sleep with you until after we're married."

"Pardon me?"

"You heard me right. I don't intend to sleep with my bride until after the wedding."

I said, "Oh?" I thought maybe I'd wandered into the middle of a Victorian novel. "Nobody abstains from sex before marriage."

"You will, my love, assuming you'll say yes when I ask you to marry me."

"This is the craziest thing I ever heard, JJ. You want to marry me, but you're not going to ask me for another four or five months. And we're not supposed to sleep together because you haven't asked me. And when you *do* ask me to marry you, we're not supposed to sleep together because we won't have been married yet."

"That's the plan, sweetheart."

I started laughing, though I didn't find it funny. "Do we sleep together *after* we get married?"

"Oh yes," he said. "Yes, indeed we do." He was utterly serious.

"I don't understand. I really don't understand. Have you looked at a calendar? This is the 1980s."

"You don't need to understand. It's a pact I made with myself. I don't intend to sleep with the woman I marry until after the wedding."

"And when's that going to be? Since you've cast me as the bride, don't you think you ought to let me in on the secret?" I was really angry now.

"Not for a couple of years. After I finish law school, I'm going to get an MBA. We'll be married when I've got the MBA."

"Just like that? You've planned my life for me. You haven't told me. And I'm supposed to just agree to it? I don't think so."

"I'm sorry to have upset you, Rachel," he said. "I really, truly am. I love you. And I know you love me. But I don't want to sleep with you because I want you to be my wife."

I started crying. Partly from anger. Mostly from frustration. He was right. I was in love with him. But except in my little fantasies right after I'd met him, we weren't at the getting married stage. Not yet. He hadn't even told me he loved me. Not in those words. And now he was informing me that we were going to be married but not for a couple of years. Weren't those the kinds of things that people in love discussed and decided together?

He parked the car and put his arms around me. I was crying in earnest now. I said, "I love you, JJ." I sobbed. "I *do* want to marry you." I sobbed some more. "But I'd like to have some say in my own life." I sobbed at length.

"There, there, sweetie," he said, kissing me on the forehead like I was a child. "I love you. It'll be all right."

The truth, I realized, was that now I *wanted* him to take me to bed. That was what people our age did when they were in love. I was in love with JJ, and I wanted him to make love to me. But I let it be all right, though it certainly wasn't. He loved me, and we were going to be married. That was the main thing.

So I bowed to his will. It would have been better if I'd forced the issue. Our lives together would have been different. But for possibly the first time in my life, I was completely spineless. It wouldn't be the last time.

It was late May when JJ finally proposed. A telegraphed move if there ever was one. Still, he found a novel way to do it. We'd gone to dinner at one of the best Chinese restaurants in San Francisco. We were talking about nothing in particular. One of our usual conversations. When dinner was over and the check came, JJ handed me a fortune cookie and told me to open it and read him what it said. What the little slip said was: "I love you, Rachel. Please marry me."

I said, "You know I will, JJ. You knew it before I did."

He kissed me and handed me a ring box. I found myself looking at a huge, square-cut diamond ring, which he put on my finger. The restaurant's owners, who'd placed JJ's message in the fortune cookie, came over to shake our hands. They'd alerted other patrons, who applauded us. As we left the restaurant, everyone whose table we passed offered congratulations. I was happy, but I think not so much over the engagement as that the waiting was over. At last.

Until he'd met me, JJ's intention had been to go East to Harvard, Yale, or MIT for his MBA. Once he'd decided that he would marry me—and before he bothered to inform me of that decision—he'd applied to Stanford and been accepted. That was his big concession; he'd stay on the West Coast.

I asked him to reconsider "the plan." I wanted to get married that summer and follow him to Stanford. Finishing at Berkeley and pursuing a career in journalism weren't any longer the first things on my mind. Getting married to JJ had taken over. But he was adamant. "We'll wait," he said. I would go on to my senior year at Berkeley and spend the following year in Santa Monica while he pursued his additional degree. Then we'd get married. I said I'd prefer to get married now. His response was "I said we'll wait, Rachel, and we'll wait." I could wait happily, or I could wait unhappily. But I was going to wait.

Did I ever think about insisting we do it my way? Yeah—for maybe forty-five seconds. What can I say? I was in love, and JJ had his reasons. Getting married and leaving me behind in Berkeley or Santa Monica was no way to begin a life together. Having me in Palo Alto would be too much of a distraction. Was it logical? Yes. Did it make sense? None at all. Sense didn't enter into it.

The only person in my life who I told any of this to was Jess. From the start, I confided in her that I'd found a boyfriend and, soon, that I was in love. I said I wasn't sure yet that he loved me, but we were spending lots of time together and he was definitely "interested."

Jess suggested that JJ and I join her and Sam one night for pizza. I had to persuade JJ. Almost beg. He said he preferred being alone with me. However, once we were at the pizza parlor, JJ was charming. And Jess was in top form.

She talked about life at Mills. "A thousand young women," she said. "On Friday and Saturday nights, that translates into a thousand girls without a thing to wear. You'd think one of our benefactors would have had the sense to donate clothes closets instead of lecture halls and libraries."

Sam would be going to medical school in San Francisco in the fall, and Jess disclosed that she had applied to and been accepted at Hastings, where JJ was just finishing.

"What sort of law are you interested in practicing?" JJ asked.

"Hell," Jess answered, "I'm only going to law school so I don't have to go to work. My folks will pay for me to go to law school."

I said, "Come on, Jess. You told me when you were fourteen that you were going to go to law school."

"What I said, if I remember correctly, is that I wanted to be a lawyer or a streetwalker."

"Don't listen to her," Sam said. "Bozo's going to be one hell of a lawyer. She probably hasn't told you that she's graduating *summa cum laude* and Phi Beta Kappa."

Jess looked embarrassed.

"Congratulations, Jess!" I said, hugging her. "That's wonderful. And you're right, Sam, she didn't tell me. Jess has never wanted people to know how smart she is. Her friends, least of all."

"She's really something, your friend," JJ said afterwards. "Is she always this way?"

"Only when she's performing," I said, "but that's most of the time. It's hard to get past it, but once you do, you'll realize that Jess has a lot going on underneath. She's just made a practice of keeping it hidden. Since we were kids."

Jess's opinion of JJ was that "he's a keeper."

After I'd tried to get JJ to make love to me and had been informed it wouldn't happen until after we were married, I was too nonplussed to tell Jess the real story. What I said to her was that JJ and I were going to become engaged at the end of the school year and that we would marry when he was finished getting his MBA. If Jess thought that was unusual—and, given her relationship with Sam, she must have wondered how two people in love could decide to live apart for more than two years—she didn't say so. What she said was, "I'm very happy for you, Rache. You deserve the best, and you've found it."

So Jess knew the essentials, though a laundered version. I wish now that I'd told her everything. If I had, knowing Jess, she might have suggested, gently but firmly, that my relationship with JJ was beginning the wrong way. Jess, who'd matured a lot faster than I had, expected marriage to be a full partnership. She wouldn't have put up with taking orders, which was what I was doing.

Meanwhile, other than Jess and Sam, no one important in my life had any idea that JJ even existed. I had asked Jess not to say anything to Arlie or Laura, and I hadn't even told my parents that I had a serious boyfriend.

My plan was to take JJ home to Santa Monica to meet my family as soon as classes were over. But how was I supposed to handle the introduction? Was I to walk in the front door like the announcer on

The Today Show and say, "Ta-da, heeeere's JJ"? Did I say, "Mom, Dad, I'd like you to meet JJ Weiner—and, by the way, we're getting married"? They'd think I'd lost my mind. Although I'd said nothing up to now, I thought it would be prudent to write everybody a letter or maybe two in advance about this extraordinary guy I'd met. Then when I brought him home, they might actually think I knew what I was doing.

I was intending to become a professional writer, but I never found anything harder to write. I couldn't be natural, and I couldn't begin to make JJ sound as remarkable as he was.

I went through three drafts before I was satisfied with my letter to Mom and Daddy. When I showed it to Jess, she advised me to start over. "Too many adjectives, Rache. It sounds like a real estate ad. Super luxury house. Custom-built from the finest materials. Large, airy rooms. All stainless-steel kitchen. Beautiful, landscaped gardens. Close to schools. Overlooking golf course. Must see to believe."

"Okay, Jess. Enough already. I take your point. Back to the drawing board."

I finally settled on the simplest possible approach: "Dear Mom and Daddy, I've met this marvelous guy, and I think I'm in love." That opening and a few bare details. Less than a page. I didn't plan to tell them I was engaged until they'd actually met JJ. JJ agreed to let me put my engagement ring into a safe-deposit box at the bank until we'd made the rounds and everyone was used to the idea that we were planning to get married.

I let Yalie and Dev know that the guy I loved was from Denver and that he was a skier, too. I dropped brief notes to Arlie, Laura, and Lynetta, saying that Jess had met him and agreed he was just the guy for me.

My junior year was drawing to a close. I had JJ's law school graduation and Jess's graduation from Mills to attend. Yalie, meanwhile, was graduating from Boulder, and Dev from the University of Denver law school. Arlie, Laura, and Lynetta were also getting their degrees. If things had gone differently in Boulder, I would have been graduating, too. But then I wouldn't have met JJ, so maybe the disaster in Boulder was a blessing after all.

When the graduations were over and I arrived in Santa Monica with JJ in tow, it would not be quite accurate to say that my heart was in my mouth. More like it had jumped out of my chest and was lying on the floor, flipping back and forth like a fish on the dock. I felt that my happiness was riding on this visit. I needed my folks to love JJ and for him to think they were simply wonderful.

I needn't have worried. Mom and Daddy saw that I was in love, and they were determined to like my guy, whoever he was. The twins, who'd just finished their freshman year in college, David at UC-Santa Barbara and Noah at the University of Washington, said it was about time I had a real boyfriend. Rebecca, who was fourteen, was gaga over this beautiful man. She didn't need to say a word. It was obvious.

Mom quickly saw through me. "Okay, Rachel," she said on the morning of the second day, "you're going to marry this boy, aren't you?"

"How did you know, Mom?" I asked incredulously.

"Because I can see the way you look at him and he looks at you, and because I went down this same road twenty-two years ago with Daddy. So out with it, darling. What's the plan?"

And so I told her, and Mom told Daddy. Mom hugged and kissed JJ, and Daddy said he'd be happy to get me off his hands, which everyone understood was a lie.

Rebecca was the most excited of all. I think she was already planning on being an aunt.

Arlie and Laura greeted JJ enthusiastically. Faithful to her pledge, Jess hadn't said a word. When I told Lynetta, she said, "God, you're younger than me, and I don't even have a boyfriend these days."

Arlie, Laura, and Lynetta each had news of their own. Arlie had been accepted into Stanford's graduate school to pursue a Ph.D. in computer sciences. Like JJ, she would be starting at Palo Alto in September. Laura had broken up with Jake Shaffer and, having earned her degree in English at Santa Cruz (with honors, no less), was interviewing for a job as a script reader at one of the studios. Lynetta had been given a trip to Europe as a graduation present from her parents and would be entering UCLA Medical School in the fall. Jess, who was also in Santa Monica for the moment, had made arrangements to rent a small apartment in San Francisco, where she and Sam would live while he went to UC Medical School and she attended law school.

I planned to see Yalie and Dev and their parents when I flew to Denver to meet JJ's family, but I couldn't possibly wait until then to tell them my news. However, it came as no surprise to my Colorado family. Yalie had already grasped the real reason for my brief letter about JJ, and the rest of the family was convinced Yalie was right. Yalie understood me, better sometimes than I understood myself. I told my cousins that JJ's family was in the construction business—Hyman Weiner & Sons.

"Holy cow," Dev said. "He's one of THE Weiners."

It was my first inkling that my husband-to-be was not just well-off, as I had already come to understand. His family was extremely rich. Dev told me that Hyman Weiner & Sons was a family enterprise worth hundreds of millions, maybe as much as five or six billion. It developed properties all over the West and owned one of the largest real estate empires in the Rocky Mountain area. "Yeah, that's right," JJ admitted a little sheepishly. "I would have told you on our tenth wedding anniversary."

So I was going to be wealthy. I hadn't expected that. Would it have made a difference if I'd known earlier? Probably not. But I certainly would have had to consider whether I was in love with JJ or with JJ's money. And I guessed he'd had those same concerns, so he hadn't told me. I wondered how much else I didn't know about him.

One of those other secrets emerged as we were getting ready to leave for Denver to meet JJ's parents. His given name, he told me, frowning darkly, was Jeremy Joshua. He was called Jemmie as a child, and his mother still referred to him sometimes as Jem. He rebelled at Jeremy when he began school, and his father came up with "JayJay," which he liked a lot better. He used the initials now.

I kissed him on the nose. "That's sweet, Jemmie," I said.

He wasn't amused.

"I hate that fucking name," he told me. "It makes me feel like Little Lord Fauntleroy in a velvet collar and short pants. You're never to use it. Never! If you ever call me that again, I'll be very angry."

I kissed him again, this time on the mouth, inserting my tongue. I said gaily, "Like the ghost in Hamlet, you want me to take a solemn vow. 'SWEAR!'" I made it sound like a voice from the dead.

"You've got the general idea, Rachel. Yes, I want your promise."

I said, "Okay, I SWEAR! Never again—except maybe in the heat of battle. Just don't provoke me."

"I'm not kidding, Rachel. I never want to hear that name out of your mouth. Promise me."

For no reason that I could understand, it had become a test of wills, and I wasn't going to give in. I said, "I won't use it if you're good."

"That's not sufficient," he said.

"It will have to do." I was ready for a fight.

He glowered at me but didn't say anything. I suppose he recognized that war was imminent and had elected to retreat instead of exchanging cannon fire. I didn't understand where JJ's vehemence had come from. There was quite a bit about my fiancé that I didn't understand—that I had never understood from the beginning.

Early the next morning, Noah drove us to the airport, and we departed for Denver. Nervous as I was when I took JJ home to Santa Monica to meet my parents, it didn't compare in the slightest to how nervous I was about meeting JJ's folks. Now that I knew his parents were super-rich, I was afraid they might think I was a gold digger. The Rothschilds weren't what you'd consider rich. My family was comfortable. Daddy's parents were very well-fixed. But we weren't in the Weiners' league. I would have been anxious anyway about meeting my future in-laws but the Weiner fortune had me completely intimidated.

When our plane landed in Denver, Yalie and Dev were standing at the gate. They had decided to surprise us. They couldn't wait to meet JJ. Each of them was holding a hand-lettered sign. Yalie's sign said: "We love Rachel." Dev's sign said: "We love JJ." If I'd grinned any more broadly, my face might have cracked. After hugs and kisses all around, Yalie presented JJ with a framed "Certificate of Inspection" that she had prepared and the two of them had signed. "Welcome to the family, cousin," Yalie told him.

For the moment, I wasn't thinking about JJ's parents or about moving to his hometown after we were married. Because of Yalie and Dev, this was my home territory, too. God, how I adored the two of them.

While we were waiting for our luggage to appear, Dev told us that she'd been hired as an associate by one of Denver's leading law firms. She'd already started work. JJ said that he knew Dev's firm. It handled much of the Weiner company's legal business. "Once I come back to Denver, we might be working together," he said.

Yalie's news was that she was starting Yale Law School in the fall.

"I may have to go back to being Ya'el," she said. "Yalie, the Yalie, is a little much."

"Remember when you came to visit in Santa Monica and my girlfriend Jess named you Harvard?" I asked. "That's a possible solution. Harvard, the Yalie. Or if you don't like that idea, why not transfer to Harvard Law, and you can be Yalie from Harvard?"

"What's wrong with Ya'el from Yale?" she said.

"You're a Yalie," I said. "Not a Ya'el. And if you're determined to go to Yale, then you'll be Yalie from Yale. That's settled." I kissed her on the cheek.

"My name's Yalie Goodman, and I go to Yale Law School," she said, trying it on. "And then the man I've just been introduced to—the man of my dreams— says, 'You're kidding me. You've got to be kidding. You can't be that stupid.' And I'll answer, 'I can *so* be that stupid.' Goddam, why didn't Mommy call me something simple like Hyacinth or Begonia or …"

"Or Gonorrhea," said Dev gleefully.

Yalie burst out laughing.

"The man of your dreams will love you no matter what," I said. "I found the man of my dreams"—I took JJ's hand—"and he loves *me* no matter what, isn't that right, honey?"

"No matter what," JJ answered.

The luggage had begun coming out of the chute. When we had assembled ours, it was time for us to leave. The date with JJ's family couldn't be postponed. We'd see Yalie and Dev again in Boulder.

Once we got into the limousine that was waiting for us, JJ said, "Your cousins are really something. Present company excepted, Yalie is the most beautiful woman I've ever seen or ever hope to see."

"You don't have to be polite about present company, JJ. Yalie's the Gold Standard. Has been since we were kids. And Dev's no slouch in the looks department, either. I'm more than content to take the bronze medal."

JJ kissed me. "You're the Olympic champion as far as I'm concerned."

"Thanks, sweetie, but I wasn't fishing for a compliment. I'm not in competition with Yalie and Dev. I love them, and I hope you will, too."

JJ said, "They seem very nice. And your cousin Dev must be quite a promising young lawyer. The firm she's joined only hires the best. My father will be happy to learn that there's a member of the family at Lockhart and Case. 'That'll keep them honest,' he'll say. My father doesn't trust lawyers, not even his own lawyers. Now that I'm a lawyer, he might not consider *me* trustworthy."

I smiled and nestled into his shoulder. I felt good after seeing Yalie and Dev. That didn't last long, however. By the time the limo had left the airport, I was once again nervously anticipating the meeting with JJ's parents. The drive to their house— JJ did not refer to it as "my" house—took half an hour. The sight of the place made my heart start pounding. Behind high brick walls on a property the size of a football field was an enormous three-story mansion, by far the largest and most imposing structure in what was obviously a very wealthy neighborhood. There was a second house inside the walls, also of substantial size, though dwarfed by the main house. Even among the baronial mansions of Beverly Hills, the larger one would have been competitive.

I was to learn later that this part of Denver, north of the Denver Country Club, was at one time closed by covenant to Jews. Hyman Weiner, JJ's grandfather, had changed that. Through agents he assembled several contiguous lots, knocked down the houses that stood on them, and built the two homes that currently stood there. The larger house, which he named "Mt. Sinai," he took for himself and his wife, Bess. The smaller house, "Mt. Zion," would be occupied initially by his housekeeper and gardener. His plan was that it would be lived in eventually by one of his children. On Hyman's death at the age of seventy-one in 1974, Bess Weiner had persuaded Herman, their older son, and his wife, Vera, to move into the big house while she moved into the smaller house with her maid. The husband and wife who served Herman and Vera's needs now occupied an apartment above the garage.

All I knew at that moment, as the motorized gates swung open, was that I was about to enter the largest house I'd ever been in and that inside it were people who held my fate in their hands. Or so I thought. Unconsciously, I'd dug my fingers into JJ's left arm. He lifted his arm to his lips and kissed my hand. "Don't be afraid, sugar. They won't bite hard enough to break the skin."

The best I could manage was a strained laugh. I felt like I was about to make my stage debut on Broadway and didn't know my lines, not a single one. I must have been trembling as we got out of the car because JJ took me by the elbow and whispered "steady." I gulped hard and took a deep breath, trying to calm myself.

JJ's mother and father met us at the door. Herman Weiner greeted me with a peck on the cheek and a restrained "how do you do?" He was in his middle fifties, tall as me and JJ and trim, an avid tennis player when he had the time. JJ's mother, Vera, was trying hard to look forty but not succeeding. Every visible part of her body had been redesigned by a plastic surgeon. I was sure that was also true of several parts not currently on view. Her bleached blond hair was fixed in the latest style, and she was expensively dressed. She extended a well-manicured hand. She also said "how do you do?" It was not what could be classified as an enthusiastic reception.

I wasn't the first girl JJ had ever brought home. He'd told me that. But I was the first girl to be introduced to his parents in quite a long time. The Weiners apparently hadn't attached any great significance to that. JJ obviously hadn't told them as much about me as I'd told my parents about him before taking him home. In any case, there was no sign of recognition that JJ might be really serious about me. I don't know *what* they thought. I felt that Herman Weiner, the real estate mogul, was appraising me like a piece of property he'd been offered, not knowing that JJ had already acquired the deed. Mrs. Mogul acted if she were looking for my price tag. They were polite enough, but I couldn't help feeling that I was a commodity on display at Sotheby's prior to auction. Apparently, I would not fetch a high price.

It was fully as bad as I'd imagined, and it only got worse when I was introduced to JJ's older sister, Annalisa Garson, who was waiting in the living room with her husband. "This is my daughter, Annalisa," said Vera Weiner, and Annalisa said, "This is my husband, Dr. Allan Garson."

JJ had warned me in advance that Annalisa was a snob. It must have been clear to her that I lacked a social pedigree because all I got from her was a "nice of you to come, my dear," uttered in a tone that can only be described as dismissive. No one had ever looked down her nose at me quite so blatantly. Not even Heidi Bernstein when she was making my life miserable in fifth grade. Dr. Garson stared at me as if

I were a prospective patient whose ability to pay was in serious doubt. He nodded and mumbled something ending in "....meechoo."

I was saved from total humiliation by JJ's grandmother, Bess. I don't know if she immediately knew I was special or whether she simply felt sorry for me. My distress must have been evident. I wasn't good at hiding my emotions.

"Come sit by me, child," she commanded. She was alone on a big couch near the back wall, next to an enormous fireplace. I went over and sat down beside her.

"JJ," she said to her grandson, "this is a very pretty young lady you've brought home. I'd like you to leave us alone for a while so I can get to know her."

"I don't think she's prepared to be interrogated, Grandma," JJ said.

"That's not what I have in mind, darling boy. I see this child with a deer-caught-in-the-headlights look in her eyes, and she needs rescuing. So you just go away and let us get acquainted. Please." She made a shooing motion in his direction.

JJ retreated, and she took my hands in hers and said, "Almost twenty-seven years old and not a grain of sense about women. I hope you'll forgive my grandson for being an idiot."

I must have looked puzzled. She asked, "How old are you, child?"

"Twenty," I said. "I'll be twenty-one in October."

"I couldn't have coped with Herman and Vera when I was twenty," she said. "Let alone Annalisa. I'm seventy-nine years old, and I still have a hard time coping with Annalisa." She was still holding my hands and was now patting them. "It will be all right, dear. Don't be afraid."

I asked, "Am I so obvious?"

She smiled and touched my cheek. "Yes, dear. Maybe not to everybody, but to me. That's why I asked you to come sit with me. You just stay right here beside me and talk with me for a while. I won't let anyone bother you until you're ready."

"What should we talk about?"

"Well, JJ warned me not to ask too many questions. You just tell me whatever you'd like me to know about you."

So I sat there and told her about myself. More than I would have if she'd been asking questions.

She listened for a while and finally asked, "How did you meet JJ?"

I said, "One of my professors introduced us."

"Do you love him?" she asked.

I said, "Yes."

"Does he love you?"

"I think so," I answered. "He tells me he does."

"That's all that really matters, dear. The rest of it will fall into place."

"I wish I felt sure of that."

"You're a beautiful young woman," she said. "You're smart. I like you. Remember that. It counts for a lot in this family. You've got nothing to worry about."

I kissed her on the cheek. "Thank you, Mrs. Weiner."

"I'd like you to call me 'Grandma Bess.' Will you do that for me?"

"Of course, Grandma Bess."

She motioned for JJ to come over. She told him, "Rachel's okay now, aren't you?"

"Yes, Grandma Bess."

"JJ," she said, "it's up to you to make sure she's okay the rest of the evening. Think you can handle the job?"

"Yes, Grandma." He was looking at his shoes sheepishly, like a little boy.

She took my hand and put it in his. "Okay," she said. "Go on now. Join the others. I'll be there in a moment."

I'd been with her for fifteen to twenty minutes. JJ, his parents, and his sister and her husband had remained on the far side of the room, talking among themselves. I assume JJ had told them that Grandma Bess wanted to be alone with me. As I was to discover, Grandma Bess usually got what she wanted. No one had disturbed us. It was as if I'd been surrounded by a protective bubble, filled with restorative energy. I won't say that I was completely calm and confident when I left Grandma Bess's side, but I was no longer terrified.

"What did you and Grandma talk about?" JJ asked.

"She told me you were an idiot."

He laughed. "And after that was established?"

"I talked. She listened. She asked me if I loved you."

"And what did you say?"

"I said maybe."

He kissed me, a lover's kiss, with his arms around me.

"Grandma's okay," he said.

"More than okay. "She saved my life."

"I'm sorry, sugar," he said. "I didn't prepare the way very well, did I?"

I shook my head. "No, not very well."

When we came over to where the others were standing, Herman said, "You seem to have made a favorable impression on my mother, young lady."

Grandma Bess walked up just then, leaning on her cane. "Yes, she did," she assured him. "I *like* her. Quite a lot. Do you think you're good enough for her, JJ?"

"Probably not," JJ responded.

"Is he good enough for you, Rachel?" Grandma Bess asked.

"I haven't decided," I answered. "'Probably not' sounds about right."

Grandma guffawed and stomped her cane on the carpet, and JJ and his father laughed. Even Vera smiled. Annalisa looked as if she'd sniffed a foul odor.

Still, the tension was broken. I relaxed enough to tell JJ's parents that I had an aunt and uncle and two cousins in Boulder and that I'd been skiing in the Colorado mountains since I was a toddler. I didn't mention the interlude at CU. I'd only recently disclosed that to JJ. Almost four years after it happened, I was still ashamed of myself.

JJ mentioned that I also had family in Israel and had visited there several times. He knew that would interest his parents. Herman Weiner was a big donor to Jewish causes and had visited Israel frequently. Vera gave money to Hadassah Hospital and, it turned out, had actually met my grandfather, who was sometimes called on to speak to American visitors about Israeli medicine.

We began to talk about the political situation in Israel. I was in my element now. I'd just completed a course on the history of the Middle East and felt I really understood the dynamics of the Arab-Israeli conflict. I was unreasonably proud of my newly acquired knowledge and quite certain I knew more than any of the Weiners. (To be honest, I also thought I knew more than the people who were running things for the U.S. Government.) But I was careful—a lot more careful than I would have been around my own parents—to appear modest and to show respect for differing opinions.

I think JJ's dad liked the fact that my grandparents were Zionists and that I considered myself a Zionist too. Annalisa, on the other hand, was conspicuously uninterested in anything I had to say.

After awhile, we went in to dinner. Grandma Bess insisted I sit next to her. "You're doing just fine," she said to me as we sat down. To Annalisa, who was on her other side, she said, "How's the social climbing coming, dear?"

Annalisa wasn't taken aback, not even slightly. She looked at Rachel and said, "My grandmother doesn't like the fact that I spend my time with people she calls *goyim*. I'm not tribal enough for you, am I, Nana?"

"You might devote *some* of your energy to Jewish causes," Grandma Bess said.

"And become a Zionist like this child you seem to have adopted?" Annalisa asked, tilting her chin toward me.

"That's not the worst thing that could happen," Grandma Bess responded.

"No, thank you, Nana. As I've told you before, I prefer devoting myself to the arts."

Vera, who was at the other end of the table, intervened. "You'll have to excuse us, Rachel. This is a recurrent dispute between my daughter and my mother-in-law. It would be nice if the two of you would postpone the debate to another time. We have a guest this evening."

Grandma Bess said, "I'm an old lady, Vera. Telling the truth is one of the few pleasures I have left in life. Annalisa doesn't seem to mind what I say, do you, Granddaughter?"

"Not at all," Annalisa answered. "I take it as a manifestation of approaching senility."

I was no better at concealing shocked surprise than I had been earlier at concealing distress.

JJ whispered, "Nothing like this happens in the Rothschild household, I bet." He was certainly right about that.

The exchange between Grandma Bess and Annalisa had ended.

The astounding part was that neither seemed in the least upset by it. In fact, Annalisa appeared to be rather satisfied with herself.

She showed no interest in me, however, not during dinner and not afterwards. When she and her medical consort were ready to leave, she brushed my cheek lightly with hers and said exactly as she had at the beginning of the evening, "Nice of you to come, my dear." This time she added, "Perhaps we'll meet again." I feel certain she was hoping we wouldn't.

Grandma Bess asked me to spend the night at her house—"unless you intend to sleep with JJ."

I blushed, and Vera said, "Oh, Mother. What will the child think of us if you talk that way?" JJ said, "Go ahead, sugar. It'll give Grandma her chance to baby you."

So I retired for the night to the smaller house where Grandma Bess spent three-quarters of an hour telling me about the humble beginnings of the Weiner family. She didn't want me to be overwhelmed by the Weiner family wealth.

Just before we headed off to bed, Grandma Bess said, "My grandson won't ask my opinion, but if he did I'd tell him, 'If you haven't already proposed to Rachel, you're a fool.'" And then she added, "You don't have to say anything if you don't want to, but you're already engaged, aren't you?"

Ever the poised sophisticate, I nodded and said "yes" in a childish soprano, which was all I could manage. There were tears in my eyes. Little Grandma Bess gathered big old me in her arms, and I started weeping.

"Nothing to cry about, child," she said. "JJ's a lucky boy. And since I'm prejudiced, I think you're lucky, too."

I agreed that I was.

In the morning, when JJ came to collect me, Grandma Bess hugged him and said, "This girl's going to make some young man a wonderful wife. By any chance, are you intending to be that young man?"

JJ grinned. I squealed delightedly. And Grandma Bess said, "You'd better be good to my new granddaughter—or else! You hear me?"

JJ grinned again. I had been a huge success with the one member of the Weiner family whose opinion really mattered to JJ. On the way back to the main house, JJ said he thought his mother and father were at least halfway there.

I told him I was afraid I'd made a bad impression on Annalisa and her husband, but JJ's view couldn't have been clearer. "Annalisa would like me to marry into the British royal family, so she can hobnob with the Queen. Fuck Annalisa, and double-fuck that self-satisfied asshole she's married to."

We spent the next three days in Denver. JJ drove me all over town in his grandmother's sky-blue Cadillac. For all the time I'd spent in Colorado, I didn't know Denver at all well. Except for a compact and handsome downtown, the Civic Center, and the State Capitol, it was mostly a collection of one-story houses and low-rise strip malls strung out along the principal east-west and north-south streets and highways. There were some lovely neighborhoods away from those main roads, including especially the neighborhood where my prospective in-laws lived and the nearby Cherry Creek shopping center, but the dominant impression I got was that Denver and its suburbs had just grown and grown and grown without much of a plan. The land must have seemed endless to the people who settled there, and they simply kept extending toward the compass points. Still, with the mountains running jaggedly along the horizon to the west, it was beautiful despite all the commercial ugliness.

We'd come to Denver to visit JJ's family, but I didn't see a lot of them after the first night. There were no more formal meals. I continued sleeping at Grandma Bess's house, and I made sure I spent a few minutes each afternoon in her company. I was extremely grateful to her for getting me through that terrible first meeting. I had coffee twice with Vera, who was now very solicitous, wanting to be sure that I was having a good time. At night, JJ took me out to dinner and one night to the movies. JJ's father wasn't around during the day, but one evening when he returned from work just as we were getting ready to leave for dinner, he took me aside, where we couldn't be heard.

"You're a bright girl, Rachel," he said, "and I like the way you think. I especially like the fact that you're passionate about Israel. Vera and I own an apartment in Jerusalem, and we go at least once a year. We took Annalisa and JJ there a couple of times when they were children, but JJ's never wanted to go since. Annalisa's hopeless on the subject, of course, but I think there's a chance you might bring JJ into the fold. I'm counting on you to try."

I took that as a sign of acceptance, and I was flattered that he was asking me to do something he hadn't been able to accomplish. Once we left the house, I told JJ what his father had said to me.

He laughed. "Dad's enlisted you, has he? Brought you onto the team. Next thing, he'll put you on salary to assure that your primary loyalty is to him. That's the Herman Weiner method."

I let it pass, but I thought it was a strange thing to say. It carried an undercurrent of resentment. No, the Weiners weren't like the Rothschilds. I remembered the F. Scott Fitzgerald line: "The rich are different than you and me." Uh-huh!

JJ's Uncle Max, his wife, and his children were on vacation in France, so there was no one else I had to meet in Denver. I was eager to get to Boulder so I could introduce JJ to Aunt Ruth and Uncle Aaron. Dev and Yalie were there when we arrived, and there was an impromptu engagement party, begun with champagne toasts.

"Or would you prefer purple passion?" Yalie asked before pouring my glass. The toast she offered was, "Here's to being expelled from Colorado so you could go to Berkeley to meet a guy from Colorado."

Laughing, we all tipped our glasses and drank. And then Dev asked, "Did you know your girlfriend has a criminal record? I'll take you down to the courthouse and show it to you."

JJ answered, "I believe in rehabilitation of criminals. Marriage is part of Rachel's twelve-step recovery program, and I'm to be her sponsor."

I kissed him enthusiastically.

Aunt Ruth talked about tending Yalie and me the night of the accident. "You weren't exactly stone-cold sober as I recall, Ya'el. They probably should have expelled you, too."

Uncle Aaron recalled his part in the story of my arrest and punishment. "She wasn't, shall we say, *pleased* when she found out what her father and I did to her, but it hasn't turned out too badly, has it Rachel?"

"I'm fully rehabilitated," I said. "Right, JJ?"

This time, he kissed me.

We spent the night in Boulder and flew back to California the next day. We returned feeling we'd conquered our world. Even the harrowing visit to the Weiners had turned out okay.

In late August, JJ and I drove north to Palo Alto. I helped him settle into his apartment before classes began. Then he delivered me and my belongings to Berkeley for my senior year. We were hoping to see one another every couple of weekends. But the telephone would be our primary means of contact during the next nine months. I wasn't happy about that. Not at all. JJ had decreed that we would live apart until he finished his MBA, but although I had accepted it, I hadn't internalized it. I didn't tell JJ how I felt: that he'd simply ignored my wishes.

However, I was too busy to stew about it endlessly. I was taking a maximum load. I'd already nailed down Phi Beta Kappa and highest honors. But I wanted in the worst way to be designated the outstanding political science graduate in my class, and I'd undertaken an ambitious senior project to help my candidacy.

JJ and I talked every day, usually more than once. But the weekends together turned out to be many fewer than we'd hoped. Neither of us could take the time. Jess was living across the bay in San Francisco and was overwhelmed by her first year in law school. So I didn't see her often either. Although I had lots of friends at Berkeley, I felt lonely—as lonely as I had the year I commuted to UCLA.

Academic effort was my salvation. I worked all day every day and sometimes late into the night. I'd always been a serious student, but I outdid myself that year. Professor Ferguson told me I was producing some of the best undergraduate work he'd ever seen. The woman who taught advanced political theory told me I should get a Ph.D.. I was flattered but remained fixed on becoming a journalist after graduation. Even though I liked learning things, I had no interest in being a cloistered scholar.

I suppose I understood that not planning to continue on to graduate school would hurt my effort to be chosen for departmental honors. Professor Ferguson had certainly warned me that some members of the faculty might prefer to give the award to a student on the academic track. But I didn't want to believe that. I thought I was the best and would win the award because I deserved it.

*   *   *

On those occasional weekends when JJ and I met, I was more than ready for us to sleep together. I figured JJ would change his mind now that we were engaged. For a girl who had never enjoyed sex, I was

almost panting with frustration. But he was adamant—no sex before
we got married. And he had another year at Stanford after this one. We
could only hug and kiss up to a point. As soon as he got aroused, he'd
practically push me away.

I said to him once, "You want me, JJ. And I'm ready for you. Why
can't we make love?"

"Because," he answered me furiously. "I told you before. I won't
sleep with you until we're married. Stop bugging me about it."

I started crying. "I love you, JJ. That's all."

He dropped the angry tone. "I'm sorry, sugar. It's as hard for me
as it is for you."

Even though I was still shedding tears, I started giggling. I was
looking at the erection sticking up in his slacks.

He started laughing, too. "Okay," he said. "Hard for me. Difficult
for you." He added, "I do love you. You know that, sugar."

I acknowledged that I did. But that didn't make it any easier. I
wanted to be hugged and kissed. And I wanted to hug and kiss him
back. And that was dangerous.

It got to the point where we were better off not being alone. We
went to San Francisco to be with Jess and Sam a couple of times. JJ
brought Arlie with him from Palo Alto to Berkeley once, and all five
of us spent a weekend north of San Francisco in wine country. JJ
sent me off at night to room with Arlie. If Arlie thought the sleeping
arrangements were strange, she didn't say so—not to me at least.

I was pleased that my friends were becoming JJ's friends. But I
also knew that my friends were being used as shields against our sexual
desires. Our weekends together were just about as frustrating as they
were fulfilling. It was a long, long, long nine months.

After we'd employed Jess and Sam a couple of times to fend off
temptation, Jess grasped what was happening. "Excuse me, Rache, for
asking a question you may not want to answer. You're not sleeping
together, are you? Sam and I are your chaperones."

I hesitated before answering. I could have told her to back off.
Instead, I said, "When did you get to be so perceptive, Jess? No, we're
not sleeping together. JJ won't allow it."

"I'm probably getting into something I shouldn't, Rache. But don't
you think that's a little peculiar?"

I couldn't say another word. I held back, with considerable effort, the tears I was ready to shed and just nodded my head.

Jess hugged me and said, "I'm sorry, Rache. I don't mean to upset you. I should never have asked."

She couldn't un-ask the question, however. What she'd done, without meaning to, was to reinforce my feeling that JJ's edict was unreasonable. He wasn't concerned about how it affected me. But I didn't ask Jess, whom I'd come to consider the wisest of my friends, for her advice. Nor did I say anything to JJ. I should have done both.

*   *   *

In June, I graduated with highest honors, but the departmental award in political science went to Melanie Ashland. I knew Melanie very well. We had been rivals for the past two years, and there was quite a nasty edge to the rivalry. I felt really bad when I got the news. I didn't think it was fair. I was sure that I was the better student and that Melanie had been chosen only because she'd already signed up for graduate school. Despite Professor Ferguson's warning, I'd convinced myself that I would get the award because it was due me. If only it had been someone other than Melanie. She was such a suck-up, such a smile-in-your-face, knife-in-your-back kind of person. God, I hated her.

I still get worked up when I think about it.

Now that I was graduated, I wanted to get married and spend the coming year with JJ in Palo Alto. He wouldn't agree. "We've already been over this. You'd be a bad influence," he told me. "I'm having a hard enough time in the MBA program without Rachel Rothschild breathing in my ear."

I wanted to spend the summer with JJ, hiking and biking in the Colorado mountains. But he wouldn't agree to that, either. He intended to work in Denver over the summer, and he wanted me to start my career. We had our first real fight. I complained that JJ always wanted things his way. He said I was acting like a child and needed to grow up. I had a tantrum, proving to him, I suppose, that he was right.

We had this disagreement in the living room of my parents' house. I stormed off to my bedroom and slammed the door. I laid down on the bed and began pounding the pillow with both fists. After awhile,

JJ knocked on the door. I said, "Go away." He came in anyway to apologize. I made him grovel before I let him kiss me.

But the net of it was that we did things JJ's way. We always did things JJ's way.

All he would agree to was a week in the Colorado mountains. He invited Dev and Yalie to join us. He refused to be alone there with me. Yalie was taking the first part of the summer off after her first year at Yale Law School, and Dev could get away from Lockhart and Case for a week. They felt awkward about intruding. Since Jess had already guessed the truth, I felt obliged to tell my cousins. Resignedly, I explained that JJ insisted on chaperones and I'd rather have the two of them than a duenna. "I feel like a nun," I confessed. "But that's JJ. Even though I've told him I'm not a virgin, he won't sleep with me until we're married. Virgin or not, it's been decided. I'm to be JJ's virgin bride."

I didn't bother pretending that I accepted the arrangement willingly. I loved Yalie and Dev, but I wanted to be alone with JJ. Still, I never worked up the nerve to demand that we end this Victorian fantasy of his, nightmare of mine.

So I shut out my irritation with JJ and settled for what I'd been given. The four of us drove toward Aspen, settled in at the Aspen-Basalt Campground, and spent our days biking and hiking along the noisy, rushing Roaring Fork and Frying Pan Rivers. We also explored the magnificent Maroon Bells, with their mountain meadow floor and climbing trails. We even fished for trout, something I had never done, and we grilled our own catch. On the final afternoon, we hired a guide and took a raft trip along the Colorado River rapids outside Glenwood Springs. The trip was hell for me. I was scared, I was wet, I couldn't wait for it to end. Some tomboy I'd turned out to be! JJ, Dev, and Yalie enjoyed themselves immensely, and they teased me about being a city slicker. I bore the kidding with as much good humor as I could muster, which wasn't much.

The next morning, we returned to Denver via Boulder, where we dropped Yalie. Dev had an apartment near Cherry Creek, close to where JJ's parents lived. JJ had decided that I would sleep overnight at the Weiner compound and then fly home to Santa Monica. Herman and Vera told JJ that they wanted me to stay an extra night. They intended to take us to dinner at Green Gables Country Club with

Grandma Bess and JJ's Uncle Max and Aunt Mildred and their three children. I had to meet the rest of the family, and this was the easiest way to do it, they argued. JJ consented. He didn't ask me; he told me.

We spent part of the day at the zoo. That night, JJ and I drove alone to Green Gables. Herman and Vera brought Grandma Bess. Max and Mildred Weiner turned out to be very pleasant people, and they welcomed me warmly. More warmly than Herman and Vera had the first time I met them. But now I was officially recognized as JJ's fiancée, so that might have explained the difference. Whatever the reason, they were nice to me, and I liked them. However, I didn't much care for their three children, and I didn't make a favorable impression on them, either.

When I got to know them later, I realized that they were already jealous that their cousin, JJ, was Grandma Bess's favorite. Grandma Bess's obvious warmth toward me was anything but a plus in their eyes. The son, who'd quit college because it required too much hard work, was a vice president of Hyman Weiner & Sons. He was a lot more interested in having a good time than he was in his job. The second oldest, a girl, considered herself an artist, and her parents indulged her in that illusion. The youngest, who was attending Vassar, was twenty but seemed considerably younger—in fact, juvenile.

I hoped not to have to spend much time with these cousins. We were never going to be friends. I told JJ as we were driving back to the house that I liked his aunt and uncle.

"What did you think about my three cousins?" he asked.

"They seemed okay," I lied.

"They're not," he said. "He's playboy and a leech. Louise pretends to be a painter, but it's just an excuse for not working. And Char is a snot."

"You really love them," I said, grinning.

"Yes. The same way they love me."

"Then I'll tell you the truth," I said. "All I could think of was that I hoped we wouldn't have to see these people too often."

"Never is too often," he said. "But my uncle's a nice guy, and I'll be working with him. I won't be able to avoid running into his son. You'll see him and his sisters rarely, which will probably seem much, much too frequently."

"I think I can handle 'rarely,'" I said.

Once again I was discovering that the intense family feeling in the Rothschild clan wasn't to be found among the Weiners. In just about a year, I would be marrying into this family and moving to Denver. All I could think of was, thank God, the Goodmans will be close by. The Goodmans and Grandma Bess.

The following morning, I kissed Grandma Bess good-bye and brushed cheeks with Herman and Vera. Then JJ drove me to Stapleton Airport and off I went, more frustrated than happy after the week in Colorado. Frustration was getting to be a normal condition for me.

I'd yet to have a serious conversation with JJ about the main source of my discomfort, having my life arranged for me without my being consulted. Why not? Was I afraid of losing him? Probably. I really didn't understand the consequences of allowing a pattern to be set that would continue after we were married. Looking back, though I was a college graduate and ready to begin my career, I didn't have the force of personality to be JJ's partner in our relationship. He led, and I followed. Resentfully to be sure, but nevertheless I followed.

*   *   *

Before looking for my first job, I talked it over with Amanda Collins. She told me I could have a position at the *L.A. Times* if I wanted one, but she advised against it. She said I'd be taken on as a copy girl to begin with and when I finally graduated to reporting assignments, I'd be treated as a cub, given work that wasn't very challenging. The apprenticeship could last a year or more. Amanda said she could get me an interview with Harold Matthews, editor of *L.A. Beat*, a well-established monthly with broad readership. I would have a much better opportunity there to do what I was capable of doing.

"The *L.A. Times* is not the best school for a starting journalist," Amanda said. "Come to us after you've proven yourself, and you won't be forced to do work that's below your skill level."

A week later I was on the job at *L.A. Beat*, gathering information for the "What's On in LA-LA Land" section and writing "brights" for the front of the book, short items about Los Angeles personalities or happenings, derived from tips provided by publicity agents, ideas submitted by readers, or interviews with people identified by Harold

Matthews: movie stars, musicians, club owners, studio executives, talent agents, local businessmen, and so forth.

The staple fare was fluff about the entertainment industry. "That is the kind of writing visitors to L.A. are interested in," Mr. Matthews said, and tourists were a significant part of *L.A. Beat's* audience and the principal target of most of the magazine's advertisers. The longer articles that appeared in the magazine were occasionally written for permanent residents of Los Angeles who were neither employed in nor dependent on the entertainment industry. About one per issue was the Matthews formula.

Writing fluff wasn't what I'd trained to do, but I was pretty good at it. The front of the book was read by almost everyone who picked up the magazine, subscribers as well as tourists. Mr. Matthews liked my work so much that he wanted me to continue doing it indefinitely. Because of the advertisers, the tourists had a much more important place in Harold Matthews's judgments about editorial content than the subscribers did. *L.A. Beat* was not so much about Los Angeles as about making money for the owners, one of whom was Harold Matthews. I was doing what he thought was important work even if I didn't.

After three months, I asked Mr. Matthews to let me write an article about Moses White, the drug counselor I knew from when I was doing community service following my expulsion from CU. I explained Moe's background and—with some editing—how I knew him. Mr. Matthews wasn't enthusiastic. Drug addicts, unless they happened to be actors or rock stars, weren't popular with tourists. But he allowed himself to be persuaded that Moe White's personal story had enough human interest to attract our regular readers, maybe even some of the visitors who picked the magazine up off the newsstand or found it in their hotel rooms.

Moe White wasn't at all sure he wanted to be profiled in *L.A. Beat*, but I convinced him that the story wouldn't just be about him. It would be about the drug crisis in L.A. neighborhoods and about helping young addicts confront their demons.

Shayanna Lee was startled when I walked in the clinic's front door, representing *L.A. Beat*. It was written all over her face. She was not pleased to see me or to hear about my project. She had not been consulted, she said, and she wasn't sure she would allow it. But I had taken the precaution of clearing the idea for the article with the mayor's office and with Ms. Lee's immediate supervisor.

"Call them if you'd like," I said sweetly. And, making it sound like a concession, I added matter-of-factly, "I won't mention you or the name of the clinic, if you prefer." I had decided that the best way to rub Ms. Lee's nose in it—her *motherfucking* nose, to use Lynetta's formulation—was by *not* rubbing her nose in it.

I spent most of a day at the clinic trailing Moe around, and I took him out to lunch twice just to talk. Getting him to tell me more about himself was the hard part. He much preferred talking about his work at the clinic. Nevertheless, I finally got his story.

He'd grown up in South Central L.A., the son of a hardworking, churchgoing mother and an absent father. As a young teenager, he'd run with a neighborhood gang, dropped out of junior high school, become addicted to heroin, been arrested for armed robbery at fourteen, been packed off to a "reform school"—"a heartbreakingly usual story," he said.

A counselor who'd been a football star at California State University in L.A. helped Moe see possibilities other than life on the streets. He got Moe interested in throwing a football around and lifting weights. He also convinced him to get his high school equivalency degree. Once he was free again, Moe managed with help from his mother's pastor to get into Los Angeles Community College, where he'd "done okay" —well enough to win a football scholarship to California State and there to earn a degree in social work.

"I owe three people," Moe said. "My Mama, who never give up on me, Jamaal Jackman, who set me straight, and the Reverend Coleman. Without them, I prob'ly be in San Quentin or dead."

When I was finished at the clinic, I spent two days researching L.A.'s drug problems. That would provide the larger context into which Moe's story would be fitted.

The article I wrote described Moe's success with one addict and his failure with another and also covered the relationship between Moe's personal history and his vocation. But it was also about drug addiction in Los Angeles and the struggle to cope with it in all its manifestations—as a criminal enterprise, as a spur to robbery, assault, and murder, as a catastrophe for certain communities in the city, as a human disaster. The piece was overwrought and overwritten, and it had a lot more in it about drug addiction than fit Harold Matthews's definition of "good copy." Harold Matthews was a lazy editor, however. He took what I gave him, cut it a fraction to fit the available space, and did very little else.

Even with its defects, which were many, the article drew a lot of favorable comment. Mr. Matthews heard personally from the mayor, something that did not happen very often. A prominent civic leader wrote a letter to the editor, thanking *L.A. Beat* for "sensitive handling of a very important subject." The article turned Moe White into a minor celebrity. I heard from my contact in the department that Shayanna Lee thought she should have received a credit as Moe's boss. That pleased me. I felt I'd repaid her in a small way for how she treated me.

Next I convinced Mr. Matthews to let me write about L.A.'s public transportation system. I had used it for the better part of two years and understood something about its strengths and its deficiencies. Most of the people who read *L.A. Beat* regularly spent hours each week on the freeways but never saw the inside of a bus. Tourists weren't big customers of public transportation, either. I planned to tell readers what it was like trying day after day to get from public housing at one end of the city to a low-paying job at the other end across a sparsely connected web of transit routes.

Again, Harold Matthews was less than enthusiastic. However, I believe he had enjoyed the unexpected acclaim resulting from my previous piece, and maybe he had begun to think that an occasional article about L.A.'s problems might generate prestige locally that would be good for the magazine's reputation. So, once again, he said yes.

I knew exactly how I wanted to proceed. I told the story by tracing the daily routes traveled by a black woman from South Central who served as housekeeper for a family in Beverly Hills, a Hispanic man from East L.A. who was a janitor at a hotel in Santa Monica, and a Vietnamese man living near Korea Town who worked in a restaurant in Century City. I also explored how L.A.'s transportation system came to be the way it was and collected national statistics for purposes of comparison. Chicago's system, for example, was much more compact than L.A.'s and handled many more passengers with fewer buses. When I got all this material in place, I interviewed L.A.'s transportation chief about plans for improving area mass transit.

Harold Matthews indulged me in ways that a more exacting editor would not have. I was trying to be a serious journalist, and publishing serious journalism was not something that *L.A. Beat* was customarily accused of. My stuff was like meat and potatoes on a platter full of chocolate truffles. But once more, Mr. Mathews heard from people who were important figures in Los Angeles public life that the article was a useful contribution to the good of the city. Even one of the other owners complimented him for finding this new writer.

Amanda Collins was thrilled by my progress and told me so. "You're a natural investigative reporter, Rachel," she said. "Keep at it, honey."

*   *   *

The end of JJ's MBA program was in sight now, and I was more interested in planning our wedding than in my next byline. The wedding would take place in Santa Monica in mid-June, and I wanted a big, traditional affair: a white-tie ceremony at our temple in Westwood, with my little sister Rebecca as maid of honor, seven bridesmaids (Yalie, Dev, Arlie, Laura, Jess, Lynetta, and—strictly for protocol reasons—JJ's sister, Annalisa), and a guest list in the hundreds. I was even sending an invitation to Suzi Orbach, whom I hadn't seen since the beginning of tenth grade and hadn't heard from for more than two years.

JJ's best man would be Dr. Allan Garson, Annalisa's husband. Though JJ couldn't stand his brother-in-law, he didn't want to alienate his sister even further. Groomsmen would include Professor Tom Ferguson, who brought us together, an investment banker from New York who'd been JJ's friend since childhood, two law-school classmates, his roommate at Berkeley, and two more college friends. I thought he should have made room for my brothers, the same as I'd made room for Annalisa among my bridesmaids, but once again I didn't say anything.

My Rothschild grandparents would be flying in from Israel, bringing my cousin Avital (add one to the list of bridesmaids), and, unexpectedly, Mom's parents were also coming. I had seen them once when I was very young but didn't even remember them. The entire

Colorado clans on both sides would attend, and I was eager for my parents and my father's parents to meet Grandma Bess.

More than four hundred fifty people were scheduled to be at the wedding. Suzi Orbach would not be among them. A brief letter from her mother reported that Suzi earned a teaching certificate after college, joined the Peace Corps, and was now teaching English in Sierra Leone.

About seventy-two hours before the wedding, I began to panic. Although Mom had all the details under control, I was sure everything would go wrong. I almost had a fit when the rabbi who was to marry us rejected certain of my suggestions about changes in the wedding rituals. *How dare he!* I thought. I flew into a rage at the caterer about how the tables were to be set. "I want fish knives for the salmon!" I shouted. I broke down and cried hysterically when my wedding gown required a small repair. And the afternoon before the wedding rehearsal, I screamed "goddam you" at Rebecca when she offered an opinion different from mine on the music to be played while the wedding guests were waiting for the ceremony to begin. Rebecca turned and left the room without saying a word.

"Back to my bedroom, young lady," Mom interjected in a tone I hadn't heard since I was a child. Once the door was closed behind us, Mom said, "I've let you get away with a lot the last couple of days, Rachel. I understand about bridal nerves. But you've gone entirely too far. You're almost twenty-three years old, and you're acting like an eight-year-old. What you just did to Rebecca is disgraceful. You ought to be ashamed of yourself. She was just trying to offer a suggestion, and you spit right in her face. I want you to go out there and beg her pardon. Otherwise, you and JJ can get married in the rabbi's study, and we'll forget the big ceremony and the party."

It was an empty threat. Mom knew that. I knew that. But I stood there hanging my head during the lecture, and I was weeping before it ended. "I'm sorry, Mommy," I said. I hadn't called her anything but "Mom" in years. "I'm really, truly sorry." I went into Mom's arms, looking to be comforted. Mom told me, "There, there, baby. Everything's going to be just fine."

I found Rebecca in her room, hurt but dry-eyed. I apologized sincerely. "I'm sorry, Beck. I shouldn't have screamed at you. I know you were only trying to help. I guess it shows *I'm* the baby in this family, not you. I'll stand in the corner if you like."

We hugged, and peace was restored. On the day of the wedding, I was as calm a bride as anyone had ever seen. Certainly no one had ever been happier than I was at this moment. I was surrounded by family and friends. JJ and I were finally together. And I'd never believed more strongly in the fairy-tale ending of happily ever after.

The presence of my Horowitz grandparents was not a success. My grandfather, Rabbi Moses Horowitz, in his Orthodox garb, looked like he'd been parachuted in from the Me'a She'arim. He declined an opportunity to read one of the seven wedding blessings because he would not participate in a Reform ceremony. My grandmother, Sara Horowitz, must have felt completely out of place with her heavy Yiddish accent and determinedly unfashionable clothing. We belonged to a different world than they did.

When we were standing in the receiving line after the ceremony, my grandfather said something to Mom as he went by. I could see the lightning flash in her eyes. Though she never told me what happened, I'm sure he gave her cause to remember why she'd left home at nineteen and hadn't been to see them in twenty years. It was obvious that they disapproved of us—her, Daddy, me, my siblings. As far as they were concerned, we weren't real Jews, just wannabe *goyim*. I don't know why they came. Perhaps to reinforce their convictions about our brand of apostasy. They didn't have ten words to say to me. I said hello and good-bye to them and, in between, I ignored them. There were too many people around that I loved and who loved me to want to spend precious moments pretending to have a connection that wasn't there.

My Rothschild grandparents, on the other hand, were very important to me. I regretted not having enough time to be with them. (I didn't have enough time to be with anybody.) But I made sure they met Grandma Bess, and I introduced them to JJ's parents, reminding Grandpa and Vera that they'd met in Israel. Grandpa and Herman, JJ's dad, were having a conversation about Israeli politics when I left them.

At the wedding dinner, JJ and I made the rounds, stopping at every table. But I was eager to get away. I'd waited more than two years for what was coming next, and I'm not ashamed to say I wanted it. At the same time, I was apprehensive. I'd had sex before and hadn't liked it.

Would it be different with JJ? I hoped it would be different. I needed it to be different.

JJ and I spent our first night together as husband and wife at the Miramar, the poshest hotel in Santa Monica. I undressed in the bathroom and came to JJ in a diaphanous blue nightgown. No preliminaries were really necessary. Believe me, I was ready. But JJ was a patient lover. He kissed me deeply, and I kissed him back. He helped me out of my nightgown and kissed my naked body. He grasped my core and gently opened me. I was writhing at his touch and beginning to moan.

"Please," I said. He entered me. We found one another's rhythm and rocked with increasing intensity to a shattering climax. It was better than I'd hoped. I was exhilarated and exhausted. "I love you, love you, love you, love you," I said, until he stopped my mouth with a final kiss. We fell asleep with me on his shoulder, and when we awakened in the morning, I was still lying naked in his arms. I wanted JJ to make love to me again. My apprehension was gone. I liked sex with JJ. I loved sex with JJ.

Afterwards, we put our night clothes back on and had a leisurely breakfast in our room. In the afternoon we caught a flight that would take us overnight to Italy for a month-long honeymoon. This was my first time in Italy, and I was as excited as a little girl. We'd be visiting Rome, Capri, Positano, the Amafi Coast, Florence, the Tuscan countryside, Venice, Lake Como, Milan—all places I had dreamed about seeing. JJ had been to Italy before, and he arranged our itinerary so he could show me all the sights he loved: the ruins of ancient Rome, the fountains, the Spanish Steps, the Vatican, the Blue Grotto at Capri, the coastline along the Gulf of Salerno, the golden Duomo in Florence, Michaelangelo's *David*, the Pitti Palace, the Uffizi Gallery, the canals of Venice, St. Mark's, the Villa d'Este, La Scala, and the modern core of Milan.

It was beginning to be hot in Italy, especially in the south. But I was an eager tourist during the day, taking in all the sights that JJ had planned for me to see. At night, there was sex. We could not get enough of one another's bodies. I adored the feel of JJ's nakedness on mine. I liked having his weight on top of me. I liked having him beneath me. I liked having his head between my legs and discovered that I even liked giving him a blow job, something I'd found abhorrent when boys had suggested it to me in high school. We dispensed with condoms. I wasn't reticent about my delight. I moaned, I panted, I squealed. I raked JJ's back with my nails when we were approaching a climax. I screamed his name. This was a different me.

Everyone comes back from Italy raving about the food. Every day we found a restaurant to come back to for dinner. But, otherwise, we had little time for Italy after dark. All we wanted to do was to retire to our room and make love. Once we even had intercourse during my period. JJ told me laughingly that I was wearing him out. But I think he was at least as eager for me as I was for him. The years of restraint and frustration were over, and we were making up for lost time.

It was a glorious month. I was spectacularly happy. When it was done, we flew back to Denver from Milan via JFK in New York. We returned to a penthouse condo overlooking Cheesman Park, which JJ had purchased several months before the wedding and refurbished. I saw it for the first time when JJ opened the front door and we walked in. It was actually two apartments joined together and had more rooms than I thought we needed—a sizable living room, family room, dining room, kitchen, three bedrooms, and three and a half bathrooms. It had a large balcony outside the living room, looking toward the mountains. The view could not have been better.

JJ's mother, Vera, had furnished the place for us. It was all beautiful, but not to my taste at all. I liked modern furniture with clean lines. Vera, without bothering to ask, had done the living room in French Provincial. It was much too formal for me. I wanted to be relaxed at home, not concerned with every little scratch. But I concealed my irritation. Vera meant well, and—what the hell—I would hang a few of Mom's paintings and, as for the French Provincial, I could always tell my family when they came to visit, "This is Vera's living room, not mine."

The master bedroom held a king-size bed where I hoped JJ and I would spend a lot of time.

And one of the other bedrooms was fixed as a den-office for JJ, with a mahogany desk, a high-backed desk chair, two leather side chairs, a standing globe of the world, floor-to-ceiling bookcases, and a large TV set on its own stand opposite the desk.

We had no sooner unpacked our suitcases than JJ told me to come downstairs with him. Waiting on the driveway in front of the building was a bright silver Mercedes, the smallest sedan they made. JJ handed me the keys. "It's yours, sugar. Hope you like it."

Like it? It was the cutest little car I'd ever seen, almost a sports car. I all but jumped into JJ's arms and knocked his glasses askew when I kissed him. I was so excited that I had a hard time getting the key in the lock so I could open the door. Once JJ did it for me and I was behind the wheel, I couldn't wait to try it out.

"Where should we go?" I asked JJ. He suggested City Park, and when that turned out to be not enough, we drove west toward the mountains with the windows wide open and the air streaming across our bodies. I felt as if I could drive straight ahead to Santa Monica to show my new toy to Mom and Daddy, Rebecca, and the twins. But the adrenalin couldn't fight the jet lag forever, so I turned the car around near Golden and we went back to the apartment. Time for bed. And just as I was falling asleep, I suddenly thought that if the silver Mercedes were soft like a teddy bear, I might take it to bed with me. I began giggling. But JJ was already breathing deeply, and he didn't hear.

*   *   *

There was no immediate reason for me to find work. We had all the money we needed, JJ didn't think it was a good idea, and I wanted to enjoy being a newlywed. That turned out to be a serious mistake. I had been going to school or working for the past six years, and being at leisure in a new city in new circumstances gave me too much time to find my discomfort level.

It exposed the divergence of my interests from Vera's as well as the difference in our temperaments. I saw too much of Annalisa and found myself disliking her intensely. She was eight and a half years older than I, and she treated me like a child. Furthermore, she seemed to resent me in every conceivable way. JJ volunteered an explanation: "You succeeded at college, she didn't; you're natural, she's a twenty-four-carat phony; you're beautiful, she's not."

It wasn't that Annalisa was ugly. She was actually quite nice looking. But the same features that made JJ handsome were out of place on his sister. She was four or five inches shorter than I was, but she had sloping shoulders and an awkward gait like a whooping crane. She visited the hairdresser regularly, but her hair was naturally straight and lifeless. Her relentless social climbing and snobbery were characteristics I found ridiculous as well as off-putting.

Annalisa's husband, *Dr.* Allan Garson—I couldn't think of him any other way—was the most self-centered human being I'd ever encountered. He was an orthopedic surgeon. But even in a branch of the medical profession where arrogance appeared to be as unremarkable as antlers on an elk, Dr. Allan Garson stood out. Like his wife, he was a social climber of the worst sort. Their two daughters attended the "best" schools with the children of the most socially prominent families in Denver. While they were cute little girls, they were being raised to be insufferable.

Grandma Bess was a completely different story, of course. She'd truly elected me to be her favorite granddaughter, and I loved the old lady. But Grandma Bess was now eighty-one, and while she could be a marvelous substitute grandparent, she could not supply the companionship I needed. My cousin Dev was living in Denver, close to our condo, but she was deluged with work at the law firm. In addition, she had a new boyfriend, a young professor of political science at the University of Denver named Mark Chapman. They were just getting to know one another. So I saw much less of Dev than I would have liked. Yalie was back East, starting her final year in law school. I talked with my parents every day and kept in close touch with Arlie, Laura, and Jess. I talked only occasionally with Lynetta, who was in med school and, as she described it, "busy as the proverbial one-armed paperhanger." She said, "There's so much to learn, and they throw it at you relentlessly. Even though I'm in good shape physically, I'm tired all the time."

Without a job to keep me busy, I was restless. I played tennis most mornings or used the gym. Many afternoons, I traipsed around town in my silver Mercedes, visiting museums and other cultural attractions. It wasn't a very satisfying life.

I was looking for things to do, and that's when I began writing my autobiography. I don't know why. What did I have to write about? My life had been pretty uneventful thus far. I wasn't ever going to be famous. But I enjoyed writing, and I liked the challenge of recreating what I'd experienced when I was younger. Somewhere in the back of my mind, I was thinking *Maybe I'll write fiction some day, and a memoir will provide me with raw material.*

I wrote a couple of hours every day, but writing about yourself is lonely work. Not a lot of people to interview. It wasn't enough to meet my needs. I wanted JJ's attention. I didn't like it when he worked late in the evenings or brought a packed briefcase home on weekends. I liked it even less when he went into the office on an occasional Saturday to catch up. If I had been in charge, JJ would have gone to the office late, arrived home early, and taken three-day weekends every weekend. JJ had a fifty-million-dollar trust fund in his own name—our name—and hundreds of millions more to come. I wasn't greedy. All I wanted was JJ.

I have to admit that I made a huge pest of myself. I called JJ at the office several times a day so he could tell me he loved me. I complained endlessly about his hours and, even more so, about weekend work. He explained his responsibilities—repeatedly and with mounting annoyance. He talked about keeping the company going for our children and our children's children. I understood, but I didn't want to understand. As I've already said, I wasn't yet a grown-up. I wanted what I wanted.

I complained once too often about the amount of weekend work JJ was bringing home in his briefcase. JJ told me to shut up, and I said "Fuck you. Make me if you're man enough." The next thing I knew he had me by the wrist, and then I was over his lap and he had my skirt up and was pulling my panties down. I was kicking and screaming, "Don't you dare." When he had my bottom bared, he began spanking me with the flat of his hand—hard.

I was still fighting him, but he was much too strong. I started crying, more from the humiliation than the pain, but he kept on until I stopped struggling and gave myself over completely to my tears.

When JJ was finished spanking me, he kept me lying there across his lap while he told me, "I love you more than anything in the world, sugar. But if you're going to act immature, you are going to feel the consequences. It's up to you. You can have another spanking tomorrow or next week or never again. I'd a lot rather make love to you than spank you. Do you understand me?"

I started bawling all over again. Finally, I was able to say, "Yes, lover, I understand." And, then, though I had every right to be the aggrieved one, I said, "I'm sorry."

The next thing I knew JJ had lifted me into his arms and was carrying me into the bedroom. He laid me down on the bed, got rid of my skirt and panties, stripped off my blouse and bra, and dropped his own clothes on the floor. He took me without any preliminaries. I felt like Cavewoman After the Hunt. I wasn't ready. "You're hurting me, JJ," I said.

He pulled out of me immediately and apologized. Then he made love to me slowly and gently.

By the time he reentered me, I was completely liquid. We reached climaxes simultaneously, and I saw stars and pinwheels. After he came inside of me, I went down on him and sucked him clean, the first time I'd ever tasted his semen. I urged him to another erection. This time he took me from behind, holding my small breasts and bumping against my red bottom. When JJ spent himself the second time, I collapsed on the bed, and he collapsed on top of me. Just before we fell asleep, I told him that I loved him more than ever.

Daniel, our first child, was conceived that night. I wasn't taking the pill as regularly as I should have if I wanted to avoid becoming pregnant early in our marriage.

We hadn't talked about children yet. Still, we were ecstatic about the news. We made plans, unmade them, remade them. Once we knew it would be a boy, we spent three consecutive weekends furnishing the nursery. That could easily have been accomplished at a single store in an hour, but we were in no hurry to decide. We were enjoying the process.

I suffered from morning sickness at first. Mom flew in from Santa Monica and put me to bed for a few days. When I was back on my feet, I saw my ob-gyn and was told that I was remarkably healthy and the baby was doing just fine. We were a bit gingerly in our lovemaking after my belly swelled, but abstinence was not on the agenda. We simply found new positions, even consulting a sex manual for the purpose.

Mom and Daddy had been planning a big family seder in April, our first as a married couple. We decided not to attend. I, as the first-time mother-to-be, and JJ, the proud father-to-be, were being very careful, overly careful. Mom was very disappointed, but she accepted our decision. After all, this would be her first grandchild, and she was almost as excited as the prospective parents.

You would have thought also that this was Grandma Bess's first great-grandchild, though Annalisa had already given her two. I don't know that Grandma Bess tried particularly hard, but if she did, she wasn't terribly successful in disguising the fact that JJ was her favorite grandchild. And she had made it clear to the family that she was also extremely fond of me. So our child would be very special in her eyes. That was just another reason (as if she needed one) for Annalisa not to like me.

The baby was born in the middle of August, two months short of my twenty-fourth birthday. We had been married fourteen months. Daniel Avraham was the name we chose. He weighed eight pounds five ounces and had dark brown hair and coloring like JJ's. JJ hired a live-in nurse to be with us for the first several months, though I didn't see why.

My parents came for the baby's birth and stayed on until his bris, when it was all I could do to keep from fainting. After Mom left, I understood the advantages of having a live-in nurse. Babies were a lot more work than I had anticipated.

I was determined to breast-feed, which meant that I was up often in the middle of the night. I adored my little guy but was happy enough to have Marie Halloran bathe him and change his diapers. I'm convinced I would have done okay as a not-so-rich-man's wife but, it was definitely easier not having to worry about what it was costing to keep Daniel comfortable and me well-rested.

When Marie departed and it was just the three of us, I thought I was doing just fine. JJ, however, felt I was showing signs of harassment, so he brought in Blanca Rodriguez, a middle-aged Mexican woman, to handle household duties. She came daily. Her presence left me free to spend my time on Daniel when he was awake and on writing when he wasn't. I did my writing on a laptop computer, sitting on a chair in Daniel's room. I liked to keep an eye on him while he napped. I felt I had a little miracle on my hands and didn't want to miss a single miraculous moment—napping, for instance. I was waiting impatiently, as if for history's first baby, to see him smile, roll over, sit up, teethe, begin to crawl. I talked incessantly to him when he was awake and kissed him a thousand times a day. I loved having him suck at my breast. In most respects, I'm sure I was no different than any other new mommy except that Daniel was my sole responsibility. The writing was a luxury, and I dropped it—often in mid-sentence—the moment Daniel stirred.

Mom had warned me that some husbands subconsciously feel displaced by their children. She said to be sure to show affection to JJ as well as to the baby. That advice was unneeded. With Blanca handling the food shopping and the cooking, I had plenty of energy left at night for my husband. We made love most nights, and I was often the one who initiated it. My appetite for JJ's body remained fierce and unquenchable. I had no difficulty remembering to tell him how much I loved him. He was everything I wanted, everything. Smart, funny, good-looking, nice, and—best of all—in love with me. His being rich was no handicap, certainly. But I was absolutely sure I would have been in love with JJ if we were penniless. Our life together was quiet but joyous. We rarely went out while Daniel was an infant. I didn't feel the need. I was not at all lonely. In fact, I'd never felt happier.

I had plenty of company. Grandma Bess stopped by regularly to see the baby and to tell me how wonderful he was. Dev came once a week in the evening, bringing dinner, and she spent the entire morning with us every Saturday if she wasn't needed at the office. JJ's parents brought Shabbat dinner most Friday nights. Aunt Ruth and Uncle Aaron visited when they had reason to be in Denver. And, of course, my parents were on the phone constantly. Rebecca, who had just begun her freshman year at Berkeley, called at least twice a week. She was eager to hear the latest news about her nephew, even his sniffles. I also heard frequently from Jess, Laura, and Arlie. They were as close to me as sisters and considered themselves Daniel's aunts. Lynetta was serving an internship at a hospital in Oakland and was working even harder than she had in medical school, but even she called every couple of weeks.

Then again, I rarely heard from my cousin Yalie. Having graduated law school, she was now clerk to a judge on the U.S. Circuit Court of Appeals in Washington, D.C. Dev asked me to forgive Yalie's inattention. "She's swamped with work," Dev said. "But, more important, she's in love."

That was news. Except for the few weeks on the kibbutz when we were in Israel together while in high school, I'd never known Yalie to have a real boyfriend, let alone be in love. "Who's the guy?" I asked.

"Someone she knew at Yale," Dev said. "He's in D.C., too. And it's no coincidence. I think he followed her there. In fact, I'm sure of it."

"Has anybody met him?" I asked.

"Not yet. I get the idea that Yalie's intending to bring him to our next seder. So you'll meet him the same time the rest of us do."

"Yalie in love," I said. "I'd begun to believe it would never happen."

"Well, at least one of the Goodman girls is in love," Dev responded.

"You next, sweetie," I said, hugging her.

"Yeah. Me next," she said uncertainly.

*   *   *

Danny was eight months old when the next Passover arrived, and there was a month-long discussion within the Rothschild clan as to whether to celebrate it in California or Colorado. Either way, the logistics would be challenging. First of all, there were the baby's needs to be considered. Though the family custom for years had been to gather in Santa Monica, Danny's convenience argued for Colorado.

Mom, however, was a more accomplished *balaboste* than Aunt Ruth, who would have to take charge if it were to be held in Boulder. Aunt Ruth cheerfully admitted, "I cook okay in French, Italian, and Chinese. But I'm really lousy in Yiddish, especially on *Pesach*." So there was an argument for California.

If it were to be in California, the visitors would include me, JJ, and Danny, Aunt Ruth and Uncle Aaron, Dev and her "friend," Mark Chapman, and Yalie and her boyfriend, Richard Reiner—a total of nine people. The California roster comprised Hanna, Hillel, David, Noah, and Rebecca, and Noah's girlfriend, Alyse Windom—only six. But Yalie and her boyfriend were flying in from Washington, D.C., and it would be just as easy for them to fly to Los Angeles as to Denver. So the weight on the decision scale was about even, minor edge to Colorado.

JJ suggested the possibility of holding the seder at a Denver hotel, relieving Aunt Ruth of the burden if Colorado was selected, but nobody liked that idea, especially not Aunt Ruth. "If I ever heard a vote of No Confidence," she laughed, "that's it. Maybe you'd like to have it catered by the penitentiary in Canon City."

I really wanted to go home to Santa Monica. It just felt right. Sitting shoulder-to-shoulder around the expanded table in the Rothschild dining room, listening to Daddy run the seder and Rebecca ask the Four Questions, eating Mom's matzoh ball soup and gefilte fish—there was no other way to celebrate Passover. I could also see my girlfriends while I was there and introduce them to Daniel. That would be an added bonus.

After all the back-and-forth, my nostalgia was the deciding factor, especially because it was shared by Dev and Yalie. Like me, Yalie hadn't attended the family seder the previous year. And she'd missed two others while she was at Yale. Now that law school was over, she made it clear she was really looking forward to seder at Aunt Hanna's and Uncle Hillel's. Why should she give that up just because she was fully grown now and the family was expanding? Dev, a full-time Coloradan, was equally attached to the Santa Monica tradition.

So California it would be.

Although Mom would have liked me, JJ, and the baby to stay at the house, JJ arranged a suite in the hotel where all the other visitors would be lodged. He assured Mom that Danny would spend more time in the crib she'd rented than at the hotel, and it would reduce the load on the bathrooms. So Mom was mollified.

I met Yalie's boyfriend, Richard Reiner, for the first time in the hotel lobby as soon as we arrived. He was a dark-haired young man from Chicago, working as an aide to an Illinois senator. Taller than me. "Rachel," Yalie said, kissing him as she said it, "this is Richie, my lover. Lover, this is my cousin Rachel, one of my previous roommates." No guessing games required on these two. Yalie was announcing straightforwardly that they were a couple.

Dev was standing in the check-in line with Mark. I had been introduced to him but didn't know him at all well. While Dev had brought him with her to the seder, they were staying in separate rooms, and Dev wouldn't describe him as her boyfriend. I assumed she was being coy. It turned out that she was insecure. My normally confident cousin knew *his* status. She was in love with him. She just wasn't sure he was in love with her.

Once we got into our suite and had unpacked, I nursed Daniel for a while and put him down for a nap. Then we got dressed. When Daniel awoke, we drove over to my folks' house. We were the last ones to arrive. While everyone fussed over Daniel, I embarked on a project I'd had in mind since meeting Yalie's and Dev's boyfriends in the hotel lobby. I was determined to establish a personal connection with both of them. Yalie was living with Richie and, if I was any judge, the relationship between Dev and Mark was heading in that direction. If these men were the love interests of my two cousins, I intended to know them and charm them.

American politics was the thread that connected us. I'd studied it. Richie practiced it. Mark taught it. Although I was constantly being interrupted by the need to do this or that for the baby, I maintained a running conversation with the two of them all through the late afternoon. I assume Dev and Yalie could see what I was up to, because they found things to do in the kitchen, leaving me a free field in which to operate.

When I needed to change Daniel's diaper on the folding table Mom had installed for that purpose in my old bedroom, I was so far along in my conversation with Richie and Mark that I pulled them into the bedroom with me.

We had a lot to talk about: the eroding power of the Soviet Union in Eastern Europe, fighting in Yugoslavia, release of the Iran-Contra report, whether George H. W. Bush was up to the task of redefining American policy now that the Cold War was over, the situation in the Middle East, and that hardy perennial of political discourse, the November elections. I was having quite a lot of fun. Although he'd majored in political science as an undergraduate, JJ wasn't preoccupied with politics the way I was, so I didn't often have an opportunity to talk about the issues that really interested me.

Not realizing they were under my microscope, Mark and Richie no doubt thought they were escaping family scrutiny for the moment. And, of course, they were getting to know one another at the same time that they were getting to know me.

Mission accomplished. I found an opportunity later to tell both my cousins that I approved of their guys.

"Isn't he sweet?" Yalie asked.

"I didn't kiss him. I only talked with him. But I'll take your word for it."

Dev's comment about Mark was, "We've only dated a few times. I thought he'd enjoy coming to our seder."

"That's a pile of you-know-what," I said. "You've got your knickers in a knot over this guy, and he's crazy about you. So give it a rest, doll-face. I can see right through you, and so can everyone else."

"Okay, so I like him a little." Dev smiled shyly.

"Oh yeah. And he's pleased to make your acquaintance, too. Juliet, this is Romeo. Romeo, this is Juliet. Have a good time, but don't stay out too late."

"Don't tease," Dev said. "We haven't gotten to that stage yet." After a pause, she asked, "Do you really think he likes me?"

"As sure as my name is … What *is* my name? Oh, yes, Rachel Rothschild. Like you, doll-face? He's head over heels."

"Are you sure?" asked Dev plaintively. My cousin was in torment.

I dropped the bantering tone and hugged her to me: "I'm sure. Trust me. He loves you. And, yes, he's a wonderful guy. I can tell." All I knew for sure was that Mark was smart and had the right opinions, but he *had* to be in love with Dev, and if Dev loved him, he *must* be wonderful.

Our seder that evening was far less relaxed than usual. I was up and down with Daniel, whose only interest was in his mother's breast, and Daddy shortened the service considerably to accommodate. But there was still plenty of laughter, conversation over dinner, and song. everyone seemed to have a good time except Alyse Windom, Noah's live-in girlfriend.

Noah was in his last semester at the University of Washington. Alyse, a junior, was not yet twenty, a light-skinned black girl whose father was a mortgage banker in San Francisco and whose mother was a well-known sculptor. She said she'd been around Jewish people her entire life, but this was her first seder. It was also clear that she'd never been around Jews as anybody's girlfriend. And Noah seemed to be oblivious to her discomfort.

David, who'd finished at UC-Santa Barbara and was pursuing an advanced degree in engineering and architecture at UC-Berkeley, was at the seder alone. He paid far more attention to Alyse than Noah did. In fact, almost everyone there paid more attention to Alyse than Noah did. Maybe they'd had an argument or something just before the seder began. If so, there would have to be a lot of making up afterwards.

Rebecca, although she was in college, was still the youngest at the table, except for Daniel, and she was being a good sport about having to ask the Four Questions. However, I suspect she was mighty tired of being the butt of all the stale jokes that go with the job. Being the baby in the family has its high points and its low points, and the seder at not-quite-nineteen has to be among the lowest. I'm sure she was more than ready for Danny to replace her.

We had another seder the second night. But the crowd was much smaller. David went back to Berkeley. Rebecca went out on a date, much to her mother's annoyance. Noah said he and Alyse had other arrangements. Maybe so. If I'd been Alyse, I certainly would have made other arrangements, and they probably wouldn't have included Noah. Mom was miffed and vowed next year in Colorado, but the absence of the younger members of the family gave me an opportunity to engage Mark and Richie in table-wide conversation. Again, Dev and Yalie must have known what I was doing, parading their boyfriends in front of the family so that their best features were on display. Rachel Rothschild, strategist, at your service. I felt quite proud of myself when the evening was over.

My other plans for the California visit didn't work out too well. Jess had finished law school and was clerking for a federal judge in San Francisco while Sam completed medical school. Lynetta was in Oakland. Arlie was working on a paper that needed to be completed by the end of the week, and Laura wasn't feeling well. Arlie stopped off at our hotel one morning to admire Danny and have breakfast. She reported being "over my ears in work," but she was animated and happy. She'd gained a little weight since we saw her last and looked better than she'd ever looked. I couldn't risk exposing Danny to Laura's germs, so I went to see her alone. Laura seemed a mess, and it wasn't just the flu. Her job was going well, and she loved it. But she admitted to having an affair with a married man. She was desperately afraid that it would lead to heartbreak—hers. She knew it was stupid, she said. She knew it was wrong. She wanted to break it off. She had to break it off. But she couldn't.

Laura—Dr. Lovelorn, the advice giver—could have used some advice. But what did I know about love affairs? Only what I'd read in

Madame Bovary and *Anna Karenina*. All I offered was an unconvincing "It'll work out, honey. You'll see."

In spite of having less time than I wanted with my girlfriends, the trip to California had been a huge success. Daniel had been to his first seder. I felt that I'd made Mark and Richie feel welcome. Yalie gave me a particularly strong hug when we separated. "Thanks," she said. "I thank you. Richie doesn't know it, but he thanks you. And the children we plan to have someday also thank you. You're the best."

Dev simply said, "See you in Denver, cousin. Dinner's on us."

*   *   *

At ten months, Danny was walking, and he was speaking at a year. I was absorbed in his every accomplishment. JJ must have felt I was too absorbed. When Daniel was nearing fifteen months, JJ sat me down one evening after dinner and told me he wanted to hire a nanny. I was shocked. Why did we need a nanny, I wanted to know. "Danny already has a full-time mother," I said indignantly.

JJ said he wasn't suggesting that I was doing less than a wonderful job being Danny's mother. But he thought I ought to resume my career. He wanted me to find a part-time job in journalism—maybe twenty hours a week. It would be good for me, good for us, and, ultimately, good for our children. I said I would think about it, which I did. After about a week, I said no, not now. Maybe in another year or two.

Six weeks later, I changed my mind. Until JJ brought it up, I hadn't considered finding another job in journalism. When I said no, I meant no. But I couldn't stop thinking about it. Gradually the idea captured my imagination. I daydreamed about being known to everyone as Rachel Rothschild. Even though I'd kept my name, the people I met in Denver thought of me as JJ Weiner's wife. Aside from Dev, Mark Chapman, and maybe Grandma Bess, there was nobody in town who knew me as a separate human being.

I read the local newspapers and city magazines with sudden interest, thinking about where I might fit in. I decided that I wanted it.

Once I said yes to the idea, JJ put an ad in the newspaper for a nanny and also made some inquiries through the nursing association. There were five applicants. Hillary Marks, a young Englishwoman not yet twenty-one, was the easy first choice. While she had no experience whatever, Hillary established a mysterious and immediate rapport with Daniel. After five minutes, they were old friends. She also impressed me and JJ with her obvious intelligence. Hillary was a small young woman with delicate features and a copper-colored skin, the daughter of an English Jew and a woman whose family emigrated from India immediately after World War II. The mother converted to Judaism, and Hillary had been raised as a Jew, which was a plus.

Though not especially well-educated, she was very smart and seemed supremely competent. She had come to the United States with a girlfriend the previous year. When her friend returned to England, Hillary settled in Denver, which she'd visited and liked. We did not inquire about her immigration status. With all the illegals around, it was an obvious issue. We didn't ask, probably because we were afraid of the answer.

Hillary's presence removed any doubts I had about returning to journalism. It was not difficult for me to land a job with *In the Rockies*, the publication that was my first choice. I had excellent references from L.A. and, since money was not an important consideration, I was not just affordable, I was downright cheap.

I jumped into the work eagerly. I did some rewrites at first on items submitted for the front-of-the-book highlights section, the same sort of local gossip column that was my first assignment at *L.A. Beat*. Franklin Edwards, the editor, liked my writing and, after a couple of months, gave me an assignment covering a charity ball, which my sister-in-law, Annalisa, was chairing. I tried to beg off, pleading conflict of interest. His answer: "Nonsense. Everybody at the party will know you, even if you don't know them. It's a natural."

So, with misgivings, I went to the ball, which I would otherwise have avoided. Since I was going as a journalist, I did not insist that JJ accompany me. He hated these things. The ball wasn't a total disaster. It was worse than that. It was a fiasco. The hotel's heating and air-conditioning system had broken down after an electrical storm that afternoon, and the ballroom was oppressively warm and stuffy, with no air moving. The hotel management moved belatedly to install huge fans at the main doors, and that blew paper decorations all over the place. The storm had also complicated installation of the band's sound system. The speakers repeatedly emitted piercing shrieks that forced everybody to sit there with their hands over their ears. When the speakers weren't wailing, the music was far too loud to permit people to talk to anyone except their closest neighbors. The singer with the band had to quit halfway through the evening because she had a cold and her throat was too raw to continue. The steaks were overdone. The food service was terrible. And to top everything off, the speech by the evening's honoree, which was supposed to be brief, went on for what seemed like an hour longer than forever. Everyone had a perfectly awful time, thank you very much, and remember not to invite us again.

My report on the event was intended to be funny. I concluded it by writing, "It could have been worse. It could have been *my* party." Franklin Edwards loved it. Furious did not begin to describe Annalisa's reaction. She sent me a blistering note and screamed at JJ, calling me "that nasty little brat you married." JJ told her to "fuck off." Grandma Bess found the article very amusing and said so to Annalisa. That didn't improve things any. JJ's mother, Vera, took her daughter's side. Herman stayed clear of the fray. Uncle Max told me, "Annalisa's a pain in the ass, honey. Don't let her get you down."

It did get me down, however. The circle the Weiner family moved in was very small, and everyone in it was soon aware that Annalisa and JJ's wife were barely on speaking terms. I sent Annalisa a letter of apology, explaining that I hadn't meant to embarrass her (not consciously, at least). That did not satisfy Annalisa. Our relationship, none too good to begin with, was very strained. Because he stuck up for me, JJ also got the chill.

Unfortunately, the story drew a bagful of letters to the editor, most of them complimentary. People who had attended the ball but were not involved in staging it said they died laughing. They thought I'd described the evening perfectly. Annalisa's cohosts were as angry as she was, and the evening's honoree, whose name I had avoided mentioning, cancelled his subscription. Franklin Edwards was delighted with the number of responses and didn't mind the complaints in the least. He wanted me to do more society pieces. I was eager to do something else, anything else. I didn't want to provide Annalisa with additional reasons to dislike me, which was the almost certain outcome if I continued to find humor in the doings of Denver's socialite class.

In an effort to solve the problem, I began to bring Mr. Edwards—he was in his late sixties and, therefore, definitely *Mr.* Edwards—my own story ideas. I proposed doing a substantial piece on the local science fair, reporting on one school's efforts to foster winning entries. My idea was to focus on a school with a large minority population instead of one of the schools that customarily supplied the contest winners. I would do a story that would appear in advance of the competition and then do a follow-up story afterwards. Mr. Edwards mulled it over for several days and then gave me the go-ahead.

"You're a pretty good writer, young lady," he said. "I'm willing to give you a chance to do what you want to do. But I need to warn you in advance, I don't run things just because they've been written. I'll spike a story if I don't think it measures up. That okay with you?"

Although I have no doubt I would have been extremely unhappy if anything I wrote ended up in the wastebasket, I assured him it was okay. Clearly, it was going to be different working for Mr. Edwards than it had been working for Harold Matthews.

I put a lot of effort into the story. I wasn't a science reporter and would need help explaining what the entrants were trying to prove. However, I was very interested in issues relating to minority achievement, and I suppose deep down I saw it as an opportunity to display my enlightened social conscience. I interviewed the principal and the teachers at a high school in the Five Points area in order to select the students on whom I would concentrate. Then I interviewed each of the kids about their projects and about their ambitions. I took a large number of photographs.

Juggling it all might have been a cinch for an experienced writer, but it was the most complex journalistic assignment I'd ever undertaken. Getting it all down on paper proved harder than I anticipated. I worked long hours writing and rewriting it at the desktop computer in what had been JJ's office at our apartment and was now mine. When I showed my draft to Mr. Edwards, he sent me back to the computer to do it over. He wanted me to spend more time on the kids and less on the projects. To accomplish that, I had to do some additional interviewing.

I was quite proud of myself when the article appeared in print, and I got a lot of praise for it. JJ acted as if I'd won a Pulitzer Prize. He made a dinner reservation for the two of us at one of the city's best restaurants to celebrate my triumph and presented me with a corsage before we went. I hadn't worn one since my wedding and, before that, my high school prom. I felt wonderful.

The second article, on the outcome of the competition, was far less successful. I had to write about the winning entries and the kids who submitted them and also about "my" kids, none of whom won more than an honorable mention. Balancing the two parts of the story proved to be beyond my capability at that stage in my career. I couldn't make the pieces fit together organically, and my inability to simplify the science made my description of the projects difficult to understand. In the initial draft, the part about the losing kids had a "meanwhile, back at the ranch" feeling to it that I couldn't overcome. I felt sorry for the kids I'd interviewed for the first article, and my prose was weighed down by the sentiment.

Mr. Edwards wasn't gentle with me. "Only a small number of our readers are astrophysicists, Rachel," he said. "Let's try to explain these projects in a language that approximates English. And please spare me this sob-sister stuff. Nobody died. The kids have got a right to be disappointed at not winning, but don't render it as tragedy."

He gave me some ideas on how to improve what I'd written. I just wasn't able to execute them properly. In the end, he did some heavy-duty editing of my final draft to make it clearer and less disjointed and printed only a truncated version. I was lucky he didn't throw it away altogether. He probably would have done so if it hadn't been the second half of a story printed the previous month. I felt thoroughly chastened. It showed me how much I still needed to learn. The one good thing about it was that I knew I was working for somebody who would teach me to be a better journalist.

I confessed to JJ that I considered the second article "a piece of shit." He wouldn't hear of it. "Ah, but a girl's reach should exceed her grasp, or what's a heaven for?" he asked, paraphrasing Browning. It was oddly consoling. JJ's support made me feel the way I did when I was learning to roller-skate. You fall, you get back up, you keep trying until you do it right.

I had started at *In the Rockies* in mid-October. The charity ball that got me into trouble with Annalisa was in early December, and my write-up of the event appeared in the January issue. The science fair stories were reported and written in January and February. But writing for *In the Rockies* wasn't the only thing happening in my life—in our lives—during that period.

I tried hard to keep work in perspective. Hillary Marks was

exceptionally good with Daniel, but he remained my number one priority. I resisted working more than twenty hours a week, though that wasn't always possible. I took full responsibility at bedtime when I was at home, which was most evenings. I played with him, read to him, lay down beside him until he was asleep. I was determined to be a good mom, and I think I was.

But I also needed some recreation. Even before I started my new job, I had been talking with JJ about taking a skiing vacation in Aspen or Telluride, perhaps in early January. We would take Daniel, of course, along with Hillary. But JJ had a better idea. He suggested that we make the trip during Christmas week and turn it into a vacation with all of my bridesmaids: Dev, Yalie, Jess, Arlie, Laura, Lynetta, and their significant others, and, of course, my sister Rebecca, my maid of honor. I was thrilled by the prospect. Annalisa would not be included, needless to say.

JJ said he'd make the arrangements while I called each one to extend the invitation. I learned that Rebecca had already been invited to go to Hawaii over the Christmas-New Year's Day holiday with her roommate and her roommate's family. She didn't want to cancel that. Lynetta had to work at the hospital, and, besides, she wasn't a skier. Everyone else accepted with enthusiasm.

I was really looking forward to the reunion. Dev was the only one I saw with any regularity, though I had also gotten to know Mark, whom Dev was still describing as her "friend." I knew that Yalie had finished her clerkship and was now working for a California senator. She and Richie were living together, and Dev's opinion was that while they might wait until Yalie was pregnant, it was only a matter of time until the two of them got married. Arlie was nearing completion of her Ph.D. course work at Stanford and was starting on her dissertation. Jess, like Yalie, was done with her clerkship. She was back in the Santa Monica area because Sam—Dr. Samuel Adams—was doing his internship in Los Angeles. She'd just taken a position in a Beverly Hills firm that specialized in entertainment law. Laura had progressed from reading scripts to editing them for a major studio and was trying to maneuver her way into the production side of the business. She acknowledged—unhappily—that she was still involved with the married man she'd told me about when I'd gone to see her at her apartment at Passover.

There would be thirteen of us on the skiing trip, a baker's dozen.

Dev was coming with Mark, Yalie with Richie, and Jess with Sam. Arlie, for the first time ever, was in a serious relationship. His name was Seth Goldberg, and he was pursuing a doctorate in mathematics at Stanford. Laura was the only one coming alone.

As Christmas approached, I was in a fever of excitement. I couldn't think of anything better than being with my two cousins and three of my four closest girlfriends for an entire week. I told JJ repeatedly how grateful I was to him for having come up with the idea.

JJ said that the plan was for us to meet in Aspen. We would go there early on Friday to take possession of the lodge he'd rented and to get things set up, and the others would arrive over the next two days. On the night before we were to leave, JJ packed our things in his big car. The following morning, we headed for the mountains. We were nearing the Frisco-Breckinridge turnoff from I-70 when JJ announced that we would have to stop in Vail for about an hour. There was a man staying in Vail that he needed to see on business. For Daniel's sake, I wanted to get to Aspen as quickly as possible, but if that's what JJ had to do, okay.

As we approached Vail, JJ took the first turnoff on the eastern edge of the town. He soon came to a stop before a big, beautiful stone and wood lodge building. "Come inside," he said to me and Hillary. Since it was very cold outside, there was no choice. JJ had to get his briefcase out of the trunk, so I was the first one to the door. I knocked briskly. When the door opened into the main living room, there was Mark. Behind him were Dev, Yalie, Jess, Arlie, Laura, Richie, Sam, and another man, who had to be Seth Goldberg. They were all shouting, "Surprise, surprise."

For a long moment, I felt as if I were seeing the world through a prism, with the light bent and bathed in strange color. "What are you guys doing here?" I finally asked. "Aren't we supposed to be in Aspen?"

It was JJ who answered, "Welcome to your new ski lodge, sugar. We own this place."

"What?" I asked. "We *own* this place? How? Why?"

JJ replied, "I bought it for you six months ago."

"Why Vail?" I asked. I should have been overjoyed, but I wasn't. I could see that the others were becoming a little uncomfortable, but that didn't stop me. I could barely contain my anger.

"Because it's possible to get to Vail for a weekend," he said with a sharp edge that no one could possibly have missed. "You can't really drive to Aspen for a weekend. And you can't go to Telluride for much less than a week. That's why."

I said, "Oh?" It was not a question. That I was more than a little upset was obvious to everyone. It looked as if the entire civilized world knew that JJ owned this house in Vail before he chose to let me in on the secret. I barely had enough presence of mind to defer further discussion with him until I'd greeted everyone. Daniel was undoubtedly the only one in the lodge who didn't know that there was a storm coming. But everyone tried to steer away from it and concentrate on the grand reunion.

My cheeks were burning, and my forehead was throbbing. Still, I hugged my girlfriends and bestowed kisses on the guys, except for Seth whom I was meeting for the first time. I shook hands with him and let him kiss me on the cheek. I introduced each of them separately to Daniel and collectively to Hillary. JJ went out with Mark and Richie to collect our suitcases and our gear, and the three of them took the suitcases back to the bedrooms we would occupy during the week.

Danny announced that he was hungry, and seven women appeared ready and eager to help feed him. Dev and Yalie had collaborated on brunch. And the whole party—twelve adults and one child—was soon helping dispose of it.

The women were exchanging information about what had happened since they last saw each other. Richie and Mark were discussing politics, and the other guys, who barely knew one another, were talking about the upcoming Bowl games. Probably the only ones who were still thinking about the approaching conflict were me and JJ. At least I was. Behind the veneer of the hostess, I was steaming. All the grievances that had built up inside of me since early in our relationship were right there, on the verge of bursting through, scalding everyone in the vicinity when the pipe burst.

Once we were alone, I could no longer control myself. I demanded an answer. Why in hell had JJ bought this lodge without consulting me? He tried to explain. If we were going to go skiing regularly on weekends during the winter season and if my cousins were going to come along, Vail was a lot easier to get to from Denver or from Boulder than the resorts I favored. I listened to his logic, but I wasn't mollified.

I was on fire. It was part of a pattern. JJ bought our apartment without consulting me. Vera furnished it without consulting me. JJ surprised me with the Mercedes. This lodge was bought and furnished without me.

How could I resent JJ's generosity? Maybe I couldn't, but I did. I felt that I'd been cast as a bit player in my own life. JJ decided what was right for us. I had my premarital grievances, too: his decision that we wouldn't have sex until we were married, that I wouldn't be permitted to move to Palo Alto, that I'd go home to Santa Monica to start my career in journalism. Maybe those were all good decisions, but I felt I should have had a part in making them. I told JJ I was not prepared to let him continue making up his mind for both of us.

When I told him for the third or fourth time that I objected to being surprised this way, JJ flared. "Goddam it, I bought the house for you, the apartment for you, the car for you. What am I supposed to do? Ask your permission to give you a gift?"

"Don't be ridiculous," I said in the most biting tone I had in my repertoire. "The apartment is for *us*. The lodge is for *us*. I have a right to help make those decisions."

"Fine," said JJ, though the way he said it made clear that it definitely *wasn't* fine with him. "Next time I'll know better than to do something nice for you. I don't need this shit."

"You're being unreasonable," I said.

"Unreasonable? Is that what you call it? Unreasonable was buying this big a place so we can entertain your cousins and your girlfriends. Unreasonable was buying you a Mercedes when a VW would have done perfectly well."

It went on like this until we were both shouting. Finally, I swept a lamp off a side table onto the floor, picked up a book, and threw it at JJ's head. Then I ran out of the room crying. By the time JJ came after me to apologize, I'd left the house and was heading I don't know where. I hadn't even taken a coat.

JJ caught up with me a hundred yards down the roadway. He said he was sorry and tried to take me in his arms. I slapped his face as hard as I could. He grabbed my wrists and forced them behind me. I spit at him. I'm sure he was tempted to kill me then and there. But instead, he gripped me tight, kissed my neck, and said soothing things to me. I struggled to break free, but he wouldn't let go. I was shivering in the December cold, and so was he. JJ told me he loved me, and after a time, I stopped struggling and went limp. I felt defeated. I started crying again, but my anger had crested and was now receding. I was completely spent, a rocket that had burned all its fuel.

By the time we returned to the house fifteen minutes later, chilled to the bone, JJ had promised never to make a decision without me—not on what brand of toothpaste to buy, not on what kind of wine to order with dinner, not on what color suit to wear when we went out. And, though my eyes must have been quite red, I was smiling—barely—and saying, "You're going to make me sorry I asked to be included, aren't you?"

JJ answered, "I'll sure as hell try."

When we reentered the lodge, Jess—reliable old Jess—waved away apologies before any were offered. "Armistice Day," she declared loudly. "A moment of silence in honor of all the combatants, alive and dead." I was crying and laughing at the same time. Then Jess announced, "Silence is over. Time to party. Who wants a beer?"

Dev said, "How about purple passion for our two famous drunks, Yalie Goodman and Rachel Rothschild?"

Yalie threw a pillow at her sister, and everything was all right.

Someone had started a fire in the fireplace, and JJ and I sat down on the ledge in front of it to warm ourselves. When that was accomplished, we each had a beer straight out of the bottle, and then another. Soon everyone was talking and singing and laughing, and the unpleasant beginning had been forgotten. JJ and I sealed our peace treaty in bed that night. The only good part of quarreling was making up.

Once I'd accepted that Vail was the right place to be, I was very pleased with the big lodge that JJ had chosen. It had plenty of room. We would be able to have all the company we wanted. Furthermore, the place was divided up in a way that would permit us to close off sections when we were by ourselves or to close off our rooms and allow friends to use the rest of the lodge. I'd already decided to give Dev her own key, and Yalie would have one also when she returned to Colorado—*if* she returned to Colorado. She and Richie were vague about their plans, though it was certain that whatever they did and wherever they did it, they would do it together.

My explosion was soon forgotten, even by me. The rest of the week was great fun—except that I didn't get to do the kind of skiing I'd hoped for. My intention had been to ski with Yalie and Dev, my childhood companions on the slopes, but I hadn't reckoned with romance. Dev went onto the mountain with Mark, who could only deal with intermediate slopes, and Yalie spent most of her time on the novice course with Richie, who had never been on skis before. Since I didn't relish skiing alone, I joined Dev, Mark, and JJ on the intermediate trails. It was no hardship, of course, but I was disappointed. The skiing wasn't very challenging.

Among the others, the only one interested in doing any skiing was Laura. She signed up for lessons as a beginner. By the end of the week, she was out there with Yalie and Richie, falling down with the best of them and having a wonderful time. Jess made her position clear on the first day: "You won't ever see *me* on skis. I'm much too fond of my bones. But you can count me in on the partying afterwards." Sam stayed at Jess's side. Although they didn't seem in any great hurry to marry, Sam and Jess were never apart except when they went to work. Arlie and Seth did a lot of hiking. "No skiing for me, either," Arlie said. "I think it's one of those things you have to start when you're four."

Danny got star treatment all week. We'd brought a little sleigh for him, and the adults took turns hauling him around in it. He also enjoyed rolling around in the snow and, although Hillary hadn't seen much of it growing up, she was extremely adaptable. She rolled along with him.

*   *   *

By the time the vacation ended, Laura's mood was lighter and Arlie seemed happier than she'd been in years. Having watched Danny in action all week, Jess declared in a loud whisper, "Don't tell Sam, but I'm thinking of having him make me an unwed mother." Sam was standing by her as she said it, grinning broadly. Yalie was proud of how quickly Richie was learning to ski. And Mark and Dev, who began the week in separate rooms, ended it in the same bed. *At last*, I thought.

Shortly after the beginning of the new year, just as I'd begun working on my two science fair articles, my father-in-law announced that he and Vera were going to Israel for ten days in March. He invited me and JJ to join them, bringing Daniel and Hillary. I wanted to go. I hadn't seen my grandparents since my wedding, and I hadn't seen my two male cousins, Aunt Shoshana's boys, in nearly ten years. JJ readily agreed to make the trip, his first to Israel since he was a kid.

I thought about leaving Daniel in Denver with Hillary, but JJ categorically rejected that idea. He gave me two reasons. The first was that if something were to happen to us, our son would be orphaned. I accepted that as logical. The second reason he gave me was that I was being selfish.

That made me angry. "It's a difficult trip. New York to Tel Aviv is like twelve hours. He'll be miserable."

"And it'll be hard on you," JJ said. "Poor you."

"That's not fair. I'm not thinking about me. I'm thinking about *him*."

"If I remember correctly, Rebecca went to Israel as a one-year-old and there were four of you and your mother didn't have a nanny along to help. Isn't that right?"

He had a point, of course, though that didn't make me any less angry. I said, "Fuck you, Jemmie," and left the room. He didn't come after me. I'd struck him below the belt.

Too fucking bad, I thought.

I needed to take a walk to get rid of my anger. I slammed the apartment door as I went out. This time, he didn't come after me. Outside, it was one of those January days that Colorado gets when the sky is clear, the sun is shining, the air is crisp, and you almost don't need a coat. I made a circuit around Cheesman Park while I tried to calm down. And when I was back where I'd begun and not yet calm, I made the circuit again.

I tried to tell myself that Daniel at nineteen months would have a harder time on the trip to Israel than Rebecca did at a year. But that didn't wash. There had been four of us kids, and the twins at four and a half had been a lot worse passengers than Daniel would be. *Was JJ right about me? Was it selfishness on my part? Was I worried that having Daniel along would interfere with my vacation?*

By the time I'd gone twice around the park perimeter, I was feeling guilty. I'd had a glimpse of me that I didn't like. Though I should have been, I wasn't contrite. Instead of opening up to one another and talking it through, JJ and I were silent the rest of the day. It was settled, however. We'd take Daniel with us.

It was several weeks later that JJ took me to dinner to celebrate the publication of the first science fair article. Though maybe only subconsciously, it might have been his way of apologizing for our argument. Maybe the consolation he offered me after I flubbed the second article was also motivated in part by a need to reassure me of his love. I don't know.

The flight over to Israel at the beginning of March was as awful as I'd anticipated it would be. Hard on Daniel. He couldn't stand being confined hour after hour. Hard on Hillary because she couldn't make him comfortable. I couldn't, either, though I tried. Eventually, he exhausted himself and fell asleep on my shoulder. Hillary offered to take him from me, but I shook my head. I didn't want to disturb him. Besides, holding him that way reminded me of how much I loved him. And I didn't *want* to be spoiled. I was resolved not to be.

We arrived at Ben Gurion Airport outside Tel Aviv around midday. Herman had arranged for us to be picked up by a driver with a large van. He transported us to the King David Hotel in Jerusalem, where Herman had booked several rooms. JJ and I had a suite with a separate bedroom for Daniel's crib, and Hillary was next door. Herman and Vera stayed at their condo.

I was dead tired after the overnight flight and wanted a nap. But the phone rang. My aunt and my cousins were down in the lobby. JJ came down with me. He knew Aunt Shoshana and my cousin Avital from our wedding. But he hadn't ever met Shoshana's sons. The oldest was thirty-four now and no longer the lean young man I remembered. He was beginning to go bald. The younger one, who would soon be thirty-two, had a thick, though neatly trimmed, black beard that entirely changed the face I remembered. I'm not sure I would have recognized either one of them if I'd encountered them in the street. No spouses or children were present, which was just as well since it gave me time to become reacquainted with my cousins.

The older boy, Elon, who'd studied at the Technion after the army, now ran a chemical facility for one of Israel's biggest companies. He had married a woman from a German Jewish family that came to Israel in the 1920s. They lived on the outskirts of Jerusalem with their children, two girls and a boy. Yigal, the younger boy, hadn't gone on to college after the army. He owned a clothing store in Tel Aviv. Quite a trendy place, I'd been told. His wife was the child of an Iraqi Jewish family that fled to Israel in 1947. They had two kids, a boy and a girl. Avital had been married for two years now to a kibbutznik from the Upper Galilee whom she'd met during her army service. They were living on his kibbutz. Having begun on children before marriage, they had a boy two months older than Danny.

Aunt Shoshana had moved to Tel Aviv to be near her parents, my grandparents. She worked at the Defense Ministry. As a native English speaker with an American college education, she wrote speeches and press releases for senior officials. She was pretty high up in her department. Occasionally she was called upon to translate for those few among her bosses who weren't fluent enough in English to converse with visiting dignitaries.

I asked about my grandparents, whom I would see in Tel Aviv in several days. Aunt Shoshana said that my grandmother was "still going strong." But my grandfather wasn't.

"You've got to prepare yourself, Rachel," she told me. "His mind is failing. He might not recognize you. It depends on the day."

I wasn't ready for this news. My father hadn't warned me, and neither had Aunt Ruth. It came as a bitter shock. The last time I'd seen Grandpa—at my wedding, nearly three years ago—he seemed as vigorous and as engaged as ever. I couldn't remember how old he was. "Over eighty," Aunt Shoshana said, "nearly a year younger than your grandmother. He's not angry like some older people get with dementia. Just forgetful and confused."

Oh, boy, I thought. *This part will be tough.*

Meanwhile, Elon had invited me, JJ, Hillary, and Danny for dinner on Wednesday night. Avital, her husband, and her son came in from their kibbutz to join us. The conversation at Elon's was almost as confusing for me at the beginning of the evening as it was for JJ, Danny, and Hillary. My Hebrew was anything but good. I'd forgotten nearly everything I'd learned during the weeks Yalie, Avital, and I had spent on the kibbutz. Elon's wife spoke English reluctantly, and her kids spoke it poorly. Avital's husband knew about as much English as I did Hebrew. For the two of us to talk was like trying to kiss wearing deep-sea divers' helmets. Avital's little boy and Danny couldn't communicate at all, although that didn't seem to matter a lot. Mysteriously, gestures and signs seemed to work perfectly well.

JJ knew no Hebrew at all. However, he spoke a little German, haltingly and with an American accent. He was willing to let Elon's wife laugh at him in order to make a connection. That did a lot to relieve the stiltedness of the conversation. Since JJ was willing to expose his ignorance of proper German, Dahlia began to use her English on us, and it turned out that her command of the language was reasonably good. She kept apologizing because she was accustomed to reading English, not speaking it. Despite her thick Israeli accent, I had almost no difficulty in understanding her.

She was Elon's age; they shared birthdays and had known each other since primary school. They'd been married eight years. Dahlia had studied dentistry. But it was clear that her real vocation was motherhood. Her three kids came to her, not to Elon, every time they wanted something or had a question to ask. She had one or another of them on her lap frequently during the evening, and her love for them was obvious in the way she spoke to them, stroked them, kissed them. It was lovely to watch.

I really enjoyed the evening. I'd reestablished my relationship with Elon and gotten to know his wife well enough to look forward to seeing her again. Even though several years had passed since I'd last seen Avital, she and I had found plenty to talk about. Too bad all I carried away from my encounter with her husband was the impression that he was big and a trifle short in brainpower. Maybe it was just that I couldn't talk to him. Their son was a cute little kid, bigger than Danny and a lot more boisterous. He didn't stay still long enough for me to form any other opinion.

Before we left the house, I carefully wrote down the names and ages of the children so I'd know who belonged to whom. Thursday we spent sightseeing in Jerusalem. Herman had appointments with the Israeli charities he supported, but Vera was with us all day. Although my memories of Jerusalem were scattered and incomplete, Vera knew the city quite well, so we did without a tour guide. The driver Herman had hired took us around.

Our first stop was at the Haas Promenade in Talpiot, in the southeastern portion of the city. There, at the crest of a ridge running from east to west, stood a strikingly modern and handsome overlook, paved in cream white Jerusalem stone. "The best view in the city," Vera announced. It was certainly better than any I'd ever seen. Below us in the distance, to the north, rose the high stone walls guarding the Old

City. Within those walls the dominant feature was the golden Dome of the Rock, erected more than a thousand years ago by Muslims on the former site of the Jewish Temple. To our left, immediately below us, part of the promenade, were paths winding through a carefully terraced landscape of olive and pomegranate trees, bordered by lavender, rosemary, and wild grasses. Beyond it lay the hills, valleys, and neighborhoods of the New City.

The vista had a deceptive unity because of the near universal use of Jerusalem stone as facing for the city's buildings. We were looking at structures accumulated during three thousand years under the rulership of several different civilizations, and yet they seemed to comprise a homogeneous whole. Bathed in sunlight reflecting off the neutral stone surfaces, this was *Yerushalim Shel Zahav*, Jerusalem of Gold. JJ and Hillary were suitably impressed. To tell the truth, so was I. The Haas Promenade hadn't been there when I'd been to Jerusalem last. I had only visited individual sights. Here was the entire city stretched out before us in all its variety, in all its glory.

Daniel couldn't have been less interested. All he wanted was the stuffed animal that another small child at the overlook was holding. Hillary picked him up and took him away when he tried to grab it. He squalled momentarily, but it didn't last long. Daniel was essentially a happy child. Thanks mainly to Hillary. During the week, she was with him a lot more than I was. He rarely saw JJ except in the morning and on weekends.

From Talpiot, our driver drove us around the New City, close to the flat-roofed Knesset Building, across the campus of Hebrew University, and alongside the Israel Museum, then down the street past the Me'a She'arim neighborhood, crowded with Ultra-Orthodox men in their distinctive black clothing and black fedoras and women in long, ill-fitting dresses, with small children trooping numerously and noisily after them like ducks headed for the pond.

Everywhere we went we saw young Israeli soldiers, male and female, the age of American college kids, dressed in khaki or camouflage, patrolling, waiting for buses, sightseeing, enjoying their off-duty hours. The boys all carried Uzis dangling from their shoulders, a visible reminder that the possibility of violence was never absent. Many of the girls were also armed.

Around noon, our driver took us back to the King David Hotel for lunch. Afterward, we sent Daniel off with Hillary to take a nap. Vera, JJ, and I trod downhill from the hotel through the Yemin Moshe artists' colony to the Montefiore Windmill, built in 1857, and the adjacent Mishkenot Sha'anim, dating from 1860, the first Jewish settlement outside the walls. We entered the Old City by the massive Jaffa Gate and gradually worked our way through the teeming, commercial Armenian Quarter, savory with the smell of spices and grilling meat. We walked slowly via the modern Jewish Quarter, down to the plaza in front of the Western Wall, also known as the Wailing Wall. There, separated by a fence, men to the one side, women to the other, knots of Jews stood reciting prayers before the retaining wall to the Temple Mount, all that is left of the Temple of Solomon.

An elderly Orthodox Jew found JJ and took him to the men's side, while Vera and I entered the women's enclosure and walked to the wall. I began to weep, and I suddenly remembered seeing my Daddy in tears on our first visit to the Western Wall when I was four and a half. Like father, like daughter. When we were finished at the wall, Vera took a cab back to the King David. Though it was uphill the whole way, JJ and I walked. As we were climbing toward the hotel, JJ told me that he hadn't enjoyed his visits here as a child, but now he understood for the first time why his parents loved Jerusalem and Israel.

"I've never thought a lot about being Jewish," he explained. "Some people are Catholics. Some are Baptists. I'm Jewish. Okay. But coming here is like plugging into a power grid. Five thousand years of history, and it's *our* history."

"And it's our future, too," I said. "After the Holocaust, I don't think you can be Jewish in the modern world without Israel. All those dead Jews who believed in God, and what did it get them? Auschwitz. The Torah says, 'I have set before you life and death, blessing and curse. Therefore, choose life.' Israel is about Jews choosing to live. That's why my family is Zionist."

"Well," he responded, "I'm convinced, but let's not try explaining any of this to Annalisa."

Dinner that night was with a friend of Herman's from the Jewish Agency and his stylish wife. We met at one of Jerusalem's most popular restaurants. The cuisine was supposed to be Italian. Had it been in Italy—or, for that matter, in a major American city—the place would not have stayed in business long. It was expensive by Israeli standards, and the food was blah. That's the scientific word for it. But then, Israel isn't noted for gourmet cooking. Personally, I would have much preferred Middle Eastern fare. Perhaps our host would have preferred it too—many Israelis do—but didn't think it was refined enough for his guests.

On Friday, JJ, Daniel, Hillary, and I drove to Tel Aviv in a rented car. I knew the city well enough to find the Mediterranean, not much else. (My secret was that the sun sets in the west—even in Israel.) But I was the lead navigator in our car, so I was behind the wheel. We wandered around the city, map in hand, usually not getting to the places we were looking for. As evening approached, we were able to meet Yigal at the Dan Tel Aviv. Fortunately for me, it was situated on the drive overlooking the Mediterranean, the only landmark I knew how to locate. Yigal piloted us to Aunt Shoshana's house for Shabbat dinner.

I was dreading the prospective meeting with my grandfather. He'd always been a leading physician, articulate and knowledgeable on many different subjects. The idea that his mental capacities were falling away seemed the cruelest of all imaginable fates. But Grandpa was having one of his best days in a long time. *Of course*, he recognized me, he said indignantly when Grandma prompted him. "And this is her young man, JJ," he added triumphantly. "And this must be Daniel."

So the beginning was much easier than I had anticipated. My grandmother, who'd just celebrated her eighty-first birthday, was as spry as ever. Aunt Shoshana, unlike Aunt Ruth, was a Jewish cook, not a French cook or an Italian cook or a Chinese cook. Shabbat dinner at Aunt Shoshana's was matzoh ball soup, chicken, brisket, and kugel. She'd even made gefilte fish for us as an appetizer. It was like being at Mom and Daddy's house for Shabbat. The same foods, the same ceremonies.

Grandpa didn't say much during dinner. Grandma, after awhile, was preoccupied with her great-grandchildren, especially Danny, who she was seeing for the first time. That gave me an opportunity to talk with Yigal and Irit. Irit had learned English in school and spoke it confidently, though with an accent and imperfect grammar. Their children hadn't studied English yet, but being around their great-grandparents and Aunt Shoshana, they heard it regularly, and they seemed to understand almost everything.

Eran, a dark, wiry boy, was dressed in camouflage overalls like an IDF soldier. Irit said apologetically, "What can you do? He's a boy. He wouldn't get dressed for Shabbat."

Yehudit, on the other hand, was wearing a pink dress with lots of petticoats and had ribbons in her hair. She looked like Irit—brown hair, brown eyes, olive complexion. "This one's my _malka_, my Shabbat queen."

Irit herself was about Dev's age, four years older than me. Like her mother-in-law, she worked at the Ministry of Defense. She'd been in a headquarters unit during her army service, and her commanding officer took her with him when he was promoted to a senior staff position. She'd been there ever since. Her military connection might have had something to do with Eran's interest in soldiery. More likely, he was copying the young people he saw every day in the streets.

Yigal wasn't at all talkative. "I'm in the dress business," he said, as if that explained his silence. Irit is the talker in our family."

Toward the end of the evening, my grandfather's mind began to wander. He was asking me about my mother, and it was clear he meant Aunt Ruth, not Mom. "This is Rachel," Grandma said patiently. "Hillel's daughter." Dr. Rothschild said, "Oh yes. I knew that. I just misspoke."

I turned aside so the tears in my eyes would not show. Aunt Shoshana gently rubbed my shoulder.

Once Yigal had taken my grandparents back to their apartment, I allowed myself to weep openly. Aunt Shoshana hugged me. "I know it's hard, sweetheart. I try to keep myself strong for Grandma, but many's the night I've cried myself to sleep."

"What's going to happen?" I asked.

"It's going to get worse over time," she said, "but his doctors don't think it's Alzheimer's, merely senile dementia—_merely_. Some 'merely.' They won't speculate about the pace of deterioration. He repeats himself a lot, asks the same question he asked two minutes earlier and that you've already answered. Conversations don't go anywhere—just round and round in a circle. It's harder on Grandma than on anyone else. But he doesn't go wandering off, and he's still clever enough to disguise it most of the time."

I shuddered and shook my head vigorously from side to side, hoping to clear out a thought I wished weren't there.

"Do my father and Aunt Ruth know?"

"Yes, but I don't go into detail. They can't do anything about it from ten thousand miles away—and sharing the pain won't help Grandpa or, for that matter, Grandma."

"Do they have—you know—help? Somebody who comes in regularly? JJ and I would be glad to contribute."

"Thanks for offering, honey. But money's not a problem. The problem is that, aside from light housekeeping, Grandma won't hear of it. I do some grocery shopping for them. I'm there two or three times during the week, and they come here every week for Shabbat. Yigal goes to see them. Irit goes. Elon comes down from Jerusalem. Avital comes. They see more of us than they did when Grandpa was healthy. I think it helps—though to tell you the truth, Grandma prefers not to talk about it."

"I am *so* sorry." I said, hugging her.

"I know, sweetheart. I know."

When the time came for us to leave, JJ got directions from Yigal on how to get back to Jerusalem, and he drove. I just couldn't do it.

Now that he'd shown an interest, I thought JJ ought to see more of Israel than Jerusalem and Tel Aviv and the road between them. Avital was willing to be our guide. Taking a tour with Daniel in tow would not be easy, however, even with Hillary along. Avital was leaving her little one with a neighbor. I thought maybe I'd leave Danny and Hillary at the King David, but then I reminded myself that this was Hillary's first trip to Israel. So I suggested that Hillary join JJ and Avital, while I would stay behind at the hotel with my son.

Hillary said, "Oh, I couldn't."

"Yes, you can. It will give me a chance to play with my son. He might even begin to think I'm his mother."

The persuasion and the demurrals went on for several minutes. Finally, I said, "Enough, you're going and that's all there is to it. Not another word."

"That's so generous of you."

"Nonsense. I've seen the country before and will again some other time. Go!"

So it was agreed. JJ told me, "I'm proud of you, sugar. What you're doing is really very nice." Then he hugged me and kissed my cheek.

Was I being magnanimous? Or was I only trying to show myself that I wasn't as selfish as JJ had said I was? If I'm being honest with myself, I'd have to say it was the latter. I didn't like feeling selfish. This was my way of proving that I wasn't. And I was dissembling because I really wanted to see Israel again. It had been a long time. A long time.

JJ and Hillary would be going places, with Avital as their guide, that I remembered only dimly or not at all. They were taking the circle route to Haifa, Safed, the Galilee, Tiberias, and back to Jerusalem, the same route my family and I had traveled with Uncle El when I was six and a half. I'd seen some—but not all—of the sights again ten years ago when Yalie and I were in Israel.

So I was making a sacrifice. But, on the whole, I was glad that I'd made the decision because it gave me an opportunity to be with Daniel—and allowed me to think better of myself. I needed that.

Herman and Vera had shifted to Tel Aviv, where Herman had a series of appointments, leaving Daniel and me by ourselves at the King David. I liked being alone with Daniel. I wheeled him around in his stroller in the vicinity of the hotel. It was too hilly to wander very far afield. I chased after him when he was afoot. I fed him, bathed him, put him to sleep. Slept myself once he was down for the night. Got up early and repeated the cycle. It was a lot of fun. But I couldn't go back to being a full-time mommy. I just couldn't.

When they returned from the tour, JJ and Hillary were both full of enthusiasm for what they'd seen. Perhaps because they were there for under two hours, JJ described Avital's kibbutz, close to Lake Kinneret, as if it were the Garden of Eden. JJ was in well-traveled territory. Glamorizing the life of "the Jewish farmer" was something American Jews were fond of doing. They didn't know, and JJ didn't know, the reality that I'd discovered the summer that Yalie, Avital, and I were on the kibbutz together. The work was hard and often unpleasant. The houses were tiny. By the standards of the American middle class, to which most Jews belonged, the plumbing was crude and the opportunities for diversion limited. And communal life could be oppressive.

Avital told me later with amusement that she'd be happy to change places with JJ if he was so enraptured. She was beginning to be tired of living on a kibbutz and wasn't sure how much longer she could stand it. Her husband, she said, had spent his entire life on the kibbutz, except for his time in the army, and he couldn't imagine living in the city. "I guess I better get used to it," Avital said with a rueful smile. "I'm probably going to spend the rest of my life there."

The idea of having to ask permission of the community to breathe on your own made me shudder. But it wasn't my right to say anything. The way I saw my cousin Avital's future was that she was doomed to live her life in a Socialist "paradise" with a muscle-bound farmer for a husband. I listened sympathetically, however, and nodded.

"It's a great way to raise kids," I said.

"Yes, that's true," she said. "Arik runs all over the place. I don't have to watch him. If he gets lost, someone brings him back. Everybody on the kibbutz treats the small ones like their own. And the bigger kids watch out for the little ones. We're not always one big happy family, but for the children every adult is like an aunt or uncle and every other kid is like a cousin."

"That's worth a lot," I said.

"Yes, you're right. It's worth a lot."

I hoped it would be enough for Avital.

We flew back to Denver via New York. The trip back was as terrible as the trip over. Nevertheless, I felt fulfilled. I'd seen my entire family, met spouses and children, and introduced my husband to a place I loved. I thanked Herman and Vera for taking us.

Herman's answer was, "Maybe we'll make a Jew out of JJ after all."

I smiled. I didn't usually feel close to Herman. Are co-conspirators close?

*   *   *

Passover was rapidly approaching. I intended for us to fly to Santa Monica for the seder. I hadn't seen my brothers or my sister since last Passover, and I wanted to catch up. Yalie and Richie probably wouldn't be able to come. Yalie's job as legislative assistant to a California senator kept her exceedingly busy. However, Dev and Mark, now officially her boyfriend, were definitely coming, as were Aunt Ruth and Uncle Aaron. To make it even more festive for me, Mom had decided to invite Arlie, Laura, Jess, and Lynetta to join us, together with their boyfriends. That way I wouldn't have to go chasing around town in order to see them.

We were set to leave on Wednesday. Tuesday morning, we were at breakfast. I was in a dressing gown. JJ had on a shirt and tie, getting ready to leave for the office. Danny, in a tiny "running suit," was seated in his high chair, and Hillary was feeding him. JJ said, quite matter-of-factly, that he wasn't going to be able to go to Santa Monica. The representative of a large Swiss investor was flying in to talk about buying a Weiner property in Salt Lake City, and he had to be there. I was stunned—and then I was angry.

"How could you ruin our plans this way?" I demanded. "Can't your business be postponed?"

He said, "No, it can't. That's when he's going to be here, and I'm needed."

I was enraged. I dumped my plate off the table, food and all. I shattered my coffee cup against the wall, sending the coffee flying. I accused JJ of caring more about money than he did about his wife and child. I swore at the entire Weiner family—JJ, Annalisa, Vera, Herman, Uncle Max. Daniel began crying. Hillary scooped him up out of the high chair and took him away.

JJ told me coldly to stop making an ass of myself and clean up the mess I'd made. That only made me more furious. The next thing I knew, JJ had yanked me out of my chair, gripped me at the neck of my dressing gown, and was marching me toward our bedroom. I was struggling to evade his grasp but not succeeding. Once in our room, JJ threw me facedown on the bed and said, "You're asking for it, and you're going to get it."

He went into his closet and came out with a belt, leaving no doubt that he intended to spank me. I tried to escape and, when he stopped me, I scratched his face with my nails. He caught me by the upper arm. Then in one swift movement, I was over his lap and imprisoned by his legs. My dressing gown was up, my nightgown was up, and I was bare from the waist down.

I began crying. "She'll hear," I pleaded, meaning Hillary.

"I expect she will. You should have thought of that earlier, sugar."

He began on me with his bare hand. I was trying desperately to remain silent, but it was hopeless. By the time JJ switched to the belt, I could be heard all over the apartment. In fact, I have no doubt I could be heard all the way to Santa Fe. JJ was telling me that I was a spoiled brat and needed to be treated like one. He kept at me until I was sobbing like a child and between sobs promising to be good.

When he was finally done, JJ ordered me to go back to the kitchen and clean up the mess I'd made and then come back to the bedroom and apologize. I don't know why, but I did as I'd been instructed, down on my knees with a rag, weeping softly the whole time. When I came back to the bedroom, JJ had a tissue to his cheek to stop the bleeding where I'd scratched him. I apologized for my behavior and said I was really, really sorry for having scratched him. I lay down on the bed beside him and nestled against him. JJ said he forgave me. He hugged me, and I hugged him back. Then I began to cry again. Then I asked him to fuck me. That's the word I used.

Like the first time JJ punished me, there were no preliminaries. But this time, I wanted the sensation of being taken without foreplay. JJ felt the power of the moment also. He stripped off his clothes, then rode me and rode me until he climaxed. I wouldn't let him go. I lay there holding onto him, exhausted, wondering what had happened to me that I allowed myself to apologize after being spanked and then asked to have intercourse afterwards. I was in a daze. *What had I done? This isn't me*, I told myself. *This isn't me. This is something out of the Marquis de Sade, and it's disgusting. JJ's disgusting. I'm disgusting.*

When we finally separated, neither of us spoke a word. He went off to shower and get dressed again. I lay there naked, staring inwardly, until JJ emerged from the bathroom with a big bandage on his cheek. It didn't completely cover the scratches I'd inflicted on him with my nails. They would be visible for days. Again, nothing was said by either of us. It was now my turn in the bathroom. In the mirror, I saw the dark bruise on my upper arm where JJ had gripped me. I would need to wear a long-sleeved blouse for the next several days. What I told myself as I stood there under the spray in the shower was *It will do me good to get away.*

For the rest of the day, I avoided Hillary's eyes and Hillary avoided mine. I knew that Hillary knew what had happened up to, and maybe including, the sex. But there was nothing to be done about it. I had to trust that Hillary would keep her mouth shut. I felt that the relationship between us had been subtly altered and that I was in Hillary's power.

I was angry with myself for what had happened more than I was upset with JJ. After the spanking, I should have left the apartment. In my night clothes, if necessary. I should have demanded that he come after me to apologize instead of apologizing myself. I'd behaved badly, yes. But the worst of it was that I'd accepted the spanking as if it was what I deserved, and then I had *asked him* to screw me. I'd *asked* him.

Next morning, JJ took Danny, Hillary, and me to the airport. I doubt that he'd given another thought to the spanking episode, but I hadn't been able to get it out of my mind. I couldn't fathom my own behavior. It wasn't the tantrum. That was just a juvenile display. It was the submission and the sexual desire afterwards. *Am I really the person I've always thought I am?* I asked myself. *Am I going to let JJ dominate me?* I didn't have any answers for myself.

I wondered what Hillary might be thinking. Did she pity me? Did she have contempt for me? There was no point going in that direction, however. I wouldn't be able to guess, and I certainly wasn't going to ask.

I wasn't in a celebratory mood, not in the least. When the plane took off from the Denver airport, I might as well have been on my way to spend a weekend alone at a motel in East St. Louis. Then we landed in Los Angeles, and Daddy was waiting for us at the gate. It came over me in a rush. Denver wasn't my home. Santa Monica was home. I was going to be with my family and my friends. Though I felt like crying, I didn't. Daddy wouldn't understand, and I couldn't trust myself to explain.

It was more of a homecoming than I'd expected. At the last moment, Yalie had been able to take time off. So, except for JJ, we had a full house. In fact, the seder could have been held in a small stadium. In addition to me, Danny, Hillary, Mom, Daddy, Aunt Ruth, Uncle Aaron, Dev and Mark, Yalie and Richie, there were Noah, David, and Rebecca and their guests, and Arlie, Jess, Laura, and their guys, and Lynetta with a doctor friend—two dozen people.

It had been almost a year since I'd seen my brothers or my sister. Rebecca was nearing twenty now and was a sophomore. She seemed a good deal more grown-up than she had when I last saw her. Though Rebecca was slightly shorter than me and her hair was lighter than mine and straighter, there was no mistaking that we were sisters. We had pretty much the same body, the same shape face, and the same dark eyes. She was accompanied at the seder by Bobby Weinberg, a friend from Berkeley and only a friend. David, still at UC-Berkeley, had brought Alina Abramowitz, a freshman at Berkeley and a young friend of Rebecca, with whom he'd fallen in love. Noah was no longer living with Alyse Windom, the girl he brought to last year's seder. He'd finished at the University of Washington and was working in Silicon Valley. His date was Myra Goldman, a high school classmate from Santa Monica with whom he'd recently reconnected.

I'd seen my cousins and my girlfriends in Vail in December, of course. Dev was now living with Mark. They'd rented a house together not far from our apartment on Cheesman Park. I considered that an encouraging sign. Yalie and Richie were full of information about what was happening in the Senate, but they had nothing to say about their personal lives. They didn't seem any closer than they'd been in December to deciding what they'd do next.

Jess was, of course, with Sam. That was a permanent arrangement, though not yet sanctified by marriage. They were going to remain in the Los Angeles area. Jess had just passed her six-month anniversary at the law firm in Beverly Hills. She liked them, and they liked her. Jess said Sam had decided to specialize in plastic surgery.

"You think entertainment is the main industry in Southern California," Jess said. "Not so. The main industry is plastic surgery. The film studios are nothing but suppliers. In a couple of years, Sam will be known throughout the world as Dr. Samuel Adams, tit-maker to the stars."

Sam shook his head. "I don't know why I put up with this," he said. "I'm basically a burn specialist. The real news, however, is that we're getting married around Christmas."

I loved hearing that. "Congratulations! I wondered when you two were going to make it legal."

"I'm not sure it's a good idea," Jess said. "Legal is so *ordinary*. Is this what our mothers fought for at Gettysburg?"

"Stow it, Jess," Sam said. "She's been campaigning for marriage since our first moment together. Before our first moment together."

"That's a crock," Jess replied cheerily. "Our parents have been campaigning, and we decided resistance is futile. Might as well sign up for 'until death do us part.' And, yes, you're all invited. I'll let you know when we figure out where and when."

Arlie had no special news to impart, but she'd once more brought Seth, with whom she appeared to be very much in love. Arlie was prettier than she'd ever been. She had gained weight and now looked more like a female than a walking exclamation point.

Laura's date was Nelson Shlossberg. Laura and Nelson were really no more than acquaintances, Arlie explained in a whispered aside. "She's just tired of going places alone."

I found out later that Laura had concluded that her married lover was a creep, but she was still running to him whenever he called. She might actually leave the guy if she could only find someone else to love—or at least to like a lot. Nelson wasn't going to be her rescuer, however. Like Bruce Levy, whom she'd dated in high school, Nelson was good-looking, not too bright, and more interested in himself than he could ever be in a woman.

Lynetta was working as an emergency room physician. The man accompanying her, Dr. Jason Fishman, was a classmate from UCLA Medical School. They were merely friends. "I'm hoping he can tell me what's going on," she said, introducing him. "This is my first seder."

Daniel, the only child present, was the center of everyone's attention at the seder. Rebecca suggested that Daniel was already old enough to ask the Four Questions and offered to help. She took him into her lap and pretended he was whispering the questions in her ear and she was only speaking as his agent. Of course, Daddy then addressed the narrative to Daniel as if he were the sole audience. And that was the game that everyone played until Daniel demanded to be released from Rebecca's lap so he could run around the house with Hillary in pursuit to make certain he didn't wreck the place.

I had seated myself among my girlfriends, since this was the only time I'd see them on this trip. I would have an opportunity to talk with my siblings and cousins later on. Jess and Sam seemed deliriously happy, and I could see that Arlie's relationship to Seth was deepening. There was one disquieting note. Arlie kept telling everybody—in his presence—how smart Seth was. He didn't appear to think it was necessary to return the compliment or, in fact, to say anything particularly affirmative about Arlie. I thought maybe he was taking her too much for granted. No one needed to tell me that Laura was even more unhappy than she had been a few months ago.

Lynetta seemed to be thriving, though she was reluctant to talk about her work. Sam said, "The burn victims I deal with mostly come in through ER. And so do the people with gun wounds and bodies torn apart in auto accidents and heart attacks and cranial fractures from being mugged. And poor people who can't afford to see a private doctor. The rotation through ER was the toughest and most stressful thing I've done in medicine. If you can handle it, Lynetta, God bless you."

Lynetta shrugged. "I won't say it's fun, but I get a lot of satisfaction from being on the front end of saving peoples' lives. When I can't stand it any longer, I'll go do something else."

Her friend Jason said, "I've watched her in action. She's very good at what she does. Very calm. Very compassionate. Not like a lot of other emergency room doctors."

Lynetta waved it off. "Yes, and I leap tall buildings in a single bound. Thanks for the vote of confidence, Jason, but let's not overdo it."

We had reached the point in the seder when it was time to serve dinner. Mom had an army of assistants. Mom accepted the offers of help from Arlie, Laura, and Jess. They'd been coming to our house since they were kids and felt like they were part of the family. But Alina Abramowitz, Myra Goldman, and Lynetta Pearson were sent away. "It takes at least five meals in this house before you're allowed in the kitchen. These girls qualify, and you don't."

David welcomed Alina back to her seat with a lingering kiss that brought a chorus of cheers from the rest of the table. Alina blushed noticeably. At eighteen, she was the youngest person in the house except for Daniel. She was a very attractive girl, about five feet four inches tall, bright-eyed, dark-haired, curvaceous. Being on display in front of David's family was obviously difficult for her.

"Don't let them bother you, Lee," David said. "They're all jealous of your youth and beauty."

I witnessed the scene while bringing a cart full of food in from the kitchen. I said, "Come with me, Alina" and took her into the living room.

"Don't be embarrassed, lovey," I told her when we were out of range. "I'm sure it's difficult meeting so many people all at once and having them tease you. If you'd like, I'll tell David to keep his lips to himself in public. You have to understand: My brother is a guy, and like all guys, he can't help being an asshole at times."

Alina smiled shyly, and she kissed me on the cheek. "Call me Lee. That's what David calls me."

I winked at her. I said, "David's a fortunate fella. I'll tell him that, too."

Once the meal was over and the table had been cleared, the seder continued and the singing began. Before long, Hillary took Daniel off to bed. People began to leave the dining room table to chat in the living room. Then it was nearing midnight, and the party began to break up. Aunt Ruth, Uncle Aaron, and my cousins and their boyfriends were staying at a hotel. Alina was spending the night in Rebecca's room, and everyone else was going home.

Before my girlfriends left, I invited each of them to use the house in Vail during the summer and to come again in the winter—"before or after Jess and Sam get married." I wasn't playing at being the gracious hostess. I wanted them with me as often as possible.

The following two days belonged to family. The lone stranger in our midst was Alina. I was determined to include her in everything so that she wouldn't feel isolated. "Thanks, Rache," David said when the two of us were momentarily alone. "I really appreciate what you've done, what you're doing. Lee doesn't know it yet, but I'm going to marry her. I know she's young and she's got another three years of college after this one, but we're in love and I don't intend for us to wait."

"What will you do about college?" I asked. "She wants to get her degree."

"I've already taken care of that," David replied. "I've lined up a job with a firm in Oakland. As soon as I finish school, we're going to get married. She'll keep going to the university."

"Are you sure she'll say yes?"

"I'm sure."

"I hope you're doing the right thing," I said. "She's a lovely kid, but she's a kid. She may not feel she's ready to get married."

"She's ready to live with me, and I'm going to insist we get married."

"What's wrong with just living together?" I wanted to know. "Yalie and Richie are living together. Dev and Mark are living together. Jess is living with Sam."

"That may be okay for them. It isn't okay for me. It's too easy to quit when you have an argument, and I want to spend the rest of my life with Lee. Through thick and thin, better or worse, sickness or health, forever—all that shit."

"If that's what you want, little brother, I hope Lee wants it, too. You have the Rachel Rothschild Seal of Approval, good for one lifelong marriage. I guarantee it."

We hugged.

Before our time together was over, I found an opportunity to tell Alina, "My brother really loves you. Really, really. I hope you two stay together, Lee."

Alina said, "I'm planning on it." I liked her. She was a spunky kid.

When my cousins came over later in the day, I sat down with Dev, Yalie, Mark, and Richie in the living room. I wanted to hear more about Yalie's job on Capitol Hill. It was unusual for a young lawyer who'd just completed a prestigious clerkship not to go into practice.

Richie volunteered the answer: "Yale"—he'd created his own compromise between Yalie and Ya'el—"can't make up her mind whether to be a Supreme Court Justice or the next Senator from Colorado. She's had a taste of the court system. Now she wants to be political."

"Not exactly, but something like that," Yalie commented. "I'm not really sure I'm cut out to practice law. At least not immediately."

She hadn't been in the Senate job long but found it very exciting. "I'm doing the Senator's work on matters before the Judiciary Committee—civil rights, criminal justice, judicial nominations, immigration law—and I've also got a piece of the foreign affairs portfolio. It's a lot more fun than writing legal briefs."

"You can bet on that," Dev put in. "Never met a footnote or a law journal article I couldn't do without."

Mark commented, "Can you believe the lies this woman tells? She's passionate about the law."

"If that's your idea of passion, I better find a new lover."

My God, I thought, *I love these guys.*

I asked about Yalie's long-term plans. Why not? She could tell me to take a hike if I was being overly intrusive.

"I don't know," Yalie said. "Chrissakes, girl. Just because you got married in the playpen, that doesn't mean the rest of us will. Richie and I are having a good time, but there's no formal understanding between

us. It may last, and it may not. We could be together fifty years from
now, or we could split up tomorrow. We're certainly not ready to get
married. And if we do stay together, I can't tell you whether it will be
in Washington or Chicago or New York or someplace else, maybe even
Colorado. Right now I like what I'm doing, and he likes what he's
doing, and we enjoy doing it together. That's good enough for me."

My immediate reaction was *yeah, yeah*. I wanted Yalie to be
married, like I was. And then later—not much later—I wondered
whether I'd have married JJ if we'd lived together for a couple of years,
and I'd found out things about him and about myself that I was only
now learning. Then I thought *Stop it, Rachel. You're just making things
worse.*

In a separate conversation, I asked Dev about how she and Mark
were progressing. Dev laughed. She wasn't shy about it anymore.
"We're just getting to know one another. We're too busy screwing to
discover what sort of people we are. Ask me a year from now. Maybe
he'll be less hot for my body, and we'll find time to talk. How did you
know JJ was the right guy for you?"

"We talked *before* we screwed," I said.

"How old-fashioned," Dev said. "How boring."

"Yes, you're right about that."

And I thought to myself, remembering the spanking episode just
before I left for Santa Monica: *I'm not sure I know JJ even now. I'm not
even sure I know Rachel Rothschild.*

On the return flight to Denver, I was once again thinking about
the encounter with JJ prior to my departure for Santa Monica—my
tantrum, the spanking, the sexual excitement. I continued to be
ashamed of myself on all counts. For failing to behave like an adult.
For letting myself be punished like a bad child. And, above all, for
reacting as if it were an invitation to lovemaking. This was the second
time that JJ had spanked me, and the second time that it ended in sex,
wild sex at that.

I had to talk about it with JJ. I couldn't let it happen ever again. But
it was difficult for me even to raise the subject and even more difficult
to talk about my feelings. So, instead, I put it in writing and left the
long letter in an envelope on the bathroom counter one morning when
I was the first awake. I was wondering nervously how he'd react. What
JJ did when he came in for breakfast was to take my chin gently in his

hand and kiss me on the mouth. "I understand, sugar," he said. "It won't ever happen again."

The result was that we never did talk about what happened. Although I had "won" in some sense, my feelings remained unresolved. Maybe his feelings did also. The next time there was a serious blowup, it probably wouldn't lead to a spanking and sex afterward, but who knew what path it would follow? Stopped-up rivers seek and find an outlet when pressure builds, and hidden feelings will do the same. I knew that. I just wasn't prepared to confront it. I was the same emotional coward I'd been since the beginning of my relationship with JJ.

That crisis surmounted, though not dealt with, life moved on.

*   *   *

Back at *In the Rockies*, I suggested another ambitious project to Mr. Edwards. After my poor performance on the second science fair article, I wasn't sure he'd agree to it. I wanted to write about the transformation of Colorado A&M, the state's land-grant "cow college," into Colorado State University, an institution offering a full range of academic disciplines. He didn't say no, but he tried to discourage me. It was a much more serious subject than the magazine usually covered, he said, and it would be extremely difficult to make it interesting for the readers. I said I was ready to do it freelance and give him first crack at printing it. I also offered to bear all the expenses for visits to the school.

"You're a determined kid," he said with a half smile. "I like that. Okay, I'll let you go ahead. You'll do it on our dime. But if it isn't any good, I'll toss in the wastebasket. Can you live with that?"

As I'd done once before, I said I could. But I knew I'd be crushed if he rejected anything I wrote.

It took me the better part of two months to get a handle on the subject. I wasn't willing to crib the history of the transformation from a university brochure. I wanted to talk with students before and after and with professors who were there during the changeover. A lot of it would have to be done in Ft. Collins, where the university was located, a couple of hours north of Denver, close to the Wyoming border. That required me to be away from home for several short stretches, leaving Danny behind with Hillary.

I had fun doing the reporting. People were happy to tell me their war stories. And I'll have to say that I was glad to be away from Denver, alone in Ft. Collins. I never did get my feelings sorted out, however.

Writing the piece was hard work. I had to balance the personal and the institutional, explain how the land grant colleges came into being, why Colorado A&M had to change, how it functioned now. And I had to do it in three to four thousand words. "This isn't Hiroshima," Mr. Edwards told me. "And you sure as hell aren't John Hersey. Not yet anyway. No one will read an article about CSU that goes on forever—not even the university president." I hadn't even been alive when John Hersey wrote his report for *The New Yorker* about the bombing of Hiroshima at the end of World War II, but I'd read it in high school, so I knew what he was talking about.

When I was finished writing my story, I was sure I'd done well, but my view didn't count. I turned it in to Mr. Edwards and waited for his reaction. "It's okay," he said. "Not as boring as I expected." Then, after a pause, he said, "You did good, kid. I like it." I was enormously pleased. Mr. Edwards's approval meant a lot to me.

When I was done with the CSU article and it had been accepted, I proposed what I was sure would be a "fun" assignment, comparing the political and social styles of The People's Republic of Boulder and Colorado Springs, the home of Paleo-conservatism. Mr. Edwards approved the concept but had a warning: "When this article is printed, Rachel, I'd like to hold the number of people who discontinue their subscriptions to several hundred thousand. Try not to offend more readers than is absolutely necessary."

"I'll do my best," I said.

My intention was to keep it light, to make it funny by exaggerating the truth. Boulder politicians would appear as Quixotes and Commissars. The featured performers in Colorado Springs would be Dr. Strangelove, Ayn Rand, and the Christian Crusaders in full armor. No names of actual people would be mentioned.

I did as well as I could, and Mr. Edwards declared himself satisfied with the result, but I didn't have Jess Sherman's gift for caricature and the article got a ho-hum reaction. No one was greatly offended, but no one was greatly amused, either. I would not be the next Mr. Dooley, not even the next Dave Barry.

I was more successful with my next piece, which focused on

environmental challenges facing Colorado's many national parks. There was a sharp division within Colorado on whether there ought to be more or less environmental regulation. But I would deal with regulatory issues on another day. This article was about the effects of weather and other natural forces on the park system. Since, with few exceptions, everybody in Colorado, whether on the Left or on the Right, considered himself or herself a conservationist, there was little in the article that anyone could object to. It was simply a straightforward and up-to-date assessment—and it attracted wide praise.

I suggested a story on the state's financial condition, but Mr. Edwards rejected the outline I presented. "There's a reason, young one, that this publication doesn't call itself *Terminally Boring Magazine*. Half our readers would be asleep by the end of the second paragraph, and the rest wouldn't last *that* long. The thing you haven't learned yet is that magazine articles have got to be interesting. Some things are inherently interesting, like a juicy murder or a sex scandal. Some things can be made interesting by good reporting or great writing. The state of Colorado's financial condition would foil the combined talents of seven Pulitzer Prize winners and Tom Stoppard—and you're not yet in their league."

Seeing my disappointment, he said, "Okay, okay. I'm not going to say never, ever. But this isn't it. If you're determined to write about the state's financial condition, you'd better show me the consequences and the politics, how it affects real people, who's doing what to whom. Then I'll consider it. Okay?"

I said, "Okay." He'd shown me a mountain, and I was determined to climb it.

*   *   *

Summer was upon us now, and it would soon be Daniel's second birthday. JJ thought it was time to have another child, and I agreed. Somewhat reluctantly. I wasn't sure I was ready for a second kid. Nevertheless, I agreed. We worked at it, and unfortunately it was entirely too much like work. There was little spontaneity in our lovemaking. Although we'd supposedly settled the issue raised by the spanking, it remained in the background. I couldn't let go of it. JJ made every effort to arouse me in bed, but I wasn't ready to abandon myself to sexual passion. In the aftermath of the spanking, maybe I was afraid of it. I wasn't angry with JJ any longer, not consciously at least. I wasn't unhappy. I was merely passive. JJ certainly noticed my unresponsiveness.

"Well," he said one night after I'd scarcely moved a muscle during intercourse, "it's not exactly like our honeymoon, is it?"

I didn't answer, although my feelings were hurt. No, it wasn't like our honeymoon. Would it ever again be like our honeymoon?

We were still laboring to make me pregnant when the news arrived that my brother David had proposed to Alina Abramowitz—Lee. She had accepted, and they would get married on the Sunday before Labor Day, less than five months after I'd met her for the first time. It would be a very small wedding just north of Los Angeles in the San Fernando Valley. Alina's mother was seriously ill, and immediate family was all that could be managed.

JJ and I would go, of course, but we planned to leave Daniel with Hillary at Mom and Daddy's house in Santa Monica. David called Aunt Ruth and Uncle Aaron as well as Dev and Yalie to apologize for not inviting them. It just wasn't possible under the circumstances.

The complete guest list at the wedding on the Rothschild side consisted of Mom and Daddy, me and JJ, Noah, and Rebecca. On Alina's side, there was her father, a handsome man in his mid-forties, her mother, two younger sisters, and Alina's roommate from Berkeley. Mrs. Abramowitz was frail, plainly showing the ravages of her illness. She was bald after chemotherapy, and she was confined to a wheelchair

The ceremony took place in a small chapel in the synagogue the Abramowitz family attended. Noah was David's best man, and Alina's roommate was her sole attendant. Despite the small size of the audience, Alina asked that the rabbi conduct a full religious service. It was a poignant moment, and I wept quietly the whole time. Although the only time I'd seen the bride prior to the wedding was at the Passover seder, I felt I really knew this girl, that she was lovely and lively but vulnerable, and that she'd agreed to marry David not only because she loved him but because she needed him.

I had no idea how long Mrs. Abramowitz had been sick, but it was obvious that she was dying and that Lee was already essentially motherless. If Mr. Abramowitz was preoccupied with his wife's illness and fearful about the future, as seemed likely, she might not be getting much emotional support there, either. Mr. Abramowitz had two other kids at home to worry about. Probably the only thing he was really doing for Lee was paying for her education.

My assessment turned out to be pretty accurate. Alina was still a child, more on her own than she should be at eighteen. She loved David. That was certain. Under other circumstances, I think she might have preferred, considering her age, to live with him without marrying him. But David promised strength and stability, and Alina needed stability more than she needed her independence.

I didn't understand all of this immediately, but I understood enough. That was why I wept at the wedding while others were smiling. Mrs. Abramowitz was crying, too, but hers were happy tears. She'd lived long enough to see her oldest child married. My pal Jess had once said of my tendency to shed tears at any sentimental moment, whether happy or sad, that "Rachel will cry if you give her the phone book to read." That had become the word on me among friends and family whenever I started shedding tears: "You know Rachel. Hand her the phone book."

At the end of the wedding service, David shattered the traditional glass, and the bride and groom embraced. I was still crying when I offered David my congratulations. Thankfully, David misinterpreted my tears as tears of joy. I gave Lee an unusually fierce hug, saying "I love you," and then broke into silent sobs as I left her.

Mom was the only one who recognized that I was crying as if I meant it. When she asked me, I said, "I thought about my big wedding and this tiny one. I know underneath Alina has to be hurting. She's a child, Mom. Much more of a child than I was when I married JJ. And she's got it a lot rougher than I did. Besides, don't you know by now I'm a big crybaby?"

Mom kissed me on the forehead. "You're a very sensitive young woman, sweetheart. I suspect you're right. Daddy and I will do our best for her … for her and David."

Alina had to get back immediately to classes in Berkeley, so the honeymoon had to be postponed. I told David that the lodge in Vail was available whenever he and Lee wanted and for as long as they wanted it.

"Thanks, Rache," David said. "Even though I remember the time you tried to kill Noah and me, you're the best big sister a guy could have. I … we…… appreciate the offer. We're going to go to England for a few days during winter break. I'll suggest to Lee that we stop in Vail on the way back."

*   *   *

Less than two weeks after we returned from David and Alina's wedding, I arrived home from the office to find a message waiting from Daddy. It read "Urgent."

When I got Daddy on the line, he said, "I've got some bad news, Rache."

My entire body clenched. The last time I'd heard those words, they preceded the announcement of Uncle El's fatal automobile accident.

"It's your friend Lynetta."

"What?" I could barely get the word out of my mouth.

"She's dead."

"Oh, no!" I shrieked. "No, no. Please no." I was crying hysterically.

"I'm sorry, baby, but you had to know."

He allowed me to sob for a few moments.

"How?" I finally managed to ask.

"They found her dead in her apartment. An aneurysm apparently."

"When?" I could barely speak.

"Day before yesterday. She didn't go to work. They tried calling her from the hospital. When there was no answer, her mother went to her apartment and found her. She'd done her regular shift in the Emergency Room the previous night, gone to the gym to play basketball, showered, then went home to bed. She must have died in her sleep around 2:00 to 3:00 p.m. They doubt she knew what hit her."

"Who called?" Every word was an effort.

"Jess. Sam heard about it from colleagues. I've spoken with the Pearson family. They're devastated, of course. It's a real tragedy. Lynetta wasn't sick, had never complained."

"When's the funeral?"

"Tomorrow afternoon."

"I'll come."

"I knew you'd want to be there, Sweetie. I'm sorry I had to be the one to tell you."

He hung up, and I sat down and wept inconsolably. I couldn't come to terms with it. My friend Lynetta was only twenty-seven. She was on her way to being an outstanding doctor. She was full of life, and now she was dead. It didn't seem possible.

The next day, I flew to L.A. alone. I cried the whole way out. Mom and Daddy picked me up at the airport, and we went directly to the church, which was filled beyond capacity. Jess and Sam were there, of course, as was Laura. Arlie had flown in from Palo Alto. I recognized a couple dozen other mourners—her parents, schoolmates from Santa Monica High School, Lynetta's teammates and other friends from UCLA, and Dr. Jason Fishman, who'd accompanied her to the last Rothschild family seder.

I'd never been to a funeral in an African-American church. The service was long and unrestrainedly emotional. Lynetta's younger brother, whom I barely knew, spoke for the family. He kept his composure almost to the very end of the eulogy. How he lasted that long, I can't imagine. When he finally broke down, unable to finish, the entire congregation dissolved in tears. Since childhood, everyone who knew her had expected great things from Lynetta, and she'd fulfilled their expectations and more. Now, suddenly, she was gone, and the world was empty.

I never had a chance to say anything directly to Lynetta's family. We got to the church too late for that, and there was no opportunity at the cemetery. It was just as well. I wouldn't have been able to speak. Instead, I sent them a note. I told them that I understood that their loss was far greater than mine but that I loved Lynetta and would remember her always. Somehow, that seemed a paltry response to such an enormous tragedy. Words were my profession, but they were inadequate.

I had a difficult time after returning to Denver. I had no one to share my grief with. JJ was sympathetic, but he really didn't know Lynetta very well. I found myself sitting at the computer, unable to concentrate. I'd be having lunch, and then I was weeping. I went to sleep thinking about Lynetta. I woke up thinking about Lynetta. Every day she saved people's lives, but when her life needed saving, nobody was there.

My other girlfriends felt sad about Lynetta, but they didn't have the deep connection to her that I did. I put in a call to Dr. Jason Fishman. I don't know why. Just to touch another one of her close friends, I suppose.

He answered the phone, and I was so choked up I couldn't even say my name.

"Rachel?" he asked. "Is that you?"

"Yes." For a few moments, all I could do was weep. I finally recovered enough to say, "I'm sorry. I don't mean to cry on you this way."

"Don't apologize. It's always hard to deal with sudden death. And Lynetta was so young and so fit and so vibrant. She was a beautiful person. I assume you understood that I was in love with her."

"Oh, Jason, I'm so sorry. No, I didn't know."

"I don't think she felt that way about me. But I hoped she would eventually. Taking me to seder at your house was a good sign."

"That was the last time I saw her. At the seder. There were so many people. I didn't get much time with her."

"Regret's a normal reaction, Rachel, but life can't be lived backwards. We've got to be thankful for the time we *did* have with her." Jason Fishman, who loved her, was consoling me when I should have been consoling him.

We talked for close to an hour, trading memories. We belonged to different parts of Lynetta's life and had few moments in common. But we needed to speak about her, to share the immense loss we both felt.

Toward the end of the conversation, I said, "I think I'm beginning to understand the therapeutic value of the *shiva*," the Jewish mourning ritual. "It seemed bizarre to me when I was younger—family and friends sitting around for a week telling stories, eating, crying, saying prayers for the dead."

"Yes," Jason replied. "Whoever first said that 'misery loves company' must have just sat *shiva*. It's a way to let your grief out. What I remember especially from when my father died was the laughter on the third or fourth day. We'd gotten beyond tears and were beginning to celebrate his life, remembering the good times."

"It's a lot easier, though, when death comes at seventy-five or eighty-five," I said. "Lynetta should have had another fifty or sixty years. She went much too soon." I was crying again.

"Yes, she did, Rachel. She went far too soon for all of us."

By the time we hung up, I had cried myself out. There would be no more tears. Only the dull ache of an irreparable loss.

In the month after Lynetta's death, I went to synagogue each Shabbat to say *kaddish*, the Jewish prayer for the dead, in her memory. I wasn't a religious person. It just seemed right.

I was still going through these mourning rituals when I missed my period. Tests confirmed that I was pregnant. It was too close to Lynetta's death for me to feel joyous about anything, but JJ was enormously pleased. I wanted the baby, too, but it wasn't to be. Three weeks after the doctor gave us the news, I miscarried. I awakened with intense pains in the middle of the night, and before JJ could get me to the emergency room, I was gushing blood and the fetus was dead.

It was a blow to both of us, and the shared pain brought us together emotionally in a way we hadn't been together for many months. Sexual intercourse was forbidden for a time, but we lay together in the big bed in a tender embrace. We spoke about how much we loved one another, and once again, it was true.

After a time, the doctor said we could resume sexual relations, but he advised us to postpone trying to conceive another child because there had been "complications" and I needed time to heal completely.

We went back to making love not as an occupational requirement of parenthood but for the pleasure of it. I responded to JJ's touch and taste in a way that I'd ceased doing after the second spanking episode. It was not as intense as in the earliest days of our marriage, but the wanting was there again. He was my husband, my lover. We were back to holding hands outside the bedroom and to communicating with our eyes across crowded rooms and silently mouthing "I love you."

I hadn't felt this good about my marriage in a long time.

This was the mood we were in when we headed off to Santa Monica at the beginning of December for the wedding of Jess Sherman and Sam Adams—"Dr. Samuel Adams, Plastic Surgeon to the Rich, Famous, and Flat-Chested, and High-Powered Entertainment Lawyer Jessica Sherman," as Jess described the two of them to me, Arlie, and Laura.

JJ and I arrived two days before the wedding. I wanted to be there for the prenuptial party given by Sam's parents and for the rehearsal dinner. I was in the bridal party along with Arlie and Laura. "Einstein,

Boss Becker, and Dr. Lovelorn," as Jess had nicknamed us, would be standing there alongside Bozo at the altar. How wonderful that would be.

Shortly after we arrived at Mom and Daddy's house, I got an excited call from Jess.

"Guess what," she said. "I'm 'big with child'. I always wanted to be a pregnant bride, and I've achieved my ambition. It's going to be a boy."

"That's marvelous, Jess," I said. "I'm so happy for you. How far along are you?"

"About thirty-two minutes. No one's going to know at the wedding except you, Arlie, and Laura. Not even our parents. However, unless they're mathematically challenged—and I mean *seriously* challenged—everybody will be able to figure it out when the baby's born. We're trying to decide whether to name the little guy John Quincy Adams or William Tecumseh Sherman. Which do you prefer?"

"How about Groucho Marx, you clown?" I said. "Don't you dare give that baby a funny name. He'll be in enough trouble with you as his mother."

"Okay," Jess answered. "I'll remind you of this slander when he's elected President. But, seriously, don't panic. We're thinking about naming him Richard or Joshua. You haven't any idea how conventional Sam insists on being. He wants us to have the same last name. How does Dr. Samuel Sherman sound?"

"C'mon, Jess," I said. "Are you really going to call yourself Jessica Adams?"

"Trust me. Not a chance. We've reached a compromise. I'll be Jessica Sherman-Adams. He'll be Sam Adams-Sherman. If it keeps up, of course, our great-great-grandchildren are going to have sixteen last names and fifteen hyphens."

Jess had informed Arlie, Laura, and me that she was pregnant, but she'd kept another secret from us. When I arrived at the hotel for the prenuptial party, the very first person to greet me after Jess's mom was Suzi Orbach, my best friend in grade school and an original member of the Fabulous Five. I hadn't seen Suzi since tenth grade, and, except for holiday greeting cards, we hadn't been in touch for a couple of years. Suzi had returned from Sierra Leone, where she served in the

Peace Corps, and she was now teaching English at an inner-city high school in Cincinnati.

For the first hour of the party, Arlie, Laura, and I had no time for other guests. We were busy with Suze reminiscing about our girlhood adventures. We had been such close friends, and our hearts and memories were full. But when we reached the outer edges of what we all had in common, we discovered that Suze now lived in a completely different world than we did.

She was planning to return to Africa to teach. We didn't know a thing about Africa, and though we were polite, Africa wasn't on our radar screens. We were planning another trip to Vail. Suzi had never been to the Rockies. We had our love lives to discuss. Suzi was currently unattached, and we'd never met any of her previous boyfriends. The disconnect wasn't painful, but it was obvious to all of us. We'd moved on since tenth grade. Suzi had moved alone, while Laura, Arlie, and I—and Jess, of course—had traveled in parallel, always in contact, always sharing.

The possibility of reconnecting at any level of intensity simply wasn't there. We weren't the people we were in tenth grade. Suzi's life in Southern California, her intimacy with the four of us, was blanketed by time and distance. It couldn't be uncovered even if Suzi had wanted to, which she obviously didn't. The pain of severance was gone long since for her. She had new friends, new interests, and a different life. The rest of us had one another.

There was even a certain awkwardness. Sam was the only one of the guys who'd ever heard Suzi's name, and he'd only heard of her because Jess was determined to send her an invitation. Mom and Daddy, who were at the prenuptial party because Jess loved them, remembered Suzi very well. Our house had been her second home. But Suzi didn't know any of the other guests, not even Jess's parents, who remembered her only as a voice on the telephone during their daughter's adolescence. Despite everyone's effort to include her in our conversation, Suzi was a stranger from a different planet we'd once inhabited.

The group at the rehearsal dinner the next night was smaller. I had my first opportunity to talk with Sam's parents. Sam's dad told me that he'd been asked to be particularly nice to Arlie, Laura, and me. "Sam's exact words were 'Jess has three sisters. Her parents think she's an only child, but they're misinformed.' He said that you're especially special because you were responsible for bringing the two them together."

"My number one achievement in college," I replied. "I expect to have it engraved on my tombstone."

I was actually quite proud of myself. Jess and Sam were deeply in love, and I'd played a part in making it possible. I felt like a matchmaker from the old country watching two of her clients preparing for marriage.

The wedding itself was glorious. I enjoyed it more than I'd enjoyed my own because I was a guest and had plenty of time to talk to the other guests. To everyone's astonishment, Jess proved to be a highly emotional bride. When the bridal march began playing, wisecracking Jess, twenty-seven years old and an accomplished professional, was caught in a tidal wave of feeling that swept her forward to the altar with tears clearly visible in her eyes to those of us in the bridal party. Her voice cracked when she said "I do." She was crying when the minister pronounced them "husband and wife," and the tears were streaming down her cheeks when Sam kissed her.

Once the postwedding festivities began in an adjoining room, however, Jess was her usual self. "Good thing we're already living together," she told Sam in a stage whisper, "or I'd haul you out of here and claim your virginity."

Sam's mother was either used to Jess's raucous sense of humor or totally deaf. She was unfazed. Sam's father smiled.

JJ and I were seated during dinner with Arlie, Laura, and several of Sam's classmates from Berkeley and from med school. I'd been at school with Sam's two friends from UC, but I hadn't known them there and they were busy with each other. My focus was on Arlie and Laura.

Arlie had brought Seth with her to the wedding weekend. They weren't living together, but it was obvious that Arlie was serious about the relationship. It wasn't clear to me that he was equally committed. Again, I was bothered by the fact that Seth didn't find it necessary to tell us how wonderful Arlie was. My friend Arlie didn't have much experience with men. I hoped he was worthy of her love and she hadn't fallen in love with him simply because he'd shown an interest in sleeping with her.

Laura was there alone, but she swore she was "no longer seeing the guy I was playing around with." *Maybe she finally understands that she's the one who was being played with*, I thought.

She had told us when we were in Vail over the Christmas holiday a year ago that she was trying to work her way into the production end of the business. I asked her how that was coming.

"Okay," she said, not volunteering a thing. I found out later that she was hoping to have a job as an assistant producer on a big-budget film based on a script she'd just finished editing. The man who would direct the film said he was interested in having her, but Laura wasn't ready to talk about it because she was afraid he meant he was interested in having her ass. As it turned out, that was exactly what he meant.

During dinner, I was given an opportunity, as the matchmaker, to offer a toast. I'd written out what I wanted to say, but when I got up to say it I couldn't. Crybaby Rachel was there with that damned phone book again. My eyes were so blurred with tears I couldn't even read what I'd written. All I managed to get out was, "I love you guys." I had to hand my piece of paper to JJ to read aloud for me.

Jess came over afterwards to hug me, and I hung onto her and cried some more. "Okay, Niagara," she said. "You're gonna wash me away if you don't stop." I started laughing and crying at the same time.

"You know about me and the phone book, Jess. I'm just so happy for you."

"What are you when you're unhappy?" she asked. "The Mississippi in flood?"

She handed me over to JJ. "This woman is very damp," she told him. "She needs to be dried off."

I was still damp when we headed off to the airport to go back to Denver. It has been an oddly emotional few days for me. Jess was married, and it had been my doing in part. And she was going to have a baby. That caused me to remember the baby I *wasn't* going to have, and it made me sad. I wept some more.

Three weeks after we came back to Denver, David and Alina arrived from their honeymoon. The newlyweds had been in London for a week and had accepted my invitation to spend their second week in Vail. My intention was to meet them at the airport, give them a car, and send them on their way. I was not going to interfere with young love. But David said, "We'd like to spend the evening with you guys, if you'll have us." He added slyly, while Alina blushed, "Besides, we haven't been out of bed for more than five hours at a time since September, and we can use the rest."

I offered to take them to dinner. But Lee said, "Please, let's eat in. Order a pizza or something. I'm more interested in playing with my new nephew than I am in another restaurant meal."

So it was decided. True to her word, Lee was soon down on the floor with Danny, letting him climb all over her and pummel her while she occasionally snuck a kiss. David watched her with obvious affection. Lee's playfulness was one of the most endearing things about her. She was not yet an adult, and she didn't pretend to be. She was a college sophomore, recently turned nineteen, who looked more like she was sixteen but just happened to be married. It was like having a teenager in the house—one little kid playing roughhouse games with another. JJ, I know, considered Alina an ingratiating child.

I had a different take. I'd known Lee a total of eight and a half months, and we were together for only the third time. Nevertheless, we'd established a powerful bond. Lee seemed to have elected me to be her older sister, and I was more than happy to accept. I think I saw better than David did that Lee was a lost little girl in some ways, but I didn't have the patronizing view of her that JJ did. With Lee's mother nearing death and the foundations of her previous life collapsing beneath her, I thought her love for David had an air of desperation to it. She was holding on for dear life, and that could be dangerous when love's first fire began to die down.

I was determined to make David understand Lee's cavernous need for emotional support even if I had to hit him across the back of the neck with a crowbar. I intended to bring them back to Vail in the summer so I could spend a week or ten days with Lee—more with Lee than with my brother. *Come hell or high water,* I told myself, *this marriage is going to work. I gave David a guarantee, and I'm going to see that it's fulfilled.*

The following morning as they were getting ready to leave for Vail, Lee said to me, "Why don't you come with us?"

"Not a chance," I said. "Lovebirds don't need a chaperone. David would kill me, and the jury would applaud. You'll see quite enough of me, thank you, over the next forty or fifty years."

Off they went, and when they returned a week later, burnt by the winter sun and exhilarated, they were ready to return happily to Berkeley.

I drove them to the airport and would not allow them to board their plane until I'd extracted a promise that they would come again in the summer.

David tried to put me off. "We'll all be in Santa Monica for Passover. Don't you think we may be overdoing the togetherness bit?"

I said, "Fine. You can stay in Berkeley. Lee's the one we want. Command performance. She's *got* to come."

"We'll see," David answered.

"No 'we'll see,' mister," I said. "Lee is definitely coming. You can tag along if you want."

Alina was smiling throughout the exchange. "We'll come," she said softly. "I promise."

David shrugged. "I guess we're coming, Rache. The Wife has spoken."

"That's right," Lee said. "And The Husband listens."

David kissed her, and I felt I'd made my point.

*   *   *

Relations between me and JJ and JJ's family obeyed the calendar. Once a month we went to Shabbat dinner at Herman and Vera's house, bringing Daniel and Hillary. Grandma Bess and her companion were always there. Annalisa and her family were normally present. JJ's Uncle Max and Aunt Mildred came every couple of months, and occasionally their children accompanied them. There were often nonfamily guests. The number around the table was rarely fewer than ten, and it was sometimes upwards of twenty.

A permafrost separated me and Annalisa. We sat at opposite ends of the table, pointedly ignoring one another.

One night around the middle of February when I was there for Shabbat and Annalisa wasn't, Herman brought the matter to a head. When dinner was over and family and guests were moving toward the living room, he took my arm in his and said, "I'd like you to come with me, dear. There's something I need to talk with you about."

He escorted me into the library and locked the door behind us, which startled me.

He said, "Please sit down, Rachel."

I sat, but Herman continued to stand.

"First of all," he said, "I want you to know how pleased Vera and I are that you're our daughter-in-law and mother of our grandson."

What the hell's this about? I wondered. *Certainly not about how terrific a mother I am.*

He went on, "But I need to bring up something that's really bothering me, and it may not be entirely pleasant for you."

Oh-oh, I thought. *Whatever it is, here it comes.*

"You've got to stop this thing with Annalisa," he said. "It's unacceptable. Worse than that, it's juvenile."

"It's not my fault," I protested.

"No, it's not *all* your fault," Herman continued. "Annalisa is a difficult woman. She's treated you shabbily, and she's going to hear plenty from me—quite a bit more than you're going to hear. But it's not all her fault either."

I was defensive and beginning to be angry. "What have *I* done? Go ahead. Tell me."

"You wrote that pissy article about Annalisa's party," he said. "It may have been funny to some people, but it was guaranteed to hurt, and you goddam well knew it."

"The article wasn't my idea. I didn't want to cover the damn party."

"Don't give me that crap, girl. You wrote it, not some Sheila Shitface. You went and you wrote it, poison pen and all."

"That's not fair. I didn't even mention Annalisa's name."

"No, you didn't, and you didn't have to. Every single person in Annalisa's circle knew it was her party you were making fun of. You mocked her in front of the whole goddam city."

I started to get up and leave. "I don't want to listen to this."

Herman stepped closer to my chair, blocking me from rising. He allowed his voice to become louder and to take on a steely edge. "I'm not done with you, girl. Like it or not, you're going to listen to every word I say."

Herman could be intimidating when he intended to be, and I was intimidated. I was no longer trying to leave. Once he was satisfied that I would hear him out, Herman took a step back and reduced the volume.

"This hissy fit you two are having is at an end," he said. "That's all there is to it. I'm going to expect you to be civil to one another, even if it kills you. You don't have to be friends. But you *will* say hello and good-bye to one another, and when you're out in company, you'll kiss like sisters-in-law even if it makes you puke. If I ever get word that you've deliberately slighted Annalisa or talked about her behind her back or that she's done it to you, *there will be hell to pay*. Is that clear?"

I didn't want to answer. I just wanted to leave the room. "Is that all?" I asked.

"No, that's *not* all. I want you to say that you've heard me and that you'll behave like a lady."

I took a deep breath. "I heard you."

"Yes. And?"

"And I'll try."

"Starting immediately!"

"Yes."

"Okay, you can go now, but come kiss me before you go."

It was an order and I obeyed, though I wasn't sure why. The last time anyone talked to me this way was when I cursed Rebecca just before JJ and I got married, and my mother had been a lot less harsh with me than Herman was. I felt I'd been scolded like a schoolgirl. And, dammit, I was angry about it.

When we were on our way home at the end of the evening, I told JJ what happened. "What's he going to do if I disobey," I said defiantly, "cut off my allowance?"

"No, that's what he'll do to Annalisa," he replied. "I don't know what he'll do to you exactly. He's asked you to act like an adult, and if you don't, I suspect he'll treat you like a brat. Embarrass you in front of your friends, possibly. My father thinks he's made a reasonable request, and he expects you to act on it."

"Do you think what he's asking is reasonable?" There was an edge in my voice, I'm sure.

"Look, sugar. You know what I think about Annalisa and her asshole husband. But I try not to let it show. I don't want to turn my parents' dinner table into a war zone, and I don't want everyone in Denver saying Herman and Vera have two kids that despise each other. No point to it."

"So you want me to do what Herman asks?"

"Don't lay it off on me, sugar. You already complain that I make decisions that belong to you. What I've told you is what I do. What you do has got to be your decision."

I nodded thoughtfully. *He's got me there.*

That night, after we were in bed, I lay there thinking for a long time after JJ fell asleep. Now that I'd cooled down, I could see that Herman was right. He'd coerced me into promising, but I was going to do what he asked of me. *Who knows*, I told myself, *I may even get to like the bitch … about the time the Sahara becomes a rain forest.* I fell asleep with an inward smile.

Annalisa and I achieved a precarious, forced truce. My guess is that Herman told Annalisa bluntly what she *would* do. It would not have been a request. JJ no doubt had it right. The check Annalisa received monthly might not arrive if she failed to do as he said.

The first time we met under the new dispensation, I gathered myself and said, "Hello, Annalisa. How are you?"

Annalisa replied, "I'm fine, Rachel. And how are you?"

The two of us continued to sit as far away from one another as possible. When we could, we nodded rather than conversed. But we spoke when absolutely necessary. We exchanged a few words at the beginning of the evening and another few at the end. I pretended to smile when we greeted one another, and Annalisa pretended to smile in return. I imagined that I knew what Annalisa was thinking because it must be close to what I was thinking: *What a fucking hypocrite.* It was not quite clear to me whether I was describing myself or Annalisa. Probably myself since the preferred description for Annalisa would have been *What a hypocritical bitch.*

Herman, however, had achieved what he set out to achieve. Surface politeness prevailed, and silent daggers drew no blood.

I even learned to ask Dr. Allan Garson about his golf game, which always produced a long answer that required feigned interest but no attention and no response. Dr. Garson was so absorbed in his own narrative—on golf or any other subject—that he never noticed the glazed expression in the eyes of his audience, whether it was one person or one hundred.

I was invariably seated at Shabbat dinner next to Grandma Bess at the old lady's insistence. Her fondness for me was well-established. While it was resented by her own grandchildren, Max's kids, as well as

Annalisa, no one dared to object because Grandma Bess was the richest member of the family. I'm sure I was the one who was least concerned with that fact. My feelings for Grandma Bess were genuine.

I tried to drop in on Grandma Bess for an hour or so at least once a week, bringing Daniel along. It gave me time with my son and Hillary a little time to herself. Although Grandma Bess suffered from arthritis of the hip and knee and was beginning to lose hearing in her left ear, her mind was as clear as ever. She read incessantly, mostly history and biography but also the newspapers and *In the Rockies*. She always had a hundred things she wanted to discuss with me, beginning with my latest article, whatever it was. Grandma Bess looked for my byline as soon as the magazine appeared in her mailbox. She was my biggest fan. I might not know anything about the doings of Denver society like Annalisa did or be up on the latest fashions in the pages of *Vogue*, but I knew about things that Grandma Bess was interested in. She took my work more seriously than JJ did. He always praised what I'd written, but he rarely wanted to discuss it with me.

Grandma Bess was especially passionate about politics. Although she was a very rich old woman, Grandma Bess was a rabid Democrat and had been since 1932 when she was still young and the Weiner fortune didn't exist.

I liked being with Grandma Bess because my own grandparents were ten thousand miles away and they no longer traveled. Grandpa was too far out of it to go any further from Tel Aviv than Jerusalem. Grandma Bess helped me feel connected to a generation that had given me so much when I little and still had wisdom to impart.

My relationship with Grandma Bess was probably a source of unease to Annalisa and to Max's son and daughters. But it pleased JJ because his ties to his grandmother were very strong, and it pleased Herman because it made his mother happy.

With the frigid Arctic temperatures that prevailed between Annalisa and me having warmed to chilly, Herman appeared content. He didn't thank me, however, for the change in my behavior. What he said to me gruffly one Friday night was, "I'm glad you've been acting like a grown-up. About time."

I had been taught not to display my upthrust middle finger in company or to say "go fuck yourself" to my elders. So I did neither. As we left, I told JJ, "Your father makes me so mad I could scream."

"That's what the plains are for, sugar. Drive about fifty miles that way," he said, pointing toward the east, "and then start hollering as loud you can. Herman won't hear, and the cattle won't mind."

Despite my frame of mind, I started laughing. "And if I screamed in his ear, would he hear me?"

"Not a chance. The way it works is that you hear him." He added, in a perfect imitation of Herman's voice and manner, "Is that clear, child?"

I started giggling. "Okay. It's clear. It's perfectly clear. It's perfectly fucking clear. And I surrender."

*   *   *

April was coming up again, time for another Passover in Santa Monica. I had explained to JJ—unmistakably—how important this was to me. He promised to clear his calendar and not to allow anything to interfere. There would be no repeat of the previous year.

There was going to be a full house again. All the Rothschilds. All the Goodmans. Plus my girlfriends, who were becoming fixtures at the Passover table as they had been during sleepovers when I was a young teenager. I also got my folks to invite Jason Fishman, who'd come to last year's seder with Lynetta Pearson, but he told them that he was still in mourning and wasn't up to it.

David and Alina would be staying with Alina's family. Her mother was dying, and her father had asked them to. They'd come to Santa Monica only for the seder. Noah was working with a start-up company in Silicon Valley and expecting to be rich. At the seder, he was accompanied by another girl no one knew—Marla Shifrin, who lived in San Jose and didn't seem to have much to say for herself. Rebecca brought a girlfriend this time, her current roommate at Berkeley.

Dev and Mark were still living together, and though he didn't know it yet, she intended to be engaged. She was no longer uncertain about his affection. Mark, in turn, was becoming increasingly comfortable around Dev's family.

Yalie was 100 percent committed to her job and to Richie. Although the hours were extremely long when the Senate was in session, she didn't mind because her portfolio and Richie's were similar and they were usually working on the same thing at the same time, and their bosses were on the same committees and generally on the same side of the issues. "I love what I'm doing," she told me. "Richie loves what he's doing. We're in love with each other. What could be better?"

Jess Sherman-Adams was visibly pregnant and glowing, a picture of the expectant mother suitable for framing. Though she was working like a dog, albeit a professional dog, and Sam was extremely busy at the hospital and struggling to build a private practice as a plastic surgeon, Jess had no complaints, none at all.

"I puked bucketfuls at first," Jess said. "But now I inhale everything that's put on my plate. Before the kid arrives, I'm going to weigh a ton. Wait," she said, holding her palms out parallel to the floor like she'd just called the base runner safe at second, "I exaggerate. Three quarters of a ton." Bozo the Clown was not taking maternity leave.

Laura was working as assistant producer on a big-budget spy film but wouldn't say much about it. The price she was paying we learned later was to live with the director, Peter Bogusian, who'd given her the job. Dr. Lovelorn was in need of advice but too ashamed to seek it.

It was some time before she spilled the story to Jess, and Jess, in turn, told me. Bogusian didn't love Laura and didn't pretend to. He called her "Honeypot," which was not a term of endearment but a humiliation since that was also what he called a woman's vagina. He bought slutty clothes for her and insisted that she wear them when they went out together in the evening. He didn't mind that strangers looked at her like she was a whore. He found it amusing.

Laura was succeeding professionally, but she felt worse about herself than she ever had before. Once, she used to persuade herself that she was in love with each of her sex partners. Now she was just allowing herself to be fucked. And she'd agreed to follow Bogusian to his next film, knowing that she was asking for, and would receive, more of the same.

Arlie was there alone. She and Seth had quarreled. She told him once too often how to rearrange his life, and Seth replied that if he wanted to date the Army Chief of Staff, he'd call the Pentagon. Arlie didn't think she had anything to apologize about. She wanted Seth to apologize, and then she'd say she was sorry—maybe.

I didn't know about Laura or Arlie at the seder. Mom hadn't seated me with my three friends as on prior occasions. She'd put me next to Alina. I was across the table from Jess. However, it wasn't possible for us to talk softly to one another during the service as we had last year. Arlie and Laura were seated with Yalie, Richie, Dev, and Mark. I knew that Arlie and Laura were at the seder alone, of course, but Laura had come alone before and Arlie hadn't said anything to me about her tiff with Seth. I asked how he was doing, of course, but Arlie fended me off, claiming he was busy. I hadn't recognized that Arlie was in pain..

The seder was about to begin, but Daniel, who was nearing three, was having none of it. He squalled when Hillary tried to seat him and demanded to be let loose so he could play underneath the table. Hillary, normally serene and self-confident, was thoroughly flustered. She thought she was being judged on whether Daniel behaved or misbehaved because she was the one who was with him most of the time. Here he was proving that she was incompetent.

Rebecca was asked to recite the Four Questions as always. She grinned broadly and said, I'm not the youngest in the family any more. Lee is. It's her turn."

Alina was a good sport, but her Hebrew was weak and she hadn't read the Four Questions in years because she was the eldest child in the Abramowitz family. So she did it haltingly with David's coaching, but nobody minded.

Daniel tired of playing amid a forest of legs and got up to toddle into the living room and see what havoc could be wreaked. Hillary chased behind him. When he tried to upend a floor lamp, she swatted him on the behind, producing loud shrieks that brought JJ into the room, his lips tight and his eyes flaring.

"Don't you ever, ever do that again, young lady," he said to her sternly. "If you can't handle the child without hitting him, I'll find somebody who can."

I came into the living room while this was happening. Hillary reacted like she'd just been slapped in the face. She obviously didn't want to cry in front of JJ, so she said "excuse me" in a strangled voice and headed for the bathroom, leaving Daniel behind.

"Take Danny back to the table with you," I told JJ. "Let me deal with Hillary."

I knocked on the bathroom door, but there was no answer. I knocked again, and Hillary answered brokenly, "Please leave me alone."

"I can't do that, Hillary. Unlock the door so I can talk with you."

There was silence for a moment, and then the handle turned. Hillary was standing there daubing her eyes with a tissue, trying with obvious effort to regain her composure.

I kissed her, something that had rarely happened in the year and a half that Hillary had been a member of the Weiner household. "My husband's a brute sometimes," I said. "You remember what he did to me a year ago when I made him angry, don't you?"

Hillary appeared more than a little startled. We'd never before referred to the incident. But I was smiling.

"Don't worry," I reassured her. "He'll apologize. I'll make sure of that."

"I shouldn't have hit Daniel."

"No, you shouldn't. But I don't blame you. Daniel was out of control. I probably would have slugged him in the nose if I'd been the one chasing him."

Hillary was still wiping tears away, but there was a smile trying to break through. "Oh, Mrs. Weiner …"

"It's Ms. Rothschild, and you ought to be calling me Rachel."

"Ms. Rothschild, you don't mean that—about slugging him."

"Maybe not. But then I don't have him as many hours a day as you do, and sometimes he gets on my nerves, so I can imagine how he affects yours."

Hillary was smiling now, though her eyes were still moist. Impulsively, she kissed me on the cheek. She tried to say thanks and formed the word with her mouth, but no sound escaped.

I told her, "Go sit down at the table. Let me take care of Daniel for a while."

Hillary wasn't ready yet to move, but I took her by the hand and led her back into the dining room. Then I took Daniel from JJ's lap, giving JJ a look that meant *it's okay now, asshole, in spite of you.* I took Daniel into the living room to play hide-and-seek.

When the seder meal was about to be served, Hillary emerged and said, "I'll take him. I'm okay now."

"No," I replied. "He isn't going to eat—at least not at the table. You eat. I'll give him something in the kitchen. When you're done, and please don't rush, I'll give him to you and I'll eat."

That was how it happened. Daniel calmed down. Hillary seemed better. Crisis averted. I missed most of the service, but I'd be there for the afterdinner singing, which had always been my favorite part of the evening anyway.

I nodded at JJ as I returned to the table. The nod said, affectionately, *you are such a big schmuck.* He furrowed his brow in return, meaning *what do you want, I'm a man.*

Noah led the singing. It was his moment at the seder. His girlfriend, Marla, joined in. She hadn't made an impression on me earlier, but I sat up straight and looked at her when she began to sing. She had an extraordinary soprano voice. (I learned afterwards that Marla was in the San Francisco Opera Company chorus.) David sang harmony. Alina hummed along since she'd never learned the words. Jess, Sam, and Mark knew the Rothschild melodies and had mastered the choruses, so they were enthusiastic participants. The only people at the table who did not participate at all were Arlie, Laura, and Rebecca's roommate. I didn't assign any significance to Arlie's and Laura's silence. My antennae weren't in good working order, I guess.

It was close to midnight when everyone except the family had left. That was when Dev told me about Arlie and Laura. "Those two girls are very unhappy. Laura won't say why, but Arlie cried on my shoulder about Seth. He told her he's sick of being ordered around."

I made a face. "That's Arlie, all right. Jess used to call her Big Boss Becker. I guess she hasn't grown out of it. I'll give her a call in the morning and talk to her."

"I'm sure she'd appreciate it."

"What about Laura?" I asked.

"You got me. She didn't say much. But she sure is low in the water."

"I guess I'll call her, too. Unfortunately, Laura's lost the habit of confiding. She probably won't tell me any more than she told you."

The next morning I got hold of Arlie at the Becker household. She was ready to spill the contents of her heart all over the floor. I said I would come right over. We sat in Arlie's bedroom, and Arlie cried while I held her hand.

When the tears were done, she asked my advice on what to do about her relationship with Seth. I said, "What I'd do if I were you is put my feelings in a letter. Let it sit a day or so and then rewrite it and then rewrite it again. If you love him, tell him so. If you feel you've screwed up, admit it. Don't beg. And don't tell him he's got to apologize. Just tell him you'd like to make it work if he'll give you another chance." Even though I was skeptical about Seth, I was giving Arlie the best advice I had in me. If he wasn't the right man for her, she'd need to find that out for herself.

"What do you think will happen?"

"I don't know the answer to that, love. What I do know is that you're a sweetheart, and if Seth loves you the way you deserve to be loved, then he must be hurting too. So there's a chance. And if you and Seth do get back together, you've got to stop being Boss Becker. Men don't like being told what to do. Nobody does. It's always been your biggest fault, love—but it's your only fault. You're a wonderful person, Arlie. We've been friends since forever, and I'm an expert on you. So don't get down on yourself. Just write the letter and see if it works. If you lay your heart on the line and he doesn't accept it, he's simply not worthy of you. Try to remember that."

Arlie was crying again. "I'll do it, Rache. No wonder JJ calls you sugar. You're the best."

Next I called Laura, but all that Laura would say was, "I can't talk about it. Don't worry about me. I'll be okay."

The conversation was short. Laura was not okay. I sensed that. But I couldn't get her to talk. What was she going to tell me? *I went from being the mistress of a married man who said he loved me to living with a man who treats me like a whore?* That was the truth, the whole truth. Laura wasn't ready to face it, however, much less admit it to me.

Two weeks after Passover, I learned that Alina's mother had died. Despite her illness, death came unexpectedly. Alina received an emergency summons, but she and David weren't able to get there in time. Mom and Daddy attended the funeral but did not inform me until it was over. There was no need for me to come out to California, they said. Rebecca took off school for a couple of days and Noah flew down, so the Rothschild family was well represented at the funeral and would be throughout the mourning period, the *shiva*. After the immediate shock, Alina was okay. Her mother had been dying for a long time, and death released her from suffering.

I didn't learn until later that Alina's father said he couldn't afford any longer to pay for Alina's schooling. He was sorry, but his wife's illness had bled the family's savings and he had his other children to worry about. David wouldn't let Mom or Daddy tell me that. He didn't want me to know because he didn't want me or JJ to offer to pay. Nor would he allow Mom and Daddy to assume the obligation.

"We'll take out loans," he told them, "and we'll be okay. I've got a good job, and I want to be the one who puts Lee through school. It's my responsibility, no one else's."

Daddy accepted that, though he was now making a lot of money from his screenwriting assignments and would soon begin directing his own scripts. He would let David do his thing. He and Mom could find other ways to help out.

*   *   *

Although I was technically said to be working half-time, I was now spending thirty hours a week on my writing. One of the projects I undertook was a long piece about my friend Lynetta Pearson. It was my way both of memorializing her life and of confronting my sorrow about her early death. I began with her funeral and then worked my way backward through her career as a student athlete, medical student, and emergency room doctor. I didn't mention until the last line of the story that Lynetta was my friend and that I would miss her always.

All I really intended while writing the article was to send it to her family, to Arlie, Jess, and Laura, my parents, and a few of Lynetta's friends, including Jason Fishman. Daddy was the first to suggest that I submit it for publication either to *L.A. Beat* or to the *Los Angeles Times* Sunday magazine. I wasn't sure it was a good idea. Would I be seen as having exploited the tragedy of Lynetta's premature death for my own professional advancement?

"You normally write journalistic stuff, Rache," Daddy said. "This time you've done what creative writers do all the time—process their own experiences and emotions and transform them into art. You're telling people who never knew her that Lynetta was a wonderful person and that her death was a terrible loss. That's the important thing."

Reassured, I gave Harold Matthews first crack at printing the article and he accepted it, changing not a single word. I donated the check I got in payment to the hospital where Lynetta worked. That was one of the charities her family had selected in her memory.

I received a lot of notes thanking me for having written about Lynetta. The one from her family was filled with more gratitude than

I deserved. They were clearly having a very hard time. Jason Fishman called to thank me. It was a brief conversation because he was choking back tears, and so was I.

I wasn't making a lot of progress in my regular work at *In the Rockies*, however. I kept suggesting assignments that Mr. Edwards considered too complicated and "speaking frankly, too dull for our readers." He told me things like "This isn't an educational institution. We don't award degrees." And "You're trying to feed the readers a spinach and broccoli diet. It may be good for them, but they don't like it." And "You're not writing for the *Encyclopedia Britannica*, young lady. Please, a little more entertainment, a little less depth, and a lot fewer words."

I was persistent, however. I was determined to do serious journalism.

I had a couple of telephone conversations with Amanda Collins. Amanda told me, "You have enough experience now to get work on a newspaper like the *Denver Post* or *The Rocky Mountain News*. But you've really got to think about whether it's compatible with your lifestyle. It's very hard, Rachel, to be a part-time reporter and get plum assignments. If you're a beat reporter, you've got to be on hand when the news breaks. They'd probably make you a feature writer, and I'm not sure that's what you want to be."

"What about becoming an investigative reporter?" I asked. "That's what I'd really like to do, dig deep and write a series."

"Honey," she said, "I've got to be straight with you. Let's say you sent in your résumé to the *LA. Times* and it came to me as someone who's on the lookout for young talent. I'd certainly agree to interview you. You've got a good education, you're smart, and you've done some interesting stuff. The potential is there. But then I'd hear that you want to be a part-time investigative reporter, and I'd say, 'Whoa, I don't see enough experience dealing with tough subjects and getting to the root of things.' I'd say 'This kid needs more seasoning, and I'm not sure how we'll give it to her when she's only prepared to work part-time.' Then I might try to hire you for the farm team, let you do some things for one of our suburban bureaus, keep watching you. That's what I'd do if I were being selfish and trying to hold onto you for the future. But if I were being perfectly honest with you, what I'd say is something like, 'Ms. Rothschild, I'd love to hire you, but you're probably where you should be at this stage of your career. You need to extend the range of your reporting a bit; *show me* that you can dig all the way to the bottom of a subject and write about it persuasively. When you've done that, come back and see me, and I'll give you a job then.' In other words, honey, if I were being honest, I'd encourage you as much as I could, but I wouldn't hire you right away."

I needed to think about that. If I were in Santa Monica, I would talk it over with Daddy. But I was reluctant to discuss it with JJ. He'd encouraged me to have a career, but he didn't want to be inconvenienced by it. Part-time to JJ meant part-time, maybe a couple of days a week, at most three. I was out reporting, on the phone, at my computer, in the magazine's office almost every day we were in town—not eight hours every day but an average of six. JJ was trying to be gracious. I understood that he was trying. But I sensed that he'd prefer I devote less energy to the job and more to being his wife and Daniel's mother.

I asked to go to lunch with Dev. Although Dev and Mark were not yet engaged, Dev was already balancing a full-time career with a full-time relationship. "I wish I could advise you, Rache," she said. "Unfortunately, I don't know borscht about journalism. All I know is that women who try to practice law part-time end up on the Mommy Track. That's not a bad life. I'm not saying it is. It might look good to yours truly when I start having kids. But the unvarnished truth is that in exchange for having more time to be a mother and a wife, you get the full range of lowered expectations—at least until the kids are grown. And there's a good chance you'll be sidetracked permanently."

"I'm already working part-time."

"Yes, and I've already said I don't know borscht about journalism. All I'm saying is that in the field of law, following the Mommy Track limits you professionally. Now it's true that the big law firms are trying to accommodate because they don't want to look like male chauvinists, and it may be that there's something like that in journalism. As I say, I …"

"… don't know borscht about journalism. Yes, I've heard that somewhere before. Is that beet borscht or spinach borscht?"

We were both laughing.

I continued, "I think what you've told me is that I'll never make partner in a law firm."

"I'm not sure I will, either." We laughed again.

"You are some help, Dev. I can see why they pay you big bucks."

"Seriously, Rache. What Amanda Collins told you sounds sensible. But it also sounds as if you're getting very frustrated at *In the Rockies*. I can probably scout around and find someone who knows someone at *The Post*. That way you might be able to get a sense of what's possible there without the word getting back to your editor that you're looking for another job. Would you like me to try?"

I thought for a moment. "No, not right now. Actually, Dev, you've helped me clarify my thinking a lot. I'll stick it out awhile longer at *In the Rockies*. I'll try to come up with a few story ideas that will serve my purpose without offending Mr. Edwards's view that anything above a tenth-grade reading level is too highbrow."

"He's beginning to piss you off, isn't he?"

"Yes, although to be fair he's a very good editor and he's let me do some things I wanted to do. My problem is that I don't want to compromise with the readers even though I know he's right: 'You've got to meet the readers on their terms, not yours.' Blah-blah-blah. Maybe I should have studied law. Inability to say things simply and clearly is a virtue in the legal profession, isn't that right?"

Dev addressed an invisible audience. "How do you like this girl? Try to be helpful, try to be nice, and what does she do but insult you?"

"I'm not insulting you. I'm insulting your way of life. There's a difference."

"Rache, I *do* love you. Give me a hug. And then I've got to get back to the office."

As I returned home, I was thinking hard about new story ideas to suggest to Mr. Edwards. I was going to be a serious journalist if it killed me.

*   *   *

Summer had arrived, and I again reminded David that I was expecting him and Lee to come to Vail. David had backtracked on his promise, and Alina wouldn't force the issue. Although they'd been married almost a year, Lee wasn't yet twenty. She was letting David decide everything.

I called David. "Look, my darling brother, do we have to go through this again? I'll come to Berkeley and personally drag you back to Colorado if I have to. This isn't about you. It's about Lee. I've simply got to spend more time with her. For God's sake, don't you understand? The girl's just lost her mother, and she needs female support. I'm the one that's going to provide it."

"But… …"

"Don't 'but' me, little brother. This is not optional. It's what you are going to do. Is that clear?"

I suddenly had a picture in my mind of Herman Weiner standing in front of me in the library using those exact words. Intimidation worked, and I was succeeding in practicing it.

"Okay, okay. You've twisted my arm. Lee will be very happy. Now, tell me, who else is coming?"

"I've invited Noah. I've invited Rebecca. Yalie can't take off time right now. I'm hoping Dev and Mark will come up, at least for the weekend. I've told JJ he has the same choice you have—come to Vail or else. Mom and Daddy are certainly welcome, but you know Daddy; he's got a script to write, and that takes precedence. Aunt Ruth and Uncle Aaron will probably be up for a few days if Dev and Mark are there. I may ask Arlie. Jess is due in early August, so they wouldn't be able to come. Laura's a mystery. I'll ask, but I doubt she'll take me up on it. So, depending on whether Noah and Rebecca bring friends, and whether Arlie comes or Laura, it could be a crowd. Our place can handle eight couples easily, and if it's too many more than that, we'll rent the place next door. In the summer, that's no problem."

"What do you do up there in the summer?" David asked.

"You hike, you go mountain biking, you ride the rapids, you go to the music festival, you cook out, and—this will appeal to you a lot—you have sex."

"Now you're talking my language, Rache," he said. "We're definitely coming."

So that was settled. Rebecca's answer to my invitation was, "Yes, in a heartbeat. I'll ask my roommate to come along if that's okay."

Noah said he'd have to see if he could get away. If that proved possible, he'd bring Marla. "But that's two bedrooms, Rache. I'm ready to share. But, curse my luck, she isn't. Maybe by August, I'll have worn her down." Dev said she and Mark would try to arrange things so they could be there the whole time. Aunt Ruth and Uncle Aaron signed up for a three-day weekend.

All that I had heard from Arlie since Passover was contained in one cryptic telephone call, the essence of which was, "Bless you. It worked. I'll tell you about it when I see you." But Arlie's joyous tone told me a lot more than her words did.

I left a message on Arlie's answering machine inviting her to Vail. When Arlie returned the call, she said, "Yes, yes, yes, yes. I'm bringing my fiancé! So there. Now I've told you all."

The joy in her voice made me feel like I was Sigmund Freud on his very best day. The advice I'd provided with an almost total lack of confidence in its efficacy had obviously worked. Was it the right thing to do? That had yet to be determined.

I was sure that Jess and Sam would not come, but I felt I had to let them know I was thinking of them. So I called the house one evening, and as soon as I said hello, Jess began crying.

I said, "My God. What's wrong?"

"It's Laura, babe."

"What's happened? Is she sick?"

"Not physically. I can't begin to give you all the details. We had her over to dinner one night, and she fell apart at the dinner table. It's awful. She's living with this slimeball she's working for, and he treats her like dog shit. That's what she feels like, too."

"Why doesn't she just walk out?"

"You know Laura. She's allowed herself to believe that the garbage is where she belongs. It's pathetic. It's pathological."

"Were you able to do anything for her?"

"I don't think so," Jess said. "Not much at least. She needed to talk, and it was the most painful story I've ever listened to. But Sam and I sat there and let her get it all out."

"And then?"

"And then she left our house and went back to being dog shit. We pleaded with her to stay the night. We asked her to come live with us for a while. But she's like a death-row inmate who's decided to die. She dried her eyes, she fixed her lipstick, and off she went to the electric chair."

"What can we do about it?"

"I wish I knew, babe. Sam and I haven't talked about anything else for a week. I thought about calling her parents, but Laura told us she hasn't been to see them in nearly two years. The last time she was there, her mother called her a whore. Her brother and sister no longer speak to her. The only thing that would definitely help is for that miserable bastard Bogusian to swallow rat poison."

"I was planning on calling her to ask her to come to Vail."

"You can try. But she won't come. She's making another movie with Bogusian this summer."

I was in shock when the conversation ended. Should I call Laura? Or shouldn't I?

I couldn't turn my back on her. I had to call.

And so I did.

Laura pretended like there was nothing wrong and, no, she couldn't come to Vail this summer. Maybe next summer. Laura certainly knew it was a moral certainty that Jess would tell me what she'd learned. I suppose she felt the secret was out there and it would quickly spread to Arlie and me. But she'd done all she intended to do. She didn't want to talk about it again.

I hung up and sat there for a long time with my hands over my eyes. *Beautiful Laura. Sensitive Laura. How could this have happened?*

*   *   *

Early on a Tuesday at the beginning of August, I was awakened by an excited call from Sam. The baby had been born. They'd named him Richard Sherman-Adams. Jess was just fine.

"In fact, I held off calling until I could let you talk to her," he said. "Here."

Jess's voice, weak but unmistakably Jess, said, "I'm a mom. I knew I had it in me."

I laughed. "Bozo is back. You sweet, wonderful clown. Congratulations. Give Sam a big kiss for me. And Richard. And get your rest while you're in the hospital. You're going to need it."

"Thanks, Hon. I'll give you back to Sam."

Sam said everything was under control. Jess's mother was going to help out for the first week, maybe longer. Jess was on maternity leave from her law firm, of course. They'd already lined up someone to take care of the baby when she went back to work.

I was aware that Jess's income at this stage in their lives was considerably larger than Sam's. "High Powered Entertainment Lawyer

Jessica Sherman" was not just a joke Jess made about herself. Despite her youth, she was already considered a hotshot. Sam's practice, on the other hand, was just getting started, and he had huge medical school bills to pay. They couldn't afford for her to be away from the office for very long.

I would have liked to fly to Los Angeles to see Jess and the baby. Other than Daniel, Jess's baby was the first among the circle of my closest friends. Not just Jess, Arlie, and Laura, but Dev and Yalie as well. Furthermore, Jess didn't have any siblings to celebrate with her. But the group that was coming to Vail would be arriving later in the week, and I had things I must do before then. I promised myself that I'd go see Jess in a month or two.

Late Wednesday, I headed to Vail with Daniel and Hillary. Since there wasn't room in my car for the three of us and everything else Daniel needed, I left my Mercedes behind and drove there in a rented minivan. My cute little Mercedes was not a practical vehicle for a young mother and child, a nanny, and all the accessories. I knew that, but I was never going to give it up.

JJ would pick David and Alina up at the airport on Friday and drive with them to Vail. Everybody else was on their own.

Arlie and Seth Goldberg were the first to arrive, at midday on Friday. Arlie was wearing a diamond engagement ring and a happy grin. "You're looking at Deputy Assistant Underling Becker. No more Big Boss. Isn't that right, darling?"

Seth kissed her. "Yeah, yeah," he said. "Two positives forming a negative. This 'yes darling, no darling, whatever you say darling' will last about as long as summer snow in Sonoma." He was smiling as he said it. "All I've ever wanted is to be a member of the damn steering committee."

Arlie was back to herself. Better than herself. She sat down on Seth's lap and announced as she kissed him full on the lips, "This is where I'll be if you want me."

"I assumed as much," I said.

"I wasn't talking to you. I was talking to him."

I was pleased with Arlie's lightheartedness, such a contrast with her mood at Passover. I gave Seth a kiss. Now that they were engaged, I wanted to love Seth for Arlie's sake.

Then Daniel entered the house. He'd been out with Hillary riding his trike—his pretend mountain bike. He screamed "Arlie" at the top of his lungs and ran to her, and she took him into her lap on top of Seth's lap. There was a three-way papa, mama, and baby bear hug. She gave him a big kiss, and then Daniel wriggled off her lap and ran off to play with his toys, Hillary trailing behind.

None of the other visitors received the enthusiastic welcome given Arlie, though Daniel allowed himself to be kissed by everyone except his Aunt Rebecca, whom he called Auntie Becca and enjoyed teasing.

True to her promise, Arlie was still sitting on Seth's lap when Noah, Marla, Rebecca, and her roommate, Harriet, arrived an hour later.

Arlie told the newcomers, "Seth will have to greet you sitting down. He's got this growth on his body that prevents him from rising. Me."

Arlie was so silent the first time that Marla and Harriet had seen her that they scarcely noticed her. Now she was acting like an elephant in the living room, but with such high good humor that it was infectious. Marla, it developed, spoke as well as sang. In fact, contrary to my first impression, she had a lot to say for herself. She was a recent graduate of Oberlin College in Ohio, which was where she'd trained as a singer, and she'd immediately auditioned for the San Francisco Opera company and been accepted. She'd met Noah at the house of a mutual friend in San Jose. She lived there with her parents, keeping a tiny apartment in San Francisco for when the opera company was rehearsing or performing. And, yes, I could see from the calf-eyed gazes between them that there was a romance developing.

Harriet was from Chicago. She was a history student at Berkeley, concentrating on the Middle East. I remembered having taken a course in that field and showing off my new knowledge the first time I met JJ's parents. Like Rebecca, Harriet would be entering her senior year at UC-Berkeley in the fall.

JJ was next to arrive, with David and Alina. I gave Alina an especially warm greeting. This was the first time I had seen her since the death of her mother.

"Are you okay, Lee?" I asked. "You know how sorry we are."

Alina bit her lips. "You're all so wonderful to me. I don't know what I'd do without you."

"How's my twin treating you?" Noah asked. "He's not much, but he's the only twin I've got."

It was an old joke between them. David pretended that he was going to deliver a karate kick to Noah's head.

I said, "Boys. If you don't behave, I'm going to send you to your rooms."

"That's okay with me," David said. "Come on, Lee. You and I are off to *bed* without any supper."

He enjoyed making Alina blush, which she did every time David hinted that they might actually be sleeping together now that they were man and wife. "David," she said reprovingly, "you mustn't."

"Well, if Lee's not coming with me, I refuse to go," David said. "What about you, Noah?"

Noah looked sidelong at Marla. "If I go, I go alone. It's too bad, but that's the way it is."

Marla said, "No comment, ladies and gentlemen of the press. And you may quote me."

JJ was out on the back deck, making steaks, and Seth was willing to help if Arlie would let him up.

Arlie said, "Only for a good cause—and food's a good cause. What needs to be done in the kitchen, Rache?"

We were long since done with dinner when Dev and Mark arrived. Dev hadn't been able to get away from the office until well past 6:00 p.m. Aunt Ruth and Uncle Aaron wouldn't arrive until the next morning.

Mark brought two cases of beer along.

"I thought Daniel might be thirsty," he said.

Dev gave him a kiss. "Can't take this man anywhere."

"Do I know this woman?" Mark responded.

Dev jumped up so that Mark was compelled to catch her in his arms. She said, "Let me introduce myself."

"Oh, yes. You do begin to look familiar."

Clearly, I thought, *these two are on the verge.*

I carted Daniel off to bed about 8:30 p.m. and read to him until he fell asleep. When I returned, there were several lively conversations underway. Most of the guests drifted from one group to another at some point in the evening. They all liked one another, and that pleased me immensely. Everyone was still talking when midnight came and went.

Finally, around 1:15 a.m., David yawned and said, "That's it. I've got to go to bed."

Noah said, "That's what the CIA calls a 'cover story.' You can't fool us."

Alina was blushing again.

"Don't mind these louts," I said. "They were raised in a barnyard."

"Yes, we were," Noah said. "Right alongside Rachel Rothschild, the chicken-in-chief."

I threw a cushion at him.

David and Alina's departure was a signal for the rest of us—all except Noah and Marla, who sat holding hands, locked in earnest conversation. When I got up the next morning, the door to Noah's room was closed and Marla's was empty. He'd worn her down at last.

I spent hours with Alina during the week, sending David off to do one thing and another. I satisfied myself that she had recovered her equilibrium after her mother's death. She seemed genuinely happy as David's wife. She was majoring in political science as I had, and she was getting good grades. There was no reason for me to be concerned about her, she assured me.

"Lee," I said, "I'll always be concerned about you because I love you—and not just because you married my brother. Understand?" Her eyes filled up, and so did mine. Neither of us cried but we hugged one another fiercely.

I was right to have bullied David into bringing her to Vail. She and I had cemented our relationship. I was now convinced that she and her marriage to my brother were both going to be okay.

Our second child was conceived not long after the Vail trip. JJ and I were excited from the moment I missed my period. But we were also apprehensive because of the previous miscarriage. Although the doctor told us everything was fine, I reluctantly abandoned my plan to fly out to Los Angeles to see Jess and Sam and their baby.

It wasn't until November that we were confident enough to decide on Ariel as the name for the baby. She was due to arrive in mid to late May. We would need to prepare Daniel for becoming a big brother.

No sooner was I visibly pregnant than Grandma Bess decided that there wouldn't be enough room in our condo with two children, a nanny, and a live-in maid. The facts that there was plenty of room and we did not have a live-in maid—Blanca came in daily but did not live with us—did not figure into Grandma Bess's calculations. She announced to us that she intended to buy us a house. JJ said that was a bit much, but Grandma Bess insisted. "I can't take my bank balance with me when I die. I'd rather get some pleasure out of it while I'm still alive, and buying you children a house would give me the greatest pleasure I can imagine."

Grandma Bess's idea of an appropriate house was not exactly mine. She had us look at two estates she'd identified—huge walled-in structures with immense grounds, costing many millions of dollars. One of them had thirty-five rooms and looked as if it should have belonged to a duke. I had no difficulty convincing JJ that Daniel and Ariel shouldn't grow up in a palace. We agreed, instead, on a house in Golden, west of Denver, facing the mountains.

The house we decided on had been on the market for more than a year. It was situated at the crest of a slight hill, which dropped off sharply into a ravine on the side facing the mountains. To take advantage of the view, the architect had turned the house so that it opened out to the rear of the property. Approached by a long driveway, it looked very much like a one-story ranch house attached to a large barnlike building. The "barn" was an immense great room/living room facing the mountains. It was twenty-four feet high at the center under a peaked roof. Next to the great room, also inside the "barn" and facing the mountains, was a library, lined with bookcases requiring ladders to reach the highest shelves. The library could be opened into the great room to allow circulation of guests when there was a party. The "ranch house" contained two powder rooms, a large dining room, a kitchen, a breakfast room, an adjoining family room, and on the far end, an apartment for a maid or cook.

Below the main floor, sunk into the side of the ravine and facing toward the mountains, were three more levels. Because of the topography, the bottom level had the least amount of space available to it and the top level the most. The architect had solved the problem by putting the master bedroom on the bottom level, four guest rooms on the middle level, and the children's "wing"—five bedrooms and a large play area—on the first level just down from the main floor. In the "front yard," there was a swimming pool, a garage for five cars, an apartment atop the garage, and a large, paved parking area for guests. It was certainly an unusual house, and it was easy to see why it had not sold.

JJ thought it met our needs perfectly, and he was determined to have it. I allowed myself to be persuaded. It was far bigger than anything I could imagine owning, and I did not expect to entertain on the scale that the house permitted. Even if JJ and I had more children after Ariel, our family would still rattle around in the place. However, the house had magnificent views of the mountains. It was about two minutes away from the Interstate and nearly thirty minutes closer to Vail than anything in East Denver would have been. So on that basis—mountains in view and more mountains a couple of hours to the west—I agreed to the purchase.

Blanca announced that she wouldn't be able to work for us any longer. Golden was simply too far away from her house. JJ and I urged her to move in with us, but she declined. Instead of replacing her, we decided to rely on a three-times-a-week cleaning service. I would handle the shopping and cooking myself, perhaps with occasional help from Hillary. (That resolution didn't last long at all.)

Grandma Bess's generosity to JJ and me was received with poorly-concealed resentment by Annalisa. Grandma Bess had once again rubbed Annalisa's nose in the fact that she loved her grandson and granddaughter-in-law more than her granddaughter. When Annalisa complained to Grandma Bess, she was told, "Golden, Colorado, is not where the Denver aristocracy lives, my dear. You wouldn't be happy there." Grandma Bess said it in JJ's hearing.

No doubt, the response rankled Annalisa even further. But she didn't argue. JJ said Annalisa didn't want to jeopardize her share of Grandma's estate. "I'm sure she's already spending it in her dreams," he said.

I had begun to feel rather sorry for Annalisa. Imagine that. Although my sister-in-law had many acquaintances and gave lavish parties, she seemed to have no real friends. And her husband, *Dr.* Allan Garson, was so committed to loving himself that he had little left for his wife and children.

I was nicer to Annalisa than I'd ever been. Our greetings and good-byes now took longer than they had immediately after Herman's decree, and they had become warmer on my part. I'm sure Annalisa didn't know what to make of it. However, operating under the force of Herman's command, she was also obliged to linger and to say more than the minimum.

In retrospect, I probably wasn't doing Annalisa any favor, but I invited her to dinner at the house in Golden. That required her to invite JJ and me to one of her parties. Herman was startled by the unexpected thaw. He came into JJ's office one day and, as JJ reported it to me, this is how the conversation went.

"What the fuck is happening between Rachel and Annalisa? I didn't ask them to become asshole buddies. Annalisa must be up to something."

JJ answered, "It's Rachel's doing. Rachel is not a naturally hostile person. You told her to play nice, and she's playing nice. Simple as that. Annalisa could probably have Rachel as a friend if you got her a personality transplant. Failing that, take what you can get."

"Okay. I'll take what I can get. It's better than World War III."

Once the move to the new house was completed and additional furniture of my own taste had been purchased to fill the place, I gave serious thought to what Amanda Collins told me and to my subsequent conversation with Dev. If I was going to make the transition to serious journalism, I would have to take things into my own hands.

I hit on a plan. Instead of pushing Mr. Edwards to let me undertake assignments that he considered too esoteric for *In the Rockies*, I'd do the stories he wanted written on a schedule of ten to twelve hours a week and use the hours I freed up to begin an ambitious project that I had conceived after much thought. I wanted to write about the closure of Rocky Mountain Arsenal, the U.S. Army Chemical Corps facility north of Denver, and the effort to clean up the toxic residues left behind by several decades of producing nerve gas and other deadly chemical weapons. I intended to write about the secret work done at the facility, the testing of the lethal gas that was done at Dugway Proving Grounds in Utah, the mysterious deaths of thousands of sheep that resulted, and to the extent I could uncover it, the whole history of the U.S. Army's chemical warfare program at the arsenal and elsewhere.

I was certain it would make an interesting story if I could capture the drama of it, but I was also convinced that Mr. Edwards would say no if I suggested it. So my plan was to report it, write it, and put it on his desk when I was finished. If that project was successful, I already knew what I would do next. I was hoping to tackle the debate about closure of other military facilities in the Denver area—Lowry Air Force Base and the Fitzsimmons Army Medical Center—where the major story was what would be done with the facilities that were left behind and, especially, with the land. If I could do these stories right, I would have proved my capability as a serious journalist.

My excuse to Mr. Edwards for reducing my regular workload was my pregnancy. Of course, he couldn't object because he knew I had suffered a miscarriage the last time. I was actually working at least eight hours each weekday, sometimes more. And I might disappear into my office for a while on Saturday and Sunday. Most of that time went into my journalistic efforts. However, I was also putting several hours a week into my autobiography. I had finished writing about my college years, my romance with JJ, and our wedding, and I was now into the early part of our marriage. While I was going back into my personal history, I'd also begun devoting part of the autobiography to contemporary events—a kind of diary. Eventually, the first part would meet up with the second part. That was the intention.

I was still putting Daniel to bed at night and playing with him a little in the morning and again after lunch. I wasn't going to let work get in the way of that. But sometimes I'd go back to work after Daniel was asleep, and I often disappeared into my office during the day on Saturday and Sunday. JJ was beginning to be seriously annoyed about my extended working hours. I knew that. However, I loved what I was doing, and I was determined to stay off the Mommy Track that Dev had warned me about. Like any professional, I was working as long as I felt was necessary to get the job done.

"I thought we agreed," JJ said one evening when he came home at 7:00 p.m. and found me still working at my computer, "that you were going to work part-time. Seems to me you're spending more time on the job than I do."

"I'm doing this special piece, JJ."

"What kind of special piece?"

"About the closure of Rocky Mountain Arsenal."

"What do you know about the arsenal?"

"Not much yet. I'm just beginning to gather background material. I need to know what I'm talking about before I start doing any serious interviewing."

"Edwards gave you this assignment?" There was incredulity in his voice.

"No," I admitted. "I haven't told him what I'm up to."

"You haven't *told* him! You're working your butt off, neglecting Daniel, and you haven't *told* him."

I flared. "Wait a second, JJ. I don't like being told I'm neglecting Daniel. Don't you dare throw that kind of crap at me. It's not true. And maybe you've forgotten what you did to me right after we got married when I complained about the amount of time you were spending at the office. I haven't forgotten. What makes your work so goddam important and mine so trivial?"

"I pay the bills around here, sugar," he said. "I subsidize what you do."

I was so furious now that I wanted to slap JJ's face. I swung at him. He caught my right hand in midair. I tried to kick him in the shins, but he fended that off. He grabbed hold of me to prevent any further assault.

"I ought to paddle your ass for you," he said.

That was entirely the wrong thing to say.

"You do that, mister, and it'll be the last time you ever touch me. I'll leave you so fast your head will spin."

JJ must have known he'd said the wrong thing, done the wrong thing. He was probably just as angry as I was, but he fought visibly to bring himself under control. He said, "Look, I shouldn't have said that. I'm sorry."

I was far from being under control. "You fucking well should be. Take your hands off me."

He let go, and I barked at him, "Get out of my office, you son of a bitch."

When he did, I slammed the door behind him and locked it. I sat down on the edge of my desk, trembling with fury and suddenly weak. It took a long time for my pulse to return to normal and even longer for me to calm down enough to reopen the door.

In front of it, on the carpet, was an envelope with my name on it. Inside was a note that read, "You were right. I'm wrong. Please forgive me. I love you. JJ."

I had won, but I was not yet ready to forgive. I had nothing to say to JJ for the rest of the night. Nothing. We lay on opposite sides of the bed. JJ might have wanted to make up, but I put my back to him and pretended to be asleep until I finally *was* asleep. I did not have a restful night.

In the morning, I was still determinedly silent. I stayed in bed while JJ got ready for the day, and I ignored another "I'm sorry." I was not plotting next steps exactly, but I was determined to make JJ beg. I wanted him to take it all back, word for word, like rewinding a spool of tape, except it was his arrogance I wanted him to rewind, his sense of entitlement because he was the male and I was the female, because he was rich and I was his consort.

I wanted JJ to acknowledge that I was just as important to this relationship as he was, that I had the same rights and the same needs. One thing was certain. I was sure as hell not going to be knocked around—either physically or emotionally. And he'd better goddam well understand that.

I didn't get much done during the day. I couldn't concentrate on my work. I felt drained, and until noon I had a throbbing headache. But when JJ returned home, I was ready to answer his hello with a stiff hello and to respond to his awkward attempt at a kiss with a sideways presentation of my cheek to his lips. Neither of us said much during dinner. It was the stillness of the sickroom while the patient is recovering. And yet we were communicating after a fashion.

Without saying anything, he was saying, "I didn't mean it, I'm sorry, I love you." Without saying a word back, I was saying, "Yes, you should be, and I'm really mad at you, but I love you, too."

When we went to bed, I allowed him to curl around me from behind. Silent apologies had been offered, and they'd been silently accepted. The next morning I was prepared to listen to JJ say it aloud and to respond aloud. I made it plain that I expected a profuse apology, a down-on-the-knees apology, a begging-for-forgiveness apology. And JJ abjectly did as required. Before he headed out the door to work, he said, "I love you." I responded, "I love you, too," and we embraced.

The cyclone had come and gone. A few upstairs windows were missing, but the house was still standing.

*   *   *

Winter was approaching, and I broadcast invitations to my friends and family to come to Vail anytime they wanted. I wouldn't be going skiing myself. I was taking no chances with the baby.

But there was no reason I couldn't go to Vail. I even took over the bedroom next to ours and converted it into an office, where I could hook up my laptop computer and work while others were on the slopes.

Yalie was the first to accept the invitation. She and Richie were going to Chicago at Christmas to visit Richie's family, but they wanted to come to Vail over New Year's and stay on into early January while the Senate was still out of session. Aunt Ruth and Uncle Aaron would join them in Vail, as would Dev and Mark.

Although Dev didn't know it yet, that was when Mark intended to propose to her. He wanted to surprise her. So he asked my assistance in planning an engagement party.

I asked, "Aren't you afraid Dev will be upset because I know and she doesn't?"

"Nah, not Dev. She'll love having her family around her when it happens. You'll see."

"Are you going to tell her parents and Yalie?"

"Not right now. But, yes, right before they come up to Vail. I want Dev to be the only one who's surprised. She's been hinting that it's time to get married. It'll do her good to be the last to know. Keep her humble."

"This is cruel and unusual, Mark. I never suspected you were capable of dark plots."

"Just an all-American *goy* with wheat in his ears from the Nebraska plains, is that what you thought?"

"Something like that."

"You forget I studied politics, did my dissertation on Lyndon Johnson and the Tonkin Gulf Resolution. I learned how to be devious from a master."

"My sweet, innocent cousin. She's fallen into it."

"Yes, she has," Mark said contentedly.

"You are a mighty smug fellow, Professor Chapman."

"I can't deny it. But you want the truth? I'm a mighty fortunate fella. Dev's the greatest thing that ever happened to me. The very best. I'm just planning on having a little fun with her. I love her, and she knows it."

"When do you plan to get married?"

"As soon as the details can be arranged. Probably March or April.

But that's up to Dev and her folks. Once she says yes, it's out of my hands."

"If you don't mind my asking, Mark, what kind of wedding?"

"Jewish. I'm planning to convert. Might as well go whole hog. I guess that's the wrong way to put it, isn't it? But Dev's deeply committed, and I'm not much of a Christian. So my parents will be a little uncomfortable. I can't help that. You remember the Bible: 'Therefore shall a man leave his father and his mother and shall cleave unto his wife, and they shall be one flesh.' I'm going to cleave unto Dev."

"And be one flesh?"

"I'm counting on it."

My brothers and sister would also be coming to Vail. Their visit would be during Christmas. Marla might not be able to join Noah. It depended on the opera company. Alina and David would come as soon as her classes ended. The same for Rebecca, who was going to be alone this visit. She had a new boyfriend, but she told me the relationship wasn't at the stage where she'd feel comfortable inviting him.

Mom and Daddy had given up skiing. The last time Daddy was on the slopes several years ago, he'd torn ligaments in his knee, and he'd decided he was too old for the sport. Mom quit when he did. Their plans depended on whether I intended to be in Vail the whole time my brothers and sisters were there. They wanted to be with Daniel on this visit and to spend a couple of days visiting Aunt Ruth and Uncle Aaron in Boulder.

The Adams-Shermans wanted to come for a few days in February when Richard would be six months old. Arlie and Seth were unable to make it. Seth was getting ready for his orals, and Arlie was sweating over the first draft of her dissertation. No answer was received from Laura. Jess reported that she'd left numerous messages, but Laura wasn't returning the calls.

My work on the Rocky Mountain Arsenal story was progressing nicely when the first visitors began to arrive. I had talked to people living in the vicinity of the arsenal and had located and interviewed civilians who worked there. I'd spent time at the Denver library gathering information on the Army Chemical Corps. I had talked by telephone to reporters in Salt Lake City about the ill-fated tests at the Dugway Proving Grounds and obtained copies of news stories that had appeared on the deaths of the sheep and the denials that the Army had issued at the time.

After some asking around, I had found a woman, Anna Lopez, to live in and handle the cleaning and most of the cooking. Freed of all household duties, I sat at my desk in my downstairs office most evenings after I put Daniel to bed, while JJ tiptoed around overcompensating by acting as if what I was doing was the most important work anyone had ever done. Daniel had learned not to bother Mommy during the day when my door was closed. I saw him at breakfast and then again at lunch. And I usually put him to bed and read him a story. That was very important to me.

I had overcome JJ's resentment of my working habits, but I was blind to the fact that Hillary was also filled with resentment. Relocating to Golden, far from downtown Denver, made it hard for Hillary to have a social life of her own. Instead, she was mothering Daniel more than I was. I have to acknowledge that. Except for brief moments at breakfast and lunch and my nightly ritual of putting him to bed, he was Hillary's most of the time. Looking back afterward, I realize that it was *Upstairs, Downstairs* (except that, the way our house was arranged, I was the one downstairs). Hillary had been in the United States long enough to feel, as we Americans put it, that she was getting the short end of the stick.

I was usually sensitive to other people's emotions, but I was too busy with my project to have the slightest idea of what Hillary was thinking. Hillary, of course, wasn't talking. I was accustomed to Hillary's reticence and assumed that silence signified contentment. If I had it to do over, I would have treated Hillary less like an appliance and more like a human being. Maybe things would have turned out differently. I didn't mean to act like the Mistress of the Manor, though that's what I had done. I regret it now—deeply—and not just because my behavior toward her soon cost us Hillary's services. She was a lovely young woman and deserved better.

Even when the scene shifted to Vail after my family arrived, the amount of attention I paid to Daniel wasn't significantly greater than it had been at home. He also deserved better. I was busy with my parents and my brothers and sister. JJ was there, of course, and he loved taking Daniel out in the snow on a sled. But the most relief Hillary got on handling Daniel came mainly from the other members of the family, especially Mom and Rebecca, who leaped at any chance to take care of him, and Alina, whom Daniel treated as a large playmate, his partner at hide-and-seek and other games. I was busy being the Grand Hostess, I'm ashamed to say, and when I wasn't hostessing, I was back in my little office on the telephone or working at my computer. Daniel didn't come bother Mommy in Vail, either.

Even now, I have a hard time explaining my behavior. I guess I took Hillary for granted. The fun of being at Vail wasn't that I could spend more time with my son. It was having other people around and tuning into their lives. I should have spent more time tuning into my own life.

At the last moment, Marla had been able to make the trip. She was supposed to be performing in the chorus in *Die Fledermaus*. She said she felt guilty about playing hooky but couldn't let Noah come to Vail without her, so she had invented a grandmother on her deathbed that she simply *had* to visit. It was obvious that Marla, who had just turned twenty-three, was now totally in love with Noah and wanted to make their relationship permanent. It was equally clear that Noah liked having Marla in his bed but had no intention of settling down, let alone getting married, anytime soon.

David, on the other hand, appeared to be blissfully happy in his fifteen-month-old marriage. Lee was just twenty and a junior in college. Now that the weight of her mother's illness and death had been lifted, she was so exuberant and playful that she could easily have been mistaken for sixteen. No wonder Daniel chased her all over the house. Unlike the others, she didn't plead exhaustion after the first five minutes. She kept going longer than he could. She crawled around on the floor with him, allowed him to play rider while she acted as his horse, and took him outside for snowball fights. A lovable, overgrown child. On the surface, that was Lee.

Compared to her, Rebecca appeared to be a certified adult. She was just seventeen months older than Lee was and only a year ahead of her in school, but where Alina acted younger, Rebecca seemed older. She was pursuing a degree in accounting—an odd choice for the daughter of a screenwriter and an artist, I thought—and she was very precise about everything. Although she was the one that introduced David to Alina, I believe Rebecca felt he should have left her in the nursery to mature for another couple of years.

"Lee's such a little kid," Rebecca said to Mom and me. It struck me as more of an assessment than a criticism. "Yes, she is," Mom responded, "but she's a delightful little kid, and David's wildly in love with her. As they say in basketball, darling, no harm, no foul. She'll grow up soon enough. Youth is a disease that's eminently curable."

I had sworn off skiing for the duration of my pregnancy, and except for me, JJ was the best skier in the group. Rebecca was reasonably good and would accompany JJ on the intermediate slopes. Noah and David were also experienced skiers, but Noah had to stick with Marla, who was a terrified novice, and David was determined to protect Alina from her own lack of concern for her physical safety. Lee didn't know any more about skiing than Marla, but that didn't stop her.

"What's the worst that can happen?" she'd asked.

"You can break an arm, break a leg, fracture your skull," David said.

"Is that all?" Lee answered complacently. "You wouldn't let that happen to me, Sweet Lips."

"No, I wouldn't, but God might."

"Oh, stuff! If you think you can scare me off the slopes, you're wrong, you're wrong, you're wrong."

Lee was determined to go up the hill on the lift with the other skiers, and David had to go along as her bodyguard. Noah would stay at the bottom helping Marla remain upright. Marla was a big girl—well-endowed is the way it's said when meant as a description of a girl who's pretty, as Marla certainly was. If she had not been pretty, she would have been described as somewhat overweight. Keeping her upright required a lot more effort than it might have taken if she'd been constructed like my friend Arlie. The way I heard it was that Marla pulled Noah down about as often as he was able to steady her.

Mom and Daddy stayed at the lodge. They were happy to take JJ's place escorting Daniel around on his sled. While everybody was out, I sat in my office and worked. I had begun to write parts of the story about the Rocky Mountain Arsenal and was pleased with how it was coming. Although I shouldn't have been, I was also very pleased with myself.

By the end of the week, Marla reported that she was able to slide down a gentle slope without falling every time. Alina, meanwhile, was up on the mountain with skiers who knew what they were doing, and because it was steep, she was *always* falling down. She'd raised every hair on David's head apparently because she was willing to try maneuvers that were far beyond her capability. Lee seemed to think that falling down and being picked up was a lot of fun. David, I know, was relieved when the week was over and he was able to take her back to Berkeley with her body intact.

As soon as my brothers and sister departed, I had to get ready for my cousins. Mom and Daddy were going to go to Boulder for a few days and would then fly back to Los Angeles. They'd be in Boulder when Mark called to let Aunt Ruth, Uncle Aaron, Yalie, and Richie in on his plans. I was betting that when my parents heard about the surprise engagement, they'd return to Vail to join the celebration. Mark made his call on Saturday morning while Dev was out of the house on an errand, and of course, that was exactly what Mom and Daddy decided to do.

New Year's Eve was Thursday evening. I went up on Tuesday to get ready, and I convinced Yalie to come along. We never had enough time together. Of course, Richie was coming with us—also Hillary and Daniel.

Yalie and I knew one another so well that we could say a lot in very little time. Yalie was thriving. I could see it without being told. She claimed to be working too hard, going without sleep, eating the wrong things, and not getting enough exercise—but her attitude belied her complaints. She was plainly pleased with life. If possible, Yalie was more beautiful than ever. Her body was taut, her honey-blond hair was cut just so, falling in ringlets to just above her shoulders, and her green eyes drew people in like the pulsing sea. She was knock-'em-dead gorgeous. Whenever she walked by, men turned to stare. Did I envy her? Perhaps a little. Nobody turned to stare anymore when I went by. Unless I was in my sporty Mercedes. The car drew stares, not its owner.

One of the things we talked about on the way to Vail was my project. Richie latched onto it enthusiastically saying he might be able to help. His boss was a member of the Senate Armed Services Committee, and the committee staff could surely direct me to stores of unclassified information on chemical warfare issues. He'd arrange for the right people to speak with me.

Yalie was interested, however, in more personal questions. Just as

I could read Yalie's body language, Yalie could read mine, and my text made her uneasy. She told me I seemed unhappy.

I turned the unasked questions aside. I told her I was feeling the pressure to complete the article on the Rocky Mountain Arsenal before the baby was born, and that was all. I don't think she bought the explanation. But as far as I knew, I really *wasn't* unhappy. My relationship with JJ was back on an even keel, I thought. I was pregnant with my second child. Daniel was thriving. Hillary was a wonderful nanny. I saw my friends and family regularly. I liked what I was doing professionally. Yet, I wasn't content, and I didn't know why.

Trying to figure that out would have to wait. We needed to get ready for the big event. Mom, Daddy, Aunt Ruth, and Uncle Aaron drove up Wednesday morning. Dev and Mark arrived in the evening after work, as did JJ. There was a fire going when Dev and Mark entered. I had iced several bottles of champagne. Hidden in the pantry was a cake prepared by Denver's best baker, which had two little figures poised on skis above a mountain covered in white icing. At the bottom in red letters, it said: "Dev and Mark. Now and Forever."

Daniel went off to bed with Hillary around 9:00 p.m. About 10:00, there was an abrupt exodus from the living room by everyone except Dev and Mark. Mark told us what happened next. When we were gone, he stepped into the bathroom, lathered his hands with soap, stuck his head out the door, and called, "Would you come here for a second, honey? My hands are covered with soap, and I need you to get something out of my hip pocket."

It must have seemed a strange request, but Dev complied. What she pulled out of his pocket was a small package wrapped in silver and tied with a tiny red ribbon.

"Open it," Mark said.

Dev's eyes were filled with tears. She understood.

Mark went down on one knee while she opened the box and found the engagement ring. He said, "Marry me?"

Then she was kissing him with his soapy hands around her, nodding her head vigorously, not speaking. And suddenly the lights were on, and everyone was yelling "Congratulations" and "Surprise." Champagne corks were popping.

"You bastard," Dev said affectionately, wiping the tears away. "You set me up for this."

"Uh-huh," he said. "Let me introduce you to my coconspirators."

After hugs and kisses all around, the cake was brought out to be admired, though not to be consumed. That would happen on New Year's Eve.

Once he'd rinsed his hands, Mark had taken a seat in front of the fire. Dev had parked herself in his lap and was licking his ear, telling him she loved him, but that if he ever did anything like this again, she'd kill him. Aunt Ruth and Uncle Aaron, Mom and Daddy, and JJ and I were standing or sitting in pairs, holding hands. Richie was standing behind Yalie, holding onto her shoulders, kissing her neck.

Before the week was out, Dev and Mark's wedding date had been set for mid-March. It would be a tight fit, just two and a half months away, but it could be managed. Aunt Ruth would take charge. Mark had already called his parents in Lincoln to announce the engagement. Aunt Ruth had spoken to Aunt Shoshana in Israel to see if she could come. Dev quickly put together a list of people she wanted to invite. Mark already had his list.

They were talking about having one hundred fifty to two hundred people, probably in Denver since facilities that size weren't plentiful in Boulder.

Between making wedding plans and some skiing (not by me, of course), the week flew by quickly. I didn't manage to do a minute's work on my project, but I felt good about both my cousins.

Yalie, however, continued to be uneasy about me. I didn't know that until quite a bit later. She thought there was still tension between me and JJ. She didn't see the loving side-glances between us that her parents and mine still exchanged. She thought about saying something to Dev but decided it wasn't fair to lay that burden on her while she was planning her wedding. But if the situation wasn't improved the next time we were together, Yalie resolved to raise the matter with me directly. She was right, of course. I just didn't recognize it myself. Yet.

I could have been tired already of entertaining visitors, but no sooner had the family departed than I began looking forward to the arrival of Jess, Sam, and the baby.

The Adams-Shermans arrived Saturday morning, and there was someone else with them—Laura. I came running out of the lodge as fast as my condition would allow to fall into Laura's arms. Laura was laughing at my amazement, and laughter was a sound no one had heard from Laura in a long time. But she didn't look at all good, I noticed, even before the surprise wore off. She'd lost weight since I saw her last, and her eyes seemed to have sunken into their sockets.

My lifted eyebrows asked the obvious question. Laura said "Later," while behind her Jess made an emphatic "he's out" gesture, followed by a tiny wave that expressively conveyed "good-bye and good riddance." Conversation was deferred because I had to make a fuss over Richard, who had slept the whole way from the airport and was just beginning to stir. He was a pink-cheeked little bundle, and he was going to have red hair like his father. I took him in my arms and gave him a kiss, and Richard began bawling like he'd just seen Frankenstein's Monster. I handed him back to Jess, who lovingly quieted him and uncovered a breast to feed him. Soon he was nursing happily like a proper baby.

This was a side of Jess that I had never seen before. "My God," I said. "I wouldn't have believed it."

"Jess Sherman, Girl Mother," Jess said happily.

"You're nursing?" I asked.

"How perceptive of you, Rache. Me and a breast pump. I'm like Elsie the Cow. I leave a gallon or two in the fridge every morning before I go to the office."

I said it again. "My God. Who'd have believed it?"

"Not me," Sam answered. "Jess delegates. I would have expected her to assign nursing chores to one of the associates in her firm. Probably a male associate."

"Pooh. Hidden depths. That's me. Full of surprises."

Sam kissed her.

I steered Laura into the bedroom she'd occupy. Without putting it into words, I was again asking for an explanation.

"I left him. It got to be too much, so I left him." That was all she volunteered.

It was not a satisfactory answer. But since I was obviously not going to get any more, I said, "Good. I'm glad. And I'm glad you're here." I gave her another big hug.

Later I got a fuller story from Jess when the two of us were alone. Laura had gone into town with Sam to take more skiing lessons.

"Bogusian lent her out to a friend," Jess explained. "Like she was a piece of property. He said, 'Here, you can have her tonight. Bring her back in the morning.'"

"And Laura walked out?"

"No. Not before. Afterwards. She went with the guy. She let him screw her. She went back to Bogusian's. And two days later, she left."

"Something happen in the meantime?"

"Yes. She told him she didn't like being lent out like a library book, and he told her to get used to it because there'd be others. She cried for an entire day before she went."

"How did you find out?"

"She came to our house directly from Bogusian's. It was a Friday night, and she was still crying on Monday morning when I had to leave for the office. She told me everything. More than I can remember. More than I want to remember. You should have seen her. She was a wreck."

"She doesn't exactly look wonderful now. How's she doing emotionally?"

"Better. Not good, but better. She's not working for Bogusian, of course. She's found another job at the studio. I think she'll be okay."

"Is she still living with you?"

"No, no, no. I helped her find an apartment, took Richard in his baby carriage and went shopping with her, helped her move in. She's right around the corner from us, so we see her all the time. She doesn't talk a lot about the experience when Sam is around, but she keeps telling me things about herself that I'd rather not hear."

"Like what?"

"Don't ask, Rache. Please don't ask. She's done things you only read about in pornographic novels, and she feels dirty as a result. Or at least she *felt* dirty. I hope she's got it all out of her system now. Thank God, she's stopped talking about it."

"Poor girl."

"You're right about that, babe. Laura's been with a lot of guys, and I don't know that a one of them has ever cared about her as a person. But Bogusian took her down to Hell. Climbing out isn't easy. I don't know if she'll ever make it all the way."

"When did all this happen?"

"Right after you invited us to come to Vail. It took me the longest time to persuade Laura to come along. She believes everyone thinks she's a whore. Why she's willing to expose herself to me and, to a lesser extent, to Sam, I don't know. But she's been closed to everyone else until now."

"I'm glad she came."

"I am, too. It's the best sign yet. You remember her laughing when we drove up? It's the first time. I swear it."

"You're a good person, Jess Sherman. I'm glad Laura's got you to talk to."

"Yeah, lucky me. Dr. Lovelorn's Dr. Lovelorn. Some privilege. You know what Mark Twain said about being tarred and feathered and ridden out of town on a rail: 'Frankly, if it weren't for the honor of it, I'd rather have walked.'"

I kissed her and hugged her. "Love you, sweetheart."

"Love you, too."

Laura never did say anything revealing to me. But the week in Vail was good for her. She was exercising, eating, and enjoying herself. When the time came to say good-bye, she kissed me and said, "Thanks, Rache. I needed it, needed it a lot. I assume Jess has told you, and that's okay. I want you to know, but I just can't talk about it again. Not ever."

I said, "Be okay, sweetheart."

"I will be. As long as I've got friends like Jess and you."

"And Arlie."

"Yes, I haven't forgotten Arlie. I'll see her next. After Jess has paved the way."

Now that the last of the visits from my family and friends was over, I was prepared to admit to myself that JJ's buying this big lodge in Vail without consulting me was a wonderful idea. In addition to people I'd invited to come, we'd also hosted many of JJ's friends—most of the guys who'd been in our wedding and their wives or girlfriends—as well as several of his business associates. Taking them to Vail was a lot easier on me than it would have been to have them stay at our house in Golden. In fact, I didn't even have to be in Vail unless I wanted to be. If JJ had asked me, however, we might never have purchased the lodge. I was not willing to tell JJ that he had been right. I had him trained now, I thought, and didn't want to take any chances.

JJ, meanwhile, tiptoed around me. I recognized that much. He'd endured my wrath and experienced my gratitude, and in terms of intensity, I'm prepared to acknowledge that there was no comparison.

I don't think he'd quite figured out which surprises I welcomed and which ones bothered me. In the first year of our marriage, JJ had brought me unexpected gifts of jewelry, lingerie, a fur coat. He'd come home one night with two plane tickets to New Orleans, and we'd flown there for a long, wonderful weekend. He had stopped doing things like that. But that was okay. As long as he didn't force his decisions on me, I could live without his surprises.

We didn't talk about it. There was a lot we didn't talk about. Yalie was wrong to think that there was serious tension between us. It wasn't as simple as that. After four and a half years of marriage, we'd taken to living in parallel. JJ had his universe and I had mine, and sometimes they occupied the same space but more often they didn't. We made love infrequently. There weren't many other displays of affection. I should have understood us better. I should have understood me. But I didn't. Not at that moment.

*   *   *

With all the entertaining over, I was once more immersed in my project. Thanks to Richie's friends, whom I spoke to by telephone and who steered me to experts in the field, I was convinced I had all the information I needed. It took me two weeks of concentrated writing and editing to complete a draft that satisfied my own standards. When I was finished, I asked Amanda Collins if she would agree to read it. Off it went. Ten days later my manuscript was returned with a lot of editing marks and a lengthy letter filled with critical comments and suggestions. An entire section on the history of chemical warfare had been crossed out. "Off the point," it said in the margin.

Amanda suggested I begin with the Defense Department's initial denial of responsibility for the deaths in 1968 of six thousand four hundred sheep near Dugway Proving Ground in Utah, the result of a deliberate release of nerve gas from a low-flying plane. "You need to establish up front the Pentagon's penchant for covering up the truth on chem war," Amanda wrote. "First, it's a dramatic opening. Second, it will explain the gaps in information later in your story."

The comments added up to a less than flattering review, but I was not looking for flattery. I recalled being told by my high school journalism instructor that dealing with criticism from editors required a rhinoceros hide. Amanda's advice was good. It required me to do additional reporting and to rewrite the story completely, changing the order, dropping the history section entirely, and concentrating more on what was required to clean up the property for eventual use as an urban wildlife preserve. I had given too brief and incomplete an account of the damage left behind when the facility shut down. That was what Amanda wanted me to clarify.

Once I'd done additional interviewing, I wrote a second draft and then a third, reread that version carefully, and did some additional editing. Now I was satisfied. It was time to show it to Mr. Edwards. I was very nervous when I handed it to him. I'd put months into this project. If he told me that he wouldn't use it, I didn't have any idea what I'd do next.

Mr. Edwards gave me a reassuring smile and said, "You're a stubborn lady, Rachel. I like that. Never met a good reporter who wasn't stubborn as hell. I'll read it and let you know."

The next morning he called me at home. "Okay, kid. You've made your point. It's a fine piece of work. Needs a little editing, but I'm going to use it in the issue after next. And come tell me what else you've got up your sleeve. Since you're obviously gonna do what you're gonna do, I might as well know about it in advance."

To me, that phone call was sunshine at the top of the mountain, the best moment in my career. I had written a serious article, and it was going to be published about the time that Ariel was scheduled to be born. The gestation period for the piece on Rocky Mountain Arsenal hadn't been a lot shorter than for the baby. *I'm going to have twins*, I told myself, smiling. *One of them's a girl, and the other's a block of type.*

*   *   *

Preparations for Dev's wedding were now in high gear. The guest list had grown to a bit over two hundred. Aunt Shoshana was coming alone from Israel. Our grandmother would have liked to come, but she wouldn't leave Grandpa, who was no longer able to travel. Aunt Shoshana reported to Aunt Ruth and Daddy on arrival that my grandfather's memory was slowly fading and his physical condition was deteriorating. The bride didn't need to be told that. I could have done without the news myself. It was very painful.

Dev's plans contemplated a very small bridal party: Yalie as maid of honor, me, and Rebecca. She wanted Daniel to act as ring bearer, but I wouldn't allow it. "You're out of your head, cousin of mine. I don't even intend to bring him. Just sitting in the audience, there's a fair chance he'd wreck the wedding. Having him in the bridal party would be insanity."

Mark's older brother, a sociologist at the University of Iowa, would be best man. Dev was the only one who'd ever met him. Mark didn't want any other groomsmen. The parents on both sides would accompany their children down the aisle and be seated in the audience.

The wedding was to take place on a Sunday. Yalie and Richie couldn't get there until Friday night. That meant the rehearsal would have to take place on Saturday night after the *Havdalah* service marking the end of Shabbat, and there would be a small dinner afterwards. I offered to do it at our house, but Aunt Ruth pointed out that trekking to Golden did not make a lot of sense. Instead, they booked a room in the downtown hotel where the wedding and the postwedding reception and dinner were also to be held.

As it can in March, the weather interfered. Denver's airport was snowed in on Friday, and Yalie and Richie's plane was sidetracked to Albuquerque. They could rent a car to drive to Denver, but Uncle Aaron insisted they spend the night in Albuquerque so they would travel in daylight. He didn't want them on unfamiliar roads at night.

Despite the disruption, Dev was astonishingly calm. She was a thirty-one-year-old woman, not a child bride, and she was not going to fall apart because nature wouldn't cooperate. "Planning a wedding for mid-March in Colorado was always a stupid idea," she cheerfully admitted. However, as long as Yalie and Richie arrived unharmed before the wedding march was sounded, she was prepared to take it as it came. Whether or not the ceremony was smoothly rehearsed, she and Mark would be just as married when it was over, she said.

Yalie and Richie arrived at the hotel before dark on Saturday. They'd been on the road nearly eight hours. The highways from Albuquerque to Denver were completely clear as far north as Pueblo and had been freshly plowed from there to Denver. The two of them took turns behind the wheel, so they were not particularly tired. All they needed to do was check in and freshen up. The rehearsal and the rehearsal dinner would go on exactly as planned.

This was the first time most members of Dev's family, except for her parents, had met Mark's mother and father. Mark's brother was a stranger to all except Dev. It was a little awkward because, as Mark put it sardonically, "the only thing we've all got in common is an excessive amount of time spent in institutions of higher learning."

Mark's father, Homer Chapman, was a retired professor of economics from the University of Nebraska, and he knew a lot of Jews. But he said this was the first Jewish wedding for him or his wife, Anathea. Mark's brother, Hamilton, the sociologist, had been to another Jewish wedding, but he had no role in it other than to watch. He was afraid of doing something wrong and was, therefore, the most nervous member of the wedding party. Hamilton's wife, Flora, was a native Iowan, earnest, humorless, deeply religious. Mark said, "She's the only person in the entire Chapman family, going back to the beginning of time, ever to give a rat's ass about God." Flora was prepared, however, to be tolerant toward the Children of Abraham and forgiving of her brother-in-law's apostasy.

The others at the rehearsal dinner were Mom and Daddy, Aunt Shoshana, David and Alina, Noah, and, of course, JJ and Richie. Everyone—even the earnest Flora Chapman—had a marvelous time because Dev, the very definition of a radiant bride, insisted they must. Despite the big day ahead, the party continued until late in the evening. No one was more reluctant to leave than Dev.

She and Mark had taken two rooms at the hotel, one to sleep in and the other to serve as the bridal dressing room. JJ and I had also decided to stay at the hotel overnight so we could be with the rest of the family.

When everyone awoke on Sunday morning, it was snowing again—hard. Denver's streets were going to be a mess. Guests would arrive for the wedding in galoshes, boots, and other winter gear, but Dev wasn't concerned about that, either. Whatever it might look like outdoors, it was a bright clear day in Dev's world, and she was serene.

The wedding ceremony was an hour late getting started because guests were having a difficult time getting there, but the ceremony went off without a hitch. Mark's conversion to Judaism had been completed, and the rabbi performing the ceremony had agreed to a very traditional service, complete with the reading of the seven blessings and the bride circling the groom under the canopy. When Hamilton placed the wrapped glass to be shattered at the very end, Mark did the job with such vigor that it was felt through the feet by everyone standing nearby. Dev convulsed in laughter. She was still giggling when Mark kissed her. As they came back up the aisle, both of them were laughing like they'd just heard the funniest joke ever told. Yalie and Hamilton followed behind, and they too were laughing because Dev and Mark were laughing. Rebecca and I, who came next, were laughing because it was the thing to do. And soon everyone in the audience was laughing or wreathed in smiles, forgetting the awful weather waiting for them outside.

Mid-March it might be, with the winds blowing and the streets covered with new-fallen snow. Inside, the wedding was as sunny an occasion as anyone remembered, and the congratulations bestowed on the bride and groom were especially warm because everyone felt especially good.

Yalie, beside me in the receiving line, said, "I never saw anyone who enjoyed her own wedding as much as Dev."

"Don't look at me. I had six tantrums beforehand. Ask my mother. Ask Rebecca. However," I winked at my cousin, "the afterward part was quite good. Excellent, in fact."

"I guess there has to be some benefit from waiting. Poor me. I'll never know."

*   *   *

Another Passover was just around the corner. Before they returned to California, Mom and Daddy talked with Aunt Ruth and Uncle Aaron about what to do. Should they skip a year of family celebration? Yalie and Richie weren't going to come West again so soon. Rebecca and Alina wouldn't be able to take additional time off either, and David wouldn't come without Alina. So the issue was the availability of me and JJ, Dev and Mark, and Noah with or without Marla. Although I was approaching my due date and beginning to be uncomfortable, I said of course I'd come. Dev was also eager. She and Mark weren't taking their honeymoon until summer. Noah said he'd come if Marla would, though with Alina and Rebecca absent, he was damned if he'd be the one to ask the Four Questions. Mom was prepared once again to invite my girlfriends. I again asked her to include Dr. Jason Fishman, who'd been there once before as Lynetta Pearson's escort. I was doing it for her—and for me—as much as for him.

In the end, all the possible guests materialized: me, looking like I'd swallowed the Goodyear Blimp, with JJ, Daniel, and Hillary; Aunt Ruth and Uncle Aaron; Dev and Mark; Noah and Marla, a devilish glint in her eyes because she was in full possession of Noah's soul; Jess, Sam, and baby Richard; Arlie and Seth, who'd passed his orals and would soon receive his Ph.D.; Laura, alone and once more seeming sad; and Jason, embarrassingly grateful that he'd been remembered.

Daddy resolved the problem of the Four Questions. He took Daniel onto his lap and made a pretense of consulting him, after which he began: "Danny wants to know, 'Why is this night different from all other nights?'" He continued in that fashion in Hebrew and English through to the end. The result, of course, was that each member of the company began the recital from the *Haggadah* as if it was addressed personally to Daniel. That didn't last very long because Daniel's presence didn't last very long. He was off to play, Hillary attending.

I wasn't paying much attention to the ritual because I was trying to have a side conversation about Laura with Jess, who was seated next to me. Daddy kept shushing us until finally Jess said, "I gotta go be Jewish. Give me a call tomorrow."

When it was time for dinner, Mom wouldn't allow me to help serve the food. "I don't want you having that baby in my kitchen, darling. Just sit there, please. I've got all the assistants I need."

Jess had gone off to the living room to breast-feed Richard. However, Aunt Ruth, Dev, Marla, Arlie, and Laura lent a hand dishing out and delivering the food, while all the men remained at the table with me, talking about the prospects for peace in the Middle East. Uncle Aaron was optimistic. I was hopeful. Daddy was neither. Mark had been reading up on the topic, largely because of Dev's preoccupation with it. JJ, Noah, and Seth didn't know a lot, but that didn't prevent them from expressing opinions. Sam sat listening as if watching a ping-pong match involving one ball and multiple players. He would have liked, no doubt, to believe Uncle Aaron and me, but he seemed to find Daddy's skepticism persuasive. Jason was silent, lost in his own thoughts.

The talk continued during the first part of dinner, with Mom and Aunt Ruth supporting Uncle Aaron's optimism and Dev right there beside me—hoping. Daddy remained the only vocal pessimist. Jess, who had rejoined the party and who knew us well enough to be bold, brought the discussion to an end. "This conversation is boring enough to be on C-Span," she said. "C'mon, you guys. Let's move on to the singing."

I could see Sam poke her in the ribs. He thought she was being rude. But Jess was very much one of the family, and she knew we'd forgive her.

When the dinner was concluded and the table was cleared, the singing began. Now that she no longer felt herself a stranger, Marla took the lead with her stunning soprano. I noted that Laura was joining in and seemed to be having a good time, which was an encouraging sign.

Jason Fishman left while the singing was still going on. I could see that he wasn't up to it. I walked him to the door. He thanked me and hugged me good-bye. Of course, though I didn't mean to, I started to weep, and then felt I had to apologize. Jason made a stop sign with his hand. "Don't ever apologize for loving her," he said. "I'm only leaving now because I'm on the verge of tears myself." We hugged again, harder the second time, and then he left.

I no longer felt like singing. In fact, if my friends hadn't been there, I might have retreated to my old room to cry some more.

Instead, I sat down beside Arlie and asked how things were going. She grinned broadly. She and Seth were planning to be married in late August, before the new school year began. Seth would be on a postdoctoral fellowship, and Arlie had another six months or a year until she finished her Ph.D.. But Arlie would soon be twenty-nine and Seth was nearly thirty-five, and they didn't want to wait. I said I'd try to come.

"No one says 'maybe' to Big Boss Becker," Arlie responded. "Might as well say you'll come. I'll send the police to bring you if I have to. No way will I be married without you."

I said, "Okay, okay, Boss. I'll come. Send the police back to the station. I'll come."

"My sweet l'il irresistible force," Seth said. "Ever the commanding general."

Seth appeared to have grown accustomed to Arlie's abrupt delivery of orders, provided they were not directed at him.

Meanwhile, Jess and Sam were packing up their son, preparing to leave. Laura was going with them. As she was heading out the door, Jess whispered in my ear. "Don't forget. Give me a call tomorrow. We've got to talk."

I was ready to go myself. JJ, Daniel, Hillary, and I had rooms at the hotel, as did Dev and Mark. The last thing that I saw as I went was Noah in a darkened corner of the living room necking with Marla. *The boy is a goner*, I thought with satisfaction. *Marla's got her brand on him. It's just a matter of time.*

I called Jess the following morning at the office. Jess's secretary said, "I'm sorry, Ms. Rothschild, Ms. Sherman is in a meeting. But she told me you'd be calling and asked if it would be possible for the two of you to have breakfast tomorrow at your hotel. Is 7:00 a.m. okay?"

I groaned inwardly at the prospect of getting up so early but replied, "Of course."

I was waiting in a booth when Jess arrived. I was prepared to start immediately on the topic of the day. However, Jess said, "I'm sorry. Breakfast is a very important meal for Elsie the Cow. *All* meals are important for Elsie the Cow. Elsie won't even moo on an empty stomach." When the orders were given, Jess told the waitress she must have orange juice, a muffin, and herb tea before her omelet arrived. I said, "And I thought I had a ravenous appetite." Jess answered, "I've become an omnivore. Place anything edible in front of me, and I eat it. If it weren't for Richard draining it off, I'd soon be as big as a house. Make that an apartment building."

Once the waitress had delivered the essential first installment on Jess's meal, we got down to business. "Laura's living alone," Jess reported. "I don't think she's been to bed with anyone since she got away from that toad Bogusian. I know she's been propositioned. Bogusian has done everything he can to blacken her reputation. I assume every male who passes through the studio gates is told by the guard on duty that Laura Ludwig is a nymphomaniac. I'd love to get her a job elsewhere, and I've been asking around. No luck, so far."

"Should I give her a call?" I asked. "When we were in Vail, she didn't want to talk."

"Yes, by all means call her. I think she'd be hurt if you didn't. Will she tell you anything? I don't know, babe. She talks to me because I'm here. If you were the one who were here, she'd talk with you, and I'd be the one in the dark. I don't have magic healing powers, Rache. If I did, I'd print up cards and go into business: 'Jess Sherman. Potions Provider and Attorney at Law.'"

"Bozo, don't you ever quit? You're lucky somebody didn't clobber you at the seder Monday night. 'Boring enough to be on C-Span.' Hah! If anyone goes on cable TV, it ought to be you. I can see a permanent role for Bozo on the Comedy Channel. Jessica Sherman and the Brothers Marx."

"C'mon, you know me. I can't help myself. I don't mean anything by it. "

"Yes," I said seriously. "I know it. We all know it. You're such a softie, Jess. I'll never forget what you've done for Laura. I don't think she would have made it without you. You've been wonderful. You *are* wonderful."

"Shucks, golly gee, gosh. Even my own mother wouldn't be able to identify me from those clues."

We continued talking for nearly an hour and a half. Finally, Jess looked at her watch and said, "Oh, my God, I'm going to be late. I've got to go, Rache. Let me know how you do with Laura."

In the evening, I called Laura at her apartment and asked to come over.

I found Laura surprisingly stoic. "I made my bed. That's the appropriate metaphor, don't you think? I only make love nowadays with my vibrator."

I was startled.

Laura said, "I'm sorry, Rache. I know I shouldn't talk like that."

"It's okay."

"No, it isn't. It's the scar tissue speaking. I'm better than that."

My eyes were watering. "Oh, lovey, I wish I could help."

"You already have, Rache. The trip to Vail after the breakup was very good for me. Even though I let Jess tell you instead of telling you myself, I knew without speaking about it that I had your support."

"Are you still relying on Jess?"

"Couldn't get on without her. Consider yourself fortunate you don't live around the corner like you used to. I'd come cry on *your* shoulder when Jess's is soaked—which is a good deal of the time. You guys are the only family I've got these days."

"Still on the outs with your folks?"

"Yes. That rupture's never going to be repaired. I can't forgive my mother for calling me a whore—even if I deserved it."

"Don't talk that way, Laura. You didn't deserve what happened to you."

"Yes, I did, Rache. I earned it. I've faced myself in the mirror, and I'm just being realistic. Ever since I was a kid in high school, I've fallen into bed with every guy who asked me. Bogusian was just the worst of them."

I was in pain for her. "Please don't beat yourself up. Please! You're young. Your life is ahead of you. You've got to forgive yourself."

Laura laughed derisively. "You and Jess must have taken the same psych class. She tells me the same thing in almost exactly the same words."

"That's because we both love you. And what we're telling you is the truth. At least, it's what we believe to be the truth."

"I know that, honeybun. And thanks. I'll try. I *am* trying. Take it one day at a time. Isn't that what they say? It's a cliché, but it happens to be the only way. Sometimes I have a little too much to drink before bedtime. Sometimes I can't sleep. But I get up every morning, put on my face, and Monday through Friday I show up at the studio even though I know everybody's talking behind my back. 'Don't let the bastards grind you down.' I've made that my motto."

"You'll be okay, baby. I'm sure you'll be okay."

"I wish I had the same confidence in me that you and Jess do."

I talked again with Jess. I agreed that Laura must find work elsewhere. She couldn't continue to be around people who treated her like a slut. It only reinforced Laura's self-loathing.

I asked Daddy whether he was in a position to help Laura find work in another movie studio.

"I don't know, but I'll be glad to try," he said. "Tell her to come talk to me."

Before I go on, I need to say a word about my family's relationship to the film industry. My father began writing film scripts before I was born, and he'd made quite a good living doing it. He was best known for his romantic comedies, but he was also very versatile. The first script he wrote, the one he brought with him from NYU's film school that made his reputation, was a love story set in the Warsaw ghetto before and during the uprising against the Nazis. It was a huge critical success. And it did reasonably well at the box office. Not bad for a man in his early twenties.

That first film, *Love in the Warsaw Ghetto,* was a dark love story. The next one he wrote, *For Crying Out Loud,* was a lighthearted romantic comedy about a guy who can't make up his mind between two girls until he's about to lose the one he really loves. Audiences adored *For Crying Out Loud*, and that was the movie that made and sealed Daddy's studio reputation. He knew how to put people in movie theater seats.

Later on he wrote a couple of straight dramas—*Siberian Winter*, about the hard life of a prisoner in the Soviet gulag, and *Swiss Chocolate,* about the lonely existence of three Portuguese guest workers living in Geneva without their families. Both of those films won prizes, but neither made money, which is what counts in Hollywood. Daddy was in demand for love stories, not life stories. He wrote both light and serious love stories, and he was—is—considered the master of both forms.

Though Daddy earned his money in Hollywood, we weren't a Hollywood family. Mom didn't like the ethos of Hollywood, its superficiality, its shaky hold on reality, its low or nonexistent moral standards. My parents had a few friends in the industry—Daddy's colleagues on the writing and directing side mostly, an occasional actor. But their closest friends, the people they saw all the time when I was growing up, were from outside the entertainment industry. Most of them were couples with kids, a little older than me or a little younger.

As a child and teenager, I was very familiar with my mother's work as an artist. Her studio was at the back of the house, and her paintings were on all our walls. I went, not always willingly, to the galleries where her work was exhibited, and many of the people we knew owned one or more of her paintings. I was much further removed from Daddy's workaday world. I knew what he did, of course. But Daddy's films were definitely for adults, not children.

I was taken to see *Swiss Chocolate* at ten, but I didn't understand about Portuguese guest workers and I was bored by the desperate aimlessness of their lives. (So was the moviegoing public, I guess.) It wasn't until I was thirteen that I saw one of Daddy's sexy love stories. Arlie's parents had rented the video of *A Wartime Love Story.* Arlie snuck it out of the house one afternoon and brought it to Jess's house. The five of us—Suzi Orbach was still around—watched it in the Sherman recreation room. It was set in England in 1942–43, and the main characters were an American flier from upstate New York, the married British woman with whom he was having an affair, and her husband, an artillery officer who had been severely wounded at Dunkirk.

Although the film was chiefly about what eventually drove the lovers apart—the wife's guilt at having betrayed her husband—it had a lot of graphic sex, and the war scenes remembered by the husband were violent and bloody. My friends and I thought we were grown-up and sophisticated, but none of us had ever seen anything like *A Wartime Love Story.* We watched it through to the end, and when it was over, I discovered that every one of us felt we should have turned it off but no one was brave enough to say so.

I didn't see another one of Daddy's love stories until I was eighteen, after my expulsion from the University of Colorado and my disagreeable stint at the drug clinic. I had just finished my freshman year at UCLA at the time, and already knew I'd be going to Berkeley in the fall. Daddy took me to the premiere of *Mix and Match,* a revolving-door comedy in which three young men and three young women arrange and rearrange themselves romantically until they finally pair up the way the audience felt they should have from the opening scenes. The movie had lots of frontal nudity, lots of profanity, lots of steamy sex scenes. It featured several of Hollywood's hottest young stars, and the premiere was a big deal. My feelings about the evening were mixed. I was flattered that Daddy finally considered me old enough to see one of his sexy movies. But I was also embarrassed by seeing it in his presence. I met two of the main actresses at the reception afterwards and had a hard time looking at them because I'd just seen them naked on the screen.

Mix and Match made a lot of money for the studio, as did others of his romantic comedies filmed in ensuing years. Then, just this past year, Daddy had written *Coney Island Romance.* This one was a serious love story about two misfits who live near one another in Brooklyn, meet during the summer at the Coney Island amusement park, and eventually fall in love, though the girl initially considers the boy a nerd and the boy thinks the girl is homely. Hollywood being Hollywood, the director had hired two young actors best known for their good looks to play the lead roles. He turned them into misfits by giving her thick glasses and a fifties hairdo and him horn-rim glasses and a bow tie. Daddy fought unsuccessfully for actors who might actually look the roles. Daddy hadn't originally written any sex scenes for *Coney Island Romance.* The director wanted at least two and hired another writer to add them when Daddy refused. The director knew what he was doing, I suppose. The film did quite well at the box office, and the two stars were praised for having had the courage to play a couple of not-so-beautiful people. Daddy wasn't pleased, however. It wasn't the movie he'd written.

The experience with *Coney Island Romance* was what led Daddy to decide to be his own director. He was able to convince the studio bosses he should be allowed to direct one of his lighter sex-oriented comedies. His debut film was going to be *San Francisco Fog*, a reverse twist on the familiar plot in which the boy meets, loses, and gets the girl during ninety hectic minutes. The girl was the one who would do the meeting, losing, and getting in *San Francisco Fog*. Daddy had cast two rising young stars in the main roles and had assembled his own team of cameramen and costume and set designers to work with him on the movie.

This was the film Daddy was getting ready to direct when I sent Laura to see him. I wasn't expecting him to hire her, though that's what happened. I was simply hoping he'd give her some guidance and maybe say a good word for her to one of his friends.

When I phoned Laura to report Daddy's willingness to see her, Laura said, "I'm not sure it's a good idea, Rache. I'm not exactly a hot commodity these days, but I don't want to be hired because someone pities me."

I answered her sharply. "Don't be that way, dammit. Nobody's going to hire you out of pity. That's not how Hollywood works. Daddy can open doors, but you're going to have to walk through them on your own."

So a few days later, after I'd left town, Laura stopped by to see Daddy at home. I heard about what transpired first from Laura and then from my father. When pleasantries had been completed, Laura handed Daddy her résumé. He put it aside and said, "I'll look at this later. I'd rather you tell me about your experience, Laura, starting from the beginning, not the end."

Laura gave a fluent account of her earliest days as a script reader, sifting through screenplays to grade them for her superiors, and went on to describe the work she did as a story editor. When she got to her job as an assistant producer on Bogusian's films, she started to sound apologetic.

Daddy interrupted. "I'm not asking about Bogusian, dear. The man's a pig, and everyone knows it. Just tell me what you did on the job."

Laura talked about taking notes while Bogusian blocked out scenes, rehearsed actors, and positioned cameras with the cinematographer. She spoke about handling Bogusian's messages and phone calls, taking care of the paperwork, keeping his calendar, attending the dailies each evening. Daddy asked a few questions, and Laura answered.

When she was finished, Daddy said, "Fine. You're hired. Can you start at the beginning of the month?"

Laura simply stared at him, he told me.

Daddy said, "I'm directing my first movie. I need an experienced assistant. It's my decision, and you're the one I want."

"But, Mr. Rothschild …"

"I'm not doing this as a favor to you, Laura," he said. "You've got the kind of experience I'm looking for. I'm not going to have to guard my back with you around, and I know you'll work your heart out for me. I'm doing *myself* a favor."

Laura lost her composure entirely. She covered her face with her hands, and she started sobbing.

Daddy got up from behind his desk, came around to where she was sitting, and patted her on the head. "It's okay, honey. Everything's going to be okay. Dry your eyes and come into the kitchen. I'll have Mama Rothschild make you some cocoa—unless you'd prefer something stronger."

Laura said, "I'll take the cocoa, Mr. Rothschild."

"You might as well start calling me Hillel," Daddy said. "No one's going to call me Mr. Rothschild when I'm on the set. I can't have my assistant acting like she doesn't know me."

*   *   *

Back in Denver, I was in the late stages of pregnancy and, I thought, doing wonderfully well. Then one night I awoke about three in the morning feeling wet and sticky between my legs. When I started to get out of bed, I discovered that my nightgown and the sheets were soaked in blood. I began screaming. I was terrified, hysterical, certain I'd suffered another miscarriage.

JJ jumped out of bed. The first thing he did was to summon an ambulance. The next was to hold me close until the ambulance came, telling me he loved me and that we'd get through it. He, too, was certain that I'd lost the baby. But that wasn't what had happened.

Once the ambulance crew got me to the hospital, still covered in my own blood, the emergency room physician said that the bleeding, though it had been profuse, was now stopped. The fetus was okay. My ob-gyn, Dr. Steinberg, who arrived at the hospital minutes later, told me that he suspected that part of the placenta had separated from the wall of my uterus, causing the hemorrhage.

"I could let you get a little rest and then send you home in a day or two," he said. "But I don't think that's the way to go. Another hemorrhage could be very dangerous. I want to do an ultrasound to confirm my diagnosis, and then we'll take the baby from you by Cesarean section. How does tomorrow morning sound as a time for your daughter to be born?"

"Whatever you say, doctor." I tried hard to smile. But it had been a grueling night, and I felt like shit. Tired. Still frightened as hell by my ordeal.

After they gave me blood and I was in my own hospital room, I revived a bit physically. But even though I had been reassured that the baby would live and that I would be okay, I was in a terrible state emotionally. I'd always been very healthy, and now, suddenly, I felt vulnerable. JJ never left the hospital, sleeping in a chair alongside my bed, and he did his best to calm me, as did Mom when she arrived in late afternoon from California. But their efforts were pretty much in vain.

Ariel Weiner was born, by appointment, so to speak, at 8:03 a.m. on the fourth day of May, a Tuesday, approximately a week or ten days before the original due date. I was barely awake when I was handed my new daughter for the first time. But I kissed her and whispered, "Welcome to the world, Ariel Weiner." I fell asleep still holding her.

When I awoke, Mom and JJ were sitting by my bed looking worried instead of happy.

"Is something wrong with the baby?" I asked, a cold stab of fear in my stomach.

JJ shook his head. "She's fine."

"Then what's wrong?"

"Nothing, baby," my mother answered. "Everything will be okay."

But something *was* wrong. I was certain something was wrong.

When Dr. Steinberg came around the next morning before anyone else arrived, I asked him to be candid with me. What wasn't I being told?

"Rachel," he said, "the baby's fine, and you're going to be okay. But the hemorrhage was not a good sign. This has to be your last child." He was frowning.

I asked, "Why? What's wrong?"

"You had a bad time there at the end. You bled quite a bit. I don't want you to take any chances. You've got a son. You've got a daughter. That's enough. I don't want you to get pregnant again."

"Are you telling me it will be worse next time?"

"I can't be sure. But we can't take the chance. So I want you to close up shop. No more babies."

I began to sob.

He took my hands in his and said, "Don't cry, Rachel. There's nothing to cry about. You have two beautiful children. You're going to recover. There's been no lasting damage. Be happy with what you've got."

I nodded my head, but I was still sobbing when Dr. Steinberg left the room.

It took me awhile to absorb what he'd told me. I tried hard to reconcile myself to it. *I had two kids*, I told myself, *and I was alive. I had two kids, and I was alive. I had two kids, and I was alive.*

Later in the day, Dr. Steinberg took me back to the operating room and tied my tubes. It hit me unexpectedly hard. Not that I was planning to have a third child. But it foreclosed the opportunity, leaving me feeling somehow incomplete as a woman.

Mom remained in Denver for two weeks after Ariel was born. Once I was a little stronger, she was able to shift her attention to Daniel, who hadn't bought the notion that a baby sister was a blessing. Mom refrained from asking Daniel to admire Ariel. He was already getting enough of that from JJ. Her job was to keep Daniel happy, and she did that effectively until the time came for her to return home.

I started out by breast-feeding Ariel as I had Daniel. But that didn't last. I couldn't shake the blues that enveloped me after the trauma preceding Ariel's birth and the "tubal ligation." Let's say it straight out: after my sterilization. I had my baby, this beautiful little girl, and yet I was unaccountably sad, sadder than I'd been following the miscarriage. Sorrier for myself than I'd been in my entire life.

My mood went rapidly downhill after Mom left. By the end of the following week, three weeks after Ariel's birth, I was in really bad shape. I asked JJ to move into another room temporarily. I explained that I was having difficulty sleeping, but that was just one reason. I wanted to be able to sneak upstairs in the middle of the night to have a drink of bourbon, sometimes a couple of drinks. I almost never drank liquor, let alone craved it. But the doctor wouldn't give me sleeping pills, and the bourbon helped put me under. I didn't want JJ to know what I was doing. I wasn't eating. I really didn't want to see Ariel or Daniel or anyone else. Feeling guilty about that—and I felt dreadfully guilty—deepened my gloom. Frequently, I wept. I didn't want to talk on the telephone, but I couldn't always pretend to be asleep. So I spoke reluctantly to Mom and Daddy and then to Dev and Jess. But they were all very short conversations, and monosyllabic on my end.

Dev was the first to perceive that something was wrong. I didn't know that until after JJ had conferred with Dr. Steinberg, my ob-gyn, and taken me in to see him. Dr. Steinberg suggested I see a psychiatrist experienced in dealing with postpartum depression. He recommended Dr. Harold Drucker.

I went reluctantly. I wasn't keen on being a mental patient. Hollywood may have been full of people who saw psychiatrists, but I didn't know them—or anyone who admitted it if they did. Dr. Drucker, however, had what might be called the perfect couch-side manner. He didn't interrogate me. He simply invited me to talk about myself. He was calm and very reassuring. My feelings were a natural reaction to what I'd experienced, he said. He prescribed some medication, set a return visit in a week, and told me to call him anytime, day or night, if I wasn't coping.

I saw him first on a Thursday. The following Monday he phoned to ask how I was doing. "I was serious about your calling me, Ms. Rothschild," he said, "but not everybody believes me when I tell them that. So I thought I'd check in." It made me feel he cared.

I saw Dr. Drucker weekly for a month and then every other week for another couple of months.

Once I began to feel even a little bit better, I ought to have concentrated my energies on Ariel. I'd lost a lot of time bonding with my baby. But I wasn't on solid ground yet, far from it. Afraid that I'd slip back into the depths, JJ urged me to get out of the house. I allowed him to convince me, though I shouldn't have. He thought resuming work would energize me, and he was right about that part at least. Returning to journalism was rejoining the world. But, as I was to discover, I had not really come to grips with my emotional problems.

My article on the Rocky Mountain Arsenal had been published, meanwhile, and had drawn much favorable comment. Both the mayor of Denver and the governor of Colorado sent me handwritten notes complimenting me on my work. That contributed to my false sense of buoyancy.

The article was also noticed in Utah because of my description of the incidents at Dugway Proving Ground, and it was read by officials at the Pentagon in Washington. I knew this because Mr. Edwards received a letter from the commanding general of the Chemical Corps complaining about citation of classified information and my failure to emphasize sufficiently that new testing procedures had been instituted to protect the public. Mr. Edwards said he would publish it in slightly shortened form as a letter to the editor.

I had already explained to Mr. Edwards that I was hoping next to write articles about the Defense Department's interest in shutting down Fitzsimmons Army Hospital and Lowry Air Force Base and turning the land and facilities back for other uses. I was proposing to do a two-part series. The first would deal with factors that would be weighed in determining whether to close these particular facilities. The second would address what would be done with the land if it became available in areas once considered distant from the city, now surrounded practically on all sides by urban growth. Because it was also part of the land-use picture, I intended to include plans to convert the present Denver airport, Stapleton Field, into a residential, commercial, and industrial zone.

The first of these articles would give me an opportunity to show concretely how tough decisions are made, sometimes for objective reasons and sometimes under heavy political pressure, often as a combination of both. The second article would allow me to look at the struggle among contending parties that was likely to result if these huge and valuable properties were decommissioned and released for local use. Those who won the right to build on the land stood to make a lot of money. But there was also a public policy dimension to it: economic development, land-use issues, environmental considerations, availability of medical care for war veterans, the balance of public and private interests. Mr. Edwards thought I might be undertaking more than I could handle, but after the story on the Rocky Mountain Arsenal, he was willing to let me try.

He said, "It's going to take you months to do the story, Rachel, and it's okay with me if that's all you want to work on until you're done. If you'd like to keep your byline in front of the readers by writing some small things in the interim, that's okay, too. It's your call. Either way, I'm going to put your name on the masthead as a senior writer and give you a full-time salary. You've earned it."

Amanda Collins had certainly been right about sticking with the magazine instead of trying to get a job with the *Denver Post* or the *Rocky Mountain News*. Now that I'd gotten the go-ahead, I wanted to begin. First, however, my sister Rebecca was stopping by for a brief visit. She'd just gotten her degree from Berkeley, and Mom and Daddy had given her a trip to Europe as a graduation present. She was in Denver to see her new niece for the first time and, of course, to renew her ties with Daniel. Daniel loved his "Auntie Becca." Like "Auntie Lee," Rebecca got down on the floor to play with him and never told him what to do, unlike his mother, unlike his father, unlike Hillary. Following Mom's advice, Rebecca also avoided telling Daniel how wonderful his sister was.

I was glad to have Rebecca around and also glad to see her go. I was impatient to get started on my assignment. Three minutes after Rebecca was out the door, I was on the telephone, beginning to gather background information from local sources. Soon, I was working a full day, sometimes more.

I had no idea how much my eager return to journalism annoyed Hillary. JJ might have thought I needed to get away from domestic duties after coming out of my depression. Hillary, however, believed I should have focused on being Ariel's mother. Much later, I understood that I'd had another baby, and Hillary felt that she was now the mother of two. But Hillary never said a word to me. She must have said something to JJ, because he found and hired a local woman, a grandmotherly lady named Agnes Wilson, to come in five afternoons a week to take over some of Hillary's duties. Along with Anna Lopez, hired the previous November to handle cleaning and cooking duties, that allowed the household to function smoothly despite my incapacitation—and, to be completely honest with myself, my inattention.

If, after urging me to get out of the house, JJ felt I should have struck a more even balance between career and motherhood, he never expressed it. We'd been through that once, and he still bore the claw marks. Daniel had become accustomed to having a relatively small claim on my time, mostly at bedtime, sometimes at breakfast. Ariel didn't know the difference. So there was no one to tell me that I was sowing the wind.

I was succeeding professionally and failing in other, more important ways. I hadn't really bonded with my daughter. My husband was still tiptoeing around me. I might be finding satisfaction in my work, but I hadn't regained my equilibrium. Far from it. Still having a drink or two to calm my nerves before bed. I should have had a long, confessional talk with Dr. Drucker, but I didn't. Saying aloud that I needed more help was a step I wasn't prepared to take: I thought I could work it through on my own. Make that, I *hoped* I would be able to work it through on my own.

I deceived myself in part because I was making rapid progress on my latest project. I was again relying on Richie Reiner's friends on the staff of the Senate Armed Services Committee for guidance in learning about base-closing procedures. In addition, Richie had arranged in his boss's name to have a paper prepared by the Library of Congress's legislative reference service on the history of military base closings since the end of the Vietnam War.

I had a commitment to attend Arlie's wedding in Santa Monica in late August. Jess, Laura, and I were going to be Arlie's only attendants. But before then, I felt that I needed to spend a few days in Washington, maybe as much as a week, conducting interviews at the Pentagon and on Capitol Hill.

When I announced my plans, JJ asked, "What do you intend to do with the kids?"

"I don't see how I can take them along to Washington. I'll have to leave them here. I don't intend to be gone for more than a week."

"And when you go to Santa Monica?"

"If you'd like, I can take them along. With Hillary, of course. My parents would be glad to have them."

"And me?" JJ asked.

"Up to you. Want to join me in Washington? Or in Santa Monica? Or both?"

"I don't think so. I better stay here with the kids. It's a little early for Ariel to be flitting around the country, don't you think?"

"If you say so." I heard the undercurrent of sarcasm but deliberately ignored it.

JJ didn't say anything more. But, even though he'd urged me initially to resume working, it turned out that his views about my priorities weren't a lot different than Hillary's.

*   *   *

Daniel was four years old on August 7, a Saturday. JJ hired a pony to entertain Daniel's nursery school class. Of course, there were balloons and horns and party hats—and cake and ice cream and packages to tear open and toys to break almost as soon as they emerged from the box.

Daniel was exhausted and cranky by the time the last of his playmates left, but he was also very excited and Hillary had a hard time calming him down.

I put him to bed and read him a story. I also explained that the next morning I had to "get on a big airplane and go to work in Washington, when Cousin Yalie lives." The preparation was of little use. When I kissed him and Ariel good-bye as I prepared to leave for the airport, Daniel began crying bitterly. He was still crying as I shut the door behind me. *Deserter*, I thought. But the thought was fleeting.

I arrived in Washington in late afternoon. It was oppressively hot and humid, quite unlike the weather I'd left behind in Denver. Yalie and Richie met me at the airport. Yalie had insisted I stay with them in their little house on Capitol Hill, about six blocks east of the Capitol Building.

I collected two large suitcases from the baggage carousel, and Richie inquired lightly if I planned to stay the rest of the year.

"I brought different outfits for every day," I said apologetically. "I want to look professional."

"Don't mind him," Yalie said. "When we met, he owned three pairs of blue jeans, a brown sports jacket, and a ratty blue suit. If I hadn't thrown it out, he'd still be wearing the suit."

"I was just conserving precious closet space for you to occupy, my sweet," Richie said contentedly.

"I don't want to inconvenience you. I can live out of the suitcase," I said.

"Nonsense, you did right to bring a bunch of outfits. Clothes get messed up easily in this heat, and you can't be running off to the cleaners while you're here. Just ignore him," Yalie said, inclining her head toward Richie. "I do."

"You see what I put up with?" Richie asked. "Me, the answer to a maiden's prayer."

"Yes, you are snookums," Yalie said, kissing him square on the mouth. "But you still have to learn a lot about women and their wardrobes. So this week, please pay attention. Rachel will be your guide."

Richie laughed. "Okay, teacher. I'll go get the car. Meet me curbside."

It was a long drive from Dulles Airport into the city. Richie took the scenic route, overlooking the Potomac River, which provides a dramatic first view of the city, dominated by the Washington Monument. This was my first visit to D.C., and I was impressed, even thrilled, by the grand buildings and open spaces. I was also struck by the lush greenery. Denver was turning brown this time of the year, and the green it had was primarily the flat green of pine trees and other evergreens. Here the greens were more varied and far more vivid. Wherever there was an open space, it seemed to be overgrown with trees— unlike Colorado, where open spaces were completely empty or covered with sparse, low-lying bushes that eventually turned into tumbleweeds. And there were flowers planted everywhere.

Yalie and Richie drove me around the city's core of governmental buildings and monuments, up and down the main avenues running from the Lincoln Memorial past the Washington Monument toward the Capitol building and then along another axis from the Capitol toward the White House, where the line of sight was interrupted by the gray mass of the Treasury Building. Then we drove back toward the Capitol along the Mall beside several buildings of the Smithsonian Institution and the two beautiful structures, one classical and one strikingly modern, belonging to the National Gallery of Art. I gawked like any other tourist.

"What do you think?" Richie asked.

"I know this sounds stupid, but it reminds me of Rome."

"With all those Roman columns? I can't imagine why," Richie said drily.

"Do you get used to it?" I asked.

Yalie answered, "Hell, you get used to anything. Polar bears get used to ice floes, alligators to the swamp. There are days when I walk past the Supreme Court building on the way to my office and don't even see it."

"Yes," Richie added. "And you also get used to being at the center of power, and it ceases to be a thrill and becomes just another job, even though what you're doing is helping make the country's laws."

"But sometimes, at odd moments, yes, it still awes me," Yalie said. "I get a shiver every time I see the sculpture of Lincoln sitting there in his great chair, lit up at night after the crowds of tourists have departed for the day. And when I take someone to the Jefferson Memorial and stand there in the rotunda reading his words, they make me tear up even though I've read them before and I know Jefferson didn't live up in his personal life to what he wrote."

"The problem with being around Washington for any length of time is that you lose perspective," Richie said. "You become blasé. You grow cynical. You begin to think of politics as a high-stakes game— poker with a trillion-dollar pot. After a while you forget what brought you here to begin with. Yalie and I plan to leave before that happens to us."

"Oh?" I asked. "And where will you go?"

Yalie deflected the question. "We're not leaving yet."

We stopped for dinner at a row of restaurants within walking distance of the three House office buildings. The place we entered was filled with people in their middle twenties to early thirties. Handsome young men and beautiful young women. If there was anyone as old as forty, I didn't see them.

"Welcome to Capitol Hill," Yalie said in response to my comment on everyone's youthfulness. "Half the people up here at the staff level have been out of school for less than five years. They're all at the stage of life when they're willing to be someone else's creature, briefing the someone before a committee meeting, preparing letters for the someone to sign, writing speeches for the someone to deliver, drafting questions for the someone to ask at a Congressional hearing. Richie and I are no different than the rest."

"It's very exciting being a legislative assistant to a Senator or an important member of the House," Richie said. "You get a chance to exercise power in somebody else's name without having earned the right to do so on your own. But it's not work for a grown-up. Eventually you want to be your own person."

Yalie said that staff members who become addicted to power often move into the Executive Branch as political appointees or enter elective politics in their own names. For most others, work on The Hill serves as the base for careers in the world of Washington law firms and lobbyists.

"We're just passing through," Yalie declared emphatically. "We're not going to succumb to Potomac Fever. Neither of us wants a job lobbying for cancer on behalf of the tobacco industry or demanding the right to pollute for the oil industry."

I laughed. "Those surely aren't the only choices."

"No," she replied. "You can work for the good guys. For a lot less money. Or you can join the bureaucracy. Or you can go into one of the Think Tanks and try to make policy from the outside. None of that appeals to me. To us." She leaned into Richie, nestling against him. They'd obviously discussed their futures a lot, even though they might not have decided.

Yalie and Richie were passing through Washington. For the moment, however, they were part of the intricate network of young Hill staffers who knew people who knew people who could get things done in Washington. I was about to be the beneficiary of that network. Officials at the Pentagon who would likely ignore me if I called unannounced would be willing to see me because the appointments were arranged through a senior staff person at the Senate Armed Services Committee. That person would not have known me if I walked up to him and kicked him in the knee. He was helping because he was asked to do so by the committee's staff director. The staff director didn't know me either. He was acting on the request of the chief of staff to the Senator from Illinois, a member of the committee. The chief of staff, in turn, was doing it because Richie Reiner asked him. In similar roundabout fashion, Richie had also arranged dates for me at the Base Closings Commission and with a couple of defense experts at Washington think tanks.

Yalie's employer was a member of the Senate Appropriations Committee, and that was the entry point for my dates late in the week at the Office of Management and Budget and with the staffs of the House and Senate Appropriations Committees.

The only appointments I made on my own were with the members of the Colorado delegation, the two Senators and two members of the House. They were seeing me because I worked for *In the Rockies*. But I made sure they knew I was married to JJ Weiner. The Weiners were very important people. I didn't mind trading on that.

My schedule fell neatly into place: Monday morning at the Senate Armed Services Committee with the senior staffer who'd been helping set up my appointments, then with the staff director of the Base Closings Commission; Monday afternoon with scholars at the Brookings Institution and the Center for Strategic and International Studies; Tuesday morning with the staffs of the two Colorado Senators; Tuesday afternoon with the congresswoman from Denver, whom I expected to see personally, and with a second Colorado congressman who was on the House Armed Services Committee; Wednesday morning with the House Armed Services Committee staff and the rest of the day at the Pentagon, where I had three separate appointments. On Thursday morning, I'd go to the Office of Management and Budget, and the rest of Thursday I would spend talking with people handling defense appropriations for the Senate and House Appropriations Committees. Friday, I was going to see what staff writers at the *National Journal* and *Congressional Quarterly* had to tell me.

I had planned my outfits for these visits very carefully. I would wear an expensive summer dress and gold jewelry to meetings with the Colorado delegation (as befit a member of the Weiner family), a much less fancy dress and costume jewelry to the meetings with the journalists on Friday (I was one of them), and one of the three conservative business suits that I had brought with me, plus a tasteful pin or necklace, to the sessions with government officials and policy scholars (I was serious and someone to reckon with). And, of course, shoes to match each costume and clinch the impression.

The journalist in me had other concerns. I would have liked to record some of these sessions, but I knew from experience that microphones were more inhibiting than notepads. I had learned even when I was working for *L.A. Beat* not to open my spiral notebook until an interview was underway and the subject had relaxed his guard a little. Still, I'd discovered the hard way that interviewees had a way of denying the accuracy of quotes, so I'd become an indefatigable collector of documents: reports, studies, speeches, exchanges of correspondence, anything in black and white. When it was in writing, denials were considerably more difficult.

It was a very busy week. I conducted interviews all day long; and each evening before dinner, I transcribed my notes onto the hard drive of my laptop computer. Each night when Yalie and Richie arrived home from work, I was eager to talk. Yalie and Richie didn't know much about the Defense Department's effort to shed unneeded facilities. However, I found that I could profit from their sense of how Washington worked. My sketchy knowledge of the legislative process came from a college textbook, whereas Yalie and Richie had watched it in operation. The process wasn't mechanical. It was animated by political currents and crosscurrents that, while generally invisible, could be apprehended by those who worked inside the system. Yalie and Richie had been around long enough to understand how political pressure was manifested and how it influenced substantive outcomes. I told Yalie and Richie, in rough outline, what I'd learned, and they helped me understand the political dimension. They would appear in the article I was writing as "Washington observers" whose insights I'd quote. Was I a journalist or what!

I also had much else to discuss with my cousin. Yalie wanted to hear about Ariel and Daniel. She hadn't seen Dev or her parents since the wedding. She'd missed the seder in Santa Monica and was interested to know the latest about my girlfriends, who had become her friends too over the years, beginning with the week we all spent together in Santa Monica many years earlier.

On Friday night, after I'd finished all my interviews and we'd hit just about every other topic, Yalie asked me about JJ.

"He's all right," I said. When she persisted, I said, "We don't do much together these days. He's busy at the office, and I've got all this work I'm trying to do. And I'm going to California for Arlie's wedding, and JJ doesn't want to come."

"Look, Rache. I've got to ask. Are you and JJ getting along okay?"

"Why do you ask that?" I must have sounded defensive because I certainly felt defensive.

"Because I've had the feeling the last couple of times we've been together that you two might be having some problems."

"Yeah." I paused for a moment. I wanted to cry but was resolved not to. "It was JJ's idea for me to go back to work, but now that I have, he resents it. I don't want to be a rich man's ornamental wife. He'd like me to spend most of my time being the mother of his children. There are some other things, but that's the crux of it." In truth, I wasn't disclosing the crux of it. I wasn't prepared to talk about the central problems in my marriage with Yalie—or anyone else.

"How are the two of you handling having a second child around?"

"JJ hired an older women to help out," I said. "She comes in afternoons to relieve Hillary."

"And you?"

"Not too well at the beginning. I suppose you know I was seeing a psychiatrist for a while. But now I'm busy with my work."

"And JJ resents it?"

"Probably," I said. "He doesn't say anything." Despite my determination, there were tears trickling down my cheeks. She'd touched a nerve.

Yalie said, "I'm sorry, Rache. I didn't mean to upset you. I just want you to know I love you, and I'm here for you. Always will be." She hugged me close, and it was all I could do not to dissolve completely.

That was the end of the conversation. But I didn't get a lot of sleep Friday night. I kept wondering how many other people had figured out that JJ and I weren't altogether happy.

Saturday morning I flew back to Denver. I took with me a disc drive filled with notes and left Yalie and Richie twelve pounds of books and other reading material to be shipped via UPS.

All I could think about on the flight home was the conversation Yalie and I had the previous night. I kept asking myself *Are my emotions so damn transparent to everyone, or only to Yalie who knows me so well?*

When I returned home, expecting a huge welcome from my son, Daniel ran the other way into Hillary's arms. That didn't help my mood a lot. I'd brought him gifts, however, and he soon forgave me for having gone away. His initial reaction, however, bothered me quite a lot, especially after my talk with Yalie. I had to go away again next week for Arlie's wedding. Although we'd already had this conversation once, I suggested to JJ that maybe I should take Daniel with me, leaving Ariel at home with Hillary. Mom and Daddy would also be at Arlie's wedding, but Rebecca had returned from her postgraduation visit to Europe and she'd watch Daniel during the afternoon and evening of the wedding.

"If it's not too much for you," JJ said. Again, there was a note of sarcasm in his voice, though he was smiling.

I chose to overlook it.

JJ took Daniel and me to the airport. Daniel was upset because Hillary wasn't coming. He wanted his nanny as much as he wanted his mother, perhaps more. I tried not to think about that. I wanted to concentrate on the virtuous feelings I got from bringing Daniel along on the trip to Santa Monica. The role of harassed-parent-with-unhappy-four-year-old was an unfamiliar one, however, and I was not terribly good at executing it in the constricted space of the airplane's tourist cabin, the only spot available when I'd called to reserve a second seat. The flight from Denver to Los Angeles, which never seemed especially long, had me glancing at my wristwatch every ten minutes expecting a half hour to have passed. But it was eventually over, and once released from his seat, Daniel was back to his ebullient self. He was vocally pleased to see his grandparents and aunt, and they couldn't have been happier to have him.

How does Hillary do it? I wondered. *Maybe I'll slip him a mickey on the way home.*

*   *   *

Arlie was being married on Sunday, August 29, and I had originally talked about spending no more than three days on this visit. But once I decided to bring Daniel, Mom and Daddy prevailed on me to come earlier and not to return late Sunday as I had intended. So I arrived on Tuesday, the twenty-fourth, and I would stay until midday Monday, the thirtieth. Knowing that I wouldn't have much opportunity to talk with Jess and Laura during the wedding festivities, Mom invited them to dinner on Wednesday night. Although her husband and son had also been invited to dinner, Jess decided to come alone.

Jess had just prevailed in a big lawsuit brought against a major studio by one of her clients. Jess had rarely gone to court in her career as a lawyer. That was not what her firm specialized in. But she was wildly enthusiastic about the experience. "When the verdict came in, I felt like a matador who's just killed her first bull. If the judge had allowed it, I would have sliced off the ears of opposing counsel and presented them to the jury."

"La Senora Bozo, *la conquistadora del gran toro*," I proclaimed roundly.

"*Olé*! It's a real rush. I don't remember when I've done anything that was more fun."

"Have you told that to Sam?" Laura asked.

"Yes, I have. But what I said to him was 'I don't remember having more fun with my clothes on.'"

"Point, game, set, and match," I said.

Laura's news was simple. "I love working for Hillel. It's the best job I've ever had. By far the best."

"And how's your personal life?" I asked.

"I'm not seeing anyone. Still not ready. I might never be ready."

"Oh, pshaw!" Jess said.

"What the heck is that supposed to mean?" I asked.

"I dunno, but I've always wanted to say 'oh, pshaw!' and this seemed like a good occasion. I think it means something like 'don't hand me that crap.'"

"No, I mean it," Laura said. "I've shown such lousy judgment. I don't know that I'll ever be able to open my heart to another guy. I've gone out a couple of times, but I freeze up as soon as the conversation gets the least bit personal."

"Give it time, love," I said.

"I'm giving it time, Rache. I haven't got another choice, have I?"

"The wounds'll heal," I answered.

"And other clichés." Jess obviously felt the subject had been exhausted and that prolonging the discussion would only make Laura unhappy. She reached for her purse. "Let's talk about something else. Wouldn't you like to admire my child's latest pictures?"

After Jess and Laura left, Mom said to me, "I'm surprised at how perceptive Jessica has become. She's as funny as she ever was, but it's combined with a gentleness and wisdom I would never have expected in a thousand years."

"Amazing, isn't it? She was always a sweetheart, but she was the least serious girl I knew in high school. She began to settle down in college, and then she met Sam, and she's been growing in the most remarkable ways ever since."

"Laura is fortunate to have her as a friend."

"So am I, Mom. If I ever needed rescuing, Jess would be the one I'd turn to."

The rehearsal for Arlie's wedding was the next evening. It was to be followed by a dinner at the Miramar Hotel for members of the bridal party and out-of-town visitors. Seth's family was from Kansas City, and although his immediate family included only his parents and a younger sister, there were aunts, uncles, cousins, and family friends. Almost thirty people would be there for dinner.

Unlike my cousin Dev, who had been totally relaxed at her wedding and had enjoyed herself more than any of the guests, Arlie was clearly feeling the pressure. She was meeting most of Seth's relatives for the first time. She told us that Seth had warned her she might not like all of them; he certainly didn't. But Arlie was trying very hard to please everybody, and it was obviously costing her. I personally overheard remarks about how little she weighed. The comments were true enough, but it was extremely impolite for people whom she was meeting for the first time to say so where she might overhear them. I didn't like Seth's people at all, and I wasn't likely to see most of them, maybe not any of them, after the day of the wedding. But they would now be part of Arlie's life, and they weren't nice people. Not at all.

When Arlie came over to sit with us, Jess was the one who noticed that she was fighting off tears. Jess left the table to talk with Seth, who was on the other side of the room. She reported the conversation to us.

"What's up?" she asked after she'd pulled him aside. "Arlie's ready to cry."

"My goddam relatives. They've made her uncomfortable."

"Take my advice, Seth. Get her out of here as quickly as you can. Like now. If you have to say anything, tell your parents Arlie doesn't feel well and you're taking her home to rest. Then get her to cry for you if she's going to cry. Don't let her keep it in."

Two minutes later, Seth had Arlie by the hand and was leading her away.

At the friends' table, everyone but Jess was startled by the abrupt departure.

"What happened?" Laura asked.

"Arlie was ready to pop, and I told Seth to get her the hell out of here."

I said, "You're unbelievable, Jess. Seth's relatives are hard to like. But I wouldn't have had the nerve to do what you did."

"She's a marvel, my wife is," Sam said proudly.

Jess made no jokes. "I was afraid Arlie would erupt. And she'd be the one who would be harmed if it happened. If anyone asks, just say Arlie felt ill and Seth took her away so she could lie down."

On Sunday morning, as the wedding party was assembling, Seth told Jess, "You were right. She was a mess, and it would only have gotten worse. I kept her away from everybody but her folks for two days, and we let them think she was just under the weather. I'm sure she'll be okay today. I've told my father and mother that I'll hold them responsible if anyone says anything negative about Arlie. They'd better damn well make certain my other relatives behave."

No matter how confident brides are about their looks and their bodies, most are especially fussy about their appearance while dressing for the wedding. Arlie was at the extreme edge of fussiness. She sometimes joked about being built like a stick and weighing less than a good-sized dog. I don't think it usually bothered her. However, the experience with Seth's family must have unnerved her. Laura, Jess, and I went into the bridal room where she was getting ready, and she kept staring at herself in the mirror. Unhappily.

Jess went over to her and whispered something in her ear. Arlie laughed and kissed her, leaving a lipstick imprint that Jess had to remove with a tissue.

I asked Jess how she got Arlie to laugh.

"I told her 'Be happy, Arlie. The rest of the people at the wedding can go fuck themselves.'"

When she came into the sanctuary, walked down the white cloth path that had been laid across the carpet, and started up the steps to the altar, Jess, Laura, and I were standing there smiling at her with all the love we had for her, and Jess gave her a small thumbs-up sign. Now it was going to be okay. I hoped earnestly that Arlie was thinking *All you Goldbergs can go fuck yourselves.*

It was certainly what I was thinking.

For the entire week we were there, Daniel had the full attention of his Auntie Becca. She wasn't starting her new job with a local accounting firm until after Labor Day. Mom was almost as engaged, and Daddy played with Daniel every single evening, even on Wednesday before the dinner guests arrived. Daniel also got a lot more time than usual from me.

He was a happier child going back to Denver than he had been coming, and the plane trip home was less difficult for me than the trip out. Still, when Daniel saw JJ and Hillary waiting at the gate, he ran straight to Hillary. Only when he was in her arms did he allow JJ to kiss him also. "I guess he's figured out who butters his bread," JJ said.

I don't know if it was intended as a reproof, but that's how I interpreted it. Though I let it drop, I was hurt, even a little angry.

I was determined to devote more time to the children. That lasted for about a week. My project was a jealous lover, and it encroached on my intentions. I had to organize what I'd learned in Washington into a coherent story line, and I needed to arrange appointments on the Denver end. Even though I meant to establish a border between my work and the time reserved for family, the border was difficult to defend.

When it came time to quit for the day, I only had another five pages to read, so I read them.

I needed to finish putting some of my thoughts in writing, and it ended up taking an hour of playtime away from Daniel and Ariel. Calls that I made earlier in the day were returned at dinnertime, and the food was cold and Daniel had left the table before I was finished explaining what it was I was working on and why I wanted an appointment.

But I was trying. Instead of bolting down a cup of yogurt at my desk, I came into the kitchen to have lunch with Daniel and to give Ariel a bottle and cuddle her. I was even capable of taking an afternoon or a weekend off for no reason other than to play with Daniel or to make noises for Ariel. I felt good about it, and JJ noticed.

He said, "It's good to have you with us."

Once again, I ignored the sarcasm, though if it continued, there would eventually be a hell of a blowup between us. I didn't like being patronized.

The work, meanwhile, was progressing. Interviews on the Denver end were spread over several weeks, primarily because the story had to be assembled in bits and pieces from a lot of different sources. Along the way I discovered that Hyman Weiner & Sons was among the firms with plans to build at Lowry. I had to decide how to handle that. I'd have to disclose it somehow or risk being accused of a conflict of interest, possibly even of tilting the story to favor my husband's firm.

I didn't want to discuss it with JJ, so I raised it with Dev. "If it were me," she said, "I'd write the story the way I would if Hyman Weiner & Sons weren't involved. But since everybody will know about you and JJ, I think you have to find a place in the story to disclose the connection."

"That sounds right. But what do I do when I get to writing about how some people are going to get rich developing these properties?"

"Handle it deftly, sweetie. That's all I can say."

"Can I show it to you when I've got it written?"

"Sure. I'll be happy to read anything you bring me. But a lot of good that will do you. I'm a *lawyer*, Rache, not an editor. Show it to your editor. Tell him your problem and ask for his help. That's my advice."

It took until the middle of October for everything to come together, and I knew that I would need to fill in some blanks once the writing started. I wanted to have it completed and edited to my satisfaction by the end of November.

The writing was difficult. I had more material than I could possibly use, and one of the main tasks was to discard items that were interesting but peripheral. I would have to explain the need to reduce the fixed costs in the U.S. Defense budget by cutting personnel expenses and maintenance costs associated with unneeded facilities. Although I found them fascinating, I would avoid the details. Other than in the most general way, I didn't plan to talk about rival uses for budget dollars.

I finished a first draft of the base closing article by the first of November and then turned to the land use portion of the project. (I was again working full-time. More than full-time.) The availability of the air base, the possible decommissioning of the army hospital, and the eventual abandonment of Stapleton Airport would give planners a dream opportunity to transform Denver and its environs. Nothing on this scale had happened in Denver's entire history.

The proposal under consideration called for mixed-use urban development on most of the land currently occupied by the air base. Hyman Weiner & Sons was one of the potential builders on the site. Plans for the hospital land were a good deal more tentative, but the University of Colorado wanted to turn much of it into a new Health Sciences Center to replace its cramped and aging medical school and hospital facilities elsewhere in the city. The area to be vacated by Stapleton Airport was twice the size of the air base and the hospital combined, the largest urban redevelopment site in the country. A group called Stapleton Tomorrow had begun working years earlier on ideas for future use of the property, and a full-scale development plan was being prepared. Hyman Weiner & Sons was part of the Stapleton Tomorrow planning effort and would doubtless have a large role in development of the site.

Telling the story coherently was a challenge to my journalistic skills. The first draft, when it was completed, had a lot of weaknesses that would need to be repaired. Among those weaknesses was my handling of the Hyman Weiner & Sons connection. I hadn't done it at all gracefully in the first draft, and I knew it. Instead of dealing immediately with the problems in the second story, I went back to the base closings story to do another draft and get it ready for publication. I didn't intend to turn it in, however, until the land-use story was also ready to go. I wanted to be sure they would appear in consecutive issues and wouldn't take the risk that Mr. Edwards would approve the first article but ask for a rewrite of the second.

Once I was satisfied with the base closings article, I looked again at the land-use draft and decided that it read entirely too much like it had been written for a planning journal. Nobody who wasn't mentioned in the article would get as far as the second page. I had to get beyond planning concepts and abstract language to the lives of real people.

I decided to interview men and women who were losing their jobs at the air base and determine whether there would a place for them in the large number of new jobs expected to become available at the site. And what would they do in the meantime? Who were the war veterans that might be displaced if the hospital were closed, and what kind of medical care would be available at the University of Colorado Health Sciences Center that wasn't available now? What firms—or if that couldn't be discovered, what *kinds* of firms—might relocate to Stapleton Airport, and where were they based now?

It took another full week of interviewing to add color to the monochromatic material I'd collected earlier. The second draft of the planning piece, when I completed it, was a good deal better than the first. It was better yet when I redid it another time. I found a way to acknowledge my connection with Hyman Weiner & Sons without overemphasizing it or appearing to avoid it.

I failed to meet the deadline I had established for myself. It was now approaching the end of the year, and I suppose Mr. Edwards was wondering if he'd ever see the results of what his "ace reporter," as he'd begun to call me with only a trace of irony, had been working on these many months. I knew that he'd heard from people all over town that they had been interviewed, but he hadn't heard much from me. I didn't care to be pinned down.

I finally called him in the middle of the afternoon on Friday, December 17, to ask if he'd be in the office Monday morning. I came in bringing drafts of both articles and a small collection of possible illustrations. Mr. Edwards glanced briefly at the leads of both articles. "The January issue is at the printer's," he said, "and I've got most of what I need for February. The earliest these could appear is in the March and April issues. That leaves plenty of time," he grinned, "for them to be completely rewritten."

"I'm prepared to fight over every comma."

"My goodness. You hear this, Brubaker?" He was addressing the large black dog lying on the rug beside him. "This child came in wet behind the ears, and now she wants to be her own editor. Just for that, I'm going to change every other word."

Brubaker started at the sound of his name and then settled back down on his belly and shut his eyes.

I was smiling and self-satisfied. "I warn you: I cry easily."

"Okay. You've warned me. Now, tell me, what are you intending as an encore?"

I said I'd like to follow the next budget through the State Legislature.

"Oh? And what great truth are you planning to disclose?"

"I'd like to show the struggle between Denver and the rest of the state over how the money gets spent."

"And what exactly do you bring to the table, my dear? What do you know about the state budgeting process? Ever analyzed a budget? Ever taken a class in public finance?"

I admitted that I hadn't. But how difficult could it be?

"I'll be blunt, Rachel. Anyone who thinks deciphering a budget is easy isn't ready to do what you're proposing. Nobody without an axe to grind is going to walk you through the process while the legislature is in session. Chances are you'd be sent up a blind alley and miss the thoroughfare. You want to report on the State Legislature, find me another story idea. You want to deal with the state budget, take some baby steps before you try to run the marathon. Okay?"

Not okay. But that was the way it was going to be.

It took me until early January to come up with a story idea that would allow me to work around the edges of the budget process and still do some reporting at the State House. One of the first stories I had done at *In the Rockies* was about the transformation of Colorado A&M into Colorado State University. It made me aware of the intense competition for higher education dollars among various collegiate-level institutions, particularly Colorado State and the four campuses of the University of Colorado but also including the University of Northern Colorado in Greeley, the University of Southern Colorado in Pueblo, the Colorado School of Mines in Golden, Metropolitan State College in Denver, and other colleges in Alamosa, Durango, Grand Junction, and Gunnison.

I wanted to address those rivalries, the money scramble, and the political forces that determined the outcome. Mr. Edwards was reluctant, but he consented. I think he felt the new story idea wasn't a lot less complex than the original, but I was determined to report on budget issues and he decided to let me have a go at it. Getting the numbers on how much money was allocated to each institution wouldn't be too difficult, and at least I'd limited my ambition to a single budget item, higher education. He warned me, however, that I would have a very difficult time matching budget recommendations against amounts initially requested. State budget officers wouldn't give me the information, and college and university officials would be risking the state's displeasure if they did. I'd have to determine for each campus what percentage of its funds came from the state and where it got the rest of its money. That would give me a rough idea of the balance pursued by state officialdom.

As I began to tackle the assignment, I quickly realized that I was out at sea. I didn't care to run all over the state to collect background information, which in any case, was scarcer than on the federal level. My grasp of budget mechanics was unsure. I didn't have anyone like Yalie and Richie to guide me through the structure and unwritten rules of state government. Many members of the state legislature were suspicious of the press in general and my motives in particular, and if they were prepared to talk to me at all, they failed to volunteer much.

Perhaps I ought to postpone the story until I could deepen my understanding of Colorado politics and budgetary processes. Maybe I ought to take a course or two at the Graduate School of Public Affairs at the University of Colorado's Denver campus. A course in public finance would certainly be useful.

Much as I hated to admit defeat, I told Mr. Edwards that he was right after all. "I'm out there like a puppy chasing its tail," I said sheepishly. "You warned me I didn't know enough. I should have listened." I mentioned my interest in taking some graduate school classes.

"I want to say something to you, Rachel Rothschild. Don't interrupt until I'm finished. I told you once that *In the Rockies* is in the entertainment business, and it is. If I were sensible, I would have asked you to can this public policy stuff a long time ago. Now I ought to say, 'Okay, you've learned your lesson, young lady. Go write fluff.' But, darn it, you're too good for that. I really believe you can make a heck of an impact as an investigative reporter if you take the time to learn your way around. When I started in this business, the theory was that a reporter could cover the police beat on Monday, baseball on Tuesday, and the White House on Wednesday. That isn't true any longer. Science writers are expected to know something about science. It isn't just a matter of getting a few facts and stringing sentences together. If you're going to write about public policy, which is obviously your passion, you need to know more about process and a lot more about substance. I give you credit for conceding that you don't know it all. Wanting to fill in the blanks is a sign that you're committed to do the job right. You with me?"

I had listened thoughtfully, and I said, "So you think I ought to go back to school?"

"Part-time, yes. I want you to keep writing for *In the Rockies*. I intend to give you free rein. But, yes, I'd like you to realize your potential, and I think taking classes will help you do that. Okay?"

"Since you're being straight with me, Mr. Edwards, I've got to be straight with you," I said. "I came here with the idea of gaining experience and then moving to *The Denver Post* or *The Rocky Mountain News*. I haven't done it yet, but that doesn't mean I won't."

"Fair enough. I'll accept the task of convincing you that you can do more at *In the Rockies* than at one of the daily papers. You just go be the best you can be."

"That's the most wonderful offer any one could make me, Mr. Edwards." I said. "Thank you. I really appreciate it."

"Don't mention it, kid. Someday, I'll be proud to be known as Rachel Rothschild's editor."

I glanced away to hide my embarrassment. "C'mon, Mr. Edwards, I'll bet you tell that to all your reporters."

"You've got me there, kid. Before I begin to sound sentimental, this conversation is at an end."

In the week following my conversation with Mr. Edwards, I did two things. The first was to call the offices of the Graduate School of Public Affairs at the University of Colorado at Denver and ask for a list of courses available in the fall. I wanted to see what there was that might be of interest before I talked with the admissions office.

The second thing I did was to identify another project to pursue. I decided to write about the governance of the state's publicly supported colleges and universities. There were five different boards of regents or trustees for thirteen four-year schools. How did that system evolve? In addition, there was a separate board for thirteen community colleges and still another for two district community colleges. I wanted to hear the reasons given for wide disparities in the amounts distributed on a per resident student basis for each of these campuses. Why was it that allocations per student at Colorado State exceeded the amounts that went to the University of Colorado at Boulder, Denver, and Colorado Springs? And why was the amount per student for Adams State College greater than for either of the large universities? Why did Lamar Community College receive twice the amount per student that was given to the Arapahoe, Aurora, Front Range, and Red Rocks community colleges?

It wasn't the story I originally intended to tell. I wouldn't go directly into the budgeting process, and I'd steer clear for the time being of state politics and academic warfare. All I wanted to do was to satisfy my curiosity about how this crazy-quilt system evolved, to set out straightforwardly the disparities in funding between institutions, and to repeat what I'd been told about why those differences exist. The article I was planning wouldn't reveal any deep, dark secrets, and it might be a little on the dull side. But it would be easy to report and write, and I'd learn something I could use later.

Now that I'd surmounted a small crisis of confidence, I felt good about my plans. I might even take a class or two during the summer if anything interesting was available.

I didn't say anything about my plans to JJ. I'd tell him when everything was decided.

For the time being, I actually had some time on my hands. I went back to writing my autobiography, catching up and filling in some blanks. I wrote about my two pregnancies and everything that had happened in between. I'd been covering a lot of things—especially my work as a reporter—in diary form. By the middle of March, I was pretty near up-to-date.

I didn't take as much time as I should have with the children. I had fallen back into the pattern of treating them—and JJ—as an afterthought.

*   *   *

The next major event on the calendar was Passover. The first seder this year would fall on March 26, a Saturday night. Mom and Daddy wanted everyone to come to Santa Monica again, but there were complications. Yalie and Richie were going to Richie's family in Chicago for the first seder. Although they were free to attend a second Rothschild seder, if we had a second seder, they'd prefer doing it in Colorado, where they wanted to vacation for the week.

I suggested that the whole crowd come to Vail. "Seder on the slopes," I called it, although ski season would be nearly over. The proposal was welcomed by the Goodman family. Dev and Mark were expecting to vacation with Yalie and Richie. Uncle Aaron had a law journal article he wanted to finish, and Aunt Ruth did not regard my offer to host the event as a slur against her own culinary skills. JJ said he was glad not to have to think about schlepping eleven-month-old Ariel out to the Coast.

There was some initial resistance on the California end. But eventually everyone agreed. Daddy had finished his movie and wouldn't begin work on his next script for another month. Rebecca could get the week off. David's wife, Lee, was in her final semester of college and could use a short break. Marla was eager to return to Vail, and Noah was at the stage in their relationship where he wanted what Marla wanted.

Next I invited my girlfriends, hoping for but not expecting a favorable response. However, Arlie and Seth were the only ones to say no. Jess responded characteristically: "Richard says yes, and since he's still nursing, he's invited me to bring my tits. Sam will manage the diaper concession." Jess reported that Laura would come with them.

We didn't always have two seders. More often than not, only one. But since Yalie and Richie were going to Chicago for the first seder, we were going to have two this year. I arranged for the two seder meals to be delivered by a Denver caterer. Mom insisted on arriving three days early to prepare gefilte fish in my kitchen in Golden. She told Anna Lopez, our cook, what to order, and, yes, she'd show Anna how it was done.

The seders would take place less than two weeks after Dev and Mark's first anniversary, and everyone would want to celebrate with them. Passover cakes, however, were made without flour, and they were generally on the far side of inedible. Mom had found a recipe that sounded like it might be an exception, and that was also on her agenda.

People were coming to Vail in shifts. Aunt Ruth, Mom, and I would go up early Friday, taking Anna Lopez along to help get things ready. JJ would bring Daniel, Ariel, and Hillary late Friday afternoon. Daddy and Rebecca would arrive from Los Angeles in the evening, spend the night at Dev and Mark's house, and come up with them on Saturday morning. Uncle Aaron had rented a van and would meet David and Alina—as well as Marla and Noah—at the airport on Saturday morning. Jess, Sam, Laura, and nineteen-month-old Richard would get to Denver around noon Saturday and find their own way to Vail. Yalie and Richie were expected in Vail around mid-afternoon Sunday, in time for the second seder.

Daniel, at four and a half, was now the official "youngest child" who must ask the Four Questions, though he couldn't yet read words bigger than "cat" or "dog" and hadn't the faintest idea what it was he was being told to say. His hesitancies and mispronunciations got the seder started in an atmosphere of general hilarity. Richard, sitting in a rented high chair, began making loud rising and falling noises like a European police siren. Normally unflappable Jess offered apologies and moved to take him away from the table. but Daddy, who was presiding along with Uncle Aaron, waved her off.

"Don't you suppose that the Israelites sounded alarms when Moses mobilized them to get out of Egypt? Your son is just providing sound effects for the *Haggadah*."

Mom, who was sitting at the opposite end of the table, added, "You're at home here, Jessica. Just relax and be a member of the family."

I was seated next to Jess and squeezed her hand. Jess returned the squeeze and blew Mom a grateful kiss. Jess loved her parents a lot. But she had no other relatives—just Laura, Arlie, me, and the rest of the Rothschilds. Mom and Daddy had always treated her like another one of their children, and I know she felt like we *were* her family.

Daniel, as usual, wouldn't sit still for long. The ski lodge, large as it was, didn't have alternative spaces other than the central space, the Great Room in which the seder was taking place. It was hard to concentrate on the service while Daniel was running around the table to elude Hillary's pursuit. Richard, having quieted down temporarily, was once more in full voice, and Ariel was crying.

Daddy and Uncle Aaron exchanged glances, skipped large chunks of the narrative, and announced that it was time for dinner. Daniel came back to the table to eat, but Richard's meal was attached to his mommy and he snatched at her breast to claim it. Jess took him off in a corner to nurse. I think Jess got a genuine physical high out of holding the growing little guy to her bare breast and giving him her nipple to suck. She was still pumping milk to leave in the refrigerator when she went to the office. She never gave him a bottle when she was around. Nor was she attempting to wean him. Her plan, she told me, was to let him nurse as long as he wanted.

"Until college," she said.

Some of us thought she was crazy. Here was this high-priced lawyer who spent every evening with a nineteen-month-old kid at her breast. Why in heaven's name would she want to do that?

The answer, Jess told anyone who asked, was that, although she considered herself a feminist, she was also a woman. Throughout human history, being a woman meant being a wife and mother, and Jess wasn't about to give that up. Jess loved being a lawyer, and she was exceptionally good at it. Although she was only twenty-nine, she was on her way to becoming a powerhouse in her legal specialty. She'd been taken in as the youngest partner in her firm's history, and it was in spite of her being a woman. But having a career was not an obstacle in Jess's view to having a life. Her partners understood, as did her clients, that Jess Sherman, the professional, shut down the moment she left the office. The rest of the time she gave to being Sam's wife and lover and Richard's mother. For Jess, being a lawyer and being a woman were not in conflict. She was determined to be both.

Frankly, I marveled at how firmly Jess compartmentalized her life. No one was ever likely to accuse Jess of neglecting her duties as wife and mother. Dev, who was thinking about having children soon, told me she wondered whether she would have the strength to manage her professional and private lives as competently as Jess did. Dev was a good lawyer and well regarded in her firm. But she wasn't yet a partner, and she couldn't write her own ticket the way Jess could.

Yalie, once she and Richie arrived, was probably the only other one of the young generation to view Jess as a potential role model. Alina, though into her third year of marriage to David, was only twenty-one and still playing house. Marla was undoubtedly contemplating marrying Noah, but having a family was beyond their horizon. Rebecca was merely dating. Laura wasn't even doing that. Yalie, however, was turning thirty later in the year, and I don't think she intended to let her biological clock keep ticking forever. She was two months older than Jess, a lawyer like Jess, living with her lover the way Jess had lived with Sam before they married.

Yalie must have seen herself in Jess. She told Dev, who told me, that she liked watching Jess handle Richard and not just when she was feeding him. Jess seemed thoroughly at ease with him and with herself. Yalie said that she hoped she would be that sort of mother, though she considered it much more likely that she'd hand off her babies to a nanny the way I did. It bothered me to be told that I was the antithesis to Jess as a role model. But I also had to concede that it was accurate.

Because the main meals were being provided by a caterer, there was not a lot that needed to be done during the day on Saturday or Sunday. I used the time to catch up on the lives of my guests.

Laura reported that working with Daddy was the best experience of her life. He had recommended her to a colleague with whom she was currently doing a film. But she'd told Daddy she wanted to work with him on his next project, whenever he was ready.

No, she wasn't dating anyone. Yes, she was feeling better about herself. I avoided asking about her family, but Laura volunteered. "My mother sent me a letter." She closed her eyes tightly and frowned. After a pause, she continued, "I don't know what it said because I returned it unopened." Another pause. "Maybe that sounds vindictive, but in a way what my family did to me was more painful than anything else that happened. I can't forget, and I can't forgive."

When it was clear that Laura hadn't got anything more to say on the subject, I replied, "Nobody's judging you, Laura. Try not to look back too much. Just get on with your life."

"I'm trying, Rache. Thanks to all you guys, I may even succeed."

My sister Rebecca said that she didn't like her accounting job. "This green eyeshade stuff is as boring as everybody says. What was I thinking? I want to do corporate finance, and they've got me verifying expense accounts and shit like that." She was on the lookout for another job.

David was designing houses for a big developer. He intended, however, to move to his firm's Los Angeles office as soon as Alina finished at Berkeley. Lee, who majored in nothing practical, was thinking vaguely about taking up journalism, primarily because I was a journalist and she looked up to me. Lee was a bright kid and attractive in every way, but she still had a lot of growing up to do.

I asked her kindly, "You haven't done any journalism, have you, Lee?"

"No, not yet."

"It's not easy to get started, lovey," I said. "I began by working for nothing at the local weekly—and my editor wasn't sure I was worth *that* much."

"You think I shouldn't try?"

"No, no. I don't mean to discourage you. I just think you need to be prepared for the fact that it's a tough go. But then, I suppose the first job after college is always tough. I wouldn't know, would I? Journalism is the only thing I've ever done."

I kissed Lee on her forehead, big sister to little sister. "You'll do okay, honey. I know you will," I said, knowing nothing of the sort. But that was the obligatory conclusion to the conversation.

Noah had joined an Internet start-up firm and was expecting to be a rich man before he was thirty. He'd become a total techie. Living in Silicon Valley, surrounded by other computer-obsessed young men, Noah spoke the patois of bits and bytes like a native. Marla was continually reminding him to "say that again in English, darling."

Marla had won a major role in a production of *The Marriage of Figaro* that was to be performed in San Jose by a small local company. The San Francisco Opera Company had granted her leave for this purpose. She was hoping to earn good reviews that would lift her permanently out of the chorus.

Although no marriage plans had been announced and Noah might not know it yet, I was convinced there would be a wedding before the year was out. When Marla decided it was time, Noah would propose. He thought he was in control of his life, but he was wrong.

Yalie and Richie were taking a break before the current session of the Senate got into high gear. Richie's boss was up for reelection in the fall, and he expected to be busier than usual with duties normally belonging to aides who would be off on the campaign trail. Neither of them was prepared to talk about when they'd leave Washington or where they'd go when they did, but I sensed that they were nearing a decision.

It came out in little ways. Yalie had a list of places she wanted to visit "when we have the time." Richie expressed his distaste for the methods employed in political fundraising. "It's fundamentally corrupting to the system. It's midway between bribery and extortion. And yet, everybody does it because, unless you're rich and are able to do it out of your own pocket, you can't run for office any other way."

Yalie also talked about "settling down," which I interpreted as getting married and having children. Not that marriage and kids were impossible in Washington. Those things had been known to happen there. But I was sure Yalie didn't intend to do her settling down inside the Beltway.

Dev and Mark I knew about. They were the two I saw most often. Occasionally, JJ and I went out to dinner or to a movie with them. JJ had begun to rely on Dev for legal advice. Although there were more senior people in Dev's firm on the Hyman Weiner & Sons account, JJ respected her judgment. Once, JJ had asked Dev her opinion after a higher-ranking member of the firm had spoken. Though she tried to phrase it politely, she felt compelled to disagree with her senior colleague. Afterward she told JJ, "Please don't put me in that position again. I felt like a kid contradicting an adult. If you've got to hear my opinion, I'd prefer that you ask me to go first, not last."

Dev and Mark still acted as if they were newlyweds. They liked to maintain physical contact—linked hands, an arm around the shoulder, hip next to hip on a sofa, long romantic kisses. They called each other pet names. "Kitty-cat" was Mark's name for Dev. She called him "Papa Bear."

This, too, will pass, I couldn't help thinking. JJ and I were old marrieds now, and romance was a scarce commodity. Very scarce these days.

Once Passover was over, I did the story I had planned about differences in funding by the state of Colorado's colleges and universities. Clearly, the differences were based at least in part on politics. I avoided that element of the story because I wasn't well enough versed in Colorado politics to get to the root of it. That was another chastening realization.

Since I'd simplified what I was trying to show, reporting and writing didn't take very long. When I presented it to Mr. Edwards, he chuckled, "You don't give up easily, do you, Rachel?"

I said, "It's just a piece of the story. I'll get to the harder part when I figure out what I'm doing. But, no, I don't give up easily."

"Okay, I'll see what we've got here."

The next morning, he called me at home and asked me to come into the office. On my arrival, he handed back the article.

He was blunt. "It's much too long, young lady. I can butcher it if you'd like, or you can condense it yourself. I suspect you'll feel better about it if you do it yourself."

"What do you want me to get rid of?" I was a trifle belligerent, like most writers when confronted with editorial advice they didn't want to hear.

"I'm leaving that up to my star reporter. But let me tell you what's wrong. This will run five pages. I'm willing to give you no more than three. As to what you should cut, you've got too much boring detail about structure, too many unnecessary quotes, and too many numbers in the text. I'd say less about structure—only what's absolutely necessary. I'd use fewer quotes. And I'd put the numbers in a table, not in the text."

"Oh." I was thrown more than a little by the inventory of faults.

"Now, if it's too much like doing surgery on one of your children, I can do it for you. Your choice."

"I guess you're right. I'll be happier in the end if I do it myself."

"That's the spirit. I want you to be happy."

On many publications, editors and writers are natural enemies, like the cobra and the mongoose. Mr. Edwards got his way but tried not to appear coercive.

It took me two days to revise the story. Rather than trim the existing text, I decided to rewrite it entirely, tell it differently. I described the structure of the system in two tight paragraphs, saying little about history. I referred to the smaller four-year colleges and the two-year institutions by category and location rather than by name. I noted that Colorado State consistently received more per student than Boulder, the University of Colorado's flagship institution, and that Adams State received more than either. I cited the disparities among community colleges. But the numbers all went into a table.

There were five paragraphs quoting people inside the system as to why these differences existed, interleaved with another five quoting mostly anonymous sources who disputed the logic behind the allocations. Then there were three paragraphs explaining how Colorado's practice differed from that in California and New York. This is how I completed the article: "Colorado's public system of higher education is nourished at taxpayers' expense through a structure that owes more to history than to rational design. A neutral observer is compelled to ask whether this is the best way or the fairest way to deliver resources to Colorado's far-flung collegiate population."

Mr. Edwards called me at home at 5:30 p.m. "Much better," he said. "In fact, excellent. There's only one thing wrong. You are no more 'a neutral observer' than I'm a Knight of the Roundtable. I changed it to 'This observer.'"

"May I make a confession?" I asked. "I like the new version better than the old."

"Good. Another lesson learned. I don't pay you by the word, so tell your story as economically as you can. Always."

I gave it my best parade-ground imitation: "Yessir, sir! Thank you, sir!"

"At ease, private. Take the rest of the afternoon off."

*   *   *

Life had been proceeding too smoothly. Soon after I finished my latest article and immediately after Ariel's first birthday, Hillary announced that she'd decided to return to England. She would be leaving on Friday, June 3.

She told JJ, though not me, that she was mighty tired of being the mother in the family while "Her Ladyship" pursued a career. "All she said to me was that she was now at an age where she'd like to have a boyfriend, and that was not going to happen if she stayed where she was.

I was furious when JJ repeated what Hillary had said to him. I'm sure he meant me to be furious. At her, not at him. It was his way of showing me what I had become without having to say so himself. Though I was angry at her, I didn't say anything to Hillary. Instead, I stewed about it for several days until anger gave way to tears. Hillary's opinion of me distilled all the disquiet I'd felt about my behavior—but done little or nothing to change. I felt simply awful.

Hillary had merely spoken the truth as she saw it. Yes, I had suffered a serious case of depression, and I hadn't yet conquered it. But was that the reason I was neglecting my responsibilities as wife and mother? Or was it just an excuse? I really didn't know the answer.

I swallowed my pride and urged JJ to give her a handsome bonus as a going-away gift. I didn't trust myself to speak frankly to Hillary, so I wrote out what I had to say, neither ignoring her criticisms nor trying to explain myself. I simply extended her my warmest best wishes and thanked her for all she'd done for us and for our children. JJ included my letter in the envelope with the bonus. She answered with a short note expressing her gratitude to me as well as to JJ. We would part on friendly terms.

Hillary's impending loss to our household meant that some difficult adjustments would be required. She wasn't a replaceable widget. Ariel had been seeing much more of her nanny than she did of me. Daniel, approaching five, didn't remember a time before "Hilly" was around. JJ and I began scouting desperately for a successor. Through a Denver employment agency, JJ quickly found a Mexican lady named Consuela Garcia. She was in her early fifties, claimed to love children, and had good references, though from people JJ and I didn't know. We didn't look any further. She'd begin several days before Hillary left.

Between Hillary's announcement and her departure, JJ and I were scheduled to fly out to San Jose to take in Marla Shifrin's debut in *The Marriage of Figaro* as the boy page, Cherubino, who is in love with love. We had planned to go for a long weekend, but we decided to fly out in time for a Saturday evening performance and fly back the next day.

Marla's first aria in Act I was greeted with spirited applause. When she sang the famous *voi che sapete* in Act II, there were cheers of *brava* from the most enthusiastic members of the audience. JJ and I weren't experienced operagoers, but we had no difficulty recognizing that Marla had done wonderfully well.

Noah booked a room at the hotel where we were staying for a small postperformance party, and it became a celebration. Marla's parents, her two sisters, and an aunt and uncle were there, as were Mom, Daddy, and Rebecca. David and Lee had driven down from

Oakland, and Arlie Becker and Seth Goldberg, who lived nearby, were also invited.

Marla and Noah were the last to arrive. She was warm with excitement, still had traces of makeup on her face, and had news she couldn't wait to share. She demanded silence and announced that Noah had asked her to marry him. She was wearing the ring that he presented her with on the way over from the theater.

"This is the best day of my life," she said.

"And mine," Noah added.

The crowd, which was preparing to congratulate Marla on her triumph, now fell all over Noah as well. Marla's father offered a toast: "To my daughter, the opera star and bride-to-be, and to Noah, who loves her, welcome to our family."

Daddy responded: "To Cherubino, my prospective son-in-law." Marla ran to him and gave him a big kiss.

The party, intended to last about an hour, continued until past 1:00 a.m. Even then, Marla didn't want to leave. She'd only had a couple of glasses of champagne, but she was tipsy with love and applause. It was wonderful to watch.

My original intention had been to have brunch on Sunday with my family and dinner that night with Arlie and Seth. But those plans had to be discarded. All I had time for was a short conversation with Arlie at the party. Arlie expected to receive her Ph.D. at the end of the summer, and she would then become a full-time researcher at the nearby headquarters of a major computer chip manufacturer. She and Seth were very happy, she said, and, no, they hadn't seen his family since the wedding.

Mom was learning for the first time about Hillary's approaching departure. She offered to fly in to cushion the shock for Daniel. JJ thought that would be an excellent idea.

When the day Hillary was to leave finally arrived, I actually choked up as I hugged her good-bye. Hillary had an especially difficult time parting from Daniel, and despite his grandmother's presence, it was considerably harder on him. Somehow he understood that Hillary was not just going away for a few days, as she'd done previously. This time she would not be coming back. He was hysterical when the door closed behind her, and Mom and I had to work hard to calm him. Hillary was probably the most important person in Danny's life—and "probably" doesn't mean I believe I might have been more important. JJ might have qualified, possibly my Mom. Not me. Don't think that wasn't a bitter realization.

Mom's presence was a godsend. I was at home more than usual, but I represented routine while Mom offered diversion. However, Mom couldn't stay around forever. She had promised to be in Berkeley for Alina's college graduation.

Thus, it was up to Mrs. Garcia, Daniel's new nanny, to take over. Unfortunately, Daniel didn't want anything to do with her. He made a fuss whenever she came near him. It was an untenable relationship on both sides. He wanted Hillary back, and if not Hillary, then Grandma. Mrs. Garcia was not good at dealing with tantrums.

On a Saturday afternoon when JJ and I were both out of the house, Daniel kicked at her once too often She responded by slapping him across the face.

"She hitted me," Daniel reported the moment JJ walked in the door, his eyes streaming tears. Mrs. Garcia tried to explain, but JJ wouldn't listen. Within an hour she was gone, bags and all.

I thought JJ had been unreasonable. Mrs. Garcia's dismissal left me with a serious problem. JJ and I had another argument, and both of us said things we shouldn't. I told him he was pigheaded and a bully. He told me I was selfish. I told him he was a mean son-of-a-bitch. He told me I was a lousy mother. I told him to kiss my ass. He told me to shove it up mine.

We went to bed in different rooms that night, the first time that had ever happened except during my emotional breakdown after Ariel's birth. I didn't get much rest, and I guess JJ didn't either. At 6:00 a.m., he came into our bedroom and found me lying there crying. He asked to be forgiven. I said it was my fault, and both of us admitted to being shmucks. With the kids likely to be up soon and no one else to take care of them, it wasn't possible for us to cement the reconciliation with sex. But we hugged one another and kissed and promised never to do this sort of thing again. I felt closer to JJ than I'd felt in quite awhile. An occasional quarrel was better than keeping your feelings buried.

Still, the basic problem remained. Agnes Wilson, who was hired to come in several afternoons a week to relieve the burden on Hillary, made it clear that she was not interested in a full-time position; and

Anna Lopez, though an excellent cook, wasn't particularly good with the kids.

JJ and I discussed options. Daniel was already going to morning nursery school. That could be turned into a combination of nursery school and day care. Day care was also a possibility for Ariel. Neither could serve, however, as more than a stopgap solution. Daniel's routine had already been upset by Hillary's going, and his experience with Consuela was an unhappy one. Ariel might or might not prosper in day care, but neither JJ nor I liked the idea of entrusting our thirteen-month-old daughter to people we didn't know.

Finding another nanny might take weeks. I could see only one solution. I'd have to be the nanny until we found another.

I said, "Better find someone quick. I'm second-class help—a professional journalist but an amateur mother."

"We're agreed about that." JJ was only half joking. I knew it as well as he did.

The next hunt for a nanny was done more systematically than the one that found Consuela Garcia. The search wasn't confined to Denver. A firm JJ hired for the purpose placed ads in six major cities and within a week found four potential candidates, all with good credentials. The one who sounded like the best was another Englishwoman, Adelaide Miller. She was thirty-seven and had been caring for children of a Chicago family for the past fifteen years. The youngest child no longer required a nanny. Her employers praised her unreservedly.

Was she willing to move to Denver? Perhaps. It depended on "the situation." JJ and I were wary of making a second mistake. We invited Ms. Miller to fly out for an interview. She impressed us as completely confident of her ability to deal with any problem. Although the four children she'd been caring for no longer required a nursemaid, two of them were born while she was in the household, and she'd seen the other two through their teenage years and off to college. They were now twenty, eighteen, fourteen, and 12, two girls and two boys.

"They are my children, and they always will be," she said.

JJ and I brought Daniel in to meet her. He wasn't pleased with the prospect of another stranger entering his life, but she knew how to deal with that. She drew him into a conversation about a BandAid on his knee. Before long, he was showing her his scab and explaining how he got it. Soon he took her off to his room to show her his rock collection.

JJ and I needed no further convincing. JJ offered her a substantial increase in salary, and it was agreed she would begin in late July.

With my child-care problem on the way to being solved, I was free to make plans to attend graduate school part-time beginning in September. I had identified two courses I wanted to take, a class in public finance and a seminar on issue analysis. I intended to go to class two mornings a week and to one evening seminar. It had been more than seven years since I earned my undergraduate degree, and I was really looking forward to being in school again.

JJ thought I would take a leave of absence from *In the Rockies* and go to school full-time. But that didn't appeal to me. I wanted to keep my hand in professionally. Being a senior writer for the magazine was a big part of the identity I'd established for myself in Denver, and I didn't want to give it up. I was sure I'd be able to balance school and journalism without any difficulty.

Even before school started, I began work on another story for the magazine. This one would be about the new Denver International Airport, which was scheduled to open during the coming year. It would be the first major airport built in the United States in more than twenty years. I'd already written about plans to redevelop Stapleton Airfield, the property that would be abandoned once Denver International entered service. This was the other half of the story. I intended to write about how the project was conceived and to explore the controversies that accompanied its planning and construction.

To be candid—and despite the self-scrutiny forced on me by Hillary's criticism—it didn't occur to me that I ought to remain at home until the children adjusted to the changes in household arrangements. The children were going to be Adelaide Miller's responsibility. And JJ? Right now, I was preoccupied with perfecting my skills as a journalist. Unlike my friend Jess, I was not good at shutting the door on my professional life when the workday was done. JJ would get by. That was what I thought. If I thought about it at all, which I'm not sure I did.

PART II

ONE EVENING IN SEPTEMBER

Rachel's graduate seminar in issue analysis met at 7:00 p.m. each Tuesday in the North Classroom Building on the CU-Denver campus. Her plan was to spend the day on Tuesdays working in her office at home, eat the early dinner her housekeeper would prepare for her, and then drive to the campus, just at the edge of downtown Denver in a area known as the Auraria Campus. She had a permit to park in the large lot alongside the campus athletic fields, northwest of the building. The seminar was scheduled to end at 10:00 p.m., and she would be home by 10:30 or 10:45.

It was the first time in several years that Rachel had been in a classroom setting, and she found it oddly exciting to be a student again. One of her classmates, Clark Mason, a man about her own age, was an analyst with the state budget department. He was just the sort of person she needed to have on her side if she was ever to succeed in her ambition to write penetrating magazine articles on money issues in Colorado politics. Aside from learning what the class had to offer, getting to know Mason was her principal objective. She'd also become friendly with Nan Lucas, a social sciences supervisor with the Denver School System, and Harriet McAuliffe, a recent college graduate who was pursuing a public policy master's degree. Nan was several years older than Rachel and Harriet five or six years younger but very sharp.

The three women had been working in parallel on a case study of managed health care and its impact on the health system.

At the third seminar session, they were scheduled to make their preliminary reports. Rachel had volunteered for the assignment of examining trends over the decade of the eighties in the length of hospital stays, correlated by medical condition, the patient's age, sex, and insurance status, and whether the patient was inside or outside the managed care system. It had proved a grueling task. Data had been provided to her, but Rachel wasn't comfortable with the spreadsheet program required to assemble the material and make the analysis. Although it was only an exercise, the results were less than illuminating, and Rachel knew it. Obviously, she had a lot to learn.

Nan had the easier job of charting changes in medical costs and insurance reimbursement policies. Harriet prepared an analysis of other variables—changes of governmental policy, availability of new drugs, advances in medical technology, improvements in treatment methods—that might also have had an effect on how long patients remained in the hospital.

Rachel presented her findings apologetically. The professor, together with the other students in the class, critiqued her presentation. They were gentler with Rachel than she deserved—"a credible first effort," the professor said, after pointing out several flaws. Then there was a brief discussion of policy implications. Rachel was both humbled by her inadequate performance and stimulated by the exercise. She wanted to get together with her colleagues after class, to get some ideas on how she might have done her part better and to talk further about the policy issues, which excited her. Nan begged off. She had to be on the job early Wednesday morning. Harriet and Clark agreed to join Rachel for a beer in the downtown area a couple of blocks from the Auraria Campus. They crossed busy Speer Boulevard and walked to a late gathering place. Rachel called JJ on her cell phone to say that she'd be late coming home.

It was nearing 11:30 p.m. when they left the bar. Time for them all to head home. Still chatting, they returned to the school parking lot. Harriet's car was first and then Clark's. Rachel stood with Clark at his vehicle for another few minutes completing their conversation. When they finally said good night, he climbed into his car, and Rachel walked across the large lot to hers. She opened the rear door to her Mercedes to put her briefcase in.

Suddenly, someone grabs her roughly around the shoulders from behind and sticks his hand over her mouth. Rachel struggles to break loose. She stomps on his foot as hard as she can and scratches the hand he is holding her with. She also tries unsuccessfully to bite the hand he's using to gag her.

Voice: "The bitch scratched me."

Second Voice: "I'll fix that." A man wearing a mask, a dark shirt, and dark pants materializes in front of her, grips her right wrist, and twists it clockwise, putting pressure on the elbow and the wrist itself. Rachel feels as if the wrist might snap.

She tries to scream but can't get it past the hand covering her mouth. The sound dies in her throat.

Man in front: "If you want to stay alive, bitch, you'd better do things our way."

Her legs are suddenly liquid. Fear chases away resistance. She begins quaking.

Man in front, as she stops fighting: "That's better. Now, hold out your hands."

She holds out her hands. He snaps a pair of handcuffs onto her throbbing right wrist and then onto the left.

Man in front: "Where are your keys?"

Rachel still can't get any words past the hand over her mouth. She inclines her head slightly toward the ground where she'd dropped them.

He bends down and picks them up.

The man behind hauls her around to the rear of the car. The other guy opens the trunk, and the two of them force her in headfirst, lifting her over the bumper. Then they close the lid.

Though it is not particularly cold, Rachel is shaking all over, and her teeth are chattering. The motor starts, and the car begins moving. She is curled up in the car's small trunk, wedged hard against the trunk wall. She's crying. It takes awhile before she remembers the cell phone in the pocket of her slacks. With handcuffs on, extracting it is difficult. When she is finally able to get it out, it slips from her hands and falls to the floor of the trunk. Rachel can see nothing in the dark. She gropes around until she locates it. At last. She turns it on and, by feel and the dim light of the dial, is able to punch in 911 and send the signal. The police operator answers.

Rachel is crying so hysterically she can scarcely make herself understood. She is so terrified she can't even remember her car's make or model. "A German car," she says. "VW? BMW? Mercedes?" "Yes, the last one. Small one, with four doors. Silver." She cannot remember her license plate number. She gives her husband's name and their telephone number. It's ridiculous, but Rachel thinks *JJ will save me.* The car has been on the road for ten to fifteen minutes, moving rapidly at times. She doesn't know the direction. It has taken Rachel many minutes to remember the cell phone, to extract it, lose it, find it again, and make the call. She hasn't had 911 on the line for more than about two or three minutes when the car slows down and begins bouncing over a rough patch of ground. Then it comes to a stop. She drops the phone, afraid of what her captors might do to her if they find it in her hands. The lid to the trunk opens. Standing there are two men, the guy who handcuffed her and a bigger guy, also masked, also in black. The bigger guy has huge biceps, hairy arms, and more black hair peeking out of the collar of his shirt. The hair on top of his head is plentiful and long, whereas the smaller one is shaved bald.

They lift her out of the trunk, knocking her head against the lid of the trunk and her legs against the rim. They are alongside some sort of warehouse made of concrete blocks. There is no one else around.

The bald guy (gruffly): "March."

They prod, push, pull, and half-carry Rachel to a door at the end of the building. They force her inside. The place stinks. There has obviously been a recent fire in the building because the walls opposite the entry have scorch marks rising to the ceiling. The room they are in is longer than it is wide and dimly lit by a single ceiling bulb. It is filthy, as if it hasn't been used for a very long time, and filled with debris. They undo her handcuffs.

Rachel (tearfully, desperation in her voice): "Who … what do you want?"

The bald guy: "We want *you*, bitch. Take off your clothes."

The hairy one: "We wanna see everything you got to show, Mrs. Weiner."

The bald guy: "Shut the fuck up, you dumb bastard." (Then to Rachel) "Bitch, I told you to take your fucking clothes off."

Rachel can't do that even if she wanted to. She is crying uncontrollably and shaking.

The bald guy hits her hard across her left cheek with an open hand. "I fucking told you to undress, cunt." He strikes her a second time with the back of his hand on the right cheek. After a short pause, he backhands her again, harder than before. "Goddam you, I said get undressed."

Rachel starts to unbutton her sweater, but she isn't acting fast enough for him.

The bald guy to his companion: "Rip it off her."

The second man grips the collar of her sweater from behind and yanks. One of the buttons flies off, several others come undone, and the bald man opens the final buttons, enabling the man behind her to pull the sweater off. The bald guy takes hold of her blouse at the neck and pulls at it with both hands until the fabric yields. The bigger man does the same in back, and the blouse is gone.

The hairy guy: "Off with the bra!"

The bald one: "Or we'll take it off, and your tits with it."

Rachel can't control her fingers, and the two men are impatient. The bald man takes hold of her bra at the center. His muscles straining, he tears it in two, then yanks the bra straps from her arms. She is naked from the waist up, trying to cover herself. The bald guy grabs both nipples in his fingers and twists. She screeches with pain.

Rachel makes no move to remove her pants, so he shoves her backward. She lands hard on the concrete floor. He pulls off her shoes without bothering to unknot the laces, and then her socks. He sits down with his full weight on her thighs to undo her belt. Rachel hits him with her fists, trying desperately to beat him off. He slaps her face again, harder than ever. She is still resisting, so he hits her with his fist, landing the blow just below her left eye. She lies there stunned.

When the bald man stands up, the two of them take the legs of her pants and drag them off, her body following along the floor. The bigger man then kneels down, lifts her hips roughly, and rends her panties to remove them. Rachel tries to cover herself with her hands. She pleads for them to let her go. She'll pay them anything they ask.

They jeer at her. The big man: "You're gonna pay with your pussy, baby." The other one laughs.

The two of them take Rachel by the wrists, further hurting the one Baldy twisted earlier. They yank her to her feet, only to throw her facedown across a bed standing along the long wall. It is a fold-up bed in a metal frame with a dirty mattress without any covering. The bald one handcuffs her right wrist to the frame. He stands in front of her as he removes his pants. He is not wearing any underwear. He takes her roughly by the hair and lifts her face so he can rub his erect penis across her lips.

The bald one: "I know you'd like to suck my cock, baby. Maybe I'll let you do it after I screw you."

Then he steps behind her, separates her buttocks, and jams two fingers into her rectum. Rachel yelps in pain.

The bald man: "I'm going to fuck you up the ass, baby. You'll love it."

Rachel is screaming, but there is no one to hear. He starts pushing at her anus with his penis, forcing himself into her. Rachel thrashes around but can't get away. She feels her body tear as he penetrates the outer ring of muscle and drives into her. It takes him only a short time to spurt. When he gets off Rachel, the bigger man replaces him. His penis is thicker than the other man's, and getting into her takes a good deal of pushing at her already tortured opening. Rachel is in extreme pain and moaning like a wounded animal. He remains in her much longer than the first one did, rocking back and forth, tearing her further.

After they are done taking her from the rear, the bald man undoes the single handcuff. They turn her over, and the bald guy prepares to go at her again. She tries to fight him off, and he slaps her again, full force, across the breasts. Again and again. Though she is as dry as it is possible to be, he simply thrusts into her vagina, hurting her terribly. When he is finished, the hairy man takes over. Again, he tears her on the way in and remains on her and in her for a long time. Rachel is beyond pain now. She whimpers all the way through the frontal assault. She hurts everywhere.

The big guy finally gets off.

The bald man: "Now, get down on your knees, bitch. You're going to suck our cocks. You know, clean them with your tongue."

Dazed though she is, Rachel recoils. She can't do that.

The bald man takes out a switchblade and clicks it open. "Down on your knees, I told you, or I'll cut up your pretty face for you."

He pulls her up from the mattress, takes her by the shoulders, and pushes her down on her knees. He thrusts his penis toward her. "Open up, baby, and do me—or else." He puts his knife against her cheek.

Rachel opens her mouth. "Wider, bitch."

When she opens her mouth further, he puts his penis in. He grabs her by the hair and pulls her toward him. "Suck me, baby."

Rachel can't—but she does. "Taste me," he says. "Use your tongue. That's what it's for."

She's no longer capable of resisting.

When the bald guy is finished with her, the bigger guy takes over. Again, Rachel does what she has to do.

When the big guy's done with her, the bald man says, "Before we say good-bye, bitch, here's something else to remember us by." The two of them stand there and, one after another, urinate all over her—in her face, in her hair, on her breasts, on her crotch. Right before they walk out the door, the smaller man puts the metal cuffs on Rachel's wrists once again, this time securing them behind her back. And then they are gone.

Rachel collapses onto the floor and lies there curled up on her side in a ball, numb, sobbing. Her face is throbbing where the bald guy punched her. Her breasts hurt from being slapped. She vomits, trying to rid herself of the taste in her mouth. Every part of her body aches. She is bleeding from torn tissue front and rear. Many minutes pass— she hasn't any idea how long—before she even tries to get up. Without the use of her hands, it is very difficult, but she finally manages it by pushing on the floor behind herself with her handcuffed hands until she is able to get her feet under her and rise. Her clothes are gone. The men took them away. She looks around for something, anything to cover her nakedness. She finds a tarp in one corner of the room but, with her hands cuffed behind her, cannot do anything with it.

She has to find help. Despite being handcuffed, she manages to manipulate the knob on the warehouse door and pull it open. But the door is weighted, and as soon as she lets go of the knob, it swings shut. She fails four times to get it open. Finally, she hits on a strategy. Standing on one foot, she hooks the other behind the door after she's pulled it open. She isn't quick enough the first time to get between the door and the opening to the outside, but she finally does it on the second try, though the impact of the closing door on her foot hurts terribly.

Rachel stumbles out into the night air—over the edge of hysteria from the rape, in considerable pain from the physical damage that she's suffered, and almost exhausted from the ordeal of getting through the door. Her car is gone, along with the cell phone in its trunk. There are a couple of other warehouse buildings close by, but they do not appear to be in use either. Across the street, there is a vast expanse of chain link fence, surmounted by barbed wire, guarding a huge assemblage of truck trailers. Hundreds of them. Maybe thousands. Obviously it is a depot of some sort, though there is no identifying sign in sight. There has to be a night watchman somewhere, but she doesn't see a gate and the area immediately in front of her is lighted only by a high streetlamp.

Off in the distance, she can see a low-lying black bulk that might be a factory building, and beyond that lights moving along a roadway. She forgot to look for a telephone inside the building, and the door is now locked behind her. She wasn't thinking. She can't think.

Aside from the freight depot across the street, there does not seem to be anyplace in the immediate area where she might find a human being. She could walk around the depot fence until she finds a gate, or she can start toward the dark bulk, which is a couple of blocks away. The roadway is further off. Rachel is shoeless, and the ground in front of her is covered with gravel and broken glass. Her wrist is throbbing, and so is the foot she used to prevent the door from closing. She picks her way painfully to the street and hobbles along, sobbing aloud, unable to cover any part of her body. She is shivering badly, both with trauma and the cool night air. Once she trips and falls to her knees, scraping them bloody. She knows she was lucky not to have fallen on her face or cracked her head. Getting up, once again using her cuffed hands as leverage, is a struggle. Her strength is almost gone.

She can't see an opening in the fence around the depot. So she limps slowly on her tender feet, as carefully as possible, toward the dark bulk, which turns out to be a small, one-story factory building, also surrounded by a chain link fence. The gate is chained shut with a huge padlock. The glassed-in guard house at the entry way is empty. There are no lights to be seen. Somewhere, she thinks, someone must be patrolling. She shouts "Help!" as loudly as she can several times, but nothing happens. So she keeps on hobbling along a feeder road from the factory gate toward the lights on the roadway.

The moment she sets foot on the shoulder of the roadway, someone sees her. A huge truck and trailer flash by, brakes squealing, and come to a shuddering halt on the shoulder about one hundred fifty yards down the road. The driver, a middle-aged black man, radios the police even before leaving the cab. Then he runs back to Rachel, carrying a blanket that he keeps in the truck.

Rachel is far past the limits of her endurance, and the sight of a rescuer saps her of her remaining strength. She collapses in the truck driver's arms.

The man drapes the blanket around her and, supporting her with his own body, walks her slowly to his truck. A police cruiser arrives shortly afterward. Two police officers, a man and a woman, ease her into the back seat. Rachel is able to say her name, then passes out on the way to the hospital emergency room, where they take her with sirens blaring, having radioed ahead to say that they are on the way.

Although she is unconscious, the basic facts are obvious. The woman has been raped in a particularly brutal fashion. She has a black eye, red marks on her cheeks and body where she's been punched and slapped, and bruises everywhere. There is dried semen in her pubic hair. The smell of urine is pronounced. The police suspect that she may have suffered internal damage, but that will be for the doctors to determine.

When Rachel comes to on the way to the hospital, her hands are free. One of the officers has forced the lock on the cheap handcuffs. She is wrapped in the truck driver's big woolen blanket but is still shivering. The police try to question her, but she is in no condition to tell them anything.

The patrol car carrying Rachel arrives at the hospital after 2:00 a.m. Waiting attendants load her onto a gurney and wheel her into the emergency room. They take her into a side room that can accommodate two patients and swing curtains around her from tracks in the ceiling to maintain a semblance of privacy. She passes out again as they transfer her from the gurney to a hospital bed. The police stay around while one of the emergency room nurses does a rape kit. They are just leaving when JJ arrives. The policewoman persuades the emergency room clerk to let him in to see his wife. She needs it as much as he does. JJ is standing beside Rachel, holding her hand and crying when she comes to. She's never seen JJ cry before. He virtually falls on her, hugging and kissing her. The nurses gently move him aside. They ask him to go back to the waiting room. Someone will come get him as soon as they attend to Rachel's immediate needs.

One nurse takes a blood sample from her. A nurse's aide sponges her down, which eliminates some, not all, of the urine smell. Rachel is no better able to answer the doctor's questions than she was to answer police questions. So the doctor gives her pain medication and a sedative, and she falls asleep, sobbing to the last.

The emergency room physician goes out to the waiting room and takes JJ aside to tell him that his wife has been raped both anally and vaginally, has been torn in both places, is bleeding a bit, and is badly bruised on the inside as well as the outside. Both her left wrist and right foot are sprained and swollen, but there do not appear to be any broken bones. They'll know better after she's x-rayed. He's prescribed medication to ensure against pregnancy, he says.

The medication isn't necessary. Rachel's tubes were tied after her second baby's birth. JJ doesn't remember to say so. He can't think clearly.

PART III

ON A ZIG-ZAG PATH

Around 5:00 a.m., Rachel was transferred upstairs into a hospital room. JJ insisted on a private room. Luckily, one was empty. Rachel was asleep, unaware of the move. Her gynecologist, Dr. Steinberg, and her internist both appeared around 7:00 a.m. They looked at the chart prepared in the emergency room, did their own examinations, and gave additional instructions to the nursing staff. Rachel was barely conscious of their presence and fell quickly back to sleep when they left. She awoke once in midmorning, crying for help as if the rape were still in progress. JJ, who was sitting beside her, called in the nurse. She gave Rachel another sedative, which the doctors had authorized.

A rape counselor saw her in the early afternoon, followed later in the day by Dr. Harold Drucker, the psychiatrist who treated Rachel for depression after Ariel was born. Both asked JJ to leave the room while they talked to his wife. He asked Ms. Morgan, the rape counselor, why she wanted him to leave. She explained kindly that rape victims are often overwhelmed with shame. They were much more likely in the beginning to talk to a professional than to a family member, no matter how close.

Rachel, on pain medication, didn't say much to the rape counselor. She was alert enough to tell her that she was raped anally prior to the vaginal rape. She knew that was something the doctors needed to know. There was no way she could have told a male doctor directly.

She wouldn't have been capable of telling Ms. Morgan if JJ had been present. She did not say anything about being forced to take their penises into her mouth. She couldn't talk about that.

She said hello to Dr. Drucker when he came in and dissolved in tears. "Save me, Dr. Drucker," she begged. "Please save me."

He sat with her for a while, holding her hand, soothing her, promising to do all he could.

The policewoman who helped her the previous night, Corporal Lansing, came in to ask some questions. Rachel wasn't much help. She hadn't seen the faces of her attackers, she couldn't talk about details of the rape, and she was hazy on how she got from the site of the rape to the shoulder of the highway.

The truck driver who rescued her, Herman Washington, stopped by. He was a middle-aged family man with two grown daughters, and his sympathy for Rachel was so great that he had to keep wiping the tears from his eyes. JJ thanked him profusely and offered him money.

Offended by the offer, Washington said, "I can't take your money, sir. I wouldn't feel good about being paid to do the right thing."

"I didn't mean to insult you, Mr. Washington. I'm just very grateful to you for helping her, and I wanted to do something for you in return."

"What you can do for me is take care of her. She's gonna need it."

After Herman Washington left, the detective assigned to the case from the sexual crimes unit arrived. He told JJ that he was convinced Rachel was not a random victim. The fact that the men raped her anally as well as vaginally, urinated on her, and left her without a scrap of clothing suggested strongly to him that Rachel was sought out for abduction and assault. They took her, intending to defile her. He guessed that some sort of revenge was the motivation. (It was a long time— several weeks—before Rachel remembered that the big hairy man had called her "Mrs. Weiner" during the rape and the bald guy ordered him to shut up.)

The detective knew that JJ was a very wealthy man, an heir to Hyman Weiner & Sons, a big developer in the city and owner of one of the biggest real estate portfolios in the Rocky Mountain area. He and his family were natural targets. He got JJ to think about who might have it in for them. That led JJ to name two foremen dismissed from the construction company three weeks earlier for drinking on the job. JJ was the one who ruled that they were entitled to no more than two weeks' severance pay. Although the men were extremely angry, it had not seemed like a big deal to JJ at the time. Their drinking had endangered other workers, and they had no grounds to sue. The ex-foremen fit the limited description of the two men that Rachel had been able to give—one bigger than the other, one bald, one hairy.

The police went looking for the pair, but they had vanished. Their apartments were bare. Their banking and savings accounts were cleaned out, the money taken in cash. Based on where Rachel was found and the vague description she gave of the deserted, half-burnt warehouse where the assault took place, the police were able to locate the building and to get the name of the owner. He acknowledged giving a key to the bigger of the two rapists to "store some things" for a few days. He knew the guy from a bowling league. He had no idea where the fellow had disappeared to. The police eventually accepted his story.

Rachel's car was found three days after the kidnapping, parked on a side road off the main highway to Colorado Springs. Except for Rachel's cell phone in the trunk and some of her hair, there was nothing in the car, not a single fingerprint. The police could find no trace of the vehicles belonging to the two men. No one had seen the men near where Rachel's car was found or anywhere else. They were gone.

The best clue the police had was a package that came to JJ five days after the rape. It contained a silver Star of David on a chain. Rachel had been wearing it around her neck at the time of the rape. It was now wrapped in a piece of paper covered with swastikas. The package was postmarked Colorado Springs. The man who owned the warehouse also got his key back in an envelope from Colorado Springs.

Rachel's doctors told JJ that they would need to check Rachel's blood periodically to make sure she hadn't been infected with AIDS or any other sexually transmitted disease. The doctors thought it was quite likely that she would get a vaginal infection because she had first been raped anally. Her internist put her on a course of antibiotics. She was being fed intravenously because she refused all food. Rachel was unable to keep from crying. Her body still ached all over. There was a large, bruised swelling under her eye where she had been punched. She kept imagining that she still smelled of urine. She had not focused on the possibility that her rapists might have given her some terrible disease. It was horrible enough. She wasn't willing to see anyone except

JJ, who was spending most of the day, every day at the hospital. JJ told her about Daniel and Ariel, but she never asked the next question. She had no interest in anything beyond her hurt—less the physical damage after the first day than the sense that she had lost everything, that her life was over.

"She'll need a lot of help," Ms. Morgan told JJ after a second conversation with Rachel. "More than you can give her, no matter how hard you try. She'll probably resist going to a therapist after the first or second visit. Don't let her quit. Rape violates a woman's sense of self—any woman, any rape. Your wife has been through a particularly vicious rape. Those men were intending to destroy her, and they've succeeded for now. Getting her past the trauma isn't a job for amateurs. It may take a very long time."

"How long?"

"It could be years. It could be forever."

JJ blanched, showing the pain he felt. "What can I do?"

"Love her. She needs your unconditional love. And you may not get much back for a while. Rape sometimes poisons a woman's mind against all men, even those she is closest to. You've got to be prepared for that. She won't be able to help it. Love her no matter what."

JJ thought to himself that the men who attacked Rachel were aiming at him. Would Rachel conclude that he was somehow to blame? What he said aloud, his voice cracking, was, "I'll do whatever's needed. I love Rachel more than I love anything in the world."

Dr. Drucker, her psychiatrist, stopped by a second time. "How are you feeling today, Rachel?" he asked her.

She let loose another flood of tears. When she stopped crying, all she said was, "I want to die." She said it over and over, like a company working to establish an advertising slogan in the minds of consumers: "We try harder." "All the news that's fit to print." "I want to die."

Dr. Drucker told JJ, "Keep an eye on her. We don't want her to damage herself. We'll sedate her if need be. I'm going to write a couple of prescriptions for antidepressants. It's medicine she's taken before, but a heavier dose. The nurses will see that she takes the pills while she's in the hospital. You've got to be sure she continues taking them. She'll eventually climb out of the pit she's in, but she's having a very rough time of it. Once she stabilizes a bit, she ought to be seen three times a week for a while. She's going to need time to talk it out with a sympathetic listener, but someone who's neutral. Although Rachel knows me, I don't think I'm the right person for her right now. She ought to be seeing a female psychotherapist rather than a male psychiatrist. I have a couple of names I can give you. Once you've decided on a psychotherapist, let me know, and I'll give her a report on my findings. If the psychotherapist wants Rachel to continue on the drugs I've prescribed, she'll probably ask me to see her from time to time to balance her medications. I'd certainly like to help any way I can."

JJ mumbled his thanks. The idea that Rachel might be tempted to harm herself hadn't occurred to him. He felt as if the bottom had fallen out of his life, their life. He didn't know what to do.

Rachel's parents, Hanna and Hillel Rothschild, flew in from Santa Monica as quickly as they could, accompanied by Rachel's younger sister, Rebecca. Her aunt and uncle, Ruth and Aaron Goodman, came up from Boulder. Their daughter, Devorah—Dev—who was like an older sister to Rachel, was there with her husband, Mark Chapman. The Goodmans' other daughter, Ya'el—Rachel's pal Yalie—was on her way from Washington.

Hanna intended to be strong for Rachel but couldn't handle it. The moment she saw her daughter, she started crying and had to leave the room. The others weren't much better.

They milled around in the waiting room, hugging JJ, hugging one another. No one knew what to say after "I'm sorry." They were like children waiting to be told what to do.

JJ called Dr. Drucker to ask his advice.

Dr. Drucker said, "The short answer is 'I don't know.' My hunch based on past experience is that Rachel needs to know her family loves her but may not be able to handle having them all over her. It's probably best for them not to crowd into her hospital room and, after you take her home, not to come visit unless Rachel asks for them. Let them call you as often as they want. When you get the right opportunity, tell Rachel they've called and take your cue from her on whether she wants to see them or even talk with them. And be kind to them all. Be kind. She's going to need her family's love and support for a long time to come. They'll need to understand that they're not being rejected. For your wife, it's a matter of self-preservation, like a turtle withdrawing into its shell."

JJ relayed the message as accurately and as sensitively as he could. Hanna was devastated. Her child was going through the worst experience in her entire life, and the doctor was saying that her mother might make things worse by being overly solicitous. Ruth hugged her sister-in-law and told her, "Try not to look at it that way, Hanna. This isn't about you and Rachel. It isn't about any of us and Rachel. It's about the structure of a life that's collapsed under a young woman who just happens to be your daughter and my niece, Rebecca's sister, and Dev and Yalie's cousin. Rachel needs professional help if she's going to rebuild that structure—and we all have to take our guidance from the professionals who've seen this sort of thing before."

That evening, they had a pain-filled family conference. All the women wept. Several of the men did, too. Ruth and Aaron proposed that Hanna, Hillel, and Rebecca come stay with them in Boulder for a while. Dev and her husband Mark, who lived in South Denver, and Yalie, who had just arrived from Stapleton Airport, said they would also move temporarily into the parents' home, where they could all be miserable together. JJ said he would call them at least twice a day to report every development.

The next morning, they came in groups to kiss Rachel good-bye, to tell her they loved her and would be there when she wanted them: Ruth and Aaron, then Dev and Mark and Yalie, finally Hanna, Hillel, and Rebecca. Hanna could not speak. Hillel did all the talking, and Hanna stood there, in anguish, nodding. Rebecca gripped her mother's arm and wept silently. In the afternoon, the eight of them left for Boulder. Aaron took Hanna, Hillel, and Rebecca in the car that they had rented at the airport. Mark and Dev drove her parents' car. Yalie and her mother went in the car that Yalie had rented.

Rachel wept when they departed, but no more than she would have if they had stayed.

In Boulder, Rachel's family gathered in pain, made no easier by phone conversations with Rachel's twin brothers, David and Noah, who remained in California. They would fly in if there were anything they could do to help, anything at all. Hillel told them to stay where they were. "We're just in the way here," he said. "All of us."

"Maybe you are," replied David's wife, Alina. "But at least you have each other. We're sitting out here alone."

JJ asked the Boulder contingent to return a frantic phone call that came into his office from Laura Ludwig, Rachel's friend since junior high school. Laura learned through the grapevine at the movie studio where she and Hillel worked that he was summoned to Denver because of something terrible involving his daughter. Aaron was designated to speak with Laura. He told her the story that the family concocted to tell everyone outside the immediate family circle: Rachel was brutally beaten in a robbery and was in the hospital recovering.

Laura passed that story along to Jessica Sherman and Arlene Becker, who, like Laura, were Rachel's closest friends since junior high. Jess, however, guessed the truth. If all that happened to Rachel was a beating, the family would be at her bedside. It had to have been something worse, and the something worse must be rape. Aaron admitted the truth when Jess called to challenge him. Although her two-year-old was still nursing, Jess wanted to fly in. Aaron told her the same thing Hillel told his sons: "All visitors are in the way."

Dev took the phone next. She and Jess were both lawyers. But more than that, they were kindred spirits and had become very close through the years. Dev assured Jess that she would get regular reports that she could relay to Laura and Arlie.

"I know how much you love her," Dev said, beginning to cry. "It's awful. It's just awful."

Jess was crying on the other end. "I wish I could be there. Even to stand around and do nothing. I feel so helpless."

Dev responded, "We're all helpless. Maybe later."

Jess finally agreed, "Yeah. Maybe later."

Aaron then had to field a second call from Laura after she learned from Jess the truth about what happened to Rachel. Though she had received reports from Laura and Jess, Arlie also felt the need to touch some member of the family, even Aaron, the one she knew least well.

"Tell the Rothschilds I love them" was the message left in some form by all three of Rachel's girlfriends.

JJ needed to deal with his family. They, too, wanted to help. Grandma Bess was desolated by what happened. Herman and Vera asked to be given something to do. Even Annalisa seemed genuinely concerned.

JJ told his parents, "There's nothing to be done. The doctor has asked me to keep everyone away. Hanna and Hillel, the whole

Rothschild family, is up in Boulder. Look, do what you can for Grandma. Don't let her get sick over this. It's already bad enough."

After five days in the hospital, Rachel went home. Her eye was still somewhat swollen, as were her ankle and wrist. Her visible bruises were beginning to fade. She was still having terrible nightmares but no longer cried incessantly. Instead, she was subdued and passive. She wouldn't speak unless someone spoke to her, and sometimes not then. She did not ask who sent her the plants and bouquets of flowers that covered her hospital room. She didn't care.

She accepted her parents' removal to Boulder as the selfless act of love that JJ told her it was. She didn't truly care about that either.

An orderly brought her down to JJ's car in a wheelchair and helped her into the front seat. JJ leaned over and kissed her hands. She had never looked so frail. She'd lost weight in the hospital although she had finally started eating again—minimally.

"The kids are waiting for you, Rache," he said, trying to sound cheerful. "They were jumping out of their skin when I left the house."

"Oh," Rachel said. It was all the enthusiasm she could muster.

When JJ drove up to the house, Daniel came running, with Ariel following. They had been waiting for Mommy's arrival. Rachel kissed them but made no attempt to pick them up. Instead, she began leaking tears again.

"Mommy doesn't feel well," JJ told the two of them, though her response disturbed him. Even without any background in mental diseases, JJ could see how depressed she was, even worse than when she was suffering from postpartum depression following Ariel's birth. He helped Rachel inside and introduced her to the nurse he'd hired for the duration—however long it took.

He did not tell Rachel that Ms. Ellsworth had worked with psychiatric patients, and he had instructed Ms. Ellsworth not to reveal it. JJ thought a nurse with Ms. Ellsworth's experience might help assure that Rachel did not harm herself and might even assume a constructive role in her recovery.

Rachel asked no questions. She allowed herself to be put to bed, accepting the assistance Ms. Ellsworth provided in removing her clothing and putting on her nightgown. JJ told Ms. Miller, their nanny, to keep the children out of Rachel's room until further notice.

JJ had not been to the office since the rape. He simply had to go.

But he stayed only long enough to hand every pending matter over to his associate counsel and the outside law firm where Rachel's cousin Dev now worked. He told his father and uncle that he was taking an indefinite leave of absence. He felt he was needed at home, and he was certainly right. Although, at Ms. Ellsworth's suggestion, he would be using a bedroom on another floor, he spent most of the daylight hours at Rachel's side, breaking away now and then to play with Daniel and Ariel.

Rachel acted as if she were still in the hospital. She had no interest in getting out of bed, no interest in eating. She allowed the children to come into her room, even to climb into bed with her. But she cried when they did so, and they were soon taken away. She made an effort to smile at JJ when he held her hand or kissed her. But the smiles were not a success. The muscles moved in the right direction but didn't quite get there. Against every intention, JJ began to feel impatient with her. However, Ms. Ellsworth seemed to have all the patience in the world. She urged Rachel out of bed in the morning and helped her freshen up. She would not let her go back to bed but instead guided her into a soft chair across the room. She brought breakfast in, and though Rachel ate almost nothing, she took her upstairs to the kitchen table for lunch and dinner. She bathed her at night and put her to bed.

After several days, Rachel saw more of the children and made an effort to show them that she loved them. She tried very hard not to cry when they were nearby. Mostly, however, Ms. Miller kept them occupied in their part of the house, and JJ went to them several times a day. They were becoming increasingly insistent on being with their mother, Daniel particularly. It was obvious that Rachel wasn't yet up to playing with the kids or to cuddling them for more than a minute or two. Ms. Miller—Adelaide—hadn't been with them long enough to be able to soothe and control them the way Hillary could. JJ had the inspiration of turning the children over for a few days to Rachel's parents and her sister, Rebecca. The kids would benefit from being around their grandparents and their aunt, and Hanna, Hillel, and Rebecca might be distracted for a time from their constant focus on Rachel's situation. It turned out to be a godsend not just for Hanna, Hillel, and Rebecca, but also for Ruth and Aaron. Instead of sitting off to the side, they had been given something useful to do.

Dev had returned to Denver from Boulder and was again at work, though having a hard time concentrating on legal matters. Yalie had gone back to Washington, though her heart was in Colorado and she simply could not chase away the image of Rachel lying vacant-eyed in her hospital bed. If she could do Rachel any good, she would have quit her job in an instant.

But what Rachel needed was professional help.

Three days after her return from the hospital, JJ packed Rachel into the car and drove her to Dr. Alicia Cohen's office. She was the psychotherapist whom Dr. Drucker identified as the best on the list of three he provided.

Rachel knew where JJ was taking her. She didn't resist, but neither did she expect to be helped. She didn't care—about that or much else. The kids, yes, but being with them was an ordeal. Her family, yes, but she didn't want to see them yet. Her best friends, yes, but she didn't want to talk with them. Going to the psychotherapist was simply a chore she had to perform, willing or not.

Dr. Cohen's two-room suite was in a building close to the University of Colorado Medical Center. The suite had a small waiting room and a larger consulting room. The waiting room contained a leather couch, several chairs, a coffee machine on a long table under a wall cabinet, and alongside it, a small refrigerator. There was no receptionist.

After a few minutes wait, the door to the inner office opened, and Dr. Cohen came out. She was in her forties, a small woman, under five feet two inches in height, narrow-shouldered, small-busted, neatly dressed in a two-piece blue suit and a white blouse, serious in manner but with smile lines around her eyes and mouth. She had already spoken with Dr. Drucker and knew the essentials of Rachel's case. She'd also gotten a report from the nurse, Ms. Ellsworth.

"Please come in, Ms. Rothschild," she said, motioning subtly for JJ to remain in the waiting room. Dr. Cohen's desk stood to one side of the room. Two upholstered club chairs sat facing one another, with a low coffee table between them. Two other chairs in contrasting blue and green prints were arranged against the wall opposite the desk, and there was a couch beneath a high window in the far wall through which the sun was shining brightly. Rachel took one of the facing chairs. Before sitting down herself, Dr. Cohen asked if Rachel would like coffee, decaf, tea, or a soft drink. Rachel shook her head.

"May I call you Rachel?" Dr. Cohen asked.

Rachel nodded.

"I know you've been through a very traumatic experience, Rachel. I'm here to help you understand your feelings about what happened. Is that okay with you?"

Rachel was already sobbing. Quietly. She nodded again.

"You'll be coming to see me three times a week for a while, but I'm not going to push you to talk when you don't want to. Okay?" It was an interjection, not a question. "I want you to feel completely safe in this room. I will not repeat anything that's said here to another living soul. I'm not allowed to. I'm here to listen to anything you want to say. I may ask you some questions from time to time, but that's only to help you deal with issues, to think them through. Okay?"

Dr. Cohen's professional voice was a silky contralto, soothing, almost hypnotic. Indeed, hypnosis was one of the techniques at her disposal, though she employed it only with the subject's consent. Instinct already told her that she might need to recommend it to Rachel down the road. The young woman's slumped shoulders and expressionless eyes screamed depression. She hadn't yet uttered a single syllable. Speaking about anything important might be weeks away. Getting her to talk at all would not be easy.

Trying to engage her, Dr. Cohen began with routine personal questions. Where was she born? Where did she grow up? Who were her parents? Did she have brothers and sisters? Where did she go to school? What did she study? How did she come to Denver?

Dr. Cohen already knew Rachel's personal history. She had spent an hour on the phone with JJ getting the details. But this was the easiest way to draw a new patient into conversation. Beginning with pain was rarely feasible. And in Rachel's case, it was evident that the bridge to open communication would not be easily constructed.

So Dr. Cohen asked, and Rachel began answering, softly, mostly in half sentences, offering minimal information. The first visit passed with Dr. Cohen learning nothing she did not already know. When their time together was over, Dr. Cohen escorted Rachel back to the waiting room. The only thing she said was, "Please come at the same time on Wednesday, Rachel."

On the drive home, JJ asked Rachel how it went. "It was okay," Rachel said. "She's nice." It wasn't much of an answer, but it was the most informative pair of sentences that Rachel had strung together since the rape. JJ felt unreasonably hopeful.

On Tuesday, JJ called Dr. Cohen to arrange an appointment for himself. JJ left his cell phone number. She called him an hour and a half later. "I understand you want to see me, Mr. Weiner. I don't think that's a good idea. I would have to tell Rachel, and knowing that you were seeing me might make it more difficult for us to communicate. It's going to be hard enough as it is to get her to open up."

"That's not the purpose of my wanting to see you, Dr. Cohen," JJ said. "I want to ask you about your diagnosis and what you see as the course of Rachel's therapy."

"I'll tell you all I can tell you over the phone, Mr. Weiner. She's seriously depressed. That much is obvious. My hunches—and that's all they are at this stage—are that she's internalized feelings of shame, irrational as that may be. I have no doubt that she's completely lost her sense of security. I suspect she's lost her desire for intimacy—and I don't mean sexual intimacy, though that, too. Will she come out of the depression? Yes, I think so. How soon? I can't say. The antidepressants Dr. Drucker prescribed will help, but restoring her emotional health will take a long time. Will she readmit you and your children into her life? I think so. But that, too, may take a while. Weeks, maybe months. Will the two of you be able to have sex again? Yes, but please don't push it. Hug her when she lets you, kiss her, tell her you love her. It'll come when it comes. Will she ever be the person she was? Maybe, maybe not. I won't know that for a while. That's about all I can tell you."

"Thanks, Dr. Cohen," JJ said. "That helps a lot. Can I check back from time to time?"

"May I speak frankly, Mr. Weiner?"

"Of course."

"Once Rachel begins to talk, it's going to be very painful for her. Facing the reality of what happened will in some ways repeat the trauma. That's a necessary part of the recovery process. I can't tell you about any of it, not one word. That's the compact every psychotherapist makes with every patient, but it's especially necessary in this case. I can't do Rachel any good unless she has complete confidence in my discretion. When she's ready to admit me into her most private thoughts, I wouldn't want her to hold back because she thinks I'm talking to you on the side. You have to understand that when a woman is raped, her feelings toward the men in her life become very confused. In this case, because Rachel's rapists were taking revenge on you by destroying her, her feelings toward you are likely to be very complicated for a while. She doesn't blame you, I'm sure, but some part of her probably holds you responsible."

"Oh, God," JJ said in a choked voice.

"I don't mean to upset you, Mr. Weiner. But you need to know the truth."

"I understand. It hurts a lot, but I appreciate your candor."

"Let me leave it this way with you, Mr. Weiner. My experience with other patients in somewhat similar circumstances is that a time comes when there are things they want their families to know but can't bring themselves to say. When Rachel and I have made some real progress, I'll ask her if she'd like me to talk with you. I'll tell her that if she gives me permission, I'll call you, and if she doesn't, I won't. I hope that's satisfactory to you. It's the best I can offer. I do have one suggestion, however. Obviously, the situation is very hard on you. You might want to get help yourself from another psychotherapist. I have some colleagues I could recommend."

The idea did not appeal to JJ. But he said he would think about it.

Later in the week, after Rachel's second visit with Dr. Cohen, JJ took her to see Dr. Drucker. Dr. Drucker remained in charge of Rachel's medication. The visit didn't last very long. Dr. Drucker asked her how her depression was coming. He asked her how she liked Dr. Cohen. He asked about the children. He asked how she and JJ were doing. He asked whether she'd gone anywhere other than to the doctors or had any visitors. He asked her a question about current events. None of the questions were mere chitchat. Dr. Drucker taped the answers, which were given in as few words as possible. He intended to ask the same questions every time he saw her. Changes in her responses would provide a measurement of progress.

On this first posthospital visit, Dr. Drucker noted in her file that there had been very little improvement in Rachel's mood. She remained withdrawn, had essentially walled off the people closest to her, showed zero interest in the outside world. He increased her dosage.

On the third trip to Dr. Cohen's, Rachel finally said something about her nightmares. It was the first meaningful reference to the events of the rape. In one recurrent dream, she was back in the trunk of her car and yet somehow also at the wheel. She kept calling for JJ or her father—sometimes one, sometimes the other. But they weren't there, or they wouldn't come. The dream was pervaded by a sense of impending doom.

Dr. Cohen asked Rachel why she thought she was having this dream.

Rachel responded, "Because that's what happened to me."

Dr. Cohen asked, "What happened, Rachel?"

Rachel said, "You know, the two men."

Dr. Cohen, wanting her to be more specific, continued, "JJ? Your father?"

Rachel said, "No, the other men."

Dr. Cohen clarified, "The men who raped you?"

It was the first time in three sessions that the word "rape" had been used.

Rachel burst into tears. "Yes, them."

Dr. Cohen allowed her to cry for a minute or so, then changed the subject. She did not want to press too hard.

She went back to Rachel's personal history.

Rachel was at the University of Colorado now, a beginning freshman, rooming with her cousin, Yalie. She mentioned the drunk driving episode. She was reliving her emotions. Until now, Rachel had been answering Dr. Cohen's questions with a bare recital of facts, offering nothing about her inner life. The experience at CU was Rachel's first personal trauma. Her Uncle El's death in an auto accident was a terrible memory, but it hadn't happened directly to her. All the personal angst of her childhood and teenage years seemed serious enough when it was happening, but she barely remembered any of that now.

Dr. Cohen let her talk. Suddenly the words were flowing. Rachel's recollections seemed to be a million miles away from the topic that brought her to Dr. Cohen until she began talking about her date's hoping to have sex with her. "He wanted to fuck me," Rachel said angrily. "That's why he got me drunk. He wanted to fuck me. Bastard." Her cheeks were hot. She was crying again.

Dr. Cohen handed her a tissue. It took Rachel some time to regain her composure. Dr. Cohen thought about ending the session there. But she waited.

Rachel moved on to her arrest and being held in a jail cell. She recalled Uncle Aaron's coming to get her and the phony plea bargain that he and her father arranged with the prosecutor.

"How do you feel about that now, Rachel?"

"I don't know. I didn't have to do what they made me do. I hated them for it when I found out."

"Do you still hate them for it?"

"I don't know." Pause. "I guess not. They did it because they thought it was best for me. Maybe they were right. I don't know." She shed some more tears.

"Was it hard on you not being able to drive for two years?"

"Sure, it was hard. Living in Santa Monica? Going to UCLA? You can't go anywhere in Los Angeles without a car. The bus system stinks. I spent hours on street corners waiting for my bus to arrive." Her voice had an angry bite now.

Dr. Cohen made a note: "Anger. Good sign."

Dr. Cohen asked, "Do you blame your father and uncle for that?"

"I don't know." She was quiet for a moment. "I don't know. Maybe I needed to go through it. I've never been drunk again. I'm a careful driver. They meant it for my own good."

"Do you think your father loves you?"

Rachel choked up. She closed her eyes. She remembered Daddy hugging her when she got off the plane from Denver after her accident, and then the lecture she got from him on the way home from the airport..

"Yes." She could barely speak. Her voice was a whisper.

Dr. Cohen made another note and asked, "Do you love *him?*"

Rachel nodded vigorously. She couldn't speak at all. She was sobbing softly.

Dr. Cohen waited for her to regain a measure of equilibrium.

"Tell me a little about your community service time."

Rachel relived her experience at the drug clinic with Shayanna Lee. Tears fell as she spoke, but all the anger she felt then spilled out in a torrent. She was still talking when the session came to an end.

Dr. Cohen regretted having to interrupt her. This had been a breakthrough session. Rachel wasn't ready to confront the rape, but there would not be much difficulty getting her to talk about her life—at least up to when she married JJ. Those feelings remained to be determined.

Hillel and Hanna, meanwhile, had returned to the West Coast. Immediately after the rape, Noah and Marla Shifrin canceled their plans for a big September wedding. Instead, they would be married in mid-October in the rabbi's study with just the parents and siblings, except Rachel, in attendance. They could not postpone it further. Marla was scheduled to reprise her role as Cherubino in Kansas City in early December, and she had to be available before then for rehearsals. Rebecca, who intended to stay on in Denver, would fly to San Jose on Saturday afternoon for the Sunday morning wedding. She would return to Denver Sunday night. She was ready to quit her accounting job in any case, and caring for Daniel and Ariel was a lot more important than anything else she might do.

JJ was grateful for Rebecca's decision to return. The children didn't need him quite so urgently when she was around. Besides, Rebecca could help by driving Rachel to her appointments. JJ had to go back to work. His own sanity required it. He might have stayed away from the office indefinitely if he were helping Rachel, but he wasn't. She tensed up now every time he hugged her.

Rachel didn't mean to reject JJ's embraces, but she couldn't help it. She knew she would eventually have to take JJ back into her bed, but the thought of sexual intimacy terrified her. Though he knew he shouldn't react this way, JJ felt rejected. He was beginning to resent Rachel's lack of concern for others … okay, for him.

Rachel was unable to give the children all the attention they deserved. Rebecca, JJ, and Ms. Miller were doing nearly all the parenting, and the strain of that was also beginning to tell on JJ. He needed to be playful for them, and playful was his least natural mood. If it hadn't been for Rebecca, he didn't know how he would have been able to handle it.

Rachel was also grateful for Rebecca's presence, but she was still the younger sister and Rachel didn't tell her a thing. The one who did the most good for Rachel was her cousin Dev. She'd taken to visiting Rachel almost every evening after work, sometimes with Mark, more often alone. Although she was in the earliest stage of pregnancy with her first child, Dev was determined not to let that interfere with helping

Rachel. Her sympathy for her cousin was limitless, unlike JJ's. Dev was the older sister Rachel never had, and Rachel confided in her. She was the only person to whom Rachel confided her private thoughts, things she was not yet prepared to tell Dr. Cohen. Dev wasn't judgmental, didn't hector Rachel with advice. She carefully refrained from comment about Rachel's continuing weight loss.

Hanna, who'd taken to flying back and forth regularly between Los Angeles and Denver, was always trying to coax her daughter into eating something. Rebecca did the same. Grandma Bess, who came by a couple times a week, reminded Rachel all the time that she was "nothing but skin and bones." Rachel knew they meant well, but it annoyed her nonetheless. Everything and everyone annoyed Rachel—except Dev.

Dev gave her a shoulder to lean on and cry on. And she offered love without the slightest hint of criticism. Rachel didn't want other people around her—not JJ, not Hanna, not Rebecca, not Grandma Bess, not the kids. Only Dev.

Sometimes Rachel asked Dev to spend the night and to sleep with her in the same bed. Although Mark was at home waiting for her, Dev never declined. She simply called Mark and said she would be staying with Rachel. Those were the moments when Rachel was readiest to uncover more of the horror she carried inside. Rachel spilled a lot of tears on those nights, but they were also more therapeutic than most of her sessions with Dr. Cohen.

Rachel hadn't yet been able to tell Dr. Cohen directly about the rape, but one night she disclosed the worst to Dev. She was no longer confused about the details of what happened. She remembered it all vividly, almost as if it were happening now. She talked about the tearing of her tissue as they entered her anally, about the release of sperm into her body, about the punches and the slaps and the twisted nipples, about the thrusts into her dry vagina, about being forced to suck their penises, about the streams of urine in her face and all over her body, about trying to find help without a scrap of clothing on her body and her hands cuffed behind her.

Dev, of course, knew the clinical facts. The emergency room physicians told JJ, and JJ in his anguish told the other members of the family. But the brutal details were hammerblows. Dev was in agony, fighting hard not to break down herself. She let Rachel tell everything she wanted to tell at her own pace and comforted her as best she could. Rachel's head was on Dev's shoulder as they lay there side by side. Rachel sobbed herself to sleep with Dev patting her lovingly. And all the while, Dev's eyes and cheeks were wet with her own tears.

As in a heat exchange, Dev had absorbed her cousin's pain, and Rachel felt a little better for having told her cousin the worst.

Dev wondered whether she should let JJ know that Rachel had told her about the night of the rape. Would he feel excluded because Rachel chose Dev to confide in? She worried about it for the better part of two days. It was encouraging news that Rachel was beginning to talk. So Dev decided she should tell JJ. Should she omit the awful details? That was a harder question. Was Rachel intending for her to be the conduit? Was telling JJ a responsibility she had to bear for Rachel's sake? Dev decided she shouldn't conceal a thing.

Now it was Dev's turn to sob as she spilled it all out and JJ's turn to feel the fierce pain of listening, not to the clinical facts, but to the feelings of the victim. Rebecca, who was sitting there as Dev told the story, shut her eyes to make the world disappear and gritted her teeth to prevent herself from crying aloud.

When Dev finished, JJ was crying and hanging onto Dev like the survivor of a storm at sea grasping at a life raft. She was his support almost as much as she was Rachel's. Rebecca had her arms around Dev from behind.

Dev returned home and cried to Mark and, by telephone, to Yalie. But she needed to be strong for her parents and for Uncle Hillel and Aunt Hanna. Above all, she could not let on to JJ, and certainly not to Rachel, how much of a toll this was taking on her own emotions.

Three months after the rape, Rachel was still avoiding the subject during her sessions with Dr. Cohen. She'd moved on to her relationship with JJ, but she said far less about her love for him than about her feeling that he wanted to control everything. The matters she dwelt on were the decisions he made without her and the way he directed her life.

Did she credit or blame him for pushing her into journalism? She credited him, Rachel said, but she didn't say it immediately or convincingly.

Would she have preferred to have married him right after she graduated from Berkeley and joined him in Palo Alto? She said yes. She said no.

What did she do between college and marriage? Rachel mentioned *L.A. Beat*. Did she regret having the opportunity to begin her career in journalism? Well, no.

So, once she moved to Denver, her husband pushed her to go to back to work. Did she regret her experience at *In the Rockies*? Again, no.

Then why was she bothered about JJ's desire to see her pursue a career? She couldn't answer because she couldn't explain. She couldn't explain because she didn't know the answer.

Maybe it was her depression. Maybe it was because she'd lost control of her life. Maybe it was because she couldn't imagine anything beyond the moment.

She hadn't told Dr. Cohen about the two times JJ spanked her, though it was there at the center of how she was feeling about JJ ever since the rape. She was ashamed of those episodes and angry at JJ because of them, angrier even than she was when they happened. She had to confront it. She knew that. But she was not ready.

Instead, she talked about her high school sexual experiences, how unsatisfactory they were. She talked about fending off sexual advances in college. She didn't say anything about wanting sex with JJ before they got married. She didn't confess to the lust that possessed her during the early days, weeks, months of their marriage.

She was passive, not only in the retelling but in the moment. She had allowed JJ back into their bed, but not because she wanted him there. It had reached the point where it was "an issue." The first few times he tried to make love to her, she said, "I'm not ready, JJ." But she knew that could not continue. She allowed him to hug her and caress her. Finally, one night, she allowed him to spread her legs and try to enter her. She was totally dry. She would not allow him to finger her. He used his tongue to lubricate her as he'd done many times before in their marriage. All the while, she lay there, almost rigid, her fingernails dug into the palms of her hands. When he inserted his penis into her vagina, she began sobbing so violently that her entire body shook.

JJ should have stopped. But he was beyond stopping. So he continued to orgasm while Rachel lay trembling beneath him, wanting only for it to be over. And when it was, she had no words. All she could think of was how filthy she felt with his semen oozing out of her.

JJ lay there beside her, staring at the ceiling, scarcely able himself to avoid weeping.

JJ tried to figure what he might do to help Rachel's emotional condition. He discussed it with Rebecca, but she was at as much of a loss as her brother-in-law. Blocked from approaching Dr. Cohen, JJ asked Dev.

"She's falling apart … fallen apart," Dev responded. "I don't know, JJ. I'm worried about her sanity. I wish I knew what to suggest."

Despite the way their previous talk ended, JJ put in another call to Dr. Cohen. When she returned it, she did not rebuke him for asking. What she said was, "I wish I could tell you something useful, Mr. Weiner. Rachel's still not there. She isn't ready to talk about the rape."

"She's told her cousin Dev about it."

"Oh? How did that happen?"

"They're very close. Dev comes to visit her almost every day, and sometimes Rachel asks her to spend the night. It was during one of those nights. Rachel told her about it from start to finish, all the grim details."

"If you know, did Rachel's cousin put pressure on her to talk?"

"No, no. Dev's not like that. She's just there for Rachel. She's a lot better with her than I am. Rachel started talking, and the story rushed out of her as if a dam had broken. She cried the whole time, but she didn't stop talking. Dev told me she didn't ask Rachel a single question. It took everything she had just to listen to it."

"It's good that she told her cousin. In fact, it's very good. It means she *can* talk about it under the right conditions. It's important that she and I reach the stage where she's willing to tell me, so I can help her deal with it. Right now, that looks to be a long way off. She's still working on unresolved feelings about her past."

"Such as?"

"I'm sorry, Mr. Weiner. I've told you before. I can't go into that."

Dr. Cohen was ready to end the conversation, but JJ had something else he wanted to tell her. It was extremely personal.

"Rachel and I had sex for the first time a few nights ago. Or maybe the right way to say it is that I had sex, and Rachel was there while it happened. It was awful. She burst out crying. It made me feel like I was raping her."

"I'm not surprised. Rachel's reaction is one we see in a lot of rape victims. And your feelings are exactly what I'd expect. Rachel is a damaged person, Mr. Weiner. I may have said this to you before, I don't remember. But I'll say it again. Rape is trauma. The worst rape is father-daughter rape. That's the absolute worst. But Rachel's rape was particularly brutal—and it was, in a sense, impersonal, a revenge aimed at you but inflicted on her. She isn't going to recover from it as quickly as you'd like. There's nothing you can do to hurry the process except love her and support her. And sometimes that's not easy to do. Maybe it's not easy most of the time. Just try to remember that the rejection of sexual intimacy is a normal reaction to an abnormal experience. Think about what it would be like if Rachel had been in a terrible automobile accident and you could see all the damage that had been done, and all you could do is wait for it to heal. The difference here is that the physical damage from the rape is no longer visible. The damage is on the inside, and though you can't see it, it's got to heal like a broken bone, only you can't bandage it or put it in a cast, and it will take longer to heal than any broken bone ever takes."

"I understand what you're saying, Doctor. I'll do my best."

"I've got to go now, Mr. Weiner. My next appointment is waiting. But thank you for calling and telling me what you've told me. It suggests some avenues for me to explore."

Telling Dr. Cohen that he felt like a rapist while having sex with Rachel eased JJ's sense of guilt. He thought *It must be the relief Catholics experience after confessing their sins.* He made a vow to himself. He would not try to make love to Rachel again until she was ready.

JJ searched for ways to get Rachel reengaged with the world outside her bedroom and the office of her analyst. He suggested going back to work part-time. She said she wasn't ready. He suggested returning to school. She was not interested.

What about ten days in Vail with her cousins over Christmas and New Year's? They'd take Dev and Mark along and Rebecca, of course, leaving the children at home with Ms. Miller. Maybe Yalie and Richie would agree to come.

Rachel consented, but without enthusiasm. She wasn't interested in skiing. She could not focus on anything but her agony.

Dev was too far gone in her pregnancy to go skiing. She didn't have to be told, however, that this trip was about Rachel, not about skiing. So she and Mark would certainly come. Yalie said yes for the same reason. Richie, she reported, couldn't take the time. The truth was that being around Rachel at the moment was likely to bring more pain than pleasure, and it was Yalie's obligation, not Richie's.

So they gathered at the lodge in Vail, and there was a desperate attempt at gaiety led by Yalie. She was determined to get Rachel out on the ski slopes. They'd been skiing together since they were little, and Yalie knew that she could persuade Rachel if anyone could. Yalie was irresistible when she was in motion. Her gaiety was infectious, even when it was phony. Dev joined her in urging Rachel to head for the slopes.

Dev, rubbing her stomach, said, "I *can't* go skiing. Alexis won't let me. So, you'll have to go skiing for me."

Rachel allowed herself to be persuaded. JJ drove Rachel, Yalie, Mark, and Rebecca down to the lifts, joining them after he parked the car. The five of them rode the chairs to the top of the mountain, where they strapped on their skis to start the descent. Yalie and Rachel were expert skiers. The two cousins would ski the expert course, with Yalie deliberately trailing behind to keep an eye on Rachel. JJ, who might have gone with them, decided it was best to join Mark and Rebecca on the intermediate slopes.

Rachel was about halfway down the hill when she lost her concentration, wrong-footed a turn, went one way with her leg while her body went another, skied out of control across the course boundary, glanced off a small tree, and landed hard. Yalie saw it all happen. She was the first person to reach Rachel, who was lying on her side curled into a ball and moaning.

Yalie quickly asked, "Are you okay, Rache?" .

Rachel shook her head.

"What's wrong?"

"I did something bad to my knee."

"Which one?"

"Left." She moaned in pain.

By now around a dozen skiers had stopped to offer help.

One of those who had stopped was a nurse. She took charge, dispatching another skier to get the ski patrol. Rachel was halfway sitting up now, her teeth gritted against the pain. The nurse asked her to point out the location of the injury.

"There." Rachel made a feeble gesture in the direction of her left knee, which was bent and couldn't be straightened. The nurse gently touched the area, feeling the knee through the ski pants.

"She probably tore the ligaments. And I suspect she may have damaged her patella." Speaking to Yalie, she added, "We've got to get her to the hospital. She'll need surgery."

Rachel groaned. "My leg hurts, too."

The nurse felt again, and Rachel let out a piercing cry. "She's also got a fracture below the knee."

The ski patrol arrived to take Rachel down the hill, strapped to a flat board. She screamed when they lifted her and screamed again when they put her down.

Yalie followed the ski patrol down, trying to spot JJ, Mark, or Rebecca along the way. No such luck.

There was an ambulance at the bottom waiting for Rachel. No, Yalie couldn't come along.

Yalie needed to borrow a cell phone. She'd call Dev back at the lodge and ask Dev to pick her up so they could both go to the hospital. How to let JJ, Mark, and Rebecca know what had happened and where they'd gone? Maybe they'd show up before Dev arrived. What she would do if they failed to show, she didn't know. She told herself *I'll burn that bridge when I come to it*—a favorite expression that usually caused her to smile. But not this time.

Dev was on her way when Yalie spotted JJ. She told him what had happened and said, "If you'll tell me where you've parked the car, I'll wait here for Mark and Rebecca. You go with Dev."

JJ was stunned and too upset to think clearly. But he knew Yalie would need precise directions if she was going to find the car, and he tried to formulate them. Finally, he said, "This is stupid, Yalie. I know where the car is, but I can't tell you it's in the third row opposite the fifth pillar on the second floor of the garage. You'll wander all over the place looking for it. So you go with Dev, and I'll bring Rebecca and Mark. We're all going to end up sitting in a waiting room. So what's the difference if I'm there ten or fifteen minutes later?"

When Dev and Yalie arrived at the hospital, Rachel was already out of X-ray and being readied for surgery. By the time JJ showed up with Rebecca and Mark, half an hour had passed, and Rachel had been wheeled into the operating room.

The surgeon found them hours later, after the surgery was completed. He reported that the ligaments in Rachel's knee were badly torn, her patella was cracked, and her leg was fractured in two places below the knee. He'd repaired the ligaments. The leg fractures were uncomplicated, but she would be wearing a cast. Recovery from injuries would take a long time: a couple of days in the hospital, six weeks on crutches, then long and arduous therapy, primarily for the knee.

Only two people at a time were allowed in Rachel's room. When she returned from the recovery room, Yalie and JJ were waiting. She was barely conscious. JJ kissed her, and she gave a weak nod to acknowledge it. Her knee was heavily bandaged, and there was an IV in her arm with a drip of medication to block the pain. A nurse motioned for them to sit down so Rachel could sleep.

When she awakened again, JJ was standing there holding her hand. "Hi there, Klutz. How are you doing?"

She attempted a smile, but it ended in a grimace. Despite the pain medication, it hurt. She looked at Yalie and thought *It's your fault. I didn't want to go skiing. You made me.* And then she thought *Yalie loves me. She was trying to get me out of myself.* And then she thought *I'm to blame. I wasn't paying attention.* And then she thought *As a human being, I'm really a fucking failure.* And that's the thought that stuck.

JJ arranged to bring Rachel back to Denver in a plane equipped to handle a stretcher. An ambulance would meet the plane to take them home. Dev, Rachel's one-woman support team, accompanied them. Yalie would drive JJ's car to Denver and then catch a flight to Washington. She had to get back. Mark would drive back in his car, bringing Rebecca.

Now that she was home, Rachel's mood was blacker than ever. She felt physical pain along with emotional pain. She faced months of physical therapy. She would be making regular visits to an orthopedist that the doctor in Vail referred her to. She was already seeing a psychoanalyst as well as a psychiatrist. She was doing little for her children. She was no good for JJ. She was sucking Dev's blood to keep herself alive. No longer worth it, she felt.

At bedtime one January night, she wrote a long letter of apology to her dear ones, took the almost full bottle of pain pills sitting on her bedside table, swallowed them one by one, and gradually fell into oblivion. The last thought that crossed her mind was of her friend Lynetta Pearson, who had died such an untimely death. Would she be mourned the way everyone who knew her mourned Lynetta? It was 11:07 p.m.

JJ, who was again sleeping in a bedroom the next level up because of Rachel's injuries, entered her room shortly afterward to make sure she was covered and to kiss her good night for a second time. With a stab of terror in his gut, he realized that Rachel had attempted suicide. He called 911, began mouth-to-mouth resuscitation, and screamed for help. Rebecca, not yet asleep, heard him and came running.

Soon everyone but Ariel was up. Daniel was crying hysterically, and Adelaide Miller was trying without success to comfort him. He went to his Aunt Rebecca and climbed into her lap. Rebecca was in a panic, but for Daniel's sake she could not fall apart. JJ also needed her. He told Rebecca he had to go to the hospital with Rachel. He wanted her to stay behind for the kids. He'd call as soon as he had anything to report.

The medics arrived within ten minutes. They gave her a shot to rouse her. On the way to the hospital, they put her on a respirator and started an IV. In the hospital emergency room, Rachel's stomach was pumped, and she was restored unwillingly to life. By the time she was out of the emergency room and being wheeled on a gurney to a hospital bed upstairs, Dev and Mark had arrived. Dev was crying and at the same time trying to comfort JJ, who was so badly shaken that he was ready to bang his head against the wall. If he hadn't gone to Rachel's room, she'd still be there in her bed, no longer breathing. His beautiful young wife would be dead, and his two children would be motherless.

Yalie was on her way to Denver from Washington. Mark called her with the news; Dev was too upset to talk. Yalie said it was her fault. She was the one who talked Rachel into going skiing when she didn't want to.

Drs. Cohen and Drucker had been consulted, and after a conversation between them, it was agreed that Rachel should be transferred to another, larger hospital and admitted to its psychiatric ward.

"For how long?" JJ inquired.

"Until we're sure she's not going to try this again," Dr. Drucker said.

Rachel remained in the psychiatric ward for two and a half weeks. A psychiatric resident visited with her for an hour every day. Dr. Drucker stopped by every weekday morning. This was his territory, not Dr. Cohen's. Rachel was also being sent in a wheelchair for physical therapy twice a day.

She was no longer considered a suicide threat. She had stopped saying that she wanted to die. She told the hospital's doctor that she wanted to live. But she was still a wreck and not ready to be discharged. She apologized to JJ, Dev, Yalie, and Rebecca for the scare she gave them. She apologized to Hanna and Hillel, who flew in from Los Angeles as soon as they got the news—a week after it happened. JJ would have kept it from them altogether if that were possible. But they were accustomed to talking to Rachel several times a week; and Rebecca, who'd been taking their calls, couldn't keep saying that she was at the doctor's or at therapy or taking a bath. She simply ran out of credible lies, and JJ came on the phone and told them the truth.

Jess Sherman also knew. True to the promise she made right after the rape, Dev kept Jess informed, even about this latest terrible development. Again, there was nothing Jess, Laura, and Arlie could do to help. Only JJ was allowed to visit Rachel. Yes, Dev knew Jess would do anything for Rachel. No, really, there was nothing to be done, nothing. Dev had also talked Yalie into going back to Washington. There was nothing she could do to help, either.

"No, it's not your fault," Dev told Yalie. "Yes, it is." "No, it's not." "Yes, it is." "No, it's not." The conversation was a long one.

Hanna and Hillel were staying at the house in Golden and spending most of the day with Rebecca and their grandchildren. Almost five months had passed since the rape. Daniel and Ariel saw their mother infrequently. When JJ was with them, he was always distracted. Adelaide Miller hadn't been around them long enough to have formed a complete bond, but she was thoroughly professional and able to satisfy their essential requirements. Rebecca, however, bathed them in love, which was their biggest need. Having Hanna and Hillel around also helped the children, and having the children around helped Hanna and Hillel.

But Hanna and Hillel were more essential to Daniel and Ariel than to Rachel. Rachel's pillar was Dev. JJ persuaded Dr. Drucker to allow her to visit Rachel in the psychiatric ward, and Dev stopped by the hospital every weekday evening and stayed until told she must leave. She came for hours on the weekend. One day she brought exciting news. Yalie was returning home to Colorado in March, maybe for good. Through her political connections, she'd gotten a job as deputy to the U.S. Attorney in Denver. In a few years, Yalie was intending to enter politics and run for public office. Her boyfriend, Richie, would be joining her, though he didn't yet have a job. And, more exciting news, Yalie and Richie were engaged. They would be getting married in Boulder in September.

Rachel smiled the first real smile she'd displayed since the rape. She was going to get better, she told Dev, because she wanted to be in Yalie's bridal party. The enthusiasm, while temporary, was the most encouraging sign from Rachel that Dev had seen in five months. That was almost exactly how long Dev had been pregnant, and this ought to have been a very happy time as life quickened within her. Instead, because of what happened to Rachel, it had been the most trying period that she'd experienced—ever. Being Rachel's rock was extremely hard on Dev, though she never let on. She'd held her own emotions in so long, except around Mark, that they were building up like steam in a boiler, and when she let them loose, somebody was going to get scalded. She should have been wearing a warning sign that said "Danger" in big red letters.

The hospital psychiatrist believed it was now safe to release Rachel, and Dr. Drucker concurred. But he told JJ to empty the medicine cabinet in Rachel's bathroom as a precaution and to keep close watch on her. He wanted JJ to call him at the first sign her depression was getting worse. Dr. Drucker also spoke with Dr. Cohen, relaying his observations. Dr. Drucker would like Dr. Cohen to call Rachel's cousin Dev in for a talk. He knew about Rachel's dependence on Dev from Rachel herself, and he thought Dev might have some insights that Dr. Cohen would find useful.

Hanna and Hillel had spent nearly a month in Denver and needed to go home. They made JJ promise that if something else happened, he wouldn't ever withhold the bad news again. Unless he promised, they would be uneasy every moment. So he promised. Rebecca planned to stay on in Denver. She'd already been at Rachel and JJ's house for close to five months. She expected to be there for as long as she was needed.

The farewell was difficult for Hanna and Hillel. Both tried hard to avoid an excessively emotional display in Rachel's presence. Rachel was the only one who wept. By now that had become her natural reflex. It had little to do with her parents' departure.

The tears began flowing when Hanna and Hillel left Rachel's room and they were telling JJ and Rebecca and, above all, Dev to "take good care of her." Saying good-bye to the children was also tough. Hanna knew how much their presence meant, especially to Danny, who was older and more aware of what he was missing.

"We'll be back soon," Hillel said with false good cheer. "In the meantime, you be good for Ms. Miller, Auntie Becca. and your daddy. Hear?"

Once Hanna and Hillel were gone, Dev agreed to a meeting with Dr. Cohen. She left work early on a Tuesday afternoon and arrived at Dr. Cohen's office, and they began to talk. Dr. Cohen asked Dev to tell her anything that she felt might be helpful in Rachel's treatment. Dev spoke about the night Rachel revealed the details of the rape, and suddenly the boiler burst. Dev began crying harder than she'd ever cried in her life. She was unable to continue the story. All she could do was to shout at the top of her voice, "Those bastards. Those fucking bastards."

Dr. Cohen asked her to lie down on the couch and spoke soothingly to her until Dev subsided. After awhile, she accepted a glass of water and said she was ready to continue. In a flat, exhausted monotone, Dev recited the details that Rachel unloaded on her that night, while Dr. Cohen took notes. Dev's eyes were still leaking, but control had been restored.

When the recital was finished, Dr. Cohen asked how Rachel seemed now, after the hospital stay.

"Okay, I guess," Dev responded thoughtfully "I think the ski accident on top of everything else was just too much for her, and she just caved in. It was very bad for a time after the suicide attempt, but she's back to where she was before the accident. At least that's what I think. That wasn't too good a place, but it's better than where she's been recently."

They were done now. As she got up to leave, Dev said, "I'm sorry I fell apart on you. I couldn't help it. Most of the time, I try not to dwell on the rape. What those bastards did to Rachel was so cruel, so evil, so"—and a phrase from childhood sprang to Dev's lips—"not nice." A mirthless laugh escaped. "I haven't got the words for it, as you can see. If they're ever found, I'd like to see them undergo medieval tortures. Drawing and quartering would be much too easy on them."

Dr. Cohen offered Dev a bit of advice. "I know you do Rachel a world of good and she needs you. But don't go to her this evening. You've had enough for one day. You ought to take a day off now and again. Go away for a weekend with your husband. You won't be able to help Rachel if you stretch yourself past the breaking point. And you'll soon have your baby to worry about. He … "

"She," Dev interrupted, closing her eyes momentarily to let the thought linger.

"She shouldn't have a mother who's courting a nervous breakdown, and that's what you're doing by immersing yourself so totally in Rachel's misery."

"You do it every day for a living."

"No, I don't. I hear a lot of terrible things from my patients, and I sympathize. But I don't have an emotional stake in their troubles. In fact, I wouldn't be able to help them if I did. I've got to be able to maintain my distance. That's what being a professional requires. You're right there with Rachel, and you are fully exposed. It's essential that I not be. We're doing two different things for her. Believe me when I say it. Yours is more difficult."

Dev nodded. "Thanks for the advice. I don't know if I'll be able to follow it. Rachel depends on my being there. I don't know if I can disappoint her."

"I understand. But remember what I said. You won't be able to do a thing for her if you go over the edge."

Perhaps Dr. Cohen was right and Dev shouldn't spend so much time with Rachel. But that was to be decided on another day. Tonight, she'd go to Rachel because Rachel was expecting her and Dev wouldn't disappoint her.

She came to JJ and Rachel's home, determined to get Rachel thinking about Yalie's impending return to the area.

"Yalie called me this morning," she reported. "She and Richie are going to find a house in Boulder. She figures that's where she'll make her political career. After all, she's a native. Richie can't come until after the Senate adjourns for the summer. He's promised to stay on until then. In the meantime, I've asked Yalie to come live with us. Mom and Dad are *so* excited. They're already looking for a place for Yalie and Richie to buy."

Rachel stirred a little out of the lethargy she'd fallen into since returning from the hospital. "That's nice," she said. "Tell Yalie I love her. Tell her I'm waiting for her to take me skiing again."

It was the closest thing to a joke that Rachel had made since the accident, maybe since the rape.

"That's my girl," Dev said, giving her a hug. "And after Alexis is born, we'll celebrate with a purple passion party."

"After which I'll take Yalie for a drive," Rachel replied. She smiled one of her rare smiles, and Dev felt unnaturally pleased.

Rachel's attempt at suicide and her stay in the psychiatric ward left JJ more than ever determined to make her assailants pay for what they did. He talked again with the detectives in charge of her case. They assured him they were still working on it. It was clear they had no idea where the two men were. and the trail wasn't going to grow warmer anytime soon.

JJ decided to act on his own. He went to the Denver office of a large national detective and security agency. He wanted them to find the rapists. "I'll pay your fees and expenses and give you a substantial bonus if you find those motherfuckers. Just let me know every couple of weeks what you're up to and bill me monthly."

The private detectives said they would start by interviewing people who knew Hopkins and Bray. Presumably the police had already located and spoken to family members who either didn't know or wouldn't say where the men went. The private detectives were looking for something else: places the men might have shown an interest in visiting, hobbies that are best pursued in particular areas, a preference for sun or snow, big city life or the wilderness. Hopkins and Bray had not migrated to Pluto. They were somewhere, most likely in the United States since neither of them knew a foreign language, probably working in construction since that's how they were best equipped to earn a living.

It wasn't that the Denver police did not understand how to follow a trail, but Rachel's rape wasn't murder, and the resources of the Federal Bureau of Investigation weren't being deployed. It was just two local detectives with a lot of other things on their plate trying to find two men who covered their tracks extremely well. The agency JJ hired, on the other hand, had offices in a lot of different cities and a financial incentive to find these men.

JJ was obsessed with tracking them down. They had ruined Rachel's life. They were ruining his. They had to suffer. He already had an idea of what he would do if they were found … when they were found.

Rachel went back to seeing Dr. Cohen three times a week, fitted in, around, and between visits to the orthopedist and the physical therapist. Rebecca was her driver.

Rachel resumed telling her life story. She still refused to go near the rape, and Dr. Cohen was trying indirectly to lead her to it.

"I met your cousin," she told Rachel on one visit.

"Oh?"

"She's a lovely young woman. You're lucky to have her here."

"Where did you meet Dev?"

"Dr. Drucker asked me to talk with her."

"Why?"

"Because you talk to her, and she's a sensitive observer."

"What did she tell you?"

"She loves you, you know."

"Yes. Dev's like a big sister to me. She's the most important person in my life right now."

Dev at the moment came ahead of JJ, the children, her parents, Rebecca. She was the rock on which Rachel was trying to reconstruct her sanity.

"Did you see one another often as children?" Dr. Cohen continued.

"Yes. As often as it could be arranged. Her mother is my father's older sister, and we've always spent the holidays together."

"Am I right in remembering that Dev's sister was your roommate in college?"

"Before I got booted out." A rueful smile flickered across Rachel's face and swiftly disappeared.

Dr. Cohen made a note because she had never before seen a smile of any kind from Rachel. She was usually almost expressionless—except when she cried.

"Yes, I remember. Purple passion, as I recall."

Rachel smiled again, and Dr. Cohen made another note.

"Rachel, do you mind if I ask? What do you talk about with Dev?"

"Didn't she tell you?"

"A little, but I'd like to hear it from you."

"Well," said Rachel, "I tell her how I feel. It's not usually a lot of laughs."

"Do you talk about what happened to you?"

Rachel was silent. She took a deep breath and then another. "Yes," she said. "I've told Dev … I've told her everything."

"Was it difficult?"

Rachel's eyes were brimming. She did not want to cry and did not trust herself to speak. She simply nodded.

"Did it help you to tell Dev what happened?"

Rachel's palms were cold. Her breathing became shallow. She looked away and nodded again. Slowly. Reluctantly.

"I can see this is very difficult for you, Rachel. I won't pursue it any further just now. But we've got to come back to it. You understand that, don't you?"

Rachel nodded once more, and now she *was* crying, though silently.

*   *   *

Rebecca was embarrassed by the gratitude JJ displayed over her decision to remain in Denver indefinitely. "Please, JJ," she said. "Rachel needs someone, and I'm the only member of the family that hasn't got other obligations tying me down. I wouldn't be able to live with myself if I walked away."

Rachel just wasn't capable of mothering Daniel and Ariel now, and Rebecca willingly assumed that role. It made her feel useful. She loved the children, and they loved her. She provided them with more emotional support than they could get from Adelaide Miller or, for that matter, from JJ.

She knew she couldn't do what Dev did for Rachel. There was

going to be a huge hole in Rachel's safety net the moment Dev's baby was born. But Rebecca would be there for Rachel in other ways, and by then Yalie would be in town to help.

JJ figured that Rebecca couldn't just be Rachel's companion or act the part of maiden aunt to the kids. She had to have something else to do. He persuaded his father to offer her a responsible job in financial management with Hyman Weiner & Sons. JJ knew that she was interested in the field, and it would give her a chance to gain professional experience while she remained in Denver.

It hadn't yet occurred to Rebecca that she might eventually grow tired of being a caregiver. She hadn't thought that far ahead. But the job offer was a welcome one. Hyman Weiner & Sons was a big operation, and there would be plenty for her to learn. In fact, it would be a much better professional opportunity than any she was likely to find at home this early in her career.

The man she would be working for, the company's senior vice president for financial affairs, told her she would spend the first three months as his assistant—in effect, an intensive training period. He knew that Rebecca was JJ's sister-in-law, but he'd been told to treat her like any other professional.

Although nobody at Hyman Weiner & Sons discussed it openly, everyone, including Rebecca's new boss, had heard rumors that JJ's wife was brutally beaten by two exemployees of the company and that she subsequently attempted suicide. He did not need to be told that Rebecca was in Denver to help. He understood that the job might not always take priority, and he let her know that would be okay.

*   *   *

The date for Yalie's return to Colorado was approaching. Dev was planning a welcome-home party. It started out to be a small family event, but Dev kept adding guests: family friends from Boulder, a couple of high school classmates, roommates at CU after Rachel's sudden departure. Altogether, they would be more than fifty people. She didn't want to take it to a hotel—much too formal. It would be a tight fit at her own house, a very tight fit. Rebecca suggested having it at Rachel and JJ's big home.

Dev thought about that: *Will it be too much for Rachel? Better talk to JJ.*

JJ said it was a great idea. It would give Rachel something to do that was not medical. He would tell her.

"I wish you hadn't agreed," Rachel responded, somewhat petulantly.

"You're doing it for Dev, and you're doing it for Yalie. We can't say no. Besides, Dev's almost ready to calve, and we ought to relieve her of the work of putting it together."

That meant Rachel, not yet fully recovered from her knee and leg injuries, had a caterer to deal with and serving help to arrange. She wanted the place decorated in banners and balloons. Dev vetoed hiring musicians.

"This is a house party, Rache. Can the music. Nobody wants to hear it. Everybody wants to talk. Hell, in this family, we'll all be talking at once."

It was a small joke, and Rachel gave it a small grin. But it was another encouraging sign for Dev to grasp at.

Obeying JJ's instructions to let Rachel do as much of the party planning as possible, Dev agreed to a menu that she considered more elaborate than it should be. They could easily have gotten along with no help, and at most, they could use a bartender. Rachel, however, wasn't concerned about expense. In addition to a bartender, she hired three other people to assist Anna Lopez with handling the food and to do the cleanup. Dev kept her mouth shut.

JJ felt that having a job to do was good for Rachel. There was less *kvetching* going on than he normally had to endure, and he was grateful for that.

The day of Yalie's return to Denver arrived. JJ suggested that Rachel join the welcoming party at the airport. Rebecca would take her. Rachel agreed only because it was Yalie.

She remembered with a start how Yalie and Dev greeted her and JJ when they arrived in Denver to meet his parents. *How many years ago was that? A lifetime. I was so happy then. I'm so miserable now.*

Rachel was weeping when Yalie came out of the plane into the terminal. They might have been happy tears, but they weren't. She was crying for the life she'd lost.

Rachel was the first person Yalie hugged—ahead of her parents, before her sister.

"Hi, sweetheart," she said, kissing her, and Rachel was now bawling. Yalie represented her childhood, her girlhood, all the parts that had flown over the horizon.

Dev, who observed the scene from three feet away, sensed that what Rachel was displaying was not joy but pathology. As Yalie transferred her attention to her parents, Dev came up beside Rachel and squeezed her hand.

"I love you, sweetie," she whispered. "We all love you."

The party was a great success. Even Rachel enjoyed it. She shook off her self-pitying mood and allowed herself to be truly glad that Yalie had returned. She was the one who made the now obligatory joke about purple passion, which Yalie then explained with glee to nonfamily members.

"Rachel and I are a pair of reformed drunks. When she and I were freshmen at CU and living together, we both got skunked on purple passion. She got herself arrested for drunken driving and expelled. I caught hell from my parents and was placed on probation. And now she's blown our cover, and I'm at your mercy. You must not pass this information along to the U.S. Attorney's office. You must not reveal it to the *Denver Post* or the *Rocky Mountain News*. If you do, I'll never eat lunch in this town again. I'm a dead woman."

Rachel joined the hilarity.

Dev thought: *There are things Yalie can do for Rachel that I can't. And this is one of them.*

Dev was grateful on many levels that Yalie had come home. She wanted her baby's aunt close at hand. She was overjoyed to share her parents' hovering attention with her younger sister. Not least, Yalie's easy camaraderie with Rachel was wonderful to see. If anyone could bring pleasure back into Rachel's life, Yalie could. *Me for sympathy, Yalie for fun.*

People began leaving about 10:30 p.m. Ruth and Aaron departed at 11:30. They had to drive back to Boulder. By midnight, the party was down to Yalie, Dev, Mark, JJ, Rebecca, Rachel, and two of Yalie's college classmates. The classmates left at 1:45 a.m. But Yalie said she was ready to party until morning, and JJ and Rebecca were right there with her. Dev fell asleep on the living room couch. Mark was yawning.

Rachel began to wind down. She announced that there were beds for everyone, and she was going to use hers. Off she went.

Dev spent the night on the couch. Mark headed for one of the spare bedrooms, Yalie took another, JJ headed to his and Rebecca to hers. When morning arrived and the children started to make noise in their part of the house, the red-eyed adults slowly gathered in the kitchen for juice and coffee, tired but satisfied. Yalie had been duly welcomed home. Too bad Richie had to miss it. But he would be part of the family for many years to come. For once, even Rachel was looking ahead to good times.

Not a word had been said about celebrating Passover this year. Dev was in the homestretch of pregnancy. Rachel, off crutches, remained in fragile condition emotionally. The unspoken assumption was that they'd skip a year. Surprisingly, Rachel had other ideas.

She hadn't formulated the thought in this fashion, but her main interest was not so much in gathering the family as in finding an occasion to see Jess. Without fully realizing it, she wanted to touch Jess's stability, let it flow through her like an electric current. She hoped to receive her share of the wise and compassionate counsel that Jess gave Laura when Laura was in need.

Dev had been Rachel's only real confidante, and she was about to become a mother. The only other person who might perform a similar function was Jess. They hadn't allowed Jess to come see her; and while they'd talked, she and Jess hadn't really had an extended telephone conversation since it happened. That was how Rachel thought of the rape: *It.* And that was how Rachel thought of the people who made the decisions in her life: *They.* Everyone but Dev was included in *they*, even JJ, even her parents.

Members of the family were surprised that Rachel was up to a big seder in Denver and even more surprised that the intended guest list included her girlfriends. Although the notice was short and she'd have to rearrange an important business meeting, Jess immediately said yes. No one needed to tell her that it was important to Rachel. Laura would also be coming. There was no response from Arlie, though messages had twice been left on her answering machine.

Since no one expected Rachel to be capable of handling arrangements for the seder, Aunt Ruth volunteered, though it was not her primary skill and she was well aware of that. Rebecca said she'd help. The same caterer who delivered food to them in Vail would do so again. Once more, Hanna would fly in early to prepare gefilte fish and charoset. Anna Lopez, who watched very carefully a year ago, would get the ingredients ready.

Aunt Ruth booked a small ballroom for two nights at a downtown hotel. JJ asked Rachel if she would mind extending invitations to Grandma Bess, Herman, and Vera, even to Annalisa and her family. Rachel shrugged her shoulders. Her initial enthusiasm for having a large seder had begun to flag. She almost wished she hadn't gotten it started.

The first seder would be on Friday, April 14. That was less than two weeks off, and still no response from Arlie. JJ called her office on Monday, the third. When JJ identified himself, Arlie was very apologetic. She knew she should have called back, but she just wasn't up to it. She and Seth had recently separated after less than two years of marriage, and she wasn't able to talk to anyone about it or about anything else.

"I can't come, JJ. I wouldn't be good company."

"I'll tell you what I know Rachel would have me say. Of course, you'll come. You're family, Arlie. Everyone will be very angry with me if I allow you to say no."

"I'll only make it worse for Rachel."

"Licking your wounds alone isn't going to save Rachel from pain. You've got that wrong. She wants you and Jess and Laura to come because she needs you guys around her. She's got her own pain to share. That's what friendship is about—supporting one another in good times and in bad times."

"I don't know, JJ."

"Well, I do. You're coming if I have to fly out and bring you back tucked under my arm like a sack of flour, a very small sack of flour." It was a feeble joke.

"Oh, JJ."

"I'll take that as a yes. See you on the fourteenth."

JJ made certain that no one would be surprised about Arlie's situation. He didn't want anyone to say something inadvertently that would make things worse for Arlie than they already were. He trusted Jess, in particular, to make it easy on Arlie. *Funny, isn't it*, he thought.

The class clown has become the steadiest and most reliable member of the group. How do you suppose that happened?

This was the first time that some at the seder had seen Rachel since the terrible sequence of events that began almost seven months earlier. There was a good deal of shock at her appearance. She had lost a lot of weight for someone who was already slim. The customary luster was gone from her eyes. She hadn't exercised or been outdoors except to go on medical appointments, and it showed. Rachel was an outdoor plant moved inside and into a dark corner. She looked sickly.

Although everyone noticed, Alina found it hardest to bear. She thought of Rachel as her older sister. When she came into the hotel ballroom for the first time and saw Rachel, she ran off to the ladies' room to cry. David sent his sister-in-law Marla in after her, and soon both of them were weeping. Alina finally emerged red-eyed, fifteen minutes after she'd fled. Though warned in advance by Noah and Marla, David was almost equally shaken.

Jess gulped hard when she greeted Rachel, but her crying was done inwardly. All she trusted herself to say as she hugged Rachel and kissed her was, "I love you, sweetheart."

If the circumstances were different, Rachel's behavior toward most of the seder guests might have been considered rude. The only ones she greeted with any enthusiasm were Dev, Grandma Bess, Yalie, and her three girlfriends. She accepted hugs and kisses from her brothers and two sisters-in-law but had little to say to them, even to her protege Alina. Except for Grandma Bess, the Weiners might as well have been attending a seder in Cincinnati. Even her own parents and her aunt and uncle got little attention. Daniel and little Ariel were already used to climbing on JJ, Aunt Rebecca, and Auntie Lee and being fed by Adelaide Miller. Their mother took no notice of them at the seder— none.

In a distant sort of way, Rachel was glad to see the others: Richie, who'd come to be with Yalie, her brothers, her sisters-in-law. But Rachel had a very narrow field of vision during the seder. She wanted Jess on one side of her at the table and Dev on the other side. It was as if they were bookends holding her up. Her need to be comforted was so obvious as to be painful. Yalie, sitting directly across the table, was the only other person she talked to. Again, though she was not acting on a conscious plan, Rachel looked for Yalie to be her savior after Dev's baby was born.

The seder was very subdued. Hillel asked Aaron Goodman to preside, ostensibly as the host, but in reality because Hillel didn't feel up to it. Rebecca coached Daniel through the Four Questions, and the reading of the *Haggadah* followed without the usual jollity. All through it, Rachel had a fierce though unconscious grip on the hands of both her friend and her cousin.

During dinner, Rachel ate very little—a bowl of soup, two bites of gefilte fish, no chicken, no salad, none of the vegetables, no dessert. She did not participate in the afterdinner singing.

When the evening was over, Rachel wanted to be sure that Jess would come to see her the next day. She told her to bring Sam and their son, Richard, of course, and Laura and Arlie, but it was clear to all of them that Jess was the one she really wanted to see. Clear to all but Rachel. She didn't fully understand her own need.

JJ went to the hotel in late morning to get them. They could find their way to Golden on their own, but he wanted to speak with them ahead of time.

Rachel was in psychotherapy, he explained. As far as her doctors were concerned, she was no longer suicidal. But neither, JJ believed, was she on the road to emotional recovery.

"Don't be surprised if she doesn't ask you about yourself," he warned. "She's immersed in Rachel Rothschild." He said it lightly, but Jess detected the anger beneath.

Rachel was waiting impatiently for them. Her greeting was artificially earnest. Though he went to her somewhat unwillingly, she insisted on taking Richard onto her lap. She asked each of her friends in turn about recent developments in their lives, starting with Arlie. She had been told to let Arlie bring it up—or not. She didn't take in those instructions.

Arlie took a deep breath. "I guess you know. Seth and I have split. After the honeymoon, it was never any good. You remember how bad it was with his family at the wedding? Turns out they weren't the only ones who were hypercritical. I couldn't do anything right in Seth's eyes. We fought. We made up. We fought again. We screamed so loud the last time that we woke the neighbors." There was a pause while others digested Arlie's news. "Finally, he walked out on me."

"How long ago did this happen?" Laura asked sympathetically.

"Little over a month ago. I've wanted to tell you guys, but I couldn't work up to it."

"Is it permanent?"

"I guess so … I don't know. I won't go crawling. I've done that, but no more … I haven't heard a word from him since he left…. … I don't think I want to … I don't know."

Arlie's voice had become a near whisper. She was dry-eyed but exhausted by the recitation. She said, "Let's talk about somebody else. Please."

Laura stepped into the breach. "I'm doing another movie. Waiting for Rachel's dad to finish his script. I'm talking to some folks about directing a play."

Jess interrupted, "Whoa. That's news to me. You've been holding out on me, Laura." Normally, Bozo would have made some outrageous joke at this point, but Bozo hadn't come to Colorado on this visit.

"You don't know everything about me, Jess. Just *almost* everything." The problem was that it might not happen. She mentioned it now only because she owed Rachel a favorable development of some sort.

"What's the play?" Arlie asked. The searchlight had turned away from her own life, and she reengaged.

"One of those Neil Simon things. They're pretty near foolproof, so they may be willing to let a fool try."

"Don't say that about my friend Laura," Jess said. "She's a lot better than you think she is."

Laura smiled. "My cheering section."

Jess herself didn't have much new to report. "Tada," she said, gesturing toward Richard, "you're looking at my number one achievement. Standing in this corner, weighing thirty-five pounds, the champion child of his generation."

"C'mon, Jess," Laura said. "Tell them how you've brought Hollywood to its knees on behalf of your client what's-his-name."

"The last thing anyone wants to hear is a lawyer bragging. Calling for mercy, yes, but not bragging."

"She's doing very damn well," Sam declared proudly. "Best young attorney in town. Everybody says so."

"Pshaw," Jess interposed. "My favorite word. In other words, bullshit." She said it fondly. Sam was her biggest booster, as she was his. A couple for nearly ten years, three and a half years married, they remained deeply in love. No one could see them together and fail to recognize it.

It was Rachel's turn to say something.

What she said was, "I'm surviving. In case you didn't know, I tried to commit suicide. Turns out I wasn't very good at it." She laughed an actual laugh and added, "So surviving is a bigger achievement than it seems."

Arlie, who was sitting closest to her, took her hands and kissed them. "You're going to be all right, Rache. I know you are."

Laura told Rachel she wanted to see her alone. They went into another room.

"Look, Rache," she said. "We all know what happened to you. And I think maybe I know better than anyone else how you feel about it. You remember when you came to see me in Santa Monica when I was having problems adjusting to life after Bogusian?"

"Yes."

"You remember telling me I had nothing to be ashamed of, that I was young, that I had my whole life ahead of me?"

"Yes."

"Well, let me tell you some things that only Jess knows. When I first started living with him, Bogusian wanted me to pose for him. Pornographic stuff. Obscene. And I did it. He liked to take me out dancing. He always insisted that I wear a sheer blouse and a short skirt and skimpy underwear that he bought for me at Frederick's of Hollywood. And I did that, too. He'd have me sit beside him at the table and spread my legs so he could get to me. Push my panties aside. Finger-fuck me. Make me smell myself and suck it. And I did that, too. I hated myself, but I did it. When I finally walked out on him, he took one of those pornographic photos of me, enlarged it, and put it on his desk in a big frame to show everyone. If I could get over that, you can get over what happened to you."

"The difference is you got what you were asking for, Laura. I didn't act like a slut. I didn't ask to be dirtied."

"What did you say?" Laura raised her eyebrows incredulously. She felt as if she'd been punched in the stomach. Tears gathered in the corners of her eyes.

Rachel said, "I'm sorry. I didn't mean it."

"Yes, you did," Laura replied bitterly. "I was trying to help. I showed you how bad it was for me, and you threw it back in my face." Laura had risen from her chair and was preparing to leave. "That was mean."

"I'm sorry."

"Well, you should be." Laura walked out the door and slammed it behind her. She put her forehead against the opposite wall and began weeping.

Jess was beside her instantly. "What's wrong?"

Laura turned to Jess, hugged her, and began crying like a little child seeking comfort.

Rachel came out. She touched Laura on the shoulder.

"Get away," Laura spat at her between sobs. "Leave me alone."

Jess instinctively understood. She waved Rachel away. The wave said, "Let me try to handle this."

When Laura was calm enough, Jess asked, "Do you want to tell me what happened?"

Laura shook her head no, but an instant later she was speaking. "I told her about me and Bogusian, all those sordid little details, and she said I deserved it."

"She said you *deserved* it? I can't believe that. You must have misunderstood."

"Well, she didn't exactly say I deserved it. What she said was that I got what I was asking for. It's the same thing."

"You poor baby," Jess replied. "You poor baby." After a long pause, she added, "Listen to me, Laura. Listen to me carefully. I'm not going to make excuses for Rachel. She had no right, no right at all to make you feel bad. But you guys have been friends for a thousand years, and I'm sure you understand that right now, Rachel is not our Rachel. She's like a little animal that's been beaten and is using its teeth on people who are trying to help. She's focused on her own suffering. She doesn't want to be told that anyone else has suffered."

"Maybe you're right." Laura was drying her eyes. " How did you get to be so wise, Jess? Rachel was the brainy one. Arlie was the organizer. I was always the advice giver. And you were the comedian. Now you're the advice giver, the organizer, and the brain all rolled into one."

"No, no, no. All that's happened is that life has smiled on me. I found Sam early, and I haven't had a moment's doubt about myself since I fell in love. I have a perfect husband, a perfect child, a perfect job, and a perfect life. So it's really quite easy for me to be strong for my friends."

"Okay. So, what next? Do I walk back into the room and tell Rachel I forgive her?"

"No, it's too soon for that. Let me talk with her. She needs to understand that she hurt your feelings. It will do her good to feel guilty, maybe get her to stop believing, if only for a moment, that nobody else's pain matters, only hers. Let her come to you to apologize."

Jess went to Rachel, took her by the hand, and led her downstairs to her room.

"I did a terrible thing. I know it," Rachel said.

"Yes, you did. You made Laura feel like shit on the bottom of your shoe."

Rachel hung her head. "What should I do?"

"Honey, I love you. That's the first and most important thing I have to say to you. I know life has dealt you the Queen of Spades. I wish I could be here by your side to help you through it. But you do have to think about other people, Rache. If I were you, I'd go up there now and get down on my knees in front of Laura, in front of everybody, and beg for forgiveness. Beg. She might actually forgive you."

Rachel obeyed. Like an automaton. She went upstairs ahead of Jess into the living room, walked to where Laura was sitting, and knelt down in front of her.

"Laura," she began, not looking at her but staring at the carpet, "I'm sorry. I shouldn't have said what I said to you. I hope you can forgive me. I'm sorry. I'm so sorry. I'm so sorry."

She took Laura's hand and kissed it like a penitent. She was crying softly.

Laura took Rachel's head, brought it into her lap, and bent over to kiss it. After a long moment fighting not to shed any additional tears, Laura said, "I forgive you, Rache. How could I not forgive you?"

Jess stood there watching. When Rachel finally got up off her knees, Jess was there to hug and kiss her. "You did the right thing, babe. I'm proud of you."

Rachel began crying again. What wouldn't she give to have Jess close by?

*   *   *

Dev's baby, Alexis, was born a week after Passover. Like her father and her Aunt Yalie, she was going to be a blond. It was not an easy birth, and Alexis lay there in the nursery, a squashed-up little creature, while Dev slept exhausted in her hospital room. It would be awhile before both of them regained their natural shapes. Mark was already taking pictures through the nursery window. First-childitis. Everything would be recorded for the photo drawer.

Once she recovered her strength, Dev put her whole heart into being Alexis's mother. She'd taken three months of leave from her law firm to take care of the baby. She was up for a couple of hours most nights, yet Dev was nonetheless bright-eyed and unbelievably happy. She liked standing by the crib watching Alexis sleep. She liked nursing her. She even liked changing her diaper. Had anyone else ever experienced a miracle like this? Not likely.

"Little did I know," Mark said delightedly, "that this lawyer I married was a mommy in disguise."

Rachel, absurdly, was jealous of the baby's claims on Dev. She knew it was absurd, yet she couldn't help herself. Visiting with Jess was wonderful. Getting down on her knees to apologize to Laura was the best thing she'd done for anyone else since the rape. But the boost was temporary. Jess was back in Santa Monica. The only other person who might substitute for Dev was Yalie, and she had a new job that kept her extremely busy.

"What will I do without Dev?" Rachel said to JJ, meaning, as he heard it, *you don't do enough for me, you can't give me the help I need.* Rachel's sole focus on self, interrupted briefly during the visit from her girlfriends, was once more in evidence. It had begun to wear on JJ. He was tired of hearing Rachel's complaints. He knew he was being unfair, but he sometimes walked out of their room muttering "give it a rest" under his breath.

He admitted his distress to Rebecca, and she said, "It's gotta be tough on you. She's got Dr. Cohen to talk with—and Dev. Or at least she did until Alexis was born. You haven't had anyone to talk with. Maybe you should see a shrink yourself."

"No." JJ shook his head. "Dr. Cohen suggested that. But what am I going to say? 'My wife got raped seven months ago, and I'm tired of listening to her say she feels bad about it.' Somehow I don't think that's going to earn me points as a good husband. Maybe a nomination as Shit of the Year."

"Don't be so hard on yourself, JJ. You give her plenty of support. But right now, Rachel is insatiable. If you were as full of sympathy as the Great Lakes, she'd gulp it all down and still be thirsty. I'm not blind. She takes everything Dev gives her and everything you give her, and she wants still more. I'm not blaming her for it. That's just the way it is."

"Thanks, Beck. It helps having someone to talk to. I don't know what we'd do without you. I don't know what *I'd* do without you."

He hugged her, and she hugged back.

Yalie was spending less time with Rachel than Rachel counted on. She was living at Dev's, and in the few hours a week she was able to spare from work, she wanted to be there playing with the baby and cooing at her. Dev was the one who told her sister she must go to Rachel as often as possible.

"I need you, Yalie, but she needs you more. I was with Rachel more than I was with Mark during my pregnancy, and I can't do it any longer."

"She's got Rebecca. She's got JJ."

"Yes, she does, but Rebecca's too young, and JJ's a man. She depended on me."

"She's got to learn to stand on her own."

"Yes, she does. When she's ready."

"What makes you think I can be the next Dev Goodman?"

"All you have to be is Ya'el Goodman. That will be plenty. You're still Rachel's nearest and dearest, Yalie. There isn't anybody on this earth that she's closer to. Not me. Not Rebecca. Not Jess Sherman."

"You think she's forgiven me for taking her up the mountain so she could wreck her knee?"

"Yes, she's forgiven you. She blames herself."

So Yalie became a regular visitor at the Weiner household. Her relationship to Rachel was different than Dev's. Dev was an older sister. Yalie was more like a twin. She was a twin who'd led a different life than Rachel's, however, and there were many experiences that they did not share. Yalie had been her pal for as long as either of them could remember. Rachel didn't need a pal right now. She wanted someone to comfort her, to advise her.

The link between the two of them was quite powerful, however. Rachel absorbed what she could get from Yalie, which was quite a lot, though not quite what Rachel was looking for. Standing on her own was the other alternative. Unfortunately, Dev was right. She wasn't ready.

In her sessions with Dr. Cohen, Rachel was still walking around the edges of the rape, poking at it with a long stick. She wouldn't discuss the details, even though Dr. Cohen already knew most of them from Dev.

She had been told over and over—indirectly, directly, always gently—that she was not being punished for anything she did or failed to do, that evil exists, that her soul was intact, that her family loved her. But she hadn't really taken it in. She was still caught up in the humiliation of it, the annihilation of self. She kept thinking about stumbling down the road after the rape, stark naked and barefoot, with her hands tied behind her and the stink of urine rising into her nostrils. She was out there for the whole world to see. In her dreams, she imagined herself out there still.

Dr. Cohen had suggested that she allow herself to be hypnotized. Rachel wouldn't agree. She was afraid of her subconscious, scared of revealing it to Dr. Cohen, scared of revealing it to herself.

Her psychiatrist, Dr. Drucker, who saw her every other month to maintain the balance of her psychotropic medication, lead her through the routine list of questions he asked to measure progress and found discouragingly little. He told her it was time to rejoin the world. She ought to get out of the house, other than just to keep medical appointments, think about returning to work, get some exercise.

Rachel mentioned Dr. Drucker's advice to Dr. Cohen, and she concurred. "You have to start living again, Rachel. It's the other side of therapy."

Rachel said she'd try, she'd really try.

Going back to work would compel Rachel to start driving again. She would not be able to go near the little silver Mercedes, however. Anytime she looked at it, she remembered being locked in the trunk en route to the warehouse where the assault took place. She wanted JJ to get rid of it and buy her something else, she didn't care what. She rejected the idea of giving the car to Rebecca. She didn't want ever to look at it again.

JJ insisted she come shopping with him for a new car. He embraced the idea of getting her out of the house, and this was one more excuse.

Once they started looking, Rachel began to show an interest. She wanted something a little sportier than a sedan. Maybe a Jeep or a vehicle like it. JJ suggested a Land Rover. They could use it in Vail.

Vail! Rachel hadn't thought about Vail. Here it was the end of May, and the only people who'd been to the lodge in Vail since Rachel's skiing accident were JJ's sister Annalisa and her family. Maybe she could entice Dev to take the baby to Vail for a couple of weeks during the summer. Maybe Aunt Ruth and Uncle Aaron would come, too. Maybe her parents could come for a visit, her brothers and their wives. Maybe her girlfriends. She had intended to give Yalie a lodge key. She didn't do that, did she? It would be a good place for Yalie and Richie to go when he came for the July 4 weekend.

Once the car was delivered, the first place Rachel drove was to Dev's to see Alexis. She admired the baby extravagantly. If Dev had been less starry-eyed, she might have thought Rachel had gone overboard. However, no praise of Alexis's fine points was excessive in Dev's opinion.

Rachel next went to visit Grandma Bess. The old lady had aged visibly since the last time Rachel looked at her closely. That was the consequence of what happened to Grandma Bess's granddaughter. It wasn't just how she talked about Rachel. It was how she thought of her. Rachel wanted to be chipper during the visit and nearly succeeded. Grandma Bess had brightened considerably by the time Rachel departed.

Rachel told JJ she was ready to start attending Friday night dinner at the Weiners. She talked with Mr. Edwards about resuming her career.

She never finished the story about Denver International Airport. She was in the middle of it when the rape occurred. The airport was open now, and there was no point at this stage in rehashing what went before.

She didn't have any story ideas right now. She'd accept assignments Mr. Edwards proposed. Of course, he would be happy to have her back, Mr. Edwards told her. He wasn't sure what to do with her, however. He didn't want to overtax her by giving her anything difficult. Hoping she wouldn't think it beneath her, he suggested that she do "front of the book stuff" to begin. Although it amounted to a vote of no confidence and a demotion, Rachel agreed to it. She knew she wasn't capable of doing anything major. She wasn't even sure she'd be able to do something minor.

Rachel's renewed interest in life was also being shown at home. She'd taken to picking up two-year-old Ariel and depositing the child on her lap, though Ariel was decidedly not a lap-sitter. She got down on the floor with Daniel and his favorite books to half read and half be read to.

The flashes of light were brief, and the darkness was still there in abundance, but JJ was encouraged. Rachel remained sexually inert, but she allowed him to hug her as if she weren't repelled by the contact. He took that as a favorable sign.

Rachel started going to the offices of *In the Rockies* twice a week. JJ persuaded her, persuaded her gently, not to work at home. She needed to get out of the house.

She was back where she began, doing features. It was not challenging work by Rachel's former standard. Still, she was talking to people to gather information, and she resumed writing. What was missing was the lightness of touch that used to be present in her prose. Her mood had improved, but only from black to gray.

Rachel's first piece was limp as sodden face tissue. Though he wondered how she'd respond to criticism, Mr. Edwards decided not to baby her.

"Rachel," he said, "it's all good English, but it doesn't have any life. You can do better than this. I know you can."

Rachel took the story back. Although she felt like crying, she resisted. The words of her high school journalism instructor sprang to mind: Journalists must learn to accept criticism.

She reread her draft, then tossed it in the trash. Mr. Edwards was right. It was leaden through and through, and no amount of editing would turn it into silver.

She sat blankly in front of the computer screen, trying to come up with a different approach. Nothing suggested itself. Mr. Edwards saw her suffering and called her into his office.

"You know how to do this, Rachel. Don't take the story head-on.

Find an angle. What's the most interesting part of the story? Where's the human side? Start there."

"I don't know if I can do this anymore, Mr. Edwards."

"Of course, you can. You've been through a bad patch, but you haven't forgotten how to write any more than you've forgotten how to walk."

"You'll recall I was on crutches a long time, Mr. Edwards. I don't take walking for granted." She smiled.

He acknowledged her point. "All right, forget the darned analogy. What you did before, you can do again. You haven't lost the ability."

The peptalk seemed to have the desired effect. Rachel came at the story another way, and her prose took on a little energy. When she finished, it was okay, even pretty good. A small victory perhaps. Nevertheless, a victory.

Sessions with Dr. Cohen had moved to a better place. Rachel conversed freely about almost anything that didn't directly approach the rape. She froze the moment it appeared on the horizon. "I don't want to talk about that."

Dr. Cohen heard that sentence frequently. Clearly, the barrier must be penetrated.

"And, no, I won't be hypnotized."

Dr. Cohen only suggested it once. Rachel rejected it more than a dozen times.

Still, Rachel's willingness to talk about other things in her life opened new avenues for inquiry. Dr. Cohen asked purposefully about her relationship with the children. How did Rachel feel about knowing she couldn't have any more? Did the health issue make her feel more vulnerable?

Rachel thought about it. Did she regret being unable to have more children? No. Okay, maybe a little. Did her health worry her? That was the least of her problems at the moment.

Rachel said that she was not a proper mother. Her children were being raised by nannies and more recently by her sister. In contrast, Hanna was a stay-at-home mom. Her friend Jess also employed a nanny, but she took care of Richard herself in the mornings, after work, and on weekends. Dev, when her maternity leave ended, would follow Jess's example, not Rachel's.

"My kids run to their Aunt Rebecca if they scrape their knees, not to me. I'm the aunt. She's their mother." She said it matter-of-factly, but there was pain just below the surface and when Dr. Cohen probed, it popped out like a vole from hiding.

"Am I sorry I went back to work after Danny was born? No … yes. I don't know. A little bit of both. Part of me wants to be the successful career woman. Part of me wants to be a housewife and mother. Is it possible to regret having too much money to be a housewife?"

"Most women don't have *enough* money to stay at home."

"Yes. But for me, going to work was never about money. It was about being myself. Money made it possible for me to go be myself and to turn my children over to someone else to raise. Money gave me choices that other people don't have, and I'm not sure I made the right choice. Does that make sense?"

"Is being rich such a problem for you, Rachel?"

"I like what money buys. Being Mrs. JJ Weiner, the wife of this wealthy guy, wasn't enough for me, if that's what you mean. I wanted to be Rachel Rothschild, a separate human being with an identity of my own. I didn't understand what being Rachel Rothschild would cost me."

"Did you consider waiting until the children were older?"

"It's what I intended to do until my husband suggested I go back to work."

"Do you blame him for the fact that your children have been raised by nannies?"

"He didn't coerce me. He suggested. I made the decision …"

Dr. Cohen started to speak, but Rachel, having thought about it, continued. "… but, yes, I guess I blame him a little."

"Do you think that's fair?"

"No, but the alternative is blaming myself, isn't it?"

"Does there always have to be somebody to blame when things go wrong?"

"No."

"Then why do you feel it's necessary to blame JJ or blame yourself? Did either of you intend what's happened?"

"I guess not."

"I'd like you to think about that, Rachel. Things happen, and there doesn't have to be someone to blame. Not you. Not your husband."

"Okay, I'll think about it."

"And, to be more explicit, you don't have to blame anybody for the rape except the two men who committed it."

Rachel did not respond. She didn't want to think about the rape, even about who was *not* responsible.

*   *   *

Rachel had not been to Friday night dinner at the Weiners since before the rape. There was applause when she walked in the door and a round of hugs and kisses from the company, including Annalisa and her husband. Herman concluded the kiddush over the wine and the blessing over the bread with a separate toast: "To Rachel. L'chaim. To life."

Grandma Bess commanded Rachel to come sit beside her. No one was happier that Rachel was back in the world.

Rachel ought to have felt like a beloved member of the Weiner family. Yet the thought that pushed into her consciousness was that if she weren't a member of the Weiner family, the two men who raped her would have found another object for their rage. She didn't exactly blame the Weiners. It was simply the truth, and the truth was not setting Rachel Rothschild free. It had her in an unrelenting grip that was unhealthy for her relationship with JJ and unhealthy for Rachel herself. She might have passed her entire life without being the target of anyone's hatred.

"What if" was a path back to darkness and, despite the celebratory character of the evening, that was where Rachel ended it.

"What if" was what she talked about during her Monday visit to Dr. Cohen.

"You asked me whether I have a problem with being rich. The answer is that I wouldn't be here in your office if my husband weren't rich. It's his being rich that made me a victim."

"Spell that out, Rachel."

"You want to hear about the rape," Rachel said suddenly and with surprising vehemence. "I'll tell you about the rape. Those two men weren't after Rachel Rothschild. They were after Rachel Weiner. When they showed me their cocks and took me in the ass"—she meant to be obscene about it—"it wasn't for the thrill of it. The purpose was to take revenge on *her*. When they fucked me, when they made me suck their dicks with my shit on it, when they pissed all over me, when they left me with my hands bound behind me so I couldn't cover my tits or my pussy, the purpose was to hurt *her*, to hurt Rachel Weiner." Her voice was almost a shout, and then it fell to almost a whisper. "But it was *me* they destroyed, me." And then she continued in a normal voice. "So, yes, I have a problem with being rich. It nearly killed me, and Rachel Weiner also. Those men would have loved it if she'd committed suicide. That would have been the ultimate. But it would have taken me with her."

The volcano had finished erupting. Rachel was exhausted. She hadn't shed a tear. Now she was just numb.

Dr. Cohen allowed the silence to hang there in the air like a pall of smoke. When she spoke, she said, "Good, Rachel. You made the source of your anger as plain as it could possibly be. We've got to deal with those feelings, but they're out there now for both of us to see."

Rachel shrugged her shoulders. She didn't say a thing. She couldn't.

"I'm sorry for the pain that reaching this point has caused you. Psychotherapy can be a very difficult process at times. But I think you've broken through the barrier you constructed after the rape, and you should be glad about that."

"Glad? Glad isn't the word for my state of mind. But maybe you're right. I feel like I've passed over some kind of continental divide. Sorry about the vile language."

"That's okay. It's more than okay. The assault on you was obscene, and obscenity may be the only way to describe it properly."

"Where do we go from here?"

"We'll start salvaging Rachel Rothschild."

"What about Rachel Weiner?"

"That's more difficult. I don't think you like her very much."

"You're certainly right about that."

The regular therapy sessions continued. Dr. Cohen was helping Rachel explore her feelings about the Weiner family and, more particularly, about JJ.

Despite having shown herself the link she made between the rape and the Weiner fortune, Rachel wasn't able to adjust emotionally to this self-knowledge. She accepted intellectually that no one was to blame except the rapists. Yet she wasn't able to forgive JJ, not so much for having fired the two men who assaulted her as for having assaulted her twice himself. That was what the two spankings had become in her mind—beatings that ended in sex, sexual assaults.

She did not tell Dr. Cohen about the spankings and the sex that followed. She hadn't told Dev either. Somehow, those episodes were more shameful than the rape. She allowed Dr. Cohen to infer that the problem between her and JJ stemmed entirely from his efforts to run her life in the early days of their marriage. Dr. Cohen found that causality hard to accept. No doubt, rape might remind Rachel of JJ's attempt to dominate her. But for it to be the source of the sexual tension between them simply did not compute.

Rachel was trying again to get past her revulsion. She and JJ were once more sleeping in the same bed. She let JJ touch her, even make love to her, but she was incapable of reciprocating. She got no pleasure from sex and gave none. She wanted it to be over. Whether it was psychosomatic or because she tensed up, Rachel now experienced pain during intercourse. She submitted because JJ was her husband. But that was what it was: submission. There was no joy in it, no real love. It was sexual release for him and uxorial duty for her. She hadn't again burst out crying during the act. When he told her that he loved her, she answered, "I love you, too." But her body language made it clear that this was a rote response.

Rachel considered telling JJ to find sex elsewhere. That would be the same, however, as saying this marriage was over, and Rachel didn't want to take that step. She remembered loving JJ. She loved him, didn't she, until that night? She wanted to get over … not hatred—it's not hatred … she wanted to get over the desolation she experienced when she lay in bed next to him. They could still make it together if she got past that.

She said nothing to JJ about her feelings, and she declined Dr. Cohen's offer to speak with him. He was in the dark about the exact reasons for the distance that had developed between them. He suspected she felt that he was indirectly responsible for the rape. He'd forgotten the spanking episodes. Why should he remember them? Rachel demanded that he stop, and he stopped. He no longer thought about having made decisions without Rachel's participation. That was behind them.

Rachel and JJ were two people in a lightless room, groping but unable to find one another. Her desolation was matched by his sense of loss. At a time when Rachel was reviving, beginning again to be a professional, trying desperately to reestablish herself as her children's mother, thinking about bringing family and friends back into her life, her relationship with JJ was foundering.

Rachel wanted to celebrate her return to life—in all but her marriage—with a gathering in Vail. She'd given the place to Yalie for a reunion with Richie over the July 4 weekend. This would be the first time they'd seen one another in the nearly four months since Yalie moved back to Colorado, and Rachel didn't want to intrude on that.

However, Rachel invited her brothers and their wives to come for a week or ten days as soon as the lovers' tryst was over. Dev was approaching the end of her maternity leave, and Rachel wanted her, Mark, and Alexis to come to Vail also. She asked Yalie to come again for the weekend.

Rachel's entire household was coming: JJ, the children, Rebecca, Ms. Miller, and Anna Lopez.

Vail in summer was not the same concentrated beehive of activity as in the winter. But there was a music festival taking place, and for those who love the outdoors, there was a profusion of things to do. JJ and Rachel owned half a dozen bikes for guests, and more could be rented.

Rachel and Anna Lopez drove up around noon Friday in Rachel's new Land Rover. JJ would come up after work, bringing the two children, Rebecca, and Ms. Miller.

Marla and Noah were the first of the guests to arrive. Marla had something she wanted to tell everybody, but she was determined to wait until David and Alina arrived. So, after they'd made the necessary fuss over Daniel and Ariel, Noah was allowed to report first. His company was losing money but flourishing on the stock market, and Noah was several times a millionaire—on paper. Marla merely said that she was doing just fine, and she and Noah, nearly nine months married, were very happy together.

About an hour later, David and Alina drove up. No sooner had David brought the luggage in the front door of the lodge than Marla called for everyone's attention. "I'm performing in London in November," she declared excitedly, "and, Lee, you're coming with me. Okay?"

Her agent had arranged for her to do another Mozart role, Pamina in *The Magic Flute*, and he was angling for several engagements on the continent in the spring. The San Francisco Opera Company was considering her for a couple of featured roles, and there were inquiries from other U.S. companies that had heard of her work.

Alina was thrilled to be invited on the London trip. Marla had to be there a week in advance for rehearsals, and there were to be four performances over a period of two weeks. They'd be gone a total of three weeks.

"Can I go, Davy? Please, can I go?" she implored her husband.

"Sure you can go, dollie. I might even come myself for one of the performances. What about you, Noah?"

"You bet. I wouldn't miss it. I'm going for opening night. Marry Marla and see the world. That's the motto. Like joining the navy."

"Is there any chance you guys can come?" Marla asked Rachel.

"You want your own claque. Is that it?" Rachel answered. "Maybe. I'll talk it over with JJ. When's this opening night?"

"November 10, if that's a Friday. Please come. It will make me feel so good if you're all there. I won't be a drop nervous."

Marla suffered from stage fright at this point in her career, and they all knew it.

"Nerves of steel," David said.

"More like nerves of cellophane," Noah responded. "Marla gets stage fright at the opening of a door."

"I do *not*. Maybe at the opening of a bottle of wine."

Rachel gave her sister-in-law a big hug. "We're all very proud of you, Marla. Soon you'll be too famous to sing at the seder."

Marla was flushed with excitement.

David and Alina were living in Westwood, not too far from Santa Monica. David was designing houses for a major builder. Alina was emulating Rachel's career path. She found a local newspaper that was willing to have her contribute stories, and even though she was an absolute neophyte, she was hoping to become a journalist. She had a long way to go, much further than Rachel ever did.

Rachel wondered whether Alina wasn't overdoing the younger-sister-copying-older-sister bit. She wouldn't say it aloud, however, because she did not want to discourage her. Alina was nearly twenty-three, but it was impossible not to think of her as a kid, as a lively, lovely kid. There was something girlish and vulnerable about her. *Her editor probably looks at her*, Rachel thought, *and wonders what this cute little cheerleader is doing posing as a professional.*

Yalie came up late Friday, after JJ. She needed her own car because she had to be in the office Monday. Maybe she'd return again next Friday night. Dev, Mark, and the baby were the last to get there. They arrived late Saturday morning. Alexis could not be rushed.

"You look wonderful," David told Dev. "Motherhood really agrees with you."

"Yes, it does. Alexis is the most wonderful thing that's ever happened to me … along with Mark, of course."

"A little slow there on the second part," said Mark. "Alexis is also the best that's ever happened to *me*."

"Do you care to add to that?" Dev responded.

"What would I want to add?"

"You bastard. At least I included you as an afterthought."

"Yes, and I'll remember the slight to my dying day. Upstaged by my own daughter."

"These guys are something," Yalie said. "I come in at night, and they are both standing there beside Alexis's crib worshiping. If it keeps up, my niece is going to have a God complex by the time she's three."

"I'll have to go back to work soon enough," Dev replied. "I'm just enjoying what I've got."

Yes, Rachel thought. *I wish I was better at that. Maybe I wouldn't be in third place in my own children's lives. After Rebecca and the nanny. Make that fifth place. I forgot Mom and JJ.*

Daniel was at the stage where he liked to run around outside, and that was okay as long as someone followed after him. Doing so was Rebecca's pleasure. Now that Rachel no longer needed her quite as much, Rebecca was working full-time at Hyman Weiner & Sons. Nights and weekends were the only times she got to be with the kids. She enjoyed being with them.

In her own fashion, Rachel did, too. But they had been without her for most of the past year. Ariel never had much of her mother's time, and Daniel didn't remember when he was the primary pleasure in her life. Their expectations of her were low. Ms. Miller fed and bathed them except when Rebecca insisted on doing it or when Rachel was in her motherly mode. Rebecca was the one who constantly reminded them how wonderful they were.

Rachel received her children's relative indifference to her as a dull ache. She didn't know what to do about it. Dr. Drucker and Dr. Cohen had told her that her mental health required getting out in the world. How was she supposed to reconcile that with what would be required to reclaim a larger place in the lives of her two-year-old daughter and soon-to-be-six-year-old son?

The group at the lodge divided into the doers and the stay-at-homes. David, Noah, Rebecca, Yalie, and JJ intended to be up early Sunday and out biking, hiking, and fishing. Marla and Alina planned to do what their husbands wanted to do. Daniel wished to tag along after Rebecca and JJ. That left Dev, Mark, and Rachel to remain with Ariel, Alexis, and Ms. Miller—and to talk.

This was Dev's first real opportunity to chat with Rachel since Alexis was born. Mark looked for somewhere to sit and read, knowing they should be alone.

"How you doing, babe?" Dev asked.

"Okay, I think. I finally told her, Dr. Cohen, about the rape. We got talking about whether I had a problem being a rich man's wife, and I went off like a Mars rocket. I told her everything."

"Has it helped?"

"With some things, yes. Not with others."

"Meaning what exactly?"

"I've come to terms with the fact that they were after Mrs. JJ Weiner. I was just an innocent bystander."

"If that works for you, okay. Is it better that you were an innocent bystander?"

"In some ways. It makes the rape into more of an impersonal event, like a car that jumps the sidewalk and knocks you down. I've quit feeling I was somehow to blame."

"But it hasn't resolved everything for you."

"No, it hasn't. Being Mrs. JJ Weiner is a problem."

"Oh?" The statement alarmed Dev.

"I'm not saying JJ is to blame. Obviously he's not. But it's caused me to double back on other things, things that happened before we got married, things that happened while we were newlyweds."

"You mean like his trying to run your life? This lodge, for example?"

"You know me so well, Dev. Better than anyone."

"I don't want to pry, Rache. No more questions."

"No, no. I want to tell. Right after we got married, JJ and I had a couple of big blowups. He paddled my bare behind for me twice. Even though it hasn't happened again and won't ever happen, I can't get it out of my mind. I feel angrier today than I did when it originally happened. Does that make any sense to you?"

"Not really."

"We had passionate sex afterward. Both times. I can't explain what it's come to symbolize. It's like I was raped twice by JJ before I got raped. It's not, but it is. And I can't get rid of it. It's like a wall down the middle of our bed."

"Have you told JJ any of this?"

"No. I can't. I just can't."

"Why don't you ask Dr. Cohen to tell him?"

"I can't do that either. She doesn't know about any of this. I don't know why I can tell you these things and can't tell her, but that's the way it is. I'm going to have to get around or over the wall by myself."

"Doesn't sound like you're doing too good a job of it."

"You're right about that. Even though I'm doing better in dealing with the outside world, I'm still a fucking mess inside."

"Poor Rachel." Dev kissed her on the cheek.

"That's who I've become. Poor Rachel. That might as well be my name."

The doers returned late in the afternoon. JJ had a dozen steaks to grill for dinner, two dozen ears of corn, and enough beer to float a destroyer in the Vail Valley. Mark was assisting JJ. Anna Lopez was preparing baked potatoes and a green salad.

Ms. Miller was busy with Ariel. Rachel planned to give Daniel his bath. Dev had Alexis.

Yalie had to be back at work in Denver in the morning. She went off to take a shower and get dressed for the return trip after dinner.

Noah, David, Marla, and Alina had nothing to do but talk. The twins were in different professions but still completed one another's sentences. These two peas in a pod married to young women who neither looked alike nor acted alike. Marla was self-assured (except at the very beginning of a performance). She knew exactly what she intended to do with her life. Alina was shy and, except that she was David's wife and was patterning herself after Rachel, didn't yet know who she was, much less who she would become. Marla, the prospective opera star, had an acolyte. Her young sister-in-law, Alina Abramowitz Rothschild, all but wore a notice around her neck saying "this child needs to be protected," and Marla read it with compassionate understanding. Marla was not Alina's older sister, like Rachel, but her guardian angel and her instructor in the ways of the world.

Noah and David sat across from one another drinking beer and exchanging confidences that did not need to be exchanged since each intuitively knew what the other had to tell. Marla and Alina whispered earnestly in a corner. Marla, the elder by three years, dispensed wisdom, and Alina gladly received it.

Soon the steaks were ready and the adults reassembled, and everyone was talking at once. Yalie changed her mind. She was having too much fun. Though it would require her to get up very early, she decided to spend the night and go back in the morning. In fact, she intended to come up again Friday night for the second and final weekend of the visit.

After dinner, Dev took Alexis off to give her a bottle and put her to bed. Ms. Miller led Ariel and Daniel away. Shortly, Daniel popped back in, asking to be read a story. Although he would rather have his Aunt Rebecca, Rachel was the one who went back to his bedroom with him.

Once the kids were asleep, the conversation turned to peace negotiations between Israel and the Palestinians. Mark, Dev, and Yalie had been following developments closely since the Oslo peace process began. JJ tuned in and out. Rachel hadn't paid a lot of attention since September to anything in the news, but her interest was reviving. Informed or not, however, everyone had an opinion, even Alina, who normally avoided political discussions for fear of being discovered to be naive and an idealist.

Talks were underway on expanding Palestinian self-rule in the West Bank and Gaza. The consensus of the group was that both sides wanted peace and both sides needed peace and eventually a way would be found.

Dev remained skeptical about Yasser Arafat, however. She felt he said one thing in English and another in Arabic. Yalie was concerned about the efforts of extremists on both sides to undermine the peace process.

Alina ventured an opinion about the need to establish connections between "the next generation" on both sides, something she had recently read in the literature of The New Israel Fund. "If they keep on hating one another, how are they going to make a peace that will hold?"

Mark pointed out that relations between Israel and Egypt remained chilly twenty years after the signing of a peace treaty but at least they were not fighting.

"Yes," Dev said, "but Israel and Egypt are separated by the Sinai. They don't have to live together the way Israelis have to live with the Palestinians. Lee is right. Unless we can get past the hatred, it's going to be hard to build a lasting peace."

Mark agreed and disagreed. "Yes, Lee's right, and you're right, too. But you've got to start somewhere. An agreement is my idea of a good place to start. You've got to credit the Clinton administration for trying."

Rachel, who'd been silent through the conversation, spoke up. "Seems to me our parents used to have this same discussion. I wonder if our kids will be having it twenty-five years from now."

"Rachel, the cynic," Mark said.

"Rachel, the realist," Dev responded.

And the conversation reached its end.

It was nearly 10:30 p.m., and Yalie announced regretfully that she *must* turn in. She had to be up at 5:00 a.m. to drive back to Denver. Dev followed her. Alexis would be up in the middle of the night. Rachel quit about half an hour later, leaving JJ, Mark, Rebecca, and the twins and their wives.

The topic switched to London. Marla tried to persuade JJ and Rebecca to make the trip in November for her opening night in *The Magic Flute*. JJ said he'd have to check his calendar but Rachel would definitely come. Rebecca said she'd see if she could arrange things at the office so as to allow her to make the trip.

Alina asked what to see in London while she was there, and she got so much advice from JJ and Mark that she started taking notes. *What should she do with Marla, and what should she do by herself while Marla was rehearsing?* Marla went to London with her parents when she was a freshman in college, so she'd already done the changing of the guard, been to Parliament, Westminster Abbey, and the Tower, and traipsed hurriedly through the British Museum and the National Gallery of Art. But there were other things she hadn't seen.

Marla wanted to visit Oxford and attend a play in Stratford-on-Avon. She wanted to see the Royal Shakespeare Company perform. She had her eye on the part of Desdemona in Verdi's *Otello*, and that would require more acting than the Mozart roles that were her natural metier. Why not see the best in the world perform? Maybe she could learn something.

Neither Noah nor David had ever been to England, but they wouldn't get to London until two weeks after Marla and Alina arrived, so they'd see what their wives took them to see.

"Poor widdle henpecked twinnies," Rebecca said.

"We'll fix your little red wagon," Noah said. He and David grabbed her, put her down on the floor, and began to tickle her.

"Leave her alone, you brute," Alina cried, hitting David over the head with a pillow. He pulled her down to the floor, too, sat on her, pulled off her shoe, and tickled her foot.

The two girls were soon writhing on the floor and laughing hysterically.

"No more, no more." Rebecca could barely get the words out. "Please."

"Take it back," Noah insisted.

"Please. You're hurting me."

"Take it back."

"I take it back."

"Every word."

"Every word."

"And plead for mercy."

"Mercy, mercy, mercy, mercy, mercy. Please, please, please."

"That's more like it," he said, letting her up. "You better be careful who you call a henpecked twinnie around here."

"Yessir, yessir, your twinship."

Alina had been apologizing from the first tickle, but David refused to desist until Noah did.

"Learned your lesson, woman?" he asked.

When she was able to catch her breath, Alina replied, "Yes, I've learned you *are* a brute."

He made as if to tickle her again.

"Wife abuse," she screamed.

"You mean child abuse," David replied. "Come here, little kid," he said, grabbing her again but this time to hug and kiss her.

"Well," Mark declared, "If the children are done playing, I think it's time to go to bed."

It was past midnight. Alexis would soon demand feeding, and he'd better get some sleep so he would be able to relieve Dev.

"You heard the man. Time for beddie-bye," David declared, picking Alina up in his arms. "We'll see you in the morning."

Noah clasped Marla by the hand and pulled her toward their bedroom. The twins intended more than sleep.

JJ said he'd lock up. Rebecca, overheated from the struggle with her brothers, went into the kitchen to get a glass of water. On the way out, she met JJ in the hall. They kissed good night. And without either of them intending to, they were suddenly lip to lip and locked in a fierce embrace.

JJ was hard. Rebecca was becoming moist. Both of them were breathing hard. Both wanted it, and they didn't. Didn't prevailed—barely. And so they separated apologetically, and off they went to their own beds, feeling righteous but frustrated.

JJ vowed never to do that again. Rebecca could not imagine what had gotten into her. This was her sister's husband. It would be like incest. She stared unseeing at the ceiling for a long time before she finally fell asleep.

A month passed. A difficult period for Rebecca. She couldn't forget the narrow escape. She really should leave Denver and go back to Santa Monica, she thought. But the children needed her, and Rachel wanted her to remain. The job at Hyman Weiner & Sons was a good deal better than any she might have found at home, and she'd gradually taken on real responsibility for handling relationships with the company's bankers. Her boss promised her a considerable increase in salary if she would stay on permanently.

A possibility would be for her to stay in Denver but live elsewhere. She broached the subject, but Rachel wouldn't hear of it. "We've got this huge house, and you want to move into an efficiency apartment?

That's the silliest thing I ever heard. Besides, Daniel will never allow it. If you went away, he'd have no one to rely on but his mother, and you know she's not enough for him."

Rachel meant to be funny.

JJ understood why Rebecca wanted to move out. He told her, "Stay. Please. I promise it won't happen again."

Thus, it was decided. Rebecca would become a permanent employee of Hyman Weiner & Sons. She'd continue living at her sister's house. She hoped it wouldn't turn out to be a terrible mistake. If the circumstances had been different, she might have talked it over with her mother, her older sister, her cousin Dev, or her cousin Yalie. But there was no one to advise her, no one even to listen as she attempted to think it through. She was making potentially the most fateful decision of her life, and she was completely on her own.

*   *   *

Richie Reiner finished work in Washington and rejoined Yalie. They were staying with Dev and Mark temporarily. Richie had lined up half a dozen appointments with Denver law firms. He hadn't applied to the firm where Dev worked because that might be considered nepotism.

If he had been searching in Washington or New York, Richie would have had firms crawling over one another to hire him. He finished near the top of his class at a law school often cited as the nation's best, and his experience as a Senate staffer would have made him a very attractive applicant. Young lawyers from top law schools were a scarce commodity in Denver, and those with solid experience in Washington were scarcer still. But Denver was also a much smaller stage, and its law firms didn't necessarily need, or want, new hires with Richie's credentials.

Prospective employers looked at Richie like an aircraft engine being offered for use on a small car chassis. Only two of the six firms that interviewed him showed an interest in talking with him a second time. One of the two specialized in class-action suits, and the partner doing the interviewing was a lot more interested in having Richie join than Richie was in joining. Fortunately, the second firm had a broad general practice, and it also operated a Washington office, where

Richie's experience would be a solid plus. It was not the most exciting opportunity that Richie could imagine, but it would have to do.

Ruth and Aaron had found a couple of places in Boulder for Yalie and Richie to look at, and they quickly decided on a place in an older part of town that was a little beyond their price range. But Yalie, with an eye on her political future, was determined not to go to Longmont, Louisville, Lafayette, or any of the other communities with newer and more affordable housing outside Boulder proper.

Getting married was next on the agenda. Yalie did not want a big, fancy wedding. This was her hometown and the place where she went to college, so she could easily have a large crowd. Ruth was the one who wanted to invite half of Boulder to witness her younger daughter's marriage. Yalie wanted a smaller, more intimate service. The difference of opinion could have become a problem, but Richie offered a solution: a large reception Saturday night, followed on Sunday by a small family wedding and dinner.

"Done!" Yalie said enthusiastically. "See what Richie's learned from the Senate—the art of compromise."

Ruth was less pleased than her daughter. But she wasn't going to get anything better.

The reception was arranged for the balcony and adjoining area in the atrium of the Boulderado Hotel, a historic landmark built at the beginning of the twentieth century and recently redone. People were invited in shifts, but the space could barely accommodate the crowd of friends and neighbors whom the Goodmans invited plus Yalie's high school and college friends. Yalie was a good deal more excited than she expected to be.

Everyone who knew her thought Yalie Goodman was the prettiest girl, the prettiest young woman they'd ever seen. Everyone who saw her at the moment thought she'd never been prettier. Her green eyes that night were as brilliant as emeralds, and her honey blond hair, with its natural halo of curls, made her look as if she'd stepped out of an enchanted fairy tale to wed the handsome prince. Her happiness was obvious.

On leaving, guest after guest wished Yalie and Richie a lifetime of happiness. Yalie was more than a bit sorry that she had insisted on a small wedding and that these friends wouldn't be there to see it.

Still, when Sunday dawned, the small wedding again seemed

sensible. Yalie had two attendants: her sister and her cousin, Rachel. Richie's sole attendant was his older brother, Rob. Hanna and Hillel came from California, of course, as did the twins and their wives. The local contingent consisted of Yalie's parents, Dev and Mark, Rachel, JJ and Rebecca, and two couples among her parents' friends who had known Yalie since birth. They were joined by her father's brother, his wife, and their two unmarried daughters. That was the entire guest list on Yalie's side. Richie's parents were there, together with his brother's wife, his father's sister and her husband, his mother's brother and his wife, a cousin and her husband, and three other unmarried cousins.

Yalie, the thirty-one-year-old sophisticate, was transported by the occasion. It was as if she hadn't realized until the moment that the door opened for her to walk down the aisle that *This is It. I m really getting married.* When the service was concluded and Richie broke the glass underfoot, Yalie kissed him with a fervor that caused a murmur of laughter in the audience. She looked out with a self-conscious grin and blew everyone a kiss. Everyone not in tears was smiling and applauding.

Rachel came down from the *bimah* and ran off to the ladies' room to cry, sitting in a stall, muffling herself so no one else would hear. She was crying partly because she was happy for Yalie, but more because of her own misery.

The contrast overwhelmed her. Would she ever again be able to love JJ the way Yalie loved Richie? The answer that stared her in the face was that the love and intimacy in her marriage might be at an end just when Yalie's was beginning.

*   *   *

One year after the rape, Rachel's life had returned to normal in certain ways. She was working again, she was much more engaged with her children than she'd been in some time, she saw her cousins Dev and Yalie as often as possible, she visited Grandma Bess now and again, and she was going to the monthly Shabbat dinner at the Weiner home.

But her relationship with JJ hadn't been reestablished, especially the physical side of it. They were sleeping together, but the sex was completely one-sided. Rachel didn't respond to JJ's efforts to arouse her. She couldn't.

"I can't go on like this," JJ complained. "It's like making love to the dead. Don't you feel anything?"

"Yes. I feel how heavy you are.";

"What the fuck is that supposed to mean?"

"Nothing."

"*Nothing*! What am I, just a hunk of flesh? For God's sake, we're husband and wife."

"I'm sorry, JJ. I'm really sorry. I can't do it. I can't make love the way we used to. You have to give me more time."

"Okay, if that's the way it's got to be." His voice rose. "I'll give you more time. But this can't go on forever, Rache. I'm not made out of iron. I have needs."

She stared at him. "I'm not your damn sex toy. If you've got *needs*"—she spit the word at him—"maybe you ought to find yourself some street-corner pussy."

"Maybe I'll do just that," he answered, storming out of the room and slamming the door behind him.

After a night of seething, self-righteous anger on both sides, JJ apologized, and Rachel halfway accepted. But she also made it obvious that she wanted to avoid sex for a time and that it might be best for both of them if he went back to sleeping in another room.

"I'm working on it, JJ. I know how important it is. We used to be so good together. Maybe … no, I'm sure we can get back there again. All I can say is that I'm working on it as hard as I can. I'll let you know when I'm ready."

"I guess I can't ask for more, can I?" The note in JJ's voice was not acceptance but resignation.

They had come to an understanding, a painful understanding. They agreed to abstain from sex indefinitely. And, tacitly, they agreed that JJ could look elsewhere. JJ didn't exactly ask, and Rachel didn't exactly consent. But what happened between them was that JJ said he couldn't go without sex and Rachel told him sarcastically to find it outside marriage because she was not going to provide it.

Rachel avoided saying anything to Dr. Cohen about the scene with JJ. She felt—she knew—she had behaved badly. All she said when questioned was that she still had problems relating to JJ. Dr. Cohen asked about sexual relations. Rachel changed the subject. She did not want to talk about sex, not how she used to feel, not how she felt now.

Although she talked with Dev about the centrality the spanking episodes had assumed in her feelings toward JJ, she would not discuss it with Dr. Cohen. She was ashamed of being punished physically and of responding to it with sexual excitement. To talk about it with Dr. Cohen would be like admitting to perversion. All Rachel talked about willingly were her efforts to reenter the world. She told herself she was concentrating on the positive side, but what she was really doing was hiding—from herself as well as from Dr. Cohen—the dark corners that impeded recovery.

Rachel's first big obstacle, Dr. Cohen thought, *was dealing with the rape. She was able to talk that through with her cousin before she talked about it with me. Now she's refusing to deal with how she feels about her husband. And I suspect she isn't going to talk to her cousin about that, so I've got to find a way to make her open up.*

Dr. Cohen still wanted Rachel to agree to hypnosis, but she continued to withhold her consent. Perhaps she could be persuaded to be injected with a drug that would relax her and enable her to talk. Perhaps Dr. Cohen should suggest a joint session with JJ to discuss their relationship—or sessions with a marriage counselor.

But she needed to weigh the potential advantages against the possibility that Rachel might abandon therapy altogether. Dr. Cohen did not want to take that risk. Rachel continued to need help, a lot of it. She was far from having cleared the danger zone. So they would continue to pick their way along the path they were following and see what happened.

October arrived, and Marla and Alina were packing for London. They would be leaving on the fifteenth, more than three weeks before Marla's opening night performance. Noah and David intended to come in on November 5 and spend the week. Rachel and Rebecca would fly over with Hanna and Hillel on the seventh and return on the fourteenth. JJ planned to join them for the last couple of days.

Early reports from Alina, as interpreted by David, were that the two girls were "having a hell of a time, behaving like sorority sisters on the loose." Lee was on her own most days while Marla rehearsed. They spent the evenings and weekends together. Despite Marla's rigorous work schedule, most nights they stayed up until midnight. And Lee was dressed and gone by 7:00 a.m. each day. She was determined to take in *everything* London had to offer, not just the main tourist attractions.

She did all the touristy things she was advised to do, plus she visited St. Paul's Cathedral, took in a session of Parliament, toured the reconstructed Globe Theatre, and attended a play at the National Theatre. She quickly mastered the London subway system, her favored means of transportation, though she "loved London cabbies." She intended to go to Harrods, Saville Row, Bond, and Regent and Oxford Streets—not to buy particularly, but just to see the world-famous shops. She expected to take in a couple of matinees in the West End, stroll through Hyde Park and Regent's Park, and wander up and down the streets of Bloomsbury, Knightsbridge, and half a dozen other neighborhoods. Just to hear about it was exhausting. If she accomplished half of it, she'd be a perfect source of information the next time anyone asked about what to see in London.

Marla confessed to being a little nervous, as always before a performance, but Alina would not allow her to give in to it. She took charge of planning their evenings and weekends, and the agenda was crowded. What she didn't see of London alone, she planned to see in the evenings with Marla. She ordered train tickets for the weekends to Oxford and to Stratford, arranged for hotel rooms, and purchased two tickets for *The Merry Wives of Windsor* at the Royal Shakespeare Company's main stage .

"This is *such* fun," she declared, adding without meaning to do so, "All I saw on my honeymoon was a lot of ceilings." She reddened when she said it.

Marla laughed and hugged her. "I do love you so, Lee. You are the best antidote to stage fright I've ever found. How can I help being relaxed and happy when you're around?"

Marla's parents and her younger brother flew in on October 29. Her older brother and his wife arrived the following day. The Rothschilds were due in stages, beginning the following weekend. Unfortunately, external events clouded the visit. On November 4, the day Noah and David were to leave for London, Yitzhak Rabin, Israel's prime minister, was assassinated at a peace rally in Tel Aviv. Everyone was still in shock when Hanna, Hillel, and Rachel landed on the seventh. (Rebecca was not with them. She had to stay behind at the last minute because of a business emergency but hoped to catch the second or third performance of the opera.)

Marla was shaken by the news of Rabin's murder, and though they felt equally bad, everyone was trying to help her get on with what she needed to do. There was one player, Marla, and eleven cheerleaders, the mirror image of a football team. Alina provided the most help. Just before Marla headed backstage to get ready on opening night, Lee told her, "I want you to think about this sweet little girl in the stalls who is hearing *The Magic Flute* for the first time and doesn't want to be disappointed because Pamina is sad. I'm that sweet little girl, Marzy, and I'm counting on you to make me proud."

Lee was smiling, but her eyes were wet. The two sisters-in-law hugged, and Marla would be all right because she would be singing right at Lee in the sixth row center through the entire evening.

Pamina, the daughter of the Queen of the Night, was the hero's love interest and an important part for a young soprano. Marla handled it skillfully, earning warm applause. On her way out the stage door to meet the family, well-wishers surrounded her, telling her she was on her way to becoming a star.

Lee was the one who made her feel best of all, however. She presented Marla with a program and said, "Can I have your autograph?"

"Oh, Lee," Marla replied, embracing her, "what would I do without you? You're not only my traveling companion and roommate, you're my cheerleader."

Rachel's reaction to Marla's success was envy. She was ashamed of the emotion but couldn't suppress it. Here she was three and a half years older than Marla, and instead of being on her way to journalistic stardom, she was back writing trivial stuff for an obscure magazine. If she were happy about the rest of her life, it would be different, of course. Unfortunately, she saw Marla beaming as members of the family toasted her, and all Rachel could think of was *I wish I could be that happy about* anything *in my life—anything at all.*

JJ and Rebecca arrived in time for the second of Marla's four performances. The children and their nanny were staying with Dev and Yalie's parents. Marla's parents and brothers had already left for home, as had Hanna and Hillel. David and Noah were staying, along with Alina, until the run was over. Rachel, who had originally intended to go back when Hanna and Hillel did, decided to stay on with her husband and her sister.

Having the four Rothschild siblings together in London—"without parental supervision," Rebecca said conspiratorially—called for at least one big night out on the town, maybe after the curtain on the night of the final performance.

"Well," said Lee, "what about Aubergine or Gordon Ramsay or Le Gavroche?"

"Who is this child?" asked JJ. "How do you come to know about three of the very best restaurants in London?"

"You forget, I'm a journalist. I investigate."

"You've been investigating London restaurants?" Noah asked.

"Exactly. I went to the Concierge, and I said 'Give me the names of the three most expensive restaurants in town,' and he said 'Aubergine, Gordon Ramsay, and Le Gavroche.' Then I asked him 'Are they any good?' and he said 'How would I know?'"

"Now there's a concept," Noah retorted. "The *Alina Abramowitz Rothschild Guide to the Most Expensive Restaurants in the World*."

David said, "Don't think it wouldn't find an audience."

"Guidebooks for the filthy rich," Rebecca announced. "You're onto something, Lee."

Marla said, "Aubergine! Let's go there. I've heard of Aubergine."

"I'll make a reservation for an opera star and six awestruck admirers," said JJ.

"As the star of this event, I'll want champagne and a slipper for everyone to drink it from."

Champagne it would be. A lot of it. Too much. Now that the run was over and she was totally relaxed, Marla, who rarely consumed alcohol, was drinking rather than eating. After seventy-five minutes, she'd become giddy, in danger of getting seriously drunk. Finally, Alina firmly removed the champagne flute from Marla's hand and steered her toward the ladies' room.

"Let's go splash a little water on your face, Marzy. You're overdoing it."

Marla dutifully allowed herself to be led away.

Rebecca, watching them go, said, "I can't believe it. Our little Lee's become an adult."

"I guess so," said JJ.

"Seriously, guys," David answered. "It's time to stop underestimating Lee. Past time. I know you think I married a child, and maybe I did. But it's not true anymore."

Noah added, "David's right. Marla didn't ask her to come along as a playmate, though that too. Lee may act like a little kid at times, but beneath it all, she's very dependable. You know how nervous Marla can get before a performance. Lee relaxes her and keeps her centered."

Rebecca said, "Point taken."

Rachel hadn't participated in this conversation or in the earlier banter. All evening, it was as if she weren't there. She was silent, pensive, alone in the crowd. The others tried not to let it dampen the occasion, and for the most part they succeeded. Rachel's silences were becoming commonplace.

JJ invited the whole Rothschild-Goodman family to Vail for skiing over Christmas and New Year's. Even though they'd all just been to London, Rachel's two brothers and their wives were coming. Rebecca planned to come. Dev and Mark would bring their baby. Richie intended to be there the entire ten days. Yalie was busy, but she'd squeeze out as much time as she could Only the senior Rothschilds and the senior Goodmans said no.

Three days before their scheduled departure, Rachel told JJ and Rebecca she had decided not to go.

"You take the kids, Ms. Miller, and Anna. I'll be okay. I've got to be alone for a while."

"You're sure?" JJ didn't try to persuade her. Neither did Rebecca.

"Yes, I'm sure."

"Okay, then."

The others didn't learn that Rachel wasn't coming until they arrived.

Dev was worried. "I don't like her being home alone. Let me talk to her."

Rachel answered the phone.

"Rache. Would you like me to come be with you? Mark can take care of Alex."

"Thanks, Dev. I appreciate your concern. But I really do want to be alone."

"Rache, I've got to ask. Do you mind telling me why?"

"I need to sort out some things, like what to do with the rest of my life. Don't worry, I'm not suicidal. I'll be okay. You guys go ahead and enjoy the skiing. I'll see you when you come back." She remembered to ask, "How's Alexis?"

"Still the miracle baby. Goo-ing with the best of them."

"Good."

What Rachel wanted to think about primarily was whether to quit *In the Rockies* and go back to school. She was very discouraged about where she stood in her career. She was still doing small articles for the front of the book but couldn't work up the nerve to tackle anything harder. Her personal crisis had been precipitated by a draft sent to her by her sister-in-law Alina of an article entitled "London on $2,000 a Day." While Rachel's sense of humor wasn't at all robust these days, she could see how funny the article was. It was the prototype of the "guidebook for the filthy rich" that they talked about the night they all went to Aubergine for dinner, the night that Marla drank too much champagne.

Alina might have a long way to go as a serious journalist, but the kid could write. She had asked Rachel to comment, and Rachel's immediate reaction was *You've done it, Lee—this is a terrific piece. Not a word needs to be changed. You can sell it anywhere.* But there was a second reaction. *This is better than anything I can do. She looks up to me, and instead I ought to be getting advice from her.*

As an assessment of Alina's achievement, it was quite accurate. The article was well conceived and well written. And it was laugh-out-loud funny. She would have no trouble finding an outlet, and there would be a market for other articles in the same vein. Maybe even a book.

As a self-assessment, however, Rachel's judgment was wildly off the mark. Before the rape, she was on her way to becoming a very good journalist. She could be one still if she hadn't lost her desire and self-confidence. She was doing front-of-the-book stuff because she was afraid to tackle anything more substantial. Story ideas hid from her because she wouldn't search for them, wouldn't even allow them to come to her the way she used to. She'd become timid. Her prose wasn't as supple as it formerly was because her writing muscles were tight.

Being a full-time graduate student would allow her to quit *In the Rockies* without having to confess defeat. It would take Rachel back to where she had always been a star and give her additional skills she could use in journalism if—no, *when*—she came back to it. She could enroll at the main campus in Boulder and take classes three days a week, mornings and afternoons, never again at night. That would account for the next two years, more if she decided to pursue a Ph.D.. She didn't have to think about what she'd do when she finished school.

She also decided to quit seeing Dr. Cohen. She was no longer making any progress on the straight path, and she would never go where Dr. Cohen would like to take her. Psychoanalysts might want to explore the dark caverns of the soul seeking deposits of bat guano, but it was *Rachel's* bat guano that Dr. Cohen was trying to locate and there would be a lot of pain along the way. Too much.

Maybe she'd stay with Dr. Drucker. Medication helped. *No more time in the psychiatric ward. Better a druggie than a basket case. And the kids? What about the kids? I'll do the best I can for them. I wish I could do more. Maybe I can some day. Before they're grown up and gone.*

Three days into the ski vacation, Rachel got a call from Yalie, who was back in the office. Yalie wanted to have dinner. Rachel couldn't say no to Yalie, never could. They met at a downtown brewpub, Yalie's favorite hangout.

"Straight to the point, Rache. We're worried about you."

"Who's 'we'?"

"What sort of question is that to ask? Everyone's worried."

"You're worried. Dev's worried. JJ's given up worrying about me. I know that, and so do you."

"How can you believe that, Rache?" Yalie's eyes were full of tears. "JJ's a man. He was raised not to show his emotions. But he loves you, and he worries about you."

"Okay, I'll take your word for it. I don't have another choice, do I?"

"What's wrong, Rache? Now. I don't mean a year ago."

"What's wrong is that I'm lost. Your cousin is a lost soul. I thought I was on the road back, but I'm not. I have to make some changes."

"What sort of changes?" Yalie showed her alarm.

"Nothing all that drastic, sweetie. I've decided to take leave from my job and go back to graduate school. In Boulder this time. I've decided to stop going to the therapist. It's just a blind alley. No longer doing me any good."

"Have you talked to anyone about this?"

"You're the first to know. That's what I stayed home to do. To look at where I am. Think about options."

"Have you thought about all you need to think about?"

"I don't know. I guess so."

"Then you'll come with me to Vail when I go back."

"I don't want to go to Vail. I like being alone for a change."

"You listen to me, Rachel Rothschild. You're not alone. You're never *going* to be alone. And you're coming back to Vail with me. It's Tuesday. You can be alone tomorrow and half of Thursday. Then I'm taking you to Vail if I have to bop you on the head and throw you in the backseat."

Rachel should have been laughing. "Okay, if it's so important to you."

"It is. I'll pick you up at 3:00 p.m. Thursday. You be ready. The bad guys are lucky. I'm working half a day on Thursday and taking the day off Friday."

When they separated, Yalie phoned the lodge to talk with Dev.

"I got her to come with me Thursday. I twisted her arm out of its socket."

"What's the problem?"

Yalie repeated what Rachel told her.

Dev responded, "I don't like her planning to give up seeing her analyst. Sounds to me as if she's taking refuge from life by going back to school."

"There are worse ways to flee reality."

"Am I allowed to know what you've told me?"

"I don't know the answer to that. Don't tell the others. Let her say what she's going to say when she says it."

"Okay, sis. You've done good work. I'll be looking for you guys around dinnertime on Thursday."

The first half of the drive from Golden to Vail took place mostly in silence. Yalie's attempts at conversation drew little response. Rachel didn't mean to seem rude. She was busy studying the schedule of courses that she received from Boulder that morning. Now that she'd made up her mind to begin school during the second semester, she was actually excited by the prospect, more excited than she'd been by anything in more than a year.

She was clear-sighted enough to understand why. She was a star student before she met and married JJ Weiner. It was her root identity. It was what she did best. Going back to campus would be like going home to a more sheltered space than the one she shared with JJ and the children.

Once she decided which courses she was interested in, Rachel turned to Yalie as if she'd just remembered that she wasn't alone in the car. "So, how's the job?"

"I thought you'd never ask. Unfortunately, I can't tell you. Most of what I'm doing is secret for now. But it's very exciting stuff. I'll get to try criminal cases against some bad guys."

"Mafia?"

"The journalist in action. I'm not allowed for now to say whether the bad guys belong to the Mafia, work on Wall Street, log trees illegally in the National Forest, or just cut classes and stay out too late. As we say in the Justice Department, no comment—and don't quote me as saying no comment, not even as an unidentified source."

"Do you like it better than working on the Hill?"

"Nothing's better than working on the Hill. You feel like you're in the middle of the middle of things. But I prefer being Yalie Goodman to being 'the Office of Senator So-And-So.' Being 'the Office of' has limited shelf life."

"How's Richie doing?"

"Promise you won't repeat it?"

"I promise."

"Richie thinks Denver's a hick town, and the law firm he's with is just a very large hick law firm. But he's already handling major litigation, which he probably wouldn't be able to do in a bigger city with a major firm. So I think he'll be okay. But he's made a big sacrifice for my sake, and he lets me know it all the time."

"Sorry about that."

"Yeah, so am I. It's the biggest problem between us. I think I need to get him pregnant so he's got other things to think about."

"That sounds like a good plan. Tell me, does Richie like living in Boulder?"

"Oh, *yes*! That's the good side. He *loves* the place as much as I do. Bought himself a pair of in-line skates and a mountain bike, and he's out every chance he gets, careening up and down Boulder Canyon.

I'm hoping that the lure of Boulder will overcome the sense that he's landed in the sticks."

"That and having the most gorgeous woman in Colorado as his wife."

Yalie blushed. "I wish you wouldn't say things like that, Rache. I don't like it."

"Okay. You're an ugly crone. Is that would you'd prefer?"

"You must be feeling better, Rache. You're being your natural self—a bitch."

"Thank you, dear cousin." She turned serious. "Yes, I guess I'm feeling better now that I've made some decisions. Let's hope they're the right ones."

"Amen and amen to that. I love you, Rache. Wish I could do more to help you."

"It helps just knowing you're there for me when I need you."

Everyone was waiting when they drove up to the lodge in Vail. More for Rachel than for Yalie. Rachel was subdued, her usual state. She fended off questions. She preferred not to make a general announcement about her plans. They'd know when they needed to know.

"Sorry, guys. I had some things I really needed to sort out. I don't mean to be mysterious, but please don't ask me a lot of questions."

Dev was the one person she opened up to. "I've decided to quit work and reenroll in grad school. In Boulder this time. Right now, I'm a better student than I am a journalist."

"You'll be older than most of your classmates."

"That can't be helped. I'm as young as I'm ever going to get."

"Can't fault that logic. What else? It can't have taken you all this time to decide to go to school."

"You're not going to like it, Dev. I've decided to stop seeing Dr. Cohen."

"You're right. I don't like it. But tell me why. I need to hear 'why' from you."

"She's no longer doing me any good. I'm stuck exactly where I've been for the last six months. In fact, I've probably slid backward. I felt better about myself several months ago than I do now."

"You don't want to tell her what she needs to know. Isn't that it?"

Rachel nodded and covered her eyes. "I can't get anything past you, can I?"

"What is it that you don't want to tell her? Stop me if I'm pushing too hard."

"I can't tell her about me and JJ, Dev. I can't tell her what I've told you. Isn't that strange? You're a major force in my life, as personal as it gets. She's the neutral party. And yet, I can tell you things, deeply embarrassing things, that I can't tell her."

"I hope I'm wrong, but I think you're making a serious mistake. Forgive me for saying it, but you're still a psychological mess. You can't just run away from it."

"I can always resume."

"And Dr. Drucker?"

"I'll keep on taking the medication. I'm still what he calls 'clinically depressed.'"

"I want you to promise me something, Rache."

"What?"

"I want you to promise to come talk to me at least once a week. Not over the phone. In person. Will you promise?"

"I promise. You're going to be my backup psychoanalyst, is that it?"

"Something like that. I just want to keep an eye on you. If you're in trouble, I want to know about it. No more falling off the deep end."

"I wouldn't dare let you down, Dev."

"You'd better not. I love you, Rache." She could barely get the final sentence out.

Rachel had only one other person she needed to talk to on this visit, and that was Alina.

"Lee, that piece you sent me is just wonderful. It's very funny. I think you can turn it into a series, maybe even a book."

Alina was enormously flattered. "That really means a lot to me, Rachel. You know how much I look up to you."

"Lee, I couldn't write what you've written. You don't need to be a straight journalist. You're you. Don't try to be me. I'm not worth copying. I never was."

"Please don't talk like that, Rache. You're breaking my heart."

"Don't you start crying now. That's my game."

"I'll cry if I want to."

"Let's both stop. Come, give me a hug."

"I love you."

"Good, you're the third person that's said that to me today. I don't get tired of hearing it. I need every ounce of love I can get."

By now it was dinnertime. Rachel wanted to sit between Daniel and Ariel. That was inconvenient for Ms. Miller. She would have preferred to feed Ariel in the kitchen, and Daniel, who had to be persuaded to eat his vegetables, would also require special attention that he was unlikely to get from his mother. But Rachel's motherly moments had to be taken whenever offered.

At one point, when Rachel was attempting to put a forkful of broccoli in Daniel's mouth, JJ said, "I ought to get a picture of this for the scrapbook." It wasn't clear whether he meant to be sarcastic, but Rachel's tightened jaw showed Dev that it was received that way. *I need to speak to JJ. He shouldn't treat her that way. Doesn't he understand how fragile she is?*

The damage had been done. Rachel sat there seething through the remainder of dinner, and when it was over announced she was going for a walk. Marla wanted to come along. Rachel wanted to be alone, but she consented. She liked Marla, and along with everyone else in the family, she was proud of Marla's budding stardom. So she listened while they walked—half listened—to what Marla had to report about future plans. She would be appearing next summer in Salzburg. She had fall engagements in Paris, Vienna, and Berlin. The San Francisco Opera penciled her in for three roles during the following year, and she'd also been approached about performing with the Washington Opera.

Rachel tried to be interested, and really, truly, she was. But she didn't want to uphold her end of the conversation. She needed to deal with the fresh pain that JJ caused her. She wanted to walk it off, let the hurt subside. Instead, she was asking polite questions about the different parts Marla would be singing and hearing more about certain operas than she cared to know.

Marla wasn't oblivious to all this. She, too, was appalled by JJ's insensitivity. She asked to accompany Rachel in order to take her sister-in-law's mind off the injury. She wasn't just babbling. She was purposefully seeking to pull Rachel away from her own psyche. And, in a way, she'd succeeded. They were gone nearly an hour, trudging through the December chill, using flashlights where the light was insufficient. By the time they returned, even though she did not have a chance to work directly on her grievance, Rachel was feeling better, almost okay. She'd walked long enough to be tired, and against her initial instinct, she benefited from Marla's company.

At the very end of their walk, Rachel realized what Marla was up to all along. They were going up the path to the door of the lodge. Marla put her arm around Rachel's waist and hugged her. "I hope you're feeling a little better, girlfriend."

Rachel stopped and turned to her. "I really am stupid. I thought you came on this walk for you. You came for me, didn't you?"

Marla made a forget-about-it gesture. "Let's get something hot to drink. I'm freezing my ass off."

Rachel informed Dr. Cohen that she would be stopping therapy for the time being. Dr. Cohen told her it was a mistake. "You've still got a lot of issues to work through, Rachel. I know you've reached a plateau and think you're not getting anywhere. That's a very usual pattern in therapy. You need to keep working at it until you have a breakthrough to the next level. I'll be frank with you. I don't think you're ready to stop therapy. If it's me that's the problem, I'll be happy to recommend someone else."

"It's not you, Dr. Cohen. It's me. I don't have the stomach for it now. Maybe later."

When Rachel left the office, Dr. Cohen called JJ. "You remember that I told you I'd call when I had something to report. Well, I'm calling to tell you that Rachel told me she's quitting therapy. In my opinion, she's making a serious mistake. She's been sidestepping the things that bother her for some time now. If she keeps on doing that, I believe there's a risk she'll suffer an emotional collapse, maybe need to be hospitalized again. I think you ought to talk with her."

"I don't think I can help, Doctor. Rachel doesn't ask my advice these days, and I don't think she'll take it if it's offered. Our relationship is strained. I assume you know that."

"She's told me a little. Not all that much. That's one of her problems. She doesn't want to deal with how she feels about you."

"You and I are in the same boat, Doctor. I'm out of her life most of the time. I assume you know she's quit her job and is going back to school."

"No, she didn't tell me that."

"Typical. She is closed as a clam to everyone but her cousin Dev."

"Why do you suppose she is going back to school?"

"It's the easy way out. She doesn't have to face up to personal and professional failure."

"That's a pretty harsh judgment. What do you base it on?"

"I'd prefer not to get into details, Doctor. I live the personal part The professional piece of it is obvious. She hasn't done any serious work since the rape. I don't believe she's any longer capable of serious work."

"So you're telling me it's beyond your control."

"I'm afraid that's the case. I feel sorry for Rachel, but there's not much I'm able to do for her. She pushes me away. If you want to know what's on Rachel's mind, you ought to talk to Devorah Goodman, her cousin. She's the only one Rachel confides in." JJ made no effort to hide the bitterness in his voice.

"Would she return to therapy if her cousin told her she should?"

"I don't know. I don't know *anything* about Rachel these days."

"That's very discouraging, Mr. Weiner. The relationship between the two of you is definitely one of her chief problems. But she won't talk about it."

"Maybe I'm the one that should be seeing you."

"I'm sorry you two are getting on so badly."

"Yeah. Well. Not your fault. Not her fault. Not my fault. Not anybody's goddam fault."

She could hear him choking on the other end of the line.

"Maybe I'll try calling her cousin."

"That's probably best. I will make an effort to talk to Rachel. I'll urge her to come back. If she tells me anything, I'll let you know."

Dr. Cohen found Dev at her office.

"Yes, I know," Dev said when Dr. Cohen told her that Rachel was abandoning therapy. "I told her not to. All I could get her to agree to is to come talk to me once a week."

"Do you mind telling me why she's so willing to confide in you?"

"I don't know the answer to that, Dr. Cohen. I suppose it has something to do with the fact that she thinks of me as a big sister. She doesn't tell the same things to Ya'el, my younger sister, who's her best friend in all the world. Maybe it's because you give her an ear, and I give her sympathy."

"Well, I'm glad she's going to be talking to someone. Can we leave it this way? If you feel things are getting worse, give me a call. I'll confer with Dr. Drucker, and together we'll think of something."

"Okay, I can agree to that. Dr. Cohen, before you hang up, can I say … I'm glad you're concerned about her. So am I. I don't know if I can help her enough, but I've got to try. Poor pussycat, she's stranded up a tree and can't get down."

"Ms. Goodman, you're the nearest thing she's got to the fireman with a ladder. Good luck."

*   *   *

Thirteen years had passed since Rachel came to Boulder as an entering freshman at the University of Colorado. A lifetime ago. Two lifetimes ago. A life before the rape and a life since the rape. Rachel before the rape had matured into a sensible, competent, happy young woman. Rachel since the rape was a different person, no longer happy, searching for a way out of the dark.

She came to Boulder the first time to get an education. She returned the second time seeking salvation in the classroom. The one real bridge between the first Rachel and the second was academic facility. She still had those skills. As long as it was impersonally intellectual, Rachel could concentrate all her powers on achieving a goal. She enrolled in three classes—two lectures and a seminar. They each stood alone, not dependent on courses offered in the first half of the academic year. She was back on familiar terrain, once more the brilliant student whom professors enjoyed teaching and classmates regarded with envy. She felt more alive than at any time in the past sixteen months, though it was a feeling she wasn't completely able to carry with her when she left the classroom.

She drove up to Boulder on Mondays, Wednesdays, and Fridays, going directly north from Golden along the foothills. Occasionally, she stopped in to see her Aunt Ruth, and she had lunch a couple of times with Uncle Aaron. Tuesdays and Thursdays were devoted to reading and writing and any errands she needed to run. Saturday mornings, without fail, she saw Dev. Alexis played at their feet, occasionally demanding Dev's attention. When she was at home, Dev didn't like to confine Alexis to a playpen.

The visits were nothing like formal therapy. It was two intimate friends sitting together talking about the past week and anything else that came to mind. Dev talked as much as she listened, though the listening was far more intense. Unless Rachel acted troubled, Dev rarely asked a question. Her only objective was to sense Rachel's state of mind. They usually talked for an hour or hour and a half before lunch. Mark prepared a light meal for the three of them, and Rachel left when Dev took Alexis in for her nap.

It was quite different than the sessions with Dr. Cohen. Rachel was certainly aware that she was being "seen," but Dev put no pressure on her. They just talked, and when Rachel was down, the talk became a little more pointed. Rachel spoke with Dev almost as if Dev were an extension of herself. She confessed feelings she wouldn't confess to another person on earth. Unlike the visits to Dr. Cohen, which often ended with Rachel's feeling worse coming out than when she went in, the talks with Dev were a highlight of the week. Sunday through Friday, she stored up bits of her life to release on Saturday. And she listened. She listened to Dev's stories. She'd fallen out of the habit of listening to other people. Amazing that other people had problems. Even happy, successful, stable Dev. Rachel didn't realize that Dev exaggerated her problems for Rachel's benefit—so as to solicit advice. It shouldn't all flow one way.

Rachel was really enjoying being in school again. Three quarters of the things she had to tell Dev related to school: what she was learning, tidbits about her professors and classmates, papers she was writing. These were the kinds of conversations she remembered having with friends at Berkeley as an undergraduate. Dev welcomed her enthusiasm.

Less pleasing was Rachel's omission of references to her immediate family. She never mentioned JJ, except when they had gone to dinner with Yalie and Richie or been at the Weiners' for Shabbat. She rarely had anything to say about the children. Dev had to ask if she wanted to hear anything about Daniel's adventures at school.

Rachel's doing better, Dev noted in the journal she was keeping. *However, she continues to have a hard time relating to other people, especially JJ and the kids.*

Keeping the journal was Mark's idea. He was very proud of what Dev was doing for her cousin, and he wanted to be sure she did it right. "Keeping a record is the only way you'll be able to keep track of how she's progressing over time. You don't need to show it to anybody, but, God forbid, if there's a problem, it can be very important to her doctors."

The entries were mostly very brief: We talked about this, and Rachel said that; she was cheerful or not. Dev recorded it on her home computer in one growing file. She expected her weekly meetings with Rachel to continue for a long time, and she wanted to be able to use a search mechanism to find particular events without having to remember when they occurred.

Rachel simply didn't think about whether Dev might have better things to do with a Saturday morning, and Dev didn't mind. Being taken for granted was a large part of the strength she offered. There would be time enough to ask for thanks when Rachel recovered—*if* she recovered.

*   *   *

Responsibility for Passover this year devolved on Aunt Ruth, reluctant Aunt Ruth. Rachel claimed she was too busy with school, and there was no one else to take on the job. At JJ's insistence, the seders would be held at their house in Golden instead of at a hotel as they were when Rachel was running things.

"We've got this huge house," JJ said. "Big enough for a St. Patrick's Day parade through the living room. Might as well use it. I don't see that Rachel's ever going to entertain."

Rachel's busy with herself, and JJ's lost patience with her, Aunt Ruth thought. *I don't like it one little bit.*

Hanna would arrive early, as always, to prepare gefilte fish and charoset. The rest would be supplied by the caterer they had used twice previously. The list of invitees had expanded. Now that she had moved permanently to Denver, Rebecca wanted the same privilege as Rachel to invite friends from the West Coast. However, the only one of the three she asked who was free to come was Harriet Anheim, her former college roommate.

Altogether, there would be twenty-seven adults and six children at the seder: all the California Rothschilds, all the Goodmans, Rachel, JJ and the children, Rebecca, JJ's parents, grandmother, sister, and her family, Rachel and Rebecca's friends, Ms. Miller, and Mrs. Hartman, Grandma Bess's companion.

Rachel would just as soon have skipped Passover this year. However, as long as it was happening anyway, the main attraction for her was seeing her girlfriends. She'd been with everyone else recently, but a year had passed since she'd seen Jess, Laura, and Arlie. When they first got together in the large sitting room next to the master bedroom on the bottom floor of the house, Jess was the first to report.

"I'm pregnant again, girls. If it were up to Sam, I'd be pregnant all the time. I tell you, I married a sex maniac. Thank God."

Sam grinned contentedly. "Don't believe a word she says. She's the aggressor. Many's the night I have to ward her off with a stick."

"You promised not to tell," Jess said. She kissed him wetly on the lips.

Arlie said, "Disgusting. Stop behaving like animals in heat, you two. Have respect for the newly divorced."

Laura said, "I have to put up with this all the time. Hell for the unattached female is watching your best friend be slobbered on by her husband."

Sam responded, "If you'll notice, she's the one doing the slobbering. I'm the sex object in this relationship."

Jess agreed, "Yes, that's true. He's posing next week for *Cosmopolitan's* centerfold."

Rachel listened but did not participate. *Was I ever this lighthearted? I envy them so.*

She envied their lightheartedness, and she also envied the progress they were all making in their careers. Jess was a recognized authority on intellectual property, a major concern for the entertainment industries. She had published two articles on the subject in important law journals, and clients were now asking for her by name.

Sam said, "This baby will have to be born on Saturday so Jess can be back in the office on Monday."

Jess made a dismissive motion. "My assistant will give birth. I wanted to be there for conception, of course. That part I refuse to delegate."

Laura laughed. "You're obscene, Jessica Sherman. You must have run with a bad crowd when you were a girl."

Jess agreed, "I did. Every one a delinquent. I'm surprised they're not all in San Quentin. They were certainly headed that way."

Arlie interrupted, "Enough. Let's talk about something other than Jess's sex life. What are you up to, Laura?"

Sam said, "I'm leaving if you're changing the subject. Jess's sex life is the only part I'm interested in. I'll go see how Richard is doing upstairs in the playroom."

Arlie, as he was leaving, announced loudly, "Typical man. Thinks with his dick."

Sam thumbed his nose at her as he walked out of the room.

"Okay, Laura, you're on," Jess announced.

Laura said, "I'm fooling around trying to make a movie on my own."

Arlie asked, "Meaning?"

"I'm talking with a couple of producers about a script I'd like to direct. Hillel—Mr. Rothschild—helped convince them I'm ready."

"Don't be so fucking secretive, Laura," Jess said. "I know. You can tell them."

Laura explained, "I've got this idea for a comedy about two women who discover they've been sleeping with the same man and now he's cheating on both of them. They get together to fix him good. Most of the movie is about how they do it."

"Do you have a script?" Arlie asked.

"I did a draft. It's not as good as it needs to be. One thing wrong with it is that I've put every guy I've ever slept with into my villain. He's a cartoon character, I'm afraid. Snidely Whiplash. He invites hissing. I've got to rewrite it. But the plan is that I'd get to direct. I won't make a deal unless I get to direct."

Arlie asked again, "How close are you?"

"Who knows? They like the story idea and think they can get a couple of well-known actresses to play the leads. Are they going to trust it to a rookie director? I don't know. Hillel has told them I'm the next Billy Wilder. If they only discount his recommendation by 60 percent, my chances are good. But in this town, *every* aspiring director is touted as the next somebody or other. If they apply a 90 percent discount to what Hillel's said about me, my chances are *not* so good. We'll just have to wait and see."

Jess said, "You know, don't you, Rache, that your dad's become Laura's surrogate father? He's her chief booster."

"I've learned a lot from him," Laura admitted. "And he's made me feel like a person again. I owe him a lot, more than I'll ever be able to repay."

Rachel responded passively, as if to a call to tea. "That's nice." She meant to be more enthusiastic than she sounded. *I don't have any exciting news to share. I'm back in school, girls. Some career move!*

Laura asked, "And what have you got to tell us, Arlie?"

"I'm a capitalist!" Arlie answered. "Would you believe? I wrote a software program my boss liked. It's been copyrighted, and I got a bonus and a block of company stock as my compensation."

"What's this program do?" Laura continued.

"It's an algorithm for refining Internet searches. We've named it Sherlock. You know how you get eleven million hits on most searches? That's the haystack. Sherlock helps you find the needle. You enter your search terms as usual, and if you don't get exactly what you're looking for on the first try, you click on Sherlock and it begins asking you questions to eliminate irrelevant references. You don't need to understand Boolean logic because it does the exclusions for you."

"And people have the nerve to complain about the opaqueness of lawyer speak," Jess joked. "I didn't understand a word before or after Sherlock. Let's get to something I *do* understand. How are you doing personally, babe?"

Arlie said, "Okay. Make that better than okay. I'm happy to be rid of Seth, and I'm dating again. Nothing serious, but I'm going out weekends, and I'm having fun. It's nice not being around someone who criticizes everything you do. What about you, Laura?"

"Believe it or not, I'm living the life of a celibate. I have male friends and I go out to dinner and a movie with them, but the minute anyone starts making bedroom eyes at me, I'm gone. The next time I have sex with a guy, if there ever is a next time, it will because I married him. No more free samples. And, to anticipate your next question, nosy, there are no marriage prospects on the horizon."

Laura actually had a serious boyfriend, but she was not ready to say anything because she was afraid it wouldn't work out. She was accustomed to having relationships that didn't work out. He was younger than she was by a couple of years and an actor. And, yes, she was having sex with her young man, though it would probably have made greater sense not to. Still, Laura would not make the mistake with this guy that she'd made with others. She wouldn't allow herself to be exploited, and she refused to fall in love before he did. There would be time enough to confess to her girlfriends if that ever happened.

Jess turned to Rachel. "That brings us round to you, Rachel Rothschild. We've all been blabbing, and you haven't said a word."

"I haven't got much to tell. I quit my job. I quit therapy. And I've gone back to school. Unless you want to know what classes I'm taking and the names of my professors, that's the end of my story."

"Do you like being back at the university?" Jess asked.

"Yes. I may be mentally ill, but at least my brain hasn't atrophied."

Jess frowned. "Don't say that, Rache. You had a bad period, but you're not mentally ill."

"That's girlfriend talk, Jess. You know yourself how badly I'm capable of behaving. You saw me in action last year and scolded me for it. And you were exactly right. Well, I've still got my claws out. Watch out I don't get you with them. I go back and forth between hurting and wanting to hurt. If that's not mental illness, I don't know what is."

For a long moment, there was silence. Jess made a mental note to check with Dev. Dev would know more. Finally, Laura spoke up. "What can we do for you, Rache? We'd all like to help."

"I appreciate your concern, guys. I really do. The only thing I can think of is to come be with me in Vail this summer or come for skiing next winter. I like having company even when company doesn't like having me. If you care to talk about public finance or the theory of the public interest, I might even have something to say. As long as it's academic or theoretical and hasn't got a thing to do with real human beings, I'm quite articulate."

Jess was still frowning when the conversation ended. She didn't like what she'd heard at all.

Before the seder began, Jess looked for an opportunity to introduce little Alexis to her son Richard—as if it mattered to either child. They were in the library, next to the big living room. Mark was present, and after a couple of minutes' conversation about the challenges of raising children while working, Jess asked, "You won't think me rude, will you, Mark, if I ask for a couple of minutes alone with Dev? I need to ask her about Rachel."

After Mark left, Jess closed the door behind him.

Jess said, "You're the only one who can tell me, Dev. When we're talking, Rache sits there like a department-store dummy, like we're complete strangers. And when she finally says something, it's a downer. What gives?"

"I assume she's told you she's quit seeing her therapist?"

"Yes. But as far as I can tell, she's not a lot better than she was a year ago. How could she quit?"

"No, she isn't any better. She was for a while, but she couldn't hold onto it. I practically begged her not to quit therapy. She told me she didn't feel she was making any progress. When I couldn't convince her to continue, I made her promise to come see me once a week. So far, she's doing it."

"And?"

"And … I'm a complete amateur, Jess, and I'm incapable of being objective. But she comes and we talk. If things start to go bad, I hope I'll be able to recognize it and call in professional help."

"How do you think it's going?"

"So far? Pretty well. She loves being in graduate school. She was always a spectacular student."

"I know."

"It's like she's revisiting scenes of former triumphs."

"And personally?"

"To quote from *Hamlet*: 'Aye, there's the rub.' Her personal life is a shambles. She can't get beyond her pain. You'll see at the seder. She tries now and then to engage, but for the most part, she's there without being there, alone in the crowd. I think I may be the only person in her life that she really talks to without having her guard up."

"What about JJ? What about Rebecca?"

"Rebecca's the younger sister. Rachel's never been accustomed to leaning on Rebecca emotionally, and she isn't about to start now."

Dev didn't answer about JJ. She didn't want to talk about the strain in the relationship. It was not her place to do so.

Dev's silence about JJ told Jess all she needed to know. She plunged in. "I have something I need to tell you, Dev. It's been burning a hole in me for a long time. I assume you know that Rachel never slept with JJ before they got married?"

"Yes, she's told me that. It didn't make sense to her. It doesn't make sense to me either."

"JJ *required* Rachel to remain celibate for more than two years. She wanted to sleep with him, and he absolutely refused. I knew at the time it was happening how frustrating that was for Rachel. I didn't learn until a day or so after the wedding that JJ didn't live by the rules he imposed on Rachel."

Dev gasped. "Are you sure? How do you know?"

"JJ was at Stanford most of that time. Arlie was at Stanford, too. He was regularly screwing one of her friends, and she suspects her friend wasn't the only one."

"My God!" Dev said. "Does Rachel know that?"

"I'd be amazed if she did. If she knew, she would have told you herself. It was a major issue between them before they got married."

"Arlie knew and never said anything?"

"Not at the time. Arlie was shocked by JJ's behavior, but she didn't know what to do with the information. It wasn't as if JJ advertised. Arlie was probably the only person on the Stanford campus who knew that JJ was engaged to Rachel. And she wouldn't have known about JJ's extracurricular activities if another girl hadn't pointed out this handsome guy their friend was sleeping with."

"Did Arlie know that JJ had issued this no-sex edict and that Rachel was suffering because of it?"

"I don't think so. Not then. Once, five of us spent a few days in the wine country—me and Sam, Arlie, Rachel and JJ. At night, JJ sent Rachel off to room with Arlie. I don't know if Arlie considered that strange—or merely circumspect. You've got to remember that Arlie was still a virgin and all she really knew about boys was that they wanted sex all the time. She didn't want to hurt Rachel when she learned later about JJ's tomcatting around."

Dev sat there for a moment, processing the information. Jess waited for her to speak again. Finally, Dev asked, "How did it finally come out?"

"A day or so after the wedding, Arlie, Laura, and I were talking, and I said something like 'at least the waiting and wanting is over.'

Arlie asked what I meant, and I explained. Then she dropped the news on me like a load of bricks."

"And you kept this to yourself all this time?"

"I didn't know what else to do, Dev. I was pretty immature myself in those days. Rachel seemed deliriously happy at the beginning, and I didn't want to spoil it by raking over the past."

"And now?"

"God forgive me, Dev, I made a huge mistake. The trouble in the relationship between Rachel and JJ was there from the start. JJ forced a code on Rachel for more than two years and indulged himself. Since you're Rachel's only real confidante, I should have told you this a long time ago."

"Son of a bitch! How could he have done that?"

"The old double standard, Dev. One rule for Her, another for Him. It was cruel, and it was deliberate cruelty. You're right. JJ is a selfish son of a bitch. It took us all awhile to realize that."

Dev closed her eyes and took a deep breath. "I've got to think this through, Jess. I know Rachel has a rocky relationship with JJ, but I didn't know that JJ deceived her even before they were married. It explains a lot."

"That's why I thought I should tell you."

"What do you think I ought to do about it?"

"That's beyond my competence, babe. I don't know if telling Rachel the truth would help. It might make things worse, maybe a lot worse."

Dev took another deep breath and expelled it. "Yes, I think that's a distinct possibility. I appreciate your telling me, Jess. I really do. But right now I'm at a loss about what to do with it. If Rachel were still seeing her psychoanalyst, I'd call her and let her make the decision. I don't have to tell you that Rachel's very fragile. Telling her about how JJ behaved before they got married ... I just don't know. I've felt all along that my lack of training in this field is a handicap. Never more so than right now."

"I wish I could do something useful. I feel helpless sitting a thousand miles away, knowing that Rache is in such pain." Jess had an inspiration. "Maybe I can get her away from herself for a while. Do you suppose she'd come on vacation with Sam and Richard and me this summer? We're going camping in Washington State, a last fling before I become too pregnant to do anything but waddle around and complain."

"My guess is that she'll refuse. Rachel's never been one to go without a hot shower, and I doubt she's ready to start. But it can't hurt to ask. In fact, it will do her good. It will remind her that you like having her around. Even when she's no fun to be around."

"Shit," said Jess vehemently.

"Doubled and redoubled."

"I wish I could share the load."

"So do I. Believe me. I feel drained on Saturdays after she leaves. She's pathetic a lot of the time, and it hurts so much I could scream. But I know I've got to be there for her. She's willing to talk to me about the bad things in her life. Yalie's always been closer to her, but I'm the one she's chosen. Maybe it's because I've been here all along and Yalie hasn't. She got into the habit of telling me things."

"God give you strength, babe."

"I don't want to sound like a martyr. I'm happy to do it.… Happy's not the right word, is it? I do it because I'm able to do it and it's got to be done. I love her, and she needs me."

"You're doing what we Jews call a *mitzvah*. I don't know exactly what it means, but it's what we call it, don't we?"

Dev smiled. "You're wonderful, Jess. Would you like to be my therapist?"

"Anytime. If you ever want somebody to talk to, give me a call. Morning, noon, or night."

"Thanks for the offer. I may take you up on it. I can't really discuss it with Yalie. She hasn't been a part of it. Besides, she thinks Rachel's wallowing in her misery and I'm indulging her. Mark's there for me, but he doesn't know Rachel the way you do.

"You'd be doing me a favor if you called, Dev. It would allow me to believe I'm helping, and you can't begin to imagine how much I'd like to have that feeling."

Dev and Jess were just completing their conversation when Sam knocked on the door and told them their presence was required. The Weiner contingent had arrived, and Hanna and Ruth wanted everyone at the table to begin the seder.

Rachel took her usual place alongside Grandma Bess and across from Jess, who had taken Richard into her lap. Yalie's husband Richie was on Rachel's other side. Both Jess and Dev looked somber. Sam and Mark were the only ones who saw.

Rebecca had been coaching Daniel on the Four Questions. He could make his way through the transliteration of the Hebrew, but he had no idea what he was saying and it was slow going. Hillel and Aaron were in no hurry. They were content to let him proceed at his own pace with Rebecca's help, and they joined in the applause at his achievement when he finished. Daniel was very pleased with himself for asking the questions, though he was not much interested in the answers and soon wanted to leave the table.

As the job of reading passages from the narrative passed along the table, Rachel had to be told what page they were on when her turn came. Dev and Jess exchanged looks from opposite ends of the table. Jess, whose view of Rachel was unimpeded, saw that Rachel wasn't chatting with Grandma Bess or with Richie. Rachel had always been a whisperer at the seder, so Jess knew that Dev was, unfortunately, right. Rachel was bodily present but emotionally absent.

Dev and Jess weren't the only ones to notice Rachel's passivity. When the narrative was suspended for the seder meal, Grandma Bess told her what a wonderful job Daniel did asking the four questions and wanted to know what Rachel was studying. Richie asked for advice on Denver area cultural attractions that he and Yalie ought to visit in their spare time.

Alina came around the table to urge Rachel to go to Salzburg in the summer when Marla would be performing at the Festival. "You and I will tour the area while Marla's rehearsing. I need to collect information for another two-thousand-dollars-a-day story, and it would be wonderful to have a *real* journalist along to help."

JJ, across the table sitting one place away from Jess, said, "That's a great idea. You ought to do it, Rachel. It will do you good to go away for a few weeks. Maybe Rebecca and I will fly over and join you for one of Marla's performances."

"Well, maybe. I'll think about it."

Alina sent Marla around to extend the same invitation. "We'd have a wonderful time, Rache. And I could sure use some additional support. This is a big one for me. All kinds of important people in the music world will be there. You know me, I'll be nervous as a mouse in a houseful of cats. You'd be doing me a favor, honey. Say you'll come."

"You're sweet to ask. I promise I'll think seriously about it."

"I'm going to count on you. Don't disappoint me."

Hanna asked Rachel into the kitchen to help. Rachel followed her in. "Mom, you remember me, Rachel Rothschild? I'm the girl you named 'the kitchen klutz' when I was sixteen. You haven't wanted me anywhere near the kitchen during Passover for as long as I can remember. You guys must think I'm really, really stupid. Grandma Bess couldn't care less what I'm studying but wants to know all about my classes. Yalie is a native, and Richie needs me to tell him about what to see around here. Marla can't sing another note without my help. Alina can't write unless I go with her. And all of a sudden, I'm needed in the kitchen. Next thing you know, Annalisa will be asking me how to arrange a party."

Hanna laughed. "We're that transparent, are we? Everyone's trying to get you out of the doldrums, Rache. It breaks everyone's heart to see you so …"

Rachel interrupted, "… acting like a zombie. I know. Look, Mom, I appreciate what everyone's trying to do for me. I really do. I went back to school to help get over it. And I will. I'm just not there yet. You have to be patient with me." She added lightly, "It won't help me *or* you if 'the kitchen klutz' wrecks the place. So thanks for asking me, but I think you ought to draft somebody else to assist. What about Ariel? She'll probably do a better job than I would."

Aunt Ruth, who'd been listening, said, "I recommend Alexis. At least when she drops things, she's close to the ground."

Rachel hugged her aunt and her mother. Hanna kissed her tenderly and sent her back to the dining room. "Okay, sweetheart. You're right. We're better off in the kitchen without having you underfoot."

All the attention prodded Rachel out of the lethargy that possessed her earlier in the evening. When dinner was over and the singing started, Rachel joined in, even displaying some enthusiasm. Yalie suggested that the two of them sing a spiritual they used to do together as children but hadn't sung at a seder in fifteen to twenty years. Yalie started, and Rachel harmonized. Soon Marla was adding coloratura decorations at the high end of the scale, and even Grandma Bess joined in. It was the evening's highlight, everyone said, though it was not the song or the performance that made them feel that way. The real reason was the temporary light shining in Rachel's eyes. Even Ms.

Miller, whose emotional connection to Rachel was minimal, noticed the difference.

All the visitors left. So did Rachel. She went downstairs to the bedroom in the big house in Golden to sleep, but the Graduate School in Boulder was her place of refuge from the vicissitudes of being alive and in pain. People were harder to deal with than ideas. People wanted you to talk when you didn't feel like talking, smile when you didn't feel like smiling. People expected you to take their feelings into account when all you cared about were your own feelings. Ideas didn't make those kinds of demands. You met them, and they took you in. You didn't need to explain. You didn't have to pretend. Like rug vendors, they unfolded their secrets for you to examine, to admire, to take away.

In her current frame of mine, Rachel's classes provided all the company she required. She didn't need to know a thing about her classmates. And they didn't need to know a thing about her that she chose not to tell, and she didn't choose to tell them much. Her identity was Rachel Rothschild, Graduate Student. One of her professors remembered that she used to write for *In the Rockies*. "Used to," Rachel confirmed to him. "I'm not doing that any more."

She didn't answer personal questions, or she answered them cryptically. "Do you live around here?" "Yes." "Where did you get your undergraduate degree?" "On the West Coast."

"Are you married or single?" Silence. She'd taken to leaving her wedding ring in her dresser drawer.

The reticence disappeared during classroom discussions. Rachel was as quick as she ever was to find the root of an intellectual issue, and she wasn't reluctant to be the first to express an opinion. She always did enjoy being the smartest kid in the class. If contradicted by one of her classmates, even by the professor, Rachel was prepared to defend her position vigorously when she was sure she was right—and she was *always* sure that she was right. She asked penetrating questions. She still had the journalistic gift for persistency when dissatisfied with first responses.

As long as the interaction was on an intellectual plane, Rachel was capable of making connections. She continued classroom discussions over lunch, willingly talked about books on the professor's reading list. She took to having coffee regularly with one of her classmates in the seminar on the theory of the public interest, an intense young man named Louis Short with an undergraduate degree in philosophy. He was concentrating on political theory, and the course played more to his strengths than Rachel's. He was more familiar with the literature and had been over some of the same ground in other courses. Rachel liked pitting her superior intelligence against his superior knowledge. Talking with him was stimulating, and she enjoyed being flirted with. Rachel hadn't said anything about being married, and Louis Short didn't ask since he really didn't care.

Louis Short was younger than Rachel by nearly five years, a smooth-featured, dark-haired man with long hair tied in a ponytail and a neatly-trimmed, reddish-brown beard. After almost every class, they walked over to the Starbucks at Broadway and University, near where Rachel's Land Rover was parked. He had a grande double latte, she a grande latte. Rachel paid with her American Express card. That was established at the start. She had money. He didn't. Rachel was flattered by the attention. She liked him. He reminded her that she used to be considered attractive. He made her feel like a woman again.

Once her Uncle Aaron walked into the coffee shop, and Rachel introduced them. Although nothing had happened between her and Lou, she felt strangely guilty, surprised during a liaison. Perhaps it was because the conversation had moved from the intellectual and impersonal to the romantic. Lou told her how lovely she was. "The Queen of Beauty," he called her.

He was constantly inviting her back to his apartment. The tone was light, a joke between them, yet he clearly meant it. She should have told him *not on your life* and stopped seeing him after class. But she didn't say it. Instead, she began to wonder whether her aversion to sex wasn't simply an aversion to JJ. Maybe she could do it with someone else. *Maybe Lou.*

One day when he made the usual joke, she said okay. Her heart was pounding in her chest. "Where do you live?" she asked in a wispy voice.

"In an apartment north of town," he said. "Out 28th Street." He licked her ear, surreptitiously touching her breast through the fabric of her blouse. "Come on."

They used her car. He didn't have one. She would bring him back later to pick up his bicycle. He was touching the inside of her thigh as they drove, close to the crotch.

"You'll make me lose control of the car."

"I want you so bad."

"I want you, too." She didn't really mean it. *I'm experimenting. That's all. I need to get laid. That's all. Lou's a nice guy. That's all.*

It wasn't warm, but Rachel was perspiring. Her heart was racing. She could feel the pulse throbbing at her temples.

Lou gave her directions. She parked on the street outside his apartment building. He led her by the hand directly into the bedroom and began to undress. Rachel took off her shoes and socks, unbuckled her slacks, and let them drop.

"Leave your panties and bra on, Beauty. I want to be the one to take those off."

She was down to her lacy silk panties and bra, and he was stripped to his shorts. He took her in his arms and kissed her neck. He reached behind her and undid her bra, lowered the straps, and took it from her gently, then began reverently to kiss her small breasts.

She moved to lie down on the bed.

"Wait. I want to take your panties off while you're standing."

He got down on his knees and kissed her bare feet. Slowly he lowered her panties and kissed her opening. He put his hands on the globes of her buttocks and pulled her toward him, so that his face was against her. He flicked her clitoris softly with his tongue.

Slowly, he rose, kissing her breasts again, licking at her nipples while she held his head to her, then he scooped her up and carried her over to the bed. He dropped his shorts, displaying his erection, and asked her to kiss it. She did that, putting her lips to his penis, using her tongue, nibbling at his scrotum.

She was moist, and he was able to enter her in one smooth stroke. As he did so, Rachel surprised herself by starting to sob. *I don't want this. Why am I doing this?*

"I made a mistake," she said. "Please. I can't do this."

"I can't stop."

"Please. Please." She tried to push him off. When he wouldn't be pushed, she started hitting at him.

He grabbed her wrists and pinned them to the bed over her head, all the while thrusting at her, thrusting at her.

She was impaled but trying to buck him off.

"Act like you want it, Beauty, cause you're gonna get it."

It was hopeless. He was too strong, too determined. It continued and continued and continued until he stepped up the pace and, with a cry, spent himself in her. After a moment, he rolled off her.

She was weeping softly now.

"How could you? I asked you to stop."

"Yeah. You licked my prick and kissed my balls, and then you wanted me to stop? That's cock-teasing carried to a new level."

"You raped me."

"Why don't you go to the police? I'm sure you can explain to them how you got to my bedroom and got fucked without having a mark on you."

"I have to get out of here." She used a tissue to wipe up the semen leaking from her vagina and reached for her bra and panties.

"No, no, these belong to me. A souvenir. You're a third-rate piece of ass with first-class taste in underwear. I want to remember you, Queen of Beauty." He was mocking her now.

She slapped his face with all the force she could muster.

"I ought to beat the shit out of you. But I'm not going to give you a reason to claim you were raped. Just get dressed and get the hell out of here, bitch."

Naked beneath her blouse and slacks, Rachel returned to the Land Rover. She sat there behind the wheel a long time, crying. *What have I done? Why did I do that? What became of my self-respect?*

On the way back to Golden, she went off the main road to find a bar. Inside, she sat on a high stool, asked the bartender to pour her a shot of bourbon, and swallowed it with a shudder. She drank a second shot, then a third, paid her bill, and headed for home. She felt the liquor entering her system as if intravenously. She hadn't been behind an automobile wheel drunk since her freshman debacle in Boulder—*how many years ago?* But the pain was dulled. Maybe she'd be able to forget that today happened. *It'll never happen again. Never. Never.*

Saturday arrived. Rachel wanted to avoid seeing Dev this week, but when she called to make an excuse, Dev was too attuned to Rachel's moods to be taken in.

"You've got to come," Dev said. "Today especially. You're upset. I can hear it in your voice."

Against her will, she found herself in Dev's study. Though she had intended not to, she confessed what happened. Tears rolling down her cheeks, she admitted allowing herself to be bedded by a classmate. More than allowing. She admitted to wanting it.

"I needed to know, Dev. I needed to know whether it was JJ … or me. I found out it was me. But too late to make him stop. And he kept my underwear. Like some kind of trophy to mount on the wall. 'I fucked Rachel Rothschild.'" She screamed the last sentence and dissolved, laying her head on Dev's lap like a child seeking comfort from its mother.

"It's okay to cry, sweetheart. It's okay." Dev patted her lovingly until the crying stopped. "It's not the end of the world, Rachel. You needed to find out. I understand."

"What if he tells? I'm afraid he'll tell everybody—all his male friends, people who know me."

"Having sex with you after you said no isn't going to make him look good. It's not politically correct, and CU is a PC campus. I think he'll keep his mouth shut." Dev didn't think anything of the sort. But Rachel's worrying about gossip behind her back wasn't going to help her emotionally. *If there's gossip and it gets back to her, we'll deal with it then.*

"I felt so bad, right after that I stopped at a bar on the way home and got drunk. I haven't been drunk since the time with Yalie. I needed to forget."

"Burying it isn't the way to go, Rache. You need to forgive yourself. Look at it this way. You ran an experiment, and the experiment failed, blew up in your face. I'll say it again: 'It's not the end of the world.'"

"I guess not," Rachel conceded. "But I feel pretty bad about it. I haven't had a decent night's sleep since it happened. I was stupid and slutty. Going home naked underneath, all I could think about was being out there after the rape without any clothes on. Only this time I asked for it. I went back to this guy's apartment *wanting* him to fuck me."

"No more, Rache. You're beating yourself up."

"Am I supposed to feel *good* about it?"

"That's not what I'm saying, and you know it. What happened, happened. You've got to move on. Learn and move on."

"I'll try." There were tears in her eyes, but she wasn't crying. She was fighting to maintain control.

"That's my girl."

Rachel sat there exhausted, her eyes closed.

"Do me a favor," Dev said. "You need to rest for a while. Let me take you back to the guest bedroom and have you lie down. Maybe you'll fall asleep. It will do you good."

Rachel allowed herself to be persuaded. Dev gave Alexis to Mark and followed Rachel into the bedroom. Rachel took off her shoes and lay down on the bed. Dev lay down beside her and held her, and before long Rachel fell asleep. More than an hour passed before she awakened. Dev and Mark were having lunch. Alexis was in her high chair, her face smeared with food.

"How do you feel, honey?" Dev asked.

"A lot better. The last thing I remember was lying there in your arms. I must have fallen asleep in seconds. You were right, Dev. You're always right about me."

"We've been together a long time. All your life, all of mine that I can remember."

"You're the only one of us who's together right now. If I'm ever together again, it will be because of you."

Although he was in the middle of eating, Mark got up to leave the table. He didn't want to interfere with the conversation.

Rachel stopped him with her raised hand. "It's all right, Mark. I've told Dev everything I need to tell her today. She's a better analyst than my analyst. You're married to a remarkable woman."

"Yes, I am." He was holding Dev's hand and kissing it. "She's remarkable in many ways."

"I know what it must be costing the two of you to have me here every Saturday morning, but it's saving my life. I didn't want to come today, Mark. Maybe you knew that. I didn't want to come because I had something to tell her I didn't want to tell. But I came because she made me come, and I told her, and I feel like I'll make it because Dev knows."

"I'm glad to help, Rache," Dev said. "I'm glad to be *able* to help. It's no imposition, and even if it were, I'd still be doing it. You're my mission, sweetheart."

"I'd better go before I begin crying again. I'll flood this place if I start."

And so she left, and she cried all the way back to Golden, tears that purged the accumulated emotional dirt left behind by Louis Short and dislodged during her visit with Dev. *God Bless, Dev. Bless her and keep her from harm.*

Lou Short wouldn't let her forget, however. He sat next to her if there was a seat vacant. When there wasn't, he winked at her and took another seat. She tried to ignore him, but when he spoke directly to her, she couldn't avoid answering or people would begin to talk.

She considered quitting the class. But if she did, she'd be telling him *You can hound me out of graduate school just by following me around from class to class.* She had to stick it out.

It affected her performance. She was flustered. She no longer spoke up in class the way she normally did. She imagined that he'd told every other guy in the class. She remembered hearing about the signs in the boys' bathroom at high school: "For a good time, call Bunny Schwartz." She was afraid that there might be a sign in a men's room somewhere: "For a good time, call Rachel Rothschild." For the first time she understood how Laura must have felt when that rat director Bogusian was advertising her as his slut.

What could she do? *What did Laura do? She got a job with Daddy.* She told herself ruefully, *That won't work for me, will it? Daddy doesn't run an alternative university up the street.* Unless she was prepared to go home and confess to JJ, there was nothing to be done. She couldn't charge Short with sexual harassment. He had the panties and bra to prove he screwed her. For all she knew, he was planning to tell JJ himself. She'd be lucky if all he meant to do was to keep reminding her how whorishly she behaved.

Stiff upper lip. That was the only answer. Tell Dev on Saturday. Shake it off like a dog coming in out of the rain. He'd get tired of the game eventually if she refused to hand him his daily victory.

"You've got the right idea," Dev said when they met. "You mustn't show him that he's got you on the run. Close your eyes when you see him, take a deep breath and, if you can do it, smile. He's mud on your boots, sweetheart. Think about him that way, and that's what he'll become. He isn't worthy of your pain."

Rachel took Dev's advice. She looked straight at Short and thought, *You're scum. You can't get to me. You're an asshole.*

It seemed to work. When she quit acting intimidated, he stopped getting pleasure from trying to make her squirm. Three weeks after the day at his apartment, she no longer panicked when she saw him.

He still had a nasty surprise in store for her, however. In an envelope on her desk at home, with "PERSONAL" written in big red letters, she found a photo of her bra and panties and a note saying, "I'm thinking about sending these to your hubby. They still smell of you, Beauty. Want to buy them back?"

The letter arrived on a Tuesday. In a surge of fear, she called Dev immediately and asked if she could come to Dev's that evening. She brought the photo and note with her.

Rachel was desperate. "What should I do, Dev? He's going to destroy me."

"I don't think so, Rache. I could be wrong, but my guess is that he's trying to blackmail you back into his bed. If he wanted to tell JJ, I doubt he would have warned you."

"But what am I supposed to *do*?"

"Well, one thing you're *not* going to do is to give in to him. If we're agreed on that …"

Rachel nodded her head vigorously.

"… then I can see two possibilities. One is to call his bluff. Let him do what he's going to do. He might tell JJ. He might not."

"I don't think I could stand it, waiting for the other shoe to drop. And if he ever did tell JJ, I wouldn't be able to handle it. I just couldn't. What's the alternative?"

"The other possibility is for me to pay him a visit as your lawyer. I can tell him he's given you absolute proof of attempted blackmail, for which he'll go to jail, and if he carries out the threat he's made, we'll sue him for every cent he's got or ever hopes to have. I'll scare the living shit out of him."

"Will it work?"

"We won't know for sure until we try. I think I can handle this guy for you, Rache, but I've got to have your help. I'll need a day, maybe two days, to do some research and prepare some legal documents. I know you'd rather not, but you've got to go to class and acknowledge in some fashion that you got his message. He's looking for that acknowledgment. You don't have to speak to him unless he speaks to you. A meaningful nod will do if you look frightened enough. He has to be persuaded that you're terrified about what he might do. If he says anything to you—and my guess is that he will—beg him for a few days to think it over. Don't be defiant. Beg. If he sets a deadline, agree to it, whatever it is. We'll work within the deadline. Think you can do that?"

"I'll try," Rachel answered. She was holding a tear-soaked handkerchief that she'd twisted into a knot.

"Good."

Dev planned to make Short believe that Rachel was desperate, maybe desperate enough to go to her husband and confess her indiscretion. Dev was JJ's lawyer, and she'd encourage Short to believe that she was acting on JJ's behalf. If Short wanted proof that she worked for JJ, she'd tell him to call JJ's office and ask his secretary, who would confirm the relationship. Dev wouldn't exactly be lying, but Short needn't know that Rachel was the client in this matter, the only client.

At the next class session, Short took a seat next to Rachel. For Rachel to look frightened by him was no great acting feat. Just before class ended, he passed her a note. It read: "I'm waiting for your answer, Beauty. Meet me at Starbucks. Buy us the usual."

She arrived at the coffee shop before him. She bought a grande double latte for him and a grande latte for herself and paid with a credit card. He arrived ten minutes later.

"How nice to find you here, Beauty. You and I need to have a little talk. Would you like to come back to my apartment?"

"Please. Don't make me do that."

Short grinned crookedly. "We'll see later what you'll do, won't we, Beauty? I need your answer."

"Please, Lou. I need some time. I've got to think."

"Of course you do, Beauty. Would you like another ten minutes?"

"Please. I'm begging you. Give me until next week. Please."

"You want until next week? I can't do that, Beauty. But I'll tell you what. You go into the ladies' room and bring me back your bra and panties, and I'll give you until Friday afternoon. How's that?"

Rachel hadn't expected the demand. "Please. Don't make me do that. I'm begging."

"That's the price, Beauty. If you'd rather not do it here, you can do it back at my apartment. Which will it be?"

Rachel didn't have to pretend that she was crying. She went into the ladies' room, locked the door, and took off her brassiere and panties. She brought them back to Short. He sniffed the crotch of her panties. He did not hurry to put them away.

Rachel was in agony. "Please, Lou. Don't show anybody. I promise. I'll tell you by Friday afternoon. Just don't show anybody."

"Yes, you will, Beauty. I'll be expecting to hear from you. You'd better not disappoint me, or you'll be one very sorry little girl."

Rachel left the coffee shop on the edge of hysteria. As soon as she got back to her car, she phoned Dev at her office. Rachel could scarcely speak, and what she said couldn't be fully understood.

"Calm down, sweetheart," Dev told her. "Take a deep breath. Tell me what happened."

"He gave me only until Friday afternoon—and Devi … Devi … Devi …"

"What, baby?"

"He made me give him my bra, my bra and panties. My bra and panties! Otherwise, he wanted my answer right away. So I gave them to him. I'm so ashamed. I'm so ashamed."

"That miserable cocksucker! Baby, don't cry. I'm ready for him now. I'll crush him like an insect."

When she was done talking to Dev, Rachel started home. She was trembling as if ill and once more felt in need of a drink, of several drinks, to dull the pain she was in. She stopped at the same bar she visited after her tryst with Lou Short. She was wobbly with drink before she felt ready to go home, and when she entered the house and JJ saw her, it was evident to him that she was drunk.

"My God, Rachel. What's gotten into you? You're …"

"Needed a drink. Sorry."

"You *should be* sorry. Please get the hell out of here. I don't want the children to see you this way. Go to your room. I'll get Rebecca to help put you to bed."

"Don't need help. Don't want help."

But Rebecca arrived anyway. Although Rachel tried to conceal it, Rebecca saw that she was braless. Rebecca followed her into the bathroom, but Rachel refused to undress. She couldn't undress in front of Rebecca. Rebecca tried to help her, but Rachel pushed her off. "Go 'way. Lemme alone. G'outta here."

"Oh, Rache. You ought to be ashamed of yourself. What happened to your bra?"

"Thass my business. Go away, dammit. Go away."

"JJ's right. You *are* sickening." Rebecca left, slamming the door behind her.

Rachel fell down on her bed, aware that she'd disgraced herself before her sister as well as before her husband. But at least Rebecca didn't know that she was without her panties. It was bad enough that she couldn't explain how she lost her bra.

That evening, Dev phoned Lou Short. When he picked up, she said, "This is Devorah Goodman. I'm Mr. J.J. Weiner's attorney, and I'm calling about the letter you sent his wife, Rachel Rothschild. You've heard of Mr. Weiner—Hyman Weiner & Sons?"

Short already knew the Weiner name. "Yeah? What about the letter?"

"I have a copy in front of me, Mr. Short. You've committed an act of blackmail, using the U.S. mail, and I will send you to jail for it unless you cooperate."

"Bullshit, lady."

"Oh? We'll see about that. I'll be waiting for you Thursday morning at 9:00 a.m. in the breakfast room at the Boulder Marriott. I'd advise you to be there, or I will go straight to the police and we'll see who's bullshitting whom. You can also expect a civil suit for five million dollars. My fees are very high, so I don't think small. My prediction is that you'll be panhandling on Pearl Street when I get done with you. See you at nine Thursday." And she hung up.

Thursday morning, dressed in her most businesslike black suit, Dev arrived at the Marriott at 8:45 a.m. She waited in the car until 9:05 a.m., then strode into the restaurant grasping her expensive leather briefcase, which held the draft of two documents she had worked on most of Wednesday.

She found Short and sat down opposite him. Without saying an unnecessary word, she took out the first document and laid it on the table facing him.

"Read this," she said. Then she waved the waitress over and ordered juice, a bagel, and black coffee. "You want anything, Mr. Short? Or have I given you indigestion?"

What she handed him was a statement of charges with a long list of legal citations obtained during a couple of hours in her firm's library.

She could see Short becoming increasingly alarmed. She had him pegged correctly. A natural bully without the stomach for a fight.

When he was done reading, he said, "What do you want from me?"

She reached into the briefcase and pulled out the second document. It was essentially a promise to refrain from further communication with Rachel Rothschild or JJ Weiner and to return Rachel's personal property in exchange for agreement not to pursue criminal charges for blackmail or to file a civil suit. "We'll go to the courthouse, sign it, and have it notarized. You can deliver Ms. Rothschild's property to me—*all* of it, Mr. Short—by registered mail at this address, together with all photographs and negatives. If you fail to deliver any part of it by close of business Tuesday, we'll assume you want all the trouble I'm prepared to give you." She handed him her card.

"Why should I do it?" The defiance was pro forma. Dev had seen others pretend bravado just before caving.

"You'll do it because otherwise I'll cut you into little pieces, Mr. Short. And it will give me the greatest pleasure to do so."

Short said in a pleading tone, "We go to the same classes together. We participate in the same discussions. How am I supposed to stop communicating with her?"

"No personal conversation. No phone calls. No e-mail. No letters. We're not stopping you from going to class."

"Okay. I'll sign."

"Good. I thought you would."

An hour later, the document was signed and notarized, and Dev was on the phone to Rachel. "It's over, babe. He turned tail and ran like a rabbit. I think he must be all the way to Kansas by now."

Rachel ought to have felt more relieved than she did. She escaped from Louis Short, but she'd given JJ another reason to be angry with her and Rebecca must surely be wondering how she came to not be wearing a bra. Should she tell Rebecca that she stopped wearing bras altogether, or leave the question unanswered? Unanswered was probably best.

Rebecca's words—"JJ's right. You *are* sickening" —pursued her. She couldn't get them out of her head.

The end of the term was approaching. Rachel and Short were still in the same theory seminar. She thought about quitting and decided not to, and he was damned if she was going to drive him away. It was impossible for them not to participate in the same discussions. There was an edge a serrated edge to any conversation involving both of them. Where Short might previously have said "Rachel has a good point," he now asserted that "Ms. Rothschild doesn't understand" what the author of the moment had written. Rachel's reply was "Mr. Short is, as usual, wrong." Others in the seminar would have had to be inanimate objects not to recognize the poison flowing between them. An in-class referee would doubtless have awarded the most points on their exchanges to Rachel. She prepared what she intended to say in advance. The discussion took place on grounds she'd chosen, and as in basketball, she enjoyed the home floor advantage. Short couldn't be sure where she was going. He was looking to knock her off stride. She wouldn't concede a thing, however. They'd both taken to exaggerating their differences, making themselves look faintly ridiculous.

After one clash, Professor McDermott told Rachel he'd like to see her in his office after class. When she arrived, he asked her to sit down and offered her a cup of tea, which she accepted.

"I don't want to know what's happened between you and Louis Short," McDermott said. "But you're acting like a couple of juveniles, and it's got to stop. I won't have my seminar turned into a battlefield. Settle your scores elsewhere, please, not on my time. Okay?"

Rachel reddened. "Yessir. I'm sorry. It won't happen again."

But it did happen again because Professor McDermott hadn't had the same conversation with Short. Rachel made a point about something John Rawls wrote, and he disputed it.

"Mr. Short is entitled to his point of view," she said. He persisted, and she was forced to answer, "I don't happen to agree." He pressed on, and she answered, "I don't want to fight about it, Mr. Short."

"You don't want to discuss it because you know you're wrong."

Professor McDermott intervened sharply. "That's enough, Louis. Please take the junior high school routine to the playground. Not in here, please."

Short was plainly startled. "I'm sorry. I was trying to make a serious argument. I suppose I got carried away."

"You suppose right. We've all heard more than we care to hear of your quarrel with Ms. Rothschild."

Short defended himself. "My quarrel isn't with Ms. Rothschild. It's with her ideas."

"Fine. We've still heard quite enough. Now, let's move on."

Rachel made a face at Short also worthy of junior high school, and Short gave her a dagger stare. But that was the end. For the remainder of the school year, they made an effort to avoid participating in the same discussion.

Rachel was empty when classes were done at term's end. She was facing summer without anything to keep her interested. She declined Jess's offer to take her with them on a camping trip. Although she'd gone camping once years earlier with Arlie, Laura, and Lynetta Pearson, Rachel hadn't been since and wasn't interested in trying it again. Marla and Alina had urged her to come to Salzburg, and JJ told her to go. She could do a couple of articles for *In the Rockies*. Her name was still on the masthead as a senior writer. But she didn't have anything she cared to write about.

She ought to spend the summer with Daniel and Ariel. Leaving them to go off with Marla and Lee would be another act of self-indulgence. She couldn't imagine, however, being alone with the kids for two or two-and-a-half months. Ms. Miller was taking five weeks off, and that would mean being *really alone* with the children much of the time, feeding them, bathing them, dressing them. She'd get a little relief from the woman who regularly relieved Ms. Miller, of course, but not all that much. Hiring a full-time nanny while their mother was around would be a sort of confession of incompetence or indifference.

The prospect of boredom compounded by anxiety and a sense of guilt—that was Rachel's state of mind. She told it all to Dev, flagellating herself as a rotten mother. Dev soothed her, consoled her, counseled her. After an agonizing hour, Rachel concluded that the best thing for her to do was to go to Vail with the children for the five weeks Ms. Miller was away and then to fly to Europe to join Marla and Alina in Salzburg. She wanted Dev to come to Vail, too.

"If I could, I would, sweetie. I have to be at work, though. The best I can promise is that Mark and Alex and I will come up for a weekend or two while you're there. What about JJ?"

"I don't know. JJ and I haven't had a lot to say to one another since I came home drunk. I suppose he'll come up weekends to see the kids. Maybe Rebecca will come along, though she's mad at me, too. She loves being with the children. And I'm sure they'd rather be with her than be with me."

Dev responded abruptly, "Stop that, Rache! Don't you *ever* get tired of 'woe is me?'"

Rachel was shocked. Her lip was trembling. "You *asked* me to tell you everything. I don't have to keep coming if you don't want to listen."

"I'm sorry, Rache." Dev knew she'd hurt Rachel's feelings. "I shouldn't have said what I said. I *do* want to tell me everything. Sometimes I'm not a very good listener, I guess."

Rachel was in tears. "Don't judge me, Dev. I won't be able to bear it if you judge me, too."

"And I can't take it when you cry." Dev handed her a tissue. "I won't if you don't. Deal?"

Rachel wiped her eyes and tried to smile. "Okay. It's a deal."

Rachel left for Vail on a Tuesday morning. She purchased a small bicycle for Daniel. She intended to teach him to ride a two-wheeler the way Hanna taught her to ride when she was small. It was one of the episodes of childhood that she remembered most vividly. She wanted Daniel to remember the way she remembered. She purchased a small trailer for the back of her own bike, very much like the one Hanna had when she was a baby, so that she could take Ariel along once Daniel was able to ride by himself. She picked up a dozen new toys that she would dole out gradually during the visit, and she'd also taken a pile of books, some for her to read to Daniel, some for him to read to himself. Luckily, she kept a closet full of clothes in Vail because, with all the extra things she was taking for the children, there was barely room enough in the Land Rover for a couple of suitcases.

It was actually fun for about a week: Rachel dressing the children in the morning, making breakfast and feeding them, running after Daniel holding onto the back of the bike until he gained enough confidence to ride on his own, playing peekaboo with Ariel and hide-and-seek with Daniel, feeding them lunch, putting Ariel down for her nap, driving them into town to ride the big lift to the top of the mountain, taking the kids for ice cream, running around after them in the open air, going home for dinner, bathing Ariel and putting her to bed, reading to Daniel and lying beside him until he fell asleep and sometimes, exhausted, falling asleep when he did. She might actually be their mother if she tried. And even enjoy it—briefly.

But no one came up on the first weekend, and there was no relief from the daily routine. She couldn't read the books she brought for herself because the children constantly wanted this or wanted that. Ariel was three and toilet trained but prone to accidents, especially at night. Rachel was accustomed to changing urine-soaked sheets approximately never. Daniel was after her ceaselessly to admire his athletic prowess, which was negligible, or his drawings, which were utterly unintelligible. Ariel wouldn't eat what she was given. Daniel had the yechs for vegetables, especially when green. Feeding him was even more of a struggle than feeding his sister. Both children scattered their toys all over the place and couldn't be persuaded to pick them up. Going grocery shopping with them was an ordeal. Ariel demanded to be held, and Daniel wanted candy and sugared cereals with cartoon creatures on the box. "I won't eat that" was his constant refrain.

None of the neighboring houses were in use. There were no other children around. Rachel, who was a loner most of the time, wanted a little adult companionship. Although she was loathe to admit to Rebecca or JJ that she couldn't manage alone, Rachel called Rebecca and pleaded with her to come up the following weekend. "The kids are driving me crazy," she said apologetically. When Rebecca arrived along with JJ late Friday, Rachel willingly yielded the mothering responsibilities to her younger sister, telling herself that the kids would be hers again Monday and she needed to relax a little in the meantime. It wasn't a good weekend, however, because she and JJ were barely speaking since the night she arrived home drunk, and her relationship with Rebecca was also frayed. She'd given both of them another reason to think she was incompetent.

Rachel asked Dev to come the following weekend. While she couldn't turn the children over to Dev the way she turned them over to Rebecca, it helped to be caring for Daniel and Ariel alongside Dev, who was caring for Alexis. She saw how loving Dev was toward Alexis, how calm, how unhurried. She would have liked to be that way with her children. *I was that way with Daniel when he was a baby, wasn't I? Before JJ persuaded me to hire a nanny and make a career.* But then she thought: *Dev has a baby, a nanny, and a career. Jess has a baby, a nanny, and a career. Why can they manage it, and I can't?*

Watching Dev with Alexis should have been a joy—an inspiration, even—but, instead, it was depressing. Rachel fought against it, but it enveloped her. By Tuesday morning, she was feeling so down about things that she put in a call to Dr. Drucker. He said he wanted to see her as soon as she came back to town, but in the meantime, he prescribed a second medication for her to take twice daily.

"I need you to call me back on Friday to let me know how you're feeling," he said. "Will you do that for me?"

"Yes."

"And Rachel? Are you still seeing your cousin?"

"She was here over the weekend, and we were together a lot. But we didn't have our usual every Saturday talk."

"How long since the last one?"

"Almost a month."

"Do me a favor. Call her tonight, and do it over the phone. You can't keep it all cooped up inside of you."

So, at night, after both children were asleep, Rachel called Dev at home. Rachel explained that she was depressed and was calling because Dr. Drucker told her to. Rachel wasn't very talkative, and it could have been a very short conversation, except that Dev skillfully drew her out. Once she began, the words spilled out in a torrent. Rachel confessed that being with Daniel and Ariel heightened her feelings of inadequacy. The children got on her nerves. Dev told her that her reaction to being with the kids twenty-four hours a day was natural.

"I'm only around Alexis a couple of hours a day Monday through Friday," Dev said. "If I work a little late, sometimes she's already asleep when I get home. I'm not with her all that much. Still, there are plenty of times on the weekends when she's too much for me. I'm sure Jess would tell you the same thing about herself and Richard. You've got to stop thinking you're the only woman who finds that being a mother can be very difficult at times. Don't you think I wouldn't like to have a little time for myself instead of changing diapers? No, never! C'mon, Rache, don't be so hard on yourself. Mothers are allowed to be frustrated. Wives are allowed to be frustrated. Frustration is part of the human condition. Sometimes the major part."

"JJ and I aren't talking any more, Dev, not much anyway. Ever since I came home drunk. And Rebecca is pissed at me."

"I know, sweetheart. Rebecca has talked to me about your coming home without your bra."

Rachel had a sinking feeling. "What does she think?"

"She's disappointed in you."

"There's more, Dev. Don't sugarcoat it. What did she say? Exactly."

"I'd rather not."

"Don't baby me, Dev. Let's hear it."

"Okay, if that's what you want. She said, and I quote, 'Can you imagine? Rachel's out showing her tits in a bar like a streetwalker.'"

"Oh, God. What did you tell her?"

"Nobody, not even Yalie, not even Mark, hears anything about you from me, Rache. I listened. All I said was, 'That's really unnecessary, Beck, and cruel. Don't say it. Don't even think it. Rachel's your sister, and she's a wonderful woman. But she's also having a hard time emotionally.'"

Rachel, blanching though she knew Dev couldn't see her, asked, "How did she react?"

"She said, 'I guess you're right. I'm sorry. But I do get exasperated with her.'"

"So, what am I supposed to do?"

"I don't think there's anything you can do, sweetie. What happened, happened. Look at the good side. You're through with Louis Short. The part about the bra will blow over. And I think Rebecca may even take what I said to heart."

"And JJ? What's he got to say?"

"I can't answer that, Rache. I see him all the time on business, but he knows you talk to me and I won't tell him anything. So he doesn't talk to me about you. As to what he thinks, I haven't the vaguest idea. I can ask him, of course, but all he'd tell me is what he'd like you to hear."

They talked for nearly two hours, until nearly midnight. Dev finally said she had to stop because she had to be up at 6:00 a.m.

"Call me again tomorrow night, Rache. Talk yourself out. I can't come up this weekend, but I'll be there the weekend after next, and I'll get Mark to care for the kids so you and I can be alone. I shouldn't have allowed you to be on your own this long."

"Here I am, thirty years old and still in need of a babysitter. I knew I'd become dependent on you, Dev, but I guess I didn't understand how much until Dr. Drucker asked me—*ordered* me—to call you."

"I want to help, sweetie, but it's late and I've got to go now. Call me tomorrow."

"I will. You can be sure of that."

Talking to Dev was Rachel's escape valve. She had to articulate what was bothering her, and like goblins under the bed at night, her frustrations were chased away by the light that Dev provided.

The additional medicine prescribed by Dr. Drucker also improved her mood. And then Rebecca and JJ arrived again for another weekend, and the burden of taking care of the children wasn't all Rachel's for a couple of days. She took long bike rides by herself, went to a movie by herself, did a little clothes shopping. Although relations with her husband and sister were cool, the blackness lifted a little. By the time Dev, Mark, and Alexis drove up the following weekend, Rachel felt she'd regained control, and being her children's mother once again seemed possible.

In fact, when Ms. Miller returned to resume responsibility for Daniel and Ariel, Rachel had almost forgotten how bad things seemed for a while. She might even like to do it again sometime—not too soon, but sometime.

*   *   *

Marla and Alina had already been in Salzburg for ten days by the time Rachel arrived. They had a two-bedroom suite in a luxury hotel. Marla was rehearsing the part of Blonde in Mozart's *Abduction from the Seraglio*. She'd also be singing Mozart's *Exultate Jubilate* with the festival orchestra. Lee was playing her usual role: keeping Marla from becoming too tightly wound. However, she was also gathering material for her next couple of two-thousand-dollars-a-day articles. She had everything she needed to write on Salzburg and the surrounding area. And she'd taken Marla along for a three-day weekend in Vienna to scope out the scene there. With all the research she did in advance on the Internet, Alina was able to accomplish what she needed to accomplish in very short order.

Rachel was joining a going enterprise, and Alina Abramowitz Rothschild, whom everyone until recently considered the baby of the family, was its chief executive. Alina had been running Marla's life outside the opera house and concert hall, and she knew exactly what she would have Rachel do. "You and I will drive down to Vienna on Thursday. I've got some more work to do there. Then we'll meet Marla at the airport on Friday and fly to Budapest for the weekend. She'll come back Sunday night. You and I will stay on Monday in Budapest, spend Tuesday in Vienna, and drive back to Salzburg Tuesday night."

The opera and concert schedule began later in the week, and Alina and Rachel would be there to applaud their sister-in-law. Noah and David would come for a week of the run. Marla was already accustomed to following Alina's lead, and Rachel fell meekly into line. She'd never been to this part of world. Neither had Alina, of course, but having discovered her vocation as a comedic travel writer, she'd learned how to find out what to see, where to stay, where and what to eat, how to get around, and what in the vicinity must be visited. Marla and Rachel were the beneficiaries of her knowledge. Alina was still as bubbly as a teenager and immature in some ways. But she'd grown enormously in self-confidence, and Marla and Rachel accepted her guidance because she really did know what she was talking about.

Rachel had been there for three weeks and Noah and David had already come and gone by the time JJ and Rebecca arrived. They would stay long enough to see Marla perform, and Rachel would go home when they went home. Rebecca was moving into the suite with Marla and Alina. Rachel and JJ would stay together in a room with a large double bed. It was the first time they'd occupied the same bed in many months, and it was awkward—as if they weren't husband and wife, but male and female acquaintances compelled by circumstance to occupy the same room. Rachel couldn't even bring herself to undress in front of JJ.

They lay as far apart as possible and slept facing in opposite directions. During the time this arrangement continued, they did not exchange as much as a single embrace. They made an attempt to be pleasant, especially when the others were around, but after they'd talked about how the children were when JJ and Rebecca left home and what Rachel, Alina, and Marla had been doing, they didn't have a lot to say to one another.

Summer was ending. Marla had been warmly applauded by audiences and critics. Her future, at least as a Mozartian, was assured. Alina had one more stop to make—gathering information on Prague—and Marla would be the one at leisure on this part of the trip.

Rachel, JJ, and Rebecca returned to Golden. Rachel was preparing for the fall term. Her first visit with Dev in a month was nearly free of angst. She had enjoyed herself, she reported.

"How was it once JJ arrived?" Dev asked.

"Okay."

"No tension between you?"

"No more than usual—in fact, less."

"And now?"

"Now? Back to school."

"Are you happy to be going back to school?"

"All summer I've been a fish out of water, Dev. I'm going back to my element, the only place, God help me, that I really belong."

Toward the end of the spring term, her first as a graduate student on the Boulder campus, the chairman of the department of political science had called Rachel in to suggest that she consider getting a doctorate. "You're an extraordinarily able student, Ms. Rothschild," he said, "exactly the kind we want to have in our Ph.D. program." At the time, Rachel said she was flattered, but the answer was no. He asked her not to reach a firm conclusion but to think it over.

The more Rachel thought about it during the summer, the more appealing it became. She had begun classes in Boulder with the intention of getting a master's degree in public policy because that was what she had been doing on the Denver campus before the rape. She had simply picked up where she left off. But as she reflected on it, Rachel acknowledged to herself that she might never return to journalism, her original motive for enrolling in the public policy program. Maybe her desire to explore issues facing local and state government would revive one day. Right now, the main reason she was going to school was to go to school.

She drew up a mental balance sheet. On the one hand, she had no desire to teach and didn't consider herself a scholar. On the other hand, as a candidate for a doctorate, she would be taking a much wider variety of courses and she could stay on campus indefinitely—probably six or seven years. That would allow her to postpone a reckoning on what to do with her life after the university. She thought about it and thought about it and eventually came to a decision toward the summer's end. The weight, she concluded, was on the side of taking the doctorate. Thus, as the time neared to sign up for fall classes, Rachel made a date to see the chairman and told him that she'd changed her mind and was ready to commit to the Ph.D. program.

She hadn't the least idea of what she might do as a dissertation topic. She wasn't even sure what her field of concentration would be. However, as she explained to Dev when they were together, making the decision to go for a doctorate was the most decisive and comforting action she'd taken in a long time. Instead of equipping herself for a phantom career in journalism, she now had something positive to work toward. Dev suggested that Rachel sit down with Mark. As a political scientist himself, he could serve as an informal adviser. That sounded like a good idea. After lunch, when Dev took Alexis in to play for a while and then to put her down for her nap, Rachel talked with Mark about her plans.

The fields she knew most about were American government and public policy. However, as an undergraduate, she took courses in comparative government and liked them quite a lot. She was also interested in international relations and, except for the presence of Louis Short, enjoyed the class she took last semester in political theory.

Mark told her, "During the first year, you'll have to take courses in research methodology and data analysis, regardless of what field you decide to work in. Though I doubt you're going to enjoy mastering symbolic math, you can't read the journals these days without it. It's become a standard part of the armamentarium. I have to admit I'm prejudiced. I think use of mathematical formulas to describe political conduct imparts an illusion of precision that has led the profession in the wrong direction. However, you can't avoid learning how to use it if you're going to succeed as a political scientist these days."

"What about the major fields within political science?"

"You needn't make your mind up immediately, Rache. Since you have to show competence outside your primary area of concentration, you can afford to do a *little* looking around—emphasis on the word 'little.' My guess, if you want it, is that you'll end up concentrating on American government or public policy. Those are your strong suits. Colorado isn't the best place on earth to study international relations. There are some good people in Boulder, but distance from the two coasts hurts a lot. Don't take my word as gospel on any of this, however. In the end, you've got to decide for yourself because you're the one who has to live with it."

"Thanks for the advice, Mark. I really appreciate it. Would you mind if I checked in from time to time?"

"I'd love to help if I can, Rache. You're *my* cousin too, you know."

Although her class schedule for fall fully reflected her decision to study for a doctorate, Rachel hadn't said anything at all to JJ about her intentions. She was not sure why. Yalie knew, not from Dev or Mark, who were closemouthed about anything Rachel told them, but from Rachel herself. She made arrangements to have dinner with Yalie and Richie in Boulder one evening, primarily to catch up on what they were doing. Yalie reported that she was going to be the lead prosecutor in an upcoming major trial involving money laundering and bank fraud, and Richie was litigating a private antitrust suit one of his firm's clients had brought against a competitor in the telecommunications business. Both of them felt as if they were on the frontlines, fighting on the right side, a privilege lawyers didn't always enjoy.

In turn, Rachel told them her news. Yalie took it in and said, more bluntly than she should have, "You're putting life on hold, aren't you, Rache? That's what it's about."

"I guess so."

"What's JJ got to say?"

"I haven't told him yet."

"You haven't *told* him? I don't like the sound of that. What's going on with the two of you?"

Rachel didn't care to tell Yalie what she'd told Dev about the troubles in her relationship with JJ. She was afraid Yalie would be critical.

"I want to be surer about what I'm intending to study before I tell him. I don't want JJ to conclude that I'm 'putting life on hold.'"

"Ouch. I shouldn't have said that, Rache. I don't mean to be critical. It's just that I want so much for you to be well again."

"I know you do, love. And I'd like to oblige. I really would. But you're probably right. Working with ideas is easier for me than dealing with my emotions. So I *am* dodging life in a way."

"Just don't run away from those who love you." She meant JJ.

"I'd never run away from *you*. I'll love you always, Yalie."

"And I'll always love you back."

The conversation continued but tailed off into inconsequence. Having exposed a nerve, Yalie didn't probe further. The last thing she wanted to do was to make Rachel feel bad. Rachel didn't want to say more than she already had about her inner feelings. Dev was the *only* one who needed to know.

Both Yalie and Rachel were disquieted by their evening together. Yes, they loved one another. But Yalie was uneasy because Rachel seemed so fragile. And Rachel's love for Yalie was tinged with envy because Yalie knew what she wanted and Rachel didn't.

Still, the decision to go for a doctorate imparted a welcome degree of stability in Rachel's life. Academically at least, it had given her a greater sense of purpose. She had a whole list of prerequisites to satisfy. Until she settled on her fields of concentration, she could legitimately take any course in the graduate catalog for political science, and she also had an excuse for taking advanced classes in Spanish to satisfy her language requirements. Instead of risking the accusation that she was an intellectual dilettante, an accusation she sometimes leveled at herself, she could say to everyone, including herself, that it was all part of her Ph.D. studies.

Although she was commuting from Golden, Rachel was considered in residence on the Boulder campus. Mornings on Mondays, Wednesdays, and Fridays weren't enough. She had a late seminar on Monday and an afternoon class that met Tuesday and Wednesday. She decided to stay over in Boulder on Mondays at Aunt Ruth's. She ought to be staying with Yalie, of course. She told herself there was more room at Aunt Ruth's, but the real reason was that she would be babied by Aunt Ruth, not scrutinized.

JJ was a bit surprised by the increased amount of time Rachel was spending in Boulder. "You're practically living there," he said. It was merely an observation, but Rachel heard it as an accusation.

"Yeah. I'm taking a heavier load this semester."

"I'm glad you're occupied. You seem happier."

"Occupied, yes. Happier, I don't know."

"I mean you've got fewer complaints."

"Yeah. Fewer complaints means not having to listen."

"We always end up here, don't we, Rachel? How I've failed you."

"I'm sorry, JJ. It's not your fault. I can't get over the hump, and I keep looking for someone else to blame. You just happen to be standing there in the line of sight. Look, if I'm spending more time in school, it's mainly because school takes me away from myself, and that's better for both of us."

"I suppose so. But please try to find some time for the kids, Rachel. They need more of you than they're getting."

"Speaking of places where we always end up."

"Oh, shit!" And he stomped out of the room.

Rachel sat there for a moment, empty. She wanted to be on better terms with JJ. *He's my husband. I just can't have sex with him. It isn't as if I don't want to. I love him—or I used to. The least I owe him is a civil tone.*

She went after him to apologize. Finding him took a few seconds, but that was long enough for Rachel to decide she should tell him about going for a doctorate. *Might as well do it now. It will help him understand why I'm spending more time in Boulder.*

"I apologize for what I said and how I said it, JJ," she said when she caught up with him. "I hate myself when I act that way, and I don't blame you for being mad at me."

"I'm not really angry with you, Rachel." He was. "I'm frustrated. I should be the one apologizing. I'm not as understanding as I should be, as I'd like to be."

She came to him and they hugged, as friends hug, not as lovers. He kissed her cheek, and she kissed his.

"I probably should have told you earlier, JJ. I've decided to go for a doctorate. That's why I'm spending so much time in Boulder. I'm in my first year resident's program, and the courses I've got to take aren't available at the times I'd like."

JJ was surprised and upset. "You've been doing this for at least six weeks. Don't you think you owed me this explanation a little earlier? You might even have talked with me before you did it. I'm not exactly a stranger, for God's sake."

"I'm sorry, JJ. You're right. I probably should have asked you. I *certainly* should have told you."

"Why didn't you?"

"I don't know, JJ. I think maybe because it's an area of my life that I control. Mostly I'm not in control. I haven't been in control since it happened. Taking a Ph.D. is something I could decide for myself. Does that make any sense to you?"

"I guess so…. Maybe you can understand how I feel, Rache. I feel shut out of your life. It isn't a good feeling."

"I'm sorry, JJ. I'm really sorry. I'm sure it's hard on you. Someday it will be better for both of us."

They hugged again, this time with a faint stirring of ardor. It was the first time they'd connected in the nearly five months since Rachel came home drunk from the meeting with Louis Short. They both felt better, but the feeling was fleeting.

*   *   *

Rachel was sitting in her research methodology class on a Wednesday afternoon in mid-November when the door opened and one of the departmental secretaries walked in and made a beckoning motion at her.

Rachel followed her out the door.

"Your Aunt Ruth called. She needs to talk with you."

Having left her cell phone in the car, Rachel ran ahead to the political science department office and called her aunt's number.

Rachel asked, "What's wrong?"

Ruth was crying. "It's Grandpa," she said. "He had a heart attack. Aunt Shoshana called. I'm leaving for New York at 7:00 p.m. this evening."

"Is Grandpa going to be okay?"

"I don't think so, darling. It's pretty severe. I'm not sure he'll be alive when we get there."

"Who else is going?"

"Your Daddy. Your Mom. Uncle Aaron. Dev wants to go. I'm trying to talk her out of it. It would be much too hard on Alexis."

"I'm going with you. If Dev wants to come, she can leave Alex at our house with Ms. Miller. Alex will be fine there. What about Yalie?"

"She's trying to make arrangements at her office. I don't know about your brothers or your sister. Your folks asked me to find you. They were going to talk with Rebecca and Noah and David."

"Would you get whoever's making arrangements for you to make them for me, too? I'll go right home and pack. Just tell me when and where to meet you."

By the time Rachel arrived home, Rebecca had packed for both of them. When they got to the airport, the group numbered six. Dev left Alexis with Mark to take to Rachel's house. Yalie dumped her work on one of her colleagues. There were nine on the plane out of New York. David had come with Hillel and Hanna. Noah would be on a later flight.

Though they would need several vehicles to get them all to Tel Aviv, Elon, Aunt Shoshana's eldest son, was waiting for them at the airport. Albert Rothschild was still alive but not likely to survive the night. Hilda Rothschild insisted on remaining at his side. Elon reported that Hilda was exhausted "but holding up as well as can be expected." Shoshana was at the hospital with Yigal, her second son. Avital and her brothers' wives, Dahlia and Irit, were at Shoshana's apartment, preparing food for the visitors.

Ruth and Hillel wanted to go directly to the hospital to see their father, and Elon agreed to take them. The others would be transported to the Dan Tel Aviv and would afterward go to Shoshana's. Hanna expected to take charge of the household. Aaron would help Yigal make "the arrangements." If Albert died tonight, he would be buried tomorrow.

It was approaching midnight when Ruth and Shoshana arrived at the apartment, bringing Hilda with them. Hilda was eighty-seven and too tired to argue. The visitors hugged her and kissed her but got little response. Hilda's head and heart were at Albert's side. They'd been married almost sixty years, and this was the end.

Hillel remained at the hospital. Elon, Yigal, and Avital left to join him. At 3:00 a.m., having slept enough to make it possible, Rachel, Dev, and Yalie headed to the hospital to take over the vigil. They were to be relieved at 6:00 a.m. by David and Rebecca, plus Noah, if he had arrived by that time.

At 4:35 a.m., a nurse emerged from Albert Rothschild's room to summon Rachel, Dev, and Yalie. Their grandfather was about to die. He'd been disconnected from the heart monitors. The three young women stood beside him, speaking softly to him though he could not hear, watching his labored breathing. And then the breathing stopped. According to the clock on the wall, it was 5:16 a.m. One by one, their cheeks wet, Albert's granddaughters bent over him to kiss his forehead, offering their last good-byes, and they emerged stiff-legged and exhausted from his room, not quite knowing what to do.

Finally, Dev asked, "What do you think? Should we call first or just go to Aunt Shoshana's?"

"Someone's got to call the hotel to let them know," Yalie replied. "David and Rebecca must be getting ready to leave for the hospital."

Rachel said, "I don't know if it's good or bad that Grandma wasn't here when it happened."

"She knew it was the end when she left here with Mom and Aunt Shoshana. " Dev wiped her eyes. "She knew she'd never see him alive again." And she started sobbing. Yalie and Rachel hugged her.

Yalie said, "It's better this way. We were here to love him to the end." She also began crying. "But it's not as hard for us."

Rachel remembered, "The last time I saw him … before this … he got confused, thought your mom was my mother. In a way, that was even harder for me than watching him die. He wasn't Grandpa any longer."

Dev called the hotel and spoke to David. Noah still hadn't arrived. Then the three young women took a taxi to Shoshana's, dreading, above all, the task of telling Hilda that her husband, their grandfather, was dead. Only Hilda, Hillel, Ruth, and Shoshana remained at the apartment. Elon, Dahlia, Avital, and Avital's husband, Uri, were staying with Yigal and Irit at their house north of the city.

Hillel answered the door and understood immediately. He hugged his daughter and two nieces. Though it was his father, he was the one doing the comforting. The young women tried hard, but unsuccessfully, not to cry again. Shoshana emerged from her bedroom, followed by Ruth. Ruth's daughters went to their mother. Rachel and Hillel hugged Shoshana.

"Mama just now fell asleep," Ruth said. "I don't want to wake her up."

Shoshana answered, "I think we've got to, Ruthie. She'd be upset if we didn't. You and Hillel and I should go in to her together."

A few moments later, there was a chorus of sobbing from the back room where Hilda had been sleeping. Albert's three children joined their mother in mourning their father's death.

Burial was swift in the Jewish way. Hillel and Ruth would remain in Israel for the week of *shiva*, the ritual period of mourning. Hanna stayed with her husband. Aaron needed to get back to his law school classes. Two days after the funeral, he caught a flight back to the United States, taking Rachel, Dev, Yalie, David, Noah, and Rebecca with him.

While the rest of Albert's American grandchildren were able to remember the good times, Rachel sat numbly, staring out the window. Another part of her life was over. She didn't mean to think that way or to feel sorry for herself. She just did. Feeling sorry for herself was Rachel's default mode.

*   *   *

It was immediately after Thanksgiving. Everyone was home. Rachel was back in Boulder, where she belonged, a star in the academic firmament. The light she gave off was dazzling and, to some of her classmates, seriously annoying. In a different setting and in a different way, Rachel was where she was as a young teenager, before Jess Sherman ridiculed her behavior, compelling her to be less boastful. She was not blatantly showing off as she did then, but she *was* showing off. Her classroom comments displayed unnecessary erudition. She was not content to offer a simple answer to a question. She needed to show how much more she knew than was required. It was the technique she perfected while earning top grades as an undergraduate at Berkeley. Then, however, it was done in term papers and written course examinations. In seminars, it came across as exhibitionism.

Although her additional knowledge still impressed professors, it didn't earn many points with fellow students. One of her classmates in the seminar on American political institutions, Marjorie Andrews, satirized it as "Rachel Rothschild's standard comment on what Laski had to say about what Bryce had to say about what de Tocqueville had to say, with a little St. John de Crevecoeur thrown in." Those to whom she repeated this caricature found it hilariously apt.

"Why don't you give it a rest, Rothschild," another of her

classmates, Robert Crawford, said to her one day after she performed one of her usual star turns.

"Give what a rest?"

"It gets a little old listening to you show how much more you know than the rest of us. Everybody knows how smart you are. You don't need to demonstrate it every time you open your mouth."

"Oh, I'm sorry." She turned her head away and began to cry.

"Shit.... ... I apologize, Rothschild," Crawford said self-reproachfully. "I didn't mean to hurt your feelings.... Well, yes, I guess I did. But I didn't think you'd cry about it.... Here." He untied the bandanna around his neck and handed it to her.

Rachel was trying not to be conspicuous in a hall full of students. She accepted his bandanna and, in a voice that was barely audible, she excused herself. "I've got to go to the ladies' room."

Crawford was waiting for her when she emerged. Her eyes were red, but she was no longer crying. She handed him back his bandanna.

"Listen, Rothschild—Rachel. I feel like a twenty-four-carat son of a bitch. Would you come have coffee with me? I'd like to talk to you."

Rachel said no, but he said "please" in such a sheepish manner that she eventually consented. He wanted to be forgiven for his cruelty, and she really would like to explain herself. Crawford suggested the Starbucks at Broadway and University. Though it was the closest place, Rachel asked to go elsewhere. That was where she used to have coffee with Louis Short. They found another place on the Hill. Rachel tried to pay, but Crawford insisted. "Consider it my inexpensive apology," he said. Fifteen minutes stretched into a half hour and then into an hour and an hour and a half. Robert Crawford was a sweet young guy from Texas who had just entered graduate school after working four years as a high school teacher in Houston. He'd like to teach at the college level. He admitted to envying Rachel's facility. Rachel avoided revealing much about her personal history. But, her eyes tearing once more, she said, "I guess my classroom demeanor comes across as arrogance, but the truth is, I'm so lacking in self-confidence about most things in my life that I *need* to be successful here. I'm just a playground braggart, covering a feeling of inferiority."

Crawford handed her his bandanna once again. "You shouldn't talk like that. I don't know you very well, and I obviously don't know what's gone wrong in your life, but now that I'm past the outer walls you've thrown up around yourself, I can see that you're a really nice person. You need to give more of us a chance to like you instead of resenting you."

"I'll try to do that, Robert."

"Bob, please. All my friends call me Bob. And I'd like to be your friend, Rachel."

"Thanks, Bob. I'd like that, too. I have family in Boulder, but I don't have any other real friends."

Coffee with Bob Crawford was a turning point for Rachel. He helped her see herself as her classmates saw her, and he offered to be her friend. She initially considered Louis Short a friend, of course, but there was always a flirtatious element in their relationship, even before it turned disastrous. Bob Crawford didn't flirt with her. They were simply classmates and friends. Crawford was her entry to other members of the class. He told them she was really very nice, and they agreed to give her another chance. She stopped the showy intellectual acrobatics, and that helped. She was becoming a member of the flock, a graduate student like any other graduate student trying to make a place for herself among her peers.

By the time the fall term was nearing an end, Rachel had made a comfortable place for herself. She was progressing exceptionally well in her studies. She had a few friends. Although she told no one about her previous history, word about who she was and what happened to her had begun to reach CU-Boulder from CU-Denver. *Oh, yes, Rachel Rothschild. Very smart woman. She's the one who used to write for* In the Rockies. *Remember the story about Rocky Mountain Arsenal? She's the one who did that. Do you know she's married to a member of the Weiner family? Billionaires.*

Rachel would have been very unhappy if she knew these reports were circulating. She'd like to be anonymous. No one spoke openly about the rape. But people on the Denver campus remembered the stories that appeared in the local press and that Rachel Rothschild did not return to class afterward. How long would it be before that information reached Boulder?

*   *   *

The Christmas and New Year's holidays were approaching. They would be spent in Santa Monica this year instead of in Vail as Rachel expected. The reason for the change was Jess Sherman—rather, Sara Sherman-Adams, Jess's new daughter. Jess called Rachel in early October, and it went like this:

"It's decided. You guys are coming to Santa Monica for the holidays."

"It's *decided*?"

"Yes. Snarky made the decision."

"Who's Snarky?"

"The kid I'm toting around. Sam and I have opted not to know whether it's going to be a boy or a girl until it gets here, and we're calling it Snarky until then."

"Snarky? What an awful name to give a baby."

"We needed something that wasn't gender specific, and 'It' lacks personality, you'll have to admit. Snarky has *lots* of personality."

"You're a nut, Jessica Sherman, and you've made a nut out of that sweet Sam Adams I used to know."

"Guilty, your honor. But I didn't call to be arraigned by the grand jury. I called to get your ass to Santa Monica for Christmas."

"Why not Vail?"

"Ten reasons. One, Snarky's due to arrive in November. Two, there ain't no way we're bringing a six- or seven-week-old infant to Colorado to freeze its tootsies off. Three, you've got to come admire the latest member of the Adams-Sherman family. Four, Sam and I have purchased a big new house around the corner from where your folks live, and I need you to tell me how beautiful it is. Five, I don't intend to wait until next Passover to see you. Six through ten, I *can't* wait until next Passover. I can keep going if you want."

"I don't know. I have to talk to JJ."

"Confession. I've already talked to JJ. And Rebecca. And your parents. And Laura. And Arlie. And Marla and Noah. And Alina and David. It's all arranged. You are the last to know."

"I really ought to be pissed at you, Jess, for doing all this behind my back."

"Devious and underhanded, that's me. I learned it in law school. Somewhere between Torts and Property."

"Tell me. Have Daniel and Ariel and Ms. Miller also agreed to come?"

"Of course. I spoke with Ariel last week. She's making plane reservations for the six of you."

Rachel laughed. "I'm the victim of a fucking conspiracy."

"Guilty again, your honor. But you *are* coming, right?"

"Since you've got me surrounded, I surrender, General Sherman."

"Good girl! I'm glad you recognize defeat when you see it."

And so Rachel and company arrived in Santa Monica on December 23. Rachel preferred to stay at a hotel so she and JJ wouldn't have to occupy the same bed, but Hanna would not allow it. Marla and Noah would be staying with Alina and David, so there was plenty of room at the home of the senior Rothschilds for the six from Colorado.

Rebecca would be in her room. Ariel would sleep in Noah's lower half of the twins' bunk bed, and Daniel in the upper. Ms. Miller had the guest room. Rachel and JJ had Rachel's old room.

As in Salzburg, Rachel wanted to avoid physical contact. But it was more difficult because the bed was smaller. Lying on their backs, they were flank to flank, and it was a weird feeling for both of them. Finally, JJ said, "Would you mind if I put my arm around you, Rachel? I swear I won't try to make love to you unless you want me to, but I'd like to hug you."

Rachel's consent was wordless. She shifted her body in his direction. He passed his left arm under her neck and gingerly placed his hand on her shoulder. After awhile, she took his other hand and guided it to her breast. "Kiss me," she said. "Please." He kissed her. She could feel his erection against her, and she almost wanted him. And then she remembered Louis Short, and she shuddered. JJ felt the shudder and removed his hand from her breast and then his arm from underneath her, and the tender moment was past. Neither of them slept at all well.

Next morning, Jess Sherman was on the phone early. "I've been up since 5:00 a.m. with Sara," she reported to Rachel, "and I've waited as long as I can. Pull on a sweat suit, babe, and come on over. Sara wants to meet you. We're two blocks north and one block west."

"After breakfast."

"Now, dammit! I've got breakfast for you, more than you usually eat. *Please.*"

Please did it. Rachel told everybody she was headed to Jess's, and Rebecca said she'd like to come along. She was trying to reestablish a sisterly relationship. The two of them walked the short distance to Jess and Sam's new home, a large two-story house in beige stucco with a red tile California roof and a blue BMW convertible parked in the driveway. Jess was waiting for them, cradling the baby in her arms. Sara Sherman-Adams was a beautiful, robust-looking infant with her father's red hair and her mother's dark eyes. She was sleeping contentedly.

Rachel said, "She's gorgeous, and so are you, Jess. You look positively wonderful. Where's the happy father and brother?"

"Out buying groceries. Sam's been doing all the shopping since the baby was born, and he takes Richard with him to make sure it takes longer than it should."

Rebecca asked, "Are you back at work, Jess?"

"Not yet. I decided to wait until after New Year's. You can lie all you want about how good I look, but I still need a lot of rest. I've forgotten how exhausting a baby can be, and having Richard around doesn't make it easier."

"How does he feel about having a sister?" Rebecca asked.

"Approximately the way Microsoft feels about other software manufacturers. Richard prefers being a monopolist."

Rebecca said, "He'll adjust. When I was small, the twins didn't try to kill me more than twice a week."

"And now it's down to once a week?" Bozo asked.

Rachel stepped in, "Knowing you, Jess, Richard isn't wanting for attention, and neither is Sam."

Jess replied, "True. Sam and I are already in rehearsals for a third kid."

"Gutter mouth," Rachel said.

"You have a lot of nerve. You're the one who pushed me into bed with Sam the very first time."

Rachel grinned, an infrequent occurrence. "But I thought you'd eventually come up for air."

"I promise you we do breathe occasionally. I can't help it if I've got a healthy sex drive."

Rebecca interrupted. "Enough of the pornography channel. Didn't you say something about breakfast?"

"There's juice in the refrigerator, fresh bagels, cream cheese, lox if you'd like, and a pot of coffee Sam brewed right before he left. Help yourself."

Rebecca asked, "Should I fix a plate for you?"

"I've already eaten. But I'm nursing, so the answer is yes."

They were just finishing when Sam and Richard arrived. Although it had been eight months since he saw her last, Richard went straight onto Rebecca's lap. Sam received a hug and a kiss from Rachel and congratulations from both women. Rebecca was cuddling Richard and said she'd collect her kiss from Sam later on.

The two Rothschild women were still there in late morning when JJ put in an appearance, bringing Daniel and Ariel. Before lunch, Laura and Arlie arrived unexpectedly, bringing a large bag of sandwich makings from the delicatessen. Soon they disappeared into the kitchen, along with Rebecca, to prepare food for the company. Jess had gone into Sara's room to nurse her quietly, and the other three children were playing in Richard's room. Sam showed Rachel and JJ the house, which was about thirty years old but completely refurbished.

Sam said, "We wanted a place where we could stay forever. We looked in Westwood, which is a lot closer to where we work, but Jess really wanted to live in Santa Monica. This is her home, and this is where she wants to raise our kids. We found this place through a realtor. It needed a new kitchen, new bathrooms, more closet space, and some things we haven't gotten around to yet. But it's already comfortable."

Rachel looked around admiringly. "It's amazing. Your kids can go to the same elementary school I attended, and then on to Lincoln Middle School where Jess, Laura, Arlie, and I met, and then to Santa Monica High."

"That's the whole idea," Sam replied. "Jess wanted our kids to feel rooted."

Rachel asked, "Who would ever have expected my friend Jessica Sherman to grow up to be a matriarch?"

Sam said, "Not me. The girl I fell in love with was the person you called Bozo the Clown. Jess knocked me off my feet from the first moment I met her but I truly had no idea she was the kind of person she's become. I'm as astounded by her as you are."

"You're a lucky man." JJ was thinking … *I used to feel lucky.*…

Sam agreed, "Yes, I am. Jess is the best in every way." He laughed.

"But please don't tell her I said so. I like to keep her on her toes, thinking she can do better."

Rachel thought *I wish JJ felt that way about me. I wish I felt about JJ the way Jess feels about Sam.*

At lunch, Rachel asked for updates from Laura and Arlie. Laura was starting to film her movie about the two women punishing a guy that claimed to be in love with both of them while he was having sex with yet another woman. "It's coming along okay," Laura said. "But the problem is that right now it has a split personality. I can't make up my mind about the ending. I can't decide whether I've got a comedy or a tragedy on my hands. Is the guy an oversexed schlemiel who should end up marrying one of the women after he's been properly chastised, or is he this hateful prick who deserves worse than he gets? I can't fucking make up my mind."

Jess said, "I vote for oversexed schlemiel. That's 97 percent of the men on the face of the earth."

Arlie took a different position. "Hateful prick. I know about hateful pricks, and so do you, Laura."

Sam said, "I'd like it if someone here would have the good grace to say, 'present company excepted.' You intended to say that, didn't you, Jess?"

Jess answered complacently, "Surely you don't object to being called 'oversexed,' do you, cream puff?"

Laura ignored the byplay. "You've convinced me. Oversexed schlemiel it is. I'll let him find true love in the end with one of his tormentors."

"When do we get to see it, Laura?" Rebecca asked.

"After it's finished. That means in the can and edited. I won't feel it's finished until Hillel sees it and he tells me it's finished."

"You really have become our father's third daughter, haven't you, Laura?" Rachel was happy that Laura was getting ahead with her father's help.

Laura was dead serious. "No question about it. I hope you guys don't mind. Everybody needs a mentor, and he's mine. Though he won't admit it, I wouldn't be where I am without him. He picked me up when I was down, restored my self-confidence, taught me almost everything I know, and he continues to be the best friend I've got in the business. He's a wonderful man, your father. Maybe I should say 'our father', if it's okay with you. He and your Mom have become my surrogate parents."

Arlie said, "Maybe I shouldn't ask, Laura, but are you still on the outs with your parents?"

"Yes. Please don't ask for details. I don't want to think about it. That's another reason I'm so dependent on Hillel … and on Hanna, too. They look after me, and God knows there are times when I need looking after." This was another one of those times. Laura wouldn't say so, but the boyfriend that she hid from them at Passover was no longer part of her life. It wasn't the most painful breakup she'd ever suffered because she never allowed herself to fall in love with him. But she was once again without male companionship.

The spotlight next turned to Arlie. She'd completed another ambitious software project called Concierge. It was an algorithm that functioned as a personal shopper. It was capable of finding any merchandise or service available over the Internet from clothing to airline tickets to automobiles. The user told Concierge what he or she was looking for, and the program brought the information directly to the computer screen. "For example," Arlie explained, "there are dozens of airline, hotel, and travel sites. You can visit them individually to find what you want at the best available price, or you can commission Concierge to do it for you. Say you want to go to New York from L.A. in March, see a couple of plays, stay at a medium-priced hotel in the East 50s, and eat at a Chinese restaurant one night, at a steak house the next night, and at a French restaurant the third night. Concierge can provide you with a list of choices and make the arrangements for you in a matter of minutes, quicker and more efficiently than any travel agent. It can buy a car for you, visit every bookstore on the Internet to buy the book you want at the best price, tell you what's available in your size and at your price from all the dress stores that have Internet catalogs."

"Hell of an idea. How will it make money?" Jess asked.

"I do technology. The business plan isn't my department, so I can't answer the question. But I hope people will use it because it's an elegant idea, even if I have to say so myself. And if there's a market, I'll get to do more things like Sherlock and Concierge. You can't imagine how much fun it is." She stopped. No one asked about her personal life, which was just as well, because she was not ready to talk about her warming relationship with one of her former professors at Stanford.

Rachel started, "Okay. You don't have to ask. I know it's my turn. There isn't much to tell. I've started working on a doctorate in political science. Period. I don't know what I'll do with the doctorate if I get it. I don't know what branch of political science I'll concentrate on. What I'm studying to begin with is a lot of technical stuff—research methodologies, data analysis—things of no intrinsic interest to anyone outside the field. And there's nothing else going on in my personal life. Okay?" She said it with some asperity.

Arlie responded, "No one's trying to upset you, Rache. We've always been interested in one another. You'd be very unhappy if we weren't interested in you."

Rachel apologized for her tone. "Sorry. You're right. It's just that I feel like a little kid who comes in for show-and-tell with nothing to say. I used to have an interesting life, and now I don't."

There was an uncomfortable silence. Finally, Jess spoke. "I don't think you fully understand, Rache. The four of us are friends for life. It would be a pretty shallow friendship if we weren't prepared to support one another in bad times as well as in good times. This isn't show-and-tell, babe. It's sharing. And every one of us has something to share every time we sit down together. If you're in pain, it's important we know that. You remember when you were at Berkeley and I was at Mills? My life was a shambles then, and you were the one I leaned on. We've been through Bogusian with Laura and Seth Shithead with Arlie. Right now, you're the one that needs help, and we're here to give it. Please don't push us away."

It wasn't an entirely accurate summary. Jess hadn't told anyone about her brief lesbian affair at Mills until it was over. Laura concealed her most recent relationship. Arlie was silent on her new love interest. But these details did not count. Jess swept Rachel's defenses away with her insistence that honesty with one another was the foundation of their friendship. Rachel was sobbing, and her three friends were hovering affectionately around her. Laura had an arm around Rachel. Arlie was holding her hand. Jess made soothing noises like those she bestowed on Sara. Rebecca sat to the side, weeping. She pushed away the memory of Rachel's drunkenness and the missing bra. She felt very sorry for her sister.

Rachel was beginning to recover. "That's the best lecture I ever sat through, Jess. I guess I need to learn how to be more reliant on you guys."

"Look, babe. I know we're a thousand miles away, but we're here for you. Yes, you can count on us."

"I'll try to remember that."

"Do." Laura and Arlie murmured their agreement. Rebecca dried her tears.

Jess and Sam invited everyone to their house on Christmas Day. Jess's parents insisted on having it catered. They didn't want Jess exhausting herself. In addition to Laura, Arlie, and the Rothschild clan, Jess invited Arlie's parents, the Beckers, but not Laura's. She knew Laura would walk out if her parents showed up.

Rachel hadn't seen the Shermans or the Beckers in years except at weddings, but they were important figures to her when she was a teenager, the parents who didn't understand her friends during the same period when Hanna and Hillel didn't understand her. They told her how good she looked, which might actually be true since Rachel had regained the weight she lost in the months after the rape and was a very pretty young woman when she was animated and engaged, as she was now. To describe Rachel as happy would be going entirely too far, but she was ungloomy, a considerable step up from her usual off-campus demeanor.

Having caught up with her friends' parents, Rachel shifted her attention to her brothers and their wives. When Rachel crossed the living room to where they were sitting, Marla and Alina were discussing plans for Marla's spring tour of Europe. Marla was scheduled to appear in Edinburgh, Barcelona, Paris, and Berlin. Alina was talking about nearby cities that could be visited to do research for additional material for her travel series.

Noah was participating in the planning. He was proud of Marla's achievements, even though her success meant that they were apart much more than he wanted. Marla was an aspiring opera star when Noah met her, and being a frequent bachelor was implicit in their marriage vows. David, however, was an unhappy listener. He never anticipated that Alina, his dependent young bride, would be piling up frequent flier miles as Marla's companion and accomplished travel writer. He was proud of Alina, too, but he hated, hated, hated sleeping alone. Some tension was developing between them because David felt neglected and Alina thought he was being selfish.

Rachel took David with her into another room, removing him from the conversation. She asked what he was up to professionally. He was working on a large office building complex in downtown L.A. Rachel asked if he would be interested in commissions outside the L.A. area. When he said yes, Rachel suggested that he talk with JJ. Hyman Weiner & Sons used a lot of different architects. "No reason for you to sit at home pouting while Lee's out touring the universe," she finished.

"What did you say?"

"I know everyone thinks I'm a basket case, and I am, but I'm not completely blind, love. I can see that you're not happy with Lee's being away so much."

"Am I that obvious?"

"Uh-huh. Look, little brother, I'm a bad one to be giving advice. I know that. But you'd be making a huge mistake if you try to pressure Lee into staying home before she's got enough material for her book."

"I didn't marry a travel writer."

"No, you didn't. You married an unformed little girl who had no idea who she would become. Lee's just now growing up, David, and you've got to let her finish the process. I don't doubt that she'd quit running after Marla if you insisted. She loves you too much for a showdown. But she'd also resent the hell out of it. So, please, don't test her. Let her complete her book. She needs it. And you'll be happier in the end because of it."

"What makes you think there won't be another book after this one and another after that?"

"Lee's not that way. She's just not that way. You married her before she had a chance to prove herself. That's all she's doing now is proving herself. She's in love with you, David. Can't you get that through your thick skull? For God's sake, she's only twenty-four years old. Most girls her age haven't begun to think about marriage. If she were your girlfriend instead of your wife, you'd be waiting patiently for her to get this two-thousand-dollars-a-day stuff out of her system before the two of you got married. The thing is, you got married first, and she's just now getting it out of her system. Lee's not going to spend her life running all over the world. She's in love with you, asshole."

"I love her, too, Rache. And I miss her. How much longer is this going to go on?"

"Not much longer, I'd guess. She's got most of what she needs for her book. And she'll come home to write it. If you're smart, you'll use that time to make her *want* to stay home after the book is done. Now that she knows how to do it, she'll find other things to write about that don't involve so much travel."

"Okay, sis. I hope you're right. God, I hope you're right."

"Trust me. I'm stupid about a lot of things, including my own life. But I'm right about Lee. You haven't forgotten, have you, about all those times she talked to me like I was her big sister? I know who she is. I really do."

"You're good to do this, Rache. We were sure as hell headed for a blowup. And I guess you're right. I might win. But I'd probably lose by winning. You've made me a lot smarter. I hope I can act on it."

"You will, love. I know you—almost as well as I know Lee." She kissed him, an infrequent gesture between them. "I just want the two of you to be happy."

Besides the tension of sleeping in the same small bed with JJ, Rachel had another problem staying at her parents' home. Hanna was her mother, and although she didn't mean to be critical or disapproving, she was—or perhaps it was only that Rachel thought she was. Mainly, it had to do with Daniel and Ariel. Hanna rushed to do things for them, and Rachel took that as criticism of the fact that she didn't. Hanna commented that Ms. Miller worked very hard, and Rachel understood her to be saying, "You should be doing more." Hanna took Daniel down to Santa Monica Beach to go bike riding, and Rachel thought *he should be doing that with me.*

Even in the best family situations, relations between a mother and her female child go through several distinct stages from birth until the child enters her forties: dependency, rebellion, separation, reconciliation, and—if all the stars are in conjunction—harmony. The relationship between Rachel and her mother had regressed. Rachel was again in the early stages of separation, and it was crossed with a revival of adolescent conflict. Rachel felt as if she were being judged and found inadequate.

At the beginning of the visit, Hanna was mostly unaware that she was getting on Rachel's nerves. She didn't tiptoe around the way she did when Rachel was fourteen and in full-blown rebellion. She was acting like a grandmother around her only two grandchildren and like a loving mother around an emotionally fragile daughter. Hanna meant to be supportive; Rachel interpreted it as trying to take over. Hanna intended to be solicitous; Rachel saw an absence of confidence in her judgment. Hanna offered advice; Rachel perceived it as condemnation.

If he had been paying attention, Hillel might have made things easier between mother and daughter. He went off to the studio, however, to look at Laura's unfinished film and to offer advice on the final editing. As often happened when he was engrossed in a project, he might be in the room, but he was not necessarily present. He was thinking about how Laura should handle the editing so it was consistent on all counts with the upbeat, revenge-seeking-girl-marries-oversexed-schlemiel-with-whom-she's-in-love conclusion that Laura selected. Since Hillel was oblivious, Laura had no idea that she was taking him away from a more fundamental editing job, recutting the family drama so that it turned out all right in the final scenes.

JJ saw things a lot more from Hanna's vantage point than from Rachel's. Rebecca might have been the intermediary except that she hadn't yet established an adult relationship with her mother either and, besides, her own patience with Rachel was exhausted.

*   *   *

A week together in the same household under these circumstances was entirely too long. Rachel turned irritable, and Hanna felt as if she was once more dealing with a none-too-well-behaved adolescent. As the visit neared an end, not screaming at one another took all their energy.

Hanna declined an invitation to the New Year's party at Sam and Jess's house, saying this was the last opportunity she'd have to be with Daniel and Ariel. The real reason was that she'd had quite enough of her daughter's company. It was nearly 1:00 a.m. when Rachel, Rebecca, and JJ came home, and the flight back to Denver departed at 2:00 p.m. on New Year's Day. The last good-byes were warm enough, but Hanna was not sorry to see Rachel go. There would need to be a cooling-off period before they could come together again without an overlay of antagonism between them.

Back at the university at the beginning of the new year, Rachel added an intensive course in second-year Spanish to her schedule. She would need to be on campus five days a week in the mornings for her language classes, and she had late afternoon seminars twice a week. In addition, her professors were after her to decide on her fields of concentration for her Ph.D. and to start doing serious research. She had intended to reserve more time for her family, but she hadn't made that clear to her advisers and they were treating her like a full-time student. In fact, because she was considered so promising, she was being asked to do more than most other students. She was working nights and weekends to keep up.

The only inviolable item on her personal schedule was the weekly visit with Dev. She talked about cutting the visits back to once every two weeks, but Dev was adamant: "You made me a promise when you insisted on quitting therapy, and I won't let you renege on it, Rache. You got into a very rocky situation last summer, and I can't sit by and let that happen again."

"I haven't got time every Saturday, Dev."

"You'll make time. You'll call if you can't come. It's what we agreed to, and I'm holding you to it. If I thought you were ready to cut back, okay. But you're not. You return from California and tell me you almost came to blows with your mother and this week you're ready to swim the Hellespont without water wings? I can't allow it, Rachel."

"You're not my boss," Rachel said testily.

"No, I'm not your boss, sweetie pie. I'm just the designated listener, but you've got to come talk to me or I can't do the job."

"Do you want out, is that it?"

"Goddam it, Rachel. Stop trying to provoke a fight. I do what I do because I love you. I've got to do it my way because that's the only way I know how to do it. Okay?"

"Are you telling me I haven't got any choice in the matter?"

"That's exactly what I'm telling you, my darling." She took Rachel's hand and smiled.

Rachel sat back, her eyes wide open. "Well, I guess we've reached an understanding. I do what you tell me to do."

"Exactly."

"Gee, if Dr. Cohen had talked to me that way, I'd probably still be seeing her three times a week."

"I'm glad you've seen the light, sweetie. Shall we get started?"

"Anything you say, doctor."

Rachel made no further attempt to resist. She knew she couldn't get on without Dev's support, and if Dev said she had to come every Saturday, she'd come every Saturday. Everything else would have to wait.

But, of course, time for JJ and the children didn't have the same priority. She didn't ignore them, not deliberately anyway, but she did not have a lot of space for them on her agenda. Nor did she give much thought to leisure. JJ might take the children to Vail for ten days in late January or early February, but Rachel would be lucky to get to Vail on the weekends while they were there—and then only if Dev agreed. If she got to Vail any other time—with Dev and Mark or with Yalie and Richie—she'd be at her computer while they were out on the slopes.

She was as busy as she ever was during her days at *In the Rockies.* Yet she wasn't strained by the effort. In fact, she was functioning as smoothly as a trained athlete doing daily exercises. This was her territory, and she knew exactly what to do and when to do it. She had about decided on American government as her primary field of concentration, with public policy as her secondary field and law and politics as the third. Mark was right about her direction.

She even had an idea of what she might do as a dissertation topic. She'd like to analyze the impact of direct government devices like initiatives and referenda on interest group politics and on the behavior of state legislatures, comparing states like California that used these devices freely with states like New York, which did not. She wasn't ready yet to seek approval of a dissertation topic. She was simply thinking ahead.

Dev wished she better understood what to make of the difference between the purposefulness Rachel displayed in her intellectual pursuits and the aimlessness she manifested in her private life. It was as if she were two entirely different people. The one was obviously in retreat from the other.

But what am I supposed to do with this insight? I haven't got the knowledge or the skills. Dev worked hard at seeming confident during their weekly meetings, but it was a bluff. *All I'm doing is keeping her from tumbling into the abyss. I'm really not doing a thing to help with her demons.*

Dev didn't give herself the credit she deserved. While it was true that Rachel was succeeding in one part of her life and not in the other, she might not have been doing so well at CU-Boulder without Dev. Rachel could not have handled Louis Short alone. She might have allowed herself to be blackmailed or she might have fled campus altogether in order to get away from him. The decisions she made about her Ph.D. studies also owed a lot to Dev and Mark's counsel.

*   *   *

Just three and a half weeks after the second semester began, Rachel discovered that she was the target of campus gossip. Several people knew that Rachel dropped out of CU-Denver more than a year before she came to Boulder. Someone had heard about a woman who was accosted on the Auraria campus after a public policy seminar and raped. Someone else had gone to the trouble of locating a story in *The Denver Post* about an unidentified woman who was raped and beaten and left naked in the Denver warehouse district. And Louis Short contributed the information that Rachel Rothschild probably provoked the rape; she was a prick-teaser. (He asked, of course, not to have his name mentioned.)

Rachel heard about it from her friend Bob Crawford. He insisted she join him for coffee after class, saying "There's something I need to tell you." Once they were seated, he explained, "I hate to be the one, but you've got to know. Someone found a newspaper story about a woman who was abducted from the Denver campus and raped, and the rumor is that it was you."

Rachel sat for a long moment in shocked silence. She took a deep breath. "It's true."

"There's more."

Rachel was breathing rapidly and shallowly. "What more?"

"I hate to speak it. They say you invited it by your behavior."

Rachel revolved her head on her neck, her eyes shut tight. "Oh, my God. Isn't it bad enough I got raped? Why would anyone say a thing like that? These guys came up behind me in the parking lot. I never saw them before. They dumped me into the trunk of my own car, took me out into the warehouse district, and took turns raping me. Invited it? How could anyone believe that?"

"Not me. I didn't believe it for a single second. But I thought you had to know."

Rachel was moaning like an injured animal. People were turning around to stare. Bob took her hands, and she squeezed, letting her pain and outrage escape through her fingers. Eventually, she calmed down enough to thank him for telling her and asked him to please leave her alone. She'd be all right, she assured him: "I've got to absorb what you told me."

After several minutes, she left the coffee shop, headed straight to her car, and drove to Dev's house. Mark was there with Alexis. Dev hadn't yet returned from work.

Mark looked at her with alarm. "What's wrong, Rache? You look awful."

"When do you expect Dev?"

"Ten minutes, maybe. What's wrong?"

"I need Dev, Mark. I *need* her. I can't talk to anyone else."

"Can I get you something? A glass of water?"

Rachel answered, "I could really use a shot of whiskey."

Mark got it for her, and she gulped it down. Her heart was still racing when Dev walked in, alarmed to find Rachel there.

"What's wrong?"

"I've got to talk to you, Dev. I don't know what to do."

Dev escorted her into the den. Rachel had a difficult time repeating what Bob Crawford told her. She was agitated, angry, ashamed, frightened. The part about her having "invited it" was the worst. How could anyone make up a lie like that? How could anyone repeat it?

Dev came over to sit beside Rachel on the couch. "I've been afraid of something like this. The distance between Denver and Boulder is too small for the rumors not to have spread eventually. Having the story follow you around has got to be the worst feeling in the world, Rache. The one thing I'm sure of is that you can't let it run you off the campus. Even if it costs you, you've got to go back with your head held high."

"I can't do it, Dev. I won't be able to handle it. I can't."

"You can and you will because you must. You can't give up the life you've chosen just because the story's around."

"They're saying I asked for it."

"I think there's a way to deal with that. Do you trust the guy that told you? What's his name again?"

"Crawford. Bob Crawford. I haven't known him long, and I don't know him very well. But I think he was honestly trying to help me."

"Is it okay if I have a talk with him?"

"What for?"

"Two things: First, I'll ask him to squelch the rumors with the facts, a brief version of the facts. Second, I'll ask for his help in finding out where people got the idea you asked for it. If that son of a bitch Louis Short had any part in it, I'll run him off campus, I swear I will."

"I don't know, Dev. Maybe I just ought to drop out of school."

"You can't run from it, Rache, unless you plan on running forever. And how will you feel if you quit the one part of your life that's been giving you satisfaction? You'll feel like shit, that's how you'll feel. I can't let you do that, sweetheart.

"What if your way doesn't work?"

"It might not. If it doesn't, we'll find another way. We'll do whatever it takes."

Several days later, by arrangement, Dev met Robert Crawford at her sister Yalie's house in Boulder. She told him the story of what happened to Rachel, not in all of the raw detail, of course, but with enough of the background to explain that Rachel's attackers had deliberately sought her out in an act of vengeance against her husband.

"They set out to destroy her, and they succeeded. You see a side of her where she's almost whole, the intellectual side. But two and a half years after the rape, she's still an emotional wreck. The rumor that's going around could be the end of her. I'm not exaggerating. She's a complete mess."

"What can I do to help?"

"What you can do is to go back to the person who told you the story and tell him or her the truth. Ask that person to repeat the true story to the person he or she heard it from and to keep on going until everyone who's heard the story or spread the story knows what actually happened. Ask them *not* to say anything to Rachel—just don't look at her as if she's a freak. And if possible, I'd like your help in getting to the source of the lies about her behavior. They originated somewhere, and I'd like to know where."

"How am I supposed to do that?"

"I don't know if you can. But somewhere along the line, there's someone who first heard the lies from the person who told them. In fact, my hunch is that there are a number of someones who heard the lie from the original source. The person wouldn't have been content to tell it just once. The intent was to get it into circulation."

"You think you know who it was, don't you?"

"I have a suspicion, yes. It has to be someone who's got it in for Rachel, and there's one person who fits the description."

"Who's that?"

"I'd rather not say. I don't want to be accused of planting the idea or circulating gossip against the person." Dev didn't even want to specify the gender.

"I can certainly do the first part. I heard the story from two different people. I'll tell them both what you've told me and ask them to take it back up the line. I can't guarantee the second part. I doubt anyone is going to tell me where they got the story, and even if they do, there's going to be a disconnect somewhere."

"I'm sure you're right. But I'd appreciate it if you tried. It's awfully damned important to Rachel's mental health."

Crawford did his part. The rumor was no longer spreading in its most virulent form, though the effect of having told the truth is that *everyone* in the department now knew the story. The rape had followed Rachel to Boulder, and it watched her unblinkingly wherever she went. But no one identified Louis Short as the source of the slander.

Dev offered to have it out with Short anyway and accuse him of violating the agreement they made by trying to blacken Rachel's reputation. "It might work. He did it. I have no doubt about that. But it's very different than it was when I bulldozed him the last time. I haven't got any evidence to threaten him with."

"You're telling me it's not the way to go, aren't you?"

"Yes. That's what I'm doing. The problem with confronting him is that all he has to do is ask 'Who told you?' I can say 'Never mind about that,' but if he demands an answer, I haven't got one. He can deny being the source, and the only recourse we'd have then would be to brand him as a blackmailer."

"And then everybody would know what he was blackmailing me about. I'd end up losing in order to win."

"That's what I'm worried about, sweetie. A pyrrhic victory. We've got two things to use against him. One is the agreement. I could break him if I could show he violated it. But we haven't got any proof. The second weapon is the blackmail letter, and that's a double-edged sword, Rache. A double-edged sword."

Rachel sighed. "Well, so much for anonymity of the rape victim. I guess having the real story in circulation is better than having everybody think I invited it."

"I know it's not much of a consolation, Rache."

"No, it certainly is not."

A week later, Rachel reported to Dev that she was having nightmares again, was avoiding contact with her classmates, and no longer participated in classroom discussions unless asked a direct question. Dev finally did what she'd been building up to for some time. She asked Rachel to return to seeing her therapist.

"Rache, I know you don't want to, but you've got to go back to Dr. Cohen. Do it for me if not for yourself, sweetheart. I'm afraid. I think you've entered a danger zone and I may not be able to walk you through it."

"I trust you, Dev. I'm not afraid as long as you're with me."

"You don't understand, Rache. You may not be afraid, but *I am*. I'm afraid of failing you. I'll never be able to forgive myself if I let you down." Dev was the one fighting tears. "I love you, Rache, but love isn't enough. You've got to have professional help."

"I'll ask Dr. Drucker for more medicine."

"Do that if you want, Rache. But drugs aren't a complete answer. Look, I don't want to say this, but you leave me no choice. I think you're right on the edge of a breakdown. You're having a hard time at home, you had a hard time when you were in Santa Monica, and I see you losing your grip on the one area of your life where you've really been doing well. You may end up back in the hospital. I can't do it for you, sweetheart. I'm begging you. Please go to see Dr. Cohen. Come see me, too, but don't make me do it alone. *I don't know what I'm doing. I don't! I don't!*"

"Please don't cry, Dev. That's my department." Long pause. Dev was wiping her eyes. "Okay, if it's so important to you, I'll go see Dr. Cohen. Would you come with me on the first visit?"

"Of course I will. I'll come with you every time if necessary. I'm not going to abandon you. I'm just calling in reinforcements."

Dr. Cohen rearranged her schedule to make room for Rachel and Dev. Rachel asked Dev to explain the situation. Dr. Cohen listened thoughtfully, making notes.

"And this rumor about Rachel's having invited the rape, do you have any idea where that came from?"

"We don't know for sure, but there's one guy in her class who has it in for her."

"Dev is shielding me, Dr. Cohen. You might as well know the truth. I went back to this guy's apartment with him once."

"You had sex with him?"

"Yes and no. I intended to. I wanted to see if I could. And then I changed my mind, and he forced me. Afterward," —she had a hard time getting it out— "he kept my underwear. Then he tried to blackmail me. He sent me a photograph" —she took a deep breath and continued—"of my panties. He threatened to tell my husband. He wanted to force me" —another difficult moment— "back into his bed. Dev scared him off."

"And you think he spread the rumor to get back at you."

"We think so, but there's no proof."

"And now you feel like you can't face your classmates because of what they've heard?"

"Yes, that's it exactly. It's not just that they know about the rape. That's bad enough. I keep thinking about how I disgraced myself with this guy. I got over blaming myself for the rape. You helped me get over it. But I am to blame for him. I asked for sex before he forced me. I forgot it for a while, and now I can't."

Dev stood up. "You don't need me anymore. I ought to go."

Dr. Cohen said, "Rachel?"

"I'd rather you stayed, Dev. You brought me here. You know more about me at this stage than I know about myself. You can save us a lot of time by telling Dr. Cohen why I act the way I do."

"That might be useful. Do you want to listen, Rachel, or would you rather not?"

"I'm not afraid of anything Dev might say, but she might be franker if I'm not in the room."

"How long do we need, Ms. Goodman?"

"I'm not sure I like the idea of speaking behind Rachel's back."

"You're not speaking behind my back, Dev. I pretty much know what you think. The only reason for my being out of the room is that I don't want you to pull any punches for fear of hurting my feelings. I'd like her to know what you think."

"Okay. I'll need twenty minutes or so. That's all."

Rachel moved into the waiting room. She sat there blankly, numbly, slumped in a chair.

More than an hour passed while Dev told Dr. Cohen all she could about Rachel's state of mind. Dr. Cohen took notes and asked a number of questions. Then Dev said, "There's something else you ought to know that I'm sure Rachel's concealed from you. And there's a piece of it that Rachel herself is unaware of."

"That sounds serious."

"It is. Rachel agreed to marry JJ during her senior year in college. They were 'engaged' for more than two years. During that period, JJ insisted that they refrain from sleeping together, though it was something Rachel was initially ready to give and later really, really wanted."

"Was Rachel a virgin at the time?"

"No, she wasn't, and she told JJ she wasn't. But that didn't matter to JJ. He insisted."

"Well, that's certainly unusual. What's the part that Rachel doesn't know?"

"It turns out that JJ didn't live up to the code he imposed on Rachel. He slept around freely while he was at Stanford."

"How do you know about it?"

"One of Rachel's closest friends was at Stanford when JJ was there, and she found out that he was sleeping regularly with a friend of hers."

"She told you this?"

"No, not directly. The thing is that Arlie, the girl who was at Stanford, hadn't been told about the sexless relationship between Rachel and JJ. She learned about it after Rachel and JJ were married from Jessica Sherman, another of Rachel's closest friends. Rachel may have mentioned her to you. Arlie told Jess, and not so long ago, Jess told me."

"Spell out for me what you think it means."

"Look, Dr. Cohen, I know that Rachel has told you very little about her relationship with her husband. I'm guessing that she will be more open about it now. I don't know if she'll take it all the way back to her premarital frustrations, and even if she goes there, she doesn't know that JJ lived by different rules than he imposed on her. That knowledge might well shatter what remains of their relationship."

"I'm asking a slightly different question. What weight do you put on Rachel's having been deceived from the very beginning of the relationship?"

"My opinion? I think JJ Weiner is a smart, charming skunk who built his marriage to my cousin on a shaky foundation of unreasonable demands and deliberate deception." Dev spat out the last sentence with uncharacteristic vehemence. "No, I'm not a neutral observer."

"I appreciate your assessment and your honesty. I'll try to treat what you've told me as carefully as it deserves to be treated."

"Are we finished now?"

"Yes, but please have a cup of tea and compose yourself before I bring Rachel in."

Dev did as she was told. She felt almost as exhausted as a marathon runner at the finish line.

When the door to the outer office was opened, Rachel looked up with the same blank stare she had when the door closed. The passage of so much time seemed not to have registered.

Dr. Cohen said, "Sorry, Rachel. I asked a lot of questions. Your cousin's been extremely helpful. You were right. She understands you exceptionally well. Exceptionally well."

"Where do we go from here?"

"I'd like to spend another hour alone with you now, and then we'll decide how often I need to see you. I want you to continue your weekly visits with Devorah. She's able to do things for you that I can't. I will want your permission to talk with her from time to time. On this understanding: I won't ask her to repeat anything you tell her. All I want is her judgment on how you're progressing to compare with my own. Is that okay?"

"Yes. If it's okay with you, Dev."

"It's okay." She was starting to leave. "Rache? Thanks for coming."

Rachel turned to Dr. Cohen, "Imagine. She's thanking me." She told Dev, "I owe you my life."

The cousins hugged, and Dr. Cohen motioned Rachel to a chair.

"Your cousin thinks you went home with this man as a kind of test. Do you think she's right?"

"I don't know that I fully understand why I did it, but yes. I hadn't been able to have sex with my husband. Still haven't. I thought maybe …"

"… maybe you could it with another man?"

"Something like that."

"And you blame yourself for it?"

"Yes."

"Do you also reserve part of the blame for your husband?"

Rachel was surprised. "Yes. Yes, I do. I hadn't thought about that."

"Look, Rachel, we've lost a lot of time. I think your cousin is right. You're in a danger zone. You're desperate because you thought you turned the page when you went to Boulder. Now the story's caught up with you, and you've got this man chasing after you making you feel guilty, not just for what happened between the two of you but for the rape itself. It's blighted the idyll you've been experiencing in graduate school. Does that sound right to you?"

"I guess so."

"These aren't my insights; they're your cousin's. She's a very smart woman."

"Yes, she is."

"But she's wrong on one count, in my opinion. Getting this guy off your case wouldn't bring everything back to equilibrium. The fundamental problem is still the conflict between you and your husband. You went to Boulder to escape the conflict. You revisited it as a result of the episode with this other man. Your cousin patched that up for a time, covered it over. But the rumors about the rape and the lies have brought the whole thing back. And you can't run from it any longer. I think that's where you are. These last developments have destroyed the illusion of security that you created for yourself. Right now you don't have a lot of options. You can have an emotional relapse, or you can face the central difficulty."

"My relationship with JJ?"

"Yes. I felt like you dodged it the whole time you were with me earlier. Do you agree?"

"There are things I couldn't bring myself to tell you, yes."

"Those are the things we've *got* to talk about now, Rachel. I need to know what's happened between you."

"I don't know if our relationship can be salvaged, Doctor."

"That's not a question I'm trying to answer. My job is to help you understand your feelings and come to terms with them. Right now they're ruining your life, Rachel."

"What am I supposed to do?"

"To start with, I want you to tell me about you and JJ. I want you to start at the beginning and tell me everything, including things you might have told me before, because I suspect you may have left a lot out. Am I right?"

"Yes."

"And when you've done telling me everything, if we're still not getting to the heart of it, I want you to agree to undergo hypnosis."

"I'm afraid of being hypnotized, Doctor. I'm afraid of losing control."

"I understand that, and I'm not saying it will be necessary, but I want you to agree to be hypnotized if I think it's needed."

"Why don't we wait and see?"

Dr. Cohen knew she had the upper hand. "This isn't a negotiation, Rachel. The reason I need you to agree in advance is that you must have an incentive not to hide the truth from me. I want you to know that I intend to get at the truth one way or another."

"And if I won't agree?"

"I'll give you the names of other therapists if you lack confidence in my judgment."

"You want me to start over with someone else?"

"No, I want you to continue with me. But you must help me to help you."

Rachel, in anguish, conceded defeat. "Okay, Doctor. You win."

"Winning's not the point, Rachel. It's a matter of having the tools to do the job."

Rachel took a deep breath. "I never wanted to do this, Doctor, but there's a way to save a lot of time. I have this autobiography I began writing long before the rape. It's got just about everything in it. My entire life. It's sitting there on my hard drive."

"You've had this all along?"

"Yes. I didn't volunteer it earlier for the same reason I'm afraid to be hypnotized. It's got things in it I've been trying to keep private."

"Have you been hiding these things from your cousin as well as from me?"

"No … yes … I guess the honest answer is yes. There are some things about my relationship with my husband that I haven't been willing to tell anyone—not even Dev. Shameful things."

"But you've written about them?"

"Yes."

"You couldn't talk about them, but you could put them in writing?"

"It was cathartic in a way. At the time. Before the rape. I haven't written anything since the rape. Not a word. I think when I was doing it, I also had it in the back of my mind that I might someday write a work of fiction and cannibalize some of the incidents and convert my feelings into the feelings of the characters."

"And you're willing to turn this autobiography over to me now?"

Rachel nodded.

"Unedited?"

"Yes. Unedited."

"Good. Can you have it to me by this weekend?"

"I guess so."

"One thing, Rachel. I've got to be straight with you. Once I've read it, we're still going to have to talk about it. It's the only way for you to process your emotions. It's not going to be painless."

The tears were rolling down Rachel's cheeks. "I know."

And so Rachel added a couple of paragraphs at the very end to what she'd written before the rape in her autobiography, printed out her manuscript, and delivered it.

Dr. Alicia Cohen
745 Colorado Blvd.
Suite 433
Denver, Colo.

Dear Dr. Cohen:

I started writing this autobiography several years ago to have something to do before my first child was born. After awhile, it became a kind of diary. I wrote the last little bit yesterday afternoon, bringing it up to just before what happened to me happened. Reading it will tell you almost everything there is to know about me, my family, my relationship to my husband. A lot of the dialogue is made up, of course. But it's as close to true as my memory could make it. I should have given it to you at the beginning, but I just wasn't ready then to strip myself naked in front of you. I was hoping to retain some dignity. I've given up on dignity.

Sincerely yours,
Rachel Rothschild

The following week, they began at the beginning. Over a period of weeks, with much pain and many tears, Rachel found herself answering questions about her initial impressions of JJ, their courtship, their engagement, his refusal to have sex with her before marriage and insistence that she begin her career, their first visit to Denver, the wedding, the honeymoon, the ecstatic sex, the spanking episodes, her disputes with JJ over his efforts to control their life together, the conflict with Annalisa and the confrontation with JJ's father, the birth of the children, the postpartum depression, the cooling of passion before the rape, the rape, the bad sexual experiences afterward, the sleeping apart—everything. She didn't attempt to spare JJ or to spare herself. She admitted to the times before the rape when she resented his attempts to dominate her. She conceded that she was both repelled and thrilled by being spanked. She searched her emotions and acknowledged that she blamed JJ for the rape. It was his wealth that made her a target, his harsh treatment of the two dismissed foremen that caused them to seek her out as an act of revenge. She said she'd become frigid since the rape but blamed JJ for lacking patience and tenderness.

She began to understand how unforgiving she felt toward JJ. Although she'd said again and again since the rape that it wasn't JJ's fault—and thought she meant it when she said it—the emotional truth was that she blamed him then for what happened then and blamed him now for her current predicament. She didn't hate him. That would be too harsh a way to summarize her feelings. But her resentment ran exceptionally deep. It was down there where there was no light and the surface currents were not felt.

And the children? Rachel couldn't explain how she felt about the children. She knew she didn't give them the attention they deserved. Why wasn't she the loving mother she was initially to Daniel? Why did she have so little time for Ariel? Why didn't she mind that they ran to Rebecca or to Ms. Miller instead of to their own mother? "I'm just not a good mother" was the only answer she could give. It just wasn't one of the skills she was handed. She said that she loved her children. No, she didn't resent them.

"Rachel, we've come to the point where I want you to undergo hypnosis. You're telling me what you believe is the truth, I'm sure. But I think there's something deeper going on, and I have to get at it."

"Please, Doctor, don't make me."

"You promised, Rachel. Now's the time. I've got to insist."

And so, reluctantly, Rachel allowed herself to be hypnotized. The exploration, spread over three sessions, confirmed Dr. Cohen's hypothesis. Rachel's attitude toward the children began with the postpartum depression after Ariel's birth. That was caused in part by having her tubes tied, leaving her with a sense of incompleteness. And then her attitude toward Daniel as well as Ariel was overtaken by her subconscious desire to roll the clock back to before her marriage to JJ. Yes, she might marry JJ all over again, but the terms would have to be different. She would never, never, never allow herself to be dominated. She might have children, but not as quickly as she had Daniel. In her own way, she loved the kids, but she loved them ambivalently. It was love overlaid with resentment directed at their father. Her flight to Boulder was an escape from the confines of her marriage, and the children were part of what walled her in. She wanted to be free—and she wasn't. Every night she returned to her luxurious prison, the only inmate in a house full of wardens. Daniel and Ariel were among her guards. Even when they were with Ms. Miller or frolicking with Rebecca, they reminded her of all that was wrong in her life.

Dr. Cohen did not tell Rachel what Dev had told her about how JJ behaved while they were engaged and she was forced against her will to abstain from sex. Dr. Cohen did not think it would help Rachel to know that now. It might never help.

Rachel had only recently begun to see Dr. Cohen again when Passover arrived. She was not pleased to see it come. The traditional gathering would be a burden. It would be one thing if she could pick and choose among the guests, but the list was fixed in concrete. Except for Marla and Alina, who were in Europe on Marla's four-city tour and Alina's fact-gathering expedition to a dozen nearby locations, *everybody* was coming: Hanna, whom Rachel would rather not see so soon after their uncomfortable time in Santa Monica over Christmas, Hillel, her brothers, the Goodman clan, Jess and her family, Laura, Arlie, the Weiners, Rebecca's friend Harriet Anheim and her live-in boyfriend, Jonathan Fink, and another friend of Rebecca's, Marilyn Seeman.

Rachel talked with her cousin Dev. "Would you do me a big favor, Dev? Would you tell Jess, Laura, and Arlie that I'd rather not talk about my situation. Every *Pesach* we have this catch-up session where the spotlight moves from one to the other, and I don't want my moment in the spotlight. I love them and they mean well by me, but I don't want to answer any questions. You can tell them about the rumors if you want to. I guess I'd like them to know I'm upset. I just don't want to be the one who tells them. Does that make any sense to you?"

"Sweetie, whatever you want makes sense to me. Do you want them to tell you what they're doing?"

"I guess so. These guys are so much a part of me. I don't want to hurt their feelings by telling them I'm not interested. But you're right about me, love. I'm in a bad place, and I don't have energy for anyone but me. I hope you'll make them understand."

"I'll sure try."

Dev invited Jess, Laura, and Arlie to meet her in the library. "Guys, Rachel asked me to tell you something. She's had a bad time recently. She'd rather not talk about it."

Jess asked, "What happened, Dev? Can you tell us that?"

"The story about what happened to her in Denver migrated to Boulder with a nasty twist. There's a guy in one of her classes that has it in for her, and he's made it sound as if Rachel got raped because she invited it—you know, blaming the victim for having loose morals."

Jess took a deep breath. "That's awful."

Arlie and Laura had their eyes closed tight. Neither spoke.

Dev agreed, "It sure is. Anyhow, Rache is damn near falling apart, poor baby. I practically forced her to go back to her analyst. I told her I was in over my head and asked her to do it for my peace of mind."

"And she couldn't refuse you." Laura observed sympathetically.

"No, she couldn't. I hated putting it on that basis, but it was the only way I could get her to go."

Jess asked, "Will she keep coming to see you now that she's back with the analyst?"

"Yes. That was part of the deal I made."

Arlie winced. "I can't imagine how hard this must be for you."

"I won't pretend that it's been easy. Alexis is two this month, and it's been going on since long before she was born. Still, Rachel is my responsibility. It's as simple as that. I do what I have to do. I don't think about it."

"We've had this conversation before, babe," Jess interposed. "I remember telling you to call me if you needed support yourself. You never called, and I'm ashamed for not having called you. We've all let you carry the burden alone."

"Not entirely, Jess. You told me something I really needed to know, and I've passed that on to Rachel's analyst." Arlie and Laura looked puzzled. They had no idea what Dev was referring to. "Besides, I really don't mind being Rachel's confessor. I don't want to pose as some kind of martyr. I've got Mark. I've got Alexis. My sister's here. My folks are less than an hour away. I have lots of help when I require it."

Jess answered, "I'm sure you do, babe. But I'm talking about me. Outta sight, outta mind—that's not being a friend. From now on, I'm going to make a pest of myself. Is that okay?"

Dev laughed. "Sure. Maybe I ought to issue weekly bulletins."

Arlie laughed too, letting off tension. "Or establish a Web site. I can help with that."

"Let's not get carried away with the humor of Rachel's situation," Jess said, an undercurrent of anger in her voice.

Arlie was offended. "That's a hell of a thing to say. Especially from someone who's forever making tasteless jokes."

"Whoa, guys," Laura said. "Stop it. We're not going to get anywhere taking it out on one another. That isn't going to help Rachel."

Jess apologized, "You're right, Laura. I'm sorry, Arlie … Dev."

Arlie nodded, "Forgiven."

Dev said, "Nada. I understand. It's worst for Rachel, but it's not easy for anyone who loves her. Lashing out is natural."

Jess answered quietly. "Not hard to see why Rachel relies on you, Dev. You're the most understanding soul I know. But can I ask you something? Are we supposed to forego our usual ritual of telling each other what we're up to?"

"No, not at all. Just don't ask Rachel to take a turn." Dev deliberately ignored Rachel's statement that she didn't have energy for anyone but herself. *I can't let her drift away from her friends.* "I'll go get her."

Shortly, Dev ushered Rachel into the room.

Jess pretended a jollity she didn't feel. "Okay, Laura, tell us about the film."

"It will be out in September. Thanks to Hillel, the producers liked the final version. They think it might do very well at the box office. They've asked me to write and direct another film."

Arlie asked, "What kind?"

"A female buddy picture ending in marriage with the guys that done them wrong. Another oversexed-schlemiel-gets-caught movie, this time featuring *two* oversexed schlemiels instead of one. You know Hollywood. Anything worth doing once is worth doing at least twice more. The second oversexed schlemiel is what passes for originality. I'm not sure I'm going to sign."

Jess feigned incredulity. "The first time around, Laura, you were down on your hands and knees begging for an opportunity. Now you're not sure you'll condescend to give them a second chance at your services?"

"Something like that. I'd prefer not to repeat what I've already done. I'm not exactly a hot property, yet but I think I can do something different and get it financed by these folks or someone else."

Rachel asked, "What does Daddy say?"

"He's encouraging me to try my wings. Right now he's looking at my second screenplay. The one I'd like to do."

"Which is?" Arlie inquired.

"Not a comedy. It's about a young woman who's victimized by an older man, kills him, and goes to prison for it. Except for the killing part, it's the autobiography of Laura Ludwig."

Arlie raised her eyebrows. "Are you really okay with that?"

"I'm over Peter Bogusian if that's what you're asking. He isn't even the protagonist. The script's about the girl … me. A natural pushover who finally understands what she's allowed to happen to herself."

Jess said, "I hope writing it was therapeutic, Laura. I can't imagine it's going to be featured on the Comedy Channel."

"No, not likely. It's pretty heavy-duty. But, yes, writing it helped me work out a few knots. I'm not only over Bogusian. I'm over every other guy I ever slept with—a cast of thousands. Okay, hundreds. I haven't felt this good in a long time."

"Lucky you." Rachel didn't mean to say that. It just slipped out.

Laura, Jess, and Arlie exchanged glances.

Arlie asked, "And what about you, Jess?"

"A very short story. Sara is four and a half months old. Richard will be five in August. We allowed more time between them than we should have. We don't intend to make that mistake again."

Laura followed. "What about your law practice?"

"That's what got in the way of having a second child sooner. I won't allow it to get in the way of having a third."

Laura said, "But you've been so successful."

"I'm not quitting the law. I'm just getting my priorities straight. We want three kids at least, maybe four. I'll be thirty-three this year. If we decide on four, I'll be at least thirty-seven, thirty-eight when the last one is born. I'm not waiting until my ovaries are on Medicare. Besides, as I've told you guys every time the subject comes up, I enjoy rehearsals."

Arlie asked. "Are your partners okay with that?"

"About rehearsals?"

Arlie responded, "Stop it, Bozo. You know what I mean."

"My partners don't have veto power. They don't ask my permission every time they screw their wives. I don't want to sound full of myself, but I'm too valuable to them for anybody to give me a hard time. There's nobody else in the firm who knows shit about cutting-edge intellectual property issues. When I was on pregnancy leave, I still guided our activities in that area. They'll do it my way. No worries on that score."

Rachel listened to Jess, as she had every time they had been together in the last few years, with a complex mixture of admiration and envy. Jess's self-confidence was unshakable.

Laura asked, "Arlie, what's happened with Concierge?"

"It's doing okay. We've created a Web site and sold advertising. The technology's also being licensed to other sites for them to use with their customers."

Laura continued, "And what are you working on now?"

"*Big* announcement! This isn't what you were asking, but I've been saving it for this moment. I have a boyfriend. In fact, I'm getting married again—at the beginning of June."

Even Rachel joined in the congratulations.

Jess commanded, "Details!"

"His name is Jeff Hamilton. He teaches computer science at Stanford. We were friends in graduate school. We've been living together for a couple of months now."

Jess was startled. "And you've kept this secret?"

Arlie responded, "Uh-huh. Including in December when you told Rachel how we never kept secrets from one another. He hadn't moved into my apartment yet, but we'd already made love a bunch of times."

Jess said, "I ought to make you stand in the corner."

"You've got to see my point of view, Jess. I already made an ass of myself with Seth. I didn't want to risk doing it again. Once we got together, I thought of calling or writing, but I figured Passover when we were all together would be the right time."

Laura asked, "What do your folks have to say? Hamilton isn't exactly a Jewish name."

Arlie said, "They're coming around. Their Jewish son-in-law turned out badly. I think they'll give Jeff a chance. Unless they want to disown me, they haven't got any other choice. We're getting married no matter what."

Jess put in, "Good for you, Arlie. I married a *goy*, and we're doing just fine."

"Yes, but you're Jewish enough for two, and I'm not."

Jess said, "Well, as long as he's circumcised."

Laura asked, "Why don't you just ask straight out whether he's a good fuck?"

Arlie blushed. "He is."

Rachel's mind wandered to the last time she had sex—with Louis Short—and, *before that, when was it? And the last time it was good, when was that?* It was not a healthy line of thought.

Although it was his house, JJ relinquished the job of running the seder to Hillel, and that relieved Rachel of the unwelcome role as hostess. She took her customary position in the middle of the table next to Grandma Bess and opposite Jess. Her brother David claimed the other seat next to her. He wanted to tell her what he'd heard from Alina about her trip with Marla.

Not counting Molly and Jacqueline Garson, Annalisa's two teenage daughters, there were five children around the Passover table under the age of eight. Daniel, at seven and a half, was the only one of them with the faintest idea of what was happening. Once he'd asked the Four Questions, his willingness to pay attention diminished sharply. Under the circumstances, Hillel, Uncle Aaron, and Herman Weiner agreed upon an abbreviated service. As it was, a lot of shushing was going on. Finally, Hanna spoke up. "You know, we want the kids to enjoy Passover. There's time enough for them to learn what it's about as they grow older. Ariel, why don't you come here and sit in Grandma's lap? Jess, if Richard needs to talk, let him. He's not bothering anybody."

Aunt Ruth said to Dev, "I can take Alexis, darling."

"No thanks, Mom. Yalie's got dibs on the princess if she's going anywhere. Maybe you'd like to give Jess a little help with Sara."

"Don't trouble yourself, Mrs. Goodman. That's what Sam is here for, aren't you, babe?"

Daniel asked, "What about me?"

Hanna said, "You're a big boy, Daniel. But you can come sit on my lap, too, if you'd like."

"No, I wanna play," Daniel answered. He wandered off. Rebecca stopped Ms. Miller from following. She'd get Daniel when it was time for dinner.

The reading of the *Haggadah* up to the meal was completed quickly and without disruption from the children. Hanna had given the right instructions. Richard was a chatterer, but he disturbed no one. In fact, most of the adults were smiling from listening to him ask questions about what was happening in his piping little voice.

"Who's Pharaoh?" he asked. "What's a slave?" "What does plague mean?" "Are we Jewish?"

The answer he got from Jess to the final question was "Sorta. We belong, all of us, to this big family, don't we?"

The Rothschilds and the Goodmans all agreed. "You certainly do,

Richard," Hillel answered for all of them. "You, your mommy, your daddy, your little sister, Aunt Arlie, Aunt Laura. We all love you."

Richard appeared satisfied. Jess grinned and mouthed "Thank you," followed by a kissing gesture to the entire table.

Rachel was not looking forward to the start of the meal. It would force her to engage in conversation with her seatmates, and she didn't have anything she wanted to say, not even to her brother.

Grandma Bess would be ninety this year, and she was getting to be hard of hearing. The Weiner brothers had been talking with her doctor about whether to trouble her about getting a hearing aid. Her mind was completely unaffected but communicating with her took a bit of shouting, and she was reluctant to require that in a crowd, so her attempts at the table to talk with Rachel were mercifully few. She merely told Rachel that she'd like to see her more often. Rachel hadn't been at all attentive recently.

On Rachel's other side, her brother David had a lot to talk about. Alina and Marla were in Barcelona now, having completed the visit to Edinburgh. Alina visited Majorca, Valencia, Grenada, and the Costa del Sol doing her two-thousand-dollars-a-day research. He was expecting to meet the travelers when they headed to Paris. Noah had already been over—twice—to hear Marla sing the part of Eurydice in Gluck's *Orpheus and Eurydice* in Edinburgh and to hear her on opening night in Barcelona as Fiordiligli in Mozart's *Cosi Fan Tutte*. Noah and David were going together to Paris right after Passover, where Marla would be doing another Eurydice in Offenbach's *Orpheus*. Hanna and Hillel would be going, too. Noah, Hanna, and Hillel would accompany Marla to Berlin, where she'd be alternating the roles of Papagena and Sarana in *The Magic Flute*. David and Alina would stay behind to spend ten days in France, Belgium, and Holland, and then Alina would join Marla in Berlin for a few days while Noah, Hanna, and Hillel returned to the United States. Marla's versatility was amazing the opera world, and Alina was managing her life off the stage.

David said, "You gave me good advice, Rache. Lee wants us to go to Europe for about three weeks later this year, and then she'll have what she needs for her book. She says Marla will have to get along without her after this. She's ready to have a baby when she's done writing."

"That's nice."

"Our trip in the fall will be a little crazy. Oslo, Stockholm, Helsinki, Geneva, Rome, Naples, Capri, Florence."

"That's a lot."

"Yeah, but it's worth it. She'll have been everywhere she needs to go except Madrid, Lisbon, Athens, and St. Petersburg. She'll get what she can on those cities over the Internet and fake the rest. At least, that's her intention. If she needs to visit those places before the book's done, I'll take her to see them. Anything so we can get to having a baby. I'll take her to the moon if that's required."

"I'm glad it's working out, Davy."

David was undeterred by Rachel's brief answers. "You were right. Now I hope you'll figure out a way to make Marla settle down long enough for her and Noah to start a family."

"Marla's not ready."

"Well, I'd be very unhappy if it were me."

"Noah's Noah, not you. He knew what he was getting into."

"Well, that's true. Marla never hid her ambition to be a star. She's succeeding, and I guess Noah's happy for her."

"You'll be with him on the way to Paris. Ask him."

"What about you, Rache? Are you going to come over to see Marla perform?"

"I can't take the time, love."

"What about Rebecca? Is she going to be able to come?"

"I think so. She's talked about going to Berlin, and maybe Paris if it's possible to see performances in both places on one trip."

"What about JJ?"

"JJ is talking about taking Daniel to Paris and maybe London."

"Why London?"

"To see the changing of the guard."

"That would be wonderful. Daniel's old enough to see it and remember it. Will JJ take Daniel to the opera to hear Marla?"

"I don't know. Ask him."

David hadn't particularly noticed that he'd done most of the talking and heard very little in return. But Dev had her eyes on Rachel and could see that she was not saying much and her body language was screaming *All right, David, enough, go talk to somebody else.*

Dev let Alexis down to play and walked around the table to where Rachel and David were sitting.

"Be a good boy, Davy, and exchange places with me. I need to talk to Rachel for a few minutes."

David, of course, did as requested.

"I could see you wanted rescuing, sweetheart. Is it really so bad?"

"I don't want to talk, Dev. God forgive me, not even to my brother. Only to you."

"That's why I came round. You're still in pretty bad shape, Rache. We need to talk about that after everybody's gone. Okay?"

Rachel nodded. "Thanks, Dev. I love you."

Dev took her hand and kissed it. "I know you do, sweetheart."

Yalie didn't have a lot to say to Rachel at the Passover seder. She was more annoyed with Rachel than she was sympathetic these days. She didn't know about Louis Short. She didn't know that the rape followed Rachel from Denver to Boulder. All she knew was that more than two and a half years had elapsed since the rape, and it was time for Rachel to stop asking for pity. She was abusing Dev, who had a full-time job and a baby, and who spent altogether too much time changing Rachel's diapers.

Yalie kept the annoyance under wraps. Other than Richie, the only person she said anything to was her mother, and Ruth absolutely let her have it.

"I'm really surprised at you, Ya'el, and disappointed. You can't know what Rachel's gone through, and you're judging her, and you want Devi to judge her, too. Devi's been with Rachel every step of the way. If anyone has the right to decide whether Rachel's being self-indulgent or needs more help, it's Devi, not you. Have a little humility, baby."

"I'm sorry, Mommy. I'll keep my mouth shut. I won't say anything to Dev. I sure as hell won't say anything to Rachel. But how I feel is how I feel. You know how much I love her."

"Yes, you love her. But she got inconveniently raped, and then she tried to commit suicide after she smashed her knee following you down the mountain. And you want her to behave like nothing happened."

"That's not fair, Mommy." Yalie was both furious and defensive. "I don't deserve to be blamed for her attempting suicide."

"No, of course, you don't. But you shouldn't have taken her skiing, baby. The accident was a huge, huge setback. And after it, you went back to Washington, and Devi was the one who picked up the pieces.

and she's been holding Rachel together ever since. The least you ought to do before you leap to conclusions about where Rachel is or ought to be is to ask your sister how Rachel's doing."

"There's no use talking to you. You don't care what I think."

"I'm sorry, baby. I'd just like to see that fine legal mind of yours showing a little human kindness."

The conversation didn't change Yalie's opinion. It just caused her to withhold it, to swallow it instead of spitting it out. She saw Rachel as someone who lacked the discipline to overcome her injury. People fractured joints all the time. Some worked like hell to regain full range of motion, and some didn't. Those who didn't ended up being permanently invalided. Rachel was one of them. Her injury, the ski accident aside, wasn't physical, but the same principle ought to apply. Rape was terrible, but rape victims recovered. Rachel wasn't helping herself to recover.

Yalie and Richie were no longer going out regularly with Rachel and JJ. Rachel was busy at school, and she and JJ rarely went anywhere together these days. Yalie was working long hours in the U.S. Attorney's office, and all she wanted when she was off duty was to be with Richie. Rachel still came to their house in Boulder occasionally to eat dinner or spend the night, but it was more habit than genuine connection. Rachel didn't have a lot to say when they were together, and Yalie wasn't the sympathetic audience she used to be. So Rachel sat quietly at the dinner table when she was at their house while Yalie and Richie talked to one another. Sometimes Rachel listened, and often she didn't.

Yalie didn't speak to Dev about Rachel. Having been burned once when talking to her mother, Yalie didn't care to raise the subject with Rachel's number-one supporter. *They're all blind. All of them,* she thought.

Hanna forgot about her conflict with Rachel during the Christmas-New Year's holidays, even if Rachel hadn't. Although all four of her children were at the seder, Rachel was the child she watched most closely, the one she took special care of when it came time to serve the Passover delicacies: the matzoh ball soup, the gefilte fish, the beef brisket, the matzoh farfel. Rachel was the child who required the most help. Rachel would have had to be utterly unconscious not to recognize the love that was being directed her way, and the effect was to soften the shell she had covered herself with every time her mother got on the phone the last few months. *Mommy was just terrific with Ariel and Daniel and the other kids at the seder. I guess she meant well at Christmas. I shouldn't have fought with her.*

There was no formal reconciliation between mother and daughter, but by the time Hanna was ready to return to Santa Monica, Rachel was again filled with love for her. She didn't expect Hanna to understand her situation fully, and that was okay. She had Dev and Dr. Drucker, and—although she wasn't wild about the idea—she once again had Dr. Cohen.

A week after Passover, Rachel received an invitation to Arlie's wedding in Palo Alto on June 8, a Sunday. It was to be a very small wedding—immediate family and a handful of friends. Accompanying the invitation was a handwritten note from Arlie: "Please come, Rache. Please. Please. Please."

Rachel wasn't eager to go, but she really couldn't refuse. Although Marla wasn't due back from Europe until the following week and Noah had invited Rachel to stay at his house, she arranged to share a room with Laura at the hotel where the wedding dinner was to be held. Jess was coming with Sam, Richard, and Sara, mainly because she was still nursing Sara. Sam and the kids wouldn't be attending the wedding.

The moment they were together, Laura wanted to tell Rachel about her new movie. "Your dad gave me a terrific idea. Instead of killing the guy who's misused her, the heroine—i.e., *me*—is now just daydreaming about killing him, which is sure as hell what I daydreamed of doing to Bogusian and a couple of other guys. The trial and imprisonment are also daydreams. It's been transformed into a romantic comedy. In the end, she finally gets together with a guy who's entered her daydreams as the arresting officer, the prosecutor, and the warden of the jail she's assigned to. *I* should be so lucky."

Rachel was more interested than she was at Passover. "Sounds adorable. Are you ready to film?"

"No, no, no. Your dad's idea required me to do a complete rewrite of the script. And getting the daydream sequences right is *very, very* tricky. I've also had to introduce the next boyfriend and work him into the daydreams, and that hasn't been easy. I've just finished a draft, but it still needs work before I show it to your dad again."

"Do you have money for the production?"

"No problem. The same people who financed my first film have signed on. They like the daydream murder, daydream trial, and daydream jail, even though her—i.e., *my*—second boyfriend isn't the oversexed-schlemiel type. Once I've got the script right, the rest should be a cinch. I've got some ideas on who should play me and who should play the guy I end up with."

"You're really fixated on this being your story, aren't you? This isn't just a running joke."

"It's my story alright. It began as my tragedy. And now it's my comedy. I poured my hatred for Bogusian into the tragedy, and I'm the comedy."

"You don't mean that."

"Oh, I do. You can't imagine how therapeutic it's been to see myself as a hopeless idiot looking for love in every dark closet. I actually feel now as if I might recognize the right guy if he happened along."

"Maybe I ought to write a screenplay."

"You could do worse."

"I already have."

The wedding ceremony for Arlie Becker and Jeff Hamilton was to be performed in a side room next door to the small ballroom where the dinner would be held. A total of twenty-seven people were invited. Besides Laura, Jess, and the members of the Becker family, Rachel knew none of the others. They were either Jeff's relatives or people Arlie and Jeff knew at Stanford or at Arlie's lab.

The Beckers were Jewish, of course, and the Hamiltons were Presbyterians. Arlie and Jeff decided a secular service would be best. The woman who officiated at the wedding was a judge. Both sets of parents accepted the compromise.

It was a quietly happy affair. Jeff Hamilton seemed to be everything that Seth Goldberg wasn't. He said Arlie was a genius and adorable and a terrific human being as well as everything anyone could possibly want as a lover. He was maybe a year or two older than she was, which would make him thirty-four or thirty-five, five feet nine inches tall, brown-haired, brown-eyed, with glasses, slightly built, looking a little uncomfortable in a suit. Arlie wasn't as thin as she used to be. She might actually weigh 110 or 115 pounds now. She still looked vaguely elongated, almost tall, not at all wide.

But it had been a long while since she looked as radiant as she did right now. Rachel, Jess, and Laura sat there during the ceremony, side by side, each lost in memory about their years together with Arlie, each glad that she'd found someone worthy of her love. Jess wished for Arlie to be as happy as she was. Laura wished that she could find someone like Jeff—not necessarily an intellectual but someone nice, someone steady, someone who was both loving and willing to be loved. Rachel wished she, like Arlie, could have a fresh start.

*   *   *

It was summer. The school year had ended. Rachel was again at loose ends, intending to spend a little time in Vail, perhaps with the children. JJ had been to Paris and London with Daniel. Rebecca had left for Paris and then Berlin for a couple of weeks.

Five weeks after her return from Berlin, Rebecca took Rachel aside. "I've got something I need to tell you, Rache. Please sit down."

"Sounds serious."

"It is." She blurted it out with some effort. "Rache, I'm pregnant. I got the test results today."

"My God! Who's the father?"

"That really doesn't matter. He isn't going to marry me if that's what you're thinking. He's already married."

"Oh, you poor child. Did you know?"

"Did I know that he was married? Yes. It's the way it is. I'm pregnant, and he's married."

"What you going to do? Will you have an abortion?"

"No. I'm going to have the baby, and I'm going to raise it."

"Where do you plan to go?"

"If you mean, am I going to run off some place to 'hide my shame,' that's not what I'm intending to do. There are lots of single women having babies these days. I'm going to be one of them."

"So you're planning to stay in Denver?"

"Yes. Denver's my home now. *This,*" she gestured, "is my home. I hope it can continue being my home."

Rachel hugged her. "Of course, this is your home, Beck. I hope I can be as good an aunt to your child as you've been to mine."

"Thanks, sis. I hoped you'd say that. Being surrounded by family—by you and JJ and the kids—is what I'm used to. I don't know how I'd cope if I had to go elsewhere."

"We've got all the room in the world, Beck—for you, for your child. I don't need to ask JJ. If I *wanted* to put you out, he wouldn't let me. He loves you."

"Yes, we're lucky. He loves all of us."

It would be awhile before Rebecca's pregnancy began to be noticeable. They debated—Rachel, JJ, Rebecca—what to tell Daniel and decided to wait until he asked. He was eight now, and the question would certainly come. The answer would be straightforward: Aunt Rebecca is having a baby. And if he pressed, the answer would be that she was having it alone. Time enough, years from now, for him to be told that Aunt Rebecca wouldn't identify the father, that the baby is "ours."

JJ suggested to Rachel that it might be best, if Rebecca would agree, for the two of them to adopt the child. It would forestall a lot of questions. The child would still be Rebecca's but have legal status as a member of the Weiner family.

JJ said, "The child may think it's got two mommies, but at least it will also have a daddy."

"That's very generous, JJ."

"Your sister's happiness is important to me. Important to us. This family couldn't get on without her."

"Whether or not she agrees, I'm sure she'll be pleased with the offer."

"So it's settled?"

"Between us, yes, it's settled. It's up to Rebecca."

"Good. I won't bring it up with her until the time is right. But I'm sure she'll see the advantages."

Rachel gave him a kiss. "It hasn't been easy for us these last couple of years, JJ. But you're a good man, and I'm grateful to you."

Soon, Rebecca was experiencing morning sickness and extreme fatigue. She was a very healthy young woman, and this was the first time she ever remembered feeling this ill. Nothing was fundamentally wrong, the obstetrician assured her, but she ought to take it easy for a while until her body adjusted. Rachel suggested that Rebecca come to Vail with her. "It will do you good. We'll take the children and Ms. Miller along, but I'll see to it that you get the right food and plenty of rest." Caring for her sister gave Rachel a sense of purpose she hadn't had, outside school, for a long time.

"I was gone sixteen days to Paris and Berlin, Rache. I can't take more time off."

"Sure you can. I know the boss, Beck. Herman will approve it, and your supervisor will understand. He has to. You've got to take care of yourself. It will only be a couple of weeks. You'll see how much better you feel in the fall."

Rebecca allowed herself to be persuaded. JJ said Anna Lopez would go along to do the cooking for them. "It's been awhile since Rachel did anything other than boil water," he said lightly. "I don't think we ought to depend on her to cook for a pregnant woman. Do you agree, Rache?"

"I suppose not. It's certainly true that I'm a stranger at the stove. Still Rachel, the kitchen klutz."

Rachel drove up to Vail Friday afternoon with Rebecca and Anna Lopez. JJ brought Ms. Miller and the children later in the day. JJ would go back late Sunday and return the following weekend. Rachel expected to be away two to three weeks. She would have to talk with Dev by telephone each Saturday. Even though she was seeing Dr. Cohen again, she was still keeping her weekly date with Dev. Dev insisted, and Dr. Cohen concurred. "It's especially important you check in with me if you're going to be away three weeks, sweetie," Dev told Rachel. "Since you won't be seeing Dr. Cohen while you're gone, I need to know you're okay. I don't care if all we talk about is the weather. You've got to call."

"Remember, once, when I told you that you're not my boss? I was wrong. You *are* my boss, Dev. I do whatever you say."

Dev was pleased that Rachel was able to make a mild joke about it. "Good. Saturday morning. Every Saturday. Two minutes, ten minutes, an hour, two hours. Doesn't matter. Just check in, sweetie."

Daniel was at the age now where he needed other kids to play with. Luckily, there was a family two doors away with two boys, one a couple of years older than Daniel and the other a year younger. The older boy was glad to have a second kid to boss around, and Daniel was more than willing to share his toys and accept direction. The Weiner-Rothschild lodge had two sundecks on two different levels that allowed Rebecca to rest outdoors in the mornings. She was still puking regularly, and a morning nap in the open air was very restorative. Rachel wouldn't allow Ariel to intrude on her, even if she had to be the one to entertain her four-year-old. After a week, Rebecca was already beginning to feel better. She suggested they drive into the village. It would be a good change of pace for the children, and she wanted to look around for some loose-fitting clothing that she could wear once she started to bulge.

Rachel and Rebecca had been living together now for nearly three years, but Rebecca was always the care-giver. This was the first time since they were small that Rachel looked after her younger sister, and she felt good about it. *Maybe that's what I need, a little responsibility for someone besides myself. So what about caring for the children? Oh, shit. There I go again.* And now she didn't feel quite so good.

She mentioned all of this to Dev, making sure the door was closed so she couldn't be overheard. It was Saturday, and JJ was sitting out on the deck with Rebecca.

"We were in town the other day, and I was shopping for maternity clothes with Beck. I really felt good about taking care of her. And then it hit me that I wasn't doing a very good job of taking care of my own children."

"You've got complicated feelings about the kids, sweetie. That's why Dr. Cohen asked you to be hypnotized, right?"

"Right."

"You'll get those feelings untangled after awhile, and then you'll do okay again with the kids."

"God, I hope so. Daniel's eight, and Ariel's four. They deserve a mother." Her voice was anguished.

"Easy, darling. Easy. You'll get there."

"It's almost three years, Dev. Am I ever going to be a whole person again?"

"Dr. Cohen says you're making progress, sweetheart. Next time you see her, why don't you ask for an assessment. Let her tell you."

"Why is she willing to talk with you when she wouldn't talk to JJ?"

"It's different is the answer, I guess. I report to her, and in turn, she says a little about how you're doing. She doesn't tell me what you tell her, and I don't ask. Besides, I'm not a part of the equation in the sense that JJ is. I bet you never talk to her about me, am I right?" Dev was joking, but Rachel responded seriously.

"I tell her all the time that you've saved my life. I tell her that I've taken countless hours from you during the past three years."

"I didn't mean it that way, darling. I meant that if you've got problems, they're not with me. I'm not in the equation. So there's not the same risk of betraying confidences. And, besides, I'll say again, we don't discuss what goes on in your sessions. I know you underwent hypnosis because *you* told me that. Remember? She hasn't said a word about it. If you listened in when I spoke to her, you'd see. The talk's mostly one-way. I report and she listens, occasionally throwing out a crumb of information for me to pounce on."

"So she hasn't said anything about what I told her under hypnosis about me and the kids?"

"I know what you told me, sweetheart. That's it."

"I guess I need to tell her about feeling good about Rebecca and bad about the kids."

When the summer ended, Rachel returned to school. She was almost back to where she was before she learned that gossip about what happened to her in Denver was circulating within the department. The therapy sessions with Dr. Cohen helped a lot, but the weekly visits with Dev were the best thing she had going for her. They were a weekly oasis in time, like the Shabbat service attended by Jews more observant than she was.

Only occasionally did it occur to Rachel that she was taking a chunk of Dev's limited time at home with her husband and child. Dev allowed her to believe that the sessions imposed no burden, when in fact Dev was often emotionally drained after Rachel left. It was difficult to seem utterly composed when her own emotions were often seething just below the surface. She couldn't let go because her equanimity was the foundation Rachel depended on.

In early October, Dev learned that she was pregnant with her second child. Mark was after her to see Rachel less often. Maybe once every two weeks for a while. Then once a month. Dev needed to conserve her energy and Rachel was back with Dr. Cohen. Why did the weekly visits with Dev remain necessary?

"I'm sorry, honey. I don't want Rachel to think I'm walking out on her."

"How could she ever think you're walking out on her, Dev? Nobody has given her what you've given her. Three years of your life, doll. She can't go on forever depending on you to hold her up. It's not even good for her."

"I'll talk to Dr. Cohen about it, honey. That's the best I can do. When Dr. Cohen says it's okay, I'll start to taper off. I promise you if at all possible that we'll be down to once every few weeks by the time the baby's born."

"Look, doll, if you can't do it, I'll talk to Rachel. I don't think she understands how much you're chewed up by seeing her."

"Please don't, Mark! The last thing I want is to make her feel guilty. And if I *do* cut back—okay, *when* I cut back—I'm going to invite her to come be with us socially. As often as possible. She's my cousin, sweetheart, and I love her. I want her around."

"I understand, baby. I'm not telling you to keep her away. I just want you to stop giving blood once a week, 'cause that's what you're doing."

Dev sighed. "Well, you're right about that."

Rachel, meanwhile, was fully engaged with her studies. She was planning to take seminars in her primary field of concentration, American government. She'd do a seminar on the presidency and another on the U.S. Congress, as well as a class on the political economy of American politics. She'd take a couple of courses in public policy, her second field, and a class in constitutional law, the third area in which she would have to show competence. Louis Short was with her in one class, and the first time she walked in the door and saw him, she experienced a chill. However, she knew she could not afford to run like a startled deer every time their paths crossed. So she took her seat across the room, and she met his gaze without turning away. She even steeled herself to participate in the same discussions he was in without any display of anger or other emotion. It was exceedingly difficult, but she managed, a fact that she reported proudly to Dev when they next met.

"I don't even flinch when I see him anymore, like I would if I saw a snake. I won't look away either. I think—well, more like I hope—he's beginning to get the idea that I'm not afraid of him anymore."

"That's good, sweetie. I'm proud of you. And how's the class going—as compared to your other classes?"

"You *are* shrewd, Dev. The professor told me the other day he didn't think I was doing as well as I'm capable of doing. Maybe having Short there flusters me more than I think it does. Maybe it's the energy I spend *not* being afraid of him. I don't know."

"You won't be over it altogether, Rache, until you don't even think about his being there."

Rachel said ruefully, "I'm a long way from having reached that stage, love. A long way."

"Is this guy going to be around the department the whole time you're there?"

Rachel laughed without amusement. "He doesn't exactly confide in me. But, yes, I think so. We're at about the same stage in our studies. He's in a different field, thank God. And that means we'll be in fewer classes together as time goes on. But I'll still see him around. There's no way to avoid that unless I stay away from all the graduate student hangouts."

"You don't want to do that, sweetie."

Dev was hoping Short wouldn't bother Rachel again. But he'd certainly be on the lookout for an opportunity.

"If he ever bothers you, you'll let me know, won't you? I haven't given up on the idea of driving him off campus if he gives me an excuse."

Rachel laughed again, a tiny little laugh. "Bother me? He already bothers me, Dev. You mean if he harasses me, don't you, like trying to pinch my butt?"

"Call it what you want. I mean if he does something outrageous, though I really doubt it will take the form of a physical assault. I think what he'd like to do is to cut you down, humiliate you, make you cry."

"I've shed all the tears over Louis Short that I ever intend to shed."

"Good! Let's make sure it stays that way."

*			*			*

Marla was appearing during the fall and winter seasons in three operas with the San Francisco Opera Company. She was scheduled to sing Dido in Purcell's *Dido and Aeneas*, Idamante in Mozart's *Idomeneo*, another "trouser" role for soprano, and Anne in Stravinsky's *The Rake's Progress*. These were starring roles, and Marla wanted everyone to come admire her. Even Rachel agreed to fly out for a weekend to see her as Dido. Alina would not be providing moral support for these engagements. This was home territory for Marla, and Noah and her parents would give her all the help she needed. Besides, Lee and David were heading off to Europe in mid-October to do the eight-city tour of Scandinavia, Switzerland, and Italy required to complete Lee's book.

Rebecca, who was over her regular bouts of nausea and felt quite good, would go to San Francisco when Hanna and Hillel did. Although she'd begun to show, she hadn't yet told her parents that she was pregnant, so the visit would certainly have its difficult moments.

"How are you going to handle it?" Rachel asked.

"I don't know. I'll tell them I'm pregnant and try to ride out the storm as best I can."

"Our mother will not handle this well."

JJ said, "Rebecca will do okay. Don't make her more nervous than she already is."

"I'm not the first one we know to have gotten pregnant without being married."

"Yes, but you'll be the first not to have a husband when the baby comes."

Rebecca flared, "Don't be so goddamed self-righteous, Rachel. At least I have someone who makes love to me. What have you got?"

Rachel turned away like someone who's had her face slapped. "That was unnecessary."

"If I thought it was unnecessary, I wouldn't have said it."

JJ intervened. "Stop it, girls. This is *our* baby, not just Rebecca's baby. We've got to pull together."

Silence.

JJ added, "It would help if you apologized, Rachel."

"I'm sorry, Beck. I was out of line."

"Yes, you were."

JJ said, "Rebecca! You shouldn't have said what you said either."

"I'm sorry." Deep breath. "I'm sorry, Rache."

By the time Rebecca left for San Francisco, Rachel had already been to see the opera and returned. When Rebecca came back, Rachel asked, "How did it go, Beck?"

"It was worse than I imagined. Mommy cried when I told her. For the longest time. Then she called me a 'tramp.' Then she told me I ought to have an abortion, and I started crying. I told her I intended to have the baby, that I want the baby, and then we were both crying.

The whole hotel was awash by the time we finished. From the lobby to the penthouse."

"It must have come out okay, or you wouldn't be making jokes."

"Yeah, it came out okay. Daddy was very good, and Mommy came around. I told them the baby is a girl and that I intend to name her Ilana after Grandma. That helped. I also told them that you and JJ plan to adopt the baby. And that helped, too. What the hell, it's their grandchild, and I'm still their little girl. But I don't mind telling you it was a tough couple of hours

JJ said, "You poor kid. Somebody should have been there with you."

Rachel snapped, "Yeah. Like the baby's father."

"That will do, Rachel," JJ responded with an edge in his voice. "She's had a tough time. You don't have to make it worse."

Rachel asked, "Did you tell Noah?"

"Yep. After Mommy and Daddy, that was easy. What he said was 'Whoever knocked you up is your business.'"

"Delicately put."

"I'll tell Davy when he and Alina come back from Europe."

"What do you want to do about your aunt and uncle and your cousins?" JJ inquired.

Rebecca replied, "I'd rather not go through it with anyone else just yet."

JJ said, "Would you like me to tell them?"

Rebecca looked relieved. "Would you? I'd be grateful."

By the time Rachel saw Dev next, she'd already heard from JJ.

"I understand you and JJ are going to adopt Rebecca's baby. Are you okay with that?"

"Yes. JJ suggested it, and it's the best solution."

"Does Rebecca understand that she's doing something that's irrevocable? With you all under one roof, it's likely to be as complicated as it is odd. Legally, the baby will be yours and JJ's, not hers. She won't be able to exercise parental authority in any legal sense."

"I don't know whether she understands all the ramifications, Dev. But I'll know that Rebecca is the baby's mother, and I'll let her make the necessary decisions. So it won't be a real problem."

"I hope not, Rache. But things happen, and you and JJ ough

to be sure that Rebecca understands the legal consequences of your adopting the baby."

"I'll make sure she does," Rachel said, though she had no intention of raising the issue.

"Do you intend for the baby to be Ilana Weiner or Ilana Rothschild?"

"That hasn't been decided. JJ's suggested Ilana Rothschild-Weiner. But it's up to Rebecca."

"Well, I hope you'll all be happy together."

"Thanks, Dev. I hope so."

Dev, although she was apprehensive for some reason she hadn't been able to define for herself, said lightly, "You know, Beck's not the only one who's going to have a baby."

Rachel, immediately understanding what was coming, responded, "Oh?" She said it without enthusiasm.

"I'm pregnant, too. Due the end of May. Another little girl."

"I'm very happy for you, Dev." But she wasn't. Rachel wasn't ready for Dev to have another baby.

A week passed, and Rachel was again at Dev's. It had been a bad week. Rachel knew she had reacted poorly—selfishly—to Dev's news. She berated herself about it. Now she was determined to be happy for her cousin.

"I've been thinking about the baby, Dev, your baby. Can I ask you a favor?"

"Of course, Rache."

"I'd like to be the baby's godmother. I know you didn't bother with a godmother for Alexis. And Yalie is ahead of me in line. But I'd really, really like to be godmother to your baby, Dev." There were tears in Rachel's eyes. "It would mean so much to me. I want to give back in some way for everything you've done, are still doing, for me."

Dev was also teary. "I'd be honored to have you as my baby's godmother, Rache. No need to talk about 'giving back.' It would be just another bond between us, sweetheart, but an important one to me."

"And to me. I'm so grateful to you, Dev."

"Don't say another word, please, or I'll start bawling."

They hugged one another, dried their eyes, and turned to other things. But Rachel had already covered the main business of the visit.

She knew she had acted badly the previous Saturday. Being the baby's godmother was more than an act of repentance, however. This is *Dev's* baby. This little girl would have Rachel's love and protection—*for as long as I live*, she told herself. And she told herself determinedly that she intended to live a long time. And to be happy.

*　　　*　　　*

It was early November. Rachel returned home from Boulder in late afternoon to find a police cruiser parked in the driveway. Alarmed, she sprinted to the front door. Rebecca greeted her.

"There are a couple of detectives here from the Denver Police Department, Rache. They want to talk to you about the two guys who raped you. They've been located in Miami. A bunch of men took them out and castrated them. The police think JJ had it done."

"Are they dead?"

"No, they're in the hospital and a lot worse for wear, but they're alive. Anyway, that's what the police want to ask you about."

Rachel went into the library off the living room, where the two detectives, Detective Logan and Detective Sgt. Albertini, were waiting.

Albertini took the lead. "Sorry to bother you, Mrs. Weiner, but I need to ask you about your husband's movements during the past few months."

"Why don't you ask him?"

Albertini answered, "We've already spoken with Mr. Weiner several times in the last ten days. He hasn't told you?"

"No, he hasn't told me. I haven't been well. Not since the rape. Maybe he didn't want to upset me."

Logan said, "So you don't know that the two rapists, Hopkins and Bray, were located in Miami eight months ago by a team of detectives your husband hired?"

"Eight months ago! You can't be serious."

Logan answered, "Perfectly serious, Mrs. Weiner. Your husband didn't tell you?"

"No. No. Certainly not."

Albertini asked, "Do you have any idea why he might have kept it secret from you?"

"I don't know. Maybe he was trying to shield me."

Albertini continued, "Would you have wanted them arrested once they were located?"

"Of course. After what they did to me, I'd like to see them in jail for the rest of their lives."

Albertini was skeptical. "Mr. Weiner says he didn't have them arrested because he wasn't sure you would have been able to stand up to the rigors of a trial."

Rachel, sensing where this was headed, backed off a bit. "Well, it certainly would have been hard for me. I was a patient in a psychiatric ward for a while after the rape, and I'm currently under the care of both a psychiatrist and a psychoanalyst. So he may have felt my condition was too fragile for me to testify in a rape trial."

Logan was equally skeptical. "Wouldn't you think he'd have asked your doctors?"

"Why are you asking me? Why not ask him?"

Logan said, "We already did."

"And what did he say?"

Logan responded, "He told us he didn't think of it. Mrs. Weiner, your husband has been out of town on several occasions during the past eight months. If you can tell us, where did he go—and when?"

"He has a calendar at the office. Surely, you've seen it."

Albertini pressed her. "Please answer the question, Mrs. Weiner. We'd like to hear from you."

"The only big trip he's taken was to Paris and London with our son."

Albertini asked, "When was that?"

"April. May. I don't know the exact dates."

Albertini continued, "How long was he gone?"

"A week. Ten days. I don't know."

Albertini persisted, "Did he go anywhere except Paris and London?"

"No. My sister-in-law was performing with the Paris Opera, and JJ—my husband—took our son to see her. Then they went to London so our son could see the changing of the guard and the Tower of London. Things like that."

Albertini went on, "What about other trips?"

"He takes short business trips all the time. We have a home in Vail.

He's going out to San Francisco to see my sister-in-law with the San Francisco Opera Company. You've got his calendar. Look at it."

Albertini said, "We have, Mrs. Weiner. But calendars can be doctored. That's why we're asking you."

"Oh. Why would he doctor his calendar?"

"I'll leave that to your imagination, Mrs. Weiner," Albertini replied drily. "If you don't mind, I have some other questions. Have there been any phone calls that have come into the house in the last few months from someone with a foreign accent?"

"Not that I know of."

Albertini asked, "Do you usually answer the phone?"

"Not usually."

Albertini pursued the line of questioning. "Who does?"

"My husband when he's home. My sister. Our housekeeper. The children's nanny."

Albertini continued, "Is there a reason you don't answer the phone?"

"I told you. I've been ill. I don't like to talk on the phone if I don't have to."

Albertini set off in a new direction. "Do you maintain a savings account separate from your husband's?"

"Yes."

Albertini asked, "How much money do you have in it?"

"I don't know. What business is it of yours?"

Albertini said, "We can subpoena your account if we have to, Mrs. Weiner. It will be easier for all concerned if you help us."

"What's my savings account got to do with anything?"

Albertini answered, "Your husband paid for the services of the detectives out of his personal funds—about 1.7 million dollars in all. That corresponds with what the detective agency's books show as having been received. We think it would have cost half a million, maybe more, to have these guys castrated. We're looking for the source of that money."

"You think JJ arranged to have them castrated?"

Logan cut in, "We're *sure* he did, Mrs. Weiner, and we're going to prove it."

"I don't have that kind of money in my personal accounts. Never did." She was about to volunteer that she and JJ owned this house paid for by JJ's grandmother, when it came to her that if JJ needed a large sum of money, Grandma Bess would willingly provide it.

Albertini asked, "If you needed money, Mrs. Weiner, where would you go for it?"

"I'd go to my husband, Sergeant. I wouldn't have a need to go anywhere else."

The questioning continued for a while, but Rachel had told them everything she intended to tell. She needed to talk to JJ.

When the policemen left, Rachel found JJ downstairs in the den.

"What's this all about JJ?"

"I assume they told you. Someone had Hopkins and Bray castrated. They think I did it."

"Did you?"

"Of course not."

"They said you found these guys eight months ago in Miami. Is that true?"

JJ admitted it. "The detective agency I hired found them. Working for a Miami construction company."

"And you didn't have them arrested?"

"I intended to. But then I thought they'd be brought back here to Denver and there would be a trial, and you'd be forced to testify in open court. I couldn't put you through that."

"Shouldn't you have consulted me?"

"I did what I thought was best. I didn't want to put your mental health at further risk. You were pretty near the edge six months ago, if you'll recall. You're not exactly on firm ground now."

"So, once again, the mighty JJ Weiner has made a decision for Rachel Rothschild."

"Shit, Rachel. What should I have done? Told you we had these two guys cornered and should we bring them to justice or let them roam free? A great question to put to someone who's standing on the threshold of a room with rubber walls."

"Fuck you, JJ. Just fuck you."

She walked out and slammed the door behind her.

On Saturday, Rachel told Dev what happened. She wanted Dev's support and also a little legal advice.

"I've got to tell you the truth, Rache. I already knew. JJ brought me into it when the police came calling. Made me promise not to say anything to you for the time being. Lawyer-client privilege. My hands were tied."

"Oh God, Dev. I thought I could depend on you."

Dev felt hurt and guilty. "You *can*, Rache, but you've got to understand. I could have pretended to be surprised when you told me. I didn't, because the last thing in the world I'd do to you is fail to be honest."

Rachel responded sharply, "Can you at least tell me what they asked about?"

"I shouldn't say anything. But they think JJ did it and they're searching for proof that he arranged it and paid for it."

Rachel said again, pointedly, "And?"

"They haven't found anything. JJ's accounts are perfectly in order. There's nothing—no phone records, no suspicious travel—to show he had anything to do with it."

"But he did it. I know he did it. He had them tracked down. He's known where they were for eight months."

"Yes, that much they know. JJ paid a detective agency to find them, paid them a lot. His accounts reflect payments to the detective agency. The police have been trying to determine whether the detective agency might have arranged on JJ's behalf to have them castrated. The detective agency vigorously denies it. I don't think that's a very likely scenario. They'd be putting their whole business on the line if they did anything like that."

"What about some individual in the agency?"

"They've explored that angle, too, I think, and come up dry."

"Have they found any of the people who did it?"

"The castration? My understanding is that there were five or six people involved. The Miami police have two of them in jail. They're minor figures in the drug trade. The thing must have been arranged through the ringleaders for a substantial sum of money, probably a quarter of a million, maybe more. The two men in custody got ten thousand dollars each in cash before and ten thousand dollars after. The paymaster was a tall man who spoke English with a foreign accent. The police found the hotel where he stayed, but he used a phony name and he's vanished. They don't have as much as a fingerprint. The people at the hotel say he sounded British but not quite. Might be from South

Africa or New Zealand or Australia, possibly from Ireland or someplace in Britain where they don't sound like they graduated from Oxford."

"Who told you all this?"

"I made some inquiries. I got some of it from the Miami newspapers. Richie helped. His firm has contacts in the Denver police department."

"You think JJ did it, don't you?"

"JJ says he didn't, and he's my client."

"He claims he didn't have Hopkins and Bray arrested because he was protecting me from having to face them in court. That's bullshit! I know JJ. If he wanted those guys arrested, he wouldn't have thought one second about how it would affect me. In fact, he would have convinced himself that putting them behind bars would do me good. He wanted to find them so he could have them castrated."

"I'm glad you're not the prosecutor, Rache. You may be right, but all that has to be proved in court, and they don't have any evidence to show that JJ did *anything* after the detective agency found them."

"Well, I bet I know where he got the money." Rachel was sure it came from Grandma Bess. Somehow JJ had the money laundered and transferred to an offshore bank. Maybe Switzerland. JJ could have found a way to do that while he was in Paris. He spent ten days out of the country.

"I don't want to hear how you think it could have been done, Rache. I'm acting as JJ's attorney in this matter. I didn't want to. I asked him to find someone else—Richie, for example. But he insisted."

"That filthy bastard! He knows how much I rely on you, and he wanted to take you away from me, drive a wedge between us."

"JJ can't drive a wedge between us, sweetie. Nobody can."

"That's where you're wrong, Dev. He can, and he did. I feel really bad knowing that you knew and didn't tell me."

Dev, in anguish, replied, "Couldn't tell you, Rache. *Couldn't.*"

"That's what I mean. He likes having you under his control. Another assistant to JJ Weiner."

"*Don't*, Rache. *Please.*" She was close to tears.

"I'm not mad at you, Dev. I understand about professional ethics. He's the one I'm angry with."

"You forgive me?" It was a plea.

"Yeah. I'm unhappy, but I forgive you. I'm nothing without you, Dev. I hope you'll remember that."

Her eyes still brimming, Dev tried to reassure Rachel, but she wasn't able to speak. Instead, she held her head while the tears rolled down her cheeks. She'd have to tell JJ that he couldn't rely on her to keep secrets from Rachel. *Rachel's too important to me*, she thought.

"Will you be able to offer me legal advice if I need it?"

Dev's sense that she'd somehow betrayed Rachel was complete. "I don't think I can." Her voice was barely audible. "Not on this."

"That son of a bitch!"

"Oh, God. l I'm sorry, Rache." She was sobbing now.

At home Rachel headed straight for the library where JJ was working. "You miserable bastard," she began. "You had to take away the one person I depend on. That's so like you."

"Ah, so Dev told you that she's known about the police inquiry, did she? I told her she ought not to."

"Dev's not a liar like you are."

"Come off it, Rachel. Damn you! Dev is my lawyer. The police are after my ass, and I needed her help."

"One, you could have found another lawyer. Two, you didn't have to instruct Dev to keep it secret from me. Three, you're a miserable fucking bastard!"

"I didn't want to worry you."

"Oh yes. Always thinking about me. How touching. I'm sure you had those guys castrated for me!" She was shouting.

"I didn't do it."

"Don't give me that shit, JJ. I know you. I know how you got the money to pay for it. I have half a mind to tell the police."

"I didn't do it, Rachel. There isn't any money."

"You got it from Grandma Bess. She wouldn't deny her grandson a lousy million bucks or two, would she? She spent ten million dollars to buy you this house."

"Buy *us* this house. You and me and the children."

"The children. Another line of defense. You wouldn't have Hopkins and Bray prosecuted because of me, and the ten million dollars wasn't for you. It was for me and the children. JJ, you make me sick!"

"You're not going to say anything to the police." It was half a statement, half a question.

"No, I'm not going to say anything to the police. Even though you had them castrated for your sake and not for mine, I can't say I'm unhappy that they got what they deserved. But tell me, JJ, how did you do it? Where did you stash the money? Where did you find the arranger, the paymaster, this foreigner with the British accent?"

"Dev's got a big mouth. I'll have to remember that in the future." He became angry himself. "But if you want the truth, okay. Yes, I had it done." He raised his voice. "I wanted to pay them back for what they did. An eye for an eye. Having them arrested and extradited wouldn't have been enough. You don't need to know the details. What you don't know can't hurt me."

"Don't worry. I'm not going to tell anybody. Not even Dev. She prefers not knowing that you're guilty."

"Look, Rache, I'm sorry about keeping Dev from telling you. I shouldn't have done that."

"No, you shouldn't. You damaged the most important thing in my life, my relationship to Dev. You made it impossible for her to give *me* legal advice when she's the one I'd naturally turn to."

"Well, don't blame Dev for the canons of ethics."

"I don't. You're the one I blame."

"Why not? You blame me for everything else that's gone wrong in your life."

Hopkins and Bray were recovering from the mutilation. A couple of detectives arrived from Miami to take their turn questioning JJ. He continued to deny everything. The Denver police made no progress in finding any connection between JJ and the gang of men who performed the castration.

JJ hadn't intended to admit his involvement to Rachel. It just came out during the argument. He didn't want to upset Rachel further, so he released Dev from any obligation not to talk with her about developments in the case. Rachel didn't tell Dev about JJ's confession. *She kept secrets from me, and now I'm keeping secrets from her. But she's JJ's lawyer. I don't want her to carry the burden of knowing what I know.*

Rachel asked, "Is this investigation going to go on forever, Dev?"

Dev felt she must answer Rachel's questions. "No, not forever. But the Miami police think they know who the paymaster was. A South African soldier of fortune who now lives in Australia. They got some likely names and photographs from Interpol and showed them to the people at the hotel and to the two suspects they've got in custody. The people at the hotel picked out this fellow. His real name is Alistair Hobson. The name that was signed on the hotel register was Noster Johns. The two people in custody claim they never met him. It probably wouldn't be very healthy for them to say anything else."

Rachel was startled. "They're trying to link this guy to JJ?"

"That's the idea. There's nothing on this end to show that JJ was ever in touch with him. They've been through phone records at the office, at the house, on JJ's car phone. They took his desktop computer and his laptop, looking for e-mail exchanges. Zero. The Australian police have spoken with Hobson. He was in the United States for a long time and didn't return until late-October, but he's denied everything, and they haven't got enough to extradite him—no sudden increase in his bank account, no lavish spending, no tie to JJ. He insists that he was nowhere near Miami, and he's got hotel bills showing he was in New York City when it happened. And, of course, JJ hasn't been to Miami in the past year. And the only time he was in New York was en route to Paris with Daniel."

"So they've got nothing on JJ."

"Nothing."

"Where else can they go looking?"

"They'll root around for a while. They might put enough pressure on the two thugs in Miami for them to tell what they know. Maybe the police can identify others involved in the castration. But I doubt they'll get anything on the people who did the arranging. It seems a safe assumption that none of the guys who actually did it can provide sufficient hard evidence against Hobson, even if they're willing to talk, which I doubt. My guess is that the case will eventually move to the back burner, and that'll be the last we'll hear of it."

"I hope so. I wouldn't want JJ to go to jail."

"Even though you think he did it?"

"Even though I'm *sure* he did it. I haven't got any sympathy for those two pieces of shit after what they did to me."

"Nor do I, sweetheart. But taking the law into your own hands, which is what JJ's accused of, is still a serious criminal offense. If they're able to prove it, JJ could go to jail for a long time, as could any accomplices."

"What accomplices?"

"Anyone who aided and abetted. By helping set up an offshore bank account or acting as the go-between with Hobson."

"Who might have done that?"

"I hope we'll never know, Rache. I hope we'll never have to ask ourselves that question."

But since Rachel knew that JJ was guilty, she was bound to ask herself that question. It couldn't be avoided.

*   *   *

The Christmas and New Year's holidays came and went. There was no family gathering this time, not in Santa Monica, not in Vail, not in Golden. The excuse given was that Rachel was too busy to superintend arrangements in Vail or Golden, and Rebecca was too far along in her pregnancy to travel to Santa Monica.

Jess Sherman didn't buy the excuse. Going to Vail didn't require a lot of arranging, and unless there was a medical problem, less than seven months wasn't when an expectant mother was too big to travel. She suspected something was wrong. She'd been talking regularly to Dev since Passover, and on one of her calls she asked why the holiday visits were being canceled. Dev said there was nothing wrong, yet she seemed unaccountably flustered. That was not at all like Dev.

That evening, Jess phoned Rachel at home.

"I don't mean to be nosy, babe," Jess began, "but Dev is upset and she won't say why. Is there anything I can do to help?"

Rachel, after a moment, answered, "Promise not to tell my folks?"

"I promise."

"The two men who raped me were discovered in Miami. Someone had them mutilated. And the police think JJ did it. They've been investigating for more than a month. The Denver police came to the house and interrogated me."

After a moment's silence, Jess asked, "Have they found anything?"

"I don't think so. Dev is his lawyer. She's in the middle of it."

"And can't say a thing. That explains why she was so agitated. She's not an experienced liar."

"No, she's not. Between her loyalty to me and her professional obligations to JJ, she's pulled apart. It's really tough on her. I feel like a skunk, Jess. I can't give her up. JJ shouldn't have put her in this spot. He could have found another lawyer."

"You can't begrudge him the lawyer of his choice, babe."

Rachel sighed. "I guess not."

"As a lawyer, I shouldn't say this, Rache, but I hope that if JJ did it, he gets away with it. Those guys deserved to have their balls cut off. I assume that's what happened when you say they were mutilated."

"Yes. A gang of men grabbed them and castrated them. I don't know any of the details, and I don't want to know."

"I asked before whether there's anything I can do. You didn't answer."

"Except for not telling my folks, I don't know what you can do from Santa Monica, Jess."

"Would you mind if I say something to Laura or Arlie?"

"If you see them, okay. Don't make a special effort to tell them. The fewer people that know, the better. I'd rather it didn't get around."

"Rache, I know this is going to sound crazy. I've *got* to see you, babe. When do your classes resume?"

"Mid-January."

"Would you mind if I came in for a few days right after New Year's?"

"Would you bring Sam and the kids?"

"No. You don't need the distraction, and I don't want it. All I want is to be with you, Rache."

"I'm doing okay. There's no need."

"It's not your need I'm talking about. It's mine. I feel so goddam fucking helpless sitting out here in la-la land. I need to touch you."

Rachel laughed. "Look who's looking to me for comfort. Jess, you and Dev are the two most stable people I know. Maybe I should say *were* because, between us, JJ and I have made a nervous wreck out of Dev. Maybe you'd like us to do the same for you?"

"Reverse psychotherapy. There's a concept. Look, pencil me in on your calendar. I'll come in late on Friday the second and stay until Monday morning. Date?"

Rachel replied affectionately, "It's a date, Bozo. Bring your straitjacket. You'll need it for the trip home."

JJ wasn't pleased to learn that Jess knew about the investigation or that she was coming for the weekend. *Jess is too damn smart. Who know.*

what she might figure out? But, of course, he didn't say any of this. There had already been enough harsh words between him and Rachel lately. He also thought he might have made a mistake choosing Dev to represent him in this matter. *She's a damn good lawyer, even though she's not a specialist in criminal law. But her personal loyalty is to Rachel, and she knows too damn much about our marriage. And she's bound to be over here when Jess comes, and God knows how those two will play off each other. Rachel's enough of a problem without Jess and Dev in the picture.*

Sure enough, Dev was the one who went to the airport to pick Jess up and bring her to Golden. In fact, Dev invited herself for the night. Mark would bring Alexis over in the morning, and they'd spend the day. Dev and Jess had been talking all the way from the airport, mostly about Rachel, some about the investigation, and finally about their children. Dev was four months pregnant with her second child, and although Jess's second child, Sara, was just a year old, Jess said she intended to get pregnant again soon.

"I was an only child, Dev. I envied Rachel the fact that she had two brothers and a sister, where I had no one else in my family. I grew up thinking four is the right size family, and I've convinced Sam that's how many we should have. I'd like to have another baby when Sara's about two and the fourth two years after that. What about you?"

"I don't know yet. This one's another girl. I think Mark would like to have a son. We'll need to talk about it after this one is born."

"What are you, Dev, thirty-six, thirty-seven?"

"I was thirty-six in September."

"I assume you'll include your obstetrician in that conversation. You want to be damn sure he thinks there's no risk."

"Yeah, I know. That's a consideration."

"It sure as hell ought to be—not *a* consideration, but the *principal* consideration. I'm sure Mark won't want to risk your health."

"I appreciate your concern, Jess. We're not there yet. The baby isn't due until late May, and it will be another year, year and a half before we're ready to decide on whether to have another."

"Look, you can tell me to fuck off if you want to, but I'd like to hear a promise that you won't get carried away just because Mark wants a boy."

"Don't worry, sweetie, I'm not going to do anything crazy. What I ought to do is send you to have this conversation with Yalie. She's so wrapped up in her work I'm afraid she'll wait too long before she and Richie try to have kids."

"They want kids?"

"Mañana is when they want kids, not anytime soon."

"I can get you some literature to give her. Through Planned Parenthood. I'm on the local board. That's why I'm so fixated on the subject."

"You've just demonstrated conclusively that you're an only child, Jess. The last person on earth that Yalie would listen to about something like this is her older sister. She'd listen to our mom before she'd listen to me."

"I have an idea. I'll send the literature to her in a plain brown envelope. She'll open it thinking it's pornography."

Dev giggled. "Feeelthy pictures of aging egg ducts. Can you arrange for this plain brown envelope to be postmarked from Paris?"

"That's a different generation, babe. Pornography is a dot-com business these days, the most successful of *all* dot-com businesses. It's a lot more likely to come from Portland, Oregon, or Portland, Maine, than Paris, France."

"Yeah, well, I'll talk to my obstetrician, and if he gives me a skull-and-crossbones warning, I'll take my life in my hands and pass it on to Yalie. If I do that, would you like to help pay for my hospital bill?"

"That bad, huh?"

"That bad."

They arrived at the Weiner home in Golden just as the conversation reached this end. Rachel saw them come. She'd been looking out the window every few minutes for the past forty-five minutes. She grasped Jess in a particularly fierce hug.

"Hey, babe, I need these lungs for breathing."

"I'm so happy to see you, Bozo. I didn't realize how much I'd miss everyone until nobody showed up for the holidays."

"I missed you, too, snookums. That's why I'm here. How are you doing?"

"You've just been talking to Dev. You tell me how I'm doing."

"Bitchy as ever. I see your analyst hasn't cured you of that, has she?"

Rachel hugged her again. "God, it's wonderful to have you here

Jess. You don't know how good it makes me feel for you to come see me."

Jess was misty-eyed. "I'm glad you feel that way, babe." Now she was smiling and teary at the same time. "I don't know why I thought about it over Christmas, Rache, but you're the one who brought Sam and me together, and I was just overwhelmed by this feeling that I *had* to see you with my own eyes to be sure you're okay. I've gotten so wrapped up in my own life that I've neglected you."

"You'll do a lot more for me if you make me laugh, Bozo, than if you make me cry. I'm pretty good at crying on my own. Right, Dev?"

Dev agreed, "You're the champ, sweetie."

Jess directed her answer at Rachel. "I've got to be in the mood to be funny."

"Okay, then tell me about Laura. Tell me about Arlie."

"Well, Arlie and Jeff are doing fine. They came down to Santa Monica for the holidays, and they were over at our house for dinner. Along with Laura. I've never seen Arlie any happier. And she's got another software project under development. This one's called 'Junk Yard Dog.' She claims it will knock most of the advertising shit out of your e-mail inbox and close those goddam pop-up windows before they open."

Dev smiled broadly. "God bless her if it works."

Rachel said, "She'll sell a billion copies."

"And probably earn the undying hatred of the shit-manufacturing-and-distributing industry," Jess added.

Rachel asked, "And Laura?"

"Her film starts production at the beginning of February. She says your dad thinks she's got a real winner. Hasn't he told you?"

"No. He's never carried stories among us kids, and he treats Laura like she's another of his children."

"He's done wonders for her, Rache."

"My Daddy's a terrific guy, Jess. Laura's his protege, and he's very proud of her."

"And one more item. Laura is dating again. A friend of Sam's. He's a little older than Sam, but they knew one another at medical school. We introduced them at a party at our house."

"Is it serious?"

"Too early to know. He's been married before. Has a six-year-old boy. Still licking his wounds. He's not jumping into anything rashly, and neither is Laura. But they seem to enjoy each other's company. The fact that they come from separate worlds is a plus. Laura's had it with men from the film industry, and Chuck Wardman isn't even a moviegoer."

"Let's hope it works out."

"Yeah. Laura's had a difficult time with men, hasn't she? Ever since we were girls and the men in her life were boys. She was what the guys called 'an easy lay' in high school. And I think she always got the worst of the relationship."

"As I recall, you were pretty boy-crazy in high school."

"That's a nice way to put it, and it's true. But I've been out of circulation since I turned twenty. I never once looked at another guy after I met Sam. On the other hand, Laura kept on bed-hopping and never met a guy who really loved her back."

Dev asked, "Is this going to be different?"

"If it ever gets to that stage, yes, I think so. Chuck Wardman is no Don Juan. In fact, he's afraid of getting his heart broken. His wife ran out on him."

Dev shook her head, "Sounds like the scenario you have in mind is two emotional cripples find each other and fall in love."

"Cripples is a little harsh. I'd say walking wounded. But, yes, that's the general idea."

Rachel was curious. "Does Laura know what you've got in mind?"

"I don't have a sign on the front door offering matchmaking services for singles, if that's what you're asking. And I haven't put a release form in front of her to sign. But we made no effort to hide our intentions. It wasn't a big party. Five couples and a pair of singles. I think Laura knows perfectly well what Sam and I are doing, and she'd have told us to get lost if the very thought offended her. And the same for Chuck Wardman."

Rachel said, "If there's a wedding, make sure I get an invitation."

"As far as I know, they haven't gotten to the first serious kiss. But keep your calendar open, babe. Keep it open."

Jess asked JJ if she could talk with him privately. JJ would have rathered not, but there was no polite way for him to refuse. They met in the library.

Jess said, "I hope you won't mind a little free advice, JJ. Rachel' not at all happy that you've picked Dev as your attorney in this matter, and I don't believe Dev's any too pleased to have the assignment. She'll do her very best for you, and she's an extremely competent lawyer. But she's a civil lawyer, and this is potentially a criminal matter. Furthermore, you've complicated relations between Rachel and Dev in ways that are unfair to both of them."

"This is not your affair, Jess. My butt is the one that's on the line, and I have the right to make arrangements that are good for me. Rachel's already voiced her objections to me. If she's got something more to say, tell her to talk with me directly. She doesn't need an emissary."

"I'm not here at her request, JJ. I'm here as a friend. Of Rachel's, first of all. But I'm also Dev's friend and yours."

"Okay, thanks for your friendly advice. Is there anything else?"

Jess held up her hands, palms out in a gesture that meant "Have it your way." "I've told what I had to tell you. The only other thing is make sure you've got a criminal attorney in reserve. You may need one."

"Who asked you to say that, Rachel or Dev?"

Jess replied angrily, "Nobody asked me to say any of this, JJ. Nor did anyone ask me to say 'Take your head out of your ass, mister.'"

She left the room, steaming. Except to say good-bye, those were the last words she had for JJ during the visit. She didn't say a thing about her confrontation with JJ to Rachel. From the cab that took her back to the airport for her return to Santa Monica, she made a cell-phone call to Dev.

"I had a brief conversation with JJ, Dev. I think he knew exactly what he was doing when he got between you and Rachel. He's very cocky, babe, very self-centered, maybe too clever for his own good. He's quite capable of doing what he's accused of doing. And he's quite capable of using you to serve his own hidden agenda. Watch out, Dev. Watch out for Rachel's sake, and watch out for yourself."

Dev said thanks, wished Jess a safe flight home, hung up the phone, closed her eyes, and rubbed them underneath her glasses. *What in hell do I do now?*

Rachel returned to school. She was having a hard time concentrating. The Denver police were still nosing around, trying to find a link between JJ and Alistair Hobson, the soldier of fortune believed to be the man who arranged for the mutilation of Bray and

Hopkins. They hadn't been able to find a thing, and JJ assured Dev that they wouldn't.

How ironic, Rachel thought, *I know he's guilty, and he maintains to Dev that he's innocent. Dev's telling me things she probably shouldn't as JJ's lawyer, and I'm concealing the truth from her.*

Rachel wouldn't tell Dev the truth because she thought Dev would have a hard time defending a client that she knew for a certainty was guilty. *Dev would make a terrible criminal lawyer. She's too pure-hearted. That's one of the reasons I love her.* Moreover, Rachel didn't want the truth discovered. *I'm glad those two guys have suffered the way I suffered. Well, glad isn't the right word. But it evens the score in a way that sending them to jail would never do.*

And yet the act of vengeance didn't make her feel any closer to JJ. It drove them further apart. Because of Dev. Rachel reconciled herself to the fact that Dev was doing her lawyerly duty, trying desperately not to let it affect relations between the two of them. It was the strain that JJ imposed on Dev that made Rachel furious.

She didn't say a lot about this to Dr. Cohen. Nothing about the investigation. However, she explained that JJ asked Dev to be his lawyer in a matter that also affected Rachel and now Dev couldn't be Rachel's lawyer because of a potential conflict of interest. It was tearing Dev apart—another grievance against JJ.

"And you're angry with him because of the emotional burden he's placed on your cousin?"

"Mainly, yes."

"That's a good sign, Rachel. Do you realize that this is probably the first time since I began seeing you shortly after the rape that you've thought first about somebody else's feelings instead of your own?"

"I hadn't considered it, but you're probably right. Still, Dev's so much a part of my life, it's almost as if I'm thinking about me."

"Don't try to minimize it, Rachel. It may be a baby step, but it's a step. You ought to be pleased that you're able to externalize your feelings. Even a little. It's healthy development."

The next time she saw Dev, Rachel reported what Dr. Cohen told her.

"You see, love, you help me even when you don't know you're doing it. I worry about how this business with JJ is affecting you, and all of a sudden that's a good sign."

"All the same, I wish I'd told JJ no when he asked me to be his lawyer on this."

"You tried to say no, Dev. You've got too soft a heart."

"Too soft a head, you mean."

"Soft-hearted, soft-headed. I love you just the way you are."

"Loved for being a dope. That's me."

"You're sure as heck no dope, my love. I'm sure JJ had mixed motives when he turned to you, but one of them is that you're a darned good lawyer."

Dev teased her, "'Heck,' 'darned'? Rache, I don't believe I've heard you avoid a four-letter word since you were fourteen."

Rachel smiled. "It's what one does in the presence of a saint."

"Okay, okay. St. Devorah. Somehow I don't think the church is ready for that. But I appreciate the nomination, sweetie."

"Now that we've restored me to full mental health, what can you tell me about the investigation?"

"I think they've gotten exactly nowhere, Rache. Hobson denies everything, and they haven't got enough to extradite him. They haven't been able to find any mysterious funds that might have been used to pay him or the guys who did the deed. They haven't been able to establish any kind of link between JJ and Hobson. They haven't gotten anything out of the two guys in Miami. According to what we hear, they won't take a plea bargain. They'd probably get their heads blown off if they ratted on anyone else in the drug ring they belong to. The police are at a dead-end."

"They're still sure JJ did it?"

"They're sure JJ did it, and they're sure Hobson was the middleman, but they haven't got enough evidence to do anything about it."

"So JJ's in the clear."

"Not really. Not until the statute of limitations has run. But the police have pretty much exhausted their leads, and unless something turns up, I doubt we'll be hearing much from them in the future."

"Well, thank God about that. I wouldn't want to see JJ prosecuted."

"Do you still love him, Rache?"

"I really can't answer that question. As you know better than anyone, Dev, I'm pissed at him a lot of the time. I'm furious about what he's done to you. I can't remember the last time we had sex.

But we'll have been married ten years this coming June. He's still my husband, and I'm still hoping things will get better between us. Is that love? You tell me."

Rebecca's baby, Ilana, was born on March 8, a Sunday. Hanna and Hillel arrived two days earlier in anticipation of the birth. Hanna regretted her reaction to the news of Rebecca's pregnancy and was trying very hard to be enthusiastic about the baby's arrival. This was her youngest child bringing her third grandchild into the world. Hanna was making a determined effort not to think about the fact that Rebecca was unmarried and that the baby's father had no intention of acknowledging her.

Ilana turned out to be a beautiful, dark-haired, dark-eyed little girl, looking exactly like her mommy did as an infant. Hanna wasn't entirely sure how she felt about Ilana's being adopted by Rachel and JJ. *Won't it be a little peculiar for the birth mother and the adoptive mother to live together under the same roof? Will Ilana know that Rebecca is her mother, or will they try to conceal it? Daniel's old enough to know that Ilana belongs to Rebecca. What will happen when he tells Ilana and she's old enough to understand?*

JJ assured her it would all come out right: "Rebecca's an integral part of our household, and the baby will be, too."

"That's okay while Ilana's little. What about when she gets a little older?"

"Daniel and Ariel don't make a big distinction between Rachel and Rebecca. They're accustomed to having both their mother and their aunt around. In fact, let's face it, the last couple of years, they've gotten more from their aunt than they have from their mother. Ilana won't lack for attention or affection. We'll work it out."

"How will your parents treat her?"

"Like any other grandchild. I'll see to that."

"I don't mean to interfere, JJ."

"Of course not, Hanna. I understand your concerns. Rebecca and Rachel are your daughters. Ilana's your granddaughter. Don't worry, I'll—we'll—take care of them."

"I'm counting on you, JJ. I feel fortunate to have such a wonderful son-in-law."

Rachel didn't hear about this conversation, not from her mother and not from JJ. She was at the hospital Sunday morning when the baby was born. Ilana was beautiful and Rebecca was happy and resting easily. But Rachel didn't feel extraordinarily excited by Ilana's birth although the child was her niece and would legally become her daughter. Rachel was actually more engaged with the impending birth of Dev's baby, her goddaughter. Dev might not be due until late May, but Rachel was already buying little things for the baby. Permanent things. A silver rattle, a silver cup, a silver spoon. She was envisioning the day when she'd be able to buy Dev's child her first fancy dress.

On Monday, the day after Ilana's birth, Rachel returned to Boulder as she did every Monday when school was in session. After this term, she'd only need a couple more classes to complete course requirements for her doctorate. Then she'd be ready to take her written exams and start work in earnest on her dissertation.

Rachel was actively considering the possibility of teaching a beginning class in the fall for freshmen and sophomores. The department was after her to do that. Not that she needed the money, of course, but they'd like her to have the experience. Her major professor, the man who helped formulate her dissertation prospectus, hoped Rachel would join the faculty in a couple of years. Professor Collingsworth was Rachel's principal booster.

The CU campus remained the cynosure of Rachel's identity. Her work at *In the Rockies* belonged to a distant past. She had no present interest in returning to journalism. She was not quite sure what she'd do with her doctorate once she had it. *Maybe I'll be able to turn my dissertation into a book. That would be nice. Maybe I'll teach after all. Uncle Aaron and Mark have nice lives. They get to spend all their time on intellectual matters. Apart from faculty meetings, of course. And grading. And advising students. And teaching a bunch of kids when to come in out of the rain. Well, at least there are* some *moments spent on intellectual matters.*

Once again, Rachel would have preferred to skip the big Passover seder, but once again, that was out of the question. It was a fuller house than ever. Almost forty people. Six Rothschilds from California, including Alina and Marla, who were absent last year. Marla was in rehearsal for her final role of the season with the San Francisco Opera Company, but the first night of Passover fell on a Friday night and it corresponded with the Easter weekend, so she was able to get away. Jess, Laura, and Arlie wouldn't miss it. Jess brought Sam and their two

children, of course. Arlie persuaded Jeff to come with her; this would
be the first seder he'd ever attended. Laura arrived alone. She and
Chuck Wardman continued to date, but it was a lukewarm relationship
and, reported Jess disconsolately, "not going anywhere fast—they've
both got their defense systems on full alert." Rebecca also had friends
coming from California: Harriet Anheim, Jonathan Fink, and Marilyn
Seeman, who were at the seder last year, plus Louise Lipman, another
of Rebecca's college classmates.

On the Colorado end, there were seven in the Goodman
contingent—seven and three-fourths counting Dev's unborn second
child, eight in the Weiner family, including Grandma Bess's nurse,
and seven members of the Rothschild-Weiner household—Rachel,
Rebecca, JJ, three children, and the children's nanny. Rebecca didn't
appear to be in the least discomfited by the fact that she was showing
her month-old daughter off without a husband anywhere in sight.
She was very matter-of-fact about it. "It was an accident," she told her
college friends, "and marriage was not a possibility, but I'll be twenty-
seven in June, and there was no way I was going to have an abortion.
I'm happy. She's beautiful, and I'm the mommy. Being the Scarlet
Woman is actually kind of fun."

"Are you going to keep seeing the guy?" Harriet asked, more than
a bit untactfully.

"Yes," Rebecca said. "Does that sound shameless? Well, I am. I
love him."

*   *   *

Rachel and her friends had their usual preseder information
exchange. Unlike last year, Rachel was willing to take her turn. In fact,
she was first up, because they all knew what happened in Miami and
they were eager to be brought up-to-date.

"The police have left JJ alone for a couple of months. Looks as if
they've run out of things to ask about. We're working on the assumption
that this is pretty much the end of the line for the investigation."

Jess wanted to know, "Is Dev still handling things for JJ?"

"To the extent there's anything to handle."

"How are you dealing with the dual loyalty question?"

"It's much less of an issue now that the heat has died down. You can ask Dev, but I don't think she's as conflicted as she was. But I'm still pissed at JJ for putting her in that position."

"Yeah, I dumped on him in January because of it. We've barely spoken since."

Laura interceded. "Well, if JJ did it, my hat's off to him. I wish I had a guy cared enough about me to do something like that."

Rachel said, "I hate to tell you, Laura, love, but you don't know what you're talking about. JJ did it for himself, not for me. He wasn't going to let those guys get away with defiling his property."

Laura was shocked. "Is that what you think, Rache? His *property?*"

"Yes, it's what I think. I'm sorry to disillusion you, Laura. It was pure revenge—no love in it, not a drop."

Arlie said, "That's terrible."

"Yes, it is."

Arlie responded, "I meant it's terrible that you feel that way."

"Oh? I guess Jess is the only one who's ever glimpsed that side of JJ—the cruel, self-centered side."

Laura said, "How awful for you, Rache."

Rachel took a deep breath and smiled wistfully. "Well, now you have some idea why I'm still a mental patient three and a half years later—and a long way away from getting better."

"Guys, I apologize for starting us down this track," Jess interjected. Let's move on. Laura, tell us how the film's coming."

Rachel whispered, "Thanks, Jess."

Laura said, "The filming will be done by the end of the month. Unlike the first time, I've known exactly what I wanted. Putting it together will be tricky, though. It's a matter of maintaining a balance between the narrative and the daydream sequences. No doubt, I'll need Hillel's help before I'm through. Thank God for Hillel."

Arlie said, "I'm sure it's going to be great, Laura."

Laura replied, "Great is an overused adjective, Arlie. I'd like it to be good, and I'll settle for okay."

Jess commented, "You're much too modest, Laura."

Laura said, "We'll see. Now, before you ask, I'm not in love, and no one's in love with me. I have a guy I see from time to time. Jess can tell you all about him because she and Sam brought us together. He's a nice enough man, but he's as afraid of getting serious as I am. So don't hold your breath. And don't ask any questions. That's all there is. Arlie?"

"Ten months married and still going strong. You should see me around Jeff. No more Boss Becker. She's gone. I don't even venture an opinion until Jeff has expressed his. And what I almost always say is 'Yes, dear.'"

"Come on, Arlie," Rachel said, "You haven't undergone a personality transplant. You're exaggerating."

"Yeah, I am," Arlie admitted. "But the truth is, I no longer feel the need to be in charge all the time. I'm very happy to share."

Jess said, "It's wonderful to see you so relaxed and happy, Arlie."

Arlie grinned. "It's wonderful *being* so relaxed and happy. I'd begun to think it would never happen."

Laura said, "Maybe there's still hope for me."

Arlie deliberately ignored Laura's comment. "What about you, Jess? What gives?"

Jess said, "I was afraid you'd never ask. The news is I'm having a third child around the middle of December … we're having, that is."

Rachel asked, "Is this another Snarky? No information about whether it's a boy or a girl until it shows up?"

Jess answered, "Since we've already got one of each, I think we're going to go with medical science this time. I'm having a sonogram later this month. I'll send everybody an e-mail the moment I know."

Laura said, "You've been saying you intended to have another when Sara was two. You did it!"

"It didn't just happen, ladies. Sam and I have been working on it diligently and enjoying the work."

Arlie said, "You're disgusting, you know that?"

Jess responded, "Why, thank you, ma'am. I try to be. I'm happy to know I'm successful."

"You'll keep on practicing law?" Rachel asked.

Jess replied, "Until the end of November. And then I'll take a couple of months of pregnancy leave and be back at work by the middle of March if everything goes according to plan."

Laura said, "Super-mom, super-lawyer, the only one of us who's got it all."

"It helps to have a super-husband," Jess said. The luckiest day o my life was the day Rachel arranged a double date for herself and me with Sam and what's-his-name."

Rachel mused, "God, what *was* his name? I can see his face. We had a world history class together. He asked me out on a date, and I asked him if he had a friend for Jess. Craig! That was his name. Craig …? Craig …?"

Jess shouted, "Walker! I remember you telling me afterward that you thought he was babyish."

Rachel agreed, "Yes. And you and I were so very, very grown-up."

"It wasn't as if he and Sam were such big buddies," Jess explained. "They lived in the same dorm and Sam had a car. That was the main thing."

Arlie said, "Well, hurray for the internal combustion engine! Without it, Jessica Sherman might be a desiccated old lady teaching second grade somewhere in the San Fernando Valley."

Jess was unusually serious. "No joke. Meeting Sam changed my life. When I was at Mills, it was popular to say that women don't need men except to have babies—and artificial insemination can take care of that. I half believed it. And maybe it's actually true for some women. But I wouldn't be who I am without Sam."

"I never heard such sentimental drivel." Arlie was light-hearted, and it showed. "You're a disgrace to womanhood, Jessica Sherman. What would Simone de Beauvoir have to say?"

Rachel laughed. "As I recall, she was getting laid regularly by Jean-Paul Sartre, and he wasn't as cute as Sam Adams."

"Getting laid is just a part of it, girls. A *very, very, very* important part, to be sure," Jess replied and then turned serious again. "You guys aside, he's my best friend, my strongest supporter, my biggest fan. There's something you guys never completely understood about me. I didn't particularly want to be smart in high school. I wanted to have a boyfriend, and boys didn't care for smart girls. Especially Michael Cohen. Then, I became a student at Mills where there weren't any boys around. I didn't mind being smart there. But it was Sam who helped me grow up. I've never had to pretend around Sam. He was proud of me."

Laura said, "In short, she loves him. Take it from me, love's no small thing when you haven't got it."

Rachel looked off into space. *You're right about that, Laura.* The conversation went on, but Rachel ceased listening.

The seder this year was unusually boisterous. The tumult began with the children. First, Daniel asked the Four Questions. He didn't need any help now. But then Ariel, who was almost five, insisted on having a turn, and she had to be helped through it word by word. Then Richard, who was almost a year older than Ariel, wanted to do it. Sam, wisely, put the boy on his lap and whispered the words in his ear while Richard repeated them.

When Richard had finished, Hillel said, "Alexis, Sara, Ilana? Do any of you want turns? What about your next baby, Devi? Or can we get on with the answers?"

Alina asked, "What about me? I used to be the youngest in this family. Isn't generational discrimination against the law? It ought to be."

Aaron asked, "Why don't we *all* do the Four Questions together?"

David said, "Good idea!"

They started reading it in English, and Jess interrupted.

She announced, "You guys do the English, and I'll do it in Hebrew."

She started reading the transliterated Hebrew, stumbling over the gargling "ch" sound.

Noah said, "You read Hebrew like a *goy*, Jessie."

"She *is* a *goy*, you dummy," David countered.

Jess replied, "Now you tell me. After all these years. Didn't I have a bat mitzvah? Or was that Rachel's? I forget."

Sam added, "After all these years of going to *seder*, our *kids* certainly think they're Jewish. Reformed maybe, but certainly Jewish."

"You're Jewish as far as I'm concerned, Jess," Rachel responded.

Aaron said, "Ah, the great rabbinic authority, Rachel Rothschild."

Hillel was impatient with the by-play. "Enough, already, dinner won't be served until midnight if we don't get to the answers."

The children, however, weren't interested in the answers, now that their part was concluded. So Daniel, Richard, and Ariel trooped off to play, and Alexis ran after them. Sara began wailing because she'd been left alone by the big kids, and Ilana was crying because she was hungry.

Hillel, Aaron, and Herman Weiner pushed quickly through the

narration to dinner. As the meal began, Rachel was seated in her usual position at the table, next to Grandma Bess and across from Jess and her family. This year, however, she'd asked Yalie to sit on her other side. There was an unspoken strain between the two cousins, once closer than sisters. Rachel wanted to reestablish the bond.

Rachel asked, "So, how's your work coming, Yalie?"

Yalie answered, "Doesn't Dev tell you? I've been on the job for three years now, and I've yet to lose my first case. You'd think my sister would do a little bragging."

"I don't give her much of a chance to talk."

Yalie frowned. "No, you wouldn't. Anyway, I work too hard, but I can't imagine doing anything else with my life right now."

"What about Richie?"

"He's gotten so he likes the firm. He gets to handle a lot of litigation, and since they've got their tentacles everywhere in the state, he's traveled to parts of Colorado I've never even been near."

"You never get to go along?"

"No. That's the bad part of being married to a trial lawyer. He's away quite a bit, and I'm not able to be a camp follower. I'd love to see him in action."

"Why don't you come to dinner when he's gone? Or we could go out together. I miss seeing you, lovey."

Yalie avoided an answer. "How are you doing now, Rache?"

"School's going great. I may do some teaching in the fall. Follow in your dad's footsteps."

"I meant how are you doing personally?"

"Better. I'm beginning to recognize myself when I look in the mirror."

"Do you mind if I ask you something, Rache?"

Although she minded, Rachel said, "Okay."

"You're seeing your analyst again. Why do you keep leaning on Dev?"

"Dev and the doctor agreed to it."

"Maybe they did. But, Chrissakes, Rache, Dev's about to have another baby. She hasn't got time to be your nursemaid."

"If it's too much for her, all she has to do is say so."

"Dev's a softie. She's never been able to protect herself."

"I don't know if I can get on without her."

Yalie voiced disgust. "Me, me, me. What about her?"

Rachel held it in as long as she could. She got up and ran to the bathroom in tears. Yalie started after her. Ruth, who'd been watching Rachel and Yalie through it all, followed Yalie, motioning to everyone else to remain seated.

"What did you say to her, Ya'el?"

"I'm sorry, Mommy. It's my fault. Let me handle it."

"Please be a little kinder, baby. She's still very fragile."

Feeling chastened, Yalie tried the bathroom door. It was locked. She rapped on the door.

"It's me, Rache. I'm sorry."

Rachel was crying. "No, you're not."

"Open the door, honey. Please. I apologize. I shouldn't have done that. Please forgive me. Let me in." She knocked again.

Rachel turned the door handle. "It's open." She was seated on the toilet seat with her head resting on the sink. She was still crying.

"I don't know what got into me, Rache. I don't mean to be so critical."

"Well, you were! I don't need to be told that I only think about 'me, me, me.' I *do* care about other people, especially about Dev."

"All I meant to be saying, Rache, is that it's going to be very hard for Dev to be attentive to you once the baby comes. You're going to have to be more self-reliant."

"I've leaned on Dev for so long that I don't know if I can stand up by myself anymore."

"Maybe I can take her place when the baby's born. Why don't you come talk with me?"

Rachel shook her head. "You're not a good substitute, Yalie. You're the smartest person I know, but you're not the most sensitive. I don't know if you don't understand how easily I bruise or if you don't care. Either way, I'm afraid of being hurt by you. I really, truly am."

Yalie was crestfallen and teary herself. "Can I confess something, Rache? Mommy bawled the hell out of me a year ago for lacking compassion toward you. I didn't like it one little bit. I can see now that she was right. I feel terrible about what I said, and a lot worse when you tell me that you're afraid of me." Yalie started sobbing in earnest.

"I thought I was the only crybaby in this crowd. Me and Ilana."

Yalie rubbed her eyes and tried to smile. "Guess not. Luckily haven't ever done this in court." She burst out crying again. "Oh, Rache, forgive me. Please. Please."

"Of course, I forgive you, Yalie. I think you're like a desert cactus, spiky on the outside and sweet on the inside. It's just I'm not in condition to risk the spikes to get to the sweetness."

"I'll try to do better, Rache. Don't give up on me."

"Give up on you? I would never give up on you, lovey. But will you do something for me?"

Yalie was still weeping. "Yes, of course."

"Don't be too hard on me, Yalie. That's all I'm asking."

Yalie couldn't say anything. She just nodded her head repeatedly.

*   *   *

At the end of May, Jennifer Chapman was born, Dev and Mark's second child. Tests showed that Jess was also going to have a girl, and, defying superstition, she and Sam picked out a name for her: Zoë Sherman-Adams.

Dev was in labor for twenty-two hours with Jennifer. She refused a C-section, but it was an exceptionally difficult birth and when it was over, she was thoroughly exhausted. Ruth moved in to care for Alexis and stayed on for ten days to give Dev time to regain her strength..

Dev expected to be out of the office about a month. Mark insisted she take at least three months off. He hired a housekeeper so that Dev would have no responsibilities other than to rest and care for the children.

Rachel, eager to have a role in her new goddaughter's first days, visited as often as her classes allowed, sometimes early and sometimes late. If she arrived in late afternoon, she brought dinner so she could eat with Dev, Mark, and the housekeeper, but the main purpose of being there was to feed Jennifer a bottle if it was time for her to be fed, hold her, rock her if she needed rocking, watch her sleep if she was sleeping. Dev wasn't nursing Jennifer. She was spending a lot of her time making sure that Alexis didn't feel displaced.

Although Rachel was around more often than usual, Dev was no longer "seeing" her. On reflection, Rachel decided that Yalie was right. She couldn't continue burdening Dev with that responsibility. Reluctantly, she suggested that their weekly sessions be ended.

"Suspended," Dev replied. But after the hard birth, it was unlikely that the weekly visits would be resumed anytime soon, if ever. Instead of unloading her complaints, Rachel made cheerful conversation with Dev and Mark. When Dev asked about how she felt, Rachel's response was "What matters now is how *you* feel."

It was pure bravado on Rachel's part. She was miserable without Dev's support. The visits with Dr. Cohen were clinical, devoid of the love that Dev provided. Rachel was now stopping in to have lunch a couple of times a week with Aunt Ruth, ostensibly to talk about Dev and the baby. In reality, she was seeking another source of human warmth and affection. She was also seeing Yalie when there was an opportunity, but it was almost like an experiment, tentative and fearful on both sides. Rachel was acutely afraid of being hurt, and Yalie was being unnaturally sweet to avoid even the slightest possibility of giving pain.

Looking at it objectively, Rachel understood that she was chasing a will-o'-the-wisp. But she couldn't help herself. In those 'half-conscious moments before sleeping and waking, she imagined talking to Dev about this or that problem.

Finally, she brought it up with Dr. Cohen. "Now that Dev isn't available, I don't have anyone I can talk to. I'm afraid of slipping back into depression."

"You've mentioned a girlfriend that's like Dev. What's her name?"

"Jess. Jessica Sherman."

"Would it help if you talked with her occasionally?"

Rachel brightened. "Why didn't *I* think of that? Of course, it would help."

That night she called Jess.

Rachel asked, "Bozo? You know how you've said you're frustrated being a thousand miles away and unable to help?"

"Yes."

"Well, I think you're soon going to regret it. I need to talk to somebody from time to time, and with Dev out of commission, you're elected."

"If that's what you want, Rache, it's okay with me. Just remember it can't be like it is between you and Dev. There's a lot in the last four years I know nothing about."

"Yeah. Unfortunately, I know *all* about it. Just ask."

"Okay, when do we do this?"

"I've been seeing Dev once a week on Saturday morning for about an hour and a half."

"That sounds okay. Can we do it first thing? Say 8:00 or 9:00 a.m. Pacific time? I'll save the errands I usually run on Saturday for later in the day."

"You're good to do this for me, Jess."

"Babe, I wish like hell it weren't necessary. But it is, and I'm here for you."

Jess became the repository of Rachel's secrets. Jess was the one who heard about Rachel's insecurities, her struggle to reconstruct a loving relationship with Yalie. But Rachel also wanted to cover old ground. Jess didn't know a lot about her problems with JJ preceding the rape, and Rachel told her, although Jess wondered why. The one thing that Jess carefully avoided was telling Rachel about JJ's sleeping with other women at Stanford before they got married while insisting that Rachel refrain from sex, even with him. Jess didn't know how Rachel would respond to that news, but she was sure it wouldn't be good.

However, Jess wasn't as deliberately passive as Dev tried to be. Jess asked more questions, offered more advice. But she was patient and astute. She understood that even before the rape, Rachel was a bit of the proverbial "bird in a gilded cage" —super-rich but confined. Jess had witnessed the overbearing-son-of-a-bitch side of JJ's personality. She could imagine how it grated on Rachel, who always had a rebellious streak, even when they were girls together. She knew about JJ's carrying on at Stanford, more evidence of how self-centered and controlling he was. Not a nice person at all, Jess believed, though she didn't say that to Rachel.

The weeks passed. Jess became ever more deeply immersed in Rachel's marital history, in her resentments. Rachel told Jess about the spankings. She recounted the rape, every brutal detail. Without tears this time but compulsively, as if purging herself of the memories. She told Jess about her inability to have sex with JJ, about her encounter with Louis Short. She withheld nothing.

Jess inquired gently. "Why do you feel the need to confess to me about this fellow Short, babe? It's ancient history. You could easily omit it."

"I don't know, Jess. Why did Laura tell you about the shameful things Bogusian did to her? Maybe I'm seeking absolution."

"But Dev's already absolved you, hasn't she?"

"Yes."

"Then why show me your dirty linen again? Why wallow in it?"

"I committed adultery, Jess. You have to understand that about me. I did a bad thing, and I suffered for it. I'm still suffering."

"Okay, babe. I see that. I see where you're coming from."

Rachel also told Jess about her ambivalent feelings toward the children, disclosed under hypnosis to Dr. Cohen.

"It's hard for me to comprehend, Jess, and harder to live with. Loving them and resenting them at the same time. I work on overcoming the resentment, and then every time I go out of my way to show them affection, it feels phony. *I* feel phony."

"How do you feel about Ilana? Any different than you do toward Daniel and Ariel?"

"Ilana's a sweet little baby. She really is. JJ and I have taken the preliminary steps toward adopting her. But her mother's right there in the house with us, and legal status apart, she's my niece, not my daughter, and she always will be. She's Rebecca's child, and even though I love her, I don't want to get between her and Rebecca. It's very confusing."

"Any idea who the real father is?"

"None. Rebecca won't say, and I've stopped inquiring."

"Is she still seeing him?"

"Presumably. She doesn't show any interest in having a boyfriend."

"I suppose it's her business."

"She's twenty-seven, Jess. If she's in love with a married man, there's nothing I can do that will change it."

Rachel didn't have a lot to say about current events. She didn't have a need to do so. Her life seemed to be on a fairly even keel. Summer came and went. She was back on campus teaching an introductory course about the American political system to entering freshmen. Her cousin Dev was feeling okay again. Her goddaughter Jennifer was doing wonderfully. Rachel was becoming more comfortable around Yalie, and Yalie wasn't acting as artificially sweet as she initially did. She was seeing Dr. Cohen less frequently at Dr. Cohen's suggestion. She was actually feeling pretty good about herself. It was as close to serenity as she'd ever come in the last four years.

The birth of Jess's third child, Zoë Sherman-Adams, was imminent. On the Saturday before the baby was due, Jess told Rachel, "I think this office is going to be closed next week, babe. You can talk to my answering machine if you want. I'll have Zoë call you back to tell you how much she weighs."

Rachel laughed. "With you as her mother, I wouldn't be at all surprised, Bozo. Seriously, though, would you ask Sam to call me when the baby's born? No matter what the time is. I'd *love* to be awakened at 3:00 a.m. to hear that mother and daughter are doing fine. Okay?"

"I promise, babe. After my parents and Sam's, you'll be the first to know."

The call arrived four days later at 11:30 p.m. Sam was excited. "Zoë's a redhead, Rache. Jess asked me to be sure to tell you that paternity is certain."

"That's Jess all right. Who else would be making jokes with the umbilical cord still attached?"

"Isn't she wonderful!"

"You got the best one of the Fabulous Four, Sam. Absolutely!"

Two Saturdays later, the phone rang at Rachel's house, and it was Jess. "I'm sitting here nursing Zoë, and I thought it's time for me to resume my job as counselor."

"You're special, Jess. You really are. But I'm okay. I'm really okay. I haven't felt this good about myself in four years. You've already got one baby. I think I can toddle along without you for a few more weeks."

"Okay, sweet potato. If you're sure. But don't hesitate if you need me. It's no big deal. Zoë won't mind. And Sam's perfectly capable of preventing Richard from killing Sara."

"Are the other two okay with the baby?"

"Sara doesn't know that Zoë's not a doll, and Richard's already used to playing second fiddle. Third fiddle isn't a lot different."

"Yeah, I'm sure he's starved for love and affection. What are you going to do about work, Jess?"

"Don't know yet. I'm not doing anything for the first month. Then I'll try working out of the house for a while. If that pans out, I may not go back into the office until Zoë's at least twelve weeks old. I don't want my clients to think they can get along without me, but Zoë comes first."

"You're a marvel, Jess. I don't know how you do it and still manage to seem so composed."

"Fake it, babe. That's how I do it."

"If there's anything you aren't, Jess, it's a fake. *I'm* the fake."

"Don't, Rache. Do me a favor, and *don't*! I haven't been through what you've been through. None of us have been through what you've been through. You look at me and see perfection. I look at me and see luck. I'm lucky to have friends like you, lucky to have Sam, lucky to have found a profession I'm reasonably good at, lucky to have three beautiful children. Life's filled with random occurrences, doll baby. I struck gold, and you got hit by a falling safe. Don't punish yourself. Okay?"

"I guess the long-distance counselor was needed after all, wasn't she? I'm some stable personality."

"Listen to me, Rachel Rothschild. You're getting there. I've seen an improvement just in the few months we've been talking. When Dev stopped being available to you every Saturday, you acted like the roof caved in. Now I offer to resume, and you tell me to take my time. That's progress, babe. I don't take any credit for it. None at all. But I see it. From what you've told me, Dr. Cohen sees it. You're not forbidden to talk to Dev, are you? Ask her what she sees."

"You really think I'm coming out of it?"

"Definitely! Your mood is lighter. You're more interested in the world outside yourself. I think having a goddaughter has been great for you. You lost Dev temporarily, but you gained Jennifer. Reconnecting with Yalie has made a difference. And you're getting quite a bit from those kids you're teaching. I have high hopes for you, Rache. I really do."

                    *   *   *

Rachel felt a lot better when she hung up. *Thank God for Jess and Dev. If I'm ever whole again, they'll be the ones who've made it possible.*

Shortly after the beginning of the year, the bomb dropped. Hopkins and Bray filed a fifty-million-dollar damage suit against JJ in the Denver courts. Their lawyer, Thomas Lord Fitch III, made certain that the Denver media heard about the filing. Everybody in Denver and Boulder who wasn't already aware that Rachel had been raped now knew the story. Reporters ran all over the place ferreting out details of the rape, the mutilation of the plaintiffs, and the unsuccessful police effort to prove that JJ did it. They knew about the soldier of fortune, the team of drug-connected criminals who actually did the job—almost everything there was to know.

Rachel refused all interviews. She tried to hold onto the tiny bit of privacy left her. The media kindly omitted the fact that she was confined to a mental ward briefly after an attempted suicide. But that and the anal rape were about all that was not revealed. She suffered a huge setback emotionally. She spent a tearful couple of hours with Dev when the story broke. Dev convinced her to return to campus when the new term started. Coming back was a struggle. The only comments she heard were sympathetic and supportive, but no one needed to tell her that everybody was talking about it. She was teaching another beginning course in American government, and every time she saw two students huddled together, she was certain they were talking about her.

In addition to seeing Dev, she'd spoken several times—at length—to Jess, and her visits to Dr. Cohen increased once more to three a week. It was taking every ounce of strength she had to hold herself together. Even Yalie was clucking over her, worried about her emotional state.

JJ insisted that Dev handle the case. "You've been my attorney all along. I need you now more than ever. I won't force you to withhold information from Rachel, but that's it, Dev. That's the only concession I'll make. If you don't do this for me, I'll take every scrap of business away from your firm."

"You don't need to blackmail me, JJ."

"I'm not blackmailing you, *cousin*. I'm just letting you know where I stand. I *need* your help."

"This is not my area of expertise."

"I know that perfectly well. Bring in help if you want to, but I want you to be in charge. I trust you. You ought to be complimented by that."

Dev truly didn't have to be blackmailed. If JJ really wanted her, knowing her limitations, she would unquestionably have felt obliged

Norman I. Gelman

to do it, much as she would have preferred not to. The threat to cut off her firm's relationship to Hyman Weiner & Sons simply proved how ruthless JJ was capable of being when he wanted his way. Dev didn't need any further proof that Rachel was right about JJ's drive to dominate. Suddenly, unwillingly, and without the direct knowledge that Rachel had, Dev was sure that JJ did what he was accused of.

The Denver attorney on the other side was Thomas Lord Darrow III, a tub of a man about fifty-five years old with a reputation for playing rough. Darrow was not the name he was born with. At birth, his last name was Augusto, Thomas Augusto. Augusto served him through law school, but when he went into practice, he wanted a more distinguished name. So he had it changed. He figured Thomas was okay for a lawyer. Darrow he took from Clarence Darrow of the Scopes trial. Lord sounded English and snooty. The III suggested ancestry—Choate maybe, if not Harrow or Eton.

Thomas Lord Darrow III was no more refined or capable, however, than Thomas Augusto, and big-time clients were not impressed by his implied lineage. He was a lone operator, a scrambler. But he was a street fighter, an adversary not to be taken too lightly when legal scholarship was not a consideration. He'd gained some local notoriety in a couple of successful personal injury suits. Darrow's counterpart in Miami was George Patterson, who also specialized in personal injury cases. Whoever sent Hopkins and Bray to Darrow and Patterson must have figured that their injuries were as personal as it got.

Dev's take on her two adversaries was that Patterson would be the easier one to deal with. Darrow carried a chip on his shoulder the size of a telephone pole. He relished fights against the legal establishment, and Dev's firm wore its blue-chip label proudly. In addition, bringing JJ Weiner to his knees would do great things for Darrow's reputation. Already, he was reveling in the publicity.

Patterson, on the other hand, appeared to be in it strictly for the money. Dev made an appointment with Patterson to come see him in Miami.

Patterson wanted to know, "Why don't you talk with Darrow? He's there in Denver."

"Mr. Darrow likes playing to the grandstand. Check me if I'm wrong, Mr. Patterson, but I think his main interest is Thomas Lord Darrow III. I'm sure he doesn't care a lot about you, and I'm not convinced he cares about your clients. I want to talk to you about what's in your clients' interest—and yours."

Patterson agreed to see her. Two days later, they were meeting in a fancy suite Dev had booked at a leading hotel in downtown Miami. She meant to impress him.

"Let's play the cards faceup, Mr. Patterson. Your levers in the case are two: One, you can play havoc with JJ Weiner's reputation, and two, you can force his wife to take the witness stand and describe what happened. I think you—George Patterson—believe we'd pay you and your clients a lot of money to preserve Mr. Weiner's reputation and keep Ms. Rothschild off the stand. The problem with that plan is that your associate in Denver has all but destroyed one of your levers. He's already inflicted grave damage to Mr. Weiner's reputation by spreading the story all over the media. Damaging him is no longer an effective threat. The damage has been done. I won't deny that the threat to call Ms. Rothschild as a witness is an important lever. But consider this. The only reason Hopkins and Bray haven't been extradited to Denver to face rape charges is Ms. Rothschild's unwillingness to testify against them. If she's forced to testify in the civil suit, I can promise you there'll be a criminal case, and I can promise you Ms. Rothschild will be a witness. Your clients may win the civil suit if you can produce convincing evidence that my client caused them to be castrated, but frankly, they're rapists and they aren't going to get a lot of sympathy from the jury. I'll see to that. If they get any money, it's not going to be a huge amount. And whatever money they get, they'll have a big problem spending it in prison, and that's where they'll be for a long, long time."

"So what are you suggesting?"

"What I'm suggesting is that taking this case to trial is—without question—a losing proposition for your clients, and it may not net much for you. Darrow may gain from the publicity, but it will be at your expense and theirs. The alternative is to settle the case. If your clients agree to withdraw the suit, I'm prepared to offer them a generous settlement and assurance that Ms. Rothschild will continue to refuse cooperation with the criminal case. You'll have earned a substantial fee, and it's up to you whether you want to share any of it with Darrow after he undercut your whole strategy."

"What are we talking about here?"

"I believe I can persuade Mr. Weiner to pay them each five hundred thousand dollars plus attorney's fees."

"That's not enough for the pain and suffering."

"You give me a figure."

"I can't without talking to my clients."

"Talk to them then. The offer's good for a limited time only. Then they'll have to take their chances with a jury and the police."

"How long?"

"I'll get a little sun tomorrow and go back to Denver Thursday afternoon. If I don't hear from you by Thursday morning, the offer's withdrawn."

"I'll call you."

Dev wasn't a sun worshiper, and she would have liked to leave for Denver immediately to get back to Jennifer, Alexis, and Mark. But that was not the way the game had to be played. So she would spend the day sightseeing in Miami, where she'd never been before. She hired a guide to take her around.

Dev enjoyed riding through South Beach with its restored Art Deco facades and busy outdoor restaurants. After that, however, the tour quickly paled. Maybe it was the oppressive humidity … or the women in shorts and men in pastel pants … or the billboards advertising shows with performers who were surely dead. Perhaps it was simply the disagreeable mission that brought her to Miami. Whatever the reason, Dev had seen all the coconut palms, blue-water inlets, and shopping streets she cared to. She had the guide take her back to the hotel, where she collected a telephone message from Patterson, took a cool shower, went for a swim in the outdoor pool, showered again, and changed into fresh clothes. Now she was once more ready to play in the dirt. At 5:05 p.m., she called Patterson at his office.

"My guys will settle for one and a half million dollars each."

"That's way too much, Mr. Patterson. I'm prepared to guess that a jury will give them much less than that once they've heard about the rape and listened to my eloquent plea on behalf of all women not to penalize a grieving husband and father for something he had nothing to do with. And God knows how much they'll need to spend to defend themselves in a losing battle against the rape charges. Because they *will* lose, and they *will* go to jail. The only reason we're prepared to settle this case at all is that it will forestall some inconvenience for Mr. Weiner and some agony for Ms. Rothschild."

"Okay, a million and a quarter."

"Too much, seven hundred fifty thousand dollars."

"A million each."

"You're a tough bargainer, Mr. Patterson. Okay. Be here at 9:00 a.m. I'll prepare the papers. You tell me how to have the checks made out. We'll have the signing tomorrow afternoon at the bank. Your clients will have to be there. I want their signatures witnessed."

"It's a deal. We'll be there."

Dev hung up the phone and shut her eyes. She'd done what she came to do and for the amount she told JJ would be necessary. Why did she feel sullied by the transaction?

*   *   *

Neither Rachel nor JJ was interested in hosting another large Passover celebration. Instead, Hanna and Hillel would hold the seder at their house in Santa Monica. JJ begged off. Passover and Easter were very close together this year, and JJ wanted to spend a long weekend in Vail "doing absolutely nothing." He said he needed the time to recuperate from the strain of fending off the lawsuit. Rachel was working very hard to recover her balance. Dev and Jess convinced her that attending the seder would help. She'd be immersed in the love of friends and family.

The Weiners would not be coming to Santa Monica, but it would still be a large gathering, augmented by two new little ones, Dev's Jennifer and Jess's Zoë. Marla was once more in rehearsal, this time in Chicago for the part of Mimi in *La Boheme*, but since the seder came just before the long Easter weekend, she agreed to fly to Santa Monica to meet Noah. Alina was temporarily at leisure. Her book was due out next month, and the publisher had arranged for her to do a fourteen-city book tour. After that, she and David intended to go on a "vacation-vacation," no scrounging for two-thousand-dollars-a-day information, just luxuriating in the sun along the Cote d'Azur in France. Whatever she did next, Alina promised David it wouldn't be another travel book.

"No more peripatetic Lee," David announced with satisfaction.

"From now on, she works at home. She's promised to travel no further than the library."

Rachel's pals were all coming. Jess was still delaying her full-time return to the office. She was going in two or three times a week to meet clients and otherwise worked from home. She wanted to keep doing that if possible. She liked being available to the children during the day, even though it was difficult to persuade Richard that a closed door meant "Mommy's working." Arlie and Jeff, married nearly two years, were beginning to be anxious about Arlie's failure to conceive. Laura was still dating Chuck Wardman. Jess thought they'd eventually get married—just because it was a comfortable relationship. Neither was passionately in love with the other. Meanwhile, Laura's last film earned warm notices from the critics and made a pretty good showing at the box office. She'd have no trouble attracting backers for her next project.

Rebecca's friends would also be there, though not in the same configuration as last year. The women—Harriet Anheim, Louise Lipman, and Marilyn Seeman—were the same. But Harriet had broken up with Jonathan Fink and she was coming alone, while Louise Lipman was now living with Jason Epstein and bringing him with her.

The seder was the same raucous affair as last year. Once again, the Four Questions were recited seriatim by Daniel, Ariel, Richard, and The Company. Jess had made a determined effort to master the "ch" sound in Hebrew and, as Noah put it, "is now qualified to be a Jewish child." There were eight children at, or near, the table now. Rebecca's Ilana— now Ilana Rothschild-Weiner—was a year old, talking a little, and able to totter around by herself when she was allowed out of the many laps that wanted to hold her. Jennifer was at the crawling stage, but Dev didn't want her scooting around on the floor, picking up things, and putting them in her mouth, so she was incarcerated in a playpen. Zoë was too little to do much of anything, but Jess needed to keep an eye on her to protect her from sister Sara's desire to demonstrate her love for the baby by hugging her until she cried. The bigger kids—Daniel, Richard, Ariel, and Alexis—quickly lost interest in the proceedings and disappeared into the family room, where Hanna had thoughtfully collected a pile of toys for them to occupy themselves with.

Rachel was enjoying herself. The nightmare of the past couple of months had receded. Once more, she felt alive and almost well. She'd seated herself, however, between Yalie and Dev and across from Jess, and all she needed was Dr. Cohen at the table to have her entire support system present. She and Yalie were again in tune with each other. Although Dev was the one Rachel relied on during the crisis over the lawsuit, she had Yalie's unmixed sympathy. That was something Yalie hadn't previously offered since returning to Denver. Rachel had dinner at least once a week with Yalie and Richie at their place in Boulder. Often it was Richie who prepared or brought in the meal because it was a stretch for Yalie to get home in time. She was still the hotshot prosecutor on an unbroken winning streak.

Rachel acknowledged to herself that she was happy the Weiners weren't in Santa Monica. The monthly Shabbat dinners weren't taking place as regularly as they used to. Rachel's schedule was often the excuse but not the reason. JJ simply didn't want to go. Rachel hadn't made a special visit to see Grandma Bess in months and months, and the old lady was miffed at her in spite of Rachel's best efforts to explain that she was busy preparing for her comprehensives. "You could find time if you wanted, young lady," Grandma Bess had said more than once. And, of course, Rachel felt guilty.

When the Passover narrative reached that point, Rachel, the kitchen klutz, was allowed no part in serving the meal. Hanna and Ruth dished out the food, and the other women delivered it. With her female companions gone from the table, Rachel took little Ilana in her lap, but her mind was elsewhere, thinking about JJ's absence.

Daniel was the only one who actively complained about his not being there. Rachel suspected that more than half the people at the seder accepted that he deserved some solitude after all he'd been through. She thought the rest—herself included—simply didn't miss him. Jess certainly didn't. Dev wouldn't say, of course, but Rachel thought she had quite enough of JJ while she was acting for him on the case involving the two rapists. She was convinced that Yalie and Richie actively disliked her husband, partly on her account but largely on his.

Rachel was happy JJ stayed in Colorado because that meant she didn't have to share her room and her bed with him. The last time they did that in Santa Monica, it hadn't turned out very well. Rachel was beginning to think she would never resume physical relations with JJ.

Dr. Cohen helped her understand how deeply rooted her resentment of him was. Instead of fading from her mind, the two spanking episodes loomed larger than ever. He abused her. He treated her like he owned her, and the vengeance he took on the two rapists was because they'd damaged his property. *Simple as that.*

Rachel's reverie ended when all the women returned to the table. Jess asked how school was coming.

"I'll be done with almost all my course work by the end of this semester. I'll take my comprehensives in the fall, and assuming I don't flunk out, I'll start doing research on my dissertation topic around the beginning of next year."

"Are you going to continue teaching?"

"I don't know for sure. I've got to talk to my adviser about that. I've surprised myself. I really enjoy teaching. But I don't know if it will interfere too much with preparation for my comprehensives. And then, once I start work on my dissertation, I'll need to spend quite a bit of time off campus doing my research."

Yalie explained, "She's going to work on how initiatives and referenda impact on the legislative process."

Rachel cautioned, "If it's approved."

Jess asked, "I assume that means California?"

Rachel said, "Yes—at one extreme. And New York or Massachusetts on the other. A state that doesn't make much use of initiatives and referenda. For purposes of comparison."

Jess nodded. "Interesting topic. Will you have to spend time out here?"

"Mostly in Sacramento," Rachel replied. "That's where the records are. I'll also need to do a considerable amount of interviewing. What I'm really hoping to get at is whether the these alternative ways of making law allow politicians to dodge responsibility. I think that's what happens, but I need to demonstrate it. "

Jess inquired. "And in the East?"

"Albany or Boston." Rachel laughed. "I can assure you I'll spend a lot less time if it's Albany."

Mark said, "I want to stipulate that she didn't ask my advice, and I'm hurt."

Dev flicked her hand dismissively. "Don't listen to him. She told him about it, and he thinks it's a terrific idea. Ambitious. Difficult. But a good dissertation topic."

Rachel clasped her hands as if at prayer. "If I don't fall on my face."

"Yes, if she doesn't fall on her face." Mark was being facetious. He had a lot of confidence in Rachel.

Yalie made a face at her brother-in-law. "What a confidence builder you are, Mark."

Mark said, "I give mostly F's to my students."

Rachel jumped in. "I don't mind if you tell them how much you've helped me, Mark."

"Okay. Rachel owes it all to me. I take her classes for her. I write her papers for her. I coach her on what to say during seminars. I'm her Svengali."

"I guess Mark's determined not to be serious. But, yes, he's helped me a lot, including with the selection of a dissertation topic."

"I get half her Ph. D., the Ph. portion."

"I give up." Rachel smiled. Almost everyone noticed. Rachel hadn't smiled often in the past four years.

Rachel recovered better from the shock of the suit and the publicity than initially seemed likely. She was not the first rape victim whose story became public. Because of the circumstances surrounding her case, especially the revenge visited on the victims, which everyone assumed her husband did for love, she'd become a celebrity on the campus. Women's groups wanted her to come tell her story. She refused. She was not ready—might never be ready—to talk about it before an audience. She certainly wouldn't tell the truth, not about the rape itself or the reasons behind it, not about the mutilation of the perpetrators.

Rachel would have liked to retreat into the obscurity of being just another graduate student. But that was not possible. Everyone on campus who'd ever met Rachel Rothschild now knew that she was the wife of one of the richest men in Colorado. When she declined speaking engagements, she was asked to "contribute to the cause." The "cause" might be hotlines for rape victims or feminism or someone's academic hobbyhorse. Sometimes, when she was in the mood, Rachel wrote out a personal check, which uniformly disappointed the recipient because she or he thought the check was much smaller than it should be. Sometimes she suggested that a request be submitted to the Weiner family foundation. Sometimes she asked for literature and said she'd "think about it," which, of course, she never did.

Saying no was difficult for her. It was a little word, an important word, a necessary word at times. But Rachel was always a soft touch, even when she didn't have much, and now that she was richer than she had ever expected to be, she'd like to help. She really would. But like a lot of rich people, she concluded that hundreds of casual acquaintances looked at her and saw dollar signs plastered all over her countenance. And she'd become wary of the vast majority of petitioners and skeptical about the causes they espoused. She was only willing to give to things she believed in and people she trusted.

Rachel always considered herself a feminist. But she'd never been a militant. Militants believed they had a right to other people's opinions. They didn't persuade; they insisted. Rachel shied away from those types. Avoided them in college. Avoided them afterward. Now that she'd been victimized, experienced personally the feminist nightmare, Rachel saw that the militants might really have a point. But she didn't like many of them as individuals, and she didn't want to be their case in point or their heroine or their financial angel. She wanted, please, to be left alone.

Yalie counseled her. "I know it's easy to give advice when you're not the one they're after, Rache. But if you hang in there, I think it will pass. You need to practice saying 'no.' It's a simple word. N-o. Not interested. Won't do it. Eventually, they'll get the idea."

"I'm sure you've got the right idea, Yalie. I don't know if I can act on it. I keep trying to explain myself."

"That's a mistake, honeybunch. You give a reason, and they try to convince you otherwise. It's hard, though, to argue with no. Instead of saying 'I don't want to do it because …,' tell them 'I won't do it.' Period. It's the right answer to every intrusion."

Rachel leaned over and kissed her cousin. "Yalie, it's nice having you on my side again."

"It's nice being here."

PART IV

RACHEL DECIDES

The spring term was nearing an end. Rachel had a research paper she'd allowed to slide and must complete. She was working at her desk in the office adjoining her bedroom. It was after 2:00 a.m., and she was fighting off sleep. She had to keep on working for another couple of hours and needed a cup of coffee. She was walking upstairs toward the kitchen to make it when she heard a muffled cry coming from JJ's room—a woman's voice. It could only mean one thing.

She flung open the door, and there was JJ, as she'd guessed, lying naked on top of some prostitute, fucking her brains out.

"You filthy son of a bitch!" she screamed.

JJ, startled, untangled himself. Suddenly Rachel realized in horror that the woman in bed with him was her sister Rebecca. It was an ice pick thrust into her heart.

She shouted obscenities at both of them, sputtering with rage. She rushed past JJ to get at Rebecca. She scratched her sister's face with her nails, drawing blood.

JJ pulled Rachel away and got between them. Rachel succeeded in kicking his shins, but she was barefoot and it had little effect. She attempted to knee him in the testicles.

Finally, JJ got behind her, clasped her arms to her sides, and held onto her with his right hand linked to his left wrist. Rebecca had one hand to her damaged cheek and with the other was struggling to put on her pajama top and bottom. She was crying hysterically.

Rachel was loudly angry, ready to awaken the entire household. "When I told you to go find a whore, I didn't expect you to bring one into the house, and I didn't expect the whore to be my sister." She meant to wound them both as they'd wounded her.

"Stop it!" JJ commanded.

"My sister's a WHORE! My sister's a WHORE! My sister's a WHORE!"

Rebecca cried harder every time Rachel said it.

JJ twisted Rachel around violently so that she was facing him and slapped her across the face. Hard.

"Leave the room, Rebecca. Rachel and I need to talk."

Rebecca didn't *leave*; she fled, swept along by a flood of tears.

"Listen to me, Rachel. I'm not going to allow you to abuse Rebecca. She and I are in love."

"*In love*? You make me sick. You're not in love with anyone but yourself. How could you do this to me? I'm your wife."

"You haven't been my wife for four and a half years. You can't stand to have me near you."

"After this, yes. You're goddam right I don't want to have you near me. You or that immoral slut you claim to be in love with."

He slapped her again. "I told you not to talk that way about Rebecca."

Rachel was crying now at the humiliation. "How could you do this? Yes, we haven't been sleeping together. I was raped. I was *raped*! I almost killed myself. You can't imagine how much I still hurt inside. I've been trying to regain control." She could hardly breathe. She said it again. "I've been *trying*."

"Maybe you have. But all I know is that you put me out of your bed nearly four years ago and told me to go fend for myself."

"I didn't mean for you to go fuck my baby sister. You're a dozen years older than she is."

"We didn't plan it this way. It just happened."

"When?" It was a wail.

"The first time we slept together was when you went off to England to hear Marla perform. But Rebecca and I started falling in love a long time before that. We fought it as long as we could."

"Oh, God. What am I going to do?"

"Nothing. We're going to go on as if this never happened."

"You're out of your mind. I'll sue for divorce."

"You can have a divorce, provided you give up the children."

"Give up the children? Are you *out of your mind*?"

"I'm very serious. If you ask for custody, even joint custody, I'll fight you every inch of the way. You haven't done much of anything for Daniel and Ariel in a good many years. Nor for Ilana. Don't try to blame it on the rape. It began long before that, and you know it. I'll bring Hillary back, if need be, to prove neglect predating the rape. Rebecca is a lot more the mother of these children than you are."

"And I can show you're an unfit father. What will they think when they hear you've been fucking my sister?"

"What will they think when they hear about Louis Short?"

Rachel was stunned. "What do you know about Louis Short?"

"That you fucked him. That's what I know."

"How?"

"Private detectives. In case it ever came to this."

Rachel was unable to take it in. "How?"

"After that night when you came home drunk and without your bra. Credit card receipts and so forth. At the bar. At Starbucks. It wasn't difficult. You paid for a lot of coffee when you were seeing him regularly. The folks at Starbucks remembered the two of you, and the detectives found him."

"He *told* them?"

"He *enjoyed* telling the story. I have it on tape if you'd like to see it."

Rachel was in anguish. "You wouldn't use that." She knew he would.

"I intend to have the kids, Rachel."

"It wasn't what you think."

"What I think doesn't matter. You'd better worry about what Louis Short will say when I put him on the witness stand. Dev Goodman won't be able to save you this time."

"Dev?"

"Yes, I know about the agreement Dev forced Short to sign. I'll put her on the stand, too, if necessary."

"Does Rebecca know what you're up to?"

"Not in any detail, no. But she won't save you, if that's what you're thinking."

"You'd throw me in the garbage."

"Don't be so fucking melodramatic. You abandoned me before I abandoned you. You ought to be flattered. I went and fell in love with a younger and healthier version of you—the Rachel you used to be."

Rachel had a flash of insight. "God almighty. Rebecca was the go-between, wasn't she? She took the money from Grandma Bess and carried it to Europe for you. She must have flown to Switzerland from Berlin and deposited it."

"You can't prove a thing, Rachel."

"And she was your contact with Hobson, wasn't she? She set it up, arranged the payoff. You wanted vengeance, and she did your bidding. Isn't that right?"

"You always *were* a smart girl, Rachel."

"And you're a lousy, fucking son of a bitch."

"There's not a scrap of evidence. None. Dev doesn't know all that much. And she can't even tell what she does know because she was my attorney."

"You thought of everything, didn't you?"

"I tied up the loose ends if that's what you mean."

"And now? You want me to move out without the kids and see them once a week."

"We'll see what a court has to say. As far as I'm concerned, if you want a divorce, they don't have to see you ever. They'll be a lot better off with Rebecca."

"You'd try to take my kids away from me? How could you do that? I can't believe even you could be that cruel. What if I don't ask for a divorce? What did you say about going on as if this never happened?"

"We don't need to be divorced. I'm sure that will be okay with Rebecca. You may have a hard time believing it at this moment, but the only reason I didn't tell you a long time ago about Rebecca and me is that she didn't want you to be hurt. Even after she got pregnant with Ilana, she wouldn't let me tell. Better to be an unwed mother than to hurt sister Rachel."

"Ilana was yours all along."

"That's right. We didn't plan on that either, but Rebecca *wanted* my child. She would never have considered an abortion."

"And I thought she was just a *common* slut."

JJ slapped her again, harder than before. "I'm warning you, Rachel. I won't allow Rebecca to be insulted. You'll keep your tongue under control, or you'll get out of this house."

"Are you telling me you expect me to kiss Rebecca's *ass* and *stay here* and watch the two of you *fuck*?"

"I'm not asking you to kiss Rebecca's ass. You *will* have to be polite—in fact, more than polite around other people. But, yes, my idea is that we'll go on living in this house. It's plenty big enough. You'll keep on being my wife in name. Rebecca and I will move in together, and she'll be my real wife. She already is. You just didn't know it."

"That's sick. You're a mean, sick bastard."

"Maybe so. But it will work out."

"You expect me to consent to being a guest in my own house?"

"You'll go on doing what you have been doing—being involved with yourself, sorry for yourself, living by yourself in the master bedroom, playing with the kids when the mood strikes you."

"And the children? What about the children?"

"Rebecca will go on being Daniel and Ariel's aunt, paying a lot more attention to them than you do. And she'll go on pretending to be Ilana's aunt, as we agreed."

"Now I understand why you were so eager to adopt the baby. Stupid me. I thought you were being so openhearted. You two played me for a sucker, and I fell for it."

"You can see it however you like. I didn't want the baby to be branded as illegitimate, and the only alternative would have been to tell you then that Ilana was Rebecca's and mine."

"Another kindness to Rachel. Thank you so much. And what else? Tell me what other plans you have for me."

"Those depend on Rebecca. She may want another baby. I'm willing, if she is, to pretend the next baby is also your child. She can act the unwed mother again. She's done that once already. Or she can disappear for a while, and you'll disappear also. And when the baby arrives, we'll tell the world that it's yours. What does it matter? Rebecca is already mother to Daniel, Ariel, and Ilana. She'll simply be mother to another child that is ostensibly yours."

"Do you really expect me to agree to this?"

"After you've thought about it, yes. It's the best solution for all of us. For you, me, Rebecca, and the children. No family crisis outside these four walls. Your parents will never have to know. You'll live exactly as you have been living, with more money than you can possibly spend. You can come and go as you please. You can go to school full-time. Take an apartment in Boulder. Stay there as often as you'd like. I won't object. If you ever decide to do so, you can go back to work full-time. You can keep on having the seder here, keep on playing the grande dame at Vail. You'll be free to sleep alone forever. Or find some other guy to fuck. The kids will keep calling you Mommy, and they'll call Rebecca Auntie Rebecca. The only real difference is that you and I can stop pretending to one another that we have a life together. And Rebecca and I will be able to stop sneaking around."

"You're going to sleep with Rebecca in front of the children?"

"No. She's already in the bedroom next to mine. We'll simply cut a door in the wall between us. She'll go into her room at night, and I'll go into mine, and then she'll come through into my bed … our bed."

"How am I going to face everybody?"

"Nobody needs to know. Just me, you, and Rebecca. As far as the world is concerned, Rachel and JJ will be man and wife, and Rebecca will continue to be your loving sister. Lou Short will stay muzzled."

"This is sick … grotesque."

"Perhaps so, but that's the way it's going to be unless you're prepared to make a fight of it—and, in the end, lose everything. Because that's what will happen. I'll hire the toughest and meanest lawyers I can find. Tom Darrow maybe. You'll get an alimony check, but I'll see to it that you lose everything else that matters to you. I'll make sure that the agreement Dev struck with Short is voided. You won't be able to show your face on campus once he tells his story."

"You expect Rebecca to be your mistress?"

"No, I expect her to be my wife in every way that counts."

"And I'm supposed to watch this happen under my nose?"

"It's *been* happening under your nose. If you weren't so engrossed in yourself, you might have wondered how Rebecca got pregnant without having a boyfriend you ever heard her talk about. My guess is that Jess knows or at least suspects. Not much gets past her. Maybe Dev knows, though I doubt it. She's a goddam Girl Scout, much too innocent for a lawyer. Look, Rachel, if you weren't so fucking blind to anyone's emotions but your own, you would have noticed that you and I haven't been in love for a *long* time. That's the main thing. Rebecca and I would never have happened if you and I were still in love. But we aren't, are we? And let's face the facts, Rachel. You stopped loving me before I stopped loving you. You stopped loving me before the rape—maybe long before the rape. I don't know when it happened or why it happened, but it happened."

Rachel stood there, speechless and numb.

"Think it over, Rachel. I'll wait for your decision. But not forever."

Rachel, after a moment, asked, "How much time have I got?"

"A week should be enough. Two weeks at the most. You either move out and sue for divorce, or you stay on my terms. Understood?"

Rachel slowly nodded her head, eyes down and unseeing. She couldn't say a word, not "yes," not "no," not "fuck you." The conversation was over. Rachel headed toward her room as if in a trance. She had to digest what had happened.

Rebecca was nowhere to be seen.

Instead of going directly to her bedroom, Rachel started upstairs to pour herself a stiff drink. At the next landing, the childrens' level, she stopped herself. She shook her head violently as if to clear her brain of the clouds that enclosed it like a mountain top. *No,* she thought, *I'm not going to get drunk. I'm not going to give that son of a bitch the satisfaction of watching me fall apart. I'm never going to give into him. Never! And liquor isn't going to help me think it through."*

She turned around and went downstairs to the office adjoining her bedroom. She began to shut down her computer. Then she decided, *Fuck that. I'll finish what I started and maybe by morning, I'll be able to concentrate on a solution instead of spending the rest of the night stewing about JJ and Rebecca and feeling sorry for myself.*

She sat down at her computer. For the next two hours, she concentrated on the research paper which she'd been writing. She was no longer sleepy, and her mind was surprisingly clear, focused on her paper. In the main, she was able *not* to think about her predicament or even about what she saw when she opened the door to JJ's room.

Her project complete, she lay down in bed, not bothering to shed her clothing, not even her shoes. She was exhausted but she wasn't immediately able to fall asleep. Instead, she made her first decision.

Blaming Rebecca was not a useful emotion. *Leave her out of it. It's all about me and JJ and the kids. And the kids!* She meant that, she realized. She really meant *And the kids. They're mine, I'm their mother, and I can be again.*

Her second decision came soon afterwards. *I can't just go to a divorce lawyer. I need advice from someone who will understand and who won't judge my reactions. I can't go to Dev on this. Jess is the only one who can help me. I'll call her in the morning.*

That was enough to allow her to doze off for a couple of hours. Although it was a fitful rest, when she awoke at 10:15 a.m. and took a shower, she wasn't groggy. She knew what she had to do. With a towel still wrapped around her, she phoned Jess and found her working in her home office.

"Jess," she said, "I need to come see you. It's awfully urgent. If I can get on a plane today, do you have time to talk with me?"

"About what, sweetie?"

"I'm divorcing JJ."

"Wow … " After a moment's reflection, she continued, "I'll have to admit, it doesn't really surprise me, Rache. I'm sure it's the right step. You should have done it a long time ago.

"He's toxic, babe. Really bad for you in every way. I've been on the verge of telling you a couple dozen times. But I told myself you had to reach that conclusion for yourself. Problem is I don't practice law in Colorado, and I'm not a divorce lawyer. How am I supposed to help you?"

"It's very personal, Jess. I need advice that I can't get from any divorce lawyer. I can't even talk to Dev about it. You're the only person on earth who can help me." Although she had kept her emotions in check until now, Rachel began to cry.

"My God, Rache. If it's that bad, of course you can come see me. Let me know your arrival time and come straight to the house."

"Can I impose on you, Jess? Can I check into the Miramar and ask you to come to me?"

"May I ask why, Rache? We've got plenty of room. Besides, you're family."

"That's the problem, Jess. You know how much I love them but I can't have the kind of conversation I need to have with you when Sam and the kids are around."

"Okay, if that's the way it has to be. Okay. Do you want to check into the hotel and then call me?"

"No, I'll call you from the airport and you can meet me at the hotel as soon as it's convenient."

"When you said urgent, I guess you meant urgent."

"Yes, it sure as hell is."

Before 4:00 p.m., Rachel was on a United flight to LAX. By 6:30 p.m. Pacific Time, she was at the Miramar where she found Jess waiting in the lobby. They hugged. Rachel's shoulders were shaking.

"I'm sorry, Jess. I didn't intend to cry on you. You can't imagine how grateful I am to have you as a friend."

Jess had tears in her eyes. She didn't know exactly what to expect when they got upstairs. She was simply overwhelmed by seeing Rachel in such obvious distress.

Once they were in her room, however, Jess stopped Rachel before she got started. She'd made a sudden decision. "There's one thing you ought to know, babe. JJ cheated on you when he was at Stanford— while you were engaged and he was forcing you to refrain from making love."

"My God! Why wasn't I told?"

"Because when it came out, you were already married and seemed deliriously happy. Arlie knew about it and told me right after your wedding. That was the first time she heard about JJ's 'no sex' edict. And I wasn't enough of an adult to know what to do with the information. After the rape, I told Dev, and she told Dr. Cohen, and we were afraid that telling you then would destroy you. I'm telling you now so you'll understand that JJ was *never* worthy of your love. Not from the very beginning."

Rachel was silent for a long moment, thinking. "He really is a complete prick, isn't he?" she said at last. After a pause, she added, "It was all about controlling me, wasn't it ... from the start? He never consulted me. Looking back, he really wasn't concerned with what I wanted or how I felt. He was determined all along to have it his way. I wish I'd understood that early enough to have avoided marrying him. I'm glad you told me now, Jess. I really mean it. It wipes out any feeling that I might be responsible for what's happened between us."

"Good. I hoped you would react that way. Now let's get down to business."

Rachel proceeded to recite the events of the previous night, every detail. "JJ's 'solution' is no solution at all," she said at the end, "but I don't want any member of my family to know about JJ and Rebecca."

"Unless it becomes absolutely necessary?"

"I'd like for it not to become absolutely necessary. I don't give a fuck about JJ, especially after what you've just told me, but I want to figure a way out of the mess without destroying my sister."

"Well, she is to blame, you know."

"I know she is in part. But the reason Rebecca was living in Denver is that she came to take care of me and my kids after the rape. I can't forget that. I don't want to forget it. Rebecca was attracted to JJ the first moment she set eyes on him—when she was fourteen. JJ and I have been totally estranged for the last three to four years. You know that. It must have been clear to Rebecca long before it was clear to me. Rebecca has nobody, and JJ can be a charming bastard when he chooses to be; he charmed me at twenty into submitting to his dictates. You know our history as well as anyone does, better in fact than I did until a couple of minutes ago. I'm sure he charmed Rebecca into his bed."

"Um," Jess said, thoughtfully. "Yes, I see what you mean."

"Okay. Now let me set out a few guidelines. I'm absolutely not going to stay on JJ's terms. I'm going to divorce him. I'm certainly not going to give up the kids. I don't give a shit about JJ's reputation but I don't want to sue on grounds of adultery because I don't want to name Rebecca as the other woman. I don't want to make life impossible for her. If she chooses afterward to marry JJ and to identify Ilana as their child, that's up to her. I've got to prevent JJ from allowing Lou Short to tell his story all over Boulder. I wouldn't be able to deal with that. Now, how do I go about it?"

Jess responded, "Wowie, that's a big order." She paused, supporting her chin in her hand. After a moment's reflection, she continued, "I need some time to think about this, Rache. Would you do me a favor? Why don't you go down to the dining room and order us a little dinner. Not too much for me. But I'd like a beer—Newcastle or Bass Ale if they've got it. Order yourself a drink, too. Then take a little walk. I expect we're going to be here for a couple hours."

"How much time do you need?"

"Give me an hour, babe. But before you go, how close are you to Richie Reiner?"

"I see him often enough. Now that I'm spending so much time in Boulder, I eat dinner with him and Yalie pretty regularly."

"My impression is that he's a very good lawyer? Do you agree?"

"Damn good. Very versatile."

"He's the one I'd like to handle your case," Jess said. "But you'll have to ask him not to say anything to Yalie or Dev. Think he can keep a secret from his wife?"

"Yalie and Richie work different sides of the street. Neither of them exchanges professional secrets with the other."

"Good. Now go take your walk."

By the time Rachel returned, Room Service had already delivered dinner and Jess was drinking her beer and eating fried calamari.

"Finished or hungry?" Rachel inquired.

"Finished," Jess replied, "and I think I've figured a way to finish off JJ Weiner."

Excitedly, Rachel responded, "Give."

"First, you need to understand that I don't know a goddam thing about the statute of limitations on certain kinds of crimes. But there's no statute of limitations on scandal. I think we can get your soon to be ex-husband to agree to settle by threatening to expose how he took care of the two guys who raped you. With some investigative work by a good detective agency, I believe we can prove that JJ got the money from his grandmother, that the money was transferred to Switzerland by Rebecca, and that Rebecca made the arrangements with the guy in Australia who got the gangsters in Miami to cut off the rapists' balls. We'll need *proof*, however, not speculation."

"I wouldn't be able to confront JJ with that." Rachel shuddered at the very thought.

"No, I know you couldn't. We need someone who can intimidate him. That's where Richie comes in. He'll give JJ a peek at the evidence, threaten to give the police and the FBI the information on crimes that are still prosecutable, and tell JJ that you are prepared to ruin his grandmother's reputation and Rebecca's as well as what's left of his unless he agrees to a divorce on your terms."

"And what are my terms?"

"That will be up to you and Richie to decide. But, if I were you, I'd be generous and offer shared custody of the children provided you get a large financial settlement, a tape over Louis Short's mouth, and a guarantee that there will be no reprisal against Dev."

"I'd forgotten about the possible impact on Dev."

"You would have remembered sooner or later, babe. I know she means the world to you."

"You're right about that. Now what do I do next?"

"Give me Richie's office telephone number if you've got it. Eat dinner. Get a good night's sleep and show up for breakfast at my house early tomorrow morning. Sam and the kids would be furious if you came to town to talk to me and left without seeing them. But don't call your folks or anyone else in L.A. We don't want to spark anybody's curiosity about why you came to L.A. so suddenly. With luck, they'll never need to know."

"Jess," Rachel said, tearing up again, "how am I ever going to thank you?"

"By putting this all behind you and living your life on your own terms. That's how," Jess answered.

"What do I do about Rebecca?"

"Whatever feels right to you, Rache. No further attacks but no grand reconciliation either. You can try to reestablish your relationship after it's all over. Just not now."

"And JJ?"

"Tell him you're consulting a lawyer, but don't say who it is. If he asks whether you're planning on filing for divorce, say you'll tell him after you've made a decision. If he makes more threats, just tell him 'we'll see, won't we?' If it gets too nasty, pack a bag and move into a hotel. Think you can handle that?"

"With you in my corner, Jess, I'm not afraid of JJ, not even the Big Bad Wolf."

After Jess departed, Rachel drank the whiskey she'd ordered, ate a salad, undressed, donned her nightgown and got into bed. *It's done*, she thought, and then suddenly she realized *I'm free of all the damn extra baggage that's weighed me down since the rape. I'm free!* She digested that idea and then she thought, *I'm going to be okay now. At last, I'm going to be okay.* As she put her head on the pillow and began to fall asleep, she repeated the thought. *I'm going to be okay. I'm going to be okay. I'm going to be....* And then she was asleep.

Late the following morning, after Rachel had left to return to

Denver, Jess Sherman called Richie Reiner, found him in Gunnison, where he was preparing a water rights case, spoke to him for nearly an hour and got his swift agreement to represent Rachel in the divorce case. "I'm not a divorce lawyer, Jess, but I have colleagues I can consult. I'll certainly enjoy humiliating that cocksure cocksucker," Richie said. "Collecting evidence that could be used in a criminal trial is also a little outside my line but I know an FBI guy who's worked with Yale and is now in private practice. I'll ask him to handle the investigation and hire anyone he needs to back him up."

Three weeks later, Richie called JJ and asked to see him, saying it was extremely important. They met that afternoon.

"What's this about?" JJ demanded suspiciously.

"About the divorce settlement," Richie replied.

"What divorce settlement?"

Richie said: "In the words of *The Godfather,* I'm going to make you 'an offer you can't refuse.'"

"What the hell are you talking about?" JJ was belligerent.

"Let's cut the crap, JJ. I'm representing Rachel, who is suing you for divorce. I'm going to tell you what it's going to cost you if you want to be able to hold your head up in Denver and keep your lover out of jail."

"What the fuck are you up to?"

Richie grinned: "I'll spell it out for you, Mr. Clever Guy. We know exactly how you arranged to have those two guys in Miami castrated. We know where you got the money. We know who took it to Switzerland. We know who contacted Alistair Hobson. We've got the evidence to prove it. In addition to the local laws that were broken, there were also several Federal laws that were violated. If you want all of this to come out in divorce court and in the media, we're prepared to oblige. If you want to risk going to prison and to assure that other people in your family and household are prosecuted, we can make certain of that too. If you don't want either of these things to happen, you'll listen to what I'm offering."

JJ tried to keep a poker face but his eyes betrayed him. Without speaking a word, he nodded to Richie, telling him to go ahead.

"Okay, then. First, you will not contest the divorce. Second, you and Rachel will agree on joint custody of the children."

JJ started to interrupt: "Fuck that. I expect to get full custody of the kids. I can show that Rachel's an unfit mother and that she's slept around."

Richie permitted him to finish the sentence. "Allow me to continue explaining the terms of the settlement, Smart Guy, and we'll see how much fight's left in you. You've heard the first two conditions. Third, you will sign over the house in Vail to Rachel free and clear. Fourth, you will provide written assurance, backed by a twenty million dollar bond, that neither you nor your company will stop doing business with Dev Goodman and her law firm. Fifth, you will give Rachel Rothschild one hundred million dollars to be paid out on a schedule set by Rachel after she's consulted a tax attorney. Sixth, you will keep your children with Rachel in your will, which will be deposited with my firm. Seventh, you'll make certain that Lou Short continues to keep his mouth shut. Eighth, if you want to marry Rebecca, that's up to the two of you. Rachel will not interfere. Ninth, you'll pay lawyers' fees in the amount of one million dollars plus expenses incurred in our investigation."

"One hundred million dollars! A twenty million dollar bond! A million in lawyers' fees plus expenses! Where am I going to get that kind of money? You're full of shit. And Rachel belongs in an insane asylum."

"One hundred million dollars. That's the price. And I can tell you where you'll get it. You're lucky Rachel isn't insisting that you break up with Rebecca. She doesn't blame her sister for what's happened. She blames you."

"I'm not going to accept your deal."

"That may be your position now, JJ. It will stop being your position in a moment. Let me tell exactly what we've got. Our evidence is incontrovertible. We've got a copy of your grandmother's check. We know when Rebecca went to Zurich and where she stayed. We know which bank she used. We've got a record of three calls she made to Hobson on your behalf, two in Australia and one in New York. We know where and when Rebecca met with Hobson in New York City to make the final arrangements. And we have the record of calls Hobson made to her phone before and after the deed was done. We've also got a record of the calls Rebecca made to release funds from the Swiss bank where the money was deposited. We're prepared to turn that information over to the Justice Department and to the Miami police as well as the Denver police. Maybe you're not afraid of having your grandmother and your lover prosecuted. They might even be able to beat the rap. But, if this matter goes to court, we will refuse to hold proceedings behind closed doors, and we'll make sure the media get the full story, including the national media. Everyone will know about JJ Weiner's criminal activities, and everyone will know what part Rebecca played in the whole affair."

"Goddam you. I want to speak to Rachel."

"Rachel has no intention of speaking to you, JJ. I am, however, authorized to say on her behalf: 'You'd better take the deal. Next week the price goes up.'"

"You goddam fucking son of a bitch."

"Think it over, JJ. No one's going to let you off the hook. It's as cheap as it will ever be."

Five days later, after storming around, consulting a divorce lawyer, fulminating at length and trying vainly to formulate a counter-attack, JJ Weiner capitulated. He hadn't bothered talking with Rebecca. He loved her—more than he'd ever loved Rachel, in part because Rebecca was more pliant. JJ decided for both of them.

He tried to bargain, but Richie wouldn't listen. "The terms I listed are the terms you'll agree to," he insisted. "They're unreasonable," JJ replied angrily. "And I suppose you thought the terms you offered Rachel were 'reasonable?' You dug the tiger trap for Rachel, and now you're in it," Richie sneered. He despised JJ, and he didn't mind showing it.

When she got the news, Rachel called Jess: "I love you, Jess Sherman. I always have and now more than ever. You saved my life and you prevented my family from having to hear about Rebecca. Now that I'm through with JJ, I actually believe I'm going to be okay. I owe you more than I can ever pay. But I intend to send you a check for a million dollars."

"You can send it if you want, Rache, but I won't cash it. If you feel compelled to show gratitude, you can let me recuperate in Vail after my fourth baby is born early next year. It wasn't what we'd planned, but it turns out you *can* become pregnant while you're nursing. Her name is going to be Rachel Rothschild Sherman Adams after a friend of mine."

Rachel burst into tears. "Oh my God, Jess. I'm so lucky to know you."

"You unquestionably are. I admit it with characteristic humility," Bozo answered.

"I'm onto you, Jess," Rachel said, crying and laughing at the same time. "You're Bozo, the Pussycat."

At the other end of the line, Jess laughed happily. "Unmasked at last," she said. "Yes, that's who I really am. Meow."